The Vanguard Anthologies

BOOK III

By LD Roberson

"Barbarism is the underbelly of this animal called society.
In fact, it is the most dangerous carnivore in all kingdoms
from the sheer number of beings it devours every day."

First Edition, Copyright 2015

CHAPTER I

"Grace and Mercy," Driven says as he finishes another hundred plyometric handstand push-ups, keeping count on his personal heads-up display. "That's what I named them when my dad handed them to me. These guns are all I brought when I left home," Driven balances himself on one hand and taps them with the other, "except my favorite belt." He moves over to the suspended rings, walking on his hands. He presses off the ground from the handstand, grabs the rings without his feet ever touching the floor. He adjusts himself and then, finally starts his pull-up routine, music booming in the bud in one of his ears.

"Why?" Synite asks from the bench on the wall, typing in Co'mmei on a tablet projection. He and Driven are in a private gym that Driven rented out to get his daily workout in. He gets to come in whenever he is in the area as long as the schedule permits.

"Why what? I said a lot of stuff," he says between repetitions of upside-down shoulder flyes.

Touché, Synite thinks as he reiterates: "Why'd you name your guns Grace and Mercy?"

"Oh," Driven swings around, stops in a handstand and does some more presses. "Well, to be honest with you, just because it sounds cool. Grace and Mercy are things that people probably wouldn't think of when you talk about any weapons, much less guns. Maybe it's what the victim of their wrath," he says with a smile on his face, "hopes I have for them when they're looking down the barrels. Yeah! Yeah, I think I'll use that next time somebody asks! Good talk."

Synite laughs at this guy who, from what he can tell, really is his polar opposite. He believes it is a good thing to have someone similar to Driven around, reckless as he may be. His skill should hopefully make up for his attitude, Synite hopes. "Sure, kid."

"What are you writing over there?" Driven hops over to look at what his friend is doing, "That's about your lady?"

"Mostly," Synite speaks of the poetry he puts down whenever he gets the feeling or the chance. "Some are pretty terrible but I try to put my thoughts down as often as possible."

"Everything does read better in Co'mmei," Driven confirms.

"I agree," Synite loves his first language, especially the way it rolls off the tongue. "You read every language?"

"All the documented ones," Driven's brain is probably the most complex thing Synite has come in contact with outside of his own heart, "and a few that aren't written anymore but still spoken…maybe twelve or thirteen."

"I wish I could learn more languages," Synite knows he does not have the time or the dedication to do so.

"Wanna learn something more useful…like how to shoot?" Driven can tell by the lack of wrinkles around Synite's eyes that he did not grow up shooting guns. "I mean, only I can handle mine since they lock up if I'm not touching them but I have a few others on the ship!"

"Shoot at what?" He flies up to the window near the ceiling and looks out at the surrounding landscape which is made up almost completely of desert, remarking at how desolate it seems on the surface. "There's nothing but sand!"

Driven tells him, "There's a camp out to the nort. Nobody in this world owns guns, no militaries or anything. But the Regency here loves me so they say if I felt the need I could kill some wild animals or something."

"Maybe later," the Air commander says. However, out of the window on the other side of the gym is a mountain of money and the main reason Airiq Driven knows about this place.

Yar JK is not the most lush, generally beautiful planet in its system but it does have a collective ideal of wealth that runs through the veins of its beings. It is one of the most progressive planets Driven has ever set foot on and is one of the reasons he is such a great businessman. Yar JK taught him how to connect with people and sell himself and a need, not the product.

It also taught him to completely stop consuming uselessly. This entire planet is about building the best version of itself without any sort of monetary system whatsoever. Everyone helps each other and there is nothing to prove; love is the only validation these peoples need. It is not communism but collectivism: they have no anxiety and do not need money to execute business because they do not want or feel the need to take more than necessary. If someone has more space or more resources, there is no jealousy from the rest of the world because they trust each other: those who have more apparently need more to survive.

Yar JK is a world of beings that provide for each other and sleep well at night. Everyone eats breakfast, lunch and dinner. Everyone works towards improving the entire planet every day. Every able-bodied being takes time to exercise in large groups or in their homes. Crime is minimal as there is no need to steal. There is no class and there is minimal poverty. Enjoying the shortness of life is the status quo as they are all actually living fully and not just breathing. There is no cap on success as it is only measured in ideas and the work that comes from them.

"I hate ceilings," Synite floats down by Driven and then to the ground. "I hate them almost as much as I hate war."

"I can tell!" Driven goes to the ground and does some power stretches. "If I could fly, I'd probably hate them, too."

"What do you hate?" Synite asks spontaneously. He has not been given the chance to get to know someone in a long time and wants to take full advantage since Driven seems to be an open book.

"Well," the young man has to think long and hard about that, not because there are so many different things he hates but that there are so many things he loves. "I guess the thing I hate the most is," he has to stop and gather the best way to state it. "Wow! Nobody has ever asked me this before!"

"I can tell," Synite smirks.

"Shoot, now that you mention it, ceilings would probably be what I hate the most, too. But not so literally, you know?" Synite understands exactly but continues to listen. "Limitations. Anything that confines. Hell, I guess that means I'd hate walls too, right?"

"The whole building?" They have a laugh together.

"I love the gym though!" Driven qualifies. "And ships. Moving ceilings are okay."

"Not so literal, kiddo," Synite taps him on the shoulder. "Why," Synite realizes he is asking Driven *why* a lot, mainly because he does not understand him very much. "Why do you work out? You don't need to, I mean, with your Borganics and all."

"Because it's fun! It gets the fluids moving in my body and raises my awareness, among other things," the adrenaline junkie he is, Driven does whatever he can to feel a rush. "The daily dose of energy that my body gives me, and yours does, too, is much stronger when you get stronger! The feeling is great. The feeling of failure and getting strong again, enough to bounce back from that failure in moments instead of days or weeks," he wraps up his stretches, "that's why I do it!"

The gym manager comes in and greets Driven familiarly, "The early group is coming in soon, my friend. You can stay and join or teach a class or two today if you wish!"

"We have a few other things to do," Driven tells him. "But I'll come back when we're done though!"

"Maybe I'll join in too," Synite thinks aloud as he sees his reflection in the metal of some gym equipment. He looks at his father's spitting image: the little bit of stubble around his jawline and the blonde dusted through his cocoa hair. His past couple of cycles has aged him a little more than he thought they would prior to being put in a cell of dirt and tortured. *I guess that would knock the child right out of anybody.*

From the day he was brought to the Sword to now, Synite believes he has come a mighty long way. He made it to the top of the world only to abandon it for what he hopes to be his greater cause. And, this entire time, that hope is what has kept him on this path. His vision of a future without all of this strife and struggle burns as bright as it did when it was first lit under that arena. "What are you over there in deep thought about?" Driven can tell by the focused look and the shape of his brow.

"I was a slave not even two cycles ago," Synite would rather not rehash the entire situation. "I'm thinking about how I might have needed that time in my life, despite how bad it was from the outside looking in. It's nice to not have to be in that situation anymore, though. I appreciate the direction I'm heading in even if I don't know what to make of it yet."

"Man, I did not know you were a slave," Driven admits. "I just thought you, Psilos and Amethyst couldn't leave the planet without permission. That's a yarly of a different color!"

"He and I were slaves and Amethyst was a powerful figurehead to keep the rest of the world at bay," which is the best way Synite could describe the situation. "But for the three of us to be where we are now is worth all of the trouble I've been through."

Driven is impressed, "That's great man. I've never been through anything close to that but I'm sure whoever you were before is still inside you somewhere." The child that was focused on finishing school and trying to figure out what he wanted to do with his life had to be quiet for him to endure all of the pain. If he missed his former life for even one moment too long, things would have fallen apart for Synite. The torturers or one of his opponents absolutely would have smelled the weakness like hounds after a fox as they swarmed him.

He looks at himself now, a secondary school dropout (as he has never returned since his kidnapping) who fought his way out of bondage and into wealth that was quickly erased in order for him to be free. And now, here he stands in relative control of his destiny with all the power and ability to move mountains. He thinks back to when he caught Promis from the avalanche of rocks down the side of that crag on Earth 8. He thinks back to Amethyst truly moving the mountains as she shot down a huge ship with one finger. *And her whole reason for being here is me.*

In the preparatory gym recently added to the Sword, the Enslaver's varsity team warms up for their first tournament battle that takes place in about three hecu. Lone, who fought in the royale at the time of the escape, practices changing direction sharply in the sand. Lo, past member of the lower five in Atlan's Profit Circle, gets used to their team uniform, stretching and hopping about. Castra Nim, the team captain, sits in the corner of the room watching his teammates. The most movement he makes in the next hecu is scratching his nose, not to be misconstrued with picking it (so he would say if they asked).

The team sport was created and initiated with agreement from nine out of ten arenas on Earth 11. Surprisingly, it did not take very long to agree on a set of basic rules also. There can only be three active warriors per team with as many as five alternates that have to be designated outside of the respective Profit Circle teams. Only two from each team are allowed on the field at a time. They can engage any way they wish and, when one of the two starters either dies or surrenders, the third member has to wait at least two eins to come in. During this slim window of time, the winning team has the distinct advantage of being two-on-one and can try to strike a killing blow with the momentum on their side. If the second starter is eliminated before the two eins is up, the third has the opportunity to either fight for the win alone or surrender. If the second survives through the two eins, the third comes in and it is two-on-two again. This continues until one team is killed or surrenders.

One of the aspects of team battle that the Sword Report has the best time with is trading. Warriors can be put on the open market not unlike any other sport and dealt for monetary, political or team strength purposes. The only difference is that the individual warrior can reject their deal and remain loyal to their team no matter where their arena tries to send them or what other arena tries to get them. Rejections rarely occur because of the pressure from the leadership that is put on the warrior and the behind-the-scenes repercussions that are threatened if certain deals are not made. This has already happened to two of the three warriors on the Atlani team and, rumor has it, may happen again soon.

The Sword team's opponents from Nortghard are on the other side of the wall Castra rests against, going through a playbook of attacks and defenses that they have been plotting since they found out they were fighting the Atlani team. They are coached much in the same manner that Synite was when Santhia gave him intelligence on his opponents, finding weaknesses and attempting to exploit them. Arra Chinoch, S'san Zark and Wik have been practicing and perfecting techniques, trying to become a well-oiled machine of arena battle.

The Atlani team has no coach, no mapped out attacks, and no specific style. They planned, with Castra at the helm, to not plan. Their strategy is built around adaptation and solving the problem in front of them as they see fit at the time, remaining mentally flexible. After watching Synite's battles and his tremendous success, his greatest asset was being able to truly play it by ear at the end of the match. Even when he had no idea of his opponent's trump cards, he could still outmatch them because of his skill at acclimatization. They are mentally prepared for whatever should be thrown at them, so they hope, by not physically preparing for anything.

These are two different teams with two different philosophies that desire two completely different things. The Nortghard team is playing the underdog role with everything to prove in this system put in place for them to carve out potential success. They believe in practice, repetition and an air-tight approach shall win over the opposite. The Atlani team, as delivered to them by Fabric who was a captain of sorts in a past life, believes that being a true team prevails. Knowing each other as friends, caring for one another's success and knowing each other's' weaknesses inside and out of the arena are the most important things. This is partially because they care less about success on this battlefield and more about the revolution coming to Atlan in the near future.

An attendee comes into each of the preparatory gym sides at the same time to let each team know that it is time for them to make their way into the arena for the match to begin. The tournament is for the first Earth 11 team champion; the winning group will gain the title and financial perks that go along with it. Some politicians are attempting to contact other planets to see if they would make it more than merely a global sport, which is taking a while to gain traction.

Before the fight, the entire crowd gets the chance to participate in determining who is to choose the first contenders. They choose out of two opposing things: black or white, yes or no, up or down, etc. The captain of the away team then picks one of these opposing things and, if they pick the majority choice, they get to choose which of their two opponents get in the battle first. The majority choice is the one that wins which became the reason things are switched for each competition. If someone were to get wind of the winning answer before the match, that would give an unfair advantage to the choosing team.

Each warrior is announced, with the away team going first, getting the jeers of the crowd and the home team coming out last to raise their spirits again. The six of them meet in the middle of the Sword to a roar, excited to be a part of the first team tournament on Earth 11. The Sword set a new viewership record with over two billion reported watching globally. Before a single punch is thrown, the Enslaver had already made upwards of three billion Marks in revenue. It is extremely excited as shown from the masses of smoke and laughter that comes from Its corner of the skybox.

Zark meets Castra in the middle of the arena and a hologram comes up in the center, giving Zark 'hot and cold' for the majority choice. He grins, looks back at Arra and pushes his large hands through his choice. S'san Zark, a financial consultant by day, started a career as a professional triathlete, participating in the longest triathlons on Earth 11 and losing only one because he did not train as much the cycle his first child was born.

He moved from the high ranks of the triathletes to the lower ranks of Superathletes. Their demanding Supercourse of events occurs once every five cycles and takes place in both icy and hot conditions. Only ten percent of the Global Superathletic League is accepted per Supercourse and there can only be one winner.

The Supercourse goes from a beach, across a lake, through a forest maze, up a mountain and finishes at the bottom of the range. The Superathletes start the course staggered with two eins in between. They only get one bag and one set of clothing that they must carry the entire course. If anything is dropped for longer than one ein, the owner is eliminated. If an athlete is tagged or passed, they are eliminated. If an athlete loses mobility, gets knocked unconscious or dies, they are eliminated. The slowest finisher is eliminated if there are fewer than ten finishers; if there are more, those slower than the tenth are eliminated. The few that finish then have to fight royale style for the gold medal.

Zark climbed the ranks and, after seven cycles of training, got into the Supercourse. He was not favored but finished seventh out of eight, entered the royale and was knocked unconscious and therefore eliminated. He does what many losing Superathletes refuse to do and requested training from the being that knocked him out. The request was refused since that opponent felt inadequate because they did not win either.

Instead, Zark entered the Nortghard arena to get better at hand-to-hand combat. He has improved dramatically and plans on entering the Supercourse trials next cycle. He grinned at Arra Chinoch as he pushes his hands through the 'Hot' side considering her particular elementalist abilities.

CHAPTER II

The Air is crisper than usual this Fall in the Naz District, Driven's favorite place on Yar JK. It is also the eve of a new cycle which prompts the entire planet to prepare for dozens of festivals, carnivals and parades. This world may be filled with intellectuals and business beings but everyone takes five days of vacation for the Cycle Start Celebration, or Cystcel as the natives call it. It is one of the two times of cycle where decadence and indulgence is more than accepted but encouraged; the time to be completely open and free to frolic beyond the general freedom that they express on a daily basis.

Synite was used to the New Cycle's partying back on Earth Prime and is glad that he will be able to get a small taste of home even from so many lightcycles away. He had not relaxed or had any fun that did not involve some sort of violence since the last time he saw his schoolyard.

Cairo, Jr. takes some time to write as he looks out from the balcony of the condo he and Promis are sharing. He muses in Co'mmei:

> Your voice for me is as sweet as a zephyr coming in from the sea at sunset, the salty scent reminding me of that special feminine pitch that grabs my attention. Your skin is a beach of warm, caramel colored sand over my feet, the warm Suns against my cheek like the attention your hand gives when you rub down my face, those glowing orbs we travel between like your eyes for me, and just for me. They're the bright and powerful orbs that I travel between to give me life. I use their, your energy to live. I confess, I need your life for mine, to melt into when the world's tides crash down on me. I crave, I need your soul to survive, to walk next to going into the unknown horizon, to the future.

I'll probably delete this one. The street below is flooded with locals gathering supplies, building boats and cooking large animals. This is the only time that anyone eats anything that does not grow from the earth, so they indulge in many fishes, grazing animals, poultry and other herbivores. He can tell by the preparations around the Naz District that this may be a much bigger party than he had ever dreamed of back home. The entire place has the mixed aroma of seasoned steaks, saltwater and a flowering citrus fruit tree that blooms this time of the cycle.

He turns back in, leaving the balcony doors open to let the morning Air into the living room. He reads over another short thing he wrote for her:

> Artists find love in
> Between the lines. Ten
> times a day, we can
> fall for you again
> and again with no
> more effort than a
> look. We live below
> and hope to parlay
> in your presence here
> and in the next life,
> above forever. Dear
> is the love from wife
> to the art of man.
> With that, there will not
> be a thing that can
> break apart our lot.

Promis comes in the room with him and turns on her favorite morning music as he puts his tablet away. He has grown accustom to it since she turns on some kind of music every morning. "Don't you love this? This smell…and the anticipation in the air out there," Synite can feel the energy in the atmosphere and takes it in, "it truly makes every day more exciting."

"I love it more because I get to share it with someone I love," Promis declares over the thumping beat and skips over to Synite. "My parents taught me that I'm the only one who has no choice but to look myself in the eye every day and that it's my job to find someone who chooses to do it with me. I'm so glad I've found that in you," she kisses him on the cheek from her tip-toes. "All of it is making me so happy! And I feel so much better now that we're not cooped up on that ship."

"I can tell. You've even kept the room clean for ten days now," Synite laughs sarcastically. "Everything must be great!"

"Everything!" Lucky for him, she is used to his sense of humor and does not mind it. "What is this?" she picks up his tablet and sees a bunch of stuff written in Co'mmei. Synite reaches for it but she has always been good at keep-away. "This is nice!" She reads:

> While learning what I need to know about you,
> you should teach me things I won't learn in books.
> Books can only stretch the mind to a certain point.
> Point the way that leads us to the end of time;
> time to be who we need to be only for each other.
> Other than that, there's nothing else to care about;
> about two lifetimes to go before I look away.
> Away farther than I've ever been in a while.
> While learning what I need to know about you...

She looks up and Synite who is almost beet red, "Your words..." She forces eye contact. "Is this about me? Or is this just some deep poetry because you're not a shallow guy?"

"What do you think?" he snatches the tablet back and she jumps on his back, kissing him wherever her mouth lands.

"It's beautiful," she keeps kissing. "I wish I could put words together like you. I try my best to express myself otherwise but..."

"You do a pretty good job," he winks at her and she throws a pillow at him. He closes down his tablet and puts it on top of a cabinet so she cannot reach it.

"Do you have more?" she goes over to the cabinet and he steps in front of it. "You do! When are you going to let me read them?"

"Never," Synite grins. "They're my thoughts! And most of them aren't that great."

"Your thoughts about me aren't that great?" Promis crosses her arms and pouts.

Synite taps her lip, "I'm saying that some of the writing is pretty bad," he chuckles.

"Hey!" she hops onto the couch, "Can we fly today?"

Synite has been thinking about flying a lot lately as he has not done so in consideration of the fact that they are trying to be as discreet as possible here. "Psilos wouldn't agree with it. You don't want anyone to find us, do you?"

"No one'll find us! We'll be high in the sky," Promis persuades as Synite watches her skip around the room. As playful and childlike as she is right now, he still gets lost in her beautiful frame and face. She made her hair dark again when they got here and has not put on a single ounce of facial foundation since. "We don't have to go out for long. I only want to see the city from a bird's eye view!"

"We'll see," Synite tells his fair lady.

She scoffs, "That always means 'No'! Don't tell me that!"

"Really, seriously, I'll think about it. Driven and I can take a look around and see if anything would happen and I'll let you know what we think," Synite does not want to tell her that they cannot go so he will do his best to find a way for her.

"Thank you so much! I love you!" She hops into his arms and puts her hands behind his head. She pulls his face to her and gives him a quick smooch before she hops down.

"I love you, Sarah," Synite responds, then thinks of what Kraa-Nuve would say next: "now what do you want to eat?"

Driven takes a bit longer than Synite and Promis to get going in the morning and he prefers silence for at least the first half hecu of his day. Fortunately, the floor that they are occupying is uninhabited besides the condos he reserved for everyone. He had his apartment in particular soundproofed to keep Promis's music, Yelsh and Hemmen's arguing, Kraa-Nuve's morning sickness and Captain Grujek's terrible singing out of his morning routine. Even if a peep did get through, he could always shut his hearing off internally and not care.

Amethyst did the opposite and opened all of her vents since she does not mind listening to the early bustle of the District and their building. It reminds her that friends are around doing what they want to do, not what someone commands or pays them to do. That is enough to keep her from complaining throughout the days. She steps out to her balcony and notices the curtains blowing from inside Synite and Promis's living room as she is two doors over from them and right next to Kraa-Nuve. She harks their voices in the Air over the constant noise of the Naz District.

"Crazy," Kraa-Nuve sits next to Captain Grujek on a balcony as they both look down at Yelsh and Hemmen argue about what they want to eat. "How work?"

"I still dunno, be honess," Grujek gulps his morning energy drink. "Dey kno wha each otha's bout to say, but still find a ways ta argya! Ion git it!"

"Fight self?" Kraa-Nuve grunts and snorts. "Only way."

Grujek nods a bit, "S'posin' so. Jes lookin' crazier if ya do it aloud, ya kno Nuvie?"

"Know Gruj!" Kraa-Nuve has a laugh watching the twins go back and forth.

"Dey's good kids tho. Dunno what I do without 'em," he sips his drink.

"Love mine," Kraa-Nuve thinks about his own children and knows he probably would have killed a couple of them by now had they been on the ship with him. "Can't say same!"

"Ain't e'en kno Nuvie had kids," Grujek's culture is much more oriented for traditional family circles. "What 'bout woman?"

"With kids," the captains bond. "Your?"

"Her passed on when my boys was born. I miss the gal," Captain Grujek thinks of Mrs. Grujek. "Use ta look at my boys like twas dey fault her died but kid cain't choosin' ta be birthed. So, I deals."

Kraa-Nuve puts his head down, his way of showing condolences, and then looks back up to say: "Good father." They spend much of the morning talking about things they wish they could talk about more often considering their usual preoccupations that keep them from building new relationships.

"I's truly lookin' forwards to flyin' nex to ya, Nuvie," he taps Kraa-Nuve's elbow as he is too short to reach that high, spiny back.

"Same." Kraa-Nuve has not felt this type of mutual respect since his last crew was around. Kraa-Nuve remarks that he actually has not actually felt this much about anything in a long time, considering his budding friendship with Synite, a fellow captain in Grujek and how entertained he is by Driven.

There is also the noise of anticipation in the Sword for the announcement of the majority choice. "Hot wins," the announcer tells with no excitement, "and the Nortghard team gets the majority choice." Zark goes back to his teammates after nodding at Castra Nim, ready to input their choice for who starts on the Atlan team.

Above the middle of the arena, there are four empty frames going around resembling a carousel that shows which warriors are to start the match. The first being to pop up in a frame is Lone, which is not surprising to Atlan's team considering he is the least experienced in battle. Once Castra lost the majority choice, he knew Lone would be going in first but was not quite sure who he would be going in with.

Next, Zark puts himself in the beginning of the match. Castra looks back at Lone who goes through a stretching routine and hops up and down to warm up his legs more. Castra cannot tell if he is nervous but he showed extreme confidence in the royale last cycle, so this should not be much different. "Go on ahead," Lo tells him. "Let the crowd see you're ready!"

Lone nods and bounces out past Castra Nim into the arena, catching the eyes of millions but only concerned with the four he is to face soon.

Lo comes next to Castra and they stand proudly, awaiting the next announcement. "I think it'll be you," Lo smirks. "They want the two weakest out first."

"Well," Castra chuckles a bit, "they should've picked you before

Lone then, lowlander!"

"It's not about where you're from," Lo pokes back, "considering the womb you slithered out of!"

He gives a single guffaw, "I guess it's not about where you're at either since, you know, you couldn't make it in the PC by yourself. You'd be sitting around bored, making no Marks if I hadn't come to save you!"

The next face to come in a frame is Wik from the Nortghard team. Neither Castra nor Lo are paying any attention as they go back and forth with jokes to raise each other's spirit, knowing the liability Lone might be with Zark out there. Now, with Wik in the early mix, they are going to have their hands full as he is known for his powerful brain.

Wik, born and raised in Nortghard, had always wanted to be a fighter but his parents would never let him. Wik was certified as a genius at a very young age, noting that his brainpower extended past intelligence and into being able to physically control his body. He learned how to heal his own wounds by sheer thought before he was ten cycles old.

His parents, at the order of his overbearing mother, sheltered him as much as they possibly could and it showed as soon as he left after graduating secondary school at fifteen. He forewent his college career and, instead, enlisted in a program study for geniuses to experiment and develop each other. In the beginning, Wik was blown away with the things the brain was capable of on its own but, as most extreme geniuses do, he got bored. Granted, being able to compute complex scientific ideas in secs instead of hecu was great but he definitely knew there was more to accomplish.

So, he went to find beings similar to him that could manifest things by pure thought and ended up in a league of beings who claimed they could read minds. He spent very little time with them considering they were not actual telepaths but, as he left one of their meetings in frustration, he found himself being led by a voice in his mind. Sixteen-cycle-old Wik followed the voice to the basement of what looked like an abandoned building but ended up being the entrance to an underground network of apartment homes.

An elderly man met Wik in the courtyard of the entrance to this underground township and explained to him that he was the one leading Wik here through telepathy. He was so excited by this that he hugged the old man as he welcomed Wik home.

The old man, named Junz, took Wik under his wing and taught him how to connect with other's minds, delve deep in their psyches and to control the urge to destroy despite giving him the tools to do so. Wik could not get enough and exercised his mind so much that he was looked at as too advanced to stay in the township. The thing about telepaths is that, especially at their level, it is difficult for them to coexist. It is similar to how beings with high levels of certain chemical compounds, estrogen or testosterone, find it difficult to coexist with each other. The township was full of lower-level telepaths that got along well as they were not trying to out-do each other and absolutely wanted to be normal amongst beings akin to themselves.

Wik, however, strived for more and more and, after coming in conflict with Junz on too many occasions, he was asked to leave the township, which he did without hesitation.

He trained himself to dig into people's minds and quickly became an outcast of society, falling into the hands of the Nortghard authorities. He was ultimately sent to several different jails for several different reasons until a psychiatrist figured out his problem. He was sent to a psychiatric hospital and isolated for ten cycles until his abilities caught the attention of an arena team manager. He was pardoned, trained, and put into the Nortghard arena system where his mental prowess was accepted and praised.

Now, not only will he be challenged in battle, but he will have to understand his role as a team member. It has been difficult for him thus far to not go outside of the team plan, but he made the dedication to himself to win and then show his parents what a success he has become since leaving home. He joins Zark out on the black sand, his bald head shining above his hairy face.

Promis on his back, Synite lands on the top of their building after a half-hecu of flying her around. When they touchdown, she continues to embrace him and holds on tight. He turns to face her and return the endearment.

While they were in the Air, she asked him, "You know, I was wondering…what happens to the environment when you do some big wind and storm stuff?"

"What do you mean?" Synite was not sure what she meant about environment. "I'm part of it."

"I mean, there has to be some kind of residual damage when you manipulate the weather," she looked into the sky. "It takes a lot of time and buildup for natural tornadoes and hurricanes and storms and stuff to develop. If you throw a tornado down, doesn't it change the natural wind patterns and how the weather would be normally?"

"That's the thing," Synite explained. "My manipulation of it is like throwing a rock into a river. It might knock some things around and make a couple of ripples but only for a very short time." He chuckled a little bit, "You're either giving me too much credit or not giving nature enough."

She still questioned, "So, it depends on how long you use it?"

"If I were to put myself in tune with nature," he put a little more thought into it, "I could probably strengthen or weaken some of the occurrences that are already going to come up like tropical storms and similar phenomena, but that would take some practice and a lot of power." *Now that she mentions it, I kind of want to try it at some point. Maybe later.*

As they head back into the condominiums, "I love it here!" she exclaims. "I think I may want to stay here for the rest of my life. I know we haven't been here long enough to actually know how it is but," she looks up at him, "it feels like everything I've ever desired!"

"It is very different from everywhere I've ever been and it is a very nice place," he concurs. "I see why Driven and Grujek come here so often minus the whole not eating meat thing."

"But wait," she loosens her grip a little, "if there is no money here, why do they come here to sell things? There's no war. So who is he selling guns to?"

"I asked the same thing," Synite smiles. "Some of his clients simply enjoy meeting here because it's so obscure and probably the safest place in any galaxy."

"That's another thing I'm confused about," Promis's brow wrinkled. She poses the question to Driven over dinner as Synite did not have the answer for her after their flight. "What's keeping somebody, the Enslaver or worse, from coming here and sucking this planet dry of resources? It's ripe for one being with enough firepower to come take it over."

"I found this planet through of a network of war generals from several different systems who protect this land as they would their home," Driven explains. "Many of them retire here after their military careers end. Even some beings on opposite sides of a war retire here together. They know the rules of the game and that grand illusion disappears when it ends."

"You must genuinely trust us to have brought us here," Synite appreciates being here even more knowing that there can be no violence. It is a perfect departure from the life of violence on Earth 11.

"I mean, since you got out of a little war or two not long ago, I doubt you want to wreck a peaceful planet," Driven laughs while he tinkers with some smaller items from the ship and Synite nods very matter-of-factly with a smile on his face. He is not one to use trust as it can come back and bite even the most cunning of warriors.

"I think I'll go into town tomorrow and pick up a few things," Promis tells the boys. "We can have a party for Cystcel, too!"

"I think you'll want to come with me to the big ones with the Regency, too," Driven gets invited every cycle. "I already put everyone on my guest list!"

"I'll still want to go get something to wear," where there is a Will to shop, Promis finds a way. "Is it formal?"

Driven shakes his head, "Not at all! I wouldn't be going if it was!"

"I'll get a few options so I don't look out of place then," she decides. "Straight away."

"Don't forget your communicator and I'll let Desha know you want to go," Synite knows not to let her go alone. "I'm sure she does, too. Their schedule shouldn't be too tight."

"I don't think I need an escort," Promis would rather roam about freely than have to keep up with those two, "especially since I know you don't want to go. I'll be okay!"

"We already agreed on the way here that nobody would travel alone except Driven and that's only because he has a home here. The Enslaver isn't looking for him," the conflict continues.

She fails to understand the problem, "All this because I want to go shopping and have a moment to myself?"

"Let's not forget that there are still prices on our heads, Sarah," Synite reminds her. "Free does not mean reckless."

"Whatever," she scoffs and drops the conversation, the touch of normalcy getting to be too much for her, or not enough rather. "I'll ask her myself. I hope I don't walk in on them again."

"You too?" Driven gives a hearty round of hoots. "Man! Those two," he keeps his comment to himself.

"We have walked…"

"…in on them…"

"…once before too…"

"…and we never…"

"…knew people could…"

"…move that fast!" the twins add more to the queue of jokes at Proximity and Desha's expense.

"They are blindingly fast. Almost so much that I want to rip my eyes out," Synite snickers.

"At least come…"

"…burn the image…"

"…from our brains," Yelsh points at Hemmen's forehead and Hemmen knocks his hand away.

"Wait, wait," Driven goes over to them. "You said brains. You have separate brains? See! You do learn something new every day," Driven snaps and walks out between them.

"One of our…"

"…brains equals two…"

"…of yours, Driveena."

"So, we actually …"

"…are four times…"

"…smarter than you!" they yell down the hall after him. Synite and Promis share a drink of nectar, enjoying the dynamic of comedy between the bunch of them.

"You're clearly a bad person," Castra has run out of comebacks for Lo just in time. The final face comes up and it is his. "I guess they really do want to get it over with!"

"Just don't die," Lo tells him in a joking tone, knowing full well that the truth is usually said in jest. They have become good friends outside of being teammates and would rather not see one another perish.

Castra looks back and shrugs, "Gotta go sometime, right?"

"Shut up and get out there!" Lo points towards Lone. "And stay alive! You still owe me four hundred Marks!"

Castra palms his own face, "I thought you forgot about that! I might have to die on purpose--"

"Win and I'll forget about it, Castra!" Lo claps and points out again with a bit more intent than before.

Castra Nim meets Lone in the middle of the arena across from Zark and Wik, his wheels turning already. He can tell by how Zark is out in front that he wants to be the aggressor, or at least looking to kill first and probably protect Wik from the melee. Then, he sees Wik touch his temples with both index fingers. "Don't look that one in the eye," he whispers over to Lone. "He's a telepath and doesn't want hands. Let's focus on the big one first."

Lone nods, confident in himself and his captain's leadership as they wait for the announcement. Castra looks around at his favorite places to escape and trap, counting his blades. He does some geometry in his head, accounts for Lone's skills and feels completely ready. "And it begins!" the announcer proclaims.

Zark and Wik look each other in the eye and Zark's posture changes. Wik steps backwards slowly as Zark flexes and moves, his fighting technique recognizable to the Atlan team as new-style capoeira. It is an adaptation of the old fighting style that utilized constant motion and dance. New-style is less dance-oriented and much more deadly but has similar strikes.

Before Castra could blink again, Zark attempts a leg sweep that Lone is fast enough to jump over. Lone kicks down at the powerhouse and strikes his shoulder, only to bounce off of him and push Castra out of the way of a strong, swinging punch that heads his direction. Lone jolts towards Zark, behind him, and slashes across his back. Zark responds with a spinning back-hand of his own, knocking Lone across into one of the pillars in the center of the arena.

Castra charges a knife and gets in an aggressive stance but, before he can move to attack, Zark is in his face, ready for a roundhouse kick. "You're dead little man!" Zark threatens but Lone pushes off the same pillar he was whacked into and meets Zark's foot in the Air with his own.

Castra rolls back out of the way, feeling as slow as ever considering the pace Lone and Zark are fighting. He tries to keep up with them, watching from a few meters away as Lone compensates for his lack of size and strength with his amazing quickness. Castra has seen him move fast before but not quite to this blurring speed. Lone does a backflip and ends up next to him, pulls the knife from the captain's hand and heads back into the fray.

Three days prior, Lone had done the same thing in a spar against Lo when he tried to get an advantage. In that spar, he threw the knife in the Air which caused Lo to look away for a moment, knowing Castra's teleportation abilities. Lone got the advantage for the moment but Lo outlasted him. The knife was not charged so Castra could not have teleported through it but that moment of hesitation was enough for Lone.

They talked about it afterwards and Lone asked if, given the opportunity, he would mind using it the correct way and teleporting through. His response was simple: "Give me a signal!"

Lone actually fights with the charged knife against Zark for a few swings before Zark knocks it from his hand. He swings heavily at Lone's weaker arm, stepping over the still glowing knife. Lone twists and takes the hit with his stronger arm, surprised at how powerful the punch is and glad it did not break his arm.

Lone slides a couple meters across the sand before he gets back to his feet and winks at Castra. *I guess that's a signal!* Castra reaches for his shortsword, teleports to the knife, and slashes Zark across the back perpendicular to the slashes Lone had already made. Zark yells loudly at the deeper cut and swings around to give Castra a furious elbow. Castra was already low from the position he swung the blade, so Zark is surprised that he only swings through empty Air. Lone storms in and charges Zark with his forearms in the center of all his posterior gashes.

The pain shoots through Zark's body but his connection with Wik deadens it immediately. He stumbles into Castra who rolls backwards and throws Zark down. He puts the shortsword away and sweeps at Zark's head but misses as the Superathlete rolls out of his foot's way.

Lone joins Castra and they both get in an attack stance, ready for the next stage of the fight. "We hurt him a little," Castra remarks. "That move was brilliant!"

"You catch on quick," Lone dashes off before his captain can respond.

"I wonder if he'll want to try it again," Castra thinks aloud as he grabs another knife and charges it. "Two down, six to go."

CHAPTER III

Driven has been in the armory of the Pingar for quite some time now as he prepares the shipment for his meeting. Putting things together is usually one of his favorite pastimes but this particular order is very specific and needs more attention than usual. He still enjoys the scrupulousness of it though, considering the amount of Marks he anticipates earning from putting in his signature style.

Synite asked if he could take over for Yelsh and Hemmen in assisting Driven with the packaging, trying to stay busy and keep his mind off all the loss and stress they have been through since leaving Earth 11. It has been a task finding something to occupy himself so his mind does not drift too far. However, sitting and watching Driven put the finishing touches on his metallic casings, Synite's mind still wanders as he wonders what more there is in his future. Something about the meticulous way Driven works reminds him that he has to stay conscientious too, in case they do meet danger. "When are we going back to that gym?"

"After the parties," Driven does not look away from his progress. "Got the itch huh?"

"You can say that," Synite has no idea what to call it but that suffices. "Why don't you live here permanently?"

Driven has toiled over this over and over again over a dozen times, "I don't want to get too settled. I get stir crazy in places like this. I'd get sucked into doing the same thing every day and that's not how I want to live! My father told me before he died that I need to experience as much as I can because that's what the verses are here for."

"Wait," Synite had not known about this connection between them. He remembers Kraa-Nuve asking him about his name but, "Your father died?"

"That's what they told me," Driven recalls an elder bringing him the news and his own futile search afterwards. "I never saw his body or anything. He just didn't come back one time. We all assumed so since we couldn't find his ship's signal either."

"Mine was killed right in front of me, which is a huge reason I'm here," Synite laments but speaks of Cairo, Sr. with pride and respect. "I'm fortunate to have had him as long as I did though, with him being a police officer and all."

All of this conversing is keeping Driven from being as productive as he could be, "Mine was a General in the military so he didn't stay around very much," he zones in on a small detail and lets out a sigh of satisfaction when he hits it perfectly, "especially after I learned how to take care of myself. That might be another reason I'm not partial to sitting still," Driven laughs lightly to himself at the epiphany and preps his next uprade. "And my ma died when I was about twelve cycles. She wasn't around much either anyway, but I remember her arguing with my dad a lot. She was super passionate and they definitely loved each other but they split up before she died."

"Your mom wasn't around either?" Synite gathered from him saying he had to take care of himself. "Are you sure we aren't the same person?"

"Last time I checked, I was a one-of-one," Driven does not know of anyone else who has a full-integration with Borganics, especially not on his level. "I'm sure there are plenty of orphans out there. Wasn't your buddy Psilos's dad knocked off in that war, too?"

"Yeah, and I never heard him mention a mother," Synite remarks. "Well, aren't we a wild bunch of misfits?!"

Driven locks up his packages and comes out into the foyer with Synite. "You haven't seen wild yet! Tonight is going to be one for the lightcycles!"

They go back and meet up with everyone for the pre-party before taking it to the streets of Neo District to partake in the grandest of Cystcel events. This is the first time in a very long time that Cairo, Jr. could relax and have a night of careless fun with friends. There is a formal countdown for the new cycle in the District quadrangle; there are dozens of night parades that go from one block party to the next, growing in number as the night goes along; there are tons of firework displays and other pyrotechnic stunts. Everything is loud, exciting and packed with beings from all over the planet and system. Neo District is known to have the biggest celebrations on Yar JK, which is why Driven goes to them, and they did not disappoint. The premier day of the new cycle is nearly half gone before they all make it back to the condos, some coming in a little later than others.

Lo is proud of his team thus far, not itching to join in quite yet. He crosses his arms and picks his teeth some, wondering what the others will want for dinner after this match is over. Lone usually challenges him to see how many buffet plates they can put down consecutively before they cannot eat anymore. *As small as the kid is, he can certainly put some food away!* As a result, Lo thinks to himself about when Lone should take the wrapping off of his face and get loose.

And Lone actually speeds up a little after working off that huge meal they had before getting into the training area. He is deep into the fight, going toe-to-toe with Zark now, doing a great job predicting his opponent's movements, watching his eyes and hips to see where he is going and where he wants to go for his next move. Castra edges into the fight, trying to find a good spot to jump in that should give their team the advantage as opposed to hindering Lone's progress. It is difficult since he does not see what Lone sees and does not want to guess the next move; their actions are entirely too quick for him but this actually informs him of what his next objective should be.

Castra throws caution to the wind and hurtles in. Lone slides past him, causing him to pull up on his attack. Oblivious to the pain that Wik fights off for him, Zark runs at Castra, switching between clashes with the two fighters without hesitation. Lone flips over Castra's head, grabs an un-charged knife with his foot, lets it go at the top of his rotation, and catches it with his weak hand. He and Zark joust, Zark with a punch and Lone with the lifted knife.

Lone stabs his opponent in the shoulder, pulling the knife right back out as they pass each other. Zark was going to swing back at him but Wik could not deaden the pain in his shoulder early enough for him to want to push that direction. Wik has already been deadening the pain of stress from using his muscles so recklessly. Normally, at the pace they have been moving, Zark would have at least needed to break for a moment but not with Wik's mental and pain-blocking assistance. This was their plan for the entire match as it has worked extremely well in simulations but here, against the live Atlan team, things are more difficult.

Zark turns and goes at Lo again, no pain in his mind anymore, and grabs his arms at the wrists. "Can't run now!"

Lone drops the knife and watches Zark's reaction. His eyes move down to look at the dry knife barely long enough for Lone to uppercut kick him directly in the chin. Zark releases his grip and Lone is able to flip away. From the corner, Lo chuckles, glad he was not the only one to fall for that move. "Can't keep a good fighter down!"

Zark roars in frustration, letting it all hang out. A single, heavy tear falls from his left eye and plops in the sand. He wipes it away and smiles a harsh, sinister grin in Lone's direction. Lone rips off his facial wraps and smiles back, his grotesque snarling teeth shining with their red metallic sheen, taking much of the crowd off guard. Castra and Lo are the only ones in the entire world who have seen that spit-dripping smile, enthralled by the reactions of everyone and how similar the Oohs and Aahs are to their own initial sight of it.

"Yep," Castra says as he looks at his teammate for a moment, "still gross!"

Lone's red-plated teeth are in every imaginable direction, his dark gums sweating and his thick, forked tongue, matching the grayed resin around his teeth, slides across his smile. His eyes immediately become more intense and he howls back at Zark in response to his yell. His thin, yellowish lips are unable to cover his intimidating grill so the noise that comes out has absolutely no aesthetic.

"Besides how generally ugly it is," he told Lo and Castra the first time, "I can't close my mouth all the way so I had to put something over it when I was training. I had to make sure I wasn't swallowing debris all day, you know." After the initial shock of seeing a face that only a mother could appreciate, they agreed to not make too many jokes about it in his presence as that would be a distraction for Lone. However, when Castra and Lo had a little time to themselves, they had to let the pinned-up queue of jokes fly one after another for over half an hecu of tense abdominals and corner tears.

Now, they appreciate that shock factor and what it adds to their team's intimidation and initiative. Castra uses that moment to throw his charged knife right next to the dud lying by Zark. He takes the bait and goes to stomp the knife which explodes in an orange flash under his foot, burning the bottom of it. Castra sees beads of sweat fall down Wik's forehead onto his brow, not knowing what he is doing but still knowing to stop at that brow before he looks into the guy's eyes.

"I forgot Castra could explode those things," Lo says. "Genius." Castra points and laughs at Zark who gets as angry as he has ever been. Wik is doing his best to temper the monster but it is taking a lot of mental strength to deaden his emotions along with the pain coursing through his body. "This fool!" Lo laughs at Castra's contagious, high-pitched chortle and tittering.

Much of the crowd joins in the laughter, Castra slyly peeking at Wik's forehead as Zark's embarrassment rises. He can tell Wik is trying harder and harder to calm his teammate from within but it does not work and he has to let go. Wik drops to his knees, gasping and looks up, waiting for an opportunity to enter Zark's mind again.

The rush of anger and pain blankets Zark immediately and his composure completely goes out of the window. He rushes Lone, limping from the pain of his foot, much slower than he was before. Of course Lone notices and takes full advantage, dodging and then punching Zark in the nose with his strong fist. The punch turns him around, away from Wik's eyesight, and Lone claws his back again; Zark arches and grabs his back in pain, stumbling forward and laboring to breathe. He drops to one knee, his eyes lowered.

Castra runs at him, trying his best not to slip in the sand while he focuses on charging another knife. Zark gets back to his feet and, when Castra slashes, he kicks the charged knife away from him. He goes for a haymaker to Castra's face but punches through an orange mist. Before he can recover, Lone is on his back. He bites the back of Zark's neck and clenches down as hard as he can, harder even through the poor man's screams. Zark starts to flail as any being's fight or flight response would make them do, but it is too late. Lone grabs him with his claw for better balance and more pain.

Soon, Zark cannot take anymore so he drops to the ground, fading from consciousness and into the death he had so longed for. Lone cleans his mouth with his clawless hand as he gets up from the cooling corpse. Lone turns to look for where Castra is and, instead of finding his captain, everything goes black.

Promis wakes up that evening to see Synite's back, still groggy from the disruption of her semi-established sleep pattern. She does not hesitate to rub her hand across his shoulder and up the back of his neck as she is sure he is awake since he never truly sleeps anyway. He does not respond immediately but soon touches her knee with his hand. "What time is it?" She cannot tell since their balcony curtains are closed.

"Fifteen something," Synite had been up, had a bite to eat and gotten back in bed without waking her. "You snored louder than ever today."

"No way!" Promis thumps him on the back of the head. "I don't snore!"

"Keep believing that," he says as he looks back out of the corner of his eye. "Did you enjoy yourself?"

"It was too much fun! It has been so long since I could relax and let loose," she thinks the last time was her last date with Vincent. For a moment, she wonders how he is making it. "How about you?"

"Same," he thinks that it was fun but he does not get very much fulfillment from partaking in events similar to that. He is a trained warrior now and cannot help his new life. If it is not some sort of challenge or contest, it is difficult for him to honestly enjoy himself. "It's different for me, you know? I'm so used to all of the danger--"

"But that's not something we have to worry about anymore," she pulls herself closer and wraps her arms and legs around him. Despite these things being what most would call normal, Synite cannot help his feelings; he knows there has to be more than only this, feeling the pull of something powerful close to him. He cannot put his finger on it but he knows something different is near. Promis does her best to distract him from all these thoughts temporarily without much struggle. "Have you ever lived alone?"

"I went to boarding school," Synite reminds her. "We lived in dormitories but we were in apartments by ourselves. I had to pay bills and stuff with tuition money every month. Then I went to the loft attached to the Sword. So, yeah. You?"

"My sister and I have an apartment together at home but I'm usually not there obviously," as Synite could tell. "I've never had a permanent place of my own but I've taken care of myself for so long, I'm not even sure I could live with her or anyone anymore. I love her to death but I'm sure we'd kill each other," she laughs. "I send money to her thumb to make sure we split everything. She's the only one who really lives there but I'm not going to make her pay for it alone."

"Why did you ask that, Sarah?" Synite inquires.

Promis explains, eyes closed: "I wanted to know how you lived before now because, you know, you never actually know yourself until you've lived by yourself."

"I understand," Synite says, "I think I know myself pretty completely." And they rest, continuing to enjoy each other for the time being.

Driven, Grujek and Kraa-Nuve are already back to work on the Caracalla, the Pingar's crew showing their new fellow how to improve his weapon output without having to sacrifice much energy from other places in the ship. Kraa-Nuve and the Caracalla reciprocate by updating the flight systems of the Pingar to the version they use. Kraa-Nuve calls Synite to join them and they spend much of the next few days teaching each other codes, controls and shortcuts for their respective new systems.

"I'm taking one of the cars out in the morning, cappie-tan," Driven tells Grujek. "Town is about a hundred K-Ms from here. They want to meet before the exchange to make sure everything is copasetic. Should be a breeze."

Grujek nods to agree and continues the work he is doing as Synite comes around, "You mind if I come with you?"

"Sure, man. I hope you don't mind how I drive, though!" Driven gives Synite some new clothes from the closet of the Pingar for the drive. The sun is still down when they leave and, although Synite can barely see anything, Driven is speeding up the highway into town in his roadster. "I call her The Harbinger. She's one of my favorites," he has to yell over the exhaust and wind noise.

After a long silence between the two, Synite yells back: "What's under the hood?"

Driven grins, "Nothing too major: rambunctious five-turbo sync with supercharged electric motor, 7102 cubic-centimeter V10 wet engine, magnetic torque adjustments, rebuilt the carbon casings, cams, headers, boxed the pistons, and etcetera. It'll get us there."

"Yeah, nothing too major!" his sarcasm amuses Synite. "How long did it take to build?"

"A few cycles, on-and-off," Driven is very proud of his ability to enhance anything that has gears and is always excited to talk about it. "Can you drive?"

Synite had only just started learning how to drive before he was taken from Earth Prime but never learned how to operate a manual transmission. "Nothing like this!"

"Oh, man it's easy!" Driven pulls over into a large, empty lot and they switch places, Driven offering his teaching skills. "We have plenty of time so don't rush and don't worry about breaking anything. I could rebuild this whole car in a quarter cycle." It only takes Synite about a half hecu to get used to it, so Driven lets him drive the rest of the way. "I bet you want one now, right?"

"Do I?" Synite laughs. "Man does this thing go! My dad's car was stock and pretty boring. Plus, everything was automatic. I love the feel of this kind of manual control."

That is exactly why Driven built it that way; and, to get the attention that they are getting now as they pull into town, turning heads. "It's great, man. We're going to build you one when we get to a planet that has better supplies."

"Have you ever flown freely before?" Driving a car like this one is a distant second to flying for Synite.

"I've jumped out of plenty aircraft," Driven has never been afraid to live and is not afraid to die, preferring death over a life not worth living. This is something that his father drilled in him from a very young age. "Never been out flying without a cockpit though!"

"We'll go soon," Synite offers. "I have to pay you back for this!"

Driven shouts over the exhaust: "Yes!"

"No!" Castra yells across at Lone who is already frozen with a blank mind. He caught Wik's eye for a fraction of a sec and immediately was taken by his locking telepathy. "Let him go!" Castra yells without looking at Wik.

"I see you're the smart one," Wik smiles back.

"Two eins!" the announcement rings over the entire arena. "At the death of Zark, the Atlan team has two eins to end the battle by killing or making Wik surrender! With Lone frozen from Wik's powerful mind, what can Castra do to save his teammate?"

He runs in Wik's direction yelling, "I said let him go!"

"It's too late," Wik looks for the first opportunity to freeze Castra as well. "I'm not monitoring him. I knocked him out. Once it's done, it cannot be reversed. He's sound asleep now!"

Castra does a wonderful job avoiding eye contact. He fakes a straight jab and puts his other fist into Wik's cheek. "Maybe when your eyes are swollen enough to where you can't see, you'll let him go!"

The punch nearly knocks the genius out of Wik but he remains under control. Castra kicks him in the gut while he is bent over from the punch. Wik laughs at Castra's wild fighting until he catches a boot to the same jaw that was punched. He looks up at the clock that is swiftly approaching one ein, not knowing what to do to help the situation besides knock Wik out as quickly as possible as that may release his teammate.

Castra beats up on Wik as best he can, pummeling the brainiac to no avail. The moment he looks up to check the clock again, which is down below one ein now, Wik makes a mad dash away from him, stealing precious time away from the Atlan team and Lone's lifespan. Arra, the young fire elementalist and third member of the Nortghard team, is at her gate ready to storm in.

And so Castra gives chase to Wik. He is slower than he needs to be, however, and cannot catch up to the telepath, which surprises him at first but it makes sense on second thought. For someone who cannot hold a great hand-to-hand fight, it is smart for him to be able to run away. So, he charges two knives and throws the second one down by Arra's entrance. He throws the first one out in front of Wik and meets him with a clothesline.

Wik stands quickly and tries to catch Castra's eye but misses, Castra noticing next to the sheepish grin that Wik's face does not have a scratch on it from the beating he put down. *He heals fast, too? I guess that's why he has made it this far! He planned this out very, very well. Maybe we should have scouted more. Maybe we could have been more prepared.* And, to make matters even worse, he only has one charge left besides the one glowing next to Arra's entrance gate.

"Man to man," Castra says, "you're the greatest intellect I have ever faced. But that won't be enough," he preaches as he dashes over to Lone.

"Here she comes in three, two," the announcer counts down, "one!" A buzzer goes off as her gate opens.

He tackles Lone and they roll as the knife explodes at Arra's first step into the arena. It does not faze her but she uses its percussive force to go high into the Air. "Firefall!" she yells as a wave of green flames ignites from thin air and crashes down in their direction. Castra gets up and runs off and the flames go over Lone. Castra gets far enough away to not get burned and he does not look back as there is nothing to look at. There is nothing left of Lone's body where the green fire poured down.

A fury gathers in Lo at the sight. He yells from behind the glass and gets even angrier as the two-ein clock pops up. A dark blue pattern of thick lines spreads across his face as his anger swells. The crowd yells and jeers at the death of a member of their team who fought so well against the earlier opponent. For him to go out like that was not something anyone would have expected and they are almost as angry as Lo now. They yell expletives in a hundred different tongues at the Nortghard scum.

Wik revels in it though, readying his freezing technique for when Castra slips up as he is completely confident the Atlan captain will. He is forced to do the same thing Wik did and run from the kelly flames that dance around the area. It gets so intense that some of the sand hardens and collects. It is not as powerful as Synite's lightning that turned it to glass, but it reminds some of the faithful crowd of their old champion and their currently mixed feelings about him.

Castra gets behind one of the pillars, huffing from being so winded, and she blasts a barrage of fire at it. It splits the pole and misses Castra but the heatwave certainly does not. He cannot stand it long so he runs as fast as he can up the flaming V created by the pillar. Arra's fire burns through the base of the pillar and it falls in her direction. She strafes out of the way and gathers herself for another attack. She rolls up a bunch of fireballs and tosses them at Castra, the green flares dropping as non-explosive grenades. They are so intensely hot that he urgently dodges every single one of them. One gets close enough to give him a slight burn on his arm but his adrenaline kept him away.

His back is to Lo's entrance as a crescent-shaped firewave Arra calls her Green Inferno barreling towards him. He stands there, eye's closed and hands on his knees, as he is too tired to run anymore. And, even if he did, he would not make it past the edge of the inferno. Then it gets warmer and warmer, nearly unbearably. *Luckily my eyebrows are so light nobody can tell I have any, or else they would be burning off right now!*

The edges of the Green Inferno crash into the wall of the arena behind Castra, rumbling along like a stampede of green bulls. Then, suddenly, everything goes dark and cold for him. Castra slowly opens one eye and looks around, relieved but not quite sure whether he is dead or not. He exhales and his breath creates fog in front of him. "I guess I'm alive if I'm breathing, right?"

"Yes, idiot. You're still alive," the voice from behind him echoes through the igloo.

Castra turns around to Lo, arms crossed and brow crunched under the blue war pattern on his face. "Dude, what took you so long? The clock ran out five secs ago!"

"I wanted you to feel that heat," Lo keeps his serious tone but continues the jokes. "Can we finish this? I'm damned pissed off."

"Good," Castra tells him. "Channel it so we can get out of here. Too much of this sand is getting in my shoes."

Lo steps up next to him and he stands up, ready to finish the job. "You can stay down. I'll cut them down by myself." Lo is all about fulfilling vengeance as soon as possible.

Castra scoffs, "But, I want some action too!"

"You've done enough," Lo says sarcastically. "I think the fire is over."

"That green fire is pretty cool, ain't it?" Castra thinks about this statement after he spits it out. "Not cool but…you know what I mean!"

"Shut up and come on," Lo puffs out, and shatters the ice with his elbow. More fire comes and he keeps blocking it with his polar bear shield. He pulls out the hydra spear and, as soon as the fire stops, he blasts Arra with a jet of water, knocking her into the downed pillar.

Lo runs at Arra with the roar of his black lion sword as it grows from the dagger length to the meter length blade. He deflects the fireballs she throws at him and gets close enough to force her to dodge his slashes, swinging with concentration and the sword snarling with each pass. She is much less dangerous from close range as most of her fire misses wildly and Lo misses, cutting a chunk out of the pillar behind her.

Castra pulls his shortsword out and goes after Wik whose eyes are getting red as his brain is tiring out. His movements are sluggish but he still concentrates on trying to get that moment of eye contact. He can tell it is not going to work against Castra before he gets close enough to cut him, so he gets up and moves laterally around the edge of the arena. He keeps Castra's face in his sight and his back to the wall.

Instead of shooting blasts of fire at Lo, Arra puts a trail of the green flames behind her punches and kicks. This puts Lo a step back out of range for his sword so he sheathes it as he spins away from one of her kicks and pulls his spear out. It lengthens with the screech of a hydra to almost three meters and gives him the advantage. He keeps his shield on his forearm in case she decides to start blasting again, which is exactly what she does as they have backed off from each other. Her blasts are in the vein of streams from a military class flamethrower, both in pattern and intensity. Lo is fortunate that none of his weapons or clothing are flammable, especially not the weapons, but it is getting very hot as their fight heats up.

Lo sees Castra running after Wik in a beeline towards the same spot in the wall that Arra is backing him into. As he runs, he nods up at Lo and gives him a gesture to switch with him. The moment they get close enough to do so, Lo rolls away from the forest of fire being blasted in his direction and blindsides Wik with his shield.

Arra immediately stops firing in their direction as she does not want to incinerate her own teammate. And, in her moment of indecision, Castra Nim blindsides her in the back of the head with the hilt of his shortsword. The crowd bursts with excitement as their team gets the advantage again.

Wik gathers himself and Arra begins to fire at Castra again, the flames flashing brightly but not connecting as he is too close. Lo turns sideways and covers his eyes with his shield, but can still see Wik's feet. Lo gets the hydra spear out and blasts a strong stream of water through the split at the bottom of his shield, forcing it to pass through freezing temperatures. This stream packs ice on Wik's feet and he works his way up all the way to his waist and hands, freezing him where he stands. He keeps his shield high as he jogs around until he gets behind the telepath. Lo pulls the shield up on his shoulder so it shrinks back down, puts the spear away so it shrinks down too, and puts the dagger to Wik's neck.

"That's how to freeze somebody," Lo tells Wik in a quietly angry tone. "Are you ready to die, my friend?"

"No! Arra!" Wik yells out, moving enough to where the blade knicks his throat. "Arra! Arra help!" She finally hears him and stops the attack with Castra.

Arra gathers a ball of fire under her hand but before it is useful enough, Castra tackles her from behind, her chest to the sand and looking up at possibly the last moments of her career as a fighter. Castra grabs a handful of her hair and puts his shortsword to the back of her neck. "Get off of me!"

Castra drops all his weight on her and pulls her hair a little tighter, "You'll be headless, too, lady. Shut up."

"Kill her!" Lo implores. "After what she did to Lone, you're hesitating?"

Castra looks up, "She was fighting exactly like you and I, Lo!"

"Let her go!" Wik yells.

Lo punches him in the face from behind, "You're not in a place to negotiate, so shut your mouth!" The cut he opens does not heal quickly as Wik's brain is tired and he cannot focus on healing with a sharp object a few centimeters away from taking his life.

The blade snarls as Lo's anger rises. "Get it over with, Castra!"

"Wait a second," the captain orders. "I see opportunity here. If both of you surrender, you will keep your lives but you only have one choice: you have to join the Atlan team."

"What did you say?" Lo's fury growls with the lion sword. "I'm killing him and coming over there and killing her too!"

"Stop, Lo!" Castra yells. "I'm the captain of this team and you won't be on it if you don't follow my orders!"

Lo grumbles to Wik, "You are lucky he's smarter than I am or else you'd both be dead already."

"You might as well kill me," Arra tells Castra. "I am not a traitor!"

Wik yells. "I surrender! I'll be on Atlan's team!"

The crowd breaks their silence as it collectively gasps at this development. "We have a team change for the first time in history in the first match in team battle history! The regulations state that any member is able to offer and accept team trades anytime during a battle but never before. This is monumentous!"

"Arra, listen to reason! We can live on," Wik tells his former teammate. "There is life outside of home!"

"Get it over with," she tells Castra, a tear in each of her eyes as they lock eyes with a child in the crowd. That child reminds Arra of her little sister back in Nortghard and her tears roll down even faster.

Arra is the oldest of three: next is her brother, Immo, who is only two cycles younger than her, and their baby sister, Yanna who is only two cycles old. They were poor but happy and had always gotten along until Immo scorned her for leaving home to fight while their mother was pregnant with Yanna. Her father died a few cycles after Immo was born and she left because she did not get along with Yanna's father, her mother's new husband.

Immo and their mother tried to get them to bury the hatchet but he was stubborn and she was not accepting of someone trying to replace her father. The stress from all of this conflict was heavy on their mother and she was in critical condition when Yanna was born. They could not afford very good healthcare so the clinicians that delivered Yanna were unable to save their mother.

Arra has not been able to go back home and still has not seen Yanna at all. She has no idea how her own sister looks but can only imagine her to resemble her younger self. She and Immo got the dominant elementalist gene from her father so she is positive Yanna is bound for a more peaceful life than her, especially considering the situation she is in.

"Wait," she tells Castra, barely able to squeeze out the words. She mumbles something that he can barely understand through the tears and her thick accent.

"What did you say?" Castra leans down.

"I want to see my sister before I die," Arra exhales and relaxes. "I surrender and will be a member of your team."

Castra takes the blade away and stands over her, yelling to Lo, "She surrendered, too. Let's get out of here."

Lo cannot believe it but understands that his role as a captain is to do more than slaughter their opponents. Their pockets grew tremendously as well as their team. They both sheathe their swords and head into the depths of the arena.

After their initiation into the team and contract signings, Castra takes Arra, Wik and Lo to the Weapon's Rack. "I don't use weapons," Arra tells her new captain.

"If you see something you want, pick it up. You have the choice. You don't have to get anything if you don't want to," Wik tells her, the tension between her and Lo still substantial.

"Everyone, follow me," Castra tells them as they enter. He nods at Fabric who was waiting on them at the entrance to the secret cache where Synite found Gale. Fabric lets them in and pats Castra Nim on the back as they enter.

"About time you got here," a burned blade is tossed across the room and Castra catches it with his left hand.

"I figured it would take you a couple of days to wake up," Castra tells Lone as he sits on the edge of one of the inventory tables.

Lo cannot believe his eyes and neither can Wik or Arra. "How are you alive?" Lo breaks the silence and goes over to Lone, hugging the kid like a brother. "You were burned to oblivion by that," Lo looks over at Arra, "her! How are you here right now?" Then Lo looks at Castra's grin and immediately knows the answer. "Oh, you're an asshole, you know that right?"

Castra goes over to the both of them and grabs their shoulders, "I couldn't tell you in front of the crowd because this is a serious violation of a whole bunch of rules. I had to wait until they signed the secrecy forms before I could bring everyone in. I didn't tell you before because I needed your anger to finish the fight. And I didn't tell you after because you waited so long to save me from that fire after the clock was up," Castra smiles wryly and looks over at the two newest members. "You and Arra can play nice now that you know she didn't ash our buddy, right?"

Lo looks over at the female Fire elementalist, "I guess we should take her to see her sister soon."

"I'm still a little confused," Arra tells Castra. "How did you do this? His mind was locked so there's no way he could've dodged. I saw my fires pummel him."

"No, you didn't," Castra tells her. "You saw your fire pummel empty sand. I teleported him here before the fire hit him. I had a safety blade charged and waiting in case something like this had to happen."

"You're a genius," Wik tells his captain. "Even I would never have thought of that!"

"I still got a few burns," Lone snickers, "and I'll be expecting some really good food since I'll be cooped up in here for a while."

"What do you mean?" Lo was ready for him to fight by his side again.

"Well," Castra chimes in, "considering we would all be disbanded if anyone found out he wasn't dead, he's going to have to stay here for a while until we can get him off this planet."

"Really, really, extra good food," Lone emphasizes. "And a bigger bed, too."

"At least you're alive and not charbroiled," Lo says. "I'll go get us something to eat now!"

Castra stops him, "So, about that four-hundred..." Lo shakes his head and goes back into the market square to get food, as happy as he has ever been since Lone is breathing on the other side of a few walls.

CHAPTER IV

Earth Prime beings used to believe their planet was flat. Then, they believed it was the center of the universe, that theory replaced by Copernicus with the Solar System idea. With that, the heliocentric view came, which took a long time and a lot of bloody inquisitions to embrace. Next, even after these were proven false, they believed their galaxy was stationary and Prime's orbit was perfectly round. Then the cloud of asteroids that encase the solar system was found, and the Milky Way galaxy, A-Local Group, Virgo Supercluster and Universe 'A'.

Fortunately, technology combined with the spread of information has brought scientific fact, based on humanity's limited perceptive abilities, to replace these assumptions made by operators of weak telescopes. The elliptical orbits of planets and their eccentricity are a very important scientific study in modern travel, colonizing and resource gathering. Some precious metals can only be mined, some space stations can only operate and certain scientific experiments can only be performed at certain eccentricities of orbit.

The eccentricity of an orbit is the extent to which the orbit's path deviates from a perfect circle, which depends on a host of different physical properties of the planet itself, the bodies around it and the star it orbits. The higher the eccentricity, the further away the eccentricity value is from zero, which is, understandably, the value for a perfect circle. Eccentricity takes into account the orbital energy, angular momentum, central force (gravity of Sun) and reduced mass or inertial mass of the planet. Between 0.0000 and 1.0000 are elliptical orbits, those that equal one have a perfect parabolic escape orbit, and anything greater than one makes a hyperbola.

The point at which an orbit is closest to the solar body of the system is its perihelion and the farthest point is its aphelion. Depending on the average velocity of the body and the axis tilt, these orbital positions are important on large and small scales as they determine the lengths of seasons, changes in overall climate and, therefore, the personalities of inhabitants.

Those eccentricities above .0899 tend to be those uninhabitably dry planets with little to no atmosphere. For Prime's solar system, Mercury (.206) and Mars (.093) have the only eccentricities high enough to keep them uninhabitable wastelands, though there is some speculation that Mars was populated at some point in its history. This could actually be true as its eccentricity has increased .0005 every century. It has had the highest eccentricity change in the entire Milky Way.

The rest of the planets are all gaseous but, of course, only Earth Prime (.018 after the Cataclysm) has been inhabitable by carbon-based beings. The generally inhabitable range of eccentricity is .0249-.0149 and anything above or below that may have an atmosphere that is not normally breathable. So, Venus (.007), Neptune (.009), Uranus (.047), Jupiter (.048), and Saturn (.056) are well outside of the habitable range.

Most Earths fall below .020 as that is one of the requirements to apply to become a part of the Earth Union. Of course there are many more stipulations to join, such as population, gravity strength, axis tilt, ocean-to-land ratio and a dozen others. However, all of them are relative guidelines and can be deviated from with the right political motivations. For example, Earth 8 has an eccentricity of .0202 but the presence of Chalice and the strategic location (as it is next to Prophyria) gave it the nod past that limitation. Omega 2, however, has an eccentricity of .019 but has not made it through the application process for several other reasons such as low population and limited resources.

There are positive things about those arid planets with high eccentricities. In the days around their two aphelion points (when they are farthest away from their sun(s)), the precious metals and stones on these planets are in their most solid phase which makes them easiest to mine in large quantities. The number of days depends on their eccentricity and how far they are away from their sun(s) as the closer they are, the smaller their orbit, the fewer days the aphelion lasts.

For instance, Mercury is the closest planet to Earth Prime's central star and its orbit cycle takes approximately 88 Earth days. With an eccentricity of .206, the highest in the system, it spends the longest time in both aphelion and perihelion ranges. This extreme eccentricity makes the natural materials found under Mercury's surface some of the most odd and precious in those worlds.

The space station on Mercury is only open for eight days per aphelion, sixteen total per cycle, as is it not safe to move around the surface on that planet the other 72 days of its cycle. Certain scientific experiments only work as that temperature change, both rising and falling, occurs on the surface. Miners only get four half-days to mine those materials as, even though the mining is done underground, it is too dangerous to do any sort of work while the Sun is beating down on the planet's surface.

Politically, the owners of these tangible materials and scientific research get trillions of Marks in funding from governing bodies in order for their materials to be owned by a particular planet or nation. Owning these materials increases trade with other wealthy nations and/or planets, population increase, investing and, prospectively a wealthier nation, planet, system and universe. Of course, there is corruption and favoritism shown in many of the contracts given by governments to the mining companies. Hoarding occurs in many instances, especially when a planet is trying to get into the Earth system and has very little to offer otherwise.

All this talk of eccentricities only deals with two isolated bodies, one directly orbiting the other. There are as many other gravitational systems in the cosmos as there are possibilities, from complex triangular to simple octahedrons and more elegant systems such as the Klemperer rosette. The more complex the system, the narrower the window for mining at aphelion, the more valuable the materials but the less valuable the planet is in general.

After another of their long silences, something that almost seems mandatory for building new relationships, "Man, that was crazy," Synite says under his breath in reference to thoughts he was having about the footage of his fight against Lord Qor.

"Huh?" Driven asks, unaware of what Synite said.

"Nothing," Synite replies. "Thinking out loud, talking to myself."

"Tell myself I said hello," Driven smiles at his own quip. "Are you ready to work on your car yet?"

"I didn't even put a dent in that book you gave me on them," Synite has not made time for it, yet he has written another poem:

> If I had to give my life
> For someone to survive,
> Only for your future could
> I put mine on the line.
>
> If I had to meet eternity
> To give someone another
> Ein or two to breathe,
> I'd do it for none other.

If I was made to walk
Slowly through fire or ice
For you to see another day
I'd choose the same twice.

If the worlds were ending under
Our noses, between our feet,
By Gods, through love, there's
Only one place I'd be.

Driven continues the banter, "Swing a little harder!"

"I wish it was that easy," Synite sighs. "I have to read it slowly so I can thoroughly understand the art of it."

"What do you mean, the art? It's all numbers," Driven huffs. "Engineers don't think about art. Sometimes form just follows function in math and sometimes artists stumble upon engineering that works."

Synite challenges, "So, you don't believe there's a measure of art to what you do? I certainly see it."

"I'm saying that the art of it, the appreciation by the beholder," Driven drills, "that arises when the math works, when the science matches up perfectly. You can feel emotion, which I believe is the root of art, about a combination of numbers and precision."

"I don't think so. I think there's something outside of the numbers, you know? Something," Synite dares to say, "magical about it. It's inspired and inspiration. It's more than just emotion but the emotion that you cannot explain in any of the languages I know. You can't put a quantity to that."

"There's always a price to the priceless, man," Driven reminds him. "I'll take you to an auction one day! I remember reading about a priceless piece of art on your home planet, I think it was called the Mona Liza or something," Synite recognizes what Driven is talking about. "The legendary artist who did it was also an inventor and more concerned with numbers and secrets than art. Anyway, they valued the painting worth 70 billion Marks or something before it was destroyed in the Cataclysm. Valued and therefore quantified means it has a price just like there is a price to life. It's high but there is always a number."

"That's us trying to put a price on it," he rebuts. "Not everything can be bought on the marketplace. There are prices on all of our heads right now but do you think I'd kill you for the numbers on my thumb?"

Driven smiles confidently though he does not like being reminded that someone out there is after his life, "But artists and their art are nothing without Marks. Find a poor artist and I'll show you a *poor* artist. Not saying that everything that makes money is good but if you are not well recognized, is what you're doing actually art? If there's no beholder for the beauty to be in the eyes of, is it beauty at all?"

"Maybe not to the masses but there is art out there that is worth more than the price tag," Synite is precisely as confident. "I agree with you that there is math in everything. There is science everywhere. But that little extra something that we cannot define, that's art. When pieces of paper are so loved that they last centuries; when someone is working completely off of inspiration with no plan, no hypothesis, and beauty comes out," he looks straight at Driven, "numbers can't explain that or the feelings that come from it."

"Of course they can!" Driven uses a quiet enthusiasm that many take for granted. "One takes all of his or her past interactions and they boil down to very scientific, limited parameters. Things are not quite as random as we may believe. You were born from these two beings that gave you a specific range of potential. Your past either drives or hinders you. You're either prepared or not. Everything can be created from binary, in essence: a choice to either do something or nothing."

"I'm listening," Synite waits for the punch.

"Take music, for example," one of the most mathematically centered arts is great for Driven's argument. "Free form 'music' cannot be appreciated as an art. There has to be some rhythm, some pattern, or else it's merely sound rippling across the sky, which still has a scientific explanation. As for the feelings and appreciation, they come from either studying the art form and function or a universal, popular idea that 'this sounds good, so I like it' and that comes directly from what the listener was exposed to before hearing that particular music.

"If I heard a song I did not understand but enjoyed, I would view it as high art after I studied the music, the history behind the song, the artist, their struggle, and a host of other things. That didn't change what's on the page or what you hear or what performers interpret, it purely refined my view. It trained me, scientifically, to appreciate it more than I would by blindly listening," Driven is getting his point across much better to Synite now. *Ha, blindly listening.*

"I see what you're saying," *ha, see what you're saying,* Synite responds, "but there is a lot more than just what's on the page. If that were the case, the same person would be able to play the same song the same way a million times. Everyone would interpret it the same way. There is something intangible and fine about life that changes with perspective, somewhere between perception and reality."

This would never end and Driven knows it, "Interpretation is from the tons of chemical processes that take place in the brain, taking into account past experience, capacity--"

"What about love?" Synite knows he cannot argue this one. "Art and love carry similar feelings. Is love mathematic as well?"

"I don't think so," Driven sighs, "I know so. Just because it has not been explained by a direct mathematical equation does not mean it won't be eventually. Everything could be explained by math and science, numbers and equations at some point. It's simply putting something in, causing a reaction and something coming out. There is a reason chaos is a scientific law now, not simply an assumptive theory."

"I think we have to agree to disagree," Synite comes to terms with the difference between him and his newest friend. "I really don't feel either one of us is wrong, actually. We just don't agree." *It's great to bounce off of a different perspective though.*

"Agreed," Driven grins. "Usually I would keep going but the fact that you accept that I'm right too makes me okay with it."

Spoilsport marches up the ornate hallway that leads to the throne, the tail of his trench coat swaying behind him. His boots do not echo as he has such a perfect command over his body that his steps never make a sound. He knows the Enslaver can sense him though, besides actually expecting this visit. "Well it didn't end up as I originally assumed it would," he quickly admits to his financier and the usual throne attendees.

One of the elders leans forward from his chair, "You were not able to retrieve them then?"

"Hell, it wasn't for lack of trying, I'll tell you that right now," Spoilsport crosses his arms and leans against one of the stark white pillars, an intense contrast to his generally gloomy visage. "The damn guy refused, of course. Then I insisted, of course, but he stood his ground."

"Could you not forcefully bring him?" one of the regular attendees offers as the Enslaver purges Its lungs of smoke. "That's exactly why we sent you instead of a platoon of automatons."

Spoilsport usually wants to kill every attendee he talks to but after the first two, the Enslaver made him promise to leave them alone so he complied. "He is, well, was a pacifist. I guess having the elementalist power to take and give life makes you respect it a lot more than I do since I ended up offing him. Sometimes I don't know my own strength," which the attendees do not believe for one moment.

"Let us get this straight," a younger, female attendee approaches him.

"Halt," one of the older ones tells her. "We are not allowed within three meters of him. Keep your distance, young one."

"But this halfwit," of course Spoilsport's ears perk up again at this attendee's disrespect, "mercilessly killed one of five, only five, Aether elementalists in on this planet, breaching our agreement. Do we not punish this offense?" She stares directly at Spoilsport, "Do we?"

It takes a few tons of restraint for the being who is physically the strongest on Earth 11 at this very moment, not to mention the room, to stand in the face of such comments. Since he has gotten used to there always being at least one or two who speak on behalf of the less respectful aspect of the Enslaver's personality, his anger towards It has simmered. Also, since he knows the attendees are 90% Its collective mind, he would hate to show any aggression towards his boss. "Look: my bad. The guy wouldn't leave his wives, who are both super puffy pregnant. He said he'd die before he left his future children, blah blah blah. So, that happened."

"Ridiculous," that same attendee tries to continue before he interrupts.

"But," Spoilsport turns around and points at his back, "go ahead and pat me right here for bringing these two with me." The two pregnant wives of that Aether elementalist are escorted in plain view by an automaton. The attendees see no fear in these dark-yellow skinned women's eyes as they stand proudly, one holding her belly and the other with her four hands by her sides, in front of the Enslaver and next to Spoilsport. "Oh, did I mention one of them is an elementalist, too?"

"This is providential," an elder speaks slowly.

"That's what I said! I mean, not those words but," Spoilsport turns back to the crowd. "Now, we have a hybrid Aether-Earth elementalist to bring up as a warrior, and a half-breed. Don't all applaud at once," he says heading away. "I'll put them in Amethyst's old apartment for now. I know he wanted the pure one, but there are four of them left, right?"

The Enslaver chuckles heartily as the automaton escorts the two women away behind their new caretaker. "They'll be your responsibility!" the young attendee yells after Spoilsport.

"Probably not!" he yells back as he gets to the doorway "Oh," he taps one of the attendees that let him out, "go get Castra Nim and his team and tell them to meet me in the training field. I have a little exercise for them." Feeling the power under Spoilsport's hand for the first time, the attendee is so frightened that he goes immediately.

Moments later, he meets Castra Nim as he leaves the sky track that he jogs on every morning. The track is made of a similar material to the one from the Intragalactic Sprint that started from Earth 11 last cycle, but calibrated for use in an atmosphere and for beings that do not run faster than lightspeed. "You and your team have been summoned to the center of the training field, Captain. Gather them and get there before evening's end," the attendee tells Castra.

"By whom?" he asks as the attendee heads away without any answer. He does not hesitate to get Lo, Arra and Wik together, as they are the only members of the Atlan team that will be in public.

"I wonder what this is about," Arra is outspoken even though she has not completely gotten used to the way things operate in Atlan. "I don't love it."

"It doesn't matter what we love or like," Castra tells her and the other two. "This team follows the small rules so we can get away with breaking the big ones," he smiles from ear-to-ear.

"And as much as I hate it," Lo is in a very gruff mood today, "I do it, too. So, let's get this over with."

The four of them ride over to the training field as dusk settles and make their way to the center, amid the long shadows of the forested section. "Even if you try to read my mind," the smooth voice comes from the trees, "it'll quickly kick you out and you might end up comatose. I trained myself against telepaths so it depends on how threatened I feel subconsciously. But, have fun if you want to try!" Vincent Andreas 'Spoilsport' Sinclair, also known as E.A. for Escape Artist, shows his face, still leaning with his back against a tree.

Castra asks in the least disrespectful tone possible, "You sent for us, sir?"

"You're mighty sharp, Captain!" Spoilsport laughs at himself more than others laugh at him usually unless he is showing effort to sleep with them. Then he is a hoot. "Can you see the forest for the trees?"

Wik has heard this one but wonders Spoilsport's intentions on the riddle. Wik keeps quiet for Castra to lead their end of the conversation. "That depends on the vantage point. Where am I looking from?"

"Well, Captain, I know Lone is still alive. I saw what you did in the battle. Nobody else saw it because they're not as good as I am but I did," Lo is taken aback but Castra keeps calm in Spoilsport's nonchalant face. "You don't have to be stressed about it, though. I honestly don't care."

Castra feels Lo about to step forward and puts his arm out slightly to stop him from moving forward. "Then, what?"

"You're such a valiant warrior and all, saving him and keeping these two flunkies alive," and now Arra gets a little fired up. "So very cute of you. It almost brought a tear to the outside corner of my right eye." Castra can take loads of sarcasm but, the others, not so much. "Anyway, I'm only here to let you know that if he pops up anywhere, out at a bar, in a restaurant or in a shopping center public bath, anywhere the Enslaver's eye-looking things can see, pretty much anywhere on this planet, and a few others," Spoilsport is dramatic and enjoys his dramatic pauses, "I'll have to off him. Simple as that."

"Okay," Castra Nim says after exhaling deeply.

"This is, and I quote," he mocks the voice of an attendee, "'in order to preserve the integrity of the Sword of Atlan.' That's how it reads in my job description and contracts and stuff," the pragmatist in Spoilsport rears its head as well.

Lo grumbles from behind his captain, "We already know all of this, so what's the point of you bringing us out here?" his aggravation coming out.

"Whoa there, little man," Spoilsport returns, "I'm politely letting you know that if you make the mistake of letting him show his ugly, so, so ugly face anywhere," Spoilsport makes a quick throat-cutting gesture, heating both Arra and Lo up. "No questions. I mean, considering the fact that he's already fake dead, nobody would sincerely miss him if he was actually dead. Right? It's just that, well, you thought you were smarter than everybody but you missed a spot. Plain and simple: if somebody sees him, he'll be a little deader than he is now, wherever he is."

Neither Lo nor Arra appreciate his tone or take kindly to his threats, "Back off, you degenerate piece of--"

"Lo! Calm yourself," Castra turns around and whispers a few calming words to him that work.

"Yeah," Spoilsport snickers and points to the ground, "Low."

Lo pushes Castra to the side and Arra follows him as they lunge at Spoilsport who is still grinning. He lets Lo grab him by the jacket and pull him in, "Next time, ask permission before you threaten anyone from this team. Alright, boy?"

Before Lo can inhale, Spoilsport grabs his arm, swings him around and slams him into the tree behind him, all before his own feet touch the ground. The impact knocks the wind out of Lo but he does not fall. In the meantime, Spoilsport ends up behind Arra without her even noticing until he kisses her shoulder. She jumps and turns to see where he is but, fortunately for her, he is not there anymore. "So," Spoilsport leans against the same tree he threw Lo against, "you understand, right Castra?"

Wik looks around in amazement, unable to follow any of the movements that are presently happening with his eyes or his mind. "I don't think it matters," Castra says over Lo's wheezing, "but yes."

"Good. You may take your leave of me," Spoilsport always does a great job at reminding the forgetful how powerful he is. Few can feel it how Santhia did and less than a handful knows the full extent of his power; he prefers it that way. Spoilsport knows that initiative can be everything in a battle and the element of surprise can be paramount in attaining that. So, he keeps it under wraps until necessary. Then, after it is necessary, he suppresses it again and watches his victims limp away if he allows them to live long enough to walk.

"So," Synite has been meaning to mention this but wanted to build a level of rapport before attempting, "why sell weapons? Why not build vehicles or patent something less destructive and sell that?"

"Mainly because protection includes weaponized deterrents to other weapons," Driven responds, taking a leg of the driving. They are almost halfway along their trek and pouring the foundation of their relationship to come, "but also because not everyone can defend themselves by calling lightning from the sky or flying away. I'm making a living and having fun at the same time!"

"You're playing on beings fears, though," Synite reminds him. "Do you train them on how to use these weapons?"

"What they do after they purchase is up to them. I don't hold hands," *not anymore*, as he had tried having responsibility with a few clients and it still ended up turning in an unfavorable direction. "They are going to do what they want whether they deceive me about their intentions or not. Some beings don't feel safe in these modern worlds without the ability to be offensive. We do the best we can at filtering through the warmongers, though."

"I guess it'll never be completely right since most beings don't understand that owning a weapon doesn't make you powerful. It actually invites more irresponsible violence," Synite thinks about the history of war on Earth Prime and how that is exactly how many wars started and continued.

Driven speeds up, "And my thumb and maintenance won't let me stop," and then exits off the highway. "Most don't understand the weakness of having weapons either. You're always at the mercy of it and you have to be strong enough to handle it or else it means nothing."

There is always another question. "Do you train them up? Do you teach them how to be stronger before giving them the power to kill?"

"That's too much responsibility," Driven snickers. "Not my style at all. I'm making my living the best way I know how. Sales and service."

"But you use guns, too," Synite is confused and does not think he is going to understand anytime soon.

"Have you seen me use them arrantly or sporadically? I don't. I only take lives if I'm protecting one I care about. It's a shame that the offender always has the advantage," Driven reminds Synite of something his father said to him, "but that's the nature of things. That's why initiative is so important. That's the big difference between aggression, being an aggressor, and looking for perpetual initiative."

"That's eloquent," Synite can tell Driven has it all figured out.

Driven laughs through his nose, "And, I tell you here to your face, I'll never sell ammunition! Guns don't kill. Guns are the technology that makes killing easier, more efficient, louder, more intimidating, less intimate, on and on. Mine, at least."

"Where are we going?" Driven does not respond but Synite sits back and enjoys the speed until they stop across from a wide open, flat stretch of land. "I can see almost a thousand meters before there's anything out there!"

"My dad was an engineer when he first got in the military, among other things, and still went to war," Driven starts his story as they look out at the flat horizon. "During one of the battles, his plane was shot down and he floated down basically in the middle of a troop of militia men during an insurrection. He was the only one within about a thousand meters on his side of the battle and it was only him and his rifle, his side arm, a few grenades and a couple of extra clips.

"He never told me how, but he made it out of that battle a war hero, basically turning the tide single-handedly," he brags on behalf of his bloodline. "He did tell me that his gun was the main reason he was able to do what he did, though. It was like the gun was more than just a weapon; it was his protector. It took on its own personality, as if it guided those bullets itself, and I still have it in storage. He was sent on a mission to kidnap or kill the General that was prolonging the war, which he succeeding in doing, and stopped the coup that would've overthrown the more peaceful, popular leadership.

"He wasn't around much and I wish he had treated me more as you would a son rather than a science project. I still look up to him to for what he did for me and for our world regardless," Driven praises and chides at the same time. "I appreciate the ability to be reckless and the strength he gave to me through my Borganics. There's nothing I could do to honor him more than produce the best weapons and give the feeling I have for him to another son or brother or stranger."

As she sinks, she cannot help but feel it is completely her fault. Everything she has done or not done, every decision she has made or elected not to make, every life she has ended pulls her lower. This is the culmination of her mistakes, her actions done under the regimes of others. Though she felt she had no control, she went willingly into wars over differences of opinion; many of these opinions became the reaper for thousands upon thousands of beings. They went without a fight too, as they not only believed these opinions but believed in the leaders, their voices and their thoughts that made things happen. Whether they were led to blackness, Elysian Fields or the rotting wormwood is up to their ancestors' beliefs, or those forced onto them by someone else's ancestors. She sinks as their souls pull her deeper into oblivion, regardless of their choice of afterlife. She is neck deep in a sea of dark, waves of purple marbles crashing into her from both sides at once as she is the gravity that brings more death in her direction.

Amethyst twists violently out of this nightmare, gasping to catch her breath. This is what she rues and wishes she could avoid but it has come every time slumber blankets her, during every wink of sleep since they left Earth 11. She is either sinking or falling, being pulled into the earth or towards it, about to suffocate or about to crash into the unforgiving surface. This is either the way to remind her of her pain or her brain expelling these images and emotions from her mind in the only way it knows how; unfortunately for her, she, like many, is inclined to believe the former.

So, she cries tears of frustration and agony, slow tears that wet her ear and pool on the bridge of her nose before they cascade off into her hand, still warm when she catches them. A dim light enters the room from a passing vehicle and reflects from the bracelet that chokes her from around her forearm. It has her gasping from that dream, the asphyxiation from her past with that cursed band of power.

She groans at it, unable to relieve herself of that which puts no limitation on her body but chains her heart. The bracelet itself has no plans on relieving her anytime soon, for its fate has not been sealed, its job has not been completed just yet. Regardless, even though she knows it shall be necessary for the safety of her friends, if it would allow her to remove it for one moment or even detach her arm, she most certainly would. It has power against itself though: it cannot allow its host to be harmed by any means. Amethyst may not be able to harness it without the Will to do so, but the bracelet's Will protects the both of them, keeping her in one piece physically even if it shatters her mentally.

It is not sentient and cannot think for itself, but the Mars-like power to destroy needs no conscience. However, Amethyst does have one and it is a hungry conscience. It prefers to gnarl and gnaw at her core, dig and dive deeper into her soul, bore it wide enough for moons of pain to run in orbits.

She is reminded of the pain that exists there, the one created in the civil wars that killed many of her relatives. Though she was a princess of her State, there were many other States in her family's region. Every State had its own set of rules, laws, regulations, norms, customs and governing bodies. Some were led by co-founders, some were elected democratically, and some drew lots. Some of her family actually belonged to other States as well when the colonization began.

This foreign kingdom of beings had absolutely nothing in common with her and those who called her land home. That did not stop them from wanting to claim these States "uncivilized" and bringing all of the Heads of State to a conference to talk about unification and governing. Of course, at first none of them went along with it because you do not fix something that is not broken. However, the colonizers were very persuasive and coercive in that they had many different things to bribe these Heads with. Eventually, the ones who fought the most against the uniting of the States fell to their own vanity, thinking that if they ignore the advances of the colonizers, someone else has the opportunity to take advantage and they will be left behind.

Thus, new nations were born of a mishmash of cultures that barely spoke the same languages, much less agreed on who should lead. What was even more difficult was choosing how they should be led, so the colonizers did what they did best and gave them the bright idea of having one leader over all States in each particular nation, even though many of these lines were drawn so randomly in the eyes of the natives and many of the States included in these new nations had nothing in common except possibly their skin tone. And even that was a stretch in some areas.

This did not matter to the colonizers: they got what they wanted out of their reshaping of the lands and it included access to trillions of Marks worth of resources and trade. And, in the middle of this disarray, their objective completed, the colonizers left these new nations confused and with no idea how to run themselves in the new systems. The beings that agreed to the changes died wealthy but soon and the next generation was left with tons of disorder to deal with.

While the rich got richer and these new nations were being bled for their natural wealth, civil wars erupted all over. Amethyst's father ended up fighting on the same battlefield as her cousin except but on different sides. There were no winners except those who made quick Marks and deserted the homeland to enjoy the riches. Amethyst was left with a nightmare and is still trying to wake up from it today.

The nightmare from that night did not end when she woke up, however. It is her life, so she cannot expel these emotions from her heart yet, no matter how hard her brain's chemicals try. She decides that she must take a stance on it, though. Her driving force from henceforth, outside of protecting her friends, is to rid herself of the burden of unlimited power. This is the decision she must make in every waking hecu until the job is complete.

Lying around all day does not help her with this task so she gets up after she catches her breath. She gets ready for the day with her routine washing and primming, gets dressed appropriately to melt into the Naz District of Yar JK and looks for her communicator to find Desha and Promis.

When she does, her first suggestion is: "Let's go shopping!"

"Where would be the best place?" Promis asks. "The boys are going to town. Maybe we could meet them there!"

"Can you come along?" Desha looks for Proximity's approval, "Please?"

Amethyst and Promis smile over at him as well, "Oh, he doesn't want to but I know he'll have tons of fun!"

"I gotta question befoe I say a thang doe," Proximity stands with both hands out: "who gone pay?"

CHAPTER V

"Have you ever thought about who you are?" Driven asks as he helps Synite with his rifle holding technique. "Comparing yourself to the par, how good of a being do you think you are? Have you ever thought about that?"

Synite focuses on hitting the target Driven set for them some five hundred meters away from where they set up. "I've tried not to but I am now."

"I was thinking about what you did back in the mountains," Driven says with some amazement in his voice, "and I don't think that there are any beings, especially from Prime, who would've been able to do that, elementalist or not," he is not speaking down on the general public of Earth Prime, but speaking to the greatness of the man next to him.

"Is that the reputation of my people? I haven't kept up with the Prime news in a while," Synite admits. "And I obviously haven't been."

"I'm sure the culture hasn't changed that much in the last few cycles, huh?" Driven is trying to encourage his friend to rise to the next level.

Synite fires and misses the target by about a meter to the right, "Probably not." He taps the digital reload and another round locks into the chamber.

"Getting closer!" Driven speaks in a low tone, "So, from how it was before you left, if you entered that world as the man you are now, what do you think? How do you think you would be judged?"

Synite misses again about a half meter to the left, over-compensating a bit, "Having been through the Sword, I'm not sure how I would even accept the status quo." Something far away from them rustles at the loudness of the gunfire; a few other somethings join.

"I guess the better question is," Driven offers, "would you take steps to change things or withdraw from society entirely?"

Synite takes his time, breathes to relax more and hits the target on the edge. *Alright.* He lowers the rifle, "It would depend on the circumstances. I know I couldn't do it alone." He looks over at Driven who raises the rifle he picked, waits a few secs, and blasts through the target three times in a row with ease. Synite sighs at how unfair it is, "I don't know how motivated I am right now to change that; definitely not more than ridding the verses of the Enslaver."

Driven puts the rifle down, "Let's compete! Put your bolts of lightning against my guns, if you don't mind using moving targets!"

"I'm in!" Synite's competitive nature is always ready for the next challenge. They go round for round on accuracy with quick-draw, burning through the targets not unlike hit men with a purpose. They use stationary targets, targets that move laterally, skeet shoot, and randomly moving targets. Driven edges Synite slightly but only because of experience: he is acting on muscle memory and instincts built from repetition where Synite is using pure instinct and raw talent as usual. "Man, you're good!"

"I'm practiced," Driven reminds him. "This is what I do!"

Synite peers farther out, "What about that last target? Think you can hit that one?"

Driven looks, "The five kilometer one?" Synite nods at him and he grins back as he drops to one knee. He lifts the rifle up and waits, relaxing with his eyes closed. He slides his hand up from the butt to the trigger and puts his finger on top, waiting more. To Synite, it looks as if he and the gun are part of the same device: it is perfectly snug between his shoulder and his pectoral, perfectly parallel to the ground and his thigh, and perfectly angled to meet his sight five kilometers from his front foot.

In the meantime, Synite appreciates the silence of the wilderness. There is ambient sound bouncing around the field but it lends to the tranquility and relaxation they are sharing. To them, nothing else exists in this world right now except hitting the dot on the horizon that they are aiming at.

Crack! The round fires, actually taking Synite off-guard, and Driven's strength shines as he absorbs every bit of recoil. He knew he could not let the round leave with even the slightest twitch at the end of the barrel, so he braced himself and squeezed the trigger with a flutter. He stands, exhaling on his way up and looks through the scope to the target. "Missed."

"You what?" Synite barely heard what he said over the loudness of his focus.

"I missed," Driven confesses again, "about half meter short." He immediately wonders what he could have done better and how he resolves to hit it in the center next time. "Your turn!"

"I almost forgot!" Synite floats straight up and looks down, "Make sure I'm not in front of the line!"

"You're good!" Driven gets directly under him and looks through the scope while he waits for the flash to come down.

Synite puts his hand up by his head, "I think you might've hesitated a little! Count me down!" He snaps and points as the electricity webs between his fingers and wraps around his hand.

"Three," Driven goes through the countdown quickly, "two, one, shoot!" Synite closes his eyes and points as a sharp flash shoots across the field nearly at the speed of light. The single bolt splits the target in two from a few centimeters to the right of center. The sonic boom does not startle him as he had the countdown to queue it, "Bam! Great shot, man!"

Synite floats down shoulder-to-shoulder with his competitor and receives his congratulations, "There are so many people to thank for this achievement!"

"Come on now!" Driven laughs and jabs him in the arm. Then, it hits the both of them the way it hit Synite while he was waiting on Driven to shoot. The quietude, the undisturbed solace of nature waves over them. "I feel as though we could go anywhere and do anything right now, Synite. Sometimes, when I stare out into space I get this feeling. It's been a while since I've gotten it on-planet though."

"I'm glad you brought me out here," Synite shows his gratitude, "I never would have thought shooting would be so peaceful."

"Out here, away from the hustle, this is true freedom. We're only held back by the weather," Driven pauses and grins, "but I guess you can control that, too, right?"

Before the first Sun rises, before I know what time is, before my
Mind is ready for the world, you're already there. If only my pair
And your set of windows to the spirit could meet between those
Lines I keep crossing. To me, the solitary lost thing
Is sitting behind your ribs, to the left, just a little more…
Right there, that beautiful beating muscle causing unusual
Patterns and fluctuations in my spirit, begging for visitation,
For our spirits to intertwine, to interact between those lines

I keep crossing. I just can't help myself, throw my trust
For my own feelings out the window of my spirit, healing
Isn't something I seek anymore, I'd rather hurt for weeks
With you than be in bliss without. I can't hold this within
For as long as you want me to. Lord, nature has blessed you;
I wish I could be as blessed and live the known eternity
Right next to you. I know I'll stress you because I go
A little further than normal sometimes. Pardon that
Tendency of mine. I just can't help myself. But I'm fine.

I'll take my time. Of course…

Until you give me all of yours.

Unifying many of the psychologies and studies that have molded Synite into his current person is the philosophy of perspectivism. It says the vantage point of any being is molded by the events of their past; their present decisions and future are sculpted by largely affecting experiences. The future is so fragile and pinned to the consequence of so many variables that it can be quite overwhelming to those without the proper perspective on things. A being is of one dimension without knowledge of a past and cannot be judged on any intelligent basis. Without that, they have nothing to frame every image and decision with, as the past is the lens that every being sees the present in.

Perspectives differ so much that it is difficult to directly blame any being for their actions, to a certain degree, as they are a product of a host of actions of others. Looking at the whole of a particular species, there are trends and statistics that hold true throughout their history. For most bipedal beings in many universes, inequality is the norm though it is mostly based on physical attributes and ingrained stereotypes. No matter how much a population advances, grows, develops, mutates and/or evolves, the more things change, the more they stay the same.

Synite is a product of his mother leaving, his father dying, his enslavement and his taking control of his own life and stock. All of these events are related in some form and, from beginning to end, have had an effect on each other. This is a macro view of his life but even looking at day-to-day decisions works the same way. Decisions made throughout the day affect the decisions and outcomes of the evening and night, from what is consumed at breakfast to which direction he chooses to take for his daily routine and who he chooses to spend time with at dusk.

Some beings without the knowledge of such an idea blame the actions of others unduly on themselves, taking responsibility over another being's past just as they take responsibility over their present decisions. Some beings even take little to no responsibility for their own actions based on false pretenses that they can blame everything on the beings around them since they do not believe they are in control of their own lives at all. Some may completely disrespect the decisions of a being by unjustly misunderstanding their past or judging that being on the basis of their own past instead. Those beings with the knowledge of perspectivism have a much less self-abnegating response to the failure of others to work towards positive outcomes. They understand that the past is not simply old events. The past is the reason for the present and why beings look to the future.

In the majority of places, perspectivism is not a natural occurrence by any means. In order to achieve this perspective though, one must be taught by someone or go through obstacles. Many find that mentor in a parent or older sibling and are thus given the tools to navigate through the rough waters of the never-ending present in flux and chaos. They then know exactly how to avoid such things as inciting unnecessary attention that calls for thievery or the circumstances that come with living beyond one's means. Learning from other's mistakes may aid perspective but only a small amount.

In some more fortunate cases, the ideas of perspectivism are passed down from generation to generation. Those that inherit their attention to perspective and respect for other's perspectives also inherit the class to deal with catastrophe. They are not too easily rattled by familial misappropriation or betrayal by those trusted acquaintances which may not have had the best of intentions. They were taught not to take such things personally as they are not the problem but the past of the problematic is the main cause. They make themselves easy to get along with and find traversing through the largest and smallest of conflicts not so trying as to lose their composure.

This, however, is much more difficult for those who learned through the fire instead of being forewarned of it. They must have their perspective knocked into them, hopefully before it is the cause of their demise. Even when it is beaten into their psyche a few times, it may still be a frail concept unless reinforced habitually. Some beings honestly believe that doing the same thing that got them terrible results may not end up the same just because they are a little older yet not necessarily wiser. They may take little to no responsibility of their own in their current situation and continuously blame others, which is a perspective in itself unidentified by the bearer. They are blind to their spoiled natures, acting only on whims and wants and never on the good of any estate, even their own, until that fire is lit and smoldered.

Then, it becomes that moment for which they gravitate towards, the one that either kills them or turn them into something else. That turning point is crucial, in some cases, to more than only the being that it is thrust upon. The scab of a being that has destiny thrust upon them in order for them to become something more, something fearless of their own power, nearly always gains the perspective that anything is possible. They learn that there is nothing stronger or more dangerous than a fearless being, especially one with direction.

These types of perspectivists may come into contact and clash without an ounce of disrespect for the other but under the circumstances of the chaos of life. Different trees of pasts and the future meet head-on, without pause, and things undoubtedly change. Depending on the scruples of each being, this may be for the better or worse for the general public. Either way, change will inexplicably occur.

Driven gets them out of the plains and into a valley of the mountains that surround town. His tires screech around a corner towards the center of the valley and there is a group of four large beings standing in the road. Driven brakes down and four more of them run behind the car from the mountainside to their left. These eight heard the gunfire from the competition earlier, spotted them and figured they would not be much of a challenge from short range. They were not smart enough to stick around and notice Synite's ability since their main objective is taking what will get the most Marks. The leader approaches them from in front, his top arms crossed and the bottom two swaying with his walk. "Get out!" he yells in a language that only Driven's translating chip understands.

Driven looks over at Synite, "Want to stretch your legs a little?" and hops out of the car. "Alright, I'm out. Now what?"

"We want that machine and everything in it. Walk away and there won't be problems," he crosses his other two arms and scowls.

Driven's grin makes him even angrier, "Oh, you guys only want money? Man, this car is nothing in comparison to the prices on our heads!" Synite gets out of the car and goes to the back to face the four behind Driven. "Dead or alive, that guy is worth a million times what the car is."

"What are you saying to them?" Synite yells back in his native tongue.

"That they'll have to kill us if they want my property," Driven takes a few steps closer to their leader and reverts to their dialect. "So, back to you. Basically, you won't be taking him alive. He's not a pushover. And me: I'll whoop your ass before you lay a finger on that car, lowlander. So, you should probably try to take us dead because you definitely won't be taking us alive." Driven opens his arms and smiles.

"I guess they're going to want to fight for it, huh?" Synite says over to him. "I've never fought somebody with four arms before." Synite plots a few moves and reminds Driven and himself at the same time: "Remember: no killing!"

A breeze blows between Driven and the leader, Synite monitoring every movement that the vagrants make. The other three in front of Driven approach their leader's back and pass by him, going directly for the car. "Three on one? You're going to need more than that, my friend!" He flexes with his right arm, biceps and triceps.

They bear down on Driven simultaneously but he throws a right uppercut and knocks the one to his left out cold before they get close enough to touch him. The other two get a few arrant swings in before Driven gives a few perfect jabs that crouch one of them over. The last one grabs Driven's arm but still misses every punch. He pokes his tongue out at the attacker after one of the missed punches, laughing heartily to himself.

At the other end of the car, the other four each take a step forward. Synite raises a hand and a thick wind keeps them from taking another. "Whoa, fellas." They struggle against the force of the wind until they start to slide backwards on their feet, Synite leaning against the trunk of the car as if nothing is even happening. He hears a grunt and a body hit the ground from around where Driven is, then another thud.

"They're not dead, but when they wake up, they sure won't be happy!" Driven yells back to Synite.

"You are a fighter," the leader tells him, "and your friend back there uses magic?" Synite drops the wind and the four of them stop to catch their breath.

"It's a little more complicated than that, but," Driven nods with sarcastic solemnity. "Do you still want to fight or are we done here? I could use another round."

He pulls knives out with all four of his hands and points one at Driven's head, "We do not leave without what we come for. No bounty attracts me."

"Tell him to stop before it gets worse," Synite says. "I feel bad for these guys. They look like they just want Marks."

Driven laughs loud, "I asked if he still wanted to fight and he pulled knives out. What more do you want?"

"Let him go," Synite requests. "Compromise with him."

"I'm not backing down just because they didn't know what they got themselves into," Driven returns, paying little attention to the armed detractor. "Is it our fault?"

"I didn't say that," Synite sighs. "There's no point in fighting if they have no chance to win."

"You're too serious, man. Have a little fun!" Driven dodges the first attempt at stabbing, "So, I guess I should stand here and get stabbed? Or try to reason with this galoot? Your choice!" The other four prepare to attack as well, pulling out similar knives and blunt weaponry. "Matter of fact, why don't you reason with them? Oh, because you can't speak their language, right?" He dodges more slashes and stabs with his best dance moves. "This is so sad it's barely even funny!"

Synite rolls his eyes in frustration as they approach him with the firm belief that they can definitely win since there are more of them. "I guess I could have a little fun exercising," he says loud enough for Driven to hear.

"That's the spirit!" Driven continues his dance, staying between the four-armed grunt and his favorite thing on four wheels.

Synite does not go into any Hardened or elementalist state, figuring that may be too much for the four of them. He does, however, drop a spinning wind wall behind him after he puts some space between him and the car. Then, he flies up and over them and waits for them to come after him. One of them tries to get through the wind wall, and the other three rush Synite.

As he touches the wall, the knife in his hand spins away from his grasp. Confused, he tries again with his bare hand and it twists his arm around almost breaking his shoulder. More confused and angry, he tries to charge it with his other shoulder and it flips him to the ground. He belts out a wail that sounds similar to an angry infant.

"They are pretty dumb," Synite watches as he spins away from a swinging bat.

Driven knocks all four knives out of the leader's hands and open-palm slaps him across his face so perfectly that the sound startles Synite. He turns around in time to see Driven get off a backhand that turns the big guy away from him, pointing at him like a punishing parent. "Now get out of here and I promise not to run these fools over on my way!" He swings at Driven and he goes forehand again.

Synite slides between two of them that try to attack him from opposite sides and instead knock each other out in time to see the third slap. *This is the same as that time I was in the next room from a guy and his girlfriend fighting and he got slapped a few times. I guess Driven's long ponytail makes him the girlfriend.*

Moments later, they get back in the car and screech off, leaving a trail of dust to cover the groaning and unconscious victims. "You certainly are addicted to danger, huh?"

"I seek it out! Shoot, that's a small part of the reason I sell weapons. Usually living loud in a risky business comes with lagniappe run-ins with silly wannabe thieves," Driven grins, driving faster. "I grew up always needing to do something wild; always having to go out and do stuff that'd quench my thirst."

Synite thinks about the amount of trouble he got in while not even looking for it and cannot imagine how much he could have gotten in had he tried. "How'd that work out for you?"

"I made a bunch of mistakes and got into a bunch of foul-ups. I apologized after but learning from all of that has made me a very experienced man," Driven is proud of his scars. "And, I mean no offense, but you still ended up a freaking slave warrior even though you're such a nice guy."

Synite laughs at how he says it but is confused about the mentioning, "What's your point though?"

"I'm just saying it doesn't really matter because whatever is going to happen to you is bound to happen. Good and bad things happen to the good and bad alike. The 'verses are all about balance. It's because of who you are not who you think you are or who you wish you were." What amazes Synite the most about Driven is his ability to be both stirring and full of nonsense in the same conversation. "Shit happens, man. Shit happens and it's going to keep happening whether anybody likes it or not. It's nature! And that's why I keep the best weapons for myself."

 # CHAPTER VI

As they arrive at the edge of the town Driven has to do business in, it is nightfall and the moons are in mirror phase, both large crescents in opposite directions of one another. Driven gets to his parking garage, finding a space next to one of his other fleet of vehicles, and shows Synite up to his dormitory.

They meet out on the roof of the building to get the best view of the mirror moons and relax. "You have it made out here," Synite tells Driven.

"I made it," he takes in the cool night Air, pleasing to his warm Borganic lungs. "You never fully answered my question."

"Which one?" They had talked a lot along the way.

Driven, lounging, turns his head slovenly, "Who are you?" he yawns and stretches his arms, "you're not the same student kid from Bering City. You're not the slave-champion, number two in the arena anymore. Who are you now?"

Synite looks into the moons, confounded by the question. *Gale?* She does not answer immediately which is unsettling to him. "Besides being an elementalist and vanguard, I guess I'm not sure. With everything that has been happening and not being fully in control of what's going to happen next, it's hard to say."

"Nobody knows," Driven says, "it's all guessing. I mean, one plus one is three and all, but nobody really knows what's going to happen in the next moment. Some are more able to predict it but..."

"Yeah, like Psilos. He gets information from his other selves," Synite reminds him.

"But even they only have a certain range, right? They aren't omnipotent," at least from what he gathered before. "I digress. The point is, not knowing the future is a constant. It shouldn't keep you from being conscious of who you are just because you're a prisoner of time."

Eventually, as he seeks guidance from the sky, Gale breaks her silence. 'You are your decisions.' He thinks about that for a moment, "If I am my decisions, what about the choices I make even when I'm forced, when I had no choice except to choose?"

"I'd think those would be the ones that are even more revealing," Driven looks up at Synite, hoping he comes to the conclusion that he wants him to.

Synite turns to him, "How so?"

"Those are the times when your true character has to expose itself, you know?" Driven speaks with his hands, "The way you are when you react instinctively is who you are when you're not trying to be anything else! I should write that down."

"You have a point," Synite says, smiling at the touch of pride Driven shows. "I am more than exclusively an Air elementalist and member of the Vanguard," Synite agrees, "I just have to figure out my purpose."

"Create one!" Despite being younger than Synite in True Atomic Time, Driven has tons of advice. It may not always be spot on but he tries his best to encourage.

Synite appreciates the friendly enthusiasm at every turn, "That's an objective."

"If there was anything you could do right now, what would it be? I think that's another thing that defines us. Given the freedom to do anything, how would you use that freedom?" That gives Synite another set of questions to think about while he is figuring out who he is.

Being in a transitional stage in life can be harrowing for any being but, on that subject, there are some requirements for one to truly learn who and what they are, if it is a question one wishes to think about. These requirements consist of an encouraging environment, encouraging beings around them and enthusiasm from within.

One may find their God in a prison cell or pursue darkness from a monastery. The encouraging environment does not necessarily have to be a positive environment as, in many cases, a negative environment, such as slavery, could show more of one's character than working a steady, salaried job. This environment should have enough extreme moments that encourage the decision that one has no choice but to make, exposing their true character like an open wound to the pain of oxygen.

Extreme situations that challenge the subject and force them to experience something new or consistent about themselves will open them to knowledge of their core being. There should be multiple opportunities in the environment to push one outside of their comfort zone, as that is where growth happens. That allows a being to create an identity and embrace that as the truth, subject to change as more three-dimensional growth occurs.

As far as the beings that one would surround themselves with, they have to be similarly encouraging as the environment. They have to constantly and consistently challenge the subject's character without explicitly forcing them to come to some conclusion. There can be ways to lead them to come to their own conclusions about themselves without selfishly leading the subject into coming to a conclusion that may be false. That type of conclusion may cause a surface reaction that may not last into the crucial stages of life.

The presence of a mentor guide may or may not be productive, depending on the subject and the mentor, but can definitely assist in the points of early and middle development of character when a stern or encouraging voice is necessary. This is a delicate relationship though as mentors may be experiencing growth stages of their own at the same time, as many do. The bests are those that lead from the rear and allow their mentee to fight through their own problems after giving them the tools to do so. Mentors must encourage them to go on their own into the dark, so to speak, as a challenging environment but have the confidence that they can grow from that experience. That promotes more growth than being carried through rough situations by a mentor, though that may also be necessary in certain situations.

However, if the subject has the correct motivation and enthusiasm from within and a need to find their true self, some of this help may be shunned as unnecessary. The want to experience new things and learn about self is not easy to come by as many are not born with it or taught it at an early stage in life. Then, transitioning into that type of being can be even more difficult because of the upbringing, the discouraging environment and beings surrounding one's early development. Some would rather do back-breaking physical labor than look in the mirror and concern themselves of their own psychological state.

Some would also prefer to ignore their extremes of personality, searching only to be normalized amongst those around them instead of delving deeper into their own psyche. This is one of the most important of the requirements as the subject must identify their own need for change and laying a strong foundation for development, who they shall become in the future. In some cases, forces beyond any being's control will knock all of that development to the ground, as in a chaotic environment or volatile beings around the subject. They may hinder that self-fulfillment process, obstructing one's ability to actualize into the purest version of self.

To find that perfect balance between the right environments, the right beings and feeling the need takes a lot of hard work, dedication and a measure of luck. One must continuously reevaluate their surroundings and the characters that fill those surrounds and not be afraid to change both of them if they do not support the right result. One cannot be so vain as to ignore those beings, situations, milieus, and circumstances that reveal things about themselves that they might not want to know. You have to know what to hold on to and what to get rid of while not being afraid to do so without much hesitation.

These things do not have to be actively pursued for some beings as they may stumble upon who they are without knowledge of the process it takes, as many other things occur purely on accident. For others, trying to walk through this process may actually hinder the process itself as one may become more focused on the action rather than the result of learning. It is best to trust the process, strive to become surrounded with the requirements and push forward accordingly. Also, this is not an exact science, as most sciences are not. However, it can lead to some positive results in completing the objective of knowing about one's self. This process is possibly what many championship competitions and tournaments stemmed from: surrounding a subject with great coaching, a great team and motivating them to want to win goes far.

One thing that cannot be ignored, though, is when a subject with all three requirements met still falls short of their own objective. That speaks somewhat on the capacity of the being and exactly what league they consider themselves to be in. A sub-professional championship team will still lose to a professional team. Once one realizes they are meant for greatness at the highest level, they see no competition and fight no battles below them. They know that, in order to meet their destiny, they must remain in their league with the highest confidence against similar competition, literally and figuratively.

Synite has not completely accepted his status as he does not quite know what the highest league is yet. There are only two beings in his circle, four that he has ever come in contact with, that are aware of these heights. He may be exposed soon, though, which may be why Driven has been compelled to encourage him.

"I know Psilos wishes he was with us! That whole being king of an entire planet thing has to be stressful," Driven chats as they step onto the train that will take them to town. They parked in a huge lot that has room for every type of vehicle, including the Caracalla that is lowering onto a rooftop spot now.

Kraa-Nuve and Grujek step out, still chomping on native snacks and sharing in their usual guffaw. Kraa-Nuve's stately, broad frame dwarfs Grujek literally but figuratively, Grujek's gaudy clothing and accent give him the sore-thumb effect he thrives on. "Thinkin' I might got on a few too much clothes!"

"Hot," Kraa-Nuve points up.

"Havin' more'n one Sun'll do that!" Grujek tosses Kraa-Nuve a bottled drink. "I fig your scales'll need somethin'!"

Kraa-Nuve looks at the bottle, cracks it open and takes a swig. After he gulps the whole thing down, which does not take long, he looks at the bottle again, "Another?" and tosses it back to Grujek.

They chuckle together, "It'll take ya ten ta quench tha thirts eh? We gots as much as ya need, friend!"

"Twenty!" Kraa-Nuve snaps a finger twice as Grujek sends a message to his sons to bring more drinks. They have gotten used to each other and Grujek does not take any disrespect from his fellow captain's uncouth nature.

"Psilos doesn't actually feel stress the way we do, though," Synite explains. "Psilos only hurts when his people hurt. When they die, he feels it. When more are born, he feels it. Otherwise, he's pretty level-headed!"

"I guess since they're not at war anymore," Driven remembers, "he'll be alright." They step off the train after a ten ein ride into a downtown area with buildings of varying heights and sizes. It is windy and dusty but that has not stopped the casual crowds from gathering and socializing. "This is the perfect weather for business!"

Synite puts the hood part of his mantle up, "I don't breathe in the same way as other people but this still makes it kind of hard." Besides the dust, there is something else around that is making it difficult for Synite to breathe normally. He cannot quite tell what or who it is but its power is nearly suffocating. "Do you feel that?"

Driven pulls the metallic toothpick from his mouth, "Feel what?" He does not need to cover his mouth from the dust either because of the complex filters in the back of his nose and throat that do not allow anything outside of pure Air to pass into his Borganic lungs. His eyes can also filter through the cloud of dust to identify faces and places. However, he still slides on a pair of aviators to cover his eyes and make him generally look cooler than everyone else around.

Synite shakes it off and keeps walking, "Never mind." Under that blanket of fine dirt is a commercial district filled with malls, business offices, restaurants and service industry stations, all in the ultra-modern styling and customization. As the dust flattens out, the shopping crowds in the lower mall almost double in size. The closer Synite and Driven get to the taller buildings, though, the smaller the crowds get. Synite barely recognizes some of the languages that dot the Air around them. "This place kind of reminds me of downtown Atlan a little too much."

They go up to a second floor office where Driven meets a client and begins his presentation. Midway through, Driven's navy haired customer tells him, "Your product speaks for itself," as he hands her a three-dimensional projection of one of his creations. Synite stays outside of the office where they met, bouncing the door. "I love this one the most so far," she says, toting the virtual version of his triple-barreled, pistol-grip, side-loading, pump-action shotgun. Its ash and wood handle is in stark contrast to her sandy skin.

"And that's the best price you'll find right now, Ms. Thane," he shows her on his pricing guide, "especially for the custom fittings, personalized trigger and casings. This type of art does not come cheap, Ms. Thane. Trust me."

"Oh, I believe you!" She aims and tosses the projection around, "And I love the weight!"

Driven smiles in pride, "It's the best version of that product."

She loads it and fires off a virtual round into the wall, "Barely any recoil! It's so charming. It uses modern charges?"

"Both modern and artillery," he explains. "Ms. Thane, it can fit piercing rounds, beam charges, explosives or regular old shells. It is one of the pieces I am most proud of having my stamp on!"

Aria Thane puts the weapon back into Driven's pricing guide and pulls out another, "What kind of guarantee do you offer?"

Driven, nearly insulted by her even asking, "You'll never need another gun ever again, Ms. Thane." He looks over his glasses, "Never. It won't break but if it does, I'll personally fix it at no cost to you."

"I'm sold," Aria puts the other weapon back. "Do you have a Freeport in the Ligartiel System? Most of my deliveries are there."

"I don't divulge that type of information," Driven pulls his glasses back up on his face and points at her with his silver toothpick, "but I can guarantee delivery there."

"I'll take that as a yes," she smiles big, a little too big for his comfort. "If you were to have more valuable items in cache, what kind of prices would you have? Marks are no object to me," she tries to gauge his nonverbal response but he holds firm, smiling a friendly smile. "Anyway, send me two of the shotguns, that third rifle I looked at, and a good contact for ammunition!"

She puts her thumb down on the pad Driven gives her, her name scrolling across his tablet. "What do your friends call you, Ms. Thane?"

"My associates call me Roseweed but my friends call me Ria. I prefer Roseweed though," he puts in her order and it is approved with no problem. "My father and uncle used to call me Ria when they were mad at me for whatever reason, so it stuck but not to my liking!"

Synite is proud of his friend making the sale that he set out to make but the celebration is short-lived as a scream snatches his attention. The same voice from the same direction yells in Co'mmei: "Thief! Stop that beast!" The strikingly feminine visage under her hooded robes twists in the thief's direction and points Synite's eyes over to the wild-haired thing pushing through the moderate crowd, making them look like blades of tall grass that a predator is stalking through. "Someone, please!" she continues in Co'mmei.

Driven completes his transaction, "Your delivery is going to be--"

"Duty calls," Synite says back at the two of them. "I'm going!"

Driven's brow wrinkles and he shakes his head, rolling his eyes from behind his sunglasses. He yanks them off to scan the crowd as it parts for the thief's slick and dirty fur. Several beings stumble out of its way as it growls and pants, barking and yelling at those in its way.

Kraa-Nuve told him to stay under the radar out there so, instead of flying and catching the creature, he runs down the stairs and off after it. It continues to bark and snap at other beings as it makes its way to the mall's exit.

Driven puts his thumb pad away, "Thank you, Roseweed. They'll ship directly to you soon." Driven looks out at Synite chasing the creature and excuses himself with a hand gesture, "I have to go!"

"What is it?" Aria inquires. "He can't handle it?"

"I'll be in touch, Roseweed," Driven reassures her as he quickly puts his pricing guide and thumb pad in his pocket, dashing out of the office after his comrade.

"I guess this is where we start," Roseweed says, huffing as her salesman exits.

So this is why they get in so much trouble, right? He heads up to the top floor of the mall in the same direction Synite went in. There is an open window that Driven slides through and out onto the roof of the mall to get a better vantage point.

"That thing almost ran me over!"

"Watch it!"

"Hey! What's your problem?"

That thing, commonly known as a wolfrat, can care less about the feelings of the beings he is running over and through. He is trying to make it to his objective and does not mind the motivation of a good chase. It is actually more riveting this way, as he expected it to be. He barks and growls his way through the crowds, not having to look back as he is supremely confident that his pursuer is still coming.

Synite would not have done this at home before he knew he had the power to change things. This chase is to right a wrong as he thinks those who steal from helpless beings are despicable, especially from women who speak his native language. He remembers not to show his face or cause too much of a scene by using his powers considering the enormous price on his head. Yet, he is compelled to continue this chase through to the end, no matter what happens. "Just stop!"

Driven sprints across the rooftop and jumps from one level to the next, keeping the chase in his peripheral vision. He gets to a wall and kicks up the scaffolding then jumps down to a lower roof. Pieces of the clay roof materials crack under the weight of his steps but he adjusts so quickly to the different surface that he does not make a misstep.

The wolfrat runs down an alley, following his large canine head resembling a racing greyhound though he looks more like a scruffy mutt, and into the less populated section of the district which actually crosses under the path Driven is taking. He, almost caught up with Synite, jumps over that same alley from one building to the next, his trench flying behind him the same as a cape, Grace and Mercy gleaming from behind him. The wolfrat takes another turn back in his original direction and Driven crosses over them again.

The woman whose item was stolen has calmed her nerves enough to pull her hood down, her hair slicked back.

"Are you okay, lady?" a young gentleman asks.

She looks over to him and sighs, "Boys will be boys. I guess I have to buy another one." Her eyes change color in the sunlight and she heads off.

"I'm goin' change, Nuvie," Grujek gets up. "Too hot fo' all dis!"

Kraa-Nuve smiles, "Told!"

Back on the Pingar, Yelsh and Hemmen tinker with some monitoring equipment together when they see the encrypted beacons from Synite and Driven moving quickly in the same direction. "I wonder…"

"…what they're…"

"…going after." They push each other out of the way to get a better look. "I hope…"

"…this doesn't get…"

"…us in any trouble."

"Knowing those…"

"…guys, the chances…"

"…are pretty high!" Yelsh goes over to the communication tower and hails their dad.

"Lookin' like Drivy an' tha kid gettin' in some smoke down in da mall, Nuvie," Grujek says down to the Caracalla's captain who was completely relaxed until now. "Remindin' me of my days as a young'n!"

"Same," Kraa-Nuve still does not speak many words but gets his points across. He steps onto the Caracalla, "Beacons, ship. Kid running?"

"It seems so, captain. He and the fellow he was travelling with are heading in the same direction," the Caracalla reports to its master. "It seems as if they are giving chase to another being out in front of them. Do you want me to hail them to see what the situation is?"

"Wait. See." Kraa-Nuve is not patient by far but he does not want to have to cause any unnecessary drama on his vacation. "Know, Gruj?"

"Yep, Nuvie," they look on at the skyline of the city together. "I gots a bad, bad feelin' 'bout dis, too."

Meanwhile, Promis, Proximity, Desha and Amethyst stroll about in the lower shopping district without a care. For the materialistic, this area is bursting at the seams with shiny things and soft fabrics in clothiers, markets, auctions and trade areas.

Proximity, his pants a few size too big for this crowd, would much rather be in a more competitive space but does not mind being anywhere Desha is having fun. Her fun also hinges on sticking to his hip as much as she can along with shopping, of course. She sees a terra cotta pot that she adores and shows it to his sincere eyes. "Looks old!"

"I'm sure it is, babe," she nudges him. "I think it'd look nice on the balcony in the corner!"

"That ain't e'en much our place though," Proximity does not understand the value or concept of nesting to women.

"I figure since we're going to be here a while," Desha smiles at him and past him at Amethyst.

"I haven't decorated in a decade," Amethyst tries to think of the last time. "You can use my space too, if you're partial to it."

Proximity looks to his left and behind Amethyst, "Where Sarah at?"

"She went off," Amethyst points in the direction she last saw their fourth wheel.

Promis saw a flea market and wandered into the section that piqued her visual interests and smelled great too. She sticks out like a light bulb in her turquoise dress and bright blonde hair. She carouses several different types of items as the market is packed with everything from trinkets to throws. Every item she touches comes with a holographic price tag and sales pitch.

"She'll be aight," Proximity thinks about all of the trouble they have been through together and dismisses any worry. "She'n take care-a herself."

That same heterochromic iris having woman who got her purse snatched by the wolfrat steps under the tent of the flea market, brushing by Promis who is on her way to another section. Promis pays this no mind but it is a small world after all. She moves towards the corner of the market towards one of the exits and a dark, hairy hand comes over her mouth, muting her fearful objection. Her eyes grow wide and then close as she disappears out of the market.

CHAPTER VII

Synite may not know how small the world is, especially considering he is still chasing a thief that the ex-owner of the stolen object does not care about anymore. A small, winged lizard watches as they approach and scurries out of the way of their footsteps. The wolfrat runs out into another street, barely missed by a moving vehicle. He does not hesitate at all, though, and his pace does not slow. Synite pauses at the curb of the street, stopping at a wind wall he dropped. Driven is already on the other side of the street, checking to see which direction the wolfrat goes in and then making a beeline over the lower roofs.

The wolfrat ducks between some other buildings and Synite sprints around the corner not far behind. "Drop it!" The beast kicks a pile of rocks back at Synite and rounds the next corner. Synite jumps over the rolling rocks with no problem and skates through the Air to follow the wolfrat around the corner. "I hate dogs."

He throws other debris back at Synite and actually taps him a few times along the way; nothing major enough to slow the hero down but it definitely annoys him. Synite pushes himself forward faster with gusts of wind. He forces turbocharged gusts against the path of the wolfrat to slow him down, the winds whining their way against him and tripping the wolfrat up. He tumbles into a trashcan, recovering quickly and running down the nearest alley.

Synite is nearly in arm's reach now, trying to trip the wolfrat down again but he jumps over the winds this time. When he gathers his footing again, he makes another turn into a smaller alley which dead ends in a small cul-de-sac. The wolfrat looks up, the buildings too tall for him to climb and get away. He watches as Synite jogs up to him, sweating from that brisk jog. "Give it back," Synite's command is met soon with a low, intimidating growl and flashing of rows of jagged, stained teeth resting in discolored gums and drool. "Give in. I can take it by force or--"

Crash! The glass window next to the wolfrat shatters out towards them with Driven coming through before Synite can get the phrase out. It is so vivid and surprising to Synite that things are almost moving in slow motion. Without either foot touching the ground, Driven gives the thief a knockout to end all knockouts, hitting him perfectly behind the eye. The wolfrat's head nearly spins halfway around, almost far enough to break his neck, out cold before he hits the ground. Driven lands firmly on his feet next to his twisted up and unconscious victim. He pulls his shades off next to the unconscious wolfrat and looks up at Synite, "What the hell took you so long?!"

In Atlan, a crop of agents, the staff of faceless attendees and some engineers on payroll monitor those very events on their screens in the renovated broadcast wing of the Sword. They zoom in to see Driven explaining himself to Synite, though their sound is muffled. "I saw you run off and got jealous, so I finished my sale and took a more scenic route. The rooftops around here have a hell of a view!"

"And a tactical advantage, I see," because once you have the element of surprise, as neither Synite nor the wolfrat knew they were being chased, there is no plan that can defeat them.

"I do what I can," Driven and Synite look up at the same time. "You--"

"Yeah," Synite is on his guard, feeling something in the Air that was not there a moment before. Driven puts his shades back on then slides his toothpick back into his mouth. "You got it?" Driven pulls Grace from behind him and pulls the trigger. The round ricochets off two different surfaces before sinking between the shoulders of the other wolfrat. It falls from the ledge it was creeping on a few stories above them, landing on top of her comrade. Synite checks to see if she is breathing and, once he hears a wheeze, "Perfect shot!"

Driven grins, "No time for compliments." He aims as a cavalcade of over twenty more wolfrats creeps into their sight from a rooftop, barking and trotting towards the two vanguards. Twenty-plus more come around the corners of the alleyway towards the dead end Synite and Driven wait in.

"He lured us here, we shouldn't fight," Synite suggests as he picks up the purse that was snatched, still aiming to return it. "Let's move!"

Synite floats up about a meter before Driven yells up at him: "But what about the whole not calling attention to ourselves thing?"

"There's sixty of those things coming to this spot. I think that's eno--" before Synite can finish, he notices more wolfrats climbing out of the windows of the building next to them. A few fall and meet their demise in the rush but the others move on impetuously. "We're leaving!"

As Synite takes off, Driven runs down a narrow alley that is closer to them than the wolfrats. Not too long after taking that alley, he notices that none of them are chasing after him but they go past that alley, powering after Synite like rapid waters. He jogs back to that entrance and sees the end of the horde, a few stragglers trying to keep up with the group.

Soon, after pops from behind them, the back of the gang starts to drop to the ground from gunshots to non-vital areas. Driven gives chase, his Grace rose at his eye level, cracking many of them in the back of their legs. Synite hears their whimpers from out front. "Stop shooting!" he demands.

"For what?" Another drops, and then another few, whimpering like canines that are being locked out of a room. "You wanna turn around and fight?"

"Not this time," Synite tells him. "We have to go!"

"Oh, man," Driven could not disagree more. "I'm not killing them because I know how you hate it! That has to count for something."

"It does," Synite is proud of this death merchant for remaining calm, "but we can't continue here!"

Driven lowers his gun, almost pouting. "This is your show. I'll follow," he reluctantly holsters it and runs into the building, back up to a high enough floor to jump out of a window onto the roof of an adjacent building. Where he gets out, he listens for where all of the footsteps are coming from and heads that direction, climbing to higher rooftops as he goes.

Synite zooms through as fast as he can, wishing he was faster considering the wolfrats' foot speed is not too far behind his flying speed. There are a few that are faster than the others and are gaining on him, dropping to all-fours when cornering, making them nearly as fast as Synite. The difference in speed is so negligible to him that he tries to think of something to slow them down. Before he can, as he rolls to turn, he sees Driven sprinting atop a building next to him. He flies up some, out of reach of the wolfrats and next to Driven. "Where can we go?"

"We're going in the right direction," Driven does not pant or lose a step while running at full speed and carrying conversation. "I'm gonna jump! Make sure I don't land too hard!"

"Wait!" Driven picks up his pace and leaps diagonally in front of Synite, arms spread out. Synite flies up to him and catches him, caught off guard. "I had no idea you were this heavy!"

"I get that a lot!" Driven looks down, the ground close enough for him to land safely enough. "Let me go!" Synite obliges and Driven cracks the concrete below him with his initial landing. He tucks and rolls to break his fall some, pivots hard and throws a shoulder into the chest of the fastest wolfrat of the lot. He wastes no more time and breaks out running in front of the crowd and behind Synite.

"You're cutting it too close," Synite mumbles and slows down a little so Driven passes him. The next fastest wolfrat, who is nearly at Driven's heels, reaches to try and grab the tail of his coat but misses. Another one runs up by him on all fours and tries to jump and bite at the coattails but Synite catches him mid-air with a flipping uppercut kick to the jaw.

As he is flipping, Synite sees how deep the crowd of wolfrats is and is motivated to fly a little faster, passing Driven up again. "Nice move," Driven yells up. One catches up to him and he dodges a bite, grabs the snout next to him and pushes it hard into the concrete. The wolfrat rolls and crashes into the charging crowd, knocking several others down.

"How many are there?" Synite is trying to figure out the best course of action.

"Seventy-nine left. I've only taken out twenty-eight!" Synite is getting used to Driven keeping his statistics. Driven notices the little grin on Synite's face, "You got more?"

"I haven't been counting!" Synite tries to remind Driven that is not what they are here for.

"I can't believe you! I thought you'd be a little more competitive," Driven donkey kicks one in the chest and rolls, never missing a step as he hops up back in stride.

Synite scoffs, "So that's why you jumped down? We have to get away from them!"

Driven grunts back, "I was just getting warmed up though." He goes full speed and leaves the crew of wolfrats in his dust. The front of the regiment slams into a hard wall of wind and they pile up similar to cars on the highway at rush hecu. He grabs Driven's arms and flies out of the cover of the buildings and in the direction of the parking garage. "I told you I'd take you flying."

"This isn't quite how I pictured it, but thanks!" Driven responds.

"It's getting kind of late," Desha stopped Proximity and he looked around, doing a double-take at a woman with a blooming rose tattoo on her neck. "We should be getting ready to meet up with Synite and Driven." He breaks his gaze to pay attention to the situation at hand.

Amethyst went up to the two of them, "Are we leaving? I found everything I needed."

"We needa find Sarah," he responded, initiating Amethyst's disappointment. "We know, we know."

"Where did she go?" Amethyst asked with some urgency. Proximity pointed in the direction of the flea market tent and they went under it together. They searched for nearly a half hecu without causing a scene while Synite and Driven were elsewhere doing the exact opposite.

"Come in," Synite says over their communicators, everyone off the ship hearing through their earbuds and Kraa-Nuve hearing over the intercom. "Everyone meet at the rally point. Someone drew us into a trap. Watch out!" He yells down at Driven with the microphone still on. "We're on our way there now and should be there in less than ten eins."

As Synite is telling them the situation, Proximity and Desha look at each other, still scouring the market. Proximity stops short with wide eyes as he notices a turquoise purse creeping from under one of the shelves. "She gone. Sarah's gone!"

Synite looks confused as he jets to their predetermined meeting point. "You mean she left ahead of you guys? I don't understand." Driven looks disdainful of whoever would kidnap a woman amongst warriors, preparing mentally for the worst.

"He found her bag on the ground and we don't see her," Desha responds for her speechless companion.

"Don't panic," usually the person who panics first says that, "I'll find her. Everybody else, meet at the rally. Kraa-Nuve, warm up the PSL engines. This shouldn't take long."

"I'mma follow dem an' find 'er," Proximity hands his jacket to Desha but Amethyst puts a hand on his shoulder. "What?"

"Trust him," Amethyst gleans her own feelings to share them with the other two. "I do. We have to go."

"I'm not leaving without you," Desha tells him then they head off together.

"I'm coming with you," Driven yells, not expecting a response. "Captain, can you hone in on her position so we can track her?"

"Suroest," Kraa-Nuve sends a tracking dot to Synite and Driven, the latter taking a little longer to connect.

"Let's go!" Synite turns in the direction of Promis's tracking and they go back up above the lowest roofline. While they go after the blip on their radar that means more than merely a blinking light to Synite, the other three move towards the ship.

The Caracalla reports, "There are several military-grade ships locked on to our location. They should be ready to launch in three eins and their possible ETA is around six eins."

"Move!" Kraa-Nuve grabs his communicator. "Fast!" This probably is not the best recommendation to send to two of the faster beings in all of the universes. Amethyst can move very fast, which she does, but she has no chance in keeping up with Desha and Proximity even when they are not running near a quarter of their top foot speed.

They get around the corner near the shipyard and parking garages, close enough to run around them instead of trying to go straight through. Desha takes the roundabout route with Amethyst but, of course, Proximity stops. "I'm not leaving without you!" Desha yells over her communicator.

"Ya ain't gotta!" Proximity looks through the garages and back towards the town where his friend of many cycles is probably struggling for dear life somewhere and he is here, running away from it. He looks over to where Desha was, out of view now, and Amethyst passes by, looking him in the eye. He remembers her telling him to trust Synite and he thinks about all of the trials they have been through: the escape from Atlan, Omega 2, the mountains of Earth 8. This is only another wrung on the ladder for Synite's climb to truth and freedom. Proximity decides to follow the plan as none of Synite's plans have failed yet.

He does a good job avoiding everything for a while until there is a moving vehicle coming out of a garage. He does great dodging it but cannot help but slam into the parked ship behind it, crashing through the door and out the other side. After he rolls and gathers his steps, he looks back and waves, "Sorry!" Luckily for him, the faster he runs, the sturdier his body gets even though he ends up with a few bruises.

The two ladies make it to the mezzanine and board the ship in time to see Synite and Driven's indicators get right outside where Promis's is blinking from. "They stopped," Desha notices. Something crashes outside and Amethyst goes out to take a look at why there is a hole in the ship adjacent to them.

Desha steps off the ship in time to hear, "Came in a tad hot," Proximity says as he brushes himself off as he sits in the wreckage. "Tha's twice today!" Desha goes and helps pull him out and they pause as the queen jogs over to them.

Amethyst looks over to the stairs that she is sure Proximity came up. "Was something chasing you?" He does not respond but, when she looks over the edge of the mezzanine, she can see the dozens of wolfrats pour into the bottom of the parking hub like a wave through a dry valley. Some even start climbing up the outside walls and others storm up the stairwell.

"We have to fend them off, right?" Desha looks at Amethyst.

Driven and Synite stand outside of a tall, eerily abandoned warehouse about a half-kilometer away from the parking area. From the outside they can see it has very few windows and fewer style points. "In," Kraa-Nuve says over their earbuds. "Top. Time short."

'Another ambush,' Gale assumes. "There's no way it's not bad in there," Synite is assured by both the location and silence from inside.

"After you," Driven puts a hand out for Synite. "I'm sure it's sticky, hombre." He stretches and pulls Grace back out.

"The ships have launched," the Caracalla notes as the two of them head inside. "Six eins."

The higher in the building they get, the closer they get to the room she is in, the louder the growls and barks of more than fifty more wolfrat soldiers reverberate from the shadows. In the center of that room sits a young lady, her mouth wrapped with little care and familiar electromagnetic shackles clamped on her hands and ankles. Her dress is torn and dingy from being mishandled and mangled.

Promis shivers and her breathy moans are muffled by her binding, sweat and tears rolling down her face. "Shhhhhhhhhh," comes from deep in the darkness followed by an enthusiastic whisper: "They're here!" Promis cries harder as she searches the room, finally seeing the same garment of the woman whose purse was snatched by the first wolfrat. She glides a few centimeters off the ground over to Promis's side. Her face covered down to the chin, she leans down and touches Promis's shoulder: "It won't be long now, darling. Your other friends should be leaving you soon, too!"

"I can hear voices," Synite says as they trod through the dark hallway.

"Not used to fighting with a low roof over your head, I'm sure," Driven says to Synite's shrug, "but there's a first time for everything, right?" They get to some double-doors that Driven is sure leads to the room Promis is in. "No concierge?"

Promis breathes heavy in the silence and is startled by the door getting kicked in. When the dust settles, she sees Synite shoulder to shoulder with Driven who is holding Grace out, looking for a target. She moans loudly to get their attention as they did not see her or the flash of white as the hooded woman disappeared.

"Sarah!" Synite moves to go to her but before he can make it two steps, Driven puts his free hand over Synite's chest and nods at the sea of darkness behind her.

"Take a look see," Synite scans the room and notices the darkness shift, a few mustard-colored eyes gleam from behind her as the drip and pooling of thick saliva adds more gruesome tension to the already taut room. "They're not going to let this be a cakewalk."

"Can your Borganics adjust to pressure changes?" Synite whispers to Driven, confident that they can and confirmed with a nod. "Sarah, it's going to get kind of hard to breathe in here. Bear with me."

Synite fills the room with thinner Air, making it harder for aerobic sensitive beings to keep going, a power that Gale released to him recently. He hears the wolfrats coughing and wheezing but sees how it is making Promis nearly pass out, too. She shakes it off and tears fall from the strain on her body. "I don't think that's a good idea, bud. If she passes out for too long, she might have dain bramage."

"You're right," Synite releases and watches as her breathing slows back to normal.

"Four eins," The ship reminds them.

"Seems as if there's only one way," Synite pushes Driven's hand off and continues to his lady. About halfway there, he summons Gale and bashes the first attacking wolfrat across the face. Things seem to move slower for Synite as adrenaline rushes through his veins. "Here they come!" Driven lurches forward and meets one with a cross to the ribs, the crunching of bones music to his soul. He dodges another's claw and parries the next slash. The horde marches into the dim light and out past Promis, creating a wall between the vanguards and her.

A feminine laugh comes from the darkness behind them, "You can have her if you can get through them!"

"Who are you?" Synite yells back, fighting head-on through wolfrat after wolfrat with his staff swinging about. He cannot count how many of these rodent dogs there are as the room seems to be filling with them.

"Thank you for bringing my item back to me," she throws the purse out into the open, "but I've got plenty of them. You can keep it!" She laughs much louder and Synite starts to get angry.

"This is getting extremely old," Driven punches a wolfrat with the butt of the gun right before he fires a ricochet bullet towards where her laugh rings from. After it pings off three surfaces it stops and so does the rest of the room.

They all wait to see what happened; Driven completely sure he hit her until he hears the bullet tap the floor. "You think one little bullet can penetrate me? You overestimate yourself, boy!"

A wolfrat jumps at Driven from behind, grabbing his shoulders wide and pulling him in close. He wraps around the young gunslinger and takes him to the ground. Driven fires two shots away from them, rolls over and punches the beast in the gut a few times. Driven dodges another grappling attempt and pushes it into an open space. After a sequence of pings, two bullet holes smoke from its back and it drops to the ground.

Still fighting but momentarily amazed, Synite tries to fathom what his tag partner pulled off a moment ago. He does not get much time to worry about it as the both of them have their hands full. Synite takes out three of them at once and sees Promis lying a couple of meters away from him, groaning and crying as loud as she can. "Sarah!"

On the roof of the parking garage, Desha and Proximity box with the twenty-plus wolfrats that are surrounding them. Laser fire comes from the Caracalla and knocks a few vermin off the edge of the roof. "Come!" Kraa-Nuve has not shot his own guns in too long. Amethyst keeps her distance from the fight, standing on the ramp that stretches upwards to the communication room.

"Three eins before we are in range of the military ships' weapons," the Caracalla warns everyone.

"Engines," Kraa-Nuve announces over the communicators. "Meet kid out."

As the vertical takeoff engines start and push dust around the mezzanine, Amethyst hops down to get her friends. "Come in!" she demands, "We can't worry about them right now. We have to leave!" They each get one last knockout in before grabbing each other's hands and going on the ship as it swallows its landing gear.

Driven pinball ricochets his gunfire around the room, hitting wolfrat after wolfrat but getting no real headway. Synite is blasting winds around, knocking groups of two and three of them out of his way but it is not enough to get Promis. Some bullets crash out of the glass windows and the high altitude Air starts to creep in and chill the room.

"Kid!" Kraa-Nuve yells in his ear.

"I'm not leaving her!" Proximity listens to Synite's struggle next to the captain.

Driven chimes in, "We can finish this!" He grunts and boxes through a corner of the horde, utilizing the butt of Grace. He looks beyond them and sees Synite absorb Gale, sparking his electric aura. "Flashy! I love it!" Driven puts his shades back on in the middle of a punch to prepare for what is to come.

Synite stretches both arms out to his sides with his palms opened and fires off a rail of ion orbs with bolts of lightning trailing through. They zap and push back ten wolfrats at a time, clearing a path to Promis but only for a moment. That path closes as fast as it opened, frustrating them even more.

Right outside, the hooded woman saw the flashes of light and heard the whimpers that followed. The blasts sent pieces of the walls flying out and around, her mouth showing a lack of concern for any of the events. She waits until she hears more barks before smiling and whizzing away, flying out of the atmosphere and off-planet.

Driven comes to Synite's side and they lean back to back, "They have no intent on killing us or her. They're stalling, trying to make sure we don't leave. Whoever their leader is wants something else. They're distracting us."

"They're not going to get her!" Synite pushes a gust of wind through the room, knocking dust, hair and canine spit around. The wolfrats have a hard time keeping their footing, a few flying out of the windows, and Synite treads over to retrieve the captive. One of the wolfrats rides the wind and tackles Synite from the side. He drops the wind and they scurry into a crescent line of defense between Promis and her rescuers. One of the wolfrats grabs Promis and she screams a muffled, "Help!"

"Guys," Desha warns, "They're coming in fast so we're going to have to meet you in the sky. We have less than three eins to get off-planet before we have another Earth 8 situation," she looks at the screen that shows what is below, "except this time we're on top of a crowded mall."

"Get her!" Proximity demands.

The wolfrats growl aggressively at the two of them as another group gathers behind the first line and another behind that one. Driven looks over at Synite's defeated eyes looking down at Promis between bunches of dirty, shuffling feet. Driven knows what has to happen but waits for the decision to be made. Synite looks back and Driven tells him, "You gotta do what you gotta do."

"Sarah," Synite's voice shakes and she shakes her head and screams a muffled 'no' in fear. "We're going to get you no matter what. Hang in there for me!" Her cries hurt him as much as they hurt her as he turns and crashes out of the building, Driven running after with a loud, angry grunt. Synite gives Driven a lift to the rooftop and he runs alongside as Synite flies low. "You don't mind getting thrown, do you?"

They make eye contact, "I'm liking you more every moment buddy!"

They both pick up their pace and Driven jumps off the edge of the building right next to Synite. He grabs Driven's hands, spins around twice, and throws him feet-first through the glass. Driven rolls in behind the wolfrats and runs up to the crop, tackling a bunch of them at the same time. Synite flies in, surrounded by Gale's energy and bowls through a large group of them as well, close enough to brush against Promis's arm.

Driven gets to his side as fast as he can and knocks out the wolfrat that is holding Promis then grabs her hand. He pulls her a few meters but not far enough as another wolfrat grabs her by the ankles. Another comes and plops on top of her; another dives to tackle Driven to the ground but gets axe kicked; another comes at Driven's other leg; two more grab his forearm and they pull him away from their prized Promis. "Give her back!"

Synite comes blasting through as Driven shakes free of the two that are on him. She reaches for them as the one that ripped her from Driven drapes her over a shoulder and runs off with Promis in tow towards the windows. "No!" Synite pulls a strong wind inward, pushing against the progress of the wolfrat that fights to get to the window. Synite strides through the wind towards Promis's open hands but, before he can reach her, a wave of wolfrats takes him down. The wind slows down enough for the one hoisting Promis to get through it and Synite is forced to watch as they burst out of the building.

Twenty more wolfrats follow suit, creating a cascade of glass and ugly falling from the side of the building. As they crash out of the topmost floor, Synite blasts through the roof and swoops around to the side they came out of, only seeing the bunch of wolfrats falling to the ground. He flies down, fighting through them, as even more jump out as he goes through. He elbows his way to a clear area, seeing no trace of the Promis or where they could have re-entered the building. Since so many windows were cracked where all of the other wolfrats that survived crashed back through, he knows it would take way more than two eins for him to figure out where she went in, much less retrieve her. Those that did not make it whimper as they paint the pavement below.

Synite grunts loudly and retrieves Driven from the top floor, hurting inside since he could not save her with enough time for everyone to make it out safely. His grip is tight from frustration, "We could've gotten her out. We could have. We should've done more." This is truly where his relationship with Driven begins. As skittish and reckless as Driven is as his polar opposite, Synite feels as though he will be here with him for a long time.

"I know," Driven agrees, "I'm with you one hundred percent. I haven't run from a fight in longer than I can remember." Heartache and loss are nothing new to Synite but this version of it definitely is novel. *How could I let this happen? What am I going to tell everybody?* But they already know as Synite and Driven's indicators go away from the one in the middle of that warehouse.

The class-E fighters skirt under the clouds in formation, less than an ein from Synite and Driven and two away from the ship. Kraa-Nuve engages flight controls and Amethyst gets in the co-pilot chair. Proximity is frozen as he watches his friend's dot blink there, all alone. He can feel her fear and it turns into anger towards Synite. He thinks if he had not followed Synite's order, the three of them probably could have gotten her, especially with his speed.

"Bet I beat you to the ship!" Driven says over the communicator to Synite.

"Like guy," Kraa-Nuve speaks of his fondness to Driven's attitude. "Genetic."

Amethyst looks over, remembering the previous mentioning of Kraa-Nuve having some knowledge of Driven's parentage. "You know his family, don't you?"

"Couple," Kraa-Nuve says, focused on the rendezvous.

Synite sees the ship on the horizon and hears more coming from behind them. Driven hops up to a taller roof, kicks over to another building and scales the tallest one in the vicinity. He waits for the ship to get close enough and leaps onto the top. The Pingar comes up over them with a ladder hanging down and he grabs hold then climbs up into his ship. "Told you!"

Synite, still in the doldrums, flies lazily into the communication room, steps lazily and drops to his knees in the corner as the hatch closes behind him. They get off planet and the military ships neglect to follow them. Proximity barrels into the communication room, venting with every step. "I'm sorry," Synite admits his fault. "I couldn't get her out. We tried our hardest."

"But I coulda helped like I said! You…you sat there and tol' me not to! She my friend and ya said ya'd get her. Can't believe I trusted chu," Proximity does not hold back his scolding. "I coulda got her m'self for all dat!"

"Are you saying we didn't try?" Synite yells back.

"I'm sayin' she should be righ' here wif us!" Proximity steps towards the dormitories.

"I didn't just let them take her!" Synite tries to convince him past his anger. "You know we couldn't have stayed down there any longer without someone dying!"

Proximity swings around and runs up to Synite's face, "You an' dat long hair guy tol' us you could save 'er. How I'm posed to trust y'all if y'all ain't backin' up ya words?"

"I'm sure it's more complicated," Desha follows her partner as he trots out of the room. "She's our friend, too!"

"If you actually thought so much about it," Synite growls, "you could've come and got in the fight. But you didn't! You ran because that's all you know how to do!"

"As long as she's alive, we haven't failed her!" Desha yells. "I understand why you're both mad but save it for our enemies! Don't point it at each other!"

"Prepare for PSL jump," The Caracalla reports and everyone straps in. Synite takes Amethyst's place in the co-pilot station, obviously aggravated by the argument.

"Not pilot mad. Focus," Kraa-Nuve tells him. "Steady." Synite's silence is telling enough; he tries to calm back down on his own but it is not working. Kraa-Nuve gives some compassion, a trait he has rarely shown. "Been there. Couldn't save, either. No way could prepare."

"I'm supposed to be ready for anything! Santhia taught me that. Amethyst, too! Now look at--" Synite's body tenses up through the PSL jump and, during the jolt, his mind goes down a dark path. His emotions about Promis and his failure swell and, once they make it to the other side, tears stream down from his eyes. "I tried. I wasn't strong enough. I promised we would save--" his shortened breaths cut off his words.

He remembers when he was a child of maybe six cycles, looking out into the rain with his father's hands on his shoulders. "I'm sorry, son. I tried. I," his father swallowed his next words, fighting back his emotions for losing the mother of his only son.

"Why did she leave us, dad?" Synite remained calm, aided by the storm outside, but was truly upset beyond his own comprehension.

"I'm not sure," officer Nitengale's stress showed in the wrinkles around his face. "Maybe it was her nature." He kneeled in front of his son, "Some people just can't stay in one place for long times. They have to move on to new things no matter how much it may hurt the people who love them." Synite looked past his father's hurt eyes, "It doesn't matter as long as you know that I will never leave you."

CHAPTER VIII

The Sword's team has travelled all around Earth 11 to fight in the season of team battles. They remain undefeated with only one match left in the season and are preparing for the tournament-style championship that starts in sixty days.

During the season, akin to the events from the first fight, they have gained allies from five out of their eight battles. Through the battles, the Sword picked up seven that survived and are still on the active roster: NanVash, the invulnerable athlete with useful, bat-like wings; Suubai, the psionics expert; Abo Mimao, the ex-assassin with a steel Will and matching plates on his skin; Soldati Dmittri, who uses pyrotechnics and a pitchfork; Korisong, who uses sound waves to hypnotize and cripple; Orchanik G, with her elastic limbs that grow spikes when necessary; and Gith Rotugutu, a mid-level Earth elementalist who would rather crack jokes with the guys and hang out with Arra.

Arra has been instrumental to the team's new level of success. Since Wik was killed, she has shown the world how dangerous a scorned Fire elementalist can be, especially when that scorn is focused into a purpose. The rotation has changed several times as they allowed Castra to heal from a leg injury sustained in training. Lo kept his leadership position and has not disappointed whatsoever throughout.

NanVash, Suubai, and Abo have all stepped up when it counted; not that the others have disappointed at all. In his first battle with the team, NanVash gave the final blow and was the main reason Korisong and Orchanik G joined, Suubai saved Arra's life in the most recent match, and Abo Mimao has eight kills in his five battles, more than any one on their team has recorded in the full nine matches the team has fought in.

However, there is another team from the Sur K'oma region that is the group to watch out for, so the analysts on the Sword Report say. The Arena K'oma team has the leader in kills and submissions, Coldsmoke, with fourteen kills and another eighteen submissions. Their team has only taken two additions all season and would not have them had those elementalists not been the most difficult for Coldsmoke to kill.

On the surface, there is very little that is special about Coldsmoke, though, as far as flashy powers go. He is incredibly strong, but not the most powerful; incredibly quick, but not the fastest; agile, but not the most dexterous; smart, but not the most intelligent. What Coldsmoke has is the almighty x-factor: a great and powerful Will that he pushes to make a win out of nothing and outdo opponents in very simple fashions.

One of the most underrated values about Coldsmoke at the beginning of the season, though everyone respects it now, was his training and practice ethic. He trains twice a day, every day, in every training program and fight simulator that has been made available to him. His team has bought into it as well and attributes the majority of their success to his leadership outside of where blood is shed.

Castra and his entire team is out on the training grounds going through drills that they have designed based on their experiences in battle so far. They go through different rotations, seeing who is performing the best as the last season bout is in twenty days. They brainstorm with each other and outline team combinations and cues for each other to initiate the combinations together.

"You healed up yet, princess?" Lo asks Castra who directs Lo's spar with Gith from the sidelines. "You'll be coach Castra soon, eh?"

"You want me to come out there and show you?" Castra cannot hold the straight face he attempts. It quickly turns into a grimace and then a feeble attempt at holding back laughter. "I couldn't do it!"

"That's not all you can't do," Gith is very comfortable in this forested environment considering his elementalist affinity. He has become the next third jokester in their group, filling in for Lone; Lo and Castra embrace every moment of it.

"Your ex knows exactly what I can or cannot do," Castra bites back, much to Gith's chagrin.

"If you're talking about the same ex I think you're talking about, I know what you have and do not have as well!" Gith fist bumps Lo and they laugh together.

"Are we working here or making jokes?" Arra tries to get the boys back on track.

"Can't we multitask?" Lo raises the intensity of his spar and Gith's defense adjusts fast. "Our main objective here is to get more comfortable with each other's strengths and weaknesses anyway."

"One of Castra's weaknesses being his terrible jokes," Lo fires.

Gith punches at Lo with fists as hard as stone and blocks with the same power. "What better way to expose a weakness than keep the enemy distracted?"

"Oh, well excuse me for being a little more focused," Arra comes back.

Castra puts a hand up and everyone halts, "Santhia, may she rest in peace, trained Synite in hand-to-hand combat. He told me that, in every training session, she was teaching him verbally while attacking him with everything she had. Now, I'm not saying we're all going to get as powerful as him, but I know for a fact that following their training principles gives us the edge.

"They planned a ton and she knew how to plan for him because she knew all of his strengths and weaknesses," Castra limps through the group of them, touching each of his team members. "She magnified his strengths and minimized his weaknesses in every battle. The only way we can do that together is if we communicate and get better.

"So, talk to each other while you're sparring for the next hecu. Have regular conversation. Get to know each other better! I don't expect us all to love each other the way they did, but it would be nice. And the only way we can do that is if--"

"Castra Nim," a group of attendees and unrecognizable agents come up on the group.

Castra turns and scoffs from the middle of the circle, "I was in the middle of a very good speech man!"

"Our apologies for the inconvenience. However, there is a pressing matter to attend to," the attendee steps forward from the group. "If you would come with us, we have business."

"If it is any business to do with this team, you can say it in front of everyone here," Castra has grown into full command.

"If you wish," the attendee steps back and the lead agent steps forward.

Castra, like the rest of his team, does not recognize him or his clothing. "Who are you?"

The tall, thin, white skinned agent puts both of his hands forward. "Greetings, Castra Nim. I'm from Arena K'oma. I cordially announce that you've been traded to our team for a lump sum of Marks. I welcome you."

"Wait," Lo says. "Traded to K'oma? Who authorized this?"

"That was my line," Castra says. "How do you think--"

"As a fighter for the Sword in the team battles," the agent reports, "any of you can be traded at any time prior to the final tournament by management the same as how any of you can relinquish your own contracts during a losing arena match. It is in your contractual agreements and only fair that we have the ability to purchase your contract as much as you have the ability to give it away."

"So, he can just be sent away like that?" Arra, resembling the rest of the team, does not agree with this but, as warriors of fortune, exactly how much freedom should they assume they have?

"I implore you to have no feeling about this business decision," which is what members of a team filled with pride always say when they know they have dipped into the chemistry and heart of a possible opponent just by spending a few Marks, "since that is exactly what it was. And, it is done. You should report to the rails in the morning." The agent turns around and the entire mob of agents and attendees take their leave.

And the forest is silent as the team is stunned. "What are we supposed to do? We're probably going to end up--" Suubai stops. He knows nobody wants to hear it but it is true: knowing the advantage this gives Arena K'oma and their roster, this means they will more than likely end up fighting against Castra.

"Well, guys," Castra looks down and shakes his head, "what can you do when you're only a piece of paper and a price to these animals?"

"You could stay," Gith suggests. "Just putting it out there."

"I don't think they're going to let it work that simply," Castra regrets. "Not when lives and large Marks are on the line."

"We have to figure something out," Gith will not let it be.

"No," Castra has an epiphany, thinking more about the bigger picture and the real future, not solely the future of this team's success. "It'll be perfectly fine." He steps out of the circle and turns to look at everyone. "Well? Back to training! Just because I'm leaving doesn't mean you should slow down! And, if you're worried about me watching your techniques, I already know most of them like the back of my hand anyway since I came up with them. Man, I hope they thumbed enough Marks for me!" Unknown to Castra or anyone else, the rights Castra's contract was bought by Arena K'oma that morning for M50 million. His pay shall not increase from his cycle salary of M600,000.

The next day's Sword Report, which airs while Castra rides the train sur to K'oma, is littered with coverage on the trade, what it means for the future of the Sword and the tournament world in general. Many of the experts are completely counting the Sword team out of winning the championships now, some having them going out in the first round with the loss of their captain.

Castra knows otherwise but it would be difficult to defeat him and Coldsmoke on the same side of the field, which he is more than certain is part of the plan. He is sure they will allow him to get healthy, which will not take long, while he oversees their trainings and strategies. Then, once he gets healthy, put him in the rotation by the second round of the tournament since he does not have to participate in any battles before then to be eligible to participate in the possible championship.

How can I keep the advantage here? Castra already knows what he has to do in K'oma and the opportunity this is giving him as a member of the Vanguard, but this is a difficult position to be in. He is almost lucky that his injury gives him more time to assess the situation and not be distracted by developing active battle tactics.

Castra is glad he was able to give the team that last nugget during their training session. *Lo and Arra should be able to handle the motivation portion of training and leaders step up in battle when it's necessary. They'll be fine. Especially since their lives are on the line.* He hopes things move faster and thinks about what is going on with the crew of the Caracalla.

The sky is starless, the land is flat: the barren field stretches on for kilometers in every direction. There is no grass or life for kilometers in either direction across this plain and the only light is from the crescent moon. Synite is running across the field, alone, chasing or being chased by something or someone even he cannot see. *We're catching up,* he looks into the pitch black sky, kicking up dust behind him. *Why can't we fly?*

He looks into the sky that is fully populated with stars now. *What planet is this?* After running for what felt like a very long distance but not covering much ground, Synite pants like a tired dog as he slides to a stop at the edge of a chasm, deep and wide. *I feel tired. My lungs hurt. What is this?* To his left, there is no end to the chasm; to the right, there is no end to the chasm.

He lies on his stomach at the edge and looks down into it, the depths as dark as the starless, pitch black night sky that It blends in with. He gets up from his stomach and looks over the chasm at its seemingly endless darkness of depth. 'It's too far to jump,' Gale adds. 'Maybe we can try to fly.'

As Synite gets up to make an effort, he sees a female with dark red hair on the other side of the chasm. She saunters away, her hair swaying and bouncing as she picks up speed. "Wait! Wait for me!" He stands on the edge, shaking his arms out to get prepared, then squats and jumps for it.

Synite feels the tremendous sensation of gliding with no help but it only lasts a moment. He falls, watching as she disappears up the horizon of his eyes. All he sees now is darkness and all he feels is the pull of the underworld.

Before he hits the darkness, Synite gasps and his eyes open as his mind returns him from the world inside to the space outside. "Are you alright?" Promis's voice comes from behind him.

"A nightmare," he says, barely noticing the strangeness of the room around him. "Third in a row." He reaches for Promis behind him and grabs nothing but Air and bed sheet. She is absent from her position and he is actually alone in the room. "Where? Where are you?"

"I thought using her voice pattern would help regulate your heart rate," the Caracalla continues using Promis's voice to speak to Synite.

"You thought?" Synite is baffled by the ship's intelligence but is reminded that it is indeed merely a machine that does not quite understand fickle human emotion. "Next time, don't."

"Duly noted," the Caracalla's voice returns to normal. "It did work, however." Synite gets up and grabs his tablet.

> This distance between us is what people take for granted.
> It is what keeps me unsatisfied enough to fight to close it.
> My heart doesn't like it, yet it grows because of the distance.
> It's why I'm working and so motivated to be more than just great.
> It's the reason I need the world, every universe to embrace me.
> Unity is what; forever is when; everywhere.
> Your beauty is why; my power is how.

After he finishes putting his thoughts down, he heads into the center of the ship. Everyone gathered in the communication room, their dwelling drifting about in outer space, away from any detection that they know about in this far reaching area. There is an unsettling quiet wringing any spirit from the room that is quickly broken by Driven's projection, "So, is nobody wondering what the hell is going on here? I'm the only one? Big, smelly, purple oliphantus in the room!"

"Whatchu think?" Proximity already has his opinion. "Marks, man."

"Not best," Kraa-Nuve knows the mindset of most bounty hunters as he played that role once before. "Too hard."

"Right," Synite feels the same way. "Driven and I both noticed something weird about fighting those rat things. They never tried to capture us. They could've killed her in front of us, so we know that's not their objective. Their leader even told us that we could have her if we got through."

Proximity scoffs but decides to keep his comment to himself this time. Driven crosses his arms, "Yeah. They were stalling."

"A group of them attacked us, too," Desha points out. "Do you think they were trying to get one of us to sweeten their score?"

"Not Marks. Statement," Kraa-Nuve tries to get the two fastest beings he has ever met to speed up to their conversation.

"They went after the easiest target," Amethyst comments, "why her? I agree that money is an easy answer until you take into account that her bounty isn't nearly the biggest of the group and that they only garnered the attention of the few of us with larger bounties. They want our attention."

Synite brings to the table, "But, for what reason?" He looks up at Driven's projection and over at Proximity and Desha. "There were enough of them to get at least one of us and there's no telling who their leader was. She was very confident in the ability of that horde."

"I think their power was in numbers," Driven commented. "We dropped 'em one after another. They just kept coming."

Synite gets up and goes to the cockpit for a moment, his thoughts buzzing and bumping into each other, then comes back. "There must be something else, he marches in confidently. They know they couldn't get us in a straightforward fight. They didn't come at us head first with those numbers. They had to catch us off guard."

"Knew were there," Kraa-Nuve adds.

"And that's another thing," Amethyst questions. "How could they have known?"

"Isn't Atlan trying to broadcast our every move anyway?" Desha brings into the argument. "Is it safe to assume that, since we were there for so long, together, and since it has nothing to do with Marks, that the Enslaver knew?"

Kraa-Nuve hates to admit: "Must."

"Who was that trap really for?" Synite wonders. "If those things were in league with the Enslaver, they got Sarah. But, in getting her, what are they actually after? What does It want?"

Everyone looks at Amethyst almost at the same time. "We cannot assume I'm the target," she responds. "At least not immediately."

"You might be the main one, though!" Driven follows through. "You've always been the main target, right?"

"She has to be the Enslaver's main objective. I don't think the Sword would be putting up near this fuss had we left Earth 11 without her," Synite acknowledges his lack of importance in comparison to Amethyst for the future of the Sword.

"I believe the purpose of taking Promis," Amethyst does not appreciate the entire room's attention being on her, especially considering the events that just occurred, "would be to get your attention, Synite. They want your guard down."

Desha returns, "And if his guard is down, who else would they go after? Us? The other ship? The captain?"

"I hate to say it but, it has to be you, Amey," he knows she does not want it to be but it is the only conclusion he can come up with given the variables. "The Enslaver knows about your power and the emotional toll it takes on you. If my guard is down, then you'll get pulled into a fight. If you get pulled into a fight, afterwards you'll lose your motivation and your guard'll be completely down exactly like it was over the mountains on Omega 2. You almost gave up your life up there!" Synite paces and claps lightly as the light bulb burns brighter, "That's their plan! They want to send a strong pawn at us to force Amethyst to fight and then capture her. We have an idea but don't know who the strongest pawn is, so we should keep our trust at a minimum at this point. If they take her, they'll be able to take or kill any of us. She's the king of this war. That's why we need you back," Synite turns around to see Psilos's projection step in from the cockpit. He called Psilos for another valuable perspective on the situation before the conversation started but Psilos did not want to actually speak on it until absolutely necessary. He finalizes his plea, "We need your strength, yes; but most importantly, we need your sight."

Psilos watches all eyes turn to him as Synite takes his seat again. "I understand the reasoning behind your concluding argument. However, I am indeterminate and tentative that logic should be implemented when conducting against the beings you have recently run into. It could be unpretentiously about Marks, this being a stratagem to procure the higher targets, Amethyst, Synite, myself, by distracting those exact targets with an illogical action."

"Anybody else having a rough time keeping up?" Driven squints.

"King," Kraa-Nuve grunts, recognizing the voice of the leader and the validity of that voice.

"You must not restrict your arguments," Psilos reiterates. "I do wish to reunify our company as soon as the occasion avails itself, my friends. I long for your comradeship, though resolving and refurbishing my home has fulfilled some of my greatest aspirations." He looks to Amethyst, "When I reconcile a few more things here, I am determined to seek your position."

"And, in the meantime?" Driven still is not sure what the decision is. "We've talked, now what are we going to do about this threat? I hate running from fights. I feel as though I owe those rat-things some bullets," he looks over at Synite, "to their legs and arms. No killing?"

"I'm almost ready to take some lives myself to get her back," Synite grins. "I almost felt like using full power in there."

"Spirit!" Kraa-Nuve is ready for the grit to come from Synite's hands.

Proximity remains a man of few words when angry, "Whatchu gon' do 'bout it?"

"We," Synite corrects, "have to figure out where they took her and then return the favor."

Psilos inquires, "What beings had any sort of knowledge of any of your location? Were there any scheduled encounters or assignations that any being was in the know about any of your attendance?"

"Well," Driven squeaks, "there was my sale. I'm not sure how they would have made a connection between us, but--"

"That is where you should originate your inquiry. We must presuppose that any contact, especially unremitting contact, would put you in a specific place at a specific time and, consequently, would give them an event to plan around. Find that being and who they associate with; there you may discover the foundation of every part of our state of affairs," Psilos advises.

"How would they have known we were going shopping and to kidnap Sarah?" Amethyst is not sure this is the correct assumption.

Synite chimes, "I'm sure you were followed, probably more closely than the rest of us. If they knew where Driven was going to be, then they surely could've known where he was before we got there. They may have had a group waiting near where we were staying but we didn't have time to check because we had to run."

"And with the number of those things that we saw, all bases were probably covered," Driven adds. "I'll do some research since I got her thumb and get back with you all." His projection disappears.

"I implore the lot of you to keep watchful eyes on that young fellow of ours," Psilos warns the crew as his projection closes. "His reckless comportment may generate us even more misfortune."

Synite glances over at Amethyst whose sadness reflects from her glaring mahogany eyes, in contrast to her glowing, even skin. She unconsciously caresses the bracelet and, as she lowers her eyes in that same emotion, she catches herself and puts her hands flat on the table. Synite looks at her and cannot help but think of how fragile she is. Her heart, to him, is the only part of her that needs protection yet cannot be shielded. One cannot protect their heart from their own emotions.

He immediately feels apologetic for everything: for not being satisfied with earning the same life Amethyst had on Atlan, for pulling all of these beings into this maelstrom of problems, for forcing them to deal with the danger. And, he is sure that this is not nearly the end of it. To him, this may only be the beginning.

Many beings who are not enslaved may still allow the slave mentality to inhabit their hearts and everyday lives as they become slaves to one or more of many different types of things. Unfortunately, for the slaves of things, as opposed to the slaves of beings, the creators of those things may not have intended for such a relationship.

Actual slavery, enforced bondage, is one of the darkest stains on the histories of many worlds. It is a stain that cannot be cleaned as it has had both negative and positive ramifications for the beings that experienced it and the worlds they live in. Slavery has built nations, wondrous monuments, and races of strong-Willed beings that have carried civilization. Flip the coin and the brutality of slavery has sent talented lives, centuries of knowledge, the youth of families, and colorful cultures into oblivion. It has also rippled through the cultures of modern peoples, affecting the relations between enslavers and the freed cultures. It has taken the future generations of kings and forced them into cycles of mental subservience and social illiteracy, not to mention actual illiteracy.

Actual slavery of groups can end with whatever revolution frees them from bondage, an external event that changes the lives of others. Despite the crippled generations after, the act of slavery itself is over on the surface level although the enslaved and the slavers mentality does ripple throughout the generations after.

The other type of slavery, mental slavery, has its roots in addictions of many kinds and takes an internal revolution to abolish. Beings can be mental slaves to many things; from high-fashion to something as harmless as serving the needy in the community to mind-altering substances. Anything can keep a being from participating in the world outside of an enslaver. Beings may go to extremes to get or participate in whatever activity enslaves them, avoiding unnecessary social activity and development or accepting being alienated by the activity. These beings get so emotional over their mental enslaver that they may even become a slave to their own emotion as well.

Mental slaves use excuses upon excuses to not be social or go outside their comfort zone so much that some may not even realize that they are what they are. It does not matter how many other beings try to get them to actively participate in something else, they become defensive about their enslaver as it is the only thing they know as right and necessary in their life.

As mentioned before, when this mental slavery is to a creation or adaptation of another being, such as a sport or a particular food, it is difficult for someone who is not a slave to it to blame the creator and impossible for the slave not to. It is strange from the outside looking in and the finger is mostly pointed at the slave for the reason why they are that way. However, until there is an epiphany, the slave will always feel helpless at the unbreakable whim of their master.

A problem arises for the free when the masses are at the whims of the same mental master. When beings notice that thousands of other beings cannot look up for themselves as they are so focused on their mental slavery, then a revolution must be made. Eyes must be opened to the fact that there is a world outside of slavery and the choice must be given to be freed or remain. This process may take generations, high-profile deaths, or wars, unfortunately.

In the octadecaverse, there are twice as many slaves as there are truly free beings. In that number, there are twice as many mental slaves as there are actual slaves. There are twice as many isolated mental slaves who do not even acknowledge their slavery as there are grouped. A great number of beings, enough to populate an existing universe or two, can never be free because they will not free themselves from the shackles of mental slavery.

CHAPTER IX

Desha takes a seat across from Proximity in their room on the Caracalla and looks at him, all love and passion in her eyes. "I'm ready."

"Fo'?" Proximity is still a little charged from his friend getting kidnapped.

"A'mal," She kneels in front of him and grabs his hands. "I think, considering what I feel for you and the things we'll be facing in the near future, it is the perfect time."

Proximity gets on the floor with her, his heart racing a bit from nervous excitement. "What I gotta do?"

Her gaze shifts between his eyes, looking for the highest approval, "Are you sure you're ready? I don't want you to--"

"I been waitin' a good while, Desh," she could not have gotten any better response. "So, jus' tell me what I gotta do?"

"Stand up and put your back to mine," they stand at the same time, back to back, "grab both of my hands," and they interlock fingers. "Now, close your eyes, relax and embrace the feeling. No matter how it feels at first, embrace it."

In Desha's culture, even after committing their lives to each other, there is another step called Animus A'mal, which is the spiritual combining of souls, the amalgamation of two lives. The Animus/anima psychology system, from Carl Jung defines them as the primary anthropomorphic archetypes of the unconscious mind as well as the abstract symbol sets that formulate the Self. They are the elements of the collective unconscious, a domain that transcends the personal psyche. They are the masculine and feminine side inside of every being that deals in sexuality.

The only ritual is that they stand and connect, then the person who has the power to do so, in this case Desha, does an enchantment and the two committed beings' spirits are combined to where they can, after a certain amount of practice, actually combine their physical bodies as well as a collective soul.

She described this concept to Proximity after they publicized their commitment and he was nervous about it at first, as he is right now, but knew he would do anything for her no matter what the cost. For A'mal, the cost is a small portion of one's soul to be permanently tied with the other being in order to experience what Desha's family would call 'the truest form of love any couple could ever experience'. She, as per her customs, waited for her matched opposite to connect and choose to be her partner for the rest of their natural lives, as Proximity did.

This combination through Animus A'mal can only be done once by any person and only be broken by death, the main reason why she had been such a tough person to gain attention from. In death, the life expectancy of the survivor is cut in half, but in life, the life expectancy of both healthy beings is nearly doubled especially when fused.

Their Animus A'mal is an asexual combination, physically, mentally and emotionally. The more often they fuse, the better they get at it, the longer they can sustain A'mal. As they age, their A'mal does as well, in confidence, intuition and insight. Outside of being a combination, it also has its own personality with different strengths and weaknesses, its development in four distinct levels with different religious titles.

This union and separation is philosophically about the connectivity of a committed relationship and how the older a relationship is, the less time the two in the relationship can invariably spend apart. It seems like forever to the both of them for the connection to be made, a journey through spiritual paradise for the both of them. And, as they come back on this side of the spiritual realm, they are breathless together. Their gasps are in perfect time with each other. They turn and look at each other differently than before: deeper, more in tune and together.

Neither of them has to say a word as they know what they are feeling. They bask in the silence and glory of their new connection, separate from the rest of existence, heightened by their own newly unified existence.

Castra Nim follows his escort, led by Spoilsport, into his reception in K'oma. Several of the officers of Arena K'oma greet the two of them in usual K'oma fashion, with a single loud clap in front of their chests. The first few took Castra off guard but as he saw Spoilsport nod lightly at them, he mirrors the activity.

"They don't know me as Spoilsport here," he told Castra before getting out of their vehicle and heading into the uppermost level of Arena

K'oma for the reception. "Most call me Dr. Sinclair. Those closest to me call me Andrea."

Castra snickered, "Isn't that a woman's name? And by close, you mean what? I make up nicknames for people the first time I meet them. Can I call you Andrea, too? Or, how about Dreya? Oh, or Annie!"

"Shut up and follow my lead," Vincent Andreas Sinclair is one of his legal names although no one knows what name his parents gave him, or if he even had parents for that matter. Sometimes he has to remind himself as no one ever calls him the name he was given at birth. "They have strange customs. Stay calm and don't be rude, stupid ginger."

Castra was very disappointed in that attempt at a joke. "Come on now! You could've done better than that, Annie!"

Spoilsport never lets jokes get to him, considering he does not take to heart the grand majority of the things people say to or about him. "I could've, but you won't!" They stepped out of the car into a small crowd of welcomers.

Castra follows directions to the tee, as the way has been paved by Vincent, literally and figuratively, as he is one of the few financial backers for Arena K'oma as well as a few of its warriors, something the Enslaver has no knowledge of which is amazing as It seems to have knowledge of everything else. He limps along behind Spoilsport into the training arena where the K'oma team is waiting, the five of them dressed in matching burnt orange training uniforms except the leader who is in the same uniform but it is dark gray with orange detailing. "This is the team," Spoilsport says as Coldsmoke attempts to greet him; Spoilsport passes directly by the young man and off into the distance, leaving him in a shallow pool of dejection. "Your work starts now, ginger."

"Thanks, Annie." Spoilsport is gone before Castra can get the last word. "Well, guys and gals, I can't train right now but I'll gather a lot from watching you work!"

"It's customary t'introduce yourself," Coldsmoke does not give Castra the privilege of eye contact yet.

"Excuse my rudeness! I'm Castra Nim, for those who didn't read the memo," he limps across the turf towards Coldsmoke with a wide grin and meets the same lack of greeting Spoilsport gave.

"Everyone, introduce yourselves t'th'rookie," Coldsmoke trots back to the center of the training arena, running a hand back through his bowl of curly white hair.

"Bash," he follows Coldsmoke.

"Helena Rour," she follows, too.

"Usurpithy," he goes with Helena.

"Hey," the last warrior, a very tall, very thin member of the team leans down to him with a smile. "Allow me t'apologize on th'behalf of th'group. I'm Liffu, second captain of K'oma team. It's my pleasure t'meet you."

"Pleasure's all mine, Liffu," Castra claps in front of Liffu's chest and is met by a rousing laughter.

"I see you're getting used t'our customs! Very good!" Liffu nods, as the customary response to the clap greeting. "They may take a while t'let you into th'group. That's how some beings in K'oma are. Don't take it as a negative. We have a lot of pride and you're from outside."

"Believe me, I understand," Castra looks past Liffu as the rest of the team starts their training. "I didn't agree to this deal at all. If it were up to me, I'd still be looking forward to killing you!"

"Th'captain protested th'deal, too. We have t'make th'best out of it, right?" Liffu heads into the training session, too, Castra watching for their tendencies, strengths and weaknesses. He takes notes on each of them for the next few days leading up to the last battle, which K'oma's team won handily. Castra kept up with his old team in Atlan as they won their match as well and are looking good as they move into the tournament.

Meanwhile, he and Liffu become friends as he heals up and rehabilitates. The rest of the team does not agree with their fraternizing but Liffu is important to their success and believes whatever Castra can bring to the team is just as important.

Once he feels comfortable with the amount of information he has, he starts to put more weight on the leg, goes for jogs and eventually is able to plant his foot without feeling like he is going to collapse. "I'm almost ready," he tells Liffu as they go through a training gauntlet together.

"If you can make it through this, you should be able t'come in with us," which is what Liffu is looking forward to more than this finish line. "Do you think you can help us t'win the championship?"

"Definitely so," Castra tells his second captain, breathing heavily through the exercise. "There are...weak points...in the defense I've noticed...that could be fixed." Castra does not complete the gauntlet that time but the next day he does and, afterwards they rest up together. "I think the big thing for this team now, Liffu, is to go to the next level. The only way to get there is coaching, man. Not individual coaching. This team has that. It's about the team though. Specific situations, responding to change, knowing each other better than the opponent does, and being able to surprise them when they think they know more than you do."

Liffu listens intently, "I see what you're saying. Since I've been here we've depended on th'captain t'cover flaws."

"That's what I noticed! So," as Castra hears a door zip open behind them, he turns in the middle of his statement to see Coldsmoke.

"Are you ready t'fight me now?"

Liffu looks over at Coldsmoke, "We only recently got out of

th'gauntlet, captain. He needs rest!"

Coldsmoke's expression does not change. "Th'tournament starts in two weeks. Are you ready t'fight me or should I wait another lifetime?"

"Do I get to change shirts? I mean," Castra stands up to Coldsmoke, a little shorter than the captain, "your shirt is very nice. I think these sweaty clothes would be a disadvantage."

They meet in the training arena, Castra in fresh clothes with a few blunt weapons tied to his belt. "So, we're going all out or what?"

"This is a sparring match. I've killed twenty this season and none of them have been from my own team," Coldsmoke reports. "I don't think going all out, as you say, would benefit th'team as you would end up dead."

'Sheeeeeeeeeeeeee planned it all that way, Cairo!' a dark, quivering voice speaks from inside Synite. 'Why would sheeeeeeeeee go off on heeeeeeeeer own and clearly risk the weeeeeeeeeeeell-being of the eeeeeeeeeeeentire creeeeeeeeeeeeeew?' Synite rolls over in the bed that he and Promis used to share aboard the Caracalla, *She was careless! She wasn't used to being watched over, or watched. She slipped up!*

'You and I both know that isn't theeeeeeeeeeeeeeeeee truth!' the demonic voice pokes at his heart, making him feel every notion, every idea that it mentions to him.

'Who are you talking to, Cairo?' Gale interrupts his thoughts as she cannot hear the voice of the demon since Synite has not acknowledged it to her. *No one. I was just thinking about Sarah. I have to get her back soon or else I don't know what I'm going to do.*

'We know she isn't dead,' Gale points out, 'so it's only a matter of time before we get close enough to find her.' *Do you have any idea where she is? Apparently the entire octadecaverse knows where we are now, so we can't move quietly. We don't know a thing.*

"Synite!" a woman's voice calls in from the hall. He hops up reactively, thinking maybe it was her but it is Desha and Proximity.

"I got somethin' to say, bud," Proximity steps forward and puts both hands on Synite's shoulders. "Sorry for bein' mad at cha earlier. I know you hurtin' exactly the same as I am and it ain't fair for me ta blame you when none of us did enough."

"We all failed," Desha agrees with her partner. "There's no avoiding the past. Now, we have to focus on the future and finding a way to right this wrong."

"Together," Proximity adds. "We gotta do it together."

They both look on at the cold-faced young man in front of them, confused by his lack of emotion. "Thank you, but I need to be alone right now. Excuse me," Synite turns back in and the door closes itself right as

Proximity was going to tell him to wait. After completing their Animus A'mal, they wanted to try it in front of him and see what he thought. Unfortunately, for the sake of their relationship, they take his silence and sternness personally and head up to the communication room to find Amethyst instead of going in after their comrade.

Unfortunately for Synite, as much as he loves them, he needs his space. As much as he needs external encouragement, he needs to work internally to be able to accept it. The grass is only greener on the other side if one does not take good care of their own grass or if they do not appreciate the work they have put into it. And, they cannot make his life better right now, nor could they make it worse: he has full responsibility over both.

'I feeeeeeeeeeeel your struggleeeeeee, Cairo. You don't have to struggleeeeeeeee aloneeeeeeeeee! I'm heeeeeeeeeeeere for you. I am part of you now! Takeeeeeeee advantageeeeeeeeee of our reeeeeeeeeelationship!' *We don't have a relationship,* he tells the demon that he refuses to acknowledge as his but does acknowledge its presence, notifying Gale of the strange creature within. *You snuck inside me from Tsyuu because he was dying. All I am is an opportunity to you, a host for your evil.*

Evidently, in Synite's opinion, demons talk strange and about strange things: 'So, you still beeeeeeeelieve in eeeeeeeeeevil? But, I heeeeeeeeeeeeeelped you win that fight! You almost dieeeeeeeeeed, Cairo! If it wasn't for my meeeeeeeeeeeercy, all of your frieeeeeeeeeends would beeeeeeee mourning your untimeeeeeely deeeeeeeeeeath instead of ceeeeeeeleeeeeeeebrating theeeeeeeeeeeir timeeeeee togeeeeeeeeeeeeeether!' *Enough of your disrespect.* Synite tries his best to quiet his mind and push the darkness down. It fights for a while but his spirit is strong. The demon laughs and, as Synite suppresses, it trails off until completely quieted.

'I see we have a visitor,' Gale soothes Synite with her comforting blanket around his jarred spirit. 'The battle has turned within, too.' *What can we do to get rid of that thing? I don't want it inside me.*

'As far as I can tell,' she replies with an unfortunate but still reassuring tone, 'nothing. The demon is as much a part of you as I am right now. It is up to us to grow strong enough to get rid of it.' *Am I not strong enough right now to? Are we not together?*

'Currently, we cannot do battle as there is no defining line between us and the demon. It is powerful and knew exactly how to attach itself to stay inside as long as possible. If we were to try to destroy it in our present state, we may lose, I would be gone forever, as would your elementalism, and a portion of your soul would also be lost with me,' this comes to Synite as no good news at all. With Gale's help in his subconscious, he realizes that this is more of a challenge than a burden. *We can do it. If I can do the things I've done, I can fight off a little mischievous sprite. We will exorcise it.*

Gale feels his hope and spurns the doubt that he and she originally had for being able to fight this. 'As long as we stay strong, the task should only be difficult and not feel impossible,' her optimism breathing through him. Yet, he still cannot ignore the fact that Promis is gone and he could not save her when he had the chance. They were meters away and now they are worlds away. *We can and will get her back.*

"I think I've got you figured out," Castra Nim slides backwards as he and Coldsmoke break from a clash. This is round three of their battle, which they timed instead of going until either of them gets too tired or hurt to continue. "You're very interesting and unique, captain."

Coldsmoke stands slowly, his respect for the warrior across from him established by these rounds; his respect for the man is still up for debate. "What do you think you have figured out in this short time?"

Castra recalls, "I went light on offense in the first round, paying more attention to defending your attacks and getting a good judge of your movements. In the second, I did the opposite and tried to wail on you with everything I had without using complex technique. This last round, I fought comparable to how I would fight one-on-one in the arena, using my teleports, trying to catch you off-guard with tactics.

"It's very easy to see why you're so formidable in the arena," Castra continues. "You have one of the most powerful Wills I've ever come in contact with. There are only maybe four beings I've ever met that I believe could defeat you."

"And who might th'four be?" Coldsmoke wonders.

Castra sniffs and stretches, "Well, I'm not sure if you've ever heard of Lady Amethyst or Synite from Atlan."

"I have," Coldsmoke was able to watch those battles as he was never a slave. "Their Wills are tremendous."

"And I know you've never heard of Psilos because he never fought," sometimes Castra Nim does things and does not think of how smart they are until he is in the middle of doing them. This is one of those times and he can tell by how intrigued Coldsmoke is by Castra's mentioning some relationship to the Vanguard. "He is probably right up there with Amethyst, though you'd never know by meeting him."

"How would you know then?" Coldsmoke's eyes are bright.

Castra mirrors his enthusiasm, "Because he taught Synite and Synite told me! He said that Psilos was the second most powerful being on Earth 11 when they were still around."

"Wait," Coldsmoke steps closer, "second? That means he's more powerful than my coach then?"

"Your coach?" he had not made mentioning of a coach before.

"Dr. Sinclair," at first Castra does not know who Coldsmoke is talking about until he remembers the day he came here. "He's the most powerful being I've ever had th'privilege of fighting."

Castra is less surprised and more concerned about the agenda of his joining this team now, "So, Annie is your coach," he says under his breath, chuckling to himself. "How long have you known Dr. Sinclair?"

"He recruited me and brought me here almost five cycles ago," Coldsmoke confesses.

"That is interesting as well," Castra rubs his chin. "Your coach is number four."

Coldsmoke nearly blushes, "I was hoping so."

Castra can see the veneration he has for Spoilsport and wonders what type of past they have together. "I'll revisit that at a later time. Your power, on the other hand, is very strong. Are you conscious of it?"

"Sometimes I can control it so well that I can go beyond th'boundaries that my body has. Other times, I don't have t'control it at all," Coldsmoke looks to his team. "When I'm in th'arena, near th'end of a battle, things just happen t'me. I feel stronger, faster, smarter, more cunning than when I'm training or preparing for th'battle."

"That's your Will," Castra explains. "You have a reserve of Willpower that unconsciously boosts those abilities when need be. I want to help you learn how to control it completely."

"No," Coldsmoke tells him. "It is better that I can't. I don't want t'have t'think about it when things get rough in th'battles. Then, I might not put it where it needs t'go."

Castra understands but knows Coldsmoke does not completely, "I don't mean force you to have to control it all the time. I'm sure, even if you train to control it better, you'll still have those automatic bursts. I feel like, if you do learn to control it more, your power reserve should grow or get denser. Either way," Castra offers Coldsmoke his hand, "we can work to make you stronger, captain."

Coldsmoke looks down at Castra's hand, not quite sure why this stranger is making such an investment in him becoming stronger. He assumes that it must be for his own survival and, even if there is some sort of ulterior motive to it, that becoming stronger would garner the attention of his coach. He may possibly be less disappointing to Spoilsport if he learns from this Castra Nim character. Maybe, just maybe, that was his coach's entire reason for bringing Castra here in the first place. That epiphany is enough for Coldsmoke to shake Castra's hand and take the help that is being offered. If this increases his class enough and allows him to break through this glass ceiling to stand side-by-side with Dr. Sinclair, then by all means.

Castra, on the other hand, sees his partnership with Coldsmoke as one of the greatest recruiting opportunities the Vanguard has fallen into. It makes him think twice about the alignment of Spoilsport and whether he is actually working for the Enslaver or a double agent for the good side. Knowing what little he does know about Spoilsport, though, he decides that he is probably focused on his own self-interest. Castra wishes he could talk to Fabric about this right now but he needs to seize this opportunity.

Then, Castra realizes what Coldsmoke is thinking and his reason for being so resolute to train with him: he wants to be stronger for Spoilsport's attention, which is fine with Castra unless he is to be another soldier of the Enslaver. Castra Nim hopes that his powers of persuasion rule over this unrequited relationship between his powerhouse captain and the second most powerful being on Earth 11.

CHAPTER X

A small spacecraft, similar to the one that abducted Synite some time ago, enters Earth 11's atmosphere and lands in the back lot of the Sword. Two head automatons come to the ship's side gate and pull out a bound figure in tattered clothes. In the same clothes she was in when she was tied up in that warehouse, Promis is dragged up the same path Synite was dragged up to the Enslaver's throne. The grooves between the stones scrape her knees and ankles while her sweat drips below her. That perspiration has darkened spots of the beautiful dress, now ragged and torn up her legs, as well as matted her hair against her face and neck.

A head automaton pulls her by the simple shackles around her forearms since the complex ones that Synite had were not necessary as she has no power. She is almost lucid as she fades back and forth from consciousness. She shudders at every breath, feeling the room spin as she has not had anything to eat in over forty TAT hecu.

The laughter and snarling of the Enslaver from the end of the hall brings her back to the world of perception long enough for her to see the Pietre Dure of the Sword below her. It brings tears to her eyes and her whimpers make It laugh even louder. One of the female attendees trolls over to Promis and kneels next to her. "You are where you belong now, traitorous piece of phlegm!" She grabs Promis's chin and lifts her head up so she can see the Enslaver in full view, frightening her so much that she passes out from Its grotesquery.

Only sunlight from an exterior window illuminates the room she is taken to, casting long shadows across the stone. From the floor, a chair's legs and the electromagnet shackles around a petite pair of ankles are in the light. Promis's sniffling echoes around the room as a pair of wide feet come up next to hers.

The being that entered the room stops behind the chair, a loud buzzing noise swirling through the chilly room. Then, the buzz is muffled and long locks of dusty blonde hair float to the floor, chunk by chunk, until Promis's feet are nearly covered. The buzzing stops for a moment then starts back up again. This time, smaller pieces of the blonde hair float down, little by little, to join the pile. A slot in the floor opens up, the pile of hair swept to its final resting place.

After the large feet leave the room, Promis's sniffling and whimpers turn into real tears and an emotional breakdown. They took from her one of the things that signified her freedom as a being and as a woman. Though she still would be considered beautiful, no matter the length of her hair, she cannot help but lose every ounce of poise and equanimity.

The Enslaver's laugh turns into wheezing and another round of growling laughter that she hears in her dreams until she jolts awake. "Eat," a male voice says from the cell next to her. A bowl of some runny substance sits in the corner of her dingy cell. She grabs the bowl and scarfs down the food so quickly that she gags and almost regurgitates it. After she finishes and holds the food down for a while, she clutches the bowl and cries from the pang of sadness. "Where am I?" she speaks between sobs, never thinking she would be reduced to such a level. She has gone from Yar JK with love all around her to the blankness of this cell.

"The dungeon," he says back to her. She stands up and drops the bowl to her feet once she realizes where she is. The last time she was in this place, she was looking down into this same cell and encouraging a young warrior to rid himself of the slave mentality. That young warrior would become the man that she loves dearly but cannot touch. Her breathing goes shallow again and she wails out in the tune of a banshee.

The screeching of tires sounds very similar to that wail and is exactly what Spoilsport hears as he leaves the auction in K'oma. He and Driven have a similar love for fast road vehicles and fast ships but their taste is very different. He has attained, by one means or another, many of the rarest vehicles on Earth 11 in many of his exploits as E.A. and even gone so far as to purchase a few by way of his pay from the Enslaver.

"There were some interesting items in th'auction, no?" one of his investors from K'oma says from the passenger side. "Is there anything that caught your eye? I could put in a bid t'buy-out some of th'winners!"

"Nah," Spoilsport nonchalantly brushes off the commission-paid investor. "If I want it, I'll get it. I haven't had the thrill of thievery in a long time!"

The investor is privy to Spoilsport's high-level kleptomania streaks but does not prefer to talk about them. "We've talked about this, Dr. Sinclair. You can afford anything that was shown in there from top t'bottom. Why would--"

"Why pay for something when I can take it and nobody will be able to do anything about it?" This argument goes on between these two whenever he mentions anything close to stealing but Spoilsport enjoys ruffling the old coot's feathers sometimes. "I'll put them in the castle I stole next to the hangar full of other ships and vehicles I have collecting dust."

The investor snaps his fingers twice using both hands in unison, a sign similar to when a human shakes their head. "That's despicable! You're a distinguished gentleman of th'K'oma order of standards!" He looks over at Spoilsport with a straight face, which he cannot contain very long. They both break out into laughter and the investor cuts out the distinguished K'oma accent. "I tried, man. I really did! I think I had you for a second there!"

Spoilsport shakes his head, "I don't give one single shit about their secret order, let alone two. I signed up for political reasons. I wouldn't have the influence I have now without that little ploy," Spoilsport confesses to the investor.

"I figured that out when you stopped going to the meetings and started sending me," the investor brushes lint from his jacket. "It has done wonders for my career though, being in those meetings."

"Man, you're welcome. I'm glad you know I'd kill you if you told anyone. I wouldn't enjoy it if all my secrets got out. Not like I wouldn't be able to get everything that I wanted back anyway, it'd be a hell of a hassle having to do it all over again. And I'd probably have to do it even more under-the-table than I already did! Such a hassle."

"I understand," the investor switches back to the high-society K'oma accent but does not care to entertain Spoilsport's shenanigans, deadening the fear of being killed by the being who confides in him on several occasions. "I'll keep you abreast of th'next events, Dr. Sinclair," grinning with him.

"Thanks," Spoilsport drives hastily below ground to the K'oma floating railway station to park in his private garage as his private train to Atlan awaits his arrival. His rail is a level above the commercial rail liners instead of side-by-side with them so he can go straight from his road car to the train car. "Later, bud!"

"Enjoy th'trip home, doc!" His investor claps in front of Spoilsport's chest and heads down the stairs to the commercial tube station.

"Home is where the hate is," Spoilsport grabs his bag and goes to his seat, plugging in his destination key as the doors close and the engine warms. The train zooms forward and slides down to the main line in front of the next main departure. The trip is long enough for Spoilsport to have a drink, get updated on the Sword report from the three-dimensional media cylinder that is mounted on the ceiling of his car, and take a nice nap on his plush bedding.

"Isn't this a sight for sore eyes," he yawns and stretches through his sarcasm as he trots up the hall to check in with his employer. He stops about halfway and looks around, sniffing loudly. He wonders something but dismisses it before the thought goes too far.

"It is nice to see you as well," an elder attendee grins more than usual as Spoilsport gets close enough for them to actually see him.

Spoilsport sniffs again, still trying to put his finger on that familiar scent that he is unable to ignore at this point, "Pleasure's all yours."

"We are sure of that," another elder responds. "What do you have for us?"

"The trade went according to plan as I said it would," he thinks of other things while he speaks. "The Marks are transferred, Castra Nim is out of here and I need a drink." He has an idea of what the smell is now that he mentioned drinking.

The elders laugh together shortly, "And we appreciate you brokering that deal so efficiently. Your commission shall be sent immediately."

"I appreciate that," he knows exactly where to look. "Anything else?"

"Well," the elder to the right of the throne says between snores from the Enslaver, "there are a few new projects that have come up that we wish you to sign for. We need new scouting reports on the tournament teams that we could possibly be up against and our best lineups for each battle."

"So, basically," the powerhouse crosses his arms, "you want me to be Castra without getting the pleasure of throwing a punch?"

"These are the majesty, your employer's wishes," the elder reminds him, "not our personal laundry list."

"Yeah, and it's of the utmost importance which is why old Sword master is napping when I'm getting ordered around by the raisins," Spoilsport earns the first half of his name as he turns and strides towards the exit. "You know how to reach me."

As soon as he gets out of the Sword, Vincent goes to the front desk of apartment building where Promis stayed before they left Atlan. He asks the attendant there if the apartment is occupied and, as expected, it is not. He asks if she came back to a different apartment and, as expected, she is not living there at all. So, he grabs a bite to eat, as he was planning on taking her to lunch with him if she was there, and then scours the database of new apartment lessees, a list which her name is not on.

"Business has continued fairly gracefully," one of the two agents in the dining atrium says to the three attendees, "despite the problems from before.”

“Not to mention, we are much closer to recovering Lady Amethyst,” the female attendee chimes, “optimistically speaking.” At the entrance to the atrium, two beta test upgraded automatons guard the gate, halberds at their shoulders. “The media fleet has made contact with them several times. They can’t get too far without us knowing where they are and where they’re going.”

Spoilsport knew it was her smell and refuses to go back to that hall to get another whiff so he continues his search with the worst case scenario: the morgues. Her name does not come up in any of those searches but, he thinks to himself, *would the Enslaver allow her to be listed even if she was killed?*

He puts the thought of her being dead out of his mind but decides to ask around instead of letting his mind wander. He notices the glow of halberds in the front entrance to the atrium and thinks, *Why is that place guarded? I’ll have to go see!* So he stumbles towards the atrium without hesitation.

“How is it that you find them so quickly?” the agent leans closer to the female attendee. “It seems as though you might have one on the inside telling you--”

“We do not discuss such logistics with minor employees,” the attendee cuts him off.

The agents meet eyes and, “Understandably so,” is the best either of them can muster. “It seems--”

“The Majesty is not concerned with how things seem. Attribute our success to the Master’s power and reach going beyond that which many feeble minds can fathom,” she has no intention on allowing them to dig.

The other agent smiles at her, “Pretty words.”

“Where is she?” Spoilsport comes into their dining area, taking everyone off guard.

“How did he get in here?” The female attendee is strongly offended, “This is a private--”

“I don’t give a shit about your privacy or your food,” Spoilsport steps in closer. “All I need is an answer. Where is she?”

The agents look to the attendees who sit strongly in control, so they believe. “We haven’t the slightest about what you’re talking about, Spoilsport. I, personally apologize for our lack of knowledge to your cause.”

Spoilsport grabs that male attendee by his mantle and raises him off the ground with two fingers, “I expect an answer before some of you sheep start to disappear and others show up dead.”

“Are you threatening us?!” his female counterpart remains un-rattled, keeping her seat. As Spoilsport is about to answer, a platoon of the upgraded automatons stomps into the atrium and surround the table. The female attendee raises a hand to halt the charge. "Follow the attendee you have in your grasp to a less public place and we can talk about this."

"I'm not going anywhere," Spoilsport strikes fear in the hearts of the agents with his tone.

She looks over to the agents, "Excuse his intrusion--"

"You don't have to excuse me for a damn thing," he tightens his grip around the throat of the attendee. "Tell me what I want to know or his next breath is going to be his last."

"Please," the choking attendee squeaks out.

"And if you think those upgrades can touch me, you're wrong," Spoilsport qualifies. "They are no match. I've seen their developments."

"Step away from the employees and," her eyes grow wide as Spoilsport flips her male counterpart upside down and cocks his other fist back. Everyone reaches for or gets out of Spoilsport's way and the female attendee can no longer hold it in: "They brought her to the Sword!" Spoilsport catches the one in his hands and lowers him to the ground, still alive.

"Keep going," Spoilsport urges. "His life is still in my hands."

"She is alive. I'm not sure where they put Ms. Cassidy but," she approaches Spoilsport with her arms extended, "there are only two places I would imagine the master would put such a being."

He drops the attendee into her arms, flooring the both of them, and heads out. With his new knowledge, Spoilsport goes back to his previous train of thought. *If she was brought back and not killed, where would the Enslaver's diabolical ass tuck her awa*--and, before he knows it, he is back in the dungeon of the Sword, a place he said he would never revisit after spending a short stint as a resident there. He paces around, bringing back old memories that he would rather not be reminded of at any moment. He sees the automatons pacing and, after they pass each other, he sees his old cell. There is no one in that one, but there are occupants in the two cells to the right of it.

Spoilsport goes over and examines his old cell then hears a feminine sigh from the cell next to where he stands. He closes his eyes, knowing she cannot see him and does not know he is there, and prepares for the conversation at hand. He goes in front of the cell, looking down and barely recognizing the scruffy lady below him.

"I've always appreciated your natural scent," he says down to Promis. "Decided to show up unannounced huh, Sarah? How unruly."

"Wh—what?" She uses the little energy she has from the little food she digested and looks up, squinting to see beyond the bright bars. "Vincent?"

He chuckles, "In the flesh, if that's what you want to call it."

Spoilsport hides his fury well and does not misdirect it.

"I…" instead of being able to say much of anything, the tears say what she means.

"I guess there's an explanation for this," he waves a hand across the bars, "except I had nothing to do with it." He knows that the Enslaver is to blame for her being in here, but he has to let her know that she is partially responsible as well.

She sniffs as she looks through the bars at him again, "How did you know, then? How did you find me?"

"You know I have my ways," his demeanor changes a little. "Why doubt that?"

"What?" She cannot think fast enough to keep up with his conversation.

"You've doubted me this whole time, Sarah. You could've been here, safe with me. You could've been protected," he steps through the bars. "We didn't have to have any problems."

Promis is startled by him, "I don't want…"

"None of this had to happen. You could've let those kids go on about their business and you could still be here, making money and living comfortably," he stops before he seriously hurts her feelings as much as he would love to. "They even could've made it to the same point, if not better, without you in tow. That's all I'm saying."

"I wasn't going to be with you," she tells him. "You were going to protect me? Me and what other list of females?"

He crosses his arms, "Is that why you left? Because you weren't the only one? I was about to kill a guy to find you and that's what you're concerned about."

She coughs out, "What do you think that means to me?"

"Maybe it should mean that I care," he returns volley.

"And why would I want to look over my shoulder for the rest of my life?" his argument has brought back some of her mental fortitude.

"Sarah, seriously? What are you doing now except looking over your shoulder? Do you think you'd be here, in the same clothes after a few jumps through space and obviously a little tussle or two, in a dungeon cell if you had the right people looking after you?" He gives her time to think about it before stepping closer and kneeling next to her. "Are you ready for me to get you out of here?"

"No! Leave me," she pushes away from him. "I just want to be free, not under a monitor. I don't trust you. There's only one on this planet I can trust."

"You have absolutely no idea what you've gotten into," Spoilsport stands back up and turns away. "The Enslaver," he chuckles, "that monster you're so afraid of is only a piece of the puzzle. And, if you don't trust me in comparison to that thing, who do you trust?" He looks back at her. "No seriously, who? I need to know."

'And sheeeeeeeeee is with that man, theeeeee oneeeeeee who threeeeeeeateeeeeeeens your reeeeeeeelationship, right now as I told you sheeeeeee would beeeeeee,' the much more calm voice of the demon slithers through Synite's consciousness. *How could you know that?*
'I don't neeeeeeeed you to trust meeeeeeee, Cairo. But you do know that you areeeeeeeeen't theeeeeee only oneeeeeeee with deeeeeeeemons insideeeeeeeee,' it speaks so eloquently in all of its omniscience. 'Eeeeeeexcuseeeeee my rudeeeeeneeeeeeess. My nameeeeeeee is,' it takes a break, 'Thesia. Yeeeeeeees, my nameeeeeeee is theeeeee only thing I can say without streeeeeeeetching out theeeeeeee--' *I get it. Why are you inside of me, Thesia?*
'You took on a deeeeeeebt,' it reminds him. 'Until my pockeeeeeeet of souls is satisfieeeeeeeed, I'll hang around you. I likeeeeeeee you, Cairo.' Synite can feel the demon's smile, though he barely remembers how it looked the day it decided to take him as a host. 'Your soul is rich!' *As long as you know whose soul it is.*
'Theeeeeeeeeereeeeeeeeee is no mistaking it, theeeeee soul of an eeeeeeeeleeeeeeeeeemeeeeeeeeentalist.' *That is going to get super annoying,* Synite has, unfortunately, come to terms with the fact that there are now two other beings inside of him, in a way, although Gale he has accepted as part of him. *But, if you know your place, I think we can help each other. Damn, I'm glad I don't talk like you. It'd be hecu before I finished half of the things I need to say.*
'I apologizeeeeeeee for my impeeeeeeeeeedimeeeeeeeeeeent. It is not someeeeeeeeeething I can control,' Synite feels a light intoxication circulating through his body. 'Howeeeeeeeeeveeeeeeer, I do haveeeeeeeee a slight touch in how you feeeeeeeeel.' "I see," Synite says out loud, feeling the effect of the demon.
'Is it difficult to beeeeeeelieeeeeeeeveeeeeee that theeeeeeee woman who brought you out heeeeeeereeeeeeeeee would plot to beeeeeee saveeeeeeeed by a man you cannot yeeeeeeeeet kill? She planneeeeeeed heeeeeer kidnapping. Did you know, you had to know,' Synite waits for it to reveal more unfortunate knowledge, 'sheeeeeeee didn't want to beeeeeee heeeeeeeereeeeeee or with you?' Synite's eyes get a little darker and glassy, more and more as he allows the demon to slander the one he loves. 'To beeeeeee away from you and all of this was all sheeeeeeeee askeeeeeeeed for. Away from us and neeeeeeeeeeeext to him!'
Synite is unable to focus now, even as he and Amethyst have a conversation. They met the Pingar crew at a small space station off the

grid, filling up on supplies. All Synite is able to do is sulk beyond her ability to comfort him. "Doubt and hope are strangely powerful weapons," Amethyst heads down the hall towards the dock, leaving the conversation she seems to have been having by herself.

"How are they so powerful?" Synite does not let her leave.

Amethyst tries to explain the best she can, "You use them. You know how powerful they are. If it wasn't for hope for something better, a true freedom, there would be no Vanguard to speak of. You wouldn't have brought me here. It was the doubt that anyone could defeat you and the doubt that I would join you which brought you to the next level of strength and Will," she seems to know him better than he knows himself right now.

"I try and ignore 'em both," Driven chimes in as he butts in, coming down the hall. "No point in doubting yourself these days. Either you gonna win or lose and the way you feel about the game ain't gonna change that."

"Can't disagree," Synite sulks and sighs so much that Driven can't ignore it.

So, he addresses it: "You got a problem?"

"I have a feeling that she planned it all," he recites the ideas Thesia planted in him. "She didn't want to be here anymore. Now, she's with that guy back on Earth 11." Amethyst turns back to hear what Synite is talking about. "There's one who was stronger than me but not as strong as Amethyst or the Enslaver, but he works for the Enslaver. This kidnapping was obviously orchestrated by him and by her request."

Amethyst walks back up but Driven stops her, "I got this one." He puts a hand over one of his eyes. "So, you think she plotted to get kidnapped by those thugs to get away from the only guy who made her happy? Man! You gotta share whatever substance you've been abusing because I really want to try it!" Driven laughs.

"It isn't funny," Synite yells over the jollity. "You're blind if you can't see this! She helped plan our escape. How can I put it past her planning her own escape, too? I'm not dumb."

"Even if she was smart enough to plan something as complex as that, which I doubt," he emphasizes the word doubt and winks at Amethyst on the sly, "she was clearly in pain and scared when we tried to get her." 'Don't forgeeet how bold sheee was back on Atlan,' Thesia fuels the fire as Driven finishes up, distracting Synite from his point. "You think somebody would go through all that simply to be away from you?" 'Sheee had no inhibition theeen. Why should sheee haveee any now?'

"It was all part of the act," Synite is almost fully convinced. "Maybe she didn't know the details and that truly was fear we saw. Maybe all she told him was to get her away from me and protect her." 'You hit theee nail on theee heeead, Cairo!' "Yep! I should've known not to trust her from the beginning."

Amethyst walks away, saddened further by all of this. "You're gonna go crazy thinkin' that way, brother," Driven turns to follow her. "Fair warning."

'I don't think you should leeet him talk to you in that way, Cairo!' "Don't call me crazy!" Synite grabs Driven's arm and turns him back around. "I'm not the crazy one around here. You can't be trusted either! You're reckless and," Driven jerks away from Synite.

"You'd best watch who you put your hands on," Driven's temper shows. "I've been in your corner so far but if you're gonna act as if I'm the bad guy, I'll show you how bad I can be!" 'Heee knows nothing of your streeength! Show him!'

Before Synite can swing, Amethyst is between them, a hand on each of their chests. "I don't think I need to say anything, do I?" She looks at Synite as he feels the power behind her touch the same time Driven feels it. "I didn't think so."

"I'm going back to my ship," Driven steps off of Amethyst's hand. "Have fun with him."

Synite tries to walk past Amethyst after him but she stops him again. "I'm going to the ship. I'm over it," he tries to convince her.

"What's gotten into you?" she has never seen Synite act in this way and they have been around each other for a long time. "You've lost friends and loved ones before. Did you act like this then? Do you fully believe that, after showing you that she cares about you, she would leave?"

"You don't understand," he tries to go around her again.

"Then make me understand! You've saved me from myself more than once now," her gratefulness is one of her greatest characteristics. "Who have you become? This is not the friend I love and trust."

Synite begins to come off of Thesia's intoxication, "I don't know. I can't. I think I'm tired. I lose everyone that comes close to me," he can barely squeeze out the words. "What am I supposed to do?"

"We'll figure it out together; all of us," she leads when he needs her to and knows when to let him. "That's why we're together."

CHAPTER XI

The bell chimes in the front of the Weapons Rack and, for the first time, Spoilsport purposely meets eyes with Fabric. He thinks he can feel how powerful Spoilsport is but does not let it change his conduct. "May I help you, sir?"

"I believe you may," Spoilsport offers Fabric his hand as an equal. "My name is Dr. Vincent Sinclair. I love your store, although, as you probably know, that's not what I'm here for."

Fabric pushes his glasses up to show his eyes more clearly and shakes his hand, confirming what he thought. "I gathered that!" he smiles with his hand atop his completely bald head. "Did someone refer you?"

"Do you know who I am?" Spoilsport goes past subtlety on many occasions such as this.

Fabric lets his glasses fall, "Did she send you here?"

This is one of the rare cases when answering a question with another question satisfies the first question and continues the conversation. "You're the only person she trusts in this world now," Spoilsport informs. "Not me. And, I'm sure it's news to you that she's a dying tree, rotting in the elementalist's old cell right now."

"How?" Fabric's eyes try to pierce Spoilsport's but:

"That doesn't matter. Just know that I'm pissed. I'm pissed that It would do this to her but I'm not a crusader," Fabric gathered that by the dark gray jacket and boots. "And I want her out but she doesn't want it my way. So, there's that."

"What does she want, then?" would be the first question he would ask her given the opportunity.

"You know a few beings who would get a ton more satisfaction out of destroying It than I would. And, I know a way to give them their chance," he has successfully gained all the trust he needs from Fabric to move forward. "She doesn't understand quite as well as I do, but I'm in a much better position to make things happen than either one of you."

"Then what do you need me for? Weapons? Intel?" Fabric wonders why his trust is necessary for a being who says he could do this on his own.

"They might need the weapons but I certainly won't. I'm not going to do the fighting." Spoilsport walks towards the back of the store, "I need to know how big the room on the other side of that shift door is first."

"Your perception is immaculate," Fabric points out as he joins Spoilsport in the back. "I didn't know beings here were aware of its existence yet."

"It's my job to keep up with these sorts of things," Spoilsport looks around the wall. "How does it work?"

"It's complicated," Fabric does not allow Spoilsport any time to ask further. "How is the size of that room going to help get Sarah out?"

"I can do things that nobody else in this world can do. I know codes and routes to get here from outside without having to go through security checks. I set up the security checks," he laughs dryly. "I'm the invisible web that keeps Atlan together and secure but I'm about ready to let it go." Fabric feels he has somewhat the same role when it comes to Alexander's empire as Spoilsport does in the Enslaver's, except the difference in alignment of course. Spoilsport turns and crosses his arms impatiently as he looks through Fabric with his dark gray eyes. "Well?" Fabric opens the shift door and shows Spoilsport the cache where all of the weapons are housed as well as where Lone has been living. "I was wondering where you've been," Spoilsport winks at Lone.

"A place where Castra knew the Enslaver couldn't see, as you recommended." Lone does not get much more annoyed. "You planning on killing me while you're here?"

"I've changed my mind a bit about how many of the Enslaver's rules I'm going to be following from now on," Spoilsport says. "I actually didn't care before but now I'm completely apathetic. You ain't seen somebody care less than I care right now about whether you live or die. Or die again. Whatever. Leave if you want."

"Rest, for the time being," Fabric tells him with just as much influence. Lone nods as they walk past the tables, "The weapons are categorized and ordered. But, as you said, that's not even your concern."

Spoilsport asks the only thing that is important to him about this room: "How easily can you move all of this junk out of the way?"

"The floor shifts when needed," Fabric tells him, "so pretty fast, I guess."

Spoilsport stands in the middle of the room and looks around, surveying. "Show me." Fabric goes to the wall by the door and shifts everything against the back wall, closing all of the shelves against each other and tucking the tables on the end. He made sure to concentrate them in a certain corner so Spoilsport's perceptive abilities are blocked from sensing what may be on the other side of that back wall. The remaining space, then, is shaped like a thick L.

"Is that good enough?" Fabric smiles big.

Spoilsport thinks a little longer than he is used to thinking and decides that is enough. "Sure. Hey, kid!" He looks over to Lone with a droll smile, "now that I think about it, I have a little job for you now."

A few days later, Lone waits along the outskirts of Atlan as a luxury vehicle speeds toward him. It slides to a halt next to him, Spoilsport in the driver's seat and a passenger Lone does not recognize. Spoilsport presses a button to raise the door behind him and lets Lone get into the back seat. "This must be the chick I'm supposed to be watching."

Spoilsport looks into his rearview mirror at Lone and pulls off. "Her name is--"

"My name is Promis," she speaks for herself, embarrassed still at what they did to her hair. "You don't have to do this if you don't want to."

Lone huffs from the back seat. "I'm doing what he and Fabric agreed would be best for you, lady. Don't get all snappy with me about it."

"If you had any idea what was going on," Spoilsport stops her from responding to Lone, "you'd be happy to be here and alive."

"Then tell me," she demands. "If it's that important to you for me to be quiet, shut me up."

"The problem with that is the fact that I don't want to know," Lone says. "He's lettin' me live and I'm in his debt. The babysitter don't need to know where the parents are goin', just when they'll be back."

"And you can rest assured," Spoilsport smiles, "I don't care how much you talk his ears off. I'll be busy."

Synite slouches in his seat in the communication room. "I think the only thing they want now is for all of our heads to be on stakes and Lady Amethyst back as their prize," he tells the round table of the Caracalla's crew.

"I won't allow myself to be taken back under the Enslaver. My ambition is to only face that evil once more," Amethyst is determined but reluctant. "If it was a good idea, I would go back to Atlan on my own and destroy the entire place."

"That would topple everything," Synite says. "We wouldn't be any freer than we are now if you died. We would probably be worse off."

"There isn't a day I don't hope for peace, if that thing even exists," she supposes. "At this point, I'm not sure since so many out there are hoping against it. Everyone must always be prepared for war."

"We all want this to be over," Desha says.

Synite sits up a little, "I'm not here in vain."

"None of us are," Amethyst lowers her eyes, "but all of your involvement is liable to cause death to others. If I destroy the Enslaver," she hatches the idea, "but die in the process, does that not satisfy our goal?"

"No!" Synite stands. "Making sure that none of us dies is the only way to satisfy our goal! None! If any of us dies, I'll feel completely responsible. Sarah is gone now and we have no idea where because of--"

"You ain't tha only one that messed up, bro," Proximity reminds him. "We all in dis. We all failed, 'member?" He looks over at Desha, "Maybe some-a us oughta leave here, den."

"We can't second guess our reasons for coming together," Amethyst decides. "We may not have the same motivations but we all need each other to complete the greater task."

"And we need her back," Synite slumps again.

Suddenly, Captain Grujek comes on-screen: "We's gettin' attacked fellas!" His projection shakes and scatters as sparks fly in the background.

Soon after, the Caracalla recognizes the threat as well and reports: "The Pingar is taking serious damage from the long-range weaponry on six unidentified ships. A moment to recognize," the ship tries to scan.

"We need to help them, not worry about their specs right now!" Synite pleads to Kraa-Nuve and the ship.

On the Pingar, the small crew tries to salvage their damage. The twins bounce around, reconnecting cables and stopping the figurative bleeding around the ship. Driven and Grujek keep their posts, defending and navigating their property from danger as best they can.

They barrel roll, twist and turn but still take hit after hit from the rifles. Their shields get lower and lower, their maneuvering capabilities declining as fast as their shields. Flames dance from the top of the ship after two missiles slam the last of their protection away. Grujek is thrown from his seat and Driven stumbles into the cockpit with him. "Get the escape pods ready!"

"I ain't abandoning her, kid!" Grujek gets back up and mans his instrument, many of them unresponsive despite his best efforts. "She's been wif me too long for some coward, long-blast ta separate us!"

"Cap, there's too much damage," a fire erupts in the threshold between the cockpit and the rest of the ship. "We won't be able to repair it out here! We can't defend anymore! The environment stasis engine is damaged! If we don't--" the ship rocks violently as Yelsh is thrown into the cockpit, tears in his eyes. The captain runs to his son and looks out through the fire in search for his other half.

"Gruje! Out!" Kraa-Nuve's voice rings behind them. The Caracalla gets between the Pingar and the gunfire, defending the broken ship with its own shields and lasers. "Escape!"

"This is our only chance," Driven gets up and grabs Grujek's coat. "We don't have time to argue!" Driven picks up Yelsh and pushes the button to the right of the cockpit that opens up the escape pods, of which there are four.

"I's born on dis ship," Grujek grabs Yelsh's hand. "My sons was born on dis ship." Driven lowers the twin back to the floor. "Set pod and leave, Drivy. Go. Go!" Driven jumps away from them and the door to the escape pod claps closed. Driven watches the Pingar, along with the other three escape pods and the other three members of its crew, get engulfed in flames. Two strong missiles get past the Caracalla's laser streams and tear the Pingar apart. The explosion knocks Driven's pod into a frenzied spin off into the distance, eventually getting caught in the gravity of the nearest planet.

As they thrust away from the explosion and wreckage, three missiles zoom in the Caracalla's direction. "The Pingar and its remaining crew are gone, captain," the Caracalla reports.

Kraa-Nuve lowers his head similarly to the way he did when Grujek told him about his wife dying. "Together." He knows that Grujek would not have been able to deal with outliving his sons so he almost agrees with his sacrifice.

"This isn't happening again," Synite toils.

Kraa-Nuve raises his head and his attention snaps over to Synite. "Mourn after. Live first."

The captain and co-pilot start their evasive procedures, dodging artillery fire and shooting down missiles. "Their signals are jamming me and I cannot trace their origin. The missiles, however, are encoded in a language that originates from the same system that the leader of Atlan resided in before moving to Earth 11 and establishing ownership of the Sword. The structure of each missile is, however, one that was designed and produced on Earth 6."

"Expands," Kraa-Nuve shakes his head as they get out of the way of the firefight. They pick up speed but do not widen the gap enough for it to matter.

"You said its remaining crew," Synite notices. "Did someone get away?"

"An escape pod shot off," the ship tells.

"One? Which?" Kraa-Nuve demands an answer.

"I currently cannot tell who was in the pod, but it has been thrown onto the surface of this planet," which comes up in a three-dimensional map between where Synite and Kraa-Nuve sit.

"Track," Kraa-Nuve tells the ship.

As the Caracalla thrusts away, ten more missiles zoom in on the Caracalla's position. The ship goes as fast as it can but the missiles gain on them. "EVA 712!" Kraa-Nuve looks through the map.

Synite looks over, confused, "What is EVA 712?"

The Caracalla takes as much pride as Kraa-Nuve programmed it to have, "We ride the outer edge of a planet's magnetic field and use its gravitational force to catapult us in a tangential line, also utilizing the electromagnetic force to throw off enemy targeting systems." They do their best with the lasers but some of the missiles get closer.

"Strong grav," he points out the planet they are going to use.

The planet is maximized on the map and a diagram of the maneuver traces across. "The gravity on that planet is twenty-five times that of most Earths. It is indeed the best candidate."

"Let's do it then!" Synite agrees. The ship picks up speed but does not widen the gap at all. Synite and Kraa-Nuve concentrate and circumvent several strikes. "Shouldn't we slow down?"

"Dead slow," Kraa-Nuve has been in many situations where slowing down or hesitating even a little would have ultimately ended in losing of crew. "Got."

"For this maneuver," the ship explains, "you all need to be seated and fully secured." Proximity and Desha sit and strap in as the automatic belts and security rail come over them. Amethyst relaxes in the corner of the communication room with them, staying out of the belts. "I implore you to--"

"I appreciate your concern, ship," Amethyst parks in the regular chair. They await other orders if there be any, hoping it will not be another situation similar to Omega 2.

"Two eins away from that planet's magnetic field," Kraa-Nuve focuses on putting the ship's evasive codes in at the right time so they stay out of the atmosphere but still use the gravity. The next ein stretches to forever as the missiles close in and the quiet of space blankets them. It is difficult for them not to think about their fallen comrades but they do hope that whoever did get away is alive. "Proximity alert."

"Huh?" Proximity looks around as the alarm sounds, wondering what the problem is.

"The missiles are close enough to where, if they explode, the ship will be damaged," Amethyst explains to him. "Brace yourselves."

The ship is trying to conserve enough energy to complete the EVA 712, which requires a huge amount of power. "Quarter ein!" Kraa-Nuve announces in between the alarm's rings which are getting progressively faster as the missiles get nearer.

Before they know it, the ship jerks towards the planet below them and, timing as best as he can, Kraa-Nuve and the ship engage the upward thrusters. Those flames push against the raw grip of gravity and the ship keeps contact with the curve. It rides along, the Caracalla trying its best to not rip apart from the opposing forces.

The school of missiles come in fast behind them but curve down into the planet's atmosphere, less than a meter from contacting the back of the ship, and explode shortly after entering. "They missed!" Synite yells in elation but still struggles to keep the controls steady. "It feels like we're going to break in half!"

"Never!" Kraa-Nuve grunts as he pushes against one of the most powerful elemental forces. Proximity and Desha hold on to their rail tightly as the room shakes and buckles, their buckles rattling. Amethyst switches from crossing her left leg over her right to crossing her right over her left.

"It worked!" Synite relaxes his shoulders along with the rest of the crew outside of Amethyst who never tensed up to begin with. Kraa-Nuve nods and engages his controls. Elsewhere, Driven's escape pod flips towards that planet's moon that has its own atmosphere of orange and brown cloud coverage. The pod spins and tosses Driven around its cramped interior as it dips into the atmosphere below. The Caracalla pinpoints where the pod entered and blasts its front upward thrusters enough to twist them off the curve and back into inner space towards that moon. "Vector to the moon where the pod has entered placed."

Quickly, a projection of the aberrant moon comes up between them and a small dot shows where the pod dropped in. "Condition?" Kraa-Nuve closes the projection and pushes on without hesitation, ready to save whoever survived that explosion. The forward thrusters re-engage and the ship jets towards the dot on the map.

"The light atmosphere is chemically basic and, without the proper attire, everyone on this ship would melt. That pod is not made of a material strong enough to withstand the atmospherics for very long," the ship has a way of delivering information that motivates them even more. "I can hover for hecu without must damage and Psilos would have been able to survive. However, he is not present."

"I'll take care of it," Amethyst had been standing in the threshold of the cockpit for the entire report.

Synite turns to her, surprised she is there and then concerned for her safety. "The ship says you'll be melted!"

"Must I continuously prove the extent of my power to you, Synite?" She grips the bracelet, "I am helping to save comrades. Why would you object?" She looks up at the view, "Get us to that moon."

The Caracalla swoops above the moon, scanning its atmosphere with lasers to make sure there are no giant structures to run into. Amethyst sheds her flowing dress and wears her scars proudly in between the form-fitting pieces she has on. "You have to exit through the loading dock as to not allow any of that atmosphere into the core of the ship. It is poisonous to all carbon based beings and eats away at many of the materials on this side of the ship."

"We'll come through after you exit to provide cover and communication," Synite takes initiative. "You won't be alone down there."

"I can handle it," she heads towards the dock exit and climbs down. The ship hovers centimeters over the brownish cloud and, as the doors open, the vacuum of space grabs and pulls on Amethyst but she barely budges. She closes her eyes, tilts her head back and glows with a violet light as the power of the bracelet wraps her entire body like a second skin. She looks back down and jumps, shining like a purple star falling into the clouds, the ship doors shutting behind her. She drops for a moment then finally touches the surface, the haze still thick around her. She can barely see more than a few meters around and cannot tell what the landscape is or if anything is moving in the distance, much less where the pod is. "You might as well stay up there. The cloud is shallow and comes to the ground. Point me in the right direction."

"Front right," Kraa-Nuve tells her. "Light blink."

"I'll see if I can find it," she marches along the rough surface, trying not to trip or slip. The first thing she sees is the terrain curve up and plateau into what must be a crater. "Am I going the right direction?"

"Yes. Keep going and you should run into it," Synite directs.

Amethyst goes over the lip and slides down into the crater, dipping below the clouds and able to see a little beyond her face. "I can see a lot better down in this crater," she tells them. "There are a few caves but I don't see signs of anything living." The entire area is bare and there is no trace of an organism in sight. She scans the area and, in the other corner of the crater, a small green light dims slowly, strobes for a moment and then dims again. "I see it!" She trots as quickly as she can over the unstable surface, "It has a large break in the hull. I can't tell if there's any seepage but, regardless, its integrity might be compromised."

"Get over there quickly and throw it straight up! We'll hover directly over your position and catch it!" Kraa-Nuve looks over at Synite, wondering if he plans on taking care of that action. "What? I know you can do that, captain!" He turns his communication line back onto Amethyst, "Hurry! They might be dying in that pod!"

"Almost there!" Amethyst gets to it and grabs hold of the base and a large rock moves in the distance behind her. "It doesn't look like there's a hole, only a good crack and some dents. It should fit fine in--"

A giant stinger stabs at Amethyst but she dodges it, turning to see where the aggression came from. "What was that noise?" Synite yells down. "What's wrong?"

"There are three of them," Amethyst narrates what she is looking at. "They're big with wings and long tails with hooked stingers on the end. They look like giant scorpions with pincers but with a long neck and huge head with lots of teeth." The three spread their wings and let out a blood-curdling scream. "And large horns on their heads and really bad breath."

"Throw the pod!" Synite urges.

"I can't turn my back on them," Amethyst would rather take care of them first. "I'll try in a few secs!" She puts her hands out and purple shields cover her forearms then purple claymores stretch from her hands. All of this glowing weaponry looks entirely too big to be carried by someone her size. Then, the ship lines up with her position and does the only thing it can: wait.

She jets up and decapitates the largest of the three before they can even begin to attack her. "Ready?" she yells up at the ship, "It's coming in hot!" The giant scorpions claw and stab at her and she dodges what she cannot knock away. Amethyst cuts the pincers off of one of the remaining two. The other one shoots its tongues at her like a spear. She catches its tongues and slices them off, beckoning more screams, and then she grabs the other one by the claws and throws it at the one whose tongue she lopped off, toppling both of them on their sides.

Amethyst jumps back so that she is on the other side of the pod, still facing the giant scorpions. The weapons around her arms disappear so that she can get the best grip possible. They scream again as Amethyst picks up the pod and throws their dinner out into space. Unfortunately for their appetites , their catch had friends and they ruined the meal for these queen giant scorpions.

Before Amethyst can celebrate or try to get off the planet, the beheaded one snaps at her, grabbing her by the arm with its sharp pincer and then stabbing at her in rapid succession. She sees the other two come up behind it and notices that they have no eyes in the main head. She figures it might be just another appendage corresponding with the tail and claws, unimportant to their life.

The pod pops out above the clouds and Kraa-Nuve twists the ship around, opening the dock, then flipping the ship to catch it. The dock closes as quickly as the ship can and Synite pumps his fist. He goes over and pats Kraa-Nuve on the back for that great flying. "We got it, Amey! Now, let's get going!"

"Wait a second!" she chops off the pincer that had been grasping her arm and one of the other two flies up over her.

"I would say take your time but you should probably get up here," Synite responds. "Do you need help?"

"I won't be long," she reassures them. "Merely a setback!"

Synite goes back to his seat, "Woman late." Kraa-Nuve has a brash laugh at Amethyst's expense.

The other scorpion that still has a head slides across the ground at Amethyst and swings down at her, cracking the ground below all of them. The airborne one drops down on all eight legs to try and crush her but, instead, they fall through the ground and under the moon's surface. "I fe...bel...oun...th..." her transmission goes dark and Synite is confused.

"What'd she say?" he looks at the map where her signal light fades and is lost. "Ship?"

"She went below ground," the Caracalla puts up a cross-section of the planet, searching for her signal to appear. "With her body being covered by that power she has, I won't be able to penetrate it to find her signal from this far away."

Amethyst finally lands at the bottom of a dark cavern, her light being the only reason she can see anything. Before she can look around, one of the scorpions head butts her side, throwing her into the nearest wall. Another flies over to her, crashing into the wall and trying to crush her against it. Instead, she blasts right through it with an elbow, blowing it in half.

"Can we fit in that hole?" Synite requests measurements.

The ship shoots detection lasers down to where her signal was last seen and determines, "We cannot, under any circumstances, fit through there."

"But we could create a larger one," Synite suggests, trying to think of a way to get to his friend's side.

"Bury," Kraa-Nuve does not like the idea of piling the crust of a moon on top of anyone he has no hate for.

"If she has to use her power a lot, she may not come up," Synite knows that her desire to live is tied directly to the amount of power she uses. "That's why she's trying not to go all out on them, because she's alone. Let's hope it's enough."

Amethyst feels the depression rising inside her as she dodges the stabs of the scorpions' tails. The remaining one with the head slams it down at her like a wrecking ball and slides it across the ground to try and get her as well. She slices through its wings one at a time and it raises up in agony. She controls her breathing as best she can and dodges more, looking for an opportunity to jump out. It swings its tail around at her and she bends over backwards to dodge. Before she can get back upright, she sees the headless one hovering above, blocking her exit.

The other living one throws its head around and spews a steaming black liquid at Amethyst with its mouth, her blanket of sadness and self-doubt begins to warm over her as the liquid covers her. The remaining two scorpions, despite being seriously injured, await the partial digestion of their replacement meal. They circle their prey and bite at each other, vying for position to get the first bite.

Through the black shines a brilliant light that cuts through the goo reminiscent of a Sun's rays through the clouds and Amethyst ducks low. Instead of wasting more time, she jumps straight up, the liquid rolling off her, and burns through the scorpion above her. Her sword materializes and stretches to pole length; she hurls it into the mouth of the scorpion that spat on her. An axe materializes next and she throws the axe into the other's back. She flies out through the cloud into inner space next to the Caracalla.

"She is out," the ship shows her signal out near their position. Kraa-Nuve backs the ship up next to her and cracks open the hatch, trying not to open it all the way so the pod can stay secure.

Amethyst climbs in and the ship closes up behind them. "Clean and seal initiated for loading dock room." A generator kicks in and all of the space debris is filtered out and breathable Air is quickly pumped in. Amethyst goes over to the damaged pod and sees Driven, bruised and unconscious. Instead of pulling him out, she goes into the corner and sits, gathering herself. She knows the reason for this feeling and uses that knowledge to try and fight it but it only works so much.

The lights and systems of the ship start to flicker and buzz. "Bad time!" Kraa-Nuve yells at the motherboard, expecting the ship to shut down all systems as it has done before at other inopportune times. This looks a little different to him, though.

"Captain, please authenticate," the ship's voice sounds more plain than usual.

Kraa-Nuve looks confused by this request, hoping the entire system did not crash and wipe its memory. The flickering slows down and stops, immediately leveling out without the entire system shutting off for as long as he is used to. "Authentication complete."

A white rose with eighteen thorns on its stem pops up on the main screens, startling Kraa-Nuve as he has not seen that symbol in a very, very long time. "You've gained a few, Captain Kraa," a voice with a stern yet friendly tone comes from behind him. Synite turns to see who it is and does not recognize the projection at all.

"Who?" Kraa-Nuve says while turning and immediately stops in his tracks, dropping the ear piece he had in his hand. It is fuzzy for him at first but he can clearly make out the advanced military fatigue armor covered in a white, scientist's robe. "Ghost?"

"Not quite, Kraa," the projection reports as it takes off its helmet, his hark hair and strong facial features shining in Synite's mind, showing a semblance to an ally of theirs. "Your co-pilot can see me as well." Synite stares on, seeing a familiar facial structure but is not able to tell who the man is.

Kraa-Nuve looks over to Synite and asks with his eyes if the projection is telling the truth, "I see him, too."

"I'm only a programmed consciousness," the projection confesses. "My son is on your ship for the first time so that activated my appearance. From what I can tell, he is badly injured in the bay. Go down and plug him into coaxial line B-T2. There's a slot for it under his left foot."

Kraa-Nuve and Synite get up and pass the projection into the communication room. "Decon done?" Kraa-Nuve asks his ship.

"Yes, captain. All contaminants have been expelled," the Caracalla is back to normal. Desha and Proximity follow them down into the docking bay. Synite spots the pod first and dashes over to it then pulls the Driven son out. Kraa-Nuve brings the B-T2 line by Driven's limp body, yanks off his boot and plugs the cable into the slot where it fits perfectly just as the projection stated it would.

Desha notices Amethyst sitting the corner facing the wall, "Oh thank goodness you're--"

Amethyst responds plainly, "Stay away from me." She puts a hand up, "I'll stay in the room but you need to keep your distance, all of you."

Synite begins to step towards her but her gaze stops him in his tracks, a purple mist rising in that corner around her. "We're glad you're here."

"My power could've destroyed that whole damned moon in an instant," Amethyst reminds them, "possibly this whole system and everything in it, if I wanted to."

"We're glad you used it to help us," Desha teeters on the line of being bothersome.

"Where was this stupid ass power when my planet was being destroyed?" Amethyst spews her feelings, "I was too weak then and now I'm too strong. My life has been nothing except destruction!" She drops her head, "When does it end?" Desha starts to go over to her and console her but Proximity grabs her arm and stops her.

"Power redirected to assist in the healing of Airiq Driven through energizing his Borganic cells," the Caracalla reports.

The Driven father reappears next to his son, "Thank you, Kraa. Give him some time and he'll be fine."

"Who exactly is this guy, captain?" Synite steps over by Kraa-Nuve. "I mean I assume--"

"Original. Lead," Kraa-Nuve still does not know how to feel about seeing his oldest comrades, one who he has not seen alive in a very long time. "Tob--"

 # CHAPTER XII

In general, beings are complex, the products of tens of thousands of cycles of evolution, culture and technology. Some beings, depending on the eye of the beholder, are more complex than others due to their histories. For instance, the history of Earth Prime's humanity got a bit more complex with the Cataclysm. Previous to that primal event, the history of mankind was simple: a circuit of exercises in futility, attempting to dominate and control a planet that decided to push back fully. Money and power meant very little when everything was crushed, as showed by the equalizing of society underground.

It was easy to predict what mankind would honestly do in the event of a worldwide crisis such as the Cataclysm. Though that event did bring about true change, there were simple, sociological shortcuts which were made to tell, based on historical statistics, how those events would go. It is difficult to tell what each individual will do at any given time; however, focusing on the broader scope of things, the key was survival of the fittest and most prepared.

The great majority of beings have limits, both physically and mentally. Very few beings, less than one percent, are able to break those limits and push the race beyond their barriers. Those which add more complexity to culture go further than their generation deemed possible, seeming to be "before their time" or too strange to even understand during their time. Most beings akin to this change society in ways that go far beyond their lifetimes, their names becoming part of the collective history of the race. The present would not be the same without whatever contributions they brought with their lives.

Even fewer transcend the restrictions to their psychology, physiology and biochemistry. These few beings reach levels of notoriety only trumped by God and, in many instances, are categorized as gods themselves. Their feats, their myth, those who worship them throw their names into the realm of relative immortality. They become more than products of their surroundings and seem otherworldly to those who fill their world.

Unfortunately, in the same way as every other culture, the extremes of turmoil come when the gods change; when they go from being worshipped to reviled as blasphemous to the "true" higher spiritual being. Those transcendent beings are then reduced to jokes, caricatures, and simplified versions of their complex selves. They are sent below the average being, beneath the general public, and taken less seriously than the choice of what to eat in the morning.

The point here is that, in societies cultured by time and experiences, things change dramatically on the surface but deep down in the core stay exactly the same, restricted by the beings that mold and record history. This can be applied to culture, to each being inside the culture, and is not a local phenomenon either: every race of procreating beings has a history that shows tendencies, trends and repetition. Time does not change a race's colors; it changes the race's hue.

Though the Sword's infrastructure has been crippled, the population of Atlan has not changed. They are frustrated, currently, that they cannot witness every step, every violent swing that the Vanguard makes. There are beings complaining from the comfort of their homes about not having the ability to see what actually happened with Amethyst and Driven's pod below the atmosphere of that moon. They have always been an overly curious yet lazy lot even from their prehistory. Yet, in anticipation of revealing some visuals from the events, more watch and more wait purely to be entertained, unlike Fabric who watches out of concern or Spoilsport who watches for knowledge (the both of them are from elsewhere).

"Allow me, Kraa," the projection of Driven's father asks for permission from his old friend, Amethyst still frozen in her corner and the others giving him audience. "I am General Tobias Driven, codename Saga," he shows his chest plate that has his moniker 'General Saga' on it. "I, with the help of several other influential beings, founded the Eighteen Thorns of the Rose, a peace-keeping organization that, at our height, spanned the entire dark side of the octadecaverse. Your captain," the projection looks at the other members of the crew, "is also one of the original eighteen."

"I knew that was something else about you," Synite points at Kraa-Nuve as if he solved a riddle. He points back at Tobias, "That's why you knew Driven's name."

"Smarter," Kraa-Nuve sarcastically gives credit where credit is due. "Know Fabric, Chalice, Alex son. Happened rest, Saga?"

"Wait," Synite interrupts, "Fabric, our Fabric? Fabric from the Weapons' Rack in Atlan, Fabric?"

Kraa-Nuve nods, "Thorn, too."

"Is Sarah a Thorn?" Synite looks between the two of them.

"Agent," Kraa-Nuve says.

"Sarah Cassidy was in the overall organization but not high on the chain of command. She did show some promise, hence her codename," the wheels in Synite's head going 'round and 'round. "She never got the chance, though. She had only recently been introduced to Fabric when they got us."

Kraa-Nuve drops his head, "They."

"The same ones that ran you out of the central legion killed seven of us founders and a hundred more down in the organization," Tobias drops it on them. "Watch this," the projection disappears and a flat screen video comes on in his place, his face on the video. "If you're watching this recording, I'm probably dead and the Thorns have been overtaken as I predicted they would be."

"Always knew," Kraa-Nuve misses his old life but does not want to show that emotion on top of the mourning for the Grujeks that blankets the entire room.

"Old friend, I'm sorry to say that our worst fears were realized. The fact that you're seeing me right now means that there is some hope in fate. I implanted this message in my son when we installed his Borganics as a child in case the time came. Its activation was pending my death and his coming on our old ship," the recording of Tobias reiterates some things, confusing Synite yet again as to how Kraa-Nuve had friends. "With this message, there are a few documents that you should be proud I saved, including our original rosters and free company agreement," the ship notifies in a pop-up message that these documents are being uploaded. "Also, in the dossier are a few files that may help you narrow your search and locate the new Thorns which were formed and defected from several of our original comrades who also assassinated myself and our other counterparts," Kraa-Nuve is wary of the word assassinate because it claims purpose to the killings. "Yes, it's true. Our deaths were no accident. I must have been murdered soon after I figured out how and why Kinetric was killed.

"I do apologize, Kraa. I'm sorry to have to tell you these things now since I'm sure every ein has had its peril. However, you must mobilize and end this threat. I hope and suggest that you gather enough powerful allies along with my son because the road that the dossier takes you on will make you the most hunted beings in history," and, as the video ends, a young Airiq Driven trots behind his father, happy-go-lucky as ever.

The video disappears and the projection of Tobias comes back up.

"As if we aren't hunted enough!" Synite exclaims. *We'll never be able to get Sarah back. And, if she was so smart as to possibly be a Thorn, why would she react the way she did to us being chased? Wouldn't she have been used to having a target on her back by now?* He has tried to keep that thought out of his mind but, with the mentioning, he cannot help but think about her.

Kraa-Nuve walks away from the projection and over to the wall, leaning on it with one arm. Synite starts to walk by him, "Captain?" but Kraa-Nuve holds one hand up and stops him.

"Moment," the gruff pilot shows a bit of nostalgia as he shakes his head.

"Sebastian Alexander II, codename Deathrage, deceased," as Tobias lists the person, their records come up from the file, "position inherited by Sebastian Alexander III, active. Benjamin Davis Stone, codename Guerilla, inactive. Dace Starborn, codename Blueprint, defected. Hudson Clark, codename Fabric, active. Maijen Asyskik, codename Chalice, defected. N'Kala Rhoo, codename Myth, deceased. S'Waba Rhoo, codename Shadoeviper, defected."

Kraa-Nuve turns hard at this discovery, "Killed sister?"

Tobias nods through the captain's grunting and continues, "Halx Onne, dormant," Kraa-Nuve also reacts to this revelation with a sigh of relief. "Saka Nobu, codename Kinetric, deceased. Raci Islil, codename Kanabl, defected. Grey Santoro, codename Spectrewulf, deceased. Aeola Sun, codename Ravenhawke," Proximity's ears immediately perk up, remembering his interaction with her on Earth Prime's moon at the bar, "defected."

Desha looks at him, feeling his anxiety from her mentioning, "You know who that is."

"Sho glad I left her 'lone," Proximity sighs. "So, they been tryna get to us since back den?"

"Dr. Greyson Nomen, codename Crosslink, deceased," Tobias continues and Kraa-Nuve is about ready to explode with anger. "Interlocke, deceased. Bak Duluus, codename Forcible, defected. Captain Kraa-Nuve and the Caracalla, active. Finally, Skor Dasir Amembe, codename Twisted Nune, defected." Kraa-Nuve thinks about how he has lost every comrade he has ever had, nearly every friend he has ever had and that maybe he is the cursed one. First, all of the Thorns, then his next crew, now Captain Grujek and his sons: they are all gone.

He thinks that, instead of going down this road, maybe he should go home and take care of his family, which is against his very nature, but it may keep him from losing. He does not know what shall come for Synite, Amethyst and the rest of his new crew but, the way things are looking to him, loss is in his future again. And, since he has done exactly what he did not want to do and started caring about these beings, he must now prepare himself to lose them, too.

"So what does this mean?" Amethyst has calmed herself enough to approach the group. "Who are these people?"

"Something happened that I am not sure of," Tobias explains, "some sort of internal power struggle or a deception that changed the alignment of much of the organization." A list of the defectors comes up for everyone to see. "These seven I assume, led by Chalice, dismantled the original Rose and I'm afraid that it is beginning to grow again but with much darker objectives."

"This is what we all knew in the back of our minds, that we had no idea what we were up against when we left. This is it. And, we can add the Enslaver to the list of the new Thorns," Synite declares. "It has to be eighteen, right? That's eight. Who are the other ten?"

"My son came in contact with an Aria Thane, codename Roseweed," which Synite recognizes as the woman he was selling to right before Sarah was kidnapped. "She was attempting to climb the organizational ladder when the coup d'état began. It is safe to assume she has defected."

"And that woman who started the chase with those wolfrat things," Synite recalls the woman who got her purse snatched. "She has to be involved. She's the core reason why Sarah," he does not finish that statement because he barely believes it himself. Synite's emotional state reminds him of a struggle he was having as a teenager with his father shipping him off to a private school instead of allowing him to go to the local public secondary school. He sulked in his uniform as he pulled his two large suitcases floating behind him. His father was escorting him with a suitcase behind him as well. "I don't want to go."

"I know that, son," Nitengale Sr. reminded him. "You've made that clear."

Synite huffed and puffed, "Then why do I have to go?" almost to a whine.

"You should go to the best school that we can afford," his father told him for the twentieth time. "I'm trying to give you the education that wasn't given to me."

"There's more than one perfectly fine school here in Ana," Synite had done a little research and, by research, he means he asked his friends where they were going and why.

Knowing what the true issue is, Nitengale Sr. told him, "You'll make new friends. You're a good kid."

"That's not the point!" he tried to coerce, "I've had the same ones and they have my back. You want me to start over. You want to buy me better friends."

"Son," Nitengale started to feel bad but looked past his son's selling, "you'll be able to talk to your friends here anytime you want to. You can vid them when you're not doing schoolwork. I'm sure you'll text or talkie them all day anyway. So, what's the big deal? You think they won't be your friends anymore just because they're not around you?"

His father hit on one of his core insecurities, so Synite fights back, "You think that's enough. You think vids and voicemail is enough to maintain relationships. I guess so since you think that's good parenting, too!"

They both stopped in their tracks. "Not another word, Cairo!"

"Don't call me that!" his friends had been calling him Synite for a while now.

"You don't love the name I gave you?" Nitengale almost felt disrespected.

Synite started moving again, "You know, nobody calls me that anymore. Damn dad, please? It's a nickname. It's much cooler than being called Cairo."

"I don't think so," Nitengale said, catching up to his son. "Look, you'll be fine out there. You're gonna get along with a bunch of new kids and you'll feel right at home. I promise." Synite regretted that move for such a long time. Then, when his father died and he had to adjust to being a slave, it was not as bad for him to adapt to the change in environment as it probably would have been had his father not done it. Of course, at the time it seemed like the end of the world but his world was small back then. Now, the end of the world might not even be the end of the world to him.

Everyone split up and Driven is plugged into the same power source but in the dormitory Psilos used to camp in. Amethyst rests in her own room, Proximity and Desha in theirs, and Synite sits with Kraa-Nuve and the projection of Tobias in the cockpit.

"I shoulda never left her," Proximity tells Desha and she moves closer to him as they lie together.

"There's nothing else we can do right now except get ready to get her back," Desha comforts him. "We'll save her when the time comes."

"Synite was right," Proximity hates to admit. "I still feel like I needa 'poligize to 'em."

"There'll be time for that later," Desha reminds him. "Right now, we have to deal with what's in front of us and figure out how to do what we need to do."

Kraa-Nuve scrolls through the lists of deceased, defected and otherwise from the dossier that was uploaded. He goes into a deeper menu of the seven defectors and the next document outlines encounters and sightings of those few, including secret missions that they put through the system before the coup. There were also hints of secret meetings at the base of a volcano. "This is the visual proof that we had been compromised, although it was too late to process the information by that time."

There are lists and profiles of possible co-conspirators but only two names were consistent in the trends: Phixen Roon and Obburashi Anzabar. "Why? Marks? Power?" Kraa-Nuve asks Tobias.

"As you know," Tobias tries to answer, "there was a great deal of power in the original Rose and each Thorn was there to protect it. At some point, maybe these two wanted to have the power of the Rose instead of being there with us to keep it from being destroyed."

"Those two," Synite sees them show up on several different pages. "Who are they?"

"Nobody knows," Tobias warns, "which makes them probably two of the most dangerous."

"So that makes twelve," Synite counts. "But, comparable to the Enslaver, we have no idea what they can do."

"More dangerous," Kraa-Nuve agrees with Tobias. "Shroud."

Synite gets up and heads off to check on Driven. As he steps into the room, Driven is talking to a projection of his father, his face turned away. "His body is repairing itself fairly rapidly but rejecting any attempt I make at assisting," the ship tells Synite quietly.

His father's projection puts a hand on his shoulder. "All I ask is that you help them. The future depends on it."

"Whose future?" Driven scoffs. "Just because I'm in rehab doesn't mean I'm vulnerable, pop. You're not going to make me emotional."

"The future of everything! Inside you is much of the information I gathered against these fiends," Tobias tells. "You have to find the rest in the right places. Just as your body interacted with this ship, it will interact with other places that reveal more."

Driven groans as he can barely move while he heals, Synite still listening from the door. "So, you made me the key to saving the future? That was smart, pop. Real smart."

"I see you haven't lost your sense of humor," Tobias records.

"How's it going in here?" Synite asks as he finally steps in the room.

"Wonderful," Driven understands nearly every language and speaks many of them, including sarcasm. "I'm ready to run twenty marathons. Can't you tell?"

"I bet you couldn't make it twenty meters in that condition," Synite cracks back. "What is he?" he directs his question to Tobias.

"One of the wonders of science and technology," Tobias responds.

Driven strains, "And a pretty cool guy, I might add."

"Did you hear everything we talked about while you were out?"

Synite asks, looking back and forth between the two of them.

"I informed him," Tobias takes a few steps away from his son. "He has yet to decide whether or not he wants to play his part yet."

"I really, utterly hate when people, including but not limited to dead parents, talk about me as if I'm not in the room!" Driven mustered up the most enthusiasm he could.

"Whoa, man. Get some rest," Synite puts a hand on his shoulder. "This isn't the time to get offended. We need to worry about getting the beings who did this to you."

"Getting?" Driven chuckles a little. "Bro, I'm not worried about revenge on a fleet of unknowns."

Synite is confused, "They destroyed your ship and killed--"

"Dude!" Driven jerks away from Synite's arm, obviously getting better fairly quickly. "You want me to rest but you remind me of some shit that's going to piss me off? Some shit that hurt me, damn near took my life? Get out of here with that!" Synite does not respond but raises his chin and steps out of the room.

"How is he?" Desha comes up behind Synite as he heads down the hall. "He was banged up pretty bad."

"His body heals fast," Synite leaves it at that.

"Tha's good," Proximity is not far behind. "Hey, 'Nite. I, umm, wanna 'pologize real quick for--"

"Don't worry about it, Prox," he puts a hand up to stop him from throwing more emotion than he is ready to battle. "It is what it is. We both said stuff we shouldn't have said. Friends argue."

"You was right though," Proximity tries to get his apology out.

"It's the past," and Synite does not allow it. "Now, the only thing I care about is finding her. I'll sacrifice for that." The couple feels that way about each other but Synite's reason may be a little different from theirs at this particular moment. They are not surprised that he feels that way because of how he saved her on several different occasions.

"I'm happy that you've found someone you'd die for," Desha's heart is warm.

Synite sniffs and rubs his nose as a masculine reflex, "Hopefully it won't come to that." He leaves them behind and gets to the communication room with Amethyst at the cockpit's threshold. "Ship, can you give me more information on what's in the dossier?"

"Certainly," it brings up three-dimensional projections on the table of the images from the dossier and Synite sits by them. "The original 18 Thorns of the Rose came together as a group of ex-military mercenaries, including Tobias Driven, Sebastian Alexander II, Benjamin Davis Stone, Maijen Asyskik, Aeola Sun and Kraa-Nuve. They saw the need for a corporation of leaders in the octadecaverse, housing the 18 windows of power."

"It must have been pretty bad before they started," Synite grunts.

"To a certain extent, it was a chaotic bedlam after the cataclysms, so they united several different regions to take the reins and lead all kinds of beings into a positive future," the ship reads straight from the report. "There was a long time when the organization progressed and changed many things for the better. Many planets grew and good things were the trend as the organization's power increased.

"The original 18 had issues picking sides when it came to helping certain planets move into becoming self-sufficient and own their liberty. There were several instances when the vote was not unanimous about which side to help but, in the original agreements, they did agree to stay a unit when assisting and to use the full force to complete their tasks.

"The insurrection began from within the organization, apparently, but there is no evidence to suggest who, what, where, when or how. Most who saw it happen decided that the why was solely to capture the already established power structure and use it for selfish reasons. Seven of the original eighteen were corrupted and allowed a new leadership to take over.

"The new leadership has not identified itself as of yet," Kraa-Nuve comes in the room and Amethyst takes a seat next to Synite. He looks over to her and grabs her hand. "There is a lot of secrecy around the new organization, outside of the seven that ushered in this generation."

"It seems the modern Thorns have just taken over where the old guard left off," Amethyst stays subjective, "except with different leadership."

"No!" Kraa-Nuve defends his comrades. "Secret. Skewed. Agenda!"

"Of course you don't agree," Amethyst expected, "like they didn't agree with some of the things you guys did."

"Not same," Kraa-Nuve tries to get her to understand with his limited communication. "Enslaver right, good?"

"He has a point," Synite plugs in. "They were out in the open and were working towards giving others freedom. It does the exact opposite." He directs back to the ship, "What about the rest?"

"Outside of the few you have come in contact with," it convinces them of what they already assumed, "it is impossible to tell who they may be or where they may be. It is difficult to even know if they are a force of 18 or the few that are in the open."

Silence falls over them like precipitation divorcing the sky until Amethyst takes a big sigh, "Promis was right when she said we had no idea what we're up against." She looks over at Synite, "but so were you, Synite. Neither do they!"

 # CHAPTER XIII

"In the beginning of everything, before science and before history, there was only Light and Dark in perfect balance. They existed without Power or Will and in complete harmony in the first dimension, and there was no room for conflict. Things were perfect by definition: it was and still is what every being since has strived for. Light and Dark both grew Powerful together in the faultlessness of balance as they granted each other the Will to complete tasks with each other. Power was something they shared as it grew spontaneously and naturally out of their newly attained Wills.

"When they had enough Power between the two of them, they made a unified decision to build the second dimension, the Plane, together as equals and it, too, was the epitome of excellence, perfect by nature. They continued to grow more Powerful as they expanded the Plane in opposite directions. This became problematic as they could not communicate as well since they were stretching so far away from each other at such a rapid pace.

"Outside of the Plane, there was absolutely nothing, different from the nothing that most beings may perceive it to be. There was no void, no danger, no Space, just a wall on either side of the plane where nothing had yet been created. Then, being the more enterprising of the two, Light decided on its own to use its half of Power and the Plane to create the third dimension, Space. Light did not intend on deceiving Dark in doing this but made it in order to reunite without wasting effort by going backwards. Unbeknownst to Light, the balance between the two of them was immediately thrown off and Dark knew as soon as it happened. Dark could not understand why Light would go off and take the next step alone as they had done everything as equals before.

"As Light was trying to get back closer to its counterpart, Dark decided to move the same direction Light was moving in, expanding the dark side of the third dimension and moving away from Light as quickly as Light was trying to reunite with Dark. With this movement, they both gained more Power and thought very little of the Plane they had created together.

"After completing the third dimension separately, Dark's jealousy of Light's creation got too big to handle. So, Dark created the fourth dimension, Time, without the help or blessing of Light. This moment of genesis, the beginning of Time, is what most human scientists call the Big Bang. This did not balance Light and Dark as Dark assumed it would, but stretched Dark even farther away from Light at an alarming rate. Because Time was created with scorn, Dark would never be able to come to terms with Light ever again. Dark would continue along the path of Time with growing jealousy and anger over Light creating Space, along with the light of the cosmos, by itself.

"The struggle for Power between Light and Dark created much conflict over Time and Space. They both began filling each other's Space with pieces of their own Power for different reasons: Light wanted to get closer to Dark and regain the perfect balance that they had before; Dark wanted to take over Light's Space as revenge for throwing off the perfect balance. They have not been able to clearly communicate their true reason to each other as the faster Light's Power grows, the more difficult and more jealous Dark gets despite their Power being nearly equal.

"Light began to create celestial bodies in order to communicate with Dark on its behalf. Stars were born, galaxies collected, and universes exploded into existence. Planets violently found their Suns, cooling and heating over billions of cycles around their Suns. Elements came naturally with the existence of Time and Space, eventually leading to the creation of Life. However, Dark grew more jealous still at the products of Light's creations though they were all made to reach back to Dark and, instead of waiting, created Death, as a function of Time, to take back the Power Dark assumed Light was trying to use against it. Dark decided the only way to become equals with Light would be to create the opposite of everything.

"This did not work either as none of those celestial bodies or otherwise lived long enough to reach Dark. Soon, other opposing concepts were borne naturally from the interactions between all of these creations. Paradise and disaster, peace and war, creation and destruction, to name a few, continue to keep Light and Dark from interacting with each other as equals ever again.

"One of the most important, though, was the concept of limitation. Dark had created scarcity, a reason to divide things, a reason to keep things to oneself. Once Death reigned over Life and Time, beings were forced to collect things in order to take advantage of their fleeting experiences on this side of Life. Dark and Death made sure that no one would truly be able to collect enough knowledge to understand Death or what happens when Life's Time ends. This search for understanding Death evolved into Instinct and Thought which branched into Reason, Knowledge, Love, Art, everything that exists as beings try their hardest to leave a mark on Time, giving weight to their existence.

"Within its Space, Death forced beings to section off all celestial bodies into thirty-six universes that revolve around the central point where Light and Dark first split up to create the Plane. The billions of galaxies in both of the octadecaverses have more than ten trillion systems that have more than fifty trillion planets that have life. There are no true lines between the eighteen universes, only those created by the beings that have travelled to each of them. Some lives stretch eons, giving the ability for them to reach and divide the farthest reaches of space but, regardless, they all have the Dark hand of Death awaiting them at the end of their Time. Though nature, based on the relatively infinite stretches of space in the octadecaverses as they continue to expand, reflects heavily on the ways Light and Dark interacted with each other from before the beginning.

"The original Plane is now the barrier between Dark's and Light's octadecaverses, a curved wall that can only be crossed by a few bodies that are powerful enough to get through. The Power of Dark is seen in the death and swallowing of Light's celestial bodies, the almighty and unwavering gravitational pull of black holes. No forms of light (radio, infrared, visible, x-ray and gamma) stand a chance against the engulfing Power of Dark.

"Relatively recently, through the Elements that were created by the combination of Time and Space, Dark has been sharing its Power. It has been building an army of beings, led by the Elementalist Pinnacles, which will exact revenge on Light for the supposed betrayal. These Pinnacles, the four beings that can control every aspect of their Elementalist sphere, are to break the Plane and allow Dark to seep through while Light is occupied.

"Then, as far as Dark states, the four Pinnacles yearn to destroy all of Light's bodies and Dark will take over both sides tipping the balance in the favor of Dark and satisfying its vengeance. Once the Pinnacles break the Plane and Dark gets enough of Light's Space, Dark should not have any reason to let Time exist anymore. So, Dark will end Time and take Space for itself while Light keeps seeking Dark out to re-establish balance."

"Great! Keep it up," Castra Nim encourages his new teammates in the drills he is showing them. He has had to correct several of their mechanics in different stages of the drills but, overall, they are a good team and fit well with each other. It will be his task, though, to figure out how to fit into the scheme without sacrificing their chemistry or one of their lives.

"The battle is tomorrow," Castra enthusiastically reminds them in order to replace their nervousness with excitement. "We are the team to beat but that does not mean we can go in without being completely ready; and we are ready!" Everyone, including the other trainers and sparring team get in the circle to listen to his encouragement. "We have the most confidence in this world! Earth 11 won't know what hit them when we step foot in that arena, on that battlefield of glory!" They cheer him on, "There's nothing stopping us! Like every great team, the only thing that can keep us from victory is ourselves!"

Castra throws his fist up and everyone comes around to clap by his chest. They all gather in and cheer, their exhilaration amplified. However, as everyone breaks away to get some rest, the only thing Castra can think about is Atlan and how he may have to kill one of his own near the end.

Fortunately for them, the format of the tournament puts them on the complete opposite side of the bracket. So, the only chance they have to face each other in battle is if they both go undefeated, which is the way things may end up in all likelihood. And, they are allowed ten days between tournament battles and fifteen before the championship battle to recuperate and scout the next team. It gives Castra more time to worry less about having to fight his family. This will afford him time to focus more on building a stronger bond with Coldsmoke so that, when the time comes to face the Enslaver, he chooses to be on the side of the Vanguard. Liffu approaches him, "You seem concerned."

"I'm fine," Castra is not one to go on about his emotions, "just focusing."

"You won't have anything t'worry about," Liffu puts a hand on his shoulder and quickly feels the tension he is holding. "Is it your home you're worried about?"

"Not quite," Castra tries to avoid the conversation. "There are some deeper things going on over there that may be tough if any of them die."

"But if it is them that your concern sits with, I understand. Before I was a starter, it was difficult t'watch them fight without my help," Liffu recalls, "especially when someone would get killed who was here for a long time."

Castra deflects to him, "Did that happen a lot?"

"Three times before and twice after I began starting on th'main team," Liffu confesses. "It's never something you get used t'happening but it is part of th'game."

The bracket and location for the tournament were released five days ago and K'oma's first opponent is the team from SurLioln, where Batlazar was born, in the neutral arena on the island of Gol off the coast of Atlan. They are scheduled as the last fight of the first round after Atlan easily defeated Hu-est Gate Arena's finest earlier in the round.

They meet in Gol for the night match, its surface convex as it was built around a hill. SurLioln's warriors are announced first, as is customary for the lower seeded team. The five of them and their two alternates do not garner much applause, especially not in comparison to the roar of the crowd for K'oma. Bash, Helena Rour, Liffu, Usurpithy and Coldsmoke are all touted to win as the active team for Arena K'oma.

Castra Nim still garners a great applause as he waves out to the crowd from the pine in their dugout. Bash and Helena Rour join him as the starting trio of Liffu, Usurpithy and Coldsmoke march atop the slight hill to meet their three opponents, their apparel matching completely from head to toe, so much that it is nearly impossible to distinguish between them. If it was not for very slight differences in build, even the most attentive eye would not be able to tell the difference.

They don flat masks with slits for their noses and openings for their eyes; white fur over their heads, down their backs and around their waists, ankles and wrists; and a lightly armored suit that does not fit close enough to the body to tell whether each is male, female, somewhere beyond or in between. Even as the announcer calls each of their names, neither of them acknowledges their designation. They keep their eyes on Coldsmoke, Liffu and Usurpithy, analyzing them, from what Castra Nim can tell.

The Lioln team each drops into a stance quickly, then mimics the stance of their teammate to the left of them, then does it again, their stances rotating from left to right. This is a tactic that they have used successfully to further confuse their opponents and got them into this tournament with their last victory. Castra is thoroughly mesmerized by the sight despite having watched them perform it during research. "It's even better in person," he says over to Bash who is unimpressed as usual.

"Whatever," is usually the response Bash gives as he is not amused by much. "Let me know when th'bloodbath's over." He leans back and crosses his arms and legs, fully prepared to take a nap.

Castra watches the fight intently, Usurpithy conserving energy, Coldsmoke not being challenged much and Liffu not having a tough time, but not having an easy one either. After all of the enthusiastic speeches and encouragement, this team is exactly what it was before: acting as if this battle was meant for them to win without doing the work to win it. Their sense of entitlement is shown in their lack of urgency.

They have not used a single team technique and have reverted to single battles, regressing as if Castra had never even come to this team. That is exactly what Spoilsport is thinking as he watches the fight from the Sword. Coldsmoke's technique improved slightly but that is the only improvement he sees, sorely disappointed. That feeling is shared by Castra who yells out to them, "Teamwork! Leave no doubt!" Liffu seems to hear the plea as he moves closer to Usurpithy, attempting to initiate something. It falls on deaf ears, however, and puts Liffu in an even worse situation than he was in before. As he tries to get his teammate's attention, he leaves a huge opening for his Lioln warrior opponent to exploit. Coldsmoke is in range to stop his cohort from being killed but this puts the entire team on the defensive, a position that they never do well in. The warrior Coldsmoke was fighting is freed up to do what he pleases to Usurpithy, initiating a double-team.

The tide turns quickly as the Lioln team takes full advantage of the situation. They pin Usurpithy on one side of the hill, the Gol crowd confused about how this favored team is basically down in the fight. There is a rumble of concern going around the crowd, particularly for the gamblers who knew Lioln had absolutely no chance of survival.

Coldsmoke defends against the one trying to attack Liffu as he recovers. Coldsmoke's Will rises to the challenge as it usually does when the situation gets tougher. He gets noticeably faster and then grows concerned about the bout Usurpithy is in alone on the other side.

Liffu gets up and heads over the top of the hill, sliding down the other side to speed his descent. On his way down, he pulls his left arm off and spears it at one of the Lioln warrior's backs. It remains attached to him by a long ligament and, when it grabs onto the back of the warrior's fur, he jerks it back. He then throws a roundhouse kick and his lower leg detaches at the knee. The kick meets the Lioln warrior in the face, exciting the crowd again in the favor of K'oma.

Liffu retracts his appendages and slams his opponent into the ground next to him, getting more temporary cheers. Usurpithy has a rough time regaining control of his battle as he is more of a grappler. His adversary keeps distance between them, using simple long-range energy attacks that are not very powerful but are rather painful when they hit. He also seems too slow to close the distance, as Liffu and Castra can tell, so Liffu decides to return the favor and double team the one fighting Usurpithy.

He attempts another team technique with Usurpithy to get the distance closed with some success as Usurpithy is able to wrestle with his challenger. At the same time, the one Liffu left on the ground mounts his back, wraps his legs around Liffu's waist and arms around his neck. Liffu struggles to breathe, trying to pull him off. He throws his right arm off into the Air and, after it reaches its zenith, it comes down and grabs the Lioln warrior by the fur. He pulls to reconnect the arm and it works but was not strong enough to get the choking monkey off his back.

Coldsmoke is at a stalemate with his opponent as well, not understanding why. "This is the tournament!" Castra yells out to them.

"No prisoners!" which is one of the established rules of the tournament: no team can recruit or save a member of a defeated team during tournament play; they either have to surrender or die. *This is why I wanted him to learn how to control that Will of his. Now would be a good time to use it!*

The captain notices beyond his fight that he cannot see or hear the rest of his team. They are too quiet and on the other side of the hill, out of his line of sight. So, he waits for an opening and puts some force behind a dropkick that sends his antagonist into the wall. Then he dashes around to the other side of the hill to see Liffu being choked on the ground and Usurpithy wrangling in the corner.

In the moment of decision, things slow down for Coldsmoke. He can tell Usurpithy is not in a dire situation so he moves to assist Liffu. Once he gets there, he can tell his vice-captain cannot breathe so he squats over them and grabs the Lioln warrior's arms at the wrists and pulls. He sees the life go back into Liffu as he is able to breathe again, his survival instinct coming back together. It still takes a moment for Coldsmoke to pry them apart and, after doing so, applies his own chokehold around the neck of their opponent. He switches it to a half-Nelson, leaving Liffu time to catch his breath and recover. Instead of keeping the hold, Coldsmoke suplexes him over his shoulder. He drops him almost on the same spot on his back that Liffu slammed him on and it cracks one of his ribs.

The Lioln warrior curls up in pain but the one Coldsmoke left takes his place in the fight. "They're…relentless!" Liffu says as he stands back up.

"Don't forget what team this is!" Castra yells in to them. It does not look as if Liffu hears him as he has a difficult time staying on his feet. "Liffu! Gather yourself!"

"I'm…trying," he says from a three-point stance and drops down to one knee.

Castra looks over at Bash and Helena who are both still oblivious to what is going on in the fight. "Is this how you two always are?"

"We aren't out there so why get stressed out about what's going on?" Helena responds.

"Exactly," Bash cosigns. "It's best t'stay completely relaxed down here while they do their job. You're wasting energy watching."

"But these are your teammates! Your cheering might keep them focused, keep them from giving up," Castra pleads for their help. "Your warning might keep them alive! Maybe you'll notice a strategy or something."

"Neither one of us are good at that," Helena admits. "If we're not in the fight, it doesn't even make sense."

Castra fumes, "Your lack of…whatever the hell it is you're lacking right now doesn't make sense to me!"

"Whatever," Bash lies down on the bench and Helena looks away without responding. Castra can do nothing except shake his head and go back to paying attention to the fight.

Airiq Driven's relationship with his father, Tobias Driven, was not the greatest from the younger's perspective, as he previously described. Tobias installed his Borganics at such a young age that he never got the chance to have a regular childhood, which grew to become the biggest cause of friction between these two. Airiq was always being studied and monitored, tweaked here and there by his father in the limited amount of time they had together. Unfortunately, this made him feel like more of a project than a son for a very long time.

In TAT time, he is a few cycles younger than Synite but, having been through certain things at such a young age, they are about the same when it comes to maturity. Driven's urges for excitement and his daredevil attitude were genetic but he did not discover how much he loved defying physics until a cycle after he healed from his last Borganics surgery and was able to use it all full out.

It took a long time but Airiq and Tobias did understand each other: Tobias was a scientist and leader of his generation, a one-in-a-trillion type of being who needed to be respected by the masses more than only his own family and friends. He was not a fly-by-the-seat-of-his-pants kind of man since his reputation was built on his competence, professionalism and reliability. He was a certifiable genius in engineering though he was neither eccentric nor socially awkward.

Tobias made very few snap decisions and even those that he did make were completely calculated risks. He was always prepared to climb or descend branches on his decision tree and, from his earliest memories to his last, he was compelled by some internal force to be more than successful: he felt the subconscious need to be a revolutionary icon.

Airiq became rebellious and never wanted to try and live up to his father's name, although that is the only name he ever goes by. He respected his father above all else and never spoke a hint of negativity about him as he knew how that would hurt him. Most of his chiding came in the form of silence, patronizing looks and going against the grain just to do it, as most teenagers do.

He would rather use the power given to him to enjoy his life as much as possible instead of being treated as a weapon or test pilot for what would change his world. Once he knew he could, Airiq would go out on a limb to experience life to its fullest and never look over his shoulder except to see who he had passed. Things came easy to him, with the help of his father and, for that he is forever gracious.

This understanding of the rift between them kept the Drivens from pushing each other away, as many normal father-son relationships would have been strained to their breaking point under similar circumstances. It is not to be misunderstood: Tobias loved Airiq completely. He considered his son to be his greatest success even before adding the Borganics. However, Airiq was oblivious to these underlying feelings though he knew that, since his mother left, Tobias was doing the best he could at being a father and founder of the Thorns.

He heard a little bit about what his father did when he hung around the labs and went out with his father and his closest associate, Dr. Grayson Nomen, who was later recruited into the Thorns and coded Crosslink. This name was given to him by Tobias because of his relationship with Airiq and how he was a link between the two of them when they drifted apart from each other emotionally.

Crosslink was a very sensitive man, not to the point to where he was emotionally unstable but he was much attuned to being's emotional states. He was a doctor of psychology, a psychiatrist and neurologist, a master of the brain and how beings used it. He was a key in Tobias's development of Borganics in that he designed the neural links that allowed the user of Borganics to keep full control over their body.

He and Airiq got along so well because of his empathy for young Driven's situation. He explained everything to him so he would not be left in the dark by his father, and Airiq understood. Crosslink and Driven bonded so much that, when Tobias never came back, he stayed with Driven as long as he could before sending him off away from the fighting.

Driven was devastated by the loss of both of his father figures in such a short time period but knew he would have to go on with his life. So, with the tools given to him by his Tobias and Grayson, Airiq traversed his home universe, drifting along until he found a place that was comfortable enough for him to relax.

When he found that relaxation on Yar JK, he also found friendship in Captain Grujek and his sons as they met quite randomly. Driven was selling electronics, building road cars, teaching private boxing lessons and filming stunt videos at the time. Yelsh and Hemmen were fans of his stunts, noticed him on a train one day and, despite Driven thinking they were kind of strange, he took a liking to the family and they invited him to join on their next trip off-planet.

In the process of making Grace and Mercy among other weaponry, Tobias taught Airiq so much about weapons that forging his own became a nice hobby. He had learned so much about sales on Yar JK that selling his own product was a natural next step as they appealed so much to high-end weapons owners. He caught the eye of several wealthy businessmen through some of the contacts he made on Yar JK and has kept them as clients despite there being conflicts of interest sometimes. Both his father and Crosslink taught him that, in business, you must allow those with interests to resolve their own conflicts, though this idea might have caught up with him now.

There was a pair of powerful reasons for Tobias inventing Borganics. The economical reason was that their home planet was a very arid place and much of civilization was forced to live underground after a solar flare struck the surface of the planet. Millions died, nearly forty percent of the population, in the wake of the event and Tobias was bent on making a way for his race to survive and thrive on the surface again. The emotional reason was that, before the Borganics, Driven was such a sickly child, born prematurely by four weeks, and rarely got out of the house from being so weak from illnesses. Tobias wanted his son to become a strong, useful young man who could do anything he wanted to with his life.

As far as the environment goes, Tobias started engineering exoskeletons, as most scientists do who are looking for ways to stay alive in strange elements. At the same time, he worked closely with biochemists in looking for ways for Airiq to get stronger without having to take a litany of medications every day for the rest of his life. After trials and many failures, Tobias got the bright idea of doing exactly what his people had to do: go below the surface to fix the environmental problem. Thus, Borganics were born and the development began. Throughout that process, he decided that he may be able to fix his son's biological problems while enhancing the other project, killing two birds with one stone or, actually extending the life of the whole flock with something more complex than a rock.

Driven was not the first experiment, nor was he the last successful implant, but he was definitely the one most meticulously operated on. The extent of the surgeries and their requisite recovery periods were a strain on all three of them, physically and emotionally. Although there was the scientific aspect of getting his project as great as he could, that was not the main reason he never left Airiq's side. There were techs, assistants and other employees that could have monitored Airiq during recoveries and even done some of the surgeries instead of Tobias. However, he was there because he refused to leave his son's life in anyone else's hands.

The few beings that Tobias fitted the entire Borganics slate into had five procedures that took at least four hecu each. The procedures go as follows: first, genetic enhancement including installation of nanometer-sized medical robots (nanomedbots) into the endocrine system for more efficient healing and diagnostics for the other procedures, DNA treatment for immune system boosting, and cellular modification to prepare the body for the other phases; second, neurological enhancement with software installation; third, his internal cybernetics including biometric monitors, augmentation for all of the senses except for taste, and bone density restructuring; fourth, extra-sensory augmentation for echo-location, GPS tracking, wireless communication with devices, and bionic servos for the joints; fifth, muscle density augmentation, the relatively unbreakable semi-robotic indo-frame installation, hair and hair follicle replacement with motion detectors and fiber optics.

Grayson and Tobias operated on Airiq a total of twenty-eight different times, some of the procedures taking over eight hecu to complete. He was tasked with making Driven the picture perfect version of his life's greatest accomplishment and Tobias certainly succeeded in that. Driven became both the reason for and the example of a genius's work which is something very few beings can say. His body is literally a miracle mingling of art and technology that will never be duplicated.

 # CHAPTER XIV

Kraa-Nuve visits with Driven for the first time since the accident, Tobias's projection still lingering in the room. "What happened back then with you two?" he asks the captain.

"Saga saved, held line," Kraa-Nuve looks down, embarrassed by his own actions, "couldn't wait."

"If you had waited," Tobias puts a hand on Kraa-Nuve's shoulder, "there would be no possibility of a prosperous future for us. No one would have lived. You had young Alexander with you. You had to survive."

"Owe life," Kraa-Nuve finally raises his head, saddened by the fact that he is speaking from beyond the grave, only a glimmer of Tobias's actual self, and not the man.

Outside the room, a dejected Proximity passes by and Synite follows, "Prox! Hold on!"

"Ain't nothin' to say," Proximity slows his pace but does not stop for Synite. "We goin' live by her people, outta yo' way," Synite stops but Proximity keeps walking. "Soon as we see Sarah and know she safe, we leavin'."

Desha comes out to join the conversation, "We have been pretty big liabilities thus far and you know it."

Proximity turns to face Synite from down the hall, "We wanna settle down, bro. Ion wanna see no more fightin'. Not 'tween us or dem."

"What about," Synite cannot fathom right now losing any help. "What about the plans?"

"We have to do what's best for our future together," Desha reminds him. "You should do the same with you and Sarah. We'll help you with that and then," she puts her arms around her other half and gives Synite a solemn face. "Fabric should be able to take care of whatever you wanted us to do, or someone else, maybe Castra Nim or one of his teammates.”

“He still recruitin’ huh?” Proximity gives more offers for their replacements. “They got it.”

“I’ll bring it up to everyone else but,” Synite sighs and scratches his head.

“No need,” Proximity would rather they leave quietly when the time comes without any fuss. “We wanna tell you ‘cause we know how important all dis is. We love ya, bro. Don’t be thinkin’ we don’t.”

“I…I just,” Proximity walks up and puts his hand on Synite’s shoulder.

“We wanna make a family, ‘Nite,” Proximity smiles back at Desha and she looks down, grinning. “We startin’ to try and build one now and, after seein’ Sarah get took that way, ya know how I’d go nuts if it happened to Desh.” He releases and turns back to head off with her, “We sorry.”

After they head off, out of view, Synite huffs, “I’m sorry, too.” He goes back towards the communication room and Driven yawns loudly, reminding Synite that he does have other comrades.

“Man I feel like shootin’ something!” Driven shifts his body around as he gets more control back in his body. “It’s been too long!”

“Guns below,” Kraa-Nuve gets to his feet. “Welcome to ‘em.”

“Shoot I might have to live down there for a little while once I can move well enough to get out of this stupid bed,” it does not take much for someone similar to Driven to get stir crazy.

“Yours,” Kraa-Nuve feels terrible about losing the Pingar’s crew. “Moment?”

Driven still is not used to Kraa-Nuve’s shortness of speech. “What?”

“Implants,” he speaks of the Borganics. “What got?”

“I replaced his entire skeleton,” Tobias’s projection recalls, “with a polymer that is a thousand times stronger than normal bone, nearly unbreakable, and 72.1% lighter. He has a host of microcells that replaced the crop of slow-acting white blood cells and are the reason he is able to heal so quickly. Some muscle enhancing proteins and wiring were added, laced with about a million sensors of internal and external activity. He has brain and spinal cord protection casings tied in with his new skeletal system.”

“Hey, projection Dad, we’re both bored already,” Driven yawns again and looks up at Kraa-Nuve. “Know I work real well when I’m not beat the hell up.”

“Saw chase,” Kraa-Nuve nods. “Crazy.”

“He is a special boy,” Tobias remarks. “And his weapons are

definitely special."

Driven sees Synite passing, "Hey!" Synite stops and comes in. "Hey man I wanted to thank you for coming after me. Y'all didn't have to since we just met and all. I mean, I'm cool but you definitely risked a lot."

"You're family to us now," Synite goes by them. "Except to Kraa-Nuve and Psilos. They're pretty old." Kraa-Nuve whacks him on the top of his head, dropping him to the floor.

"Young smack!" Kraa-Nuve and Driven laugh together, louder and longer than Synite would normally approve of having someone laugh at him.

Things go as smoothly as a fight to the death could for K'oma: the fight regulated soon after Liffu got back up. One from Lioln is knocked unconscious and dragged from the field. Castra continues to cheer them on as Usurpithy finally starts to understand the team concept, or so it seems. Coldsmoke used their period of advantage to tire out one of the two that are in the battle while Liffu continues to recover near their bench, listening to Castra's encouragement.

As the next warrior comes in, the fight continues to move on steadily. Liffu is able to get back into the mix, creating some havoc with his ability to throw his limbs and still control his extremities. Coldsmoke and Usurpithy switch opponents so Coldsmoke can wear another one down and Usurpithy can crush them into submission, which is exactly how they get rid of their second victim, the advantage back on their side.

At the same time, Liffu gets a tad too comfortable and takes a critical blow to the side while his arm is extended, locking it up and he cannot retract it. He grabs his side with his free arm and allows for another opening which the Lioln warrior takes full advantage of, going for Liffu's head. The window of that opening closed quickly though and Liffu is able to move out of the way of the initial thrust but could not dodge the knee that came after it.

That knee hits Liffu square between the eyes and he bends over in pain, his hand over his bleeding face. The Lioln warrior drops several consecutive elbows to the back of his head and neck, further damaging Liffu's ability to move. He yells in pain, getting both Usurpithy and Coldsmoke's attention finally as they are about to throw the killing blow on the other warrior.

Coldsmoke dashes up the hill and, as he goes back down, he can only watch as his vice-captain is beaten into the ground. Liffu is unconscious, Castra looking on with concern and the entire crowd watching in disbelief. The Lioln warrior sees Coldsmoke coming out of the corner of his eye. He decides to hurry up and even things up; so, he jumps and comes down on Liffu's neck with both feet, crushing the bones and other vital internal systems housed there.

The announcer declares Liffu dead after that, stunning the crowd and angering Castra Nim. Liffu was the only being on the K'oma team that he had honestly bonded with and now he is no more. Castra drops down to the bench next to Bash and looks over, "Time for one of you to get in there."

"What?" he and Helena Rour both look up for the first time since the match started to see their vice-captain lying motionless on the side of the hill.

"What happened?" Helena Rour looks over at Castra, "Explain this to me!"

"I said, it's time for one of you to get in there!" Castra yells back. "So, either get ready or leave the others to fend for themselves!" Neither Bash nor Helena Rour were expecting to have to join in this match at all, which is why their attitudes were so poor as a reflection of their cockiness. Castra is one to believe that, if you go into a match actually thinking you are invincible, it creates a situation where the underdog has something to prove. When underdogs have something to prove and have the talent to prove it, heads roll. This is why he never lets his attitude get there, because of how foolish the two of them look at this very moment with one of their superiors killed.

Bash moves past Helena Rour to enter the match as soon as the advantage period is over. Usurpithy immediately takes out the warrior he and Coldsmoke had double-teamed to keep the odds in their favor as the final Lioln warrior comes in, a bit larger than the other four. Castra cannot move from his seat, frozen by the loss of his only friend in a very wide radius. He has to take a moment and think about the bigger picture; he puts his personal feelings aside and stands up, remembering the larger goal. "This fight has to end one way or another." Helena Rour has no words for the time being, which Castra does not mind.

Coldsmoke finally reaches and confronts the warrior that killed his vice, anger in his face. "Why do you search for revenge in this world?" the Lioln warrior speaks for the first time. "Everyone here is only out for themselves. I did not kill your comrade; I killed someone who would have killed me, given the proper opportunity. Nothing more, nothing less."

This speech stops Coldsmoke in his tracks near the bottom of the hill, "Then you should understand as well when your heart refuses to work for your battered body." Coldsmoke immediately backs up his words and clotheslines the warrior to the ground, one that would have knocked the head off of an unsuspecting victim of it. The oohs and ahhs of the crowd are reminiscent of an extremely embarrassing sports moment. The consensus is that Coldsmoke probably should get this fight over with to spare the poor fighter's time.

However, Lioln's recently entered warrior has a different idea as he runs up behind Coldsmoke. Unfortunately, Coldsmoke's Will is so high right now that there is almost nothing anybody in the arena would be able to do about it, especially with any sort of direct attack. Just as the last Lioln warrior gets into his range, Coldsmoke swings around, grabs the back of his head, and drives it into the ground, dragging it up the side of the hill.

The warrior kicks out of Coldsmoke's grasp and, as soon as his head is up to see where he is, he is met with a lariat similar to the one that dropped his teammate. His mask that was already cracked from being dragged is completely thrown off by the attack, so he immediately covers his face with his hands when he has the wherewithal to do so. Bash steps into the field as Usurpithy predictably moves over to finish off the warrior Coldsmoke left in his warpath. Castra says to himself, "It's a shame it took a death for him to take control of the match. I'll be thoroughly discussing this with him after this is over."

Only one hand covering his face now, the last warrior swings wildly to get some space away from Coldsmoke. Bash joins them at the top of the hill, ready to make an impact on the nearly completed match. The last Lioln warrior refuses to uncover his face even though Coldsmoke approaches him for the final blow.

Coldsmoke drops to one knee and gets set to throw the last punch. The ground shatters under him as he pushes off and, right before he gets in range for his ultimate punch, the warrior rises and removes his hand from his face. He reveals something to Coldsmoke that no other being will ever be able to see, something that will stay in his mind for the remainder of his time on this side of life. And, once the blow is laid upon him, his face turns to ashes.

Afterwards, Coldsmoke goes and rips off the masks of the other Lioln dead but sees only ashes. No camera got the angle to view the warrior's living face, nor does anyone understand why Coldsmoke is so adamant about seeing it again. He was interviewed later describing it as "One of the most awe-inspiring things I've ever laid waste to." He is well aware of the killing clause that forbids contact between the winning team and a survivor of the losing team under any circumstances; even despite that, the Lioln warrior that did live disappeared into exile.

"I am going to find my way in the rotation," Castra Nim gives his statement the K'oma staff and press after the match. "It was disappointing to see our vice-captain meet his demise in the battle," he cuts his eyes at Bash and Helena Rour, "and we as a team are filled with regret for losing him. However, we will move past it and be victorious regardless. Thank you."

Bash tries to approach Castra Nim, "I promise I'll--"

"I'm not here to listen to vows," Castra interrupts. In private, he completely ignores the attempts at conversation from anyone on the team except Coldsmoke who he still argues with for his lack of control. "Why did it take for them to get that far for you to take over? It's as if you were in autopilot or something. You know the rest of the matches won't be as easy as that one was for you, right?" Coldsmoke is still deeply affected by the last Lioln warrior's face, in sort of a trance over it as Castra Nim vents at him. "I told you to try and learn to control your Will but you want to force it to click on its own. You're silly for that."

"Fortune is on our side," one of the staff members comes in with a report of their next opponent.

Castra reads it to himself as the staff member awaits his facial reaction which shows a sorrowful relief. "The next team we face only had one survivor and no alternates. Therefore, we are starting the battle with a three-to-one advantage."

"And here is the report on that survivor," the staff member shows them a diagram of Hyolocke, the last warrior for Oest Mun. He is a frail young boy with the posture of a king, his eyes full of scorn for the life of slavery that has brought him to this point. He, much like Synite, was brought to Oest Mun solely to fight and his heart has grown cold because of it. He has no more sympathy and lost the ability to care, which has made him dangerous. Unfortunately for him, from a being's perspective if they care about living, his days seem to be numbered now as he is set to go up against Coldsmoke, Usurpithy, Bash, Helena Rour and Castra Nim on his own. Hyolocke has been in many a near death experience since arriving in Oest Mun but his death date has essentially been set in the eyes of the public's great majority. "The second round is twenty days from today."

CHAPTER XV

Agents and attendees circle the control room in Atlan, the crowd in a general unrest. A statistician comes into the room with a data pin which she plugs into the main view screen. "As you can see," she speaks to the crowd of colleagues, "the consensus about the recent activity is frustration due to the public's inability to monitor anything that went on in the recent conflict."

The head agent, in more decorative clothing compared to the others, steps forward to the podium. "Why is it that we don't have cameras that can withstand those atmospheres? We cannot assume that every planet they set foot on is going to be pleasant."

An attendee on the panel speaks up, "The budgetary committee thought it to be unnecessary since--"

"Is this a joke?" the head agent interrupts. "With the resources of Lord Chalice and the Enslaver, among others, budgetary concerns do not exist!"

"Excuse me," the statistician steps back up and the head agent allows her the floor. "Despite the lack of approval by our audience as a whole, the viewer ratings and numbers still went up. They were actually twenty points higher than usual after a battle they saw much more active footage from."

Everyone looks at the graphs that she posts as she points at the viewership spikes. "The numbers do not lie," an attendee says.

"Maybe it's an aberration but," the statistician remarks.

"Aberration or not," the head agent smiles, "profits were made! Give this young lady a bonus!"

"Maybe some of our viewers prefer not to see everything," another attendee puts in. "Maybe more suspense comes from the unseen."

"Is that what we need?" the first attendee asks.

"Nonsense!" the head agent discounts that notion. "It was a good change of pace. It is our responsibility to deliver footage to the masses and that is what we are going to do from here on out." He points at the corner of engineers, "Begin development of cameras able to record in harsh climates and the ships that can take them there! Do not let this happy accident happen again! Marks are no object. Build, build, build!"

Psilos's projection stands at the table, arms crossed, as the Caracalla shoots off from the Capricorn Way. "It is ill-starred that he was battered in that fashion," he speaks of Driven after having visited with him, "but he appears quite resilient; a wonder of science and technology. And from the wealth of information you have bestowed upon me based on his parentage, I am afraid of the aftermath of our subsequent conversation.

"There is much more to this than the few bounties on us," Psilos speaks his piece. "For these 18 Thorns, those appraisals are nothing in contrast to what it costs for their power to wane. This is about the fates of myriad worlds and there is no coincidence."

Amethyst, Synite and Kraa-Nuve sit around the table in the communication room. "When Santhia convinced me to leave," Synite starts, "I knew I would cross the Enslaver. That was why I knew I had to befriend Amethyst. I'm glad that friendship became true and not contingent on fighting against It, the same as one of those 'the enemy of my enemy is my friend' situations."

"As am I," Amethyst validates.

Synite sighs, "But peace and freedom are my objectives. They have been since I felt I had the power to achieve them. This," he points down at the table, "this situation we're in doesn't feel the same as either one."

"Just because it hasn't been as easy as we thought it would be," Amethyst calls, "doesn't mean it's unattainable. We have only a few more steps to take."

"And how many more of our friends do we have to sacrifice?" Synite puts his head on the table. "If the Enslaver is the head of the new Thorns, is destroying It going to end this?"

"You want?" Kraa-Nuve offers Synite. "Girl or Free?"

Synite smiles amid the seriousness, "Having both is too much to ask, right?"

"I believe what our esteemed captain is asking is, how far are you willing to go for her? Because, from what I gather, she is probably in the grasp of the Thorns," Psilos points out.

Synite's hesitation, fueled by Thesia's seeds of doubt, speaks volumes to those paying attention. "We can't leave her out to dry," which sounds a lot different from what he was saying before. "I made a commitment and I plan on keeping it."

"This boils down to us finding a way to Atlan and destroying the Enslaver along with the Sword," Amethyst blurts. "Let's stop dancing to their music."

This is exactly what Psilos was afraid of, "And if It is only an insignificant piece of the puzzle? If It has less to do with the outcome than we can evaluate with our current perspective, we are getting into something--"

"The only way to know is to find a way back there and do it," Synite literally goes and stands behind Amethyst. "The only way to find out how deep the water actually is, you know, is to jump in and touch the bottom." Amethyst looks up at the young warrior, the young leader of their movement. "What do we have to do?"

"Do Desha or Proximity have any opinion on the matter?" Amethyst looks back for them to come in.

"They said that they are along for whatever we decide as long as Sarah is brought to safety," Synite remembers how disconsolate he was after they told him their plans. "Going back seems like the only way."

"The destruction and disorganization of this threat must be our major objective. Killing the Enslaver Itself will not accomplish that task. It should be an amazing start but that, in itself, is not something we can assume will go executed as we plan it," Psilosking orates. "Now is the time that we must activate the assistance that we have been planting inside the Sword and force the revolution upon Atlan."

"Fabric," Kraa-Nuve takes the responsibility to hail his old friend.

"Do you think that he'll be able to find us a way in?" Synite hopes out loud.

"He should at least know more than us," Amethyst is certain. "He'll know the state of play down there and at least be able to give us some sort of suggestion."

"Fabric usually knows more than his colleagues think," Tobias's projection adds. "It was always his job to be able to do things that no one else could. That is why we brought him in."

"Once we solve the puzzle of getting onto Earth 11 without being obliterated, things will move forward," Amethyst puts on the table. "Then, once we get there, our objectives are in front of us: destroy both the Enslaver and the Sword and release the slaves."

"And figure out where Sarah is, of course," Synite adds, putting aside his second-guessing. "That whole system is probably crawling with Sword security. If any one of us even looks in Its direction for too long, they'll know."

"Do," Kraa-Nuve assumes. "Took Pingar long dist."

"I have studied the variable patterns and tendencies our predators have both shown and attempted, with the help of Tobias, to plot several courses that travel along blind spots," the ship reports. "I have come to the complex conclusion that no path is possible without getting caught in open space which, to put it lightly, would not be favorable for survival. In other words," the Caracalla stops.

"It does not exist," Tobias finishes.

"Could we find another ship or camouflage this one?" Synite suggests. "We could be under the guise of some other crew."

"Unfortunately, there is little room for idealism, my friend," Psilos interjects. "The sole justification of this ship still remaining intact is that Amethyst is in its population. From what I gathered from the assault that destroyed the Pingar, the Caracalla could have easily been the main target. The Sword has shown Its destructive capabilities both short and long range."

"And I doubt we could find a ship," Amethyst reminds him, "much less secretly finance one that would be capable enough to make that move in such a short period of time."

"Bloodbath," Kraa-Nuve grumbles.

"Ship," Psilos requests, "plot the entrance point that would sanction the most direct distance to Earth 11."

"Previously calculated," the star map comes up over the table, "it is from this spot outside of the system to directly over its Sur pole. However, getting to that spot is currently unmanageable without much conflict."

"I can assist enough to get you to this point," Psilos offers. "Once you get there, it may be the best bet to jump into a short PSL to the locus near the pole then fight the way on-planet. I will enact my noblest efforts to consolidate forces with you in battle personally at that point."

"I think that may be the only way," Amethyst believes. "A very, very difficult path considering we would still have an entire war to fight once we get on-planet, but a way nonetheless."

"Risk death," Kraa-Nuve seems less enthusiastic about going into battle as he used to be.

"Amethyst and I are able to operate in the vacuum of inner space and will assist in defending the ship until it lands," Psilos continues with the plans. "I am much more imperfect than she, but can do satisfactory enough."

"Are you able to hold it together that long with that much intensity?" Synite asks Amethyst. "I don't doubt you or your power at all, you know that. But, your well-being is still important considering what will have to happen."

"This is very true," Amethyst knows well of her emotional

instability after using those powers she was not born with, she puts a hand over her bracelet. "Thank you for considering."

Psilos does take her temperament into account: "Then, once we do get down, for her to keep pace with that echelon of intensity in battle would be entirely too much to--"

"We have been hailed by an unknown, untraceable caller," the ship closes the star map and brings the call projection up. "Do you wish to answer?" Caught off guard, everyone looks around at each other, not sure what to think of the timing of this. "My call screening protocols are being overridden. It is coming through."

Before anyone can respond to whether they want to answer the call or not, a flawless projection of Spoilsport struts over to the table. "The children of the Sword! Long time no see! How's the whole cat-and-mouse thing going for you guys up there?" He looks over at Synite, "You, you, you! Man, I miss your face. Quite the dramatic exit, huh guy?"

Synite steps up to his face, "What do you want?"

"Hey, don't get your knickers in a ball, kid," Spoilsport waves at Amethyst and smiles. "I'm calling to work with you."

"What makes you think we need your help?" Synite squints aggressively.

"Man, I bet if I was actually in your face, I'd be disgusted by your breath," Spoilsport cracks another smile. "But, probably the fact that she's here and you're not gave it away, considering how protective you are of her now." Amethyst looks for his reaction and the only thing Synite can hear is Thesia's I-told-you-so snicker from in his mind.

"And you are?" Psilos requests.

"Oh, excuse my rudeness," Spoilsport walks through Synite and to the middle of the table, "I was the Enslaver's gun for hire. They call me Spoilsport. I'm down here chilling on Earth 11, waiting on you guys to show up and shake things up a little so I don't have to."

"That confirms our suspicions about those beings working with the Enslaver," Amethyst points out.

"Oh yeah girlfriend! You have no idea about the web that has been weaved…woven…weavened outside of this little establishment," Spoilsport wipes his hair out of his face. "Think about how bad it could be," Spoilsport puts his hands in front of him, creating a picture frame, "which, considering who's in the room, I'm sure you already have. Then double it, warm it up for about two eins," he turns back to the crew of the Caracalla, "and maybe then you'll almost begin understanding the crap you're knee-deep in right now."

"You have to assume," Tobias says, "that everyone you oppose from here on out has some connection with the new iteration of the Thorns." Kraa-Nuve nods in agreement.

"Who's that guy?" Spoilsport doesn't recognize him as he points disrespectfully in Tobias's face then waves him off. "No matter, he's kind of right. They even tried to enlist me but, well, I don't like organization. They have rules and, me?" he shrugs. "Not so much. Rules and I don't get along too well or often. At least not other people's rules. Yeah, no."

"What's your plan?" Synite retrieves his attention.

"Well," he points at Amethyst, then Psilos and finally Synite, adding a finger each time he points at a new being, "to bring you three here; maybe one more, too. Pack light."

Synite cannot help but be skeptical. "And how do you figure you can do that? How can you, by yourself, figure out a better plan than we have already?"

"Simple, yet complicated," Spoilsport rolls his eyes. "I'm sure your plans include finding the safest way up to a certain point and then bringing out the big guns until you're down here to scrap your way through even more trouble until the Enslaver or everybody on your ship is dead." He thumbs back at Synite with a nearly disgusted look on his face, "Is he always like this? This conversation has been exhausting and I'm several lightcycles away!" No one finds him amusing, which is usually the case in these situations. "Anyway, I have my means. You have to follow every step I give you for it to work. Actually, there aren't that many steps, now that I think about it, but it'll be a success. Trust me on that."

"How?" Kraa-Nuve queries. "How trust?"

Spoilsport grins and looks over at the captain, "How do you know you can trust them?" he refers to the gumbo of a crew. Though he does not know what they have been through together, Spoilsport does make a good point for Kraa-Nuve: "Weren't you betrayed by an entire group of beings that he had no reason to question your authority before? This ain't so different." Though it feels a lot different than his original dealings with the Thorns, Kraa-Nuve understands the point. "I hate the Enslaver as much," Spoilsport continues, "if not more, than everyone on your ship. I was also a slave at one point. And, hell, you don't have to trust me, honestly; but know that the catalogue of dastardly things It has done has left a terrible, ugly, grimy taste in my mouth. And, taking Sarah was the final straw," Vincent tells them, he has their full attention now that he used her name that way.

Synite slams a hand down, "Who are you? What do you want wi--" Thesia stops him from completing the outburst and tells him to search his feelings for what he is actually witnessing. "Vincent?"

"Oh," Spoilsport laughs, holding his gut. "You got me!"

For confirmation, Synite asks: "Sarah…she's with you?"

"She was," which sets Thesia into a joyful spur. "I left her in good hands so I could come off the grid and make this call."

Psilos can clearly see Synite losing his composure, his fists clenching and his eyes darting to different parts of the room. The others in the room can see it as well as feel the temperature change that Synite's warming body causes. Amethyst stands up next to him, "Calm yourself. What's wrong?"

Synite's teeth are clenched so tight that he cannot respond as Thesia snakes through the fury inside him. Psilos moves to stand between him and Spoilsport now, certain that Amethyst can handle any outburst. "Let us hear about this plan of yours."

"It's simple," Spoilsport tries to look around at Synite and Amethyst but Psilos is too wide. "If you go where I tell you to go and do what I tell you to do, then you'll be here in no time."

"Captain," the ship says directly to Kraa-Nuve's earpiece, "Tobias sent a beacon from the ship when I allowed him access to assist me in finding a way to Earth 11. Someone responded to that beacon." Kraa-Nuve gets up and goes into the cockpit without saying a word.

"I guess he's mad that I didn't point at him, too," Spoilsport notes as Kraa-Nuve walks off.

"The more he talks, the madder I get," Synite whispers to Amethyst.

"I know," she puts her hands on his chest and he feels her strength. "There's nothing you can do from here."

Synite quickly understands, regains his temper and walks up to Psilos's side. "We will be ready."

"That's all I needed to hear!" Spoilsport goes over and pats Synite on the head. "You might be worth all those Marks you lost after all!"

Spoilsport closes the connection from inside the cache of the Weapons Rack and heads out. "Thanks for your time," he tells Fabric. "I'll be back when everything is ready."

"Here," Fabric tosses him a box. "For your troubles."

"For me? You shouldn't have!" Spoilsport opens the box and it's a custom forged knife. "Sweet! I'll try not to use this on your boy when I see him," he jokes. He heads to his office in the Sword before he gets to his domicile to deconstruct the box and the knife and look for recording or location devices. He scans thoroughly for any sort of signal that Fabric would be able to trace him with but does not find anything suspicious. What he does find at the bottom of the box, though, does intrigue him.

Back on the Caracalla, the three of them have discussed accepting Spoilsport's offer, agreeing that this plan is as dangerous as theirs, factoring in the uncertainty. Amethyst reminded them of his status with the Enslaver and his level of power in comparison to hers. "He may be able to back up his words."

"It is not that we should have misgivings about his prowess,"

Psilos comments. "It is his intent that I am concerned with."

"Same here," Synite is not sure what will come of this. "Could he actually be as angry at the Enslaver as we are? Why?"

"I doubt there is any part of that question that he wants to answer for us. Spoilsport is not one to volunteer much in the form of intel," Amethyst has never heard of him doing any talking that was not in his own interest. "Even if our objectives are temporarily aligned, he may try to get rid of us as soon as the Enslaver is out of his way."

"That's what he's using you for," Synite points out.

"Have you ever had an occupation previous to coming to the Sword?" Amethyst asks him.

"I did, back home," Synite only worked for a few weeks but he did have a job.

"Why you took the job and why you were accepted for the job may have been completely different," which is usually the case as most employees are searching for more money to pay whatever bills they have as opposed to the company that is looking for more customers and more market share. "This is a similar situation: I want this to be over with and he wants me to complete that task; for whatever reason, he can't or won't do it himself."

"We have to remain on alert," Psilos recommends. "I believe we can utilize his services as he wishes to utilize ours."

"He said four, right?" Synite recalls. "Should I wait until Driven heals to ask him?"

"I can ensure you that he is well enough to weigh that decision," Psilos believes and Amethyst agrees.

Synite heads back to the dormitories into Driven's room and he is sitting up on his own now. "You look as though you're about ready to chase more wolfrats," he grins.

Driven laughs along, boxing the Air to get the stiffness out of his limbs. "I'm getting there!" he sounds excited for every bit of exertion he is able to exhibit.

"How much longer do you think it'll be before you're back at one hundred percent?" Synite stands beside him.

"At this rate, probably a day or two," Driven senses a few more questions should follow. "What happened?"

"We're going to Earth 11 to end all of this conflict," Amethyst comes in the room after him, "and we wish to enlist your assistance in the first wave attack."

"There is only space for four," Psilos's projection pops up in the room. "I shall join you three at the jump point."

"Wait," Driven waves his hands quickly, "wait, wait. What?"

Synite turns to him, "One of the more powerful and influential beings in Atlan wishes to align with us. He supposedly has a way for us to get on-planet without any trouble."

"And you trust him?" Driven is confused. "Why doesn't he do it himself if he's got the kind of power that can accomplish all this?"

"He needs us," Amethyst is certain. "The revolutionaries we have been preparing on that planet will not move forward without their Vanguard."

"We put things in place that may actually be able to accomplish the decimation of the whole system that has been causing all of this turmoil," Synite tells. "Your vision and enthusiasm on the front line would definitely stack the odds even more in our favor."

"Do you even know what's going to be on the front lines out there?" Driven's self-preservation is trumping his urge to help, especially in his current condition.

"We have a fair idea," Amethyst knows that the Enslaver has to send his strongest forces and every automaton since she is involved. "In full disclosure, we are not sure of the extent of the Its power or Its personal guard but we are certain they will be what we have to deal with."

Driven processes, "So, you want me to help you against this unknown, possibly unlimited power force. And, you want me to trust this opportunist wildcard above all else to put us in the best situation to war with this unknown force? Does anyone else see anything else wrong with this picture?" He crosses his arms, "Even the fairest estimation shows the odds of success plus me living through it are nearly insurmountable. You want to hear the number? Doesn't matter, I'll tell you anyway: one and over five hundred thousand. And that's only for the plans to succeed, I'm not even talking about winning the fights against the beings you have no intel on," Driven shakes his head at them.

"What are the odds, from me being put into slavery and each of us being brought under the Enslaver," Synite pleas, "that we would make it this far?" Driven looks up and starts to calculate, "I don't want the actual number, man. I want you to understand that there's something more than just numbers going on here. As long as we have each other, I could care less what's against us."

That catches Driven's attention, "Art versus numbers, huh?"

"All we wish," Amethyst brings, "is that you consider committing yourself to this because we need as many allies as possible."

"And, after speaking with my other selves," Psilos comes forward to explain, "those odds you speak of are more in our favor than your number suggests. And, if you were to join us, it seems we have a ten percent chance of completing the task with absolutely no casualties, including you."

"Other selves?" Driven is confused.

"Yeah, he can basically see five hundred different versions of the future or something," Synite inaccurately reports, "by talking to himself but from different planes of existence."

"Seriously? Intense!" Driven squints at Psilos, "So, what am I going to say next?"

Synite whacks him on the arm, "This is important man!"

"Did you know he was going to hit me?" Driven hops out of the bed, grunting a little from the stiffness, and faces Psilos who gives him a quick side-eye. "I could've guessed he would but--"

"I can see different versions of the future but small episodes are unique. In my conversations with my other planar selves, these menial incidents do not come up unless they have some forbearance on larger affairs. Mostly, they do not merit having conversations with my other selves," Psilos tells Driven.

"If it makes you feel any better, I saw it coming," Amethyst snickers. "You deserved it, too."

"You have time to contemplate on it," Psilos moves to exit the room. "We are not certain when Spoilsport will invite us or the distance we are required to travel to where he needs us to be. You should search within yourself in the meantime."

"No pressure, right?" Driven responds, leaning on his hands against the side of the bed. Psilos's projection disappears as Amethyst walks through it and out of the room. Synite goes and sits on the floor against the wall, reminding him of how he would sit against the wall between his and Psilos's cells. "Any other persuasive tactics you guys want to throw at me?"

"I didn't think they were going to do that," Synite confesses. "I thought I was going to have to do all the convincing on my own, honestly."

"All that took me off guard," Driven hops back in the bed. "I mean, I'm completely grateful for the whole saving my life thing but I'm not sure I'm ready to risk my life on purpose," he shakes his head, "not to this degree."

"It sucked getting ambushed," Synite looks down, "and losing friends in that manner; I understand how tough it can be. This is big though," he looks up at Driven who looks to be in deep thought. "Being on this ship with everyone for this long has made me appreciate the simplicity of a life. I've gotten to the point where I know what I want with the rest of mine." He drapes his arms across his raised knees, "I guess that's the best question to ask yourself, right?"

"I love freedom," Driven remembers them shooting in that field on Yar JK, "and now, because of my dad, it'll be tough to get that back. I'm involved with all of this now by relation, which puts drastic limitations on my freedom."

Synite huffs, "I disagree. You can do whatever you want. You're in full control of your life. If you want to be free and go off the grid, you can."

"But that's the thing," Driven turns to face Synite, "I appreciate you guys! You're family to me now, like you said. I'd rather be free to be around you without having to fight for my life around every corner."

"Freedom comes with sacrifice," the most valuable lesson that Synite has approached face-to-face. "I had no choice but to fight in that arena. It was terrible but it taught me the value of true freedom. Sure, I didn't have to make my own decisions but even when I wanted to, I couldn't. And then it became all about the money and I hated that as much as fighting to simply stay alive.

"Now, everything is about the people I deal with and how I approach these experiences along the way. The feeling I had those first few days off of Earth 11, the feelings I had on Yar JK," Synite thinks about the same moments Driven was reminiscing on, "every life and death experience I've had since being thrown in this situation has been worth it because of these relationships and moments that I appreciate more than anything else.

"Many people say that if you told them a cycle ago that they would be where they are now, they wouldn't believe it. I'm probably the greatest example of that. It was weird at first, actually being free and," Synite gets to his feet, "it took a lot of getting used to. I appreciated it much more versus back when I was in school and just free by global standards, though still barred by social standards and responsibilities.

"True freedom comes from the heart," Synite points at his, "doing what you want to do with whom you want to do it whenever you want to and loving life every day. That's wealth. I hope you're willing to go down the rest of this road with me. I want us to be a beacon of freedom to others and show the darkest of hearts what true freedom is, being responsible for the things you love and the people who love you." Synite thinks of Santhia, "Even when you can only do so much and make mistakes, you're still responsible and still appreciate the good and bad. That's not the opposite of freedom."

"I appreciate your selflessness and I have my choice to make," Driven exhales heavily. "Right now, though, I think I'm going to have to separate myself from all this for a while. I know you guys could use my help but," he shakes his head, "all of this fighting isn't the life I want."

"I don't think it's the life any of us wants," Synite says solemnly.

"But you feel this sense of responsibility for the events on that planet that I don't and can't, Synite. That's who you are; that's a part of you," Synite can hear Driven's decision being made. "This is who I am." They have a moment of reflective silence, "It'd probably be best if I leave before y'all make your move. I'll go talk to Kraa."

We might not say the right things,
But we communicate something
Even if it's not what we mean.
We might not do the right things,
But we do them together and
Events turn into relationships.
We might not see the right things,
But we see them in each other,
Growing to love the beauty in flaw.
We might not feel the right things,
But we use our hearts ferociously
No matter how much it hurts.
The real question is, in these verses,
In this life, exactly what is right?
And what makes our experience
More or less right than theirs?
Perspective.

 # CHAPTER XVI

To be chemically, physically or mentally addicted to anything, or any combination of the three, will inevitably cause problems in a being's life. To be addicted to something productive (work, exercise, building things) may cause social problems but not necessarily be a negative in the grand scheme of things. However, to be addicted to something unproductive or even downright destructive can immediately rule a being out of having a positive future.

Beings addicted to positive or productive things may merely prefer their addictions over useless posturing or socializing for the sake of it. Both of those may be the addictions therein, but this idea speaks more to those addicted to producing things: monetary success through their adeptness in any field of work, social success through their mental or physical dexterity, power through their proficiency in less tangible aspects of life such as negotiating or creating strong business relationships.

Of course there are exceptions to every rule, beings that cross both planes and are addicted to their success but use the benefits of that success for more destructive things. Often, these being are celebrated for their exploits of excess and lifted to a public status that rivals the gods of the past. This case is rare and something that most adolescent minds reach for during their trudging through the pits of idealism. The adolescents admire or worship the celebrities who they know merely for their public acts of extravagance or buffoonery. This cultural cycle is tied by the media's portrayal of these characters and the proliferation of their addicting lifestyles.

Then, there are those who are addicted to something destructive, something cancerous, and they end up being cancerous themselves by their ties to their addiction. They are often seen as needing help to get out of their dungeon and to be washed of their sickness. The only problem is that the resulting sickness is only a symptom of their mental addiction to which there is no medical cure except induced sleep or the extreme of euthanasia. Some of these beings cross planes with the previously mentioned, depending on their occupational or accidental successes, still praised for living.

The last group that is addicted to simply unproductive things usually points at the others for their active addictions but do not realize their own faults in life. They prefer mindless droning, such as watching active beings live or debating on the lives of others, escapes from the troublesome idea of living actively themselves. Some prefer partaking in gently unproductive activities, such as eating, drinking or sex that may turn into destructive or restrictive addictions and diseases. Some prefer sleeping in excess, though they participate in no activity that merits the necessity of resting longer than their body or mind needs.

There comes a time in every beings life where they cross over the bridge from childhood to their next stage in growth. There is a period when most children are enjoying the true freedom of life so much that they dread even the lightest mentioning of sleep, no matter how necessary it is. They scratch and cry until their bodies tell them enough is enough and they are forced into slumber. This is because what they know of life is a continuous flow of pure elation.

One or a team of beings is at the child's beckoning at every moment. Even the slightest hint of a child being uncomfortable can attract a host of coddling and attention which reverberates throughout a developing child's life in later interaction. However, when life becomes filled with tasks that a child is not genetically or practically prepared to complete, that wave of elation passes over rocks of doubt and frustration. The child gets the help they need to lessen the blows and continue to love life, learns to accept and adapt to the continual difficulty of it or completely rejects the idea that life has to be difficult. Then, a choice is made internally: they will either look for other ways to change and enjoy life again or reject reality as a whole and prefer the magic of fantasy over the troubles of the world. For those who retreat to their dreams and prefer to be asleep rather than out participating in the world, there is less true enjoyment in something so alienating as sleep (by participating in socially inactive activities or inducing a state of mind that allows one to ignore reality i.e. mind altering substances, a being can be "asleep" to the universe around them).

Beings who enjoy watching others participate in active lives seek no enjoyment in life itself. Instead of becoming the topic of conversation, they only find enjoyment in keeping up with the conversation. When done in excess, it can be seen as 'living the simple life' or 'being easily pleased' which are both fallacy because they are neither truly living nor being anything. They watch life from afar, afraid to participate and are gluttons to their own nihilism towards experience. If told they would have to repeat this life an infinite number of times in the exact same way they are living, they would be grief-stricken and fall into an even further hole of pessimism instead of taking that as the opportunity to strike life.

It is possible, nearly natural, for beings to partake in many of these different facets of life without having to hold them as addictions. There is a way to participate in healthy levels of watchfulness, work, play and sleep. Most of these, even some of the destructive activities, are necessary to try at least in order to feel fulfilled with life.

The moral of this banter is that moderation, or at minimum purposeful structuring, is one of the many keys to one of the many doors to success. One should assume full responsibility over life and not fall victim to its flow. One should go against the grain once in a while, even if that means a small measure of solitude or loneliness to accomplish something greater than a numb participation of social events.

Not being entrenched or enslaved in something as to neglect everything else, defining an addiction, could lead to a more fulfilling lifestyle. Not being so chained to some activity that the cessation from it is traumatic could bring about more opportunity for enjoyment and less stress. Instead of being glued to giving attention to others, one should do something attention-worthy to feel more similar to a participant of the world instead of a spectator of its events.

Spoilsport finds Castra Nim, Coldsmoke and the rest of the team in their mess hall after coming back from burying Liffu in his home state. Their somberness and sobriety quickly annoys him but he sticks to the script. "C one and C two, I need to talk to the both of you in private."

Of course Coldsmoke goes without question but Castra Nim stops, "What is this about?"

"Are you questioning me?" Spoilsport's level of annoyance rises a bit more when those he considers underlings do not abide. "I'm in a mood today and I'm not to be messed with."

Castra Nim backs down a little, "I'm asking you if it's a team matter and, if it is, the whole team should be involved. If you're about to tell me somebody is getting traded again, I think everyone should know."

"I can tell that's not th'subject of his visit," Coldsmoke assumes by the way Spoilsport approached them. "If it was, he would've said it." He and Spoilsport leave the hall and Castra reluctantly follows.

"Thank you for joining us, your highness," Spoilsport's derision is golden. He throws the box he got from Fabric to Castra who catches it and looks back up at Spoilsport. "Open it already!"

"For me? You shouldn't have!" Castra grins at the olive branch he holds but remembers who threw it to him. He puts it up to his ear and listens.

"Bombs don't tick anymore, you idiot," another point to Spoilsport's level of annoyance. "If you didn't make me so many Marks, I swear I'd have killed you on the way here!"

Castra opens the box, "It's empty."

"Like your head!" Spoilsport yells. "Look at the bottom of the damn box!" Castra turns the box upside down, "My word, you are dumber than you look."

The inside bottom of the box falls out onto the ground, a small card stuck to it. Castra picks it up, giving sweet relief to Spoilsport's temper, and reads it, "'Tell Castra: the time is now.'" He flips the card to find some sort of identifying marking but there is none. "Where did you get this?"

"Things have been happening," Spoilsport starts his report. "There's a lot more to catch you up on but, long story short, Synite and Amethyst are coming back to Atlan and they need you to play your part." Castra is speechless, as his face shows, and Coldsmoke has no idea what is going on but knows better than to interrupt. "Apparently, part of the reason you accepted being sent here so easily, unbeknownst to me, was to recruit the other best fighter in the world. How that slipped by me is a wonder, but we can talk about that some other time."

"No!" Castra tells him. "I had no idea! I--"

"Whatever," Spoilsport tells him. "You're not as dumb as you put off to be, kid. You want him to help you free the slaves."

"So, you've been helping me t'be a better fighter so I could join your little revolution?" Coldsmoke does not appreciate being toyed with.

"It just so happens that I was charged with the task," Castra Nim tries to convince them. "I was sent here for cash to win for K'oma. If I was sent anywhere else, I'd have been doing the same thing with their strongest warriors." He looks at Coldsmoke, "We weren't targeting you specifically."

"Enough," Spoilsport is tired of the babble. "Your apologies don't matter because he's going to help you in the same way I'm helping Synite and Amethyst."

"Wait," their faces show astonishment. "What do you mean you're helping?"

"I'm working on getting them here. Fabric gave me what was in that box after I told him about bringing them back," Spoilsport thought about giving the knife to Castra but he actually does like it so he is going to keep it for himself. Coldsmoke does not agree with what is going on but he dare not go against Spoilsport if he is in charge. "Don't bother asking me why this, why that. I'm over this conversation. Start training and I'll give you the specs on your enemies as soon as I finish my digging."

"What is my stake in all of this?" Coldsmoke does not hesitate to ask. "I see no benefit in going to war t'free th'slaves of another arena. We have enough problems here!"

"It's bigger than that," Spoilsport appreciates Coldsmoke pushing back a little bit. "Atlan is the most powerful nation on Earth 11. For you to be one of the few who changed that nation is my intent."

"So, you're trying to set up your own dominance over Atlan after this is over," Castra surmises. "It would be easy for you to take command once the Enslaver is gone because I doubt anybody else would want to after the recovery."

Spoilsport shrugs, "It hadn't crossed my mind but thanks for the idea, bud!" A single bead of sweat rolls down Castra's forehead. "If I didn't hate people so much, maybe…you know what I might make the perfect leader of the new world!"

Coldsmoke laughs along with Spoilsport, "I guess we won't be winning any championships this season, huh Castra?"

"That depends on the timing of everything," he looks over at Spoilsport. "However long it takes him to do his work."

"It definitely won't take weeks. That Hyo kid is lucky," Spoilsport thinks out loud. "He might win it all with you guys and the Atlan team out of the mix."

"That would be crazy," Castra could not imagine him defending his crown next season.

"Even crazier is the fact that, after you all beat Atlan to win the championship, the management in Atlan was going to make a trade for you to come back for three Profit Circle members, if any of them survived," Spoilsport reports. "Then, since their PC would have been down two members and the team probably would have only been you, there would have been two tournaments to fill the spots. They had been hearing rumblings about some sort of revolution going on with all of the slave-warriors and decided to force them to kill each other the best way they know how: by earning profits at the same time!"

"So I was sent here to douse the revolution?" Castra rubs his chin.

"It makes sense," Coldsmoke points out. "Why send your captain elsewhere and only get Marks in return if you want to win?"

Spoilsport nods, "Either you were going to die here, kill your comrades, or die later because your team would have been very subpar in comparison to Coldsmoke and any combination." Coldsmoke can feel the esteem. "Either way, the target was the revolution and they missed it."

"Bureaucrats certainly move too slowly to actually make any impact, right?" Castra says to himself.

Spoilsport is at his exit, "Basically; because, if it were up to the Enslaver, you'd all just be executed. But, It has learned that those types of events are bad for profits and bad for controlling the minds of the public. They need sport! They need distraction!"

"So," Synite, Gale and Thesia all feel a little exhausted for more reason than one, "we sit and wait on his instructions then?"

"Basic," Kraa-Nuve continues his business as usual monitoring and schematics scanning. "Power game."

Synite hates that they, some of the most powerful beings in the octadecaverse, are sitting and waiting for orders from a freelancer. "For what though? He's doing it for his own amusement."

"There is a planet I want us to meet on," Psilos's projection customarily stands between the captain and co-pilot stations.

Synite gets excited, "That sounds like a great idea!"

"I am certain you are thirsty for a nurturing atmosphere, my comrade," even from another universe, Psilos can read Synite very well. "I am sending the ship coordinates now. It is a planet that Prophyrian nobles go to for sanctuary. As you are my guest, you will be afforded the same privileges and rights."

"I have received your coordinates," the Caracalla informs. "Warming the PSL drive."

"This'll pass the time!" Synite is much more satisfied with the in-between now.

"I am determined to see you soon, in the flesh," Psilosking closes the connection from his hall and heads down to catch his shuttle. "Are preparations for my launch taken care of as I requested?"

"Yes," the half-Giarc, half-Prophyrian driver tells him. "Everything is prepared. Your flight leaves as soon as it is safe to do so."

"I offer my gratitude for your excellence, Juikos" Psilosking pats him on the back as they start to move. "If there is anything I could do for you, do not hesitate to mention it to me."

"Things have been going along as well as I could have imagined," Juikos says. "Your rule has made this world a much better place. That is all the recompense I or anyone can take."

"That is wonderful to hear," Psilosking is very genuine with every being he comes in contact with around the globe. He is not at all a politician but a loving director and protector of his peoples. "How is your family?"

"They are well," the driver turns them through to the highway, overlooking an area of the city that had been ravaged by the war. "It took me a while to get my wife Yutrio's attention, as she is pure Prophyrian and I am not, but we got married once the war ended."

"Wonderful!" Psilosking continues building this relationship. He looks out into the rebuilding efforts that he has been pushing for in the city. "Have you borne any children yet?"

"We have twins," Juikos smiles proudly, laughing at the entirety of their lives together. "A male and female. Juiyos and Yutyos. Their personalities are starting to reflect us and shine in their own right."

"Those are beautiful names, Juikos," Psilosking enjoys hearing of children though he doubts he should have any of his own.

"Juiyos is having some difficulties fitting in at school, being one quarter Giarc and all," they get off the bridge and see Giarcs and Prophyrians resting together after a long day's work. "He says there is only one other besides him and his sister who has mixed blood."

Psilosking sighs, "These are things that I expected but they are difficult for me. I would say to seek guidance from my court, especially from those who are of mixed DNA."

"Thank you," the driver, though pragmatic, has hope that he and his family will live a relatively normal next three or four centuries despite the problems that are going to arise. "I plan to certainly take advantage of that invitation."

"I hope you do. I shall prompt them of your interest and you should receive a call with an appropriate appointment time," Psilosking begins to write his order. "It is of my main concern to repair that which this planet has been scarred from. Not only the reconstruction on the streets and in the buildings but repairing the bridge between the two cultures. You, my friend, are a stone in that bridge. It is my swelling hope that you remain steadfast throughout this transition; that your faith in me keeps you strong whether I return the same or changed."

This touches Juikos to the point of silence, one of the more revered responses a king could expect, even greater than loud praise. The thoughtful silence that lets them know their word has gone deeper than they may have intended. This was not the goal of this routine ride for a not-so-routine trip but it is good. It is something that only Psilosking could accomplish after being so inspired.

Yet, he has a feeling that there has to be more than one large roadblock in this future he envisions, as is usually the case. This is one of the times he prefers not to ask his other selves for guidance or for the path to choose, as there is only one path for him and the rest of the Vanguard to take now.

Psilosking leaves Juikos as he is escorted from the taxi to the VIB check-in for his shuttle. He then takes a short cart ride from the check-in station to the security checkpoint. Considering how similar Prophyrians look, even to each other, there are several protocols that everyone must go through every time they are to join a royal expedition. Psilosking passes them all directly behind his last steward of the shuttle.

"All hail!" a security officer has the rest of security, the only beings on the ship outside of the captains and Psilosking, stand and acknowledge him as he enters. As one of the more humble kings, he immediately tells them to take their seats and heads into the captain's chamber.

"Are the coordinates plotted?" the captains nod to their king as he receives their confidence and they, his. He moves back into the main cabin and takes his spot, strapping in to prepare for takeoff. The countdown begins; they lift into Prophyria's atmosphere at zero and catapult out of it. It is not long before the ship kicks into PSL and out towards their destination.

Grace and Mercy are quite possibly the most technologically advanced handguns in the octadecaverse, aided by the fact that they are the personal weapons of the most technologically advanced body in the same field of play. They have a .135 MAGNUM barrel that is 255mm long and use gas-operated mechanisms. Each is made of lightweight ceramics, carbon fiber, rubber, titanium and magnesium, making them a total weight of 1504 g each. They are also built melee combat without damaging systems or outer structure, able to withstand contact up to 1 kilo Newton of pure force. Of course, contact force is depending on surface qualities, penetration, velocity, energy and density of the object that the gun comes in contact with at the striking point.

Many beings speak of their guns figuratively knowing certain things like where the bullet will go and sometimes the trigger pulling itself. There is nothing figurative about these rudimentary looking pistols: they actually communicate with Driven's brain, eyes and nervous system constantly. Synite and Gale speak to each other through spiritual means and sometimes these conversations can be taken in other directions. Driven and his guns never mistake their relationship for anything outside of hitting whatever target he chooses.

Whenever he touches them, several systems automatically initiate. First, each gun has internal activation systems that only work when he puts his hands on them. The ammo lock turns off, the sonar detection and geo-location turn on, and the interaction software begins sending short and long wave signals to Driven's sensory implants. The sonar for each pistol emits tightly-focused, non-lethal waves that give him the statistics needed (wind speed, wind direction, muzzle velocity change, and other environmental factors) to enhance his shooting capabilities.

Then, there is a laser that comes from the barrel that only he can see. It shows him exactly where his shot will go if he shoots straight, throws a curved bullet in any direction, and where each ricochet, after up to four deflections per shot, will take the bullet. His eyes have advanced telescopic, mapping and x-ray vision that show him plots of that laser through up to ten surfaces that can be up to ten meters thick collectively. His Borganics have also aided him with magnifying, night vision, thermal sight, and polarized vision all activated simply by thought or need.

When he has his back against a corner he wants to shoot around, Driven does not have to turn and put himself in harm's way. He can use ricochet cover fire off opposite walls, floors or moving objects for himself or any other being. These shots are blind and require a measure of luck to hit any sort of target but that is not the true purpose of this ability. Being able to provide accurate cover fire at semi-automatic speed can save lives as much as sniping enemies from a thousand yards. He could also call a shot if he uses his both his internal echo-location as well as the guns' sonar but the accuracy is still decreased to 56.11%.

As far as curving bullets in any direction, the guns work directly with his central nervous system to move his arms and trigger finger at the perfect time to commit to the perfect shot. This allows him to fire around corners, ricochet at points he would not be able to reach with straight shots, and shoot around objects and beings he wishes to avoid. Grace and Mercy allow him to curve bullets around objects up to thirty meters wide but the accuracy decreases to 72.7%.

His precision and accuracy when using his systems go up to 99.7% on any given shot in any given environment (except a vacuum where it goes down to 94.1% and under water where it goes down to 91.2%). Both the laser sight and nervous system connection can be toggled on and off, giving him the option to go completely analog and shoot the same as a normal person. Even then, he is still an amazing shot and has won competitions without any system assistance. To aid his balance, he has sound filtration and suppression, enhanced and directed hearing, and his own internal echo location.

Another system that can be toggled is the auto-shot: each gun can independently fire without Driven having to pull the trigger. The laser systems interact with his brain and sight to lock on to a target then calculate trajectories, ricochet patterns and curved-shot patterns, giving him plenty of directions to choose the perfect shot. Whichever gun has the best angle fires without him having to pull the trigger when auto-shot is on. Most of the time, he keeps it turned off so his body does not go into full blown autopilot, killing everything he locks on to. However, he switches it on in situations where timing is crucial and he does not want the fraction of a sec it takes to pull the trigger to decrease the accuracy of him hitting perfectly or ricocheting off of a moving target. In the few situations that he has used auto-shot, Driven has only turned it on for whatever specific shot he needed it for and then turned it back off right after. This rides the line between the old adage, "Guns don't kill people, people kill people," very finely as he still prefers to call the shot for the weapon to fire.

Tobias developed these technologies with the theory that one perfect shot from the perfect shooter is more effective than 10,000 rounds that do nothing but damage the landscape or harm beings that are not the target. Their military had developed targeting software installed in drones that could do well but, without the element of human choice, they could not be nearly as effective. They could not physically go places that soft-tissue beings could or use judgment as there is no artificial intelligence that can tell right from wrong. Even replicated patterns and algorithms could not top the achievement of Borganics combined with Grace and Mercy.

The ammunition is a small caliber, armor-piercing, ricochet-capable bullet that is biometrically created from Driven's bodily waste. Each bullet is shaved when shot and a bit of the shavings store in the guns to cover the new ammunition when it is loaded in. To do a complete reload, which he rarely has to do since each gun holds one hundred fifty rounds, all he has to do is put the gun in one of the holsters for two eins as the rounds pour in.

He also has the option to use low-energy, invisible laser fire that can cut down trees and even, when held at the same spot for long enough, dig through armor. The energy for the lasers is biometric as well, coming from stored calorie intake. Each gun can hold up to five eins of constant laser fire at its lowest intensity and two eins at its highest. To give some perspective, the highest intensity equals about $1/1,000^{th}$ of the power of a bolt of lightning, using about 8 Watt-hecu of energy.

Those two options give Driven relatively unlimited sources of firepower. He can store up to ten clips worth of ammo depending on his food intake which he watches carefully. If he knows he needs more, he eats more to create more. And, his reload time is equal to the amount of time it takes to use up one gun's laser fire.

So, in a tough firefight, after using 300 99.7% accurate rounds, he can reload Grace while using a constant laser shot with Mercy, reload Mercy while using the laser shot with the loaded Grace, and then use another 300 99.7% accurate rounds. That's upwards of 3600 total bullets in one session before he is emptied, without producing anymore. Driven has come to terms with the fact that, if anyone survives through the whole 3600 armor-piercing rounds and ten eins of intense laser fire from each gun, his opponent deserves to win and he should not have started the fight to begin with.

At the end of the day, however, Driven is not even relatively immortal; he may live for some centuries but this is science, not magic. He has everything he needs to stay alive for a very long time but he can still be killed. Not even Tobias was sure how long it would take for his Borganics to deteriorate to the point to where they cannot keep him alive since they constantly repair his organs and fight off every infection automatically. And, considering the fact that he has nearly perfect weapon skills and dangerous hand-to-hand fighting skills, he will be able to protect himself from nearly anything. Tobias wanted his son to live long, flourish and make an impact.

 # CHAPTER XVII

"We have made it, my king," the Prophyrian pilot reports.

"I would prefer you did not refer to me that way while we are here," Psilos, as he is now on another planet and no longer on the land that considers him king, does not accept the title. "Only Psilos. Here, I am your equal and you should treat me as such." He looks back at the rest of the crew, "That goes for the rest of you as well."

"Alright, Psilos," one of the security officers speaks up. "Before we exit, I wish to warn you of something."

"Go on," Psilos gives his attention.

The security officer stands, "There have been rumblings back on Prophyria of a plot to, dare I speak, assassinate you. Only rumblings, I suspect, but rumblings can turn into true hunger after some time."

"That is surprising," another of the security officers speaks up, "especially considering how well he has done! The entirety of Prophyria has been unified! Who would not approve of such a thing?"

"I would assume those who would profit more from the continuation of war," Psilos has come in contact with many of that litter. "Or someone who does not approve of my desegregating actions."

"I have heard something similar," a third security officer stands. "It was from a pack of Giarc dogs that knew nothing but evil."

"And it is that thinking that has probably caused these sorts of rumblings," Psilos interrupts his bigotry. "I wish to never hear such things come from another mouth on my home. These separating words and their exposure to more generations make me cringe." He steps up before the lot of them, "You are not to carry such ideas on to the next generation. They must die along with those who have sought out action based on them. No being on that planet is any more or less vulnerable than the next. Is this our truth?”

"Agreed!" the troop steps in unison as they pronounce the second syllable of the word.

"This satisfies me," Psilos moves to the exit door and sheds his kingly regalia. "Now, let us find our way on this refuge." They all step off together into the landing dock. The ship had made a water landing, as is custom here, and docked at the edge of the Mainland. On this planet named Demor 6, the majority of its land is made of islands and over 70% of its surface is water.

The largest land mass, officially called Republica Demora, is known by the majority as the Mainland and houses offices of the State, wealthy residents who prefer to live inland, and very few tourist attractions. Psilos and company are taking their credentials to the office of the State to register as visitors and prepare the Dock Masters for the arrival of the Caracalla.

"Do you think that, when you return, someone may try your life?" the first officer speaks to Psilos. "That may be a very vulnerable time. Maybe we should call ahead for extra security measures."

"That is not necessary," Psilos hopes aloud.

"He probably already knows what is going to happen when he gets back," one of the guards says to another. "You know about his power, right?"

"I have heard," he says back.

"Actually, I have not been communicating with my other selves lately," Psilos admits. "I do not wish to alter my future based on the pasts of others even if they are alternate versions of me."

The group makes it up to the Mainland and into a small commercial district overlooking the water. This is the first time in a very long time that Psilos has sat peacefully with a few of his fellows, feeling close to equal instead of an aberration. They all enjoy some general conversation in the hecu it takes for them to be approached from behind by a familiar voice: "I've never seen so many Prophyrians in one spot without violence!"

Psilos turns and grabs Synite's arm, excited to see his greatest of friends in person again. "It has been a while for us as well, Synite."

"Unfortunately, especially considering Synite's shortening patience, the Caracalla did one of its irregular reboots before they jumped to PSL on our way here to meet you, Psilos," Amethyst apologizes to his company after they embrace. "We were stuck for several hecu!"

"It was a fortunate accident," the head of security addresses them. "It gave us an opportunity to converse with our ki..." he looks at Psilos, "with Psilos on a personal level unlike any other time. We could not have had this at home."

"Thank the ship for that," Synite stands next to Psilos and he puts his broad hand on Synite's shoulders reminiscent of how he did that first time in the training forum. The only difference is that, instead of training hard for the moment to prove himself, they are standing in front of the proof that their movement is valid. The proof steps up next to them and they all look out at the horizon, looking into the light of the past reflecting off of the rich waters of Demor.

Synite looks over at Amethyst and up at Psilos, feeling recharged from the atmosphere. "Into the future?"

They depart from Demor 6 and coast back into outer space away from the system. They drift into where Light is completely absorbed, where Dark is so deep that it swallows existence. Some stretches of space are so black that there is nothing to be reflected in any direction and nearly everything that is not illuminated by the light of the ship's thrusters disappears. If there were no location services, no predetermined direction to get through from this sea of night to the next, there would be no way. Some would consider it pure peace despite how violent an unprotected, universally weak being's end would be if they stepped into that vacuum without protection for a moment.

That violence is an infinitesimal drop in the proverbial bucket of the raw power of Dark. Without even the concept of mercy, it crushes everything that does not exert a somewhat equal force on it. Stars, planets, moons, bases, ships, and everything that exists with some stability are miracles. They are things that should not exist in the realm of Dark but Light has other plans.

A child that no one recognizes pops up in the communication room, startling Synite and Kraa-Nuve. The child has on no clothes but has no sexual organs either. However, to them, there is something strangely recognizable about the child's eyes. It pops over to Amethyst and hugs her tightly, knowing she can take the power of the hug. It is indeed a powerful hug, too.

It pops over to Psilos and looks up at him from only one meter above the floor, "You know who I am, don't cha?"

"Yes, I can see you," Psilos responds. "I was not aware that you two were capable of such things, however."

Psilos senses Synite's aggression and puts a hand up to stop him from stepping too strongly in the child's direction. He stands there with his hands out. "What the hell?"

"You will see momentarily, my friend," Psilos steps back and the child drops to its knees. Suddenly, where there was the child, there is now a fully clothed Proximity and similarly clothed Desha. Synite is disarmed by the sight, trying to understand a bit more about what happened. "For what length of time can the two of you sustain that form?"

It seems that Proximity is unable to talk as he looks at Desha from his hands and knees, short of breath. She sits with her legs crossed on the floor, "We ain't so good at it yet," obviously having absorbed a piece of Proximity's personality. "A couple-few eins for now."

"What do we call that?" Synite still does not completely grasp what happened or why there was a blindingly fast infant a moment ago but his two friends now.

"Right na," she points down, "if I 'member right, we feel like our name is A'rris. It's our first A'mal togetha. The mo' we do it, the older we get, the mo' we can hold it togetha."

"Time is everything," Psilos imparts a gem of knowledge. Desha explains to everybody what the A'mal is and what it means to them. Proximity finally joins the conversation and they are all amazed by its intricacies and how sensitive Proximity and Desha are about it.

After they finish that conversation, Psilos brings up the most pressing topic: "Was there a timetable on when Spoilsport was to guide our way onto Earth 11?"

"Wait," Kraa-Nuve tells him. "No more, less."

"I believe we should discuss a few things," Amethyst brings to the table. "We must be prepared for the worst: that he is still in the employment of the Enslaver and attempting to dupe us into believing he is temporarily on our side. If this is a trap, we must have a contingency."

"What can we do?" Synite opens the floor for ideas. "If he sends us into a star, what can we do? If we are to be arrested immediately, what can we do?"

"When we get there," Synite speaks to the crew, "if things are not quite as they should be, will we be able to fight our way out of it?" Everyone looks at Amethyst.

"There are twelve Sukayishiru and possibly one-to-two hundred automatons that are to be sent directly as soon as a threat is identified," she looks over at Psilos, "but most of them should be more tiresome than effective in battle. Then, there is the Profit Circle."

"They're on our side," Synite remembers establishing that relationship before his fight with Tsyuu. "What can these Suka-whatevers do?"

"I only know that they work in three cohesive units of four and that, alone, each of them could be in the top five of the Sword's Profit Circle," Amethyst had seen them in a training run about ten cycles ago. "Their power is strange though. I could not get a reading on their limits."

"I had never felt their presence either," Psilos admits. "What of their abilities?"

"I only got to observe one group," she tries to recall for a moment then gives up. "I can't remember exactly but each of them does have their own specific weapon and range of power."

"If Spoilsport helps us fight, he'd give us a big advantage. He probably knows everything about them as he knows everything about everything else," Synite says with a measured amount of angst. "I know we can't count on that but it would definitely be a bonus."

"We must not disremember our primary target," Psilos reminds them. "It would be foolish and assumptive to believe the Enslaver is going to go down without a fight."

Synite thinks how Santhia taught him to think, "Best case scenario, we send Castra and whoever he brings to the table to destroy the waves of automatons. Psilos can lead a charge against one of the teams of Suka-things, I can lead another one and Amethyst can lead the third one. We have to get through them, or at least get to a point where the three of us can separate from those scuffles, so we can get to defeat It as quickly as possible.

"Once the Enslaver is dead," Synite winks at Amethyst, "the rest of the forces should surrender pretty easily. Then, we call for Kraa-Nuve to come and get us."

"We gonna stay and rebuild, right?" Desha suggests.

"Not immediately," Psilos answers. "I have forces working full-time on several important areas of Prophyria. They are to assist in the rebuild of Atlan after things cool down. It would be best if those who are already there usher things until a full reconstruction is ready."

"At least the crew of this ship will need to stay out of the public light for a while," Amethyst adds.

"I agree. I don't know if I'll even want to stay period," Synite thinks beyond.

"After the Enslaver's regime is lifted," they have never heard Proximity speak so clearly, "what about the other arenas which allow for slaves?" Everyone looks at him in mild astonishment, "What?" he does not yet realize how much the A'mal has changed him.

"You have a point, my friend," Psilos smiles at him. "Our move is going to start a revolution that may spread elsewhere. Legislation will likely be enacted to investigate the dealings of every arena."

"That has to be an objective," Synite thinks out loud. "We have to change the way that world does things. We cannot have the youth sentenced to death without having a chance at life."

"That goes without saying," Proximity steps in. "However, we can't assume it'll happen that way. Someone has to make it happen."

"We'll have to cross that bridge once we get to it," Amethyst smiles with Desha as she marvels at her other half.

"There is an encrypted call incoming," the ship announces. "My contact protocols are being overridden."

A projection of Spoilsport comes up in the room, "Hey guys! I see the gang's all here! How's the waiting been going? Ready for war?" He looks up at Psilos, "You always look ready, man. I wish I was you."

Amethyst approaches him, "We have questions for you."

"Nah," Spoilsport waves her off, "I'm not ready to take questions yet. It'll be better after you guys are down here. I do have some good news, though! Maybe my reporting will answer all of your questions."

"Listening," Kraa-Nuve grumbles.

"Everything is going smoothly and I have coordinates for you," a map comes up from the table. "Now," Spoilsport clasps his hands together, "let's coordinate!" He looks around, "See what I did there?"

Synite turns his hand up, "Is that all?"

"All?" Spoilsport steps over to him, "Kid, you have no idea how much I want to slap you across your face and actually feel it! All? You know what?" Spoilsport steps off, "For your snide remarks, I'll just sit back and let you find out everything in the middle of the war. You don't need my help anyway."

"Wait," Synite tries to recover, "I didn't me--"

"Don't!" Spoilsport steps around. "It's too late for groveling, kid. What's done is done. I hope you fight well enough to stay alive. And I hope you stay alive long enough to get what you want out of this whole ordeal because I know," he pauses, "never mind. See ya!"

"What wi--" Amethyst tries to get her question in but he is already gone.

"The connection was lost," the ship reveals. "Do you wish for me to pilot us to these coordinates?"

"Where do they lead?" Synite looks at the map in front of him.

The map zooms in quickly to the destination and it is a moon named Pag, the third moon of the planet Tialian. It is far enough from Tialian right now that they will not be detected by the authorities there. "Evidently," the ship finishes scanning the files sent with the coordinates, "after we reach Pag, these files should open up for other protocols to be set."

"Type?" Kraa-Nuve is concerned about the well-being of his ship.

"They are encrypted as well," the ship tries to read anything from the file but, "and they are encoded so much that I cannot even see the size of the file. It seems the only way to get into the file is to reach Pag."

"Onward then," Psilos votes with no offers of opposition and they all prepare for the jump to PSL. Everyone on the ship, including the AI, seems anxious to see what this step brings and if Spoilsport is actually acting in a noble fashion or if he is merely a thief in a high position.

Synite wonders if it would even be considered noble if there is an ulterior motive for bringing them back. "We still need contingency."

"If anyone attacks us," Amethyst stands, "when we touch down, let me handle them. You two scatter and get a better view of things," she speaks to Synite and Psilos.

"What about the ship?" Synite looks over at Kraa-Nuve and he looks back; the whole crew is nearly stiff.

"Shields, gunking," Kraa-Nuve assures them and thumbs over at Psilos then back at himself. "Got self."

"We're together," Synite reminds him, their lives intertwined like a braid. "We'll stand behind you, Amey, no matter what." She looks over at him, the same love in her eyes that was there when he protected her from having to use her power on Prophyria. And he looks back with the same adoration from the first time they met on Atlan.

"Most certainly," Psilos joins, draping his hands on their shoulders. "We do not flee while you stand at the precipice of endangerment."

"Man that was definitely some Psilos stuff to say," Synite huffs, almost jealous. "I wish I knew how to talk in a kingly manner!"

"You'll learn," Amethyst puts a hand on his sternum.

Synite thinks aloud, "I don't know. I don't think I'd want to rule over the masses. I don't believe I want to actively influence them. I prefer to be myself and not have to watch my actions for the approval of beings who don't understand my process. I hated hearing about spectators who judged the way Santhia, Psilos and I did things, the way I fought. They would say that I should've or could've done this and that but probably never even been hit in the face before!"

"I remember the couch critics," Amethyst thinks back to her times in the arena. "They would say I needed to slow down, that I needed to give them something more to look forward to. They did not understand what you understand about me. They didn't know how heavily the violence weighs on my soul."

"Exactly," Synite and Amethyst had never completely bonded on their roots in the Sword as it had been a touchy subject for both. They must both figure this might be something either of them may not come out of alive. "The viewer very rarely trusts that there is more going on than what they see. They always think they could have done better if they were in our shoes."

"I don't think anyone except you could have done much better than I did," Amethyst cracks a smile.

Synite had been burning to ask this for a long time: "What'd you think about Lord Qor? Was he afraid of you as I thought?"

"Definitely," she laughs. "His royal façade annoyed me. Every other being who had come to second position had challenged me."

"He cited it was for political reasons," Synite recalls. "He says he didn't fight you because it would look bad."

"When the topic came up, which it did on several occasions," she remembers three in particular, "he would send his agents of annoyance and they would talk the Enslaver out of it. They always said we would both be worth more alive and fighting others than if one of us killed the other. That actually was true but the sniveling and avoiding showed his weakness more than anything."

"What about the others?" Synite continues. "Why didn't you offer to fight them whenever they got close to you? Why did you send me to other arenas instead of dominating them yourself?"

"You have to remember, I didn't care so much about the power," Amethyst tries to search back to her feelings. "I was just as much, if not more of a slave than you were, Synite. I fought because they made me fight, not because I had anything to prove. I was a tool, a marketing engine. I'm sure world domination was next on the agenda, or maybe the threat of it was enough," she looks down, almost ashamed of herself in that time.

And it makes sense to him, almost so much that he regrets asking the question. "When you think about it, we both had about the same amount of hardship in the arena, too. Similar sacrifices."

"I am glad you have come to that conclusion," Psilos commends and ushers a deepening of their relationship. "As much difficulty as we had opening you up to the culture of arena battle, plus the difficulty you had actually executing it, she had those same issues in fighting against it."

Amethyst relaxes a bit more despite their destination. "What about your fights? Did you ever enjoy it?"

He relaxes right along with her, "Which part? The fighting?"

"All of it. The grind, the training, the crowd," she thinks of everything else she hated about it, "the negotiations, the wealth, the accomplishments, the fans. I could go on."

"The only thing I know is that I really enjoyed being called a champion," Synite remembers his chest swelling, resembling a bird of prey. "Being tangibly better than the world at something made me truly feel," he takes a moment to get the right word, "validated. It made me necessary. I understand that I couldn't have gotten that without all the other nonsense but I would trade it to feel that way again. I wouldn't trade being free for being a champion, obviously, but that was worth all the blood I spilled from myself and others."

"I was fond of when you took a stand against killing," Amethyst admits, "although it made me feel terrible about all of the little purple marbles I had collected over the cycles. That defined your career path to me and, honestly, was the real reason I allowed you audience. It's completely, if you think about it, the sole reason we're here now and why you're not a little purple marble, too."

This revelation also gives Synite a measure of justification for those actions. He had begun to wonder whether or not he should have actually killed some of the beings he went up against, probably since the influence of Thesia has grown. However, that statement made him feel as though he is exactly where he is supposed to be right now. He feels that everything is happening accordingly and for a reason. With the knowledge of the Thorns and their direction, Synite believes that the reason shall reveal itself soon as well.

Their conversation continues as genuinely as it had until C announces: "We are in the system that houses Tialian and its moon Pag. Our ETA is less than one hecu." The Caracalla slows out of PSL and bullets through the solar system, maneuvering not unlike a car on the road with slick tires due to the lack of friction in the massless void of space. The rush of anxiousness almost knocks each of them down as an unusually strong gravity would. Instead of pulling them down, though, it pulls them closer together. They are the Vanguard in this revolution and this is where their legacy truly begins.

In the middle of the night, Fabric receives a short message from Spoilsport, confused by it at first but decides in his better judgment to follow directions. "I'll get right to it!" So, he gets out of bed and hastily makes his way to his store.

In the lobby of the Weapons Rack, he goes to the front door and props it open, letting the breeze in, his glasses gleaming in the moonlight. The scent of the market foods pours into the room almost instantly. He scurries to the back of the store and does his combination to open the door into the cache.

"Floor plans!" at his command, the 3D diagram of his current floor plan comes up in front of him. He slides all of the aisle racks into one corner and all of the tables against a wall then he flicks the floating 'execute' key. The floor hums as it shifts things around mechanically. He moves back into the lobby and leaves the door into the hangar ajar enough for the breeze to move through how his directions told him.

Fabric gets another message from Spoilsport as he waits at his desk for something to happen. This message is much different from the last one, but still demands something of him. This demand, however, by its nature, puts a smile of excitement across Fabric's face not unlike the one he made when he heard the original plan.

The Caracalla arrives exactly in the coordinates and drop down next to a stylish, four passenger vessel that is resting near the border of the dark and light sides of Pag. "That must be him," Synite remarks. "Can we open the instructions he sent now?"

"The files are decoding themselves as we speak," the ship responds. Everyone waits for the results of the decoding in silence, ready to cut the thick suspense. It seems to be the longest few eins that Synite has ever experienced as he gets tenser. "The instructions say, and I quote, 'Whoever's going, hurry up and get on. Then, wait.'" Everyone waits for the rest of this message they had anticipated so greatly. "That's it. Don't shoot the messenger."

Synite has never rolled his eyes so hard in his life, he believes. "I'll be right back," he dashes back to the dormitories and into Driven's room where the young man is doing one-armed, one-legged pushups. "We're going."

Driven does not stop his motion, "And you came to ask me one last time, right?" Instead of responding, Synite waits for him to answer his own question. "Good luck, Synite. And," Driven stands up to face him, "if we never see each other again, I do appreciate meeting you and our time together. You'll always be like a brother to me."

They shake hands heartily and Synite heads back up, giving Proximity and Desha the same embrace. Amethyst comes in and joins their embrace, Psilos preparing to head down to the exit. "We ain't gonna be long behind ya," Desha pitches. Proximity has never been good at these situations so he remains at a loss for words.

Synite puts on gear to survive the walk from the Caracalla to the little ship that is fresh off the auction block. He has never, in all of his travels, walked through zero gravity before. *Better late than never,* he thinks as he, Amethyst and Psilos cross the barren desert of a moon to the ship. "This thing is tiny. Are we sure about trusting Spoilsport?"

The exterior door to the ship opens showing them four seats. He and Amethyst can fit side-by-side and Psilos has to take up the back row on his own. "We have committed to this. Let us see where it goes."

"Where is he?" Synite looks around for any sign of Spoilsport and there is nothing. "Are we supposed to fly this thing?"

"You are a pilot now, Synite," Psilos boosts his confidence. "You can navigate us through space without the full assistance of the Caracalla, can you not?"

"We'll see soon I guess," the three of them board the ship and the exterior door shuts and airlocks behind them.

Spoilsport comes in as Synite takes his seat in the captain's chair, Amethyst in the co-pilot's chair and Psilos against the back wall in the other two chairs. "Sure did take you all long enough," he says.

"It is only a projection," Psilos immediately notices to quell the assumption that he will be joining them on their voyage.

"You could've just come up on screen," Synite leans back into his seat again.

"Aww, don't be a spoilsport!" the projection laughs at itself. "That was a good one! Anyway, is everyone strapped in and secure? Good! Bye-

bye!" The projection disappears as fast as it appeared in the first place.

"Wait," Synite looks around for instructions to the controls, "Where are we supposed to be going? Where is the naviga--" The ship rocks from side to side and, from where they sit, the horizon of the light side of the moon begins to sink. "We're being lifted! It's a trap! Amey!" Amethyst stands up but before she can make any move off the ship, the entire thing glows a bright white and disappears in a flash.

From the captain's seat on the Caracalla, Kraa-Nuve looks on through his main screen. Proximity and Desha look on in pure astonishment and shock, not sure what to make of the event. "Where did they go," Proximity finally yells in at Kraa-Nuve. "The bastard Spoilsport incinerated them! It's over!"

"Actually," the ship corrects, "it looks to have been a spatial, temporal tear."

"Teleport," Kraa-Nuve translates for them.

"Teleported?" Proximity storms into the cockpit with Kraa-Nuve. "To where?"

"More of the encoded message has been unlocked, captain," the ship sends the next set of details to his main screen. "What is it you wish to do?"

"Drop kid," because Driven requested to be taken off the grid. Kraa-Nuve then waves Proximity away as he reads over the message given to him from Spoilsport. "Stations! Mission!"

The professor at the front of the classroom clicked a laser pen and flipped it between his fingers. On-screen in front of the class, the word 'Teleportation' came down, projected from the ceiling. "What does this mean?" he requested participation from her crop of students.

After a long moment of unresponsive grumblings, a young lady raised her pale, blue hand meekly, "Well, isn't it similar to when you move something from one place to another instantly?"

"Can someone be more specific," the professor looked around the room for another volunteer. Cairo Jr. sat quietly attentive in the rear of the secondary school class.

A boy raised his hand and the professor offered him the floor, "I think it's when somebody, you know, wants to go somewhere, so they picture it in their head, use some magic, and then they're there!"

"And," the professor played the room well, "what is this idea of instantaneous transportation from one place to another based on?"

"Magic, like I said?" the same boy guessed.

"Sometimes, yes," the professor still reserved his actual lesson. "But, let's stay in the realm outside of magic." He paced around the room between the desks, making eye contact with some of the students including

Synite. "Where do most power users draw from?"

"Within," young Synite spat out quickly and quietly.

The professor turned to him, "Come again?"

"Within?" he repeated, bashful as ever.

The professor grinned, "Correct. Now," he went back up to the front of the room, "the thing that most assume about teleportation is that it is a magically derived phenomenon, which can be true." He picked up his air-writing pen and began the actual lesson here. "Instant transmission," he wrote as he spoke, "by destruction of an object at one point and re-creation of that object at another."

My head hurts, young Synite thought to himself and things started getting blurry for him at this point of the professor's speech, "Actually, the hallmark of a powerful teleporter is compression. You see, Einstein told us--"

Slam! The professor jerked in the direction of the loud bang as his lecture is cut off by Synite dropping to the ground with dead weight. The same young girl with the pale blue skin screamed and the rest of the class went to pandemonium. Synite shook and the professor helped get the students away from him as best he could, "Stay calm! He's having a seizure," he tapped the emergency call button on his air-writing pen. "Give him room to breathe," the call came in on his earpiece and he touched his ear. "I need an EMT for a student having a seizure in room 45-T."

Later, in her station, the nurse shined a dim light into young Synite's eyes to make sure he was completely recovered and responsive. They dilate correctly while she goes back and forth between each eye. Cairo Sr. leaned against the wall behind them as she checked his pulse. "Everything seems to be back to normal," she said.

"This isn't his first time at the rodeo," Nitengale knew his son was not embarrassed of his seizures anymore so he felt comfortable enough with telling her. "We can take it from here. He's a fighter, he'll make it."

"I understand," the nurse updated Synite's records in her system. "We'll just send him home for the day to rest that brain of his."

"We appreciate your help." Nitengale put his hand on Synite's shoulder, "Ready, kiddo?"

Young Synite nodded and got up from the chair and as they headed to the exit, "Thanks." These migraines and seizure were a somewhat normal occurrence for him after that. His dad was still the only person who was there for him consistently when he regained consciousness, never wanting to miss an opportunity to be there for his son. He noticed after a while that he never had issues during rainstorms and Nitengale would hope for rain, unusual for an officer of the law, but only because it kept his namesake's ills at bay.

 # CHAPTER XVIII

As things creep back into normal color from the monochromatic flash, Synite looks down at his hands, still not quite sure what happened or how. He tries his best to catch his breath and get his wits about him but he cannot; his entire body feels as though it was crushed and then kicked around like a crumb on the kitchen floor.

It does not hurt him though; this is a completely different sensation from pain. To Synite, it is more of a complete dizziness, bordering unconsciousness, in combination with a slowly releasing pressure on his entire body. He feels as though he is being inflated back up to his original size practically the same as a balloon.

All he can hear at the moment is the sound of his own heart and short, quick breaths. Soon enough, he can hear voices that he hopes belong to Amethyst and Psilos, and feel movement around him. The pressure on his eyes seems to release and he can vaguely make out the control panel of the tiny ship he was on before everything went white.

The pressure on his brain lifts and his senses start to return with that release. He feels something reaching for him through the Air and spins away from it then raises a hand to Amethyst, standing calmly near the exit door. "Calm down, Synite." He looks up and Psilos is still seated behind her as he is unable to stand in such a tight space. "Look," she points towards the front window.

The cloud of dust around the ship whisks away and Synite starts to see more clearly. "This place," he walks back up to where he was sitting. "I've been here before." 'Yes, we have,' Gale tells him. 'This is where we first met.' He turns back to Amethyst, "We're in Atlan! This is," and instead of waiting, he opens the exit door and steps out into the cache of the Weapons Rack.

Amethyst steps out behind him, still wary of exactly what happened. She recovered quicker than Synite but was still disoriented from the teleportation. "How did we get here?" Before she can put her second foot on the ground, her heart drops as she feels how close she is to the Enslaver again. She is certain that It cannot feel her as Its powers of perception are low, especially since It is probably sleeping. She knows though and the hatred for that being rises in her like magma during a volcanic event.

"I don't know but that was a hell of a trip," Synite remarks, still shaky but getting more comfortable considering his surroundings. His voice brings Amethyst back to the moment and suppresses her fury for the time being. Then, he sees the door that leads to the storefront start to inch open.

Fabric peeks his head in and pushes his glasses up, smiling at the sight of Synite in one piece. "I can only imagine!" he yells as he disappears back into the store. The front doors slam shut and then he dashes back in. "Synite, my boy! Welcome back!"

"I am to assume we made it?" Psilos looks out from the ship on all fours.

"I guess we can trust Spoilsport after all," Amethyst lets go of that reservation.

Synite shakes hands with Fabric and turns back to Amethyst, "For now at least since our goals are aligned. We'll see how long they stay that way."

"My apologies for the lack of communication but he required complete discretion and we didn't have time for any debate," Fabric goes to Amethyst and shakes her hand as Psilos squeezes out of the ship. "He was sure one of you might not have agreed to such a venture."

"The two of you spoke about this?" Amethyst wonders how Spoilsport would have gotten in contact with an ex-Thorn if he did not know somewhat of the new ones.

"Indeed!" Fabric does not know yet of their new information. "We planned your arrival before he contacted the ship about it." He gets to shake Psilos's hand, "And we would have brought the entire ship but it was entirely too big to fit in here. That, I must apologize for as well."

"I don't blame you," Synite voices his skepticism. "But that doesn't explain how we got here."

"It's pretty simple, guys," an orange flash followed by this unfamiliar voice comes from near the entrance door. "He teleported y'all in from across a few galaxies. That guy is something else, I tell ya!" Castra Nim puts his foot up on the wall and bows his head as he gets everyone's attention.

"Pardon him," Fabric motions to Castra. "This is--"

"Castra Nim," Synite had heard good things about his red-haired heir to the throne of the Sword.

"Nice to finally meet ya," Castra goes up to the four of them and sizes everyone up.

As he looks up at Psilos, which is a ways up for him, the Prophyrian speaks, "You are a slave?" He eyes Castra and Amethyst steps up next to Synite.

"Not for long since y'all showed up," Castra claps and rubs his hands together. "I brought a few friends, if y'all don't mind me introducing them, too." He waves and Coldsmoke steps into the room followed by Lo, NanVash, Orchanik G, Arra, Gith and Suubai. "This is the revolution."

Synite looks back at Amethyst and Psilos, trying to grasp what is in front of him. He recognizes Lo, "Where are the rest of the old Profit Circle members?"

"When the arena was restructured into a team battle," Lo steps in front of the group, "Ma'aro and Chierra were pardoned and left and, of course, Vulcarus died during your escape." Synite shakes his head at another life on his hands. "Lone couldn't be here though as that Spoilsport guy has him babysitting the girl."

Synite goes over to Fabric, "He's doing all of this to have her to himself?"

"I don't believe that is it," Fabric ponders on it for a moment.

"Then what else could it be?" Synite does not have enough intel on the man to know what direction to go in.

"I believe he knows you three won't be able to stay after the battles," Fabric considers. "That would make him the most powerful being on the Earth 11. And, the enemy of his enemy is indeed his friend."

"He wants to systematically cut ties with the Enslaver then," Synite still thinks they have to watch him as closely as possible even after this is over. "Did she know we would be coming back?"

"From what he said, yes, but she didn't want to be here," Fabric rubs his head. "I didn't ask why but I'm assuming because of the danger."

'And you should assumeeeee that it is beeeecauseeee weeee areeee heeeereeee,' Thesia had been quiet for too long. "You don't think it's because of me?"

"Ah! Not at all! And, on that note, he told me to give you this if you brought it up," Fabric hands the message key to Synite and he opens it. He goes and sits where Psilos was on the little ship as the rest of the beings in the room introduce themselves to each other. It reads:

> "Strange creatures some women are. No matter how interesting a person is, no matter how much depth of character a person has achieved, in general, these outwardly beautiful beings

are only intrigued by the fact that someone is attracted to or interested in them. They only give attention to those who show them attention, and then they get what they want from them and move on.

"They strut and fan out their colorfully feathered tails, reminiscent of the peacocks of Earth Prime, using what they have just because they have it, beautiful for the sake but with no particular cause outside of getting attention and maybe procreation.

"These beings are hollowed out by their own vanity, assuming that they can somehow find something they will never get bored with; this is sad because boredom is an indictment on one's own personality and not those who seek their attention. They shall forever search for something to fill the void inside instead of learning to be the best version of themselves and growing comfortable in their own boredom.

"Those who have constantly sought their attention can be blamed partially but the rope ends with the empty soul, not the hands reaching for it. And the most critical part that they either do not understand or choose to ignore is this: beauty fades before character. Feathers fall away and wither in time. Perfect skin and shapely bodies wrinkle and shrivel. Then, the shallowness is magnified so greatly that it overwhelms even the strongest of us."

Spoilsport's face comes up on the reading and he speaks, "This is something that I picked up, an aphorism that I believe would guide you in your next few decisions. This particular quote molded me at a certain point in my life and I believe you are reaching that point as well.

"No matter how beautiful anything is, any being, objects, or cause, remember that you may not be the right one to take it up. It may seem that way at first, as it acknowledges you for acknowledging it, but these things tend to chew beings up like cud and spit them out just the same." Spoilsport disappears and the screen goes black.

Synite thinks about it and decides not to ignore the moment anymore. He steps back into the crowd and everyone turns to him, waiting on words. "I see providence in this room," he looks at Amethyst. "I see us finishing what we came here to do. It's not only possible," he steps in the middle of them and feels the energy of the room, how powerful each person is and how high their spirits are, "but we are going to turn this world in the right direction."

"Now," Psilosking speaks, "we must plan. It is time to prepare our execution."

Everyone huddles around the ship and talks about their abilities, their advantages, disadvantages, who would work well together in teams with each other and not work well together at all. Fabric stands up, "I forgot to mention that Spoilsport has the kill switch for all of the automatons ready for when we wish to move forward. Also," he takes his glasses off, "I am willing to throw a few punches with you all if my help is needed."

"Throw a few punches? Dude," Gith chuckles, "you're old."

Synite interrupts the joke, "Don't underestimate one of the original 18 Thorns, friend," Fabric looks over at him, taken aback by this comment. "He could probably take you down pretty easily without breaking a sweat!" Synite steps over to him, "As a matter of fact, I want to fight next to you, Fabric. Is that okay?"

"Fine with me! That's less I have to do," Fabric believes Synite can indeed compensate for whatever he lacks, though he can gain a few things on his own as well. "Synite, may I speak to you in private?"

"We'll talk about it later," Synite is not ready to be distracted by admitting everything he knows about Hudson Clark. "So, what can you do?"

Back in outer space, the Caracalla snaps out of PSL and goes down to the planet that the hail that responded to Tobias's signal came from. Kraa-Nuve opens a direct line to the room Driven is in, "Kid, ready?"

"This is where you're bringing me?" Driven has absolutely no idea where they are or why he was brought here specifically.

Kraa-Nuve grins, "Dad fault. Safe drop soon."

"My dad told you to bring me here," Driven is perturbed to say the least, "and you listened?"

"Owe life," Kraa-Nuve shrugs and closes the connection as Proximity and Desha join him in the cockpit. They get down on-planet and the ship sits in the grassy field it landed in long enough for Driven to get clear of their blast zone.

As the Caracalla dashes out of the atmosphere, two trucks drive up to meet Driven. The first truck stops short of Driven's position and its driver gets out as the second truck passes. The first driver gets into the passenger seat of the second truck after it stops in front of Driven. The second driver lets the window down, a cloud of cigar smoke floating from inside, and reveals a shaved face and head wearing a military uniform.

Driven steps closer to the truck and sees no one in the passenger seat as he looks past the driver. "What the hell?"

The driver chews on his nearly gone cigar and looks over his dark sunglasses. "You look akin to your goddamn father when he was younger, boy!"

Driven scowls, "Who are you?"

The Caracalla jumps out of PSL again a while later, A'rris looking on intently at their position. "We are at the system's edge," the ship tells them.

"You made it just in time!" Spoilsport's projection fades in behind them and his voice startles A'rris which breaks them back up. "I have gifts of good measure!" He points at Kraa-Nuve's screen and a list of symbols, numeric and otherwise, scroll up and across. There is no clear pattern to either of them and they soon learn why: "These are the security clearances to get through the gates of the system. The ship should be able to pass them to the gate signal that'll try to track it when you enter system space. I haven't wormed them into the system yet. Since they generate organically, I'll have to drop that in around the time you're using them. So, time it correctly and you should be good."

"Couldn't steal?" Kraa-Nuve slightly questions Spoilsport's thievery capabilities.

"Were you listening?" Spoilsport crosses his arms, "Their system does not have codes. This is the whole solar system we're talking about here, not only on Earth 11 or in Atlan. I barely found out where to hack into! It'd be impossible to find the place to pull some codes from, at least in the amount of time I had to find it!"

Kraa-Nuve shrugs, "Give credit."

"I appreciate your consideration, captain," Spoilsport spills sarcastically. "Anyway, eventually they'll figure out who you are, so you'll have to make a good go at it after that," Spoilsport also points over at the co-pilot station. "I've sent you a coordinate to plot the fastest route to. Once you get in, go there as quickly as possible. Knowing your ship's capabilities, you should make it fine with the time you'll be buying."

"Little enough," Kraa-Nuve remarks. "Verify."

"From a previous record, these codes look as they belong to a ship that is supposed to be returning to a nearby planet and has been registered for safe passage," the ship is as astonished at Spoilsport's craftiness as the rest of the crew.

"We still don't understand why you're doing this," Proximity notices as he looks at the complex codes, "nor do we understand how you're getting all of this intelligence."

Spoilsport scoffs as his projection begins to fade away, "True thieves never kiss and tell!"

"Where you goin' man?" Desha yells as the projection disappears completely. "I still ain't trustin' of him. He got somethin' else up his sleeve."

"We too," Kraa-Nuve reassures with a grin.

CHAPTER XIX

"What are we t'do about th'freed slaves afterwards?" Coldsmoke brings up a good point to the entire group. "There will be chaos." In the several instances when slavery resulted in the creation of a society and then assimilation into that same society, relations between the ex-slave cultures and the others were difficult to say the least. Much of these oil-and-water nations never truly recover from the psychological and sociological damages done on both sides.

The majority of post-slavery societies never see true equality because of the inherently deep set classism that can be both subtly or overtly taught. Giving one side, the ex-slave or the ex-slaver, of the population any sort of privileges based on that past cripples the culture beyond repair. If any reparations are given, they should be given in conjunction with emancipation, not generations later.

Even then, after the psychological handicap is healed on both sides, which may take at least four generations, if there is any economic disenfranchisement, if there is a large wealth gap, recovery may be impossible. There would have to be privileges given to close the gap which, therein, skews equality. Now the group receiving the assistance is given a crutch and looked down upon by the rest of the population that affords them that help but does not use it themselves.

The ex-slave culture subconsciously embraces this extremely complacent attitude, already prepared for help and unprepared for building some sort of familial wealth. The issue is that, when an entire race of beings is not used to having much, there is a sweeping dichotomy for the times when some sort of fortune is received by them: they either use that fortune on frivolous things that lose value quickly to enjoy it or hoard it within a small section of the culture.

Very few understand the concept of lifting as they climb, raising the entire culture and breaking the mental chains of slavery through education and evenly spreading wealth. Instead, the burden of poverty is so heavy on their souls that they end up lost in the shuffle of exploitation. The little money they have is snatched away as prices and inflation rise faster and with less legislation than wages. Generations are lost because they cannot see a clear path to equality.

Then, the wrinkles in time show some rise above the glass ceiling, give back to their communities and try their best to assimilate their culture into equality. Unfortunately, most times this leadership is too late or caught between the ex-slaver culture pushing them down and their own ex-slave culture pulling them down, ignoring the help, and citing that change is unnecessary.

Some warriors of progress get so downtrodden that they give up and others fight prejudice to their death either naturally or by assassination. And, it also seems that some stages of progress die with their respective warriors as the slave mentality regresses when there is no one there to push it out of the depths.

As generations go by and hostility dies down, the bigotry lies dormant but does not perish. It boils behind closed doors and overflows into the streets in sporadic clashes between each side that constantly show the past never dies. Both are afraid of each other in one form or fashion, one for the threat of physical harm and the other for their power.

When those drastically different types of fear interact and deadly weapons are involved, on either side of the law, tragedy strikes. Some of these tragedies are bigger than others, some publicized and some are not. Regardless of the breadth of the impact or scale of the story, each one rings the same tune. No one is without bias, especially in post-slavery nations, and that bias, along with violent nature, takes lives in a layer of unnatural selection that lies over liberty, justice and righteousness.

The only way to truly avoid these types of clashes in an unkempt, post-slavery society is to leave it for one that has either recovered completely or never experienced the curse of slavery. There are some instances in which an ex-slave could emigrate to another post-slavery society and not feel like a statistic, such as when the adjacent ex-slaves do not resemble them in any fashion or when the ex-slave class is now the ruling class. However, it is probably more feasible to find a nation that has no qualms with the type of being the ex-slave has been made into after generations of hate-filled stares.

In Atlan, a unique opportunity presents itself, however. If the Enslaver's reign ends here, they need to usher in the next stage of society, as suggested by Coldsmoke and discussed several times over by the others. Those who are able to, whether they plan to or not, should stay and become the connective tissue, the ligaments so-to-speak, between the ex-slave culture and the popular culture as no ex-slaver culture will remain as long as the Enslaver is out of the picture. Somehow, Its material wealth should be seized and distributed amongst those with nothing in their thumb; then they should be guided into preserving their newfound wealth and integrated into normal society so that they can be looked at as equal.

"The few of us who become wanted have to make a hasty exit," Psilos reminds those who he told before and informs those who he did not. "Many of you who are able need to stay behind while I send a force for recovery efforts."

"We have to manage the chaos," Synite says, "even though I won't be around to help. Those who survive and aren't in the Enslaver's bingo book have to bear the responsibility. This world cannot be left in ruin."

New weapons in hand, "Assuming I'm still alive afterwards, I'll stick around for a while and do some work," Castra Nim looks ready for war.

"As will I," Fabric starts the snowball of responses from the willing participants.

"Somebody's got to man the fort, right?" Castra seems to be enjoying the preparation as much as he enjoys to actually fight. He laughs to himself, *I said fort! Heh.*

Synite goes over to the racks as well and gets a fitted top that goes up to his ears with long sleeves, a few pieces of body armor that he spots and a large robe similar to the one Promis gave him. He throws it on over the armor, comfortable with the layers and the weight. "Whether we win or lose, though," he stays on subject, "there'll be a bunch of slaves running around with very little direction."

"We can feel responsible but all this chaos ain't our fault, ladies and gents. That's on the system of slavers. If the system wasn't so bad, we wouldn't have to tear it down. We're, like, the agents of freedom or something." Castra scratches his chin as he picks up an electrified nightstick, "I think I'll make sure they use that in the news when this is all over!" He compares the nightstick to a long sai, shrugs, and puts both of them on loops of his pants.

"Good point," Synite channels some electric energy to be sure none of his new attire is hindering his elementalist abilities and glides over to Amethyst. "I guess I wanted to suit up, too."

"It looks cool on you," she remarks. "Very sturdy!"

The first sunrise creeps over the horizon on the same beach they escaped from more than two TAT cycles ago, which is quite a long time for someone from Earth Prime. Synite is now, by his home standards, twenty-two cycles old and possibly about to have the fight of his life at that tender age. However, he has been fighting for his life for the last five cycles so this should not feel novel to him but it does. There is something different about this one, he feels, but he has been trained well to tackle it.

As the light expands westward, the Enslaver's circadian cycle brings It conscious and, immediately, It feels a glimmer of Amethyst's presence. Shortly thereafter, all of the attendees feel it as well, though to them it is only an assumption and not an actual feeling they can trust.

For some reason, the traffic this morning is heavier than usual around the market square. The weather is fair, warm for it being so early but not unbearably so with the breeze coming off the ocean. There are no arena events today so the Sword is unusually empty. Most of those who would have been at some sort of match are either in their homes or out in the street.

The moment the shift door is opened between the Vanguard and Atlan, an attendee runs into the Enslaver's hall and kneels in front of the Its poplar wood throne. "My master, they have come! Shall we send the automaton forces first or summon the Sukayishiru?"

An elder attendee shakes a hand, "The automatons must be saved to keep the slaves in check. With Amethyst here--" the Enslaver grunts and coughs out a swirling cloud of smoke. Soon, the shadows behind the throne grow and spread in every direction; breast plate armors, gauntlets and weapons emerge from the fabricated darkness.

The twelve Sukayishiru stand ready, divided into their three groups of four by the color of their armor and their custom patterns. Each has a special mask, however, all in different writhing and horrific expressions to strike fear in any opponent. To the left is the Blood and Gold group, in the middle the Midnight and Diamond group, and to the right the Black and Onyx group.

In the Blood and Gold group, the weaponry handled includes a sickle on the point of what the angel of death would carry, a curved shortsword with an ornate hilt, a very plain flail that the bearer wishes he did not have to carry, and a morning star with a lot of large, edged spikes. The Midnight and Diamond group has the naginata bearer who previously doused the scuffle below the Sword, a large claymore with a quadruple spiked hilt, one who holds a club and mace by the chain that connects them, and finally a small warrior with a giant riveted hammer that is much taller than it is wide. The group in Black and Onyx rounds out with a sharp whip, a shield that is nearly as tall as its bearer, a falchion that he handles reversed, and a short-handled, double-edged battle axe.

The attendee in front of the Enslaver faces the squadron of masked warriors, "Your defense of this kingdom begins now." They all come around to face It, group by group, and kneel at the base of the throne. "Execute them!" The one in the Black and Onyx group with the whip stands and comes out in the middle of the entire troop. She raises her right hand, the one covered snugly in the gauntlet, and slams her fist into the ground. Capsules of darkness encase them and they disappear like a shadow when light is shined on it. The Enslaver grins at the power of the guard that shall defend the Sword, anticipating high profits from the death of the rogues.

Synite is the first to step out of the Weapons Rack, nostalgic from feeling the Air of Earth 11 flowing through him. He recognizes this breeze as one of the first he got his power from and it calms his nerves into focus. It is not strange that he feels at home here, more than he would if he were in the place he was born, since he grew into himself and made his identity here.

Everyone else except Amethyst comes out in their gear with the markings of Alexander, guns in holsters, knives in hands, other weapons and armor wrapping their bodies. They divide up into three groups to match the groups that they supposed the Sukayishiru would be in. Synite leads with Fabric and NanVash; Psilos leads with Suubai, Orchanik G and Coldsmoke; Castra Nim leads with Lo, Arra and Gith, the old Atlan team back together again.

The breeze blows Synite's hood off and, quickly, a child notices his face and taps his big brother's arm. "Look! It's Synite from the movies!"

"Sure it is," the big brother ignores the annoyance. "It's probably just a guy in costume."

"Remember," Synite turns to the group, "we have no idea what these things can do. Be on your guard and protect the person next to you at all times. We cannot afford to be careless against--"

"Excuse me! Pardon me!" and, out of nowhere, Lone comes through the Weapons Rack, teleported in by Spoilsport. He goes up to Synite, "Sorry I'm late! Give me a sec to get some stuff from inside!"

He dashes back in and everyone looks around, waiting for someone to say something. "He's cool!" Castra confirms to those who did not recognize him.

Lone pops back out the door, gear hanging off of his shoulder like a father's clothes passed down to a young son. "Shit! This ain't fitting right. It looked much cooler on the rack! Be right back!" and he goes into the Cache again, coming out after another ein in completely different gear. "Okay, I'm good! Who am I with?"

Synite looks at Castra who decides quickly, "He'll be of great assistance on your team, Synite. That evens things up a bit."

"Be of great assistance?" Lone mocks him. "Since when did you start talking that way?"

"Shut up and fall in!" Castra points him over to Synite.

"I hope you had a good meal before you got here," Lo whispers to him in passing.

"That's exactly why I'm late!" he and Lo have a laugh together. "So," Lone asks Synite, "where we headed?"

All of these people, he looks around at the morning foot traffic. *It will be hard to avoid casualties in the middle of the street. We have to get into open areas as soon as we can since I'm sure they know we're here.* "As far away from this as possible," Synite responds. "We should talk on the way," Synite tells him. 'Violence is both the cause and effect of war,' Gale tells him. 'Concentrate on the mission.' "Let's go everybody! Quickly!"

Synite's group heads Nortoest towards the plains, Psilos's Nort out of the city and Castra's Est towards the coast. "I don't think actors move like that," the little brother says.

"They're probably trained, kid. I wonder what type of event they're hosting. I didn't hear anything." Then, the boys see Amethyst come forward from the doors of the Weapons Rack, amazed by her beauty. "There's no way!"

The rest of the crowd had begun to notice the strange characters coming from the Weapons Rack as well. At the sight of Amethyst, their former queen, they are all in shock and awe. They see her perfect height, her perfect shape, her perfect hair and perfect face. They see her glowing purple bracelet and flowing garments and all know that this is the real woman. There are mixed feelings amongst the crowd, some in fear, some ready to touch the hem of her dress and bow at her feet. All know that something out of the ordinary is about to occur.

She feels the Enslaver's presence again, which is mutual for the being that held her here for so long, and knows exactly where to find It. So, she creates an iridescent purple chariot carriage beneath her feet and it carries her over the crowds to the entrance of Its hall.

The others move well in their groups behind the leaders of the Vanguard, everyone through the sky. Synite carries Fabric and Lone with wind walls as NanVash flaps his wings next to them; Psilos lets Suubai ride his back and Orchanik G carries Coldsmoke; Castra, Gith and Arra slide behind Lo on his moving bridge of ice.

Still over the crowds, clouds of black pop up on the buildings around their ice bridge. The group donning Black and Onyx clash with Castra and company over the crowd, the violence causing them to scatter into the buildings and out of the street as quickly as they can. Castra, as the least sure-footed of the group, is the first knocked to the ground and forces the rest of them to get down and defend him. They stand across from the four Sukayishiru, mentally prepared for the worst.

Psilos is met in midair by the swing of a red-bladed sickle, dodging and throwing Suubai from his back. Suubai recovers in midair, floating down with his telekinetic prowess but Coldsmoke still jumps down to keep the Sukayishiru from ambushing him and Psilos comes to his side as well. Orchanik comes down last as the crowd in front of the gate to the Sword spreads around them. The Blood and Gold Sukayishiru swarm and then stop with their backs to the gate.

A sonic boom crashes against all three of Synite's wind walls, tossing his allies around and throwing them all into the black sand of the arena. 'Theeeey areeee heeeereeee!' Thesia exclaims, excited at the threat of violence. Synite summons Gale and throws her into the sky, then has to double back and drop to the center of the arena as a wall of shadows tumbles towards them. Three of the four laced in Midnight and Diamond armor drop down and the last one, the woman with the naginata, drops in front of them facing Synite.

She raises her blade at him and he raises a hand, his eyes glowing blue as his elementalist power activates. She shoots a strong sonic blast at him and he pushes an equally strong torrential wind to meet it, his robes blowing strongly behind him. The black sands swirl and crash, showing those who do not have the ability to see the details of sonic waves and winds exactly how the clash occurs. They negate each other and the stalemate forces them to intelligently stop.

"You will all die here," she tells Synite in an unusual speech rhythm, the other captains of the telling their respective Vanguard opponents at the same time. "We cannot be defeated," the three female Sukayishiru promise in unison, their minds all connected by the source of their power. "Surrender and we may spare the lives of those who have not yet wronged our Master."

The roof of the Enslaver's hall opens up, crumbling with a stream of purple light. The chariot's rays stretch to the floor and it comes down in their path. It carries Amethyst in a painstakingly slow float towards the Enslaver's throne. The only thing on her mind is the blood of billions that are on Its wiry hands; the billions of souls lost beneath one being's hand so Its thumb could get richer. The millions that It never even knew, never even gazed upon or considered, but still took everything from. The thousands killed for the entertainment of others, thrown in dungeons and pitted against each other to fight for their lives to pass the time. The hundreds It took a personal interest in abducting to put on display, to sell, to market or to grind to dust until there was nothing left. The dozens of slaves that tried to fight the system and, despite their best efforts, never made it past their fantasies. The few in the Vanguard that are with her, supporting her right now in her undertaking, and are behind her until the very end. And Amethyst, the one who will do everything with the power It forced on her to achieve revenge for billions before and billions to come.

"You know what," Synite had an epiphany in front of everyone back in the shift room, "I think, with who we have in this room, we can afford to let Amethyst go straight to the Enslaver instead of having to get bogged down in battle."

Most of the room pondered the thought of not having her to back them up but Fabric, Castra Nim and Psilos flashed elation across their eyes. "What if we can't--"

"I don't want to hear can't!" Synite stopped whoever's voice that was. "With the teams we formed and the information we have on the enemy's tactics, I believe we could take on the entire planet and at least survive to tell about it!" He had not seen Psilos smile at a joke of his in a long time and it made him happy. *The simple things.*

They waited to hear more disdain but Amethyst offered this, "My prime objective is to rid the octadecaverse of the Enslaver. I won't leave this planet again until It is finished." She looked down at her bracelet, "My hatred of this power and for the one that put it in me has brought me back. You may never understand my unique disdain. My home was destroyed by It, all I ever knew was crushed into oblivion, and then I was a mental slave to the throne. Unless you have experienced these things, you can only fantasize and that's all I've been doing since the day Synite rescued me from this.

"And that is why," she looked up as a tear rolled from her eye, "that's why I have believed so much in everything he has done. Despite what he may think," she drew attention to Synite, "everything he has led us into has been the best. I would not follow anyone else to this edge of destiny."

"So," Gith crossed his arms, "we're supposed to go out there and rip this place a new one because we don't approve of this guy?" They paused for a moment long enough for him to decide on his own: "Good enough for me!"

"If I could interject for a moment," Castra Nim took the floor. "It may be best if we don't have a master-blaster plan to get through this battle. I mean I'm a strategist at heart but if we make it too complex, we might overthink it and suffer. I believe the best plan in this case is to trust each other and have each other's backs, especially since we won't have much time to prepare."

Synite's eyes had been locked on Amethyst since she started talking. "We are behind you completely," he stepped over to her. "No matter what you want to do, we support you. We have to. I brought you to this point in your life and you've trusted me enough to come along when you could have been here, comfortable in your perch as queen," he edged close enough to touch her. "So, we return that trust to you. That's the only plan I need."

They both looked up at Psilos, "Then it is decided," He dropped the gavel without hesitation. "We make her way and she goes to the Enslaver."

Now that Psilos said it out loud, Synite did not quite appreciate it as much as he did when he thought it up. "And, if you need help--"

"No," Amethyst does not quite know the extent of the Enslaver's power at this point but, "I don't need any help against It. You have to focus on your own tasks. Let me worry about that thing."

"I think we want to say we had a hand in defeating the Enslaver," Synite spoke on behalf of Psilos as well.

Amethyst sighed, "Getting me here would not have happened without either of you. That is enough."

"You know," Castra popped in, "with all these emotions, I doubt either of you have half as much fun in this fight as I'm about to." He turned to Fabric, "Any new toys in here?"

"Certainly! I suppose we should arm ourselves," Fabric opened his utility connection to spread the racks enough for everyone to look at the weaponry Alexander afforded them for such an occasion.

"I'll take that bet!" Orchanik G followed them to the racks. "I've been itching to try a new technique I made up!"

"Game on!" Gith headed over as well as all of the others except Coldsmoke, Synite, Psilos and Amethyst.

Coldsmoke looked at the three of them as equals, "I am Coldsmoke of K'oma. Your colleague Castra Nim has told me of your plans and I am intrigued. I have come t'you in order t'have an impact in th'revolution and prove myself worthy enough t'stand next t'you in battle. That's all."

"Your being here is abundant proof," Psilos spoke for them. "However, this will not be the proving ground. This is a true battle. Nothing is proven in war except that one force is stronger and smarter than the next. This is the cost in creating freedom."

"Hey!" Synite got everyone's attention. "I need to say something before we take steps towards moving out. If you aren't here to fight in this revolution for a reason," he referred back to Coldsmoke, "if you think this is a game for you to get a notch on your belt, or a match in the arena, you shouldn't be here. This is about changing this world."

"You speak as if you are here for more than just the woman," Coldsmoke heard from Spoilsport about Promis and Synite's relationship.

Thesia rose in Synite's stomach, "You're got damn right I'm here for more than her. This is to take away the plague of this planet, not save one being!"

"We could all die on the battlefield," Amethyst took over, "including myself. I should be dead today from fighting a much lesser foe. What he says is correct: if you're not here to change this world," she looked directly at Coldsmoke.

"I was separated from my pregnant wife because she was sent t'a different arena," he rebutted. "My child did not see a moment outside her mother's womb for me t'meet her. If this is a step in th'direction of ending th'system that took my family from me," he remained relaxed despite his strong tone, "I am indeed in th'right place."

"Good enough for me," Castra Nim yelled from across the room and continued to browse. The sounds of agreement came from the rest of the new Vanguard as Coldsmoke had in the least said enough to die a noble death in their eyes. Whether it was the truth or a manipulation remains to be seen but they had to at least assume he is bold enough to fight with them.

CHAPTER XX

"You'll have to end our lives." Synite stands up to the team of Sukayishiru proudly, Gale's thunder rumbling behind his speech. "We are here to end yours." The space between them is framed by the four pillars in the middle of the Sword. This is where Synite's life was changed from pedestrian to champion and he is confident that this shall not be where it ends.

"Let it be," the captain says and the Sukayishiru move in a trained pattern into a square formation: the captain in back, the one carrying the club and mace in front with the hammer and claymore holders flanking him.

The Vanguard responds by standing shoulder to shoulder in a straight line, preparing to clash against the unknown power in front of them. Fabric puts a hand on the arm of NanVash's wing and concentrates for a few secs. "Thanks," he tells NanVash who nods in response.

Synite turns off his elementalist power and drops into Harden then dashes forward to start the battle. The small one with the huge, diamond riveted hammer drags it across the sand to meet him in the center. He is followed by the Midnight blue claymore swordsman that NanVash decides to meet in the center with a laser sword he got from Fabric, his wings folded back. Lone lifts his bazooka and Fabric cocks his favorite quad-barreled shotgun as Synite jumps over the first swing of the hammer.

The other two battles start similarly, with the Sukayishiru getting into some sort of formation and the more active participants attacking head first. The Blood sickle and flail clash with Psilos and Coldsmoke; the whip and falchion start their jar with Lo and Gith. Most of the Sukayishiru, by the looks of things, have not underestimated the capabilities of these members of the Vanguard. They are a force that does not know moderation; they are either resting or on full attack, which is how they come out against the protagonists.

Synite notices in the middle of the fight that the one carrying the hammer is swinging it twice as fast as he was before. NanVash has not been able to land a single hit on the one with the claymore as, whenever he gets close enough, the Sukayishiru turns itself into a shadow and NanVash swings the blade right through him. *So they each have a specific power set. I wonder how complex they get.* Then, he feels the captain as she starts to move back a few steps, getting a better angle to see the battle.

The claymore swings at NanVash and he lets it hit him. The dark blue blade clangs against his body as it would another blade of the same strength and same kinetic energy, the truth of NanVash's invulnerability to physical attacks revealed. He swings and passes through a shadow, yelling "Fight me!" and waving his wings in frustration.

Synite dodges a swing of the hammer and throws an ion orb at the back of the Sukayishiru that NanVash is fighting. Instead of turning into a shadow, it dodges the energy shot, telling Synite all he needs to know. "Let's switch! I'll have an advantage against him!"

NanVash thrusts at the shadow as quickly as he can, diving through it and glides towards the other fight, ready for the swing of the hammer. Synite shoots to the sky fast and rapidly fires orb after orb down at the claymore. He dodges as best he can and swings at a few to knock them away but cannot stop them all. His armor is strong enough to withstand most of what hits him but he gets knocked down nonetheless and Synite smashes down at him with a knee. He misses the knee as the Sukayishiru alters into shadow and rolls away.

They stand up to face each other and Synite squares up to him as no other being has done before. He surrounds his fists and feet with electric energy from Gale, knowing his enemy would be unable to avoid it by being a full shadow, and goes forward quickly.

Lone sees the one with the club and mace put the handles of his weapons in his hands and the chain behind him so he aims the bazooka at him and fires the one-shot missile. The Sukayishiru captain shoots a fierce round of sonic waves and blasts that set off the missile then throws the percussion of the explosion straight up as to not distract the motions of the fight ahead. *So, she's back there for defense and a wider point of view,* Synite continues to compile information.

"Well that was unfair!" Lone does not hesitate to meet the club and mace in the middle of the pillars though. He recovered his speed and dexterity in his time away from battle and shows it very well with how he dodges the swinging mace and pounding club.

Synite forces his opponent to dodge his attacks as much as he has to dodge the Sukayishiru's razor sharp blade. He throws orbs and drops bolts of lightning as part of his combinations of electrically charged punches and kicks. The claymore is such a large sword that he has to step back from the roundhouse swings that he cannot jump over or avoid to the side. He comes down on Synite with the claymore but the elementalist spins a wind wall to stop it. It twists the blade around and tosses it up but its owner turns into a shadow and glides over to catch it in midair. Synite meets him where he caught the claymore with a barrage of ion orbs and hits him with a few even while his body is in its shadow mode.

'Moreeeee! Moreeeee!' Thesia craves the violence and Synite embraces her encouragement. He dashes quickly over to the Sukayishiru and combines the electric hand with a Rock Fist that bangs against his armor. Synite is close enough to hear him breathe and he takes advantage of that by grabbing at Synite and catching his cape, spreading the shadow over it. Synite quickly unclips the robe and tosses it to the side; it floats away as a waving shadow to never be handled by human hands again. *Something new! He can do it to himself and by touch. Fine with me.*

He swings the claymore down heavily at Synite who rolls away from it to the left then drops a lightning bolt down that misses by mere centimeters. Being that close to the bolt still hurts the warrior from both the heat and the sound. He stabs the ground below Synite, still not quite fast enough with the sword to trip Synite up.

There is a sudden sonic boom and then the sound of a metal clang from where NanVash is fighting. Synite and Lone hear the hit before they see the aftermath of him rolling and skipping across the sand, his wings wrapping him like a corn husk. Before Synite can make enough space, the hammer is coming at him much faster than when they separated. *So his strength keeps going up the longer he fights.*

Synite, not invulnerable, goes to the air and two Sukayishiru come after him: first the one with the claymore jumps onto the hammer and gets catapulted and the one with the hammer jumps high, taking advantage of the overall strength increase. They both get good swings in and Synite has to put up four wind walls to break the swing of the hammer enough to where it does not break him. It does connect well enough to knock him down, but he catches himself and lands on his hands and feet.

When they land, NanVash is back up and throws a shoulder into the Sukayishiru with the claymore and keeps charging towards the captain. She blasts sonic waves into the ground to throw sand in his face but he blocks it with his left wing. She then aims the waves at him and it slows him down dramatically but does not stop him. He pushes through and, sees the next problem coming out of the corner of his eye. "Shit." NanVash is met again with the strong swing of that hammer, bouncing him off a pillar.

Lone is having major difficulty finding an opening against the Sukayishiru with the club and mace. Many of his swings are in circular patterns, either swinging his body around or swinging the weapons by their chain. He also changes the angles at which he is throwing these weapons around, leaving him no chance at predicting their actions. "They seem to be too dumb to have much of a direct plan!"

"Don't underestimate," Synite had landed close enough to him to talk, echoing what Psilos probably would have said. "They are trained to do something. Whether they are doing it or not, well, I haven't figured that out yet." 'Knowleeeedgeeee shall preeeevail!'

NanVash rolls over by them, shaking off the latest smack, rattling his wings to get the dust and stress off. He folds them back and kneels next to Synite, looking up to the captain. "This guy gets stronger the more he swings that thing."

"I noticed that," Synite notes. "We don't know where his cap is. We'll get to it eventually, right?"

"Either his or mine," NanVash stretches, ready to take a few more hits. "You doing okay with the shadow guy, ri--" All three of the male Sukayishiru walk close to a pillar by them and melt into the shadows. "What in the world?"

"They disappeared!" Lone looks around frantically for the slightest sign of them.

So, that's another power of theirs, Synite thinks and instinctively grabs NanVash and Lone's wrists. He pulls them away from the pillars as quickly as he can, narrowly avoiding the slash of a claymore, the swing of a giant hammer, and the crush of a club and mace. All three of them were standing in a different part of the shadows for the pillars. There are so many lights over the field of the Sword that the shadows form in several different directions around the objects and their bodies. "These guys have the upper hand on us in this place. The best way for us to even things up is to learn. Stick with the guy you've had no matter how they attack us and we'll eventually figure out a weakness."

The Sukayishiru jump between the shadows, dunking into them like pools of black water that do not splash. The shadows seem too small for the warriors and their weapons to fit completely into, especially the giant hammer, but that is one of the advantages of their natural ability to travel through darkness. They confuse Lone thoroughly with the dance as he backs away from the pillars as far as he can.

It gets quiet while the Sukayishiru are below. Their captain remains still, not waiting on anything except the demise of one of her team members or a reason to defend herself. Fabric continues his spy on her and the well-being of the rest of the team as they get in what they think is a safe distance away from the shadows below the pillars.

Cloud coverage creeps up behind Fabric, moving at a decent speed as the wind dips through the arena. Fabric sees the clouds' shadows pass him and looks around, wondering what is causing it. He finally looks up,

"Synite! The clouds!"

Synite turns back and looks where Fabric is pointing, the distance between the cloud shadows and the pillars closing rapidly. *There isn't enough time for me to push them back!*

'If you had meeee heeeeelping you, weeee would haveeee seeeeeen this long ago!' Thesia tries to convince him further. *Not now!*

Synite wonders whether it is worth flying up now to push the clouds away and has a better idea. "Everybody stay on your guard," he thinks of a few routes he can go but knows that being decisive instead of hesitating is one of the most important things in battle.

Lone and NanVash see the shadows come closer as well, realizing the handicap they are going to have momentarily. Lone shakes his leg as he prepares to move as quickly as he physically can to dodge whatever is coming. The tension in Fabric's shoulders rises as the clouds cover the pillars and half of the arena becomes the shadowy playground of their opponents.

From the Sukayishiru's point of view, the surface resembles a shaded glass ceiling with the texture of the sand the shadow is covering. They can see everything and hear everything as if they were standing a few meters away though they are basically in an entirely different dimension from everyone above. Down there, their movements from place to place are nearly instantaneous, at the speed of Dark (which is slower than the speed of light by an infinitesimally small amount). They can see the topography the same way one would if they were looking down at the land and their depth perception is enhanced by their marriage to the shadows.

It seems to the Vanguard that the loudest things in the arena right now are their own heartbeats. Synite cannot feel any of their movements through the shadows as nothing is actually displacing the Air around them until one of the pops up, "Behind you!"

Both Lone and NanVash turn around to nothing. Fabric turns to make sure it was not him that Synite was yelling for, which would be perfect, sarcastically. Synite was not crying wolf, however; they actually did come up for a brief moment to put their opponents on their heels.

One of them flies by Lone and knocks him down then another comes under him with a heavy uppercut that sends him up. Synite flies over and catches him as the claymore waves under them. "It would've chopped me in half, huh?"

"Now isn't the time to think about that," Synite puts a wind wall down for him to stand on, furthering his idea to defend this attack. "NanVash, you're on your own for an ein!"

"I can handle it!" he yells back, dodging a swing of the giant hammer that looks the same as a falling tree to Synite. He dodges several swings from the mace as well, bouncing and gliding from place to place like a child playing on the sidewalk. Lone looks over the edge and back up at Synite, not understanding what could possibly fix this situation.

Synite puts a box of wind walls with the bottom opened in the middle of the pillars then flies up into the clouds. Lone sees lightning flash out of the corner of his eye, the boom of thunder shaking the entire arena. NanVash resorts to flying in an erratic path to keep the enemies off and still has to dodge. "They're too fast!"

Hold on a little longer, Synite concentrates as hard as he can to get a hold of the lining of the clouds. They start to swirl and compress, their coverage shrinking as they do. The shadow shrinks from the outside in, closing faster than it spread initially.

Below, the Sukayishiru notice the shadow closing fast and dart out, the one with the claymore jumping out above the pillars. The other two are not as resolute, one hitting the surface where Synite decides to split the cloud up. He goes back down next to the one holding the hammer, put in an unfortunate situation as they both pop up right into Synite's wind wall trap. He closes it tighter and completely dissipates the cloud coverage. They push against every surface of the wind box but not before Synite sends several powerful bolts of lightning through the top. They penetrate the wind and zap the trapped Sukayishiru, electricity bouncing around the box like lottery balls.

Far, far away from all of the fighting, Spoilsport turns on his computer bar as a waitress brings him coffee. "Anything else I can get for you right now, sweetie?" Not many restaurants on any Earth outside of Prime still use living beings for the wait and kitchen staff as opposed to projections or computer programs tied into the tables. This is one of less than ten on Earth 11 and a spot that Spoilsport frequents when he wants to taste food that somebody actually had a hand in making.

"Nope," he usually skips the pleasantries but, since she's human, "thanks. Well, actually," he stops her from going away, attracting her with his smile and eye contact, "never mind."

She smiles back, "Are you sure, honey? I can get you anything."

"Call me Vincent," he says and looks at her nametag, "and I know your name isn't Herbert so, what should I call you?"

She smiles wryly, "Sara."

Spoilsport's stomach immediately goes from the ceiling to the floor, "I prefer Herbert!" He calibrates the lights from the computer bar to his position and the lights project the screen onto his contacts. He pulls his hacking programs back up as he monitors the position of the Caracalla relative to his other troops and the system line.

First thing's first, he logs into the Atlan security systems with a set of authentications that he got from one of the lead attendees he threatened.

It works perfectly, as he had no doubt it would, and lets him into the first level of security databases. He filters through and uses some mid-level hacking skills to move past several passcode gates at once.

He makes it to level 19 before things get a bit more complicated, considering the Enslaver is the only one who can override through level 20. After about a half hecu of searching, he finds a backdoor into the one part of the security systems he needs to get in: the silent alarms, more specifically, the ones that trigger the automatons. He plugs in a "change in protocols" virus that not only blocks the automatons from answering Its silent alarms but it actually shuts down all of the automatons completely if the alarm is sent directly from the Enslaver's hand, which is exactly what they are anticipating.

Next, he moves into some light registration research to find the best place to enter phase two of his hack. Once an unregistered ship approaches a solar system with an Earth planet in the system, the authorities dock with and search the ship then scan thumbs of all passengers. Or, if the ship is registered already, they are able to move through the initial scan of the exterior of the ship without stopping.

After about a liter of caffeinated beverages, two trips to the potty and another hecu of plugging away, Spoilsport digs into the Enslaver's private code server. "Herbert!" She comes running, from behind the counter and he raises a hand at her. "What I did on this computer a sec ago deserves an award. Can I get the sweetest baked thing you have back there please?"

"Yes sir, Mr. Vincent!" she gives him a high-five.

He snaps, "Matter of fact, go ahead and make it two. It's time to celebrate!"

"What are we celebrating?" she puts a hand on her hip.

"Well," he thinks about lying to her and changes his mind, "I hacked into the most secure server on the planet. I'm about to shut down the automatic defense systems and drop some codes in so some bandits can come down and start a revolution!"

She does not believe a word of it but, "Great job! Woohoo!"

He starts to type the codes in and dance in his seat. "And, you know, it's not so much that I care about the revolution or the guys doing the work," he thinks. "I just love to steal big things!"

"I see," Sara is still skeptical. "What else have you stolen?"

"What time do you get off work? Because we'll be here all day talking about the stuff I've stolen," Spoilsport takes nearly any opportunity to toot his own horn.

She blushes, "I'll be off in about 45 eins. You gonna steal me, too?"

He thinks about the events of the past few days, his teleporting and, outside of his hatred for being an employee, Sarah being the reason for most of his involvement. "It wouldn't be stealing if you came willingly. So, maybe next time, when you least expect it."

CHAPTER XXI

The groups of civilians run away as Psilos stands strong behind Suubai, Coldsmoke and Orchanik G at the gate to the Sword. The four Blood and Gold armored Sukayishiru march slowly towards them in the distance, their backs to the gate, ruthlessly cutting down any being that is between them and their target. The one with the morningstar stands back, though he is not the captain. The one with the shortsword stops some five meters in front of him as the other two continue their approach.

The captain is on the front line of this group, bearing her long, ruby sickle with its gold-adorned hilt and handle. The determination in her walk is greatly fearsome to the regular being. Her hunched over mate, holding a flail with three long chains that he drags across the street, his steps different but striking the same impression. She is the epitome of dangerous control and he is the one whose anger runs wild to frighten even his own comrades.

The owner of the shortsword raises it in the air and with it blasts a chain of small explosions, enough to throw rock from the ground into the sky. Pieces of the wall surrounding the gate avalanche down on the beings below. Their screams prompt Suubai to throw force fields above them so the rock rolls towards the Sukayishiru responsible for them.

The one nearest the gate knocks away the falling rock with his morningstar, shattering them with little effort. He throws explosions in the Vanguard group's direction, splitting them up and shaking whatever possible formation they may have had. These explosions are smaller and meant to push them in a particular direction and then end with a larger explosion at the end of that path.

Suubai puts a force field around himself to protect from the impact and the burning as Orchanik G elongates herself to avoid the trouble.

Coldsmoke dodges the explosive trains as Psilos runs right through them, barely affected by their power. He goes for the Sukayishiru that is controlling these pyrotechnics but is met by a flying punch by the captain, which he manages to block, and a flying slash by the feral Sukayishiru, which he pushes away.

They double team him, swinging their weapons one after the other, the captain's sickle coming at him in a more direct pattern and the feral flail swinging in no sort of planned fashion at all. They are good enough to not hit each other's weapons but not good enough to hit their target. Psilos, as humongous as he is, uses his elite speed and intellect to his advantage, seemingly always a step ahead. He pushes the captain out of the way and kicks the other Sukayishiru into a neighboring building.

The pyrotechnic grasps his shortsword in his left hand and points it in Coldsmoke's direction but he rolls out of the way of the brilliant explosion sent for him. The Sukayishiru is using a bit more force with these new explosions, trying to cause some physical damage to his opponents. He knocks Suubai around behind his force shield, pushing him through sections of the battleground but not truly hurting him. Orchanik backs him up and reaches for the sword. Its owner switches hands and slashes at her lanky arm, nearly cutting it off at the wrist. She thought it may not have been as sharp as a normal sword considering its current use but the blade is still a blade.

Orchanik grabs hold of a large rock near the pyrotechnic Sukayishiru and pulls herself towards the enemy. She slingshots at their foe but misses her attempt at a drop kick. Suubai dashes in providing assistance by throwing a nice haymaker across the Sukayishiru's face but it is not enough to knock him out. He has very little hand-to-hand fight training but he has a much stronger punch than one would assume by his slim frame.

The Sukayishiru goes to strike with the sword but Orchanik grabs his arm and stops it mid-swing. She pulls them closer together and the two of them attack the Sukayishiru as a team. The enemy shows mastery with his swordsmanship, flipping it around with practiced ease. Suubai puts up shields to protect Orchanik from being sliced and Orchanik yanks Suubai out of the way of the edge. He gets Suubai in the stomach with the handle of the sword and Orchanik catches his teammate from falling down.

The swordsman takes advantage of the distraction and punches Orchanik in the back with his free, gauntlet hand. That pushes the vanguard out of a normal length arm's reach and gives him enough time to back away. Suubai has to look up as the Sukayishiru switches his sword to the other hand. "Move!"

Orchanik stretches her legs and jumps high over the explosion that comes under him. *So, as I assumed,* Suubai figures quickly, *he fights with the sword in his right and blows stuff up with it in his left, the hand with the gauntlet on it. He never would've switched hands if it wasn't for a reason.* The opponent twists and points his attention at Suubai who is already running at him.

Dashing in the opposite direction, Psilos overpowers the captain as her hands are pushing against his, completely covered and being squeezed by the Prophyrian's massive palms. He forces her arms apart but she hops, nearly breaking her shoulder, and kicks one of her hands loose. She uses that hand against Psilos's other arm so he decides to throw her into the opposite building.

Once she gets close to the building, she melts into its shadow and travels through it, coming up perfectly at the end of it. Standing at the shadow's edge, the Sukayishiru captain stares Psilos down and, before he knows it, the feral one is coming at him straight from the rubble of the other building. He swings wildly across Psilos's back and then hides in his shadow. Psilos swings around at him but he is not there until Psilos's shadow is at his back again. Then he comes out of the shadow and slashes Psilos a few times on his way up and back on his way down into the shadow.

The next time, however, Psilos does a complete turn and knocks the feral Sukayishiru all the way to by the one with the morningstar. The captain comes next to them and the one with the shortsword gets in their formation again as well. He points it and a chain of large explosions rocks the buildings and the civilians in them. They start to evacuate as quickly as they can but have to climb down piles of rubble to get back into the street.

After the rocks stop falling and the chain of explosions ends, the Sukayishiru continues swinging his morningstar horizontally overhead. It progressively gets faster as his swing gets tighter and tighter, the whirl quickly catching Psilos's attention. The circle of red above the Sukayishiru gets darker as he swings the spiked ball faster. That flat cylinder goes completely black and, with that change, the darkness spreads over the area. An impossibly dark sphere covers that entrance all the way to a few centimeters in front of Coldsmoke.

They marvel at the size and depth of that dark sphere. "Wait," Suubai steps forward bravely, so he thinks, and carefully puts his hand into the dark, pulling it back quickly after absolutely nothing happens. He then steps into the dark, disappearing from all three of their sights for what seemed like forever to Orchanik, though it was less than an ein. He emerges unharmed having never stepped more than a meter into the orb of black. "It didn't hurt or anything," Suubai reports, "you just can't see past your own nose."

The civilians run away from the darkness although the chains of the flail catch one of them and pull them back in. They scream in horror and pain after being wrapped in cold metal and dragged into true darkness, both in the visual and spiritual sense. That person would not come forward from the blackest of black spheres ever again.

Psilos sees this, and the brutality against the other civilians, as enough motivation to end those responsible, as if he needed much more. "If you have the ability to do so, join me inside this blackness so no more lives are taken unnecessarily by that heathen."

"You can see through that dark?" Suubai is only slightly surprised, more enamored than anything else.

"I am, once inside a dark place after my eyes are given time to adjust to it," Psilos tells them. "I cannot see through it but once I am inside, everything will be clear to me. My skill is in adaptation and taking advantage of even the tiniest glimmer of light."

"Why wouldn't they fight us first? What are they trying to do?" Orchanik raises as Psilos steps around him.

"Wouldn't you prefer t'fight in th'most advantageous environment for you, too?" Coldsmoke pulls his gloves off. "I'm going in with you, Psilos. I can sense their position well enough t'not need my sight."

"Our odds of winning have increased exponentially with your company," Psilos closes his eyes and his feet start to glow lightly. His internally generated luminescence, as opposed to incandescence which comes with heat, climbs up his legs and lights his entire body. The light is swallowed as he enters and it does not penetrate past the edge of the dark sphere. "Suubai and Orchanik, please provide support for the civilians," he says from inside, "until we rid the area of this darkness."

Coldsmoke stretches and bounces around to warm himself up then runs into the darkness, inhaled by the pitch black orb. He had never experienced such darkness before as, even in sleep, his brain is still stimulated by something. Here, in this the truest dark, a deep and unnatural black, there is absolutely nothing. His other senses are therefore heightened and his Will assists him in feeling where things are in the dark. He quickly feels Psilos as he is hard to miss, the Sukayishiru captain who still approaches their position steadily and one holding innocent captives in the chains of his flail.

Coldsmoke runs up next to Psilos, "We have t'assume they can see everything in this."

"Correct," Psilos affirms, "otherwise they would never have created it. This dark orb is abnormal and, in all likelihood, feels similar to home to them, from what I have gathered of their abilities in the past. They have trained vigorously for this moment for much of their time under the Enslaver. This is their execution of that preparation and it is our job to disrupt it so much that they cannot adapt. That is when we win."

"Your communication is immaculate," Coldsmoke had never

fought beside a king before. This may be one of his most fond memories when he is allowed enough time to reminisce.

"Thanks are in order but not for me, for those who taught me," Psilos sees the two Sukayishiru coming in their direction. The captain keeps her pace and other has lodged his weapon into the ground and is crawling towards them. "Are you ready?"

Coldsmoke has already dashed towards the captain and she has readied herself, the gauntlet hand out front and the sickle locked behind her, ready to slash. She sees that Coldsmoke is unarmed and swings the sickle in front of her. He lurches forward, Psilos watching the punch thrown directly towards the captain's mask.

Not only does she dodge it but she gets a nice swing in as well. Coldsmoke adjusts his punch after she throws hers, getting much closer to her face than she thought he would be able to considering how fast he was moving. To him, though, everything is in slow motion now. His adjustment moves her enough to where she has to try her hardest to move away from the punch, aborting her own.

She stumbles past Coldsmoke but makes sure to swing her sickle in his direction on her way by. He steps back fast enough for it to miss and goes at her back. He aims his warpath lariat at the back of her head and she spins away, creating space between them from the slashing sickle.

The feral Sukayishiru on all fours quickens his pace towards Psilos. He jumps through the black and Psilos meets him in the black air, forcing a sonic boom to go off behind him from his powerful speed. The boom takes everyone around off guard and they either duck or gasp in preparation of another, larger explosion. This boom is all bark and no bite though, still impressive to Orchanik and Suubai.

Psilos meets the feral Sukayishiru with a palm to his chest that knocks every bit of wind out of him first. Then, Psilos passes directly through him as he dissipates into a cloud of red and gold. He reintegrates on the ground below Psilos who is now aware of the real reason for the black orb. "As long as we are under the cloak of this darkness, they cannot actually be harmed," he yells over to Coldsmoke. "We may be able to hit them, which is why she is evading your attack. However, even if you do, they can mold themselves into the shadow and out of the way of danger."

Coldsmoke faces up with the captain and, faster than he can move, she is behind him, reaching for his arm.

Elementalists are, by definition, beings that have an affinity for and control over the forces of nature and can manipulate them with their power of Will. The same as any other aspect of life, there are some who are born with higher capacities of Will and therefore higher ceilings for their power in whatever force the elementalist can use.

In elementalist conservatories, like in any other system, there are rankings by tests and proving grounds for their abilities. Some work extremely hard to become advanced, some are born with extreme talent, some are extremely average and some have a talented Will to work hard. They use their Will to control many types of forces of nature, physical, theoretical, emotional and the full gambit of energies that encompass the octadecaverse. Some even specialize in ability sets of an element (i.e. Lord Qor, an Earth elementalist who specialized in manipulating seismic energies to such a degree that he could channel that energy into creating physical constructs of pure force).

These energies can be used for offensive and defensive means, to destroy, create and manipulate anything. At their highest levels, some elementalists could be misconstrued as gods, as most cultures attach godliness with perfection and powerfulness as opposed to true love, omnipotence and omniscience. Regardless, these mortal powers are used, in most modern cases, to fight or control society.

In a smaller scope, however, in a one-on-one battle for instance, elementalists are generally immune to any attacks or defenses that include their element and/or specialty of choice in their base element or power. One of the requirements for this immunity is advancement, of course. Once an elementalist is in tune with their power to a high enough degree, after working at it for some time or having the talent to surpass the work, they can repel its strength and force if it is less than or equal to their own. If it is low enough, this ability to repel can be used with the same ease as swatting a slow moving insect.

This concept goes the same for every elementalist in every sphere: a weaker concentration of their own type of power cannot harm them unless it is channeled through another medium. For instance, dealing with the simplest Primal forces, two Air elementalists with equal levels of Will using blasts of wind stand still in front of each other. Two flames of the same intensity from similarly Willed Fire elementalists flow through each other and do not harm the elementalists that are the sources of the flames. If a Water elementalist tries to drown another Water elementalist, it does not work unless they have a higher Will and control of the crushing weight of deep waters. Even then, it is not drowning that hurts, it is the pressure of the force pushing in from every direction.

Though actually having exactly equal levels of Will is nearly impossible, some can get close enough to where they seem equal enough. The only way to tell the slight difference would be, in the example of the flames, to ask the elementalists which one of them actually felt a little warmth from the other's fire. Or, in the example of the Air elementalists, whichever one budges slightly from the push of the wind.

On the other end, if wind picks up an object and throws it towards an Air elementalist, they are not immune. If a wave picks up poisonous pathogens, the Water elementalist is not immune; they must purify the liquid the same as anyone else. If a rock is melted and turned into lava, the Earth elementalist is not protected from the extreme heat or burning of the lava unless they specialize in such. Fire elementalists are impervious to the flame itself but not the heat once it is transferred, absorbed and pushed out by another substance.

Things get more complex when elementalists start to branch off from the general powers and specify in certain things. With the example of the Water elementalist that specifies in crushing depth forces, the only thing that comes into play is the Will to live. The defensive abilities of the being in the predicament are more important than exactly what element they control. An Earth elementalist that cannot breathe under water could survive that trap if they have the technical skill and Will to either escape or somehow harm the source of the power enough to break their Will. This is where work and experience more often than not trumps talent.

Things get even more complex when dealing with other spheres of elementalism, those that do not necessarily deal with manipulating forces than can be seen, physically felt or heard. Competing forces such as Order and Chaos, Matter and the Void, pure Will power and Energy manipulation are all forces of elementalism, just in different spheres of power. They combat similarly to the Primal sphere's poles only not as obviously, quickly or certainly. A Chaos elementalist is unbothered by levels of chaos below their own but an Order elementalist's Will naturally fights Chaos at every turn.

Then, there are exceptions, such as the Stars of each element. The Earth elementalist Stars are the top five most powerful beings in the Earth pole of the Primal sphere. This handful of beings has such powerful Wills that they are head and shoulders over every other elementalist, period. They are both talented and hardworking, have perfected offensive, defensive and manipulation skills of their element, and are to the point where they are considered artists. They begin to create new techniques and new ways of manipulating their particular pole.

The Star level is something that goes progressively higher, like technology or athletics, as new precedents are created. The first Air elementalist to manipulate weather and energies that Synite can do easily was considered a genius in their time but would barely be considered above average now. Synite has only come in contact with two elementalist Stars in his lifetime, neither of which has he battled, both of which would be able to defeat him fairly easily at the level he is currently.

And, as difficult as it may be to conceptualize or believe, there is indeed something beyond the elementalist Star level.

 # CHAPTER XXII

Castra, Lo, Gith and Arra, after making a similar, you-won't-take-us-alive type of statement with some added humor, face up with the four Sukayishiru wearing black and onyx armor, the fountain in the middle of the street between them. Only the one with the battle axe steps forward, stopping after a few meters. He looks back at his captain, the female with the whip, and she nods.

Out of nowhere, his muscles pop and expand, his arms and legs get longer, his armor stretches and head swells to fit his new dimensions. His cloak and axe get bigger and longer as well, its black blades spreading like a butterfly's wings. His new girth shakes the ground as he has to keep resetting his feet, knocking everything down that is not bolted to the floor inside the surrounding buildings. As he leans against them to stabilize, he breaks windows and caves in walls causing sections of concrete and glass to tumble to the surface. At the end of the growth, the Sukayishiru has gone from two to fifty meters tall. These members of the Vanguard know now that this is going to be more than a regular fight; this is war.

After growing that quickly, he is out of breath and on one knee. The giant labors to breathe but, soon, looks up and gathers himself. He stands up slowly, stretches aggressively and flexes at the vermin below him.

"Y'all ready?" Lo seems to be licking the relish from his chops, ready to take a crack at the big guy. "I'm ready. Let's go!" He rushes towards the mountain of a man and is nearly cut down by the axe that swings pendulum-style centimeters in front of him at a speed that neither of them would have assumed that large of a being would be capable of handling. He is moving slower in comparison to when he was normal height but covering more ground faster than he would have considering his increase in strength as well.

Castra runs and tackles Lo, thinking he would be in time to push him out of the way of the next swing but there was no second one. "Get the hell off me!" Lo wriggles away.

"I thought he was going to swing again! My fault," Castra gets up and stretches. Before they can brush the dust from their pants, the Sukayishiru captain with the whip and the man with the falchion appear in front of them, apparently having teleported there. They do not attack though; they spread out past the giant's feet.

Before they can get too far apart, he grows more, now up to seventy-two meters, thirty-six times normal height, strength and weight. He drops the pole end of the enlarged battle axe down as he adjusts to balancing and nearly crushes the Sukayishiru captain but she somehow avoids it. His every breath, every shuffle of his feet sends waves comparable to an earthquake's aftershock through the earth.

The team looks on in amazement but Castra keeps his eye on the other enemies, "Here they come!"

The giant picks up his foot and kicks over Lo, apparently not even meaning to make contact with him. However, the captain moves attached to the shadow of his foot and charges Lo with her shoulder, knocking the wind out of him. She melts back into the shadow as the huge foot swings back to its original spot, Castra rolling out of the way of the captain's kick that was meant for his back.

The giant stomps his foot down, or what seems like a stomp to everybody except him, his heel cracking the street. He leans over a bit and his shadow covers nearly everything in front of him. "Everybody get out of the shadow!" Castra runs over to pick Lo up and the others run into the light, having to look up to see how the giant is moving because the shadow moves with him.

Gith gets tripped by a hand that reaches from the shadow before he is able to get into the light. He staggers, out of control, and is covered in shadow. Arra fires a brilliant stream of her emerald blaze over his head, casting a bright light over him and limiting the Sukayishiru movement through the shadow. "Stay with me!" He gets up and runs under her fire and past the top of the giant's shadow.

The captain still ends up behind them, beyond the edge of the shadow, and swings for Gith's head. He waves a wall of mud across his body, parrying the punch. He has enough time to actually dodge the next swings and attempt to get a few in of his own. Then he pushes a wave of mud in her direction but she disappears under it, apparently dropping into its shadow, and comes up next to the giant's foot.

"She's quick," Arra comes up next to him and turns to face the giant again.

Lo regains control of his breathing and Castra gives him a hard pat on the back, "Get in the game, Lo!"

"Shut up!" he wheezes back. "There's no way I could've seen her coming!" A pile of rocks that fell from the building flies at them and Lo dives backwards to dodge, the Sukayishiru captain coming up from their shadows and slamming Castra into the ground. She dips back in next to her teammate and he telekinetically throws rocks at them. "See?"

Castra coughs and brushes himself off as he gets up, "Touché, my friend."

A big column from the building next to Arra and Gith comes in their direction but she turns it to ash before it reaches them. The ash cloud never gets close enough for the captain to travel through its shadow but the giant steps forward, his shadow getting nearer to their line. "If only they couldn't hit us in the light," Gith shrugs. More rock and glass shoot in their direction and Gith raises a wall of dirt that protects them. The telekinetic Sukayishiru kicks through it and swings his gleaming black blade at Arra. She pushes him back with dazzling fireballs the size of trucks then Gith sweeps him with a low wave of mud.

"Something else is happening!" Arra yells forward. They see the Sukayishiru with the big shield jump over the fountain and come down between the giant's legs, cracking the ground with the bottom of the shield. From that point, more rifts spread in every direction through the street. The larger split goes directly between the giant's legs and branches out. Arra and Gith get separated as the ground buckles and divorces under them, Arra having to roll out of the way and Gith jumping after nearly getting swallowed below. Another crack ruptures in Lo and Castra's direction, Lo able to tackle Castra as he grabs the tiny disc on his shoulder that expands into the polar bear shield. They come down onto an ice bridge that slides them away from the opening ground.

"Whew," Lo pushes Castra off. "And no, I'm not apologizing so don't even look over here!"

"Sometimes an apology can be the best lie to tell, Lo!" Castra bursts into laughter while sitting on the ice.

Lo is confused about the laughter as nothing has been comedic to him besides the sound of Castra hitting the ground, "What's so funny?"

"I said 'my fault' and then the ground opened up! The same as a fault! Get it?" He stops laughing at the bad joke as he tries to stand up but slips and falls right back down.

"You can do better!" Gith yells over.

"Thanks for not making me teleport us," Castra gets up and tries to get his footing again, unsuccessfully. "I guess that was your revenge for me tackling you for nothing, right?" He crawls off the ice and back onto dry ground.

He and Lo face the Sukayishiru with the whip, the captain of this team. She lets the whip down and raises her hand; Castra does not see her start the motion but Lo does. He tucks, rolls towards Castra and pulls out his knife; it stretches and roars into the black lion sword. Castra sees him rolling and looks over at the whip coming for him at a blinding speed, his hands out in front of his scrunched up face.

Lo swings the roaring sword up and it catches the whip right in front of Castra's hands, wrapping it around the blade and saving Castra's head from getting sliced in half by the sharp tip. She snatches the whip back and the sword gets thrown into the side of a building.

Castra gets to exhale finally and slaps himself on the forehead, "Damn I'm glad you were paying attention! You saved me twice!"

"Stop talking and fight!" Lo grabs the kunai from his waistband and it stretches into the hydra spear.

Castra cocks his automatic rifle and aims it at the captain, "Locked and--"

"Shut up and shoot!" Lo yells and Castra follows directions, purposely taking a backseat to the new leader of the Atlan team since he knows better about Gith and Arra's new abilities. He opens fire and she runs in the opposite direction of the giant foot behind her.

Near his other foot, Arra and Gith are split by the crack in the ground, the Sukayishiru with the falchion standing across from Arra. "We need to defeat them as fast as possible," Gith yells over to her. So she starts a spark in her hand and gathers a ball of her green flames in front of her. She puts her hands to her sides and the flame splits into two parts of equal sizes with her hands.

The Sukayishiru points the falchion at Arra and lets it go. It floats from where he released it, perfectly still, and he pounds his gloved fist into the palm of his gauntlet. The falchion darts towards Arra's heart; she parries it with a blast of flame from her hand. It shoots off looking similar to a string of emeralds being thrown into the sky and pushes the flying sword off its path enough for her not to get cut.

It comes back around and she blasts it again and again, heating the entire weapon up to a tremendously high temperature. Of course, her own flame cannot melt her, nor will any other flame, with that being her natural element. However, a scorching hot blade still hurts more and cuts cleaner than a cold one.

A few of the explosive bullets hit the giant's boot as Castra fires after the captain. They explode and do little to no damage. He quickly twists his foot to shake off the hits, still amazing the Vanguard that he can move at regular speed being so large.

Lo aims from the direction the captain is running in and blasts three jets of high-pressure water. The bullets and water are converging on her and she teleports into the air above them both as they cross paths. When she drops back down, Castra runs out of ammunition but she still has to duck under Lo's jets as he comes back across.

"We can get her if we work together!" Castra stands next to Lo, reloading. He looks over at the sword jutting from the building, "Kinda might need that at some point, right?"

"Might," Lo grunts.

"Especially for the ill-mannered frivolity we are about to partake in," Castra grins and cocks his weapon.

Lo double-takes in Castra's direction, "Where the hell did you learn that phrase?"

"I've read a few books in my lifetime," and by few he literally means three or four.

As Castra aims, Lo looks up at the giant, "So, if we're double on her, who's going after him?"

"Behind you!" Lo yells, the huge axe swinging to split Castra down the middle. Castra immediately rolls to his right and hops back to his feet, the blade nearly shaving the toe of one of his boots. He runs towards the giant Sukayishiru, gun firing with little damage done. It is more annoying to the behemoth than painful.

The axe comes again and he jukes it then has to baseball slide out of the way of the next swing. The Sukayishiru captain with the whip pops in front of him but is blasted by a stream of ice from Lo's spear. "Keep going!" Castra runs by her and a giant foot casts a comparably large shadow over him. He drops the rifle and raises both of his hands, glowing orange, hooping as he is to be stomped.

In a cloud of orange dust, the giant foot crashes through the surface of shallow water of the rocky beach. He trips, dropping his axe on the beach and it clangs against the shelf of volcanic rock. He goes down to a kneel, unaware of why his knee is dropping into a pool of water and not the street. He looks around, immediately aware of where he is but not fully sure why. He does not waste time thinking but grabs his weapon and runs back towards the war.

Back in the street, there is only a light zephyr where the giant Sukayishiru was stomping. Castra breathes heavily, snapped back into reality as the rifle taps the concrete below him. He drops to a kneel as well over the gun, exhausted by the teleportation he accomplished.

"Holy shit!" Lo jumps up and down, "That was impressive!"

Arra surrounds Gith and herself with a ring of fire to keep the Sukayishiru with the falchion and the objects he has been throwing at them at bay. That Sukayishiru's telekinetic power is strong enough for him to precisely control some of the large pieces of rock broken up when the ground split. The captain teleports out of her frozen shell and gets in front of Castra again.

She runs at him and Lo does the same. She takes a strong step forward and the whip unravels under her. Lo's eyes get wide, not knowing what he will be able to do to save his friend this time.

The closer Amethyst gets, the more anxious the Sa'arbaas Sate'Gran Nuvill Ometku gets as It was unaware she would not be stopped with the rest of Its enemies. The attendees and elders beseech like beggars in the market for her to stop but she trudges on. She is tempted to part the crowd of them, a female Moses from the Old Testament of the Bible but decides to save her energy and the stress that comes with it for the more necessary objectives.

It immediately calls for the automatons to come to Its side but, of course, they all shut off instead thanks to an unlikely assist. None of the Enslaver's many contingencies are working in Its favor at this point and It only has a few left.

"It's just you and me," she yells down the hall at the Enslaver, closing in on the throne. She hears It tapping the small touchpad on the armrest, almost frantically, but still nothing happens. "No one is coming to your side! Nothing else will get in my way! We have you trapped and," that button is to call the Sukayishiru to protect It but they cannot as they have all entered into battle with the Vanguard, "and the reckoning of history's revenge has come!"

The attendees begin to wail, fearing what she is going to do to their master, Its anxiety passed on to the underlings. They bunch up around her but she keeps wading through them, their crowding only delaying the inevitable crash.

Before she knows it, a large halberd is swinging at her head and she has to bend backwards to not get decapitated. Four head automatons storm into the room, pushing the attendees to the side and fiercely entering battle with Amethyst.

I thought he shut the automatons down, she recalls Spoilsport reporting he had taken care of that. She notices that none of the regular automatons showed up to defend, which is all he actually promised. *Either he didn't know, was careless, or knew this and neglected to warn us. Regardless,* she catches one of the charged halberds in her left hand and punches through it with her right, snapping it in half.

Amethyst takes the other half and darts it into the head of one of the other automatons. Two more come into the fight, leaving five for her to destroy now, their metal shining from the dim lights. They try to surround her but she zips through a gap in between them and forces the entire group to come at her head on which would put any platoon, autonomous or not, at an extreme disadvantage (though matching up against Amethyst in general puts the great majority of beings at a disadvantage).

As now seven head automatons skate towards her, she runs through the first one, ripping through its chest with a single charge. The other six overshoot as she continues by them and turns to mount the one farthest back at its shoulders. She perches atop it as it reaches for her head. She grabs its hand, rips it off at the wrist and then jumps off using so much force that it crushes that automaton. Then, she throws the hand at the one farthest away from her, splitting it in half at the waist.

Back to four, and they all come at her at the same time, slashing and stabbing for her life. The Enslaver both stubbornly and smartly refuses to run away because this event in its entirety belongs to Its supremacy and running from her will not save anyone in this hall, only finishing her shall stop the wrath.

She makes an exhibition out of dodging all four of those blades without getting the slightest nick or scratch. There are several times when they swing in such a sequence that it looks impossible that she could have dodged all of them but she most definitely does. They only barely graze her dress once and that infuriated her enough to crush all four of them at the same time immediately after she hears the rip. "I love this dress!"

Her back to the Enslaver, all she does is snap her fingers and the quartet of lead automatons are crunched into their own bodies by large purple pistons, compressing and imploding. The uneven crushing sound of destruction echoes through the hall, calling more attention to the Enslaver now that It is the only true obstacle in the room. She turns to It, the crop of attendees still standing between them though the pieces of automaton are all over the place. After watching what they assumed was impossible, one of the attendees says to Amethyst: "You can't!" Another grabs her: "Don't! Don't go any closer!" Yet another tries to hold her back: "This is wrong!"

"You wanted me back," Amethyst says to all of them. "Now that I'm here, you want me to leave?" She is meters away from the throne when the wailing turns into loud cries, sobbing and loathing words. "I don't care. This is my time!" They put hands and bodies in her way, protecting that which would sacrifice them, willing and prepared to sacrifice their bodies to preserve their master's.

She gets close enough to behold the Enslaver's body for only the second time in her life, disgusted by sight and smell but not enough to hold her back. Its long hands appear to have been exposed to UV-rays far too long with all of their spots and wrinkles. Those yellowed, flesh-covered pencils it calls fingers move quickly when motivated. Its thin, wiry arms hang from broad shoulders with a single, long scar across each of them. Its round torso is completely covered by a specially tailored armor that sustains and protects Its vital organs outside of their normal environment. It has a tube coming from an opening between Its two forked tongues, one black and one green, all three lying on a layer of fat that rolls from where Its neck would be.

The Enslavers two mouths open in opposite directions with rows upon rows of crooked teeth on opposite sides. They are situated outside of Its single breathing hole, almost a nostril except It uses it to smoke through. Ometku does not actually have a sense of smell, which is probably why It does not care in the least about how things, including Its own body, smell or taste. It has very thin slits for eyes and they move so erratically that they seem to hardly be used for sight in the same manner as most beings.

Its hair is asymmetrical across Its face, neck, head, arms, and probably the rest of Its body. There are sporadic horns on Its head: some longer and pointed, some stubs in comparison, the rest in between. The Enslaver has a curtain-like skirt covering where Its legs should be; the four lower appendages are actually long, thick tentacles with smaller tentacles at the end for balancing.

The Enslaver drops the cigar from Its nostril and it rolls down the neck fat and on to the skirt. It brushes the embers off before a fire starts and meets eyes with Amethyst. "Did you hear me?" She speaks lower since the wails of the attendees have died down. "Your time is up."

"Of course we heard you," one of the elders speaks from near the back wall, "but do you believe your own words?" Another elder attendee creeps forward, "Do you believe you have the poise, the conviction to step in my direction?" The third elder approaches her from her right, "Do you believe in yourself, my pawn queen?"

A younger male attendee steps in her face, "What are you here for? To end my life? To attempt what millions have tried to do and failed?" A female from right behind her laughs before speaking, "You, who I took in after your own people betrayed you? You abandon me and then come back to bite the hand that not only fed you but gave you reason to live?"

"Betrayed me?" that line stuck out to Amethyst the most. "Who betrayed me?"

The Enslaver laughs, much calmer than before this conversation, another elder speaking on Its behalf, "I guess you would not recall how your parents made a deal with me for your life. They gave up so much information against their own kind that I saw no reason to allow even one of them to live," Amethyst starts to figure out what the Enslaver's holistic control truly means, "except the one who wouldn't give up anything that would incriminate her home." The elder attendee has gotten close enough to where Amethyst can smell his breath. "You were the only one on that entire planet that didn't bend to my Will so I decided you should be the only one to survive!"

"That was not your decision to make," she looks down, recalling the last words her father told her and how she has lived those words since he died. *There is no such thing as perfect but you are as close to it as a father could ever wish for,* he said in shackles as an automaton dragged them apart. *No matter what happens to us, we do not regret anything we have done especially since we created you!* "There is nothing that any of you can say or do to stop me from this," she keeps pace through the crowd, still coming to the realization of how deep the Enslaver's control is over the beings that run every station of the Sword.

"You'll stop yourself. I don't have to do a thing!" Every attendee in the room laughs hysterically. Amethyst picks one up by its throat but he tries to keep cackling through her chokehold and the rest continue the laughter. Everyone stops dry at the same time and the one she chokes squeezes out these words: "You do not truly desire to win here, Amethyst. Your longing to see my end is faint and fleeting. You think my control over them is powerful? It has nothing on the control I have over you!"

He looks down with a grin at the bracelet on the forearm directly below the hand she holds him up with. A crew of the attendees reaches for it, "You see that?" She throws him into the reaching attendees and the pitched attendee pushes the crowd back. More come to grasp at her, "This ensures my absolute control over you! You have nothing to fight me with because your Will is weak!"

Now, instead of reaching for the bracelet, they start to grab at it, crowding Amethyst. She knocks away the first one to touch her but, where that one was, two take his place. She has to swat them off of her like a swarm of giant insects, taking care not to crush any of them for conservation of life. She does, however, bruise a few of them up in the process of clearing a path between her and the one she came back to crush.

And the path is clear, her power holding them against the black marble walls. She knows as well as the Enslaver that, now that there is nothing left between them, and their battle can begin.

CHAPTER XXIII

The captain of the Midnight and Diamond squadron runs by, blasting the wind walls from the outside with sonic waves to break them open. Her trapped teammates roll away from the rain of lightning and Synite floats back down next to NanVash, Lone jumping down soon after. The three Sukayishiru are in the light, standing across mirroring Synite's Vanguard. "Hey, guys!" Fabric yells from behind and NanVash is the only one to actually look back. "You're doing great! Keep up the good work!" He throws a righteous fist into the air and NanVash reluctantly nods back at him.

"Is that guy crazy?" NanVash swings back around, wings wide, to face up his opponents. "Because, except for Synite, we're getting beat up…a little."

"Maybe he seeing something we ain't," Lone shrugs. And with that movement of his shoulders, the Sukayishiru rush them. The same three opponents that they had been scrapping with are back in their faces in short order. NanVash meets the one with the hammer out in front, kicking him in the gut before he is able to swing. He pushes hard with his wings to keep him off the ground and pushes away from the opponent. Lone dodges the claymore's guillotine attempt, hops over him and kicks off his shoulder to meet the third one and enter the fray.

The Sukayishiru with the navy blue claymore turns to try again with Lone but he is drop kicked in the back by Synite, stumbling forward three or four meters. He rotates back to the champion of this stomping ground but Synite is not there. Instead, an electrified fist comes across his face, knocking him off of his feet and into the sand. He is below Synite's feet irreverently rolling around to create space. He swings up with the claymore a few times to fend the elementalist off and, after enough swings, he is able to get up and take on the offensive again.

'Heeee would beeee no match for us if you leeeet meeee giveeee you poweeeer!' Thesia tweets in Synite's ear. 'Noneeee of theeeeem would!' "Shut up!" He rushes his opponent and grabs his sword hand. They tussle around, almost at equal strength, until the Sukayishiru turns himself into shadow and Synite falls through. They both turn quickly: Synite shoots an ion orb at him, the blue a lot darker than it usually is on Earth 11, and the Sukayishiru swings at it as hard as he can with his sword. The orb went so fast, faster than usual, that his swinging claymore missed it and it thumped him in the stomach.

"Good hit kid!" Fabric says to himself, still keeping an eye on the captain on the other end of the Sword. *She has not moved in quite some time. I wonder what she's planning. I'm still not sure if our guys are that strong or if the Sukayishiru are toying with them for now. We'll see.*

Synite fires a few more but the Sukayishiru he is up against recovers quickly and goes back after him, claymore first. They pass by Lone in their clash, the young half-animal doing well avoiding but not so well landing any hits. The Sukayishiru with the club and mace is great at making sure he keeps enough distance so Lone does not get close enough to reach him. Lone even tries to strike the weapons with his claw but they are completely solid, almost too strong for the way they look. Even the chain seems unbreakable as he scratches at it a few times and it shows no sign of any damage.

Lone begins to focus more now on trying to get a hit in than trying to defend, swinging but leaving himself dangerously close to the sharp mace. He dodges it well enough to only get a slight scratch and gets close again, putting the Sukayishiru on the defensive. Lone hops up and kicks him in the chest three times in succession. He lands squared up and goes for a haymaker with his big fist but only connects to his chest. The Sukayishiru sees an opening, the club in his gauntlet hand, and thwacks Lone hard in the small of his back with it. The hit knocks him forward and into a roll, his eyes closed to avoid sand getting in them. The Sukayishiru just stands and waits, admiring the homerun he hit, probably smiling under his mask. Lone stops rolling and gets up with his eyes still closed.

Once Lone opens his eyes, he immediately knows something is wrong. His perception of the horizon tilts and then starts to teeter-totter, throwing his balance completely off. He is dizzy and, though he cannot tell because he cannot see himself, he is leaning every direction, trying to regain his balance. Vertigo, by contact with the club, puts this Sukayishiru in an extremely advantageous position versus Lone. "Help!"

The Sukayishiru switches weapon hands, putting the mace in his gauntlet hand, preparing for the next blow. Fabric steps forward and sees the captain step forward at the same time. "Oh?" He stops before he takes another step as Synite lands hard in the sand in front of him.

"Not yet," Synite says right before dashing past the Sukayishiru with the claymore. He quickly flies over and throws a few lightning bolts between the club and mace Sukayishiru and Lone. They stop the enemy in his tracks long enough for Synite to help Lone lean against one of the pillars.

NanVash gets closer and closer to the Sukayishiru with the giant hammer, almost within wing's reach when the Sukayishiru jumps back away from him. NanVash leaps forward with him and lands close enough for his punch to land, a rush of relief running from his fist, up his arm and into his heart. The Sukayishiru turns back at him, unfazed by the punch, and lands one of his own. NanVash gives him another two to the ribs and receives one to the sternum.

They go back and forth until the Sukayishiru knocks NanVash back with the butt of his hammer. He swings it and NanVash drops to the ground to dodge, sprawled out flat. He tries to come down with the hammer and NanVash pushes up and rolls in midair out of the way then back down to his feet. "This is getting fun!" NanVash closes the distance again and throws a haymaker across his opponent's face, excited beyond belief.

After helping Lone, Synite has to fly over a slash of the claymore then flip away from the thrust of the mace. He slaps his hands together and a booming thunderclap forces them back. Then he crosses one of the two with a lariat, his arm as stiff as stone. He blasts a strong wind at the other and follows it with a drop kick, his feet as solid as a boulder. Synite feels Thesia's presence slowly leaking into his joints, loosening him up but at the same time making him strong. 'Do you eeeenjoy this feeeeeeeling?'

Stop it, Synite pushes back like a young girl playing coy in her first flirtation. He parries the gauntlet covered fist of the enemy with the claymore, and bends over backwards to dodge the swing of the club. Thesia gives him more and he throws a sliding elbow into the chest of one of the Sukayishiru, on the verge of cracking his breastplate.

The captain takes a step forward, feeling the crack as much as her team member. Fabric steps forward as well, mocking her earlier movement. She throws her cloak away from her arm, showing her naginata and its blue chrome blade. He smiles cheesy at her, showing most of his teeth and all of his crow's feet.

No! I don't need you! He yells at Thesia. 'Weeeee will seeeeee about that!' Exhaustion blankets him and only his instinct to survive keeps that sword from slicing him across his stomach. He lazily moves away from the swing of the club but gets a scrape from the back of the mace.

Before Synite knows it, he is yanked down on all fours to the earth, his elbows struggling. His entire body tensed, his every muscle contracting almost to the point of explosion. The two Sukayishiru stand over him, admiring their prey before consuming it, as his disadvantage has demoted him an object to them now and no longer an adversary.

Instead of killing him right away, they pick him up and pin him against the other side of the pillar Lone is leaning against. They look at their captain and she puts her naginata away. The Sukayishiru with the claymore goes to the other side of the pillar and picks Lone up, holding him against the pillar with his gauntlet hand. The other holds Synite up and they both prepare their bladed weapons for a double execution.

The Sukayishiru's executions of Synite and Lone are interrupted by blindside punches that knock them at least five meters away from the pillar in opposite directions. Fabric reaches down to help his young friend though Synite's sense of gravity has been amped up by a revolving rate of increase. During the peaks, he grunts and groans in pain and during its troughs, he exhales in relief. He is forced to throw up beside the pillar but away from Fabric. "When did you even eat?"

Synite looks up at Fabric, sweaty and pale from the not-so-good feeling in his gut. "About time you decided to join the party," he says between the crushing behemoth of gravity plopping down on him at random.

'You should leeeeet meeeee cureeee us of this ill,' Thesia whispers to Synite. 'If you allow meeee room to grow in you, I will rid us of theeeee poweeeeer that beeeeeing has oveeeeer us!' Synite breathes heavily, unable to hear Fabric's speech over the rumblings of Thesia inside his head and his own pain. 'Do not beeeee stubborn! Allow meeeee freeeeedom, Cairo! Giveeee us theeeee conneeeeeection!'

You cannot have control over me, Synite tells Thesia rebelliously. *This body is not yours to command.* 'I don't wish to command you or this speeeeecimeeeeeen, this teeeeeempleeeee of poweeeeeer! You will still command! I only want you to feeeeeeel its full poteeeeeential with meeee!'

"Kid!" Fabric tries to reach Synite but, instead has to push him out of the way of the Sukayishiru's swing of the club. That swing takes a piece out of the pillar; the noise snaps Synite back to the reality in front of him. The gravity pulls away from him so rough that he flies up the side of the pillar and jerks him back down as he rolls over on top of it.

Below, Fabric axe kicks that detractor straight to the gut, forcing him away again. The claymore comes slashing at his head and he knocks it away with the back of his hand then open-palm strikes him in the chest, throwing him back several meters. The Sukayishiru recovers quickly and back into the fight, taking swings with the claymore and the butt of it as well. Fabric dodges all of the swings and blocks the strikes with the blunt end.

The Sukayishiru switches grips so effortlessly that Fabric watches his hands more than actually watching his waist or the blade of the weapon. His background is working in his favor in this particular case but Fabric's experience as a fighter has him a head above.

Hudson Clark, now known by the name Fabric, was once a recruiter for Tobias when the idea for the Thorns was originally hatched. He got the senior Driven's attention from the double life he was forced to live in his youth. Though he was not an actual criminal, in order to survive he had to build a lot of criminal connections. Members of the mob started making a lot of cash on his street fights, so they put him on retainer and then hired him as head of security.

Those connections with the nefarious side of society gave Hudson good reason to get heavy into different fighting styles outside of knocking out amateurs. The intensity of his training turned him into a peak condition fighter and earned him the name Fabric from Ben, one of his training partners, for being the metaphorical framework for building the Thorns. He got into several upper-level fighting tournaments and amassed a small fortune but importantly kept his financial life separate from the crime. There were several times when the heads of the crime family he dealt with respected him even more for "being smart" and not getting caught.

With that respect came even more connections and, after a twist of fate, his elite intellect brought down the entire crime syndicate he was linked to. After proving his worth towards progress, Tobias had no choice but to look at him. His first project was to tame the wild Captain Kraa-Nuve and bring him into the fold which created a link that was utilized more recently. Then the Thorn's project came to fruition and Tobias appointed him in the recruiting position.

During Fabric's job, he was also a trainer for the candidates who made it past the process. A prepubescent Alexander II took a distinct liking to him while he was training with his father and, after the original eighteen was established, Fabric continued to train the younger Alexander. They went on many excursions together, posing as a sleeper cell and dousing wars on several different planets, ushering in the Thorn's eventual leadership over the Earth system.

Fabric actually assisted in the stabilization of Earth Prime after the final civil war before Synite was born, right before being commissioned to Earth 11 to set up a base of operations. After a rough patch, he, Tobias and the elder Alexander decided it would be best to end the Thorns project because of the risk of having too much power under one umbrella. Tobias especially regretted how fast his project built up as they could not have seen the scale of what they were doing. They saw Earth 11 as a way to start over and began compiling surveillance on several key figures there before diving into the political arena, taken aback by the daunting power and resources of the Enslaver.

Some of the whisperings of an insurrection of the Thorns were postulation, listing primary resources, abilities, standard field practices and accounts of direct contact, but some of it was highly accurate. Then, on his first day on-planet, unfortunately, Tobias Driven was killed and the dominoes started falling from there. Fabric left immediately and, with the grown Alexander II, they were forced to begin with a blank slate. Alexander began designing weaponry and making great Marks doing so.

When enough assets were available, Alexander II delved into research and development with several projects that Fabric and another of the remaining Thorns participated in heavily. In his experimentation, he became adept at dividing someone's Will and, for Fabric, it meant giving him access to more than one type of ability. With a few extra Marks, Fabric was not only able to split his Will, but absorb a portion of another being's Will to fill those extra slots.

Fabric can take a power type, flight for instance, and instill a simpler version in one of the five sections of his Will. The power he mimics is used at whatever intensity he puts it at: if he wants to engage it completely, he fills himself with it, fifty-fifty if he has two powers he wants to control, twenty percent a piece if he allots all five slots. His mimicry is by touch and is so powerful that it only takes secs for him to absorb and eins to activate as shown by how he is mimicking NanVash's invulnerability into his fifth slot. Before the current fight with the Sukayishiru, only four other beings knew of his ability to mimic.

Fabric's trade-off is unlimited, though he has learned to prefer a specific set: supernatural physical strength, passive self-healing, low-level teleportation and an ability called timesplitter. He can, at Will and by eye contact, slow down his opponents' perceptions so much that he looks as though he is as fast as Proximity or Desha. He can also crunch his own perception of Time and get hecus worth of work done in eins. It has helped him complete the tremendous amounts of planning that it took for many important things to get done over his time including the logistics of expanding the sales of Alexander's products to the masses.

When they decided to open storefronts, they created the Weapons Rack. Fabric had the bright idea of making store number 365 in the market outside of the Sword of Atlan. He got a little bite back from Alexander but after committing to run that store himself, Fabric got what he wanted. He saw the blossoming of the Sword as an opportunity to start recruiting again though Alexander was ignorant of this intention. When Promis arrived on-planet, Fabric knew something was special about that place.

Fabric was able to find Kraa-Nuve in outer space shopping at store number 719 and reconnect with him. Then he brokered the deal that got Synite, Amethyst and Psilos out of Atlan and into their dramatic, nearly operatic chase for righteousness. He has been the glue for the Vanguard before they knew they would be a team. Right now, he holds them together on the field as well.

Fabric continues the strike against the claymore bearing Sukayishiru, holding the upper hand in defense still. Though the blade is long and wide, Fabric knows the distance needed to keep his head and limbs attached to his body. When he sees a slight opening, he makes it gaping by using his timesplitter ability, slowing the Sukayishiru to a snail's pace and making him look faster than light.

He uses this power to duck under the swing of the claymore and choke slam the Sukayishiru into the black sand. He does not release the timesplitter after that: he kicks the claymore out of his hand, kicks him away from it and then jumps on the weapon, dropping both heels and all of his strength into the weakest part of the blade. It takes four tries but the blade finally breaks and he releases the technique.

Its owner screams in pain and drops to the ground as if all of his power is taken away from him, which may be the case but Fabric refuses to let down his guard. The captain felt the destruction too, not as terribly as her teammate but enough to take her breath away and drop her to one knee.

After a sonic boom, she dashes into the mix, blazingly fast in comparison to the other three, dipping through a shadow and coming out right next to Fabric. Since she felt the pain of the claymore being destroyed, she was forced to come do something about it. She meets Fabric's forearm with the blunt end of her naginata and they slide together in the direction of her action.

 # CHAPTER XXIV

Before ever meeting up with everyone, Castra Nim went off on his own to the beach to clear his mind. He had a feeling things would go downhill pretty fast so now would be a great time to enjoy the peace of nature. He took in the cool breeze of the coastal water, the calm crash of the waves against the rocks and the low cry of the gulls. He peeled a piece of fruit with one of his smaller knives, enjoying its sweetness in combination with the salty scent of the ocean.

Castra accidentally cut his finger with the knife enough to make it bleed a little. With the sting and the sight of his own precious bodily fluid, his peace was broken by the thought of battle. This one has been looming over Earth 11 for some time now, since decades before he was even born and now he has become an essential cog in it.

He used this time alone to develop several different battle strategies for different situations against different types of beings. The tactician in him was inspired by the peace in front of him. He took the same knife that drew his blood and charges it with his teleportation energy. He gripped that very knife and threw it as far into the surf as he can, hoping it got past the shelf but doubting his arm is that good.

"That ought to come in handy," he watched the knife sink into the surf and get carried off in the tide. It drifted and rolled deeper into the water but not before it stuck in the sand.

In that same spot, moments ago, the giant foot of a Sukayishiru appeared in a flash of orange and sent the wave around it in every direction. After he recovered from the shock of being teleported against his Will, he grew to his maximum height, ninety-eight meters, and took off running back towards the battlefield, crunching the ground in his path.

Back in the street, Lo and the captain with the whip are both running at Castra, one to attack and one to defend. She lets the whip down and it rockets towards the back of Castra's head. Lo makes a split-second decision to throw his shield, not to block the whip but to knock Castra out of the way. Castra is confused as to why he is hitting the ground under his teammate's shield until he hears the powerful crack of a whip above him.

Castra rolls and picks up the shield to keep himself protected from the whip while he recovers from the exhaustion of teleporting someone twenty times his size. The whip comes again and the shield roars to stop the sharp end snap. Lo uses the time she is focused on Castra to retrieve his sword from the wall. He puts the spear away and rushes her with the sword.

The Sukayishiru with the falchion uses his telekinesis to volley boulders at Arra and Gith. Arra throws flames back to drop the momentum of the rocks, melting them with the intense green fireballs. Gith raises his hands and a fence of dirt raises from the ground with them, stopping the rocks as well as Arra did. They use their defensive tactics to get closer and Arra heats things up with a river of fire flowing straight towards the Sukayishiru. The telekinetic dodges it but the flame keeps rolling towards the one behind him that caused all of the cracks in the ground.

That Sukayishiru cowers behind his huge shield then points up. From where he points, a cascade of ice pummels the green blaze. Once he is comfortable with the temperature around him, he steps out in front of the shield next to the leaning wall of ice. He looks to the green flames bouncing around as they go after his comrade, plotting on how to go on the offensive as well.

Lo is close enough to the Sukayishiru captain to get a good swing in, pushing her around enough to keep her away from his captain. He roars along with his lion sword, swinging through and connecting with the handle of her whip. She uses that end now too offensively as Lo continues his slashes. He switches to the spear and it extends into her space, making her a bit colder and backing her up. He sees a huge opening and she teleports behind him before he can thrust the spear through her heart.

Castra has almost caught his breath, mad at how long he has been out of the mix, even angrier that he has no idea what is happening. He is glad he did what he did to get that giant out away from the battle but, for a tactician to not be aware is not what he would call his finest moment. As the exhaustion wears off, he stands up and tries to assess.

Pretty green flames and dirt flying around, I'm cool with that. Sparks flying over by Lo and he's on his feet, cool over there, too. Then, he sees the last one in the rear grabbing his shield and approaching. *What does this fella have on his mind, I wonder.*

Before Castra can wonder too long, the Sukayishiru stabs his oversized shield in the ground. From the impact, arcs of wind grow and spread in their direction. The closer they get, the bigger they get and the bigger they get, the stronger they get. Gith pushes Arra out of the way and slides in time to not get knocked out by the first round. The next one, however, grabs him and throws him high above the battle.

The telekinetic seems unaffected by the storm as the attack avoids him and the other Sukayishiru. Arra tries to counteract with her fire but the arcs of wind douse the flames before they even touch. She is nimble enough to dodge but gets pinballed between the second and third waves.

Lo runs through the forest of wind, rolling and juking them with the expert dexterity of the greatest athletes. To try and end this blitzkrieg, he blasts a stream of freezing water with his spear at the shielded Sukayishiru. The winds push the blast around but it eventually stops as the ice covers the shield. The Sukayishiru lifts the shield out of the ground and cracks the ice coverage. Gith rolls down a hill of dirt he threw down to catch himself with and, though it did help him out, it still did not feel too great.

Lo keeps marching and dropkicks the shield, knocking its owner back with it. He stays on his feet though and rushes back at Lo; he catches the shield with both hands and they lock in a two-man scrum. Lo is strong on any scale but this Sukayishiru, even though he is not the type to attack, is as strong if not stronger. If it were not for Lo's grit, the Sukayishiru would have overpowered him quickly; however, they are tied in the tackle as equals.

They start pushing their ice attacks against each other, turning into the unstoppable force and the immovable object. The ice piles up to what looks like an iceberg, high enough for the giant Sukayishiru to see the tip of it. He is smashing through the edge of the city, covering ground faster than Castra hoped he would. The sky is darkening from Gale's kneading the weather to suit Synite's intentions which somewhat plays into the hands of the Sukayishiru.

"Arra!" Gith yells, limping around the area she was in. A boulder rolls his way, controlled by the mind of the telekinetic. He puts up enough dirt to push the rolling rock out of the way, still scouring for his teammate. "Arra! Where are you?!"

"In here," she whimpers and sparks a green flash to signal him. He gets over to her, surrounding them with a dirt wall and helps her up from the shop she was thrown into. "It's getting heavy out there, huh?"

"We're doing the right thing," Gith tells her. "A cycle ago we were going nowhere, even our own corps didn't think we would survive. But, we found a way and it's out there."

"I appreciate everything that's happening, Gith," she tells him, pushing solidarity. "How long do we live in this situation? This world isn't for us. We've been put in the position as pawns and I'm not for it." She looks him in the eye as the building shakes from the dirt wall stopping large rocks from smashing through and crushing them. "How much longer are we going to do this?"

He tries not to get too caught in those thoughts, "How about we win this war and decide afterwards? I doubt we could go out there and surrender at this point," he smiles at her. "And I doubt Castra would accept our resignation in the middle of the fight!"

"Okay," Arra agrees, "as long as you promise we will talk about it when we're done."

"Survive and talk," Gith helps her up. "Got it. One foot in front the other! One step at a time! Taking life in stages!"

She steps out in front of him, "Anytime now!"

"Alright," he counts down with his hand and spreads open the dirt wall. Arra throws her emerald flames out to cover and they march back out into the street.

Everyone that has been outside the dark area at the gate of the Sword has either run, is waiting on their family member to be freed from it, or is trapped by the rocks from the explosions. The only beings who are left free of fear are Suubai and Orchanik G and they have a different problem as they both feel helpless from outside the black. They pace around its circumference and even dip their heads in to check things out, unable to operate blindly.

The Sukayishiru captain of the Blood and Gold group grabs Coldsmoke's left triceps, lifts him from the ground and throws him back into it. She swings her sickle across the ground and he slides away but still gets nicked across the leg. From that cut, every nerve in his body is shocked with a disruptive jolt. Coldsmoke growls in pain, certain that her weapon is causing this.

"Don't let them hit you!" he yells at Psilos, channeling his pain to get his warning off. "Don't let their weapons touch you!" He gets scooped up by Psilos who moved fast enough to catch him off guard considering his distraction. Behind them, a small explosion pops a crater into the ground.

Psilos puts him down, "Can you continue?"

"Give me some time," Coldsmoke jumps out of the darkness towards where Orchanik G is and his teammate stretches out and catches him.

"What's going on in there?" Suubai runs up to them, noticing Coldsmoke is in obvious pain.

"We have t'find a way t'get rid of th'darkness. We can't hit them in there," Coldsmoke reports, finding it hard to speak while he fights the pain away. "They're twice as fast in th'dark. Even with all of my Will concentrated on being faster," Coldsmoke cringes, "I still couldn't touch them," his words squeezed from a tube through a pinhole.

"The one that was in the back spinning that mace over their head," Orchanik recalls. "The darkness came from him. But we don't know where he is."

Now, Psilos is caught in the center of the triangle made by the captain, the feral one and the one with the explosive shortsword. He does the most logical thing and closes in on the one with the shortsword, taking away the long-range threat. Though that Sukayishiru is not at all an adept fighter, Psilos still finds him impossible to complete an attack against. Psilos tries to predict where his opponent will move after dodging but, before he can find a good pattern, the others close in on his position and he has to retreat.

These Sukayishiru immediately spread out and form another triangle around Psilos, knowing their advantage versus a single opponent but wary of Psilos's overall strength. Although they are a step ahead at all times, he is no slouch. He then decides, considering the nature of his opponents, he has to defy all logic.

Outside, Coldsmoke is shaking off his jitters and about to go in but Suubai stops him. "I think I know a way!"

The swordsman drops small explosions around Psilos, leaving an opening for both the captain and her feral mate to go head first at Psilos from opposite sides. The captain strikes first as the other stalks the ground, awaiting an opening. Impatient as they come, he creates his own opening after the captain turns away and dropkicks Psilos in the chest. The attack does not move him far, but enough for the Sukayishiru to feel accomplished.

The captain goes back in, Psilos being especially careful to avoid her sickle like Coldsmoke warned. He tries to gain a moment of offense but they are able to avoid his every swing and kick. The swordsman drops an explosion in at the perfect time to put him back on his heels and open things up again for the captain. She gets in a nice punch to his gut followed by a chain of kicks by the feral one. They both flip back and go for his chest at the same time, nearly knocking him over from the thrust.

Psilos uses the force and tumbles, rolling back onto his feet pretty easily. The two Sukayishiru clash with him, their gauntlets meeting his arm as he charges them shoulder first. He swings up and the feral one wraps his wrist with the chains of the flail. Psilos swings down to try and throw him into the ground but he releases on the way down and lands in a three-point stance.

The captain is already behind Psilos when her subordinate gets away. She climbs his back, the handle of the sickle around his neck, but he throws her over his shoulder. She swings the sickle behind her, narrowly missing his strong jaw with the disruptive, blood colored blade. She goes right back in, her feet not even touching the ground, swimming through the unreal darkness like a shark.

The one with the shortsword turns strangely towards the spinning morningstar. The captain comes at Psilos swinging the sickle, looking the same as a spinning saw, and Psilos sidesteps her fast enough to miss the front and back of the buzzing blade. The other berserk Sukayishiru comes behind her swinging with his attack. He lands a fierce combination of strikes and Psilos continues to land none.

Then, the unspeakable happens: the captain carves out a gash across Psilos's back and he drops to his knees. The captain puts the concave edge of the blade against the powerhouse's neck. The feral soldier springs forward at full speed to push Psilos's neck across that blade. However, before he can get there, the darkness goes away completely, dropping as a curtain would when pulled from its hooks.

Psilos leans forward and kicks back as hard as he can, knocking the captain unconscious pretty quickly. The feral one had no way to stop from his attack so he follows through instead of hesitating and meets a big problem. Psilos cocks back, sensing that he has his natural advantage again, and punches the Sukayishiru into the ground. Dust, rocks and glass bounce up with the broken body of the Sukayishiru as Psilos crushes nearly three-quarters of his bones, ruptures internal organs and destroys much of the armor. It is by far the hardest punch anyone in the vicinity had ever seen before.

The Prophyrian king stands over his victim and hears a loud, constant noise coming from where he knows Amethyst is with the Enslaver. Then, he feels one of his other selves trying to contact him so he closes his eyes for a moment so they can communicate. He looks back at where the remaining two Sukayishiru are as they are being hounded by Coldsmoke, Suubai and Orchanik G.

While Psilos was inside having trouble with the captain and deceased Sukayishiru, Suubai thought up a plan to wipe out the darkness that was keeping them from victory. "Coldsmoke, you can feel where everything is in there so you'll have to be the guide."

"What am I guiding," he gritted his teeth to mask the pain.

The three of them ran together near the gate of the Sword where they know the Sukayishiru with the swinging morningstar that created the darkness was stationed. "He never moved th'entire time we were fighting. I can't feel anything from out here but I'm sure he didn't go too far."

"I assume," Suubai told them, getting in place, "that it takes all of his attention to sustain such a technique. I know, with my force fields, if I was to have to do something that size and hold it, it'd take a lot out of me. And, for me, it'd just be a shell, so I can imagine how filling that entire space with darkness can take a ton of concentration."

"So, we'll be able to sneak up on him," Orchanik G started to get the picture.

"Not with th'other three roaming around," Coldsmoke thought about how Psilos was in there by himself with all three of them. "Whatever we're going t'do, we need t'do it fast. I'm sure Psilos won't want to hold them off forever."

"The plan is this," Suubai made her stand behind Coldsmoke and give the K'oma champion his wrists. Then, Coldsmoke stepped forward a few meters to get her arms to stretch out. Suubai surrounds Coldsmoke and part of Orchanik G's arms with a tight force shield. "Ready?"

Coldsmoke was still laboring to breathe as he prepared to run into the darkness again, "I am!"

"Yep, it's now or never," she added for good measure.

Coldsmoke sprinted into the black orb and could feel where everyone was again as soon as he crossed the threshold. Not only that, but everyone could feel his presence as well, catching the attention of the only unoccupied Sukayishiru. He threw several explosions at Coldsmoke immediately, "When you get in there, you're probably going to get their attention and, generally, the long range fighter tries to neutralize a surprise attack first."

"I hope your shield stands up to it," Coldsmoke is not faithless in general but it remained to be seen what exactly his shields could do. The explosions pushed Coldsmoke around a little but he was not knocked out by the percussion or hurt by the heat. *Good enough,* he thought as he felt the last Sukayishiru standing still not too far in front of him.

Orchanik G's wrists still in hand by his waist, he dashed towards the one with the swinging morningstar and, once he was in range, pushed Orchanik's hands towards the closer enemy, "Once you get within a meter or so, throw her arms towards the one holding the darkness. Orchanik," Suubai looked over at her, "you nod when he throws your arms and I'll open up the front of the shield."

A section of the force field around Coldsmoke opened up to let the stretching arms fly out of it. Orchanik G had to brace herself for the strength of the pull, "I'm probably going t'throw your arms pretty hard," Coldsmoke said as they plotted. "Th'pain I'm in has my control kind of shaken up." Her arms reached the Sukayishiru and wrapped around him.

"He isn't even moving!" she exclaimed from outside next to Suubai who was still concentrating on protecting Coldsmoke from the explosions. Suddenly, the swordsman was standing on the stretched out arms between Coldsmoke and the other Sukayishiru. He had moved through the darkness and landed there, raising the shortsword, about to slice Orchanik's arms.

Coldsmoke hopped on top of them too and met the swordsman

with a lariat strong enough to stop him. They both fell to the ground, Coldsmoke landing under the Sukayishiru, and Orchanik constricted his Blood and Gold teammate's body as tightly as she could. Then, to add injury to the technique, "You have to squeeze as tight as you can as fast as you can. Crush him! Break him in half!"

"What if choking doesn't work?" Coldsmoke had fought them already and felt how tough they were. "They have armor. And, if I were th'enemy, I would have planned t'get hit a little. Th'only reason they are winning is because of th'advantage he is affording them."

"I have a little trick up my sleeve, no pun intended," Orchanik tried to reassure the warrior. "Get me there and I'll make it happen!" After squeezing, she ejected steel spikes from every part of her arm that surrounded the enemy. The strong steel went through the sections of his body that had no armor and anchored in. Then she picked up the Sukayishiru, turned him upside down, and slammed him into the same section of the ground that he stood on. Needless to say, this was effective enough of a distraction to end the dark cloak that surrounded them.

Then, Coldsmoke saw the captain fly across the street and into a building. As she lost consciousness, his searing pain lifted and he was able to face up with the Sukayishiru swordsman. The boom of Psilos's mighty punch was almost as percussive as one of his explosions, shaking the ground around them and putting another crater where Psilos stood. He looks up as a couple of ships come into the atmosphere, not remembering ordering anyone from his fleet to come on planet yet.

     # CHAPTER XXV

Before Amethyst gets close enough to touch the Enslaver, It lets out a strange wail that zooms through the hall, the crescendo resembling the exhaust note from a tailpipe. The skirt of Its garment flies off and Its breastplate splits down the middle. The wood of Its throne starts to split under the extra weight as Its body extends beyond the throne area.

The shriek continues an upsurge and the dragon eyes from Porussa implanted in the Enslaver's shoulders roll open and focus. Then, Its own smaller central eye opens from where the breastplate split. Both of Its arms stretch out to four times their normal length and expand to hold up the extra girth. Its claws curve and sharpen; It grows powerful unguligrade hind legs and wide, scaly toes. The Pietre Dure below cracks under the new weight even despite the monster holding Itself up.

The Enslaver, showing Its true self, opens Its head: a Venus flytrap with rows of bladed teeth lining the opening. The teeth shine golden and the slime of saliva drips down the side of Its head. Finally, a long, thick, prehensile tail protrudes from Its spine with a single hook at the tip; the tail lowers to Its side behind the huge dragon's eye in Its shoulder, moving more of a tentacle than a tail.

The shrieking finally tapers off as the transformation comes to an end. The sheer fear factor cripples everyone in the room except Amethyst, allowing her to release her grasp from them. The Enslaver reaches over and leans against one of the pillars, growling and metaphorically licking Its chops.

The transformation shows that the Enslaver has prepared Itself for more than just leading the battle from the shadows. Though It never would lower Itself into being a warrior in the arena, if It were in the situation, It would be able to fend for Itself and possibly fight up to becoming a champion. Unfortunately for the Sate'Gran, It is up against the one being It never assumed would raise her hand against It. Even more unfortunate is that she is the same being that the Enslaver made into the most powerful within multiple star systems. Ometku assumed It may have had to go up against a Lord Qor or Synite, Lo or, at the worst, Psilos. Defending against Amethyst had crossed Its mind but not without the assistance of the Sukayishiru. For the Enslaver, this situation could not be any worse.

After not having used an eye for decades, the Enslaver has to take a moment to get used to having actual sight from Its own body and not through the eyes of the attendees. Its three eyes scan the room together and swiftly lock on Amethyst, almost giddy at the sight of Amethyst in Its face. "We hope you know what you're doing," the entire crowd of attendees says in close to unison, "because your life is coming to a rapid end."

"So, you show your true face," Amethyst speaks confidently. "You must feel your own demise coming close as well to resort to such a tactic."

'And your fear,' the Enslaver's real voice, the same one that spoke when It told the attendees to find the woman in front of them, 'shall shrink you.' Amethyst looks around to see if any of the attendees' mouths are moving but they are not. 'Your love of being my most precious of slaves will turn you into an insect!'

The Enslaver's orange eye and the bloodshot, blue dragon eyes lock on to her. "No more talk!" She takes a strong step for It and dodges one of his slender claws swiping at her. It goes up on Its hind legs and curves Its back, never taking Its gaze off of Amethyst. It claws at her repeatedly, making sure to keep her at a certain distance, but not for long. She closes too quickly for It to stop her from digging a fist into Its pelvic region.

Despite the punch that could have knocked through a brick wall, the Enslaver's eyes still do not leave their lock on Amethyst. It just takes the hit and keeps swinging at her as if nothing ever happened. A bruise spreads where she hit It as those wiry hands clasp around her. She pushes them out but Its arms expand to extremely muscular in a snap and push back in. Purple energy from the bracelet wraps her forearms and hands then pushes out like a spring to a clamp.

Amethyst has had her brute strength matched before but she never thought the Enslaver, a being that sits back on Its throne, frail yet powerful, would be able to do so. The bracelet creates a ring around her that holds the Enslaver's crushing grasp at bay. It stops trying to crush and tries instead to punch her but the ring tilts up and blocks the fist. Its arm expands and tries to force through the purple ring but it does not budge even though the ceiling and floor around it cracks from the force.

It swings a few hammer fists down at her and she rolls away like a fighter jet would during a lead attack. She zooms from under the ring and hammers It on the right breastplate then roundhouse kicks the left one. Both sides crack and pieces start to tumble to the ground. It pushes her back and spins, swinging Its hooked tail across her body but the ring catches it. She grabs the tail and it yanks her off the ground then tries to slam her back down. A purple concave bowl appears under her and she slides from one edge of it to the center.

The bowl disappears and they pull against each other, the Enslaver turning again but she keeps holding on, running along the wall behind Its back. It twists hard enough to throw her off over the crowd of attendees then jabs at her. The punch connects with the ring and sends her spinning into the ground in front of her. The Enslaver swats at her but the ring expands to block it, involuntary at this point. She had not needed any defense in such a long time that she is surprised it still works so efficiently. Ometku swings Its torso below the ring and flashes all of its razor sharp teeth, meant to stab and grind her in an upwards motion but she hops on top of the ring. All of the teeth jut around the ring but do not scathe Amethyst at all.

Its tail-tentacle reaches for Amethyst but she slaps it away effortlessly every time it swings at her. It grasps her arm and pulls her in toward its mouth but she jerks back, defying gravity, and hits the tail so hard that it releases her. She drops down in front of the Enslaver and quickly goes back up to its face. She kicks it below the breast plates five times in succession. The tail reaches around its torso to grab her, stopping her from attacking It at the mid-section, but she kicks off and perches on the edge of the purple ring that is still floating.

"Don't give up," Amethyst says to the monster in front of her. "I want you to die fighting!" She jumps horizontally off the ring and swing to punch It in the center eye but before she hits, It lowers its upper body, slicing down at her with all Its bladed teeth. She continues to follow through the punch instead of pulling back and her swing breaks a few of Its teeth in half, though one of them scratches against the bracelet.

Since she is over Its mouth, the Enslaver spews a few liters of Its yellowish, acidic saliva at her, gurgling through a scream and the sound of Its own teeth clanging against the floor. The ring slides in between her and the acid and expands to block all of the thick spit from contacting her skin. Though the spit falls back down on Its back, the monster is immune to Its own destructive juices so It stands up and swings at her with Its thick arms. She blocks the first punch on her own and the ring takes care of the next few after it contracts back to normal.

It swings Its tail back around and she allows it to grab her arm so she can grab it back. She gets the tail with two hands and jerks the Enslaver off Its feet, slamming its sides into the already cracked ceiling and floor. It kicks at her and the ring stops it though it does bend a little and pushes hard enough for her to lose grip on Its tail.

It lands hard on all fours and turns Its eyes back to Amethyst, the impenetrable hoop floating down around her. All three of Its eyes seem to be focused on something as It stands still and stares. 'I hope you do give up so we can start our rule of the octadecaverse together! I would hate to have your head and not have your heart!' The dragon's eyes contract and Amethyst feels a searing pain go through her arm around the bracelet. 'I'm inside you now! Give me back the power I loaned to you!'

The ring dims and shrinks a little as her involuntary response is deadening. Amethyst tries her best to fight the pain and the Enslaver's voice out of her body. The same wailing that was audible as It transformed only echoes through Amethyst's head this time instead of through all of downtown Atlan. She closes her eyes and grimaces as she tries her hardest to get rid of the noise and pain. The Enslaver tries to take advantage of her distraction and punches at her with all Its might but the ring feebly knocks Its fist off its path, only pushing her to the side a little. Amethyst's Will responds to her being touched, amplifying her power. The ring shines much brighter than before as she opens her eyes and they glow bright lavender. "You're going to have to do a lot better than that!"

She points at the Enslaver the same way she pointed at the ship she destroyed to ensure the Vanguard's escape from the mountains. It has seen the footage and knows to dodge when that happens; It moves enough for the stream of purple light to only slice Its leg a little. She traces across Its body with her finger, the light bends and the Enslaver rolls out of the way. She moves her arm again and, this time, does not miss: the purple laser beam divides Its tail into two nearly even pieces, one hitting the floor and the other still attached to the Enslaver's back. It groans in pain and she retracts the light.

With that same hand, she sends a shockwave through the room by merely closing her fist. Several of the remaining pillars crack from the dense push, eroding the architectural life from this hall. And, as the architecture dies, it seems the life of the surrounding city is coming to an end as well. She waves over her shoulder with a backstroke, sending another shock down the hall, picking up pieces of the floor and scattering the image of Atlan, something she hopes to complete soon.

Amethyst picks up her other hand, sweat running down the crease in her back, and points all of her fingers at the unbalanced monstrosity she used to answer to, ready to take Its life. It moves erratically, and she is unable to pinpoint a vital place to strike but, when she sends all ten beams of light, they do indeed stab through several critical points in the Enslaver's body. They go through to the floor below, freezing It from the shock of getting stabbed with such a powerful blow. Plumes of purple energy flutter and spread from her back as that blow impacts the future of this world.

Every attendee in the room looks at her as they let out the loudest groans their vocal chords can muster. The halls ring from all of the noise and Amethyst is taken aback as she sees them run to the Enslaver's side. An attendee jumps through the Air, throwing its torso over the center of the beams.

Amethyst turns the energy off swiftly enough for him to drop harmlessly into the crowd, preventing an apparent attempt at suicide. She realizes that they knew she would retract to keep from killing them since that is not her aim but does not mind giving into that tactic. Everything happened so quickly that she still is not sure where exactly she stabbed the Enslaver but she has to assume it was somewhere vital considering the response.

At this juncture in the battle, one of the more crucial points for every member of the Vanguard to go through is carving out their identity relative to the team. As the Enslaver finally reveals Its true form, nearly everyone fighting to destroy It is also fighting to define the Vanguard. After learning of the original Eighteen Thorns of the Rose, many of this new generation of revolutionaries cannot help but compare their importance to what they now consider their predecessors.

The only problem for some beings, Amethyst and Psilos especially, is that they cannot be compared. They did not make the mistakes that brought these problems into the octadecaverse and, though they were alive when the problems started, they are basically the cleanup crew for the power struggle that was created.

Amethyst, though she is the most powerful being at face value, has her own personal struggles with her peaks and valleys in emotional control. Now, as she finally feels things are going the way she wants them to, she will still have some tests to complete. Having the Enslaver hovering over her since she was a young lady has made her continuously anxious, on edge at every step and stage since the destruction of her home.

She has solidified her place as a leader and someone to look up to for the rest of the team, even with Synite and Psilos, the figureheads of the Vanguard. Since Synite's renaissance and Psilos's reclamation of his throne, Amethyst has remained the constant, the foundation of the team. She has not attempted to take over the group or assert it as her own though; she knows that all three of them are necessary for their overall success. She knows her weakness has made it impossible for her to honestly lead as the decision maker as Synite's strength has shined in the times she has faltered.

Amethyst, however, is on her way to becoming who they have relied on the most to complete a task. She was the objective for Synite to bring into the fold at one point but, after getting in, she became more than just someone they did not want to have against them. She has created her niche as the one they always want to have fighting for them.

Psilos has remained a powerful mentor for Synite and the rest of the Vanguard. Even in his absences, as he rebuilds his own home, Psilos has always been that voice in the back of Synite's mind, his equilibrium. Being a successful leader of two races and an entire planet is definitely a position any leader might aspire to be in. It has given him the experience and confidence to fearlessly mold Synite into what he needs to be for the Vanguard.

With that, Psilos has been travelling between two different worlds for a long time now. Even as a slave, he knew of his home's need for him. He said himself that he could have broken free of the Enslaver before Synite got there and before the Vanguard's inception but stayed patient because he knew his time would come to become part of something larger than his home. Psilos may have saved thousands of Prophyrian and Giarc lives had he left earlier but he opted to stay. His choice was to be an important aspect of changing the fate of Earth 11, possibly every Earth and other planet as well. He has contorted his personal feelings for prospectively affecting the greater good.

That decision has rippled through the rest of his comrades; one of the unifying virtues for every member of the Vanguard has been patience. They not only have high levels of patience with each other, allowing for their team to develop naturally and not pushing things unnecessarily; they also have patience in battle, allowing the beings on the other side of the field to show their entire hand and adjusting to win.

Another virtue consistent across the team is perseverance. Psilos did not leave and take his ability home before touching Synite. Synite did not give up on training or his pursuit of Amethyst's loyalty. Amethyst did not give up on forming the team and now impacting the revolution. Castra Nim has not given up on becoming a crucial piece and leader of the newest members of the crew.

Without Psilos, these attributes would not be part of the basic philosophy of the Vanguard. His encouragement and voice has been vital to the creation of the idea that an advance guard was necessary to complete the change of Atlan. The destruction of the Sword and its owner would have been impossible without him. And without Synite to motivate, both Psilos and Amethyst would still have been sitting in Atlan awaiting someone to ignite that change. Then, he has done something that few get the opportunity to do when faced with the circumstances: he followed through and lived to impact the world that he lived in. He put himself in the position to be the detonator for the Vanguard.

Since escaping Atlan, Synite remained at the helm and actually took on more responsibilities than he had when the survival of their plans were on his shoulders. He has taken responsibility for many of the woes that have come along the way, even for events that were not directly his fault. He is the type of teammate who always feels that, if something goes wrong, he could have done more or something else to prevent it.

This has not only made Synite the cement of the Vanguard but also the star that attracts others towards their cause. Of course, there is Amethyst and her notoriety and there is Psilos and his kingship but Synite's story, from slave to leader, has pulled many of the newer members into the fold. He attracted Promis which connected them to Fabric, Kraa-Nuve, Proximity and Desha. He was a trailblazer for Castra Nim, motivated Lo and Lone and found a friend in Driven. His enthusiasm has trickled down, leading Coldsmoke, Arra, Gith and Suubai into their circle.

Recently, with the internal toils he has been going through, Synite has been struggling to figure out who he is going to become in the future. He knows he will remain part of the family but his capacity is hard for him to call at this point. Thesia's influence and the rift that is opening between him and Promis has him wanting to separate for a while, especially considering they are extremely close to completing his main objective. Once the Enslaver is finished, which hopefully Amethyst completes, he will have some choices to make as far as where to go and who to go with on the next leg of his journey through life.

Not only that, he has become a bit of a mentor as well, trying to come out from under Psilos's shadow, so to speak. He knows Psilos has taught him very well, even back when he was just learning how to swing a punch and throw a kick with Santhia. However, he also believes that, at some point, the student has to become the teacher to be considered a true leader in the group. Synite knows that as long as they are alive, he will never be disappointing to Psilos or Amethyst. However, he is trying to think and move more under his own influence as opposed to feeling like he has to ask himself what either of them would do in his situation. It is only recently that he has felt comfortable enough within his own instinct to truly let go, even with the demon inside. He feels that, hopefully, this turns him into a better man though he still thinks that ideal is something he still has to strive for, even after everything they have been through.

He wants now, with this obstacle they have to get over, to become even more than what everyone expects him to become. People have been telling Synite that they know he will be successful, which he already has been but complacency is not something he should ever rest on. Even when he seems to be going through a rough patch, he knows that there is positive growth on the other side. Even when he is doing wonderful things, surprising everyone is still not enough. He wants for extreme success to be what the expectations are for him and still to be able to exceed them. He does not know how far his life is going to be extended or shortened by his elementalist power but his ultimate goal is to be immortal. Not in the sense that he needs to literally live forever but he wants to be immortal in that his name, his legacy will never die. He wants his grandchildren's grandchildren to know from who they came. He is one of the few beings in any world to be smart and effective but also work very hard and being the best at what he does as well.

And that is why he knows he will always stay hungry for more. That is why the Vanguard has more than just a chance at changing the octadecaverse. There are always favorable odds for this group to succeed because of the beings that comprise its roster.

 # CHAPTER XXVI

Lone squeezes his eyes closed tighter and shakes his head to try and reset his balance, still not aware of what has been happening to him. "Damn, you hit hard!" This particular Sukayishiru literally knocked vertigo into Lone with the club in his gauntlet hand. "What in the verses did they do to me?"

The Sukayishiru do not respond vocally, as only the captains are able to communicate with words. He had been completely unaware of everything going around him for the entire time he was riddled with the vertigo. The one with the club and mace's chain goes at Lone but Fabric kicks the captain away and steps between them. He meets eyes with the Sukayishiru and hits him with timesplitter, slowing him down to one hundredth of his normal pace.

Lone gets a chance to look up and sees Fabric protect him, albeit on a tilt, relieved that his time is extended. Above him, Synite struggles with the warping of his sense of gravity, Thesia still giving him drops of her intoxicating relief. *I will not give in to you!* 'Leeeet's seeeeee how weeeell you do without,' Thesia huffs and yanks the relief away.

NanVash goes back and forth with hits from the giant hammer and hits given to the Sukayishiru that is swinging it. He jumps over one of the swings, landing on top of the hammer itself. The Sukayishiru swings upward, NanVash holding on as if he did not mind being thrown fifty meters in the Air. He kicks off of the hammer, gets his control in the air with his wings, and dive bombs behind his opponent. NanVash takes advantage and sweeps him to the ground then mounts him, holding his dominant arm down with a knee.

This is NanVash's favorite position and he throws more than twenty solid punches to the body and face, landing combination after combination. The Sukayishiru tries to take the top but NanVash is trained to defend every type of escape from this angle, using his wings for more balance and leverage. He slams down with hammer fists, putting a slight crack in his armor. The captain feels it too, though she is still occupied by Fabric.

The Sukayishiru finds a tiny opening and finally kicks NanVash off, grasping the handle of the hammer to prepare for a strike. Before he leaves the Sukayishiru's space, NanVash grabs its cape and pulls himself back down, dropping both knees into his opponent's midsection. The Sukayishiru and the captain hack after the powerful gut punch, short of breath at a very inopportune time. NanVash pins him down and resets his mount, pounding down on the armored warrior as if nothing ever happened.

Feeling that there is no one coming to his aid, the Sukayishiru lets go of the hammer and whispers something unidentifiable. He grabs both of NanVash's legs and his eyes glow a bright blue. Before NanVash can release himself, he is covered in shadow, rendering him deaf, blind and nearly impossible to see for everyone else. Thrown off the Sukayishiru and into the black sand, NanVash flails his wings and puts his hands up to his eyes, trying to rip free of the shadow but there is no taking it off.

Like the shadow, fear blankets NanVash. Sight is the one sense he has always been afraid of losing and he feels helpless without it. He curls into the fetal position in the sand, wrapping himself tightly with his wings and hopes that his death comes swiftly. He thinks about his life and all of the struggles he went through to become a viable option for a team of fighters, about how being a part of something was his only dream. He was prepared to give up at several different points of his life but, now that he is so close to becoming a part of history, he knows he has to last. He knows, though this is his darkest time, he has to survive for the sake of more than only himself.

NanVash puts death out of his mind as he unrolls from his pseudo-cocoon and feels the ground, searching for some vibration that would tell him someone is moving around him. He feels nothing as the Sukayishiru is still floored next to him after using a lot of energy to execute the Dark Secret technique that left him black. Considering that, NanVash gets to his feet and yells to anyone who is listening, "Guys, I'm useless! This guy blinded me and I can't hear anything either!"

Synite hears him but does not know what he can do about it. *Not only can they fight, but their power is so dangerous that,* he refuses to think further down that line as it would lead to a defeatist attitude. He grunts and grimaces, gritting his teeth enough for to hear it. He fights the pulsating force pulling him downward enough create a wind wall to carry him down to the sandy surface. He is crouched over but on his feet, though, near enough to Fabric to where the elder statesman can hear Synite's laboring. "What'd he do to me? Gravity keeps going up and down."

"I don't know," he has to yell and grunt out his responses from the middle of the scrap with the captain, "but whatever it is, you and Lone both got hit by it," Fabric cannot tell the difference between vertigo and the randomized gravity from the outside looking in. Fortunately for the both of them, they only got hit by one of these special attacks at a time. If one were to get hit by both, which has happened to some before, the victim does not survive very long to talk about it.

"I have to do something," Synite says as the Sukayishiru with the club and mace begins to recover. "I can't just," he drops to one knee as the gravity jerks him down.

Lone slides across the sand to get beside the two of them, "It looks like mine wore off," Lone reports, leaning a lot less than he was when he was stuck against the side of that pillar.

Fabric gets on his guard and Lone comes up beside him, "We have to protect Synite!" Lone had his confidence hit by being the first down but he is up again and ready to do battle. He joins Fabric in fighting, showing a fortitude Fabric had not seen from him since the royale during the escape. Lone takes a much more aggressive approach here than he did with the other Sukayishiru, giving Fabric some time to assess the situation.

I have to do this myself! Synite struggles around, trying to assert his Will beyond the power of the pulsating gravity. He concentrates and calls for Gale to assist him in creating an energy star in the same way as he did against Lord Qor the last time he was in this position. She sends a bolt of energy down to him but he is unable to handle it.

The energy from Gale crashes into him, disrupting the other connection with Thesia, 'But you don't haveeee to, Cairo! Weeee can do it togeeetheeeeer!' the demon of knowledge tries to tighten its grip. 'I can cureeee you and you can beeeee that much closeeeeer to eeeending this war!' He calls for Gale again, 'Theeee poweeeer sheeeee holds in eeeeescrow for you has nothing on what I can giveeeee!' She tries to send more but this time he is able to roll over on his back and catch it with his hands. He ignores the bursts of gravity for as long as he can but one of them is so powerful that his own energy blows up in his face.

At what cost? And that is when the demon knows that Synite gave in. 'Theeeereeeeee is no cost in theeee opportunity to leeeead your teeeeam into victory, Cairo! This fight eeeends in theeeee bloodsheeeeed of a frieeeeend if weeeee do not act now! Theeeeeey areeeee too poweeeerful for us to ignoreee!' If Synite had ever come in contact with a salesperson before in his life, this one trumps everything he has ever heard. 'I am theeeee phoeeeenix's fireeeeeee within you, Cairo! Leeeeeeet meeeeee riseeeeeeee!'

And, with that, she feels him concede to her grip without a word. He gives up the fight against her and accepts the influx of power she has offered. The flood of energy surrounds him and lifts him high above the battle happening below. Bolts of dark blue, nearly black lightning pop around him and down into the sand sending shards of black glass flying from the contact. One of them cuts Lone across the arm and he yells up at Synite, "Hey! Be careful up there!"

Before he can shout any expletive, Synite slams into the ground beside him, throwing sand up around him. His eyes go from a dark as deep as space back to their normal blue with a blink. Lone and Fabric can feel the electricity circulating around him, his rise in power daunting. Synite stares down the captain of the Sukayishiru, "Let's get this over with."

Synite feels that, even if there were an army of Sukayishiru, he would be able to win without missing a beat. He looks over to where NanVash stands with his wings spread wide, still wrapped in darkness, and surrounds him with a cube of protective wind, lifting him out of harm's reach.

He flies over and punts the downed Sukayishiru whose weapon Fabric broke into the wall, breaking his breastplate and the horn on the back of his left shoulder at impact. When the horn breaks, his gauntlet and helmet both go to ash, combining with the sand, and the unconscious human warrior beneath the power of the Sukayishiru is revealed.

The captain sends sonic blasts at Lone who is completely back to normal again, dodging them all left and right. Synite blows through the latest sonic blast, knocking it to the side, and tackles the captain, knocking her through two of the pillars. The tackle had the force of a booming tornado behind it as shown by the swirling wind trail behind Synite.

Fabric is finding it hard to understand his abrupt rise in power but chooses to step back and observe instead of interrupting the progress. Thunder rolls and lightning dances around the sky above them, Gale still clearly connected to Synite. She sends another flash of energy down to him and he focuses the blast at the creeping owner of the club and mace. It cracks his armor wide open, throwing the captain to the side and him to the ground.

The Sukayishiru with the hammer recovers and increases his strength to the maximum. He picks up his hammer like a child's toy and, feeling as unstoppable as Synite, swings as hard as he can at him. Synite, with the help of Thesia, felt the Sukayishiru moving towards him and started to move away in time for him to dodge.

Fabric backs him up and tries to hit the powerful Sukayishiru with timesplitter to slow him down but the captain takes his attention before he is able to lock eyes with the hammer's powerhouse. Lone punches the captain as hard as he can with his bigger hand, turning her head away from the attack. Synite gets to her faster than he is used to moving and knees her in the gut. Off her feet, Synite grabs the top of the captain's head and slams the back of it into the ground. Her helmet cracks a little, strands of light brown hair poking out.

She gets up quickly though, trying to blast him back with a sonic boom spreading from her center. Synite crosses his forearms in front of him, left over right, as the boom pushes him back around two meters. Before his feet stop, he is already in her face again, using electrically-laced punches.

She kicks him back and throws another sonic wave at him but, instead of taking it, he claps his hands in front of him. The crash of the thunderclap and her sonic wave spreads laterally; Synite shows no reluctance to get back in the mix again, thinking that he has an answer for everything. Thesia's power energizes him as he feels sinfully strong and fast, light as a feather with an atomic punch. Not only does he charge them with electric energy now, but he also swings so hard that thunder rolls with every punch.

Synite flies back into her face before she can recover from the concussive quality of the thunderclap. He knocks the captain around like wheat in the breeze, his attack almost indefensible. Lone had never seen someone so powerful get handled so brutally, almost disagreeing with how rough he is on the woman. Then, he remembers that she would have readily killed him by now if he was weak enough for her to do so. His actions are immediately excused as justified in his sentimental heart.

The other Sukayishiru come to her aid, swinging with their all to get Synite off of their leader. He blocks and dodges everything, almost unconsciously. Fabric is not using his timesplitter at the moment but everything feels like it is in slow motion to Synite. He feels like a war veteran battling trainees, slamming two of them against each other.

He catches the club as its owner swings it at him then yanks it out of his hand, initiating a tug-of-war with the chained mace on the other side. Synite electrifies the weapon, passing the pain through to his opponent, causing his muscles to contract. Synite continues the electrifying until he sees the hammer coming for his head. He drops a wind wall between them as he lets go then crashes through the wall to tackle him down.

Synite steps back again fast enough to dodge the next swing of the giant hammer but not far enough for the force of it to trip him up. He uses a strong wind to pick him up again and get him in arm's reach of the Sukayishiru that is attacking him. He steps back out of Synite's range and immediately becomes the target of fifty large ion orbs. He uses the hammer to protect him as best he can but Synite gains ground on him.

The Sukayishiru rolls the hammer along the ground while taking a hit from an ion orb to create distance. Synite skies over it and continues his rapid fire. He raises his hands to charge a larger blast but the Sukayishiru jumps at him, starting to swing the hammer too. Instead of going for a blast, Synite sends a rope of electricity down and wraps it around the downed Sukayishiru. The rope begins sopping up what remaining energy they have and converting it to energy Synite can absorb. 'Your neeeeeew poweeeeeers areeeee fascinating!'

After he has more than enough, Synite releases the ropes from their drained victims and looks to direct that energy into the one attacking him. A star comes from his chest and he grabs it then pushes it directly at the Sukayishiru, who swings his hammer at the blast. The energy shocks him thoroughly and they both get to the ground, Synite not staying put for very long.

He calls for tornado winds to surround his hands and the energy he holds in them. The winds circulate and spread, lightning streaming down to meet the storm. That dark lightning weaves up his arms, wrapping them all the way up to his shoulders. The tornado in his hands grows as Gale automatically assists his elementalist energies, the force of wind not stopping the Sukayishiru from his attack.

They both swing at each other with the screams of war, the force of one thousand twenty-four men with one thousand twenty-four hammers colliding with the power of an F4 tornado. The Sukayishiru warrior clutches his hammer when he sees what it will be meeting, tightening both hands. The collision is epic, throwing sand, pieces of the columns, Lone, and bolts of energy around the Sword as if someone hit them with a vehicle. The force behind the blast throws everyone not at its epicenter into the air, some landing softer than others. The already injured captain is nowhere to be found after being buried in sand, the subordinate with the club and mace unconscious from the assault on his nervous system.

Lamentably for the Sukayishiru, the energy of his albeit extremely powerful swing declines drastically after impact but the energy of a storm is perpetual. Synite's slamming typhoon barrels through the strength of the swing, catching the hammer and its holder and throwing them both into the wall of the Sword. The impact against the wall crushes most of the bones in his body and the horn on his armor that ends his term as a Sukayishiru. His mask and gauntlet blow away in the wind along with his last few breaths.

Thesia helped him to gain enough power to turn the tide in this battle, showing their overall strength but also doing something he never wanted to do again. Even though the barbaric killing of this warrior was in his defense, he will still feel remorse over it. The Dark Secret drops from NanVash as well, giving him back his senses as its caster dies.

After the current clears, Synite finds Fabric and Lone, standing next to them as they face the two remaining Sukayishiru. *Thank you,* he reluctantly praises the demon inside him, immediately feeling regret for using her, or allowing her to use him, he is not quite sure which one happened.

"I don't know what happened, kid," Fabric tells him, eyes still locked on their opponents, "but you reached a new level out there. No one on this planet except maybe Amethyst and Psilos would stand a chance against that kind of power," and he emphasized the word maybe. "Your potential is much greater than any of us could have imagined."

"I agree," Lone looks over at Synite's dusty, bruised body. "It's like you didn't even need us from the beginning. Man! Did you not know you could do that?"

Synite has to try and hold his head up high to keep from showing the embarrassment on his face, "I didn't," Synite tries to wrap his mind around the maybe that Fabric offered. "If I did, I would've saved you all the trouble, came out here with only Psilos and Amethyst and held all twelve of them off by myself." He releases the power Thesia gave him from his control, thinking about how Psilos would not have condoned the use of the demon even to get ahead in this battle.

"Well, same as the old guy said," Lone looks back at their opponents, "you took a step up. The legend of Synite continues!" Lone makes him smile, "And glad to know you're on our side. Terribly glad. Horrifically glad!" NanVash joins them from the sky, catching his breath from behind the rest of them, with gratitude across his face.

Despite the odds of victory declining tremendously over the past few eins, the Sukayishiru do not know defeat. To raise a white flag is not something they are wired to do. The captain clutches her naginata and her last teammate grips his club and mace. As they get their feet ready to attack, two ships streak through the sky over their heads, moving next to each other. Synite looks as they double back, looking as if they are moving together and not in a dog fight, and recognizes the lead ship as the Caracalla. The other he does not recognize but, for it to be flying next to their home the Caracalla, it must be an ally.

 # CHAPTER XXVII

On the Caracalla are Kraa-Nuve, Proximity and Desha, the latter ready to execute their small portion of the plan. Aboard the other ship are two beings that nobody expected to show up: Benjamin Davis Stone and Airiq Driven, an original Thorn of the Rose and a newly proclaimed permanent member of the Vanguard, respectively.

"Yeah, I resemble him a little," Driven told Stone after Kraa-Nuve dropped him off to meet him. "Who are you?"

Stone, a man who lived quite a rough life, shifted his cigar to the other side of his mouth, "Do you know who you father was?"

"You sound as if you know him better than I ever could," Driven assumed by the way Stone was talking. "What's your name?"

He pulled the cigar out, "Call me Stone, chibi Saga."

"Sergeant Ben Stone," Driven grinned, putting two and two together fairly quickly considering his extensive memory bank. "I guess you don't go by guer--"

"Not anymore, kid," all of the playfulness from before wiped away from Stone's face like rain from a windshield. "Stone. Just Stone."

"Works for me," Driven knew better than to take a war veteran back to times they wish to leave unremembered. "So, why'd Kraa-Nuve drop me here to you? Is he trying to reclaim me into his little group of revolutionaries?"

"I don't know nothing about a revolution," Stone admitted, "but I heard you got some friends who need your help."

Driven is as friendly as the next salesman but, "Forcing me to put my life on the line for a cause I don't understand isn't a very friendly thing to do, don't you agree?"

"I also don't know much about what y'all went through either," Stone continued his disclosure. "The only thing my friend Kraa told me is that your friends, the ones you've been with at war and peace, the ones who saved your ass when it was about to be an alien entree," he pointed in the sky, "they need your help now more than ever and probably gonna keep needing it until we all perish. Does that sound about right, chibi Saga? Because I know your dad would give me permission to kick your ass if he knew you were abandoning your friends."

Driven uncrossed his arms, "Are you--"

"Did I say I was done talking?" Stone crossed his to show he means business. "Was permission granted for your rebuttal? I think not!"

Driven looked confused, "I mean, you paus--"

"Are you calling me a liar? Not in a thousand full moons of Earth Six has anybody," Stone's tone temporarily went to soft, "and I do mean anybody," and back to yelling, "called Stone, Sergeant Benjamin Davis, a liar and lived to learn the truth!"

"I wasn't calling you a liar!" Driven tried to vocally overpower him and possibly gain an ounce of respect that way. "It was an observation!"

"Oh, you're real observant huh?" Stone put his arms behind his back, "You prefer to watch instead of being out there in the mud with your fellow warriors, right? You'd rather let them all die with each other and be the only one at the funeral, right?"

Driven was astonished at this stranger's level of discourse. Stone is the type of being, or so Driven assumed, who does not care to study his way into or out of things but is the best at what he does. "No, I wouldn't," Stone knew that might strike a chord with the youngster.

"Then what are we waiting for?" Stone gathered his things and Driven followed him to his ship, one that he is certain is faster and more capable than the Caracalla. They got to the dock and walked under the shadow of a magnificently powerful looking craft, "His name is Gallyntheis."

"That's a noble name," Driven examined it from the outside, making a list of the mechanical and weaponry setups he recognizes. "I guess we better hurry if we're going to catch up to Kraa-Nuve," Driven recommended after seeing the engines.

Stone stopped and looked back, "You talking down on my ship, son? This young man has been to hell and back more times than you pissed your pants as an infant and grown man combined!"

"No! Umm," Driven's bluntness might get him in some trouble with this guy. "I'm only challenging you as Kraa-Nuve would've wanted me to." Driven waited, holding eye contact with Stone's cold face.

"Yeah," he chuckled and scratched the back of his head, "that old coot probably would!" They boarded the Gallyntheis and blasted off before long, tracing the path the Caracalla left for them.

"So what's the plan exactly?" Driven asked as they passed through the outer system line, all security shut down by Spoilsport. "We storm in like we own the place and wreck shop?"

"Basically," Stone grinned as he starts learning to appreciate Driven's style as it reminds him of a mix of him and Tobias. "Exactly how I like it. We help where help is needed, assist in the rebuilding effort, maybe find a nice Ulqueusian restaurant," Driven has never had Ulqueusian food before but generally is not afraid to try anything twice. "You know, the usual vacation stuff after the battle is over." Stone remembered the feelings he had in the hundred times he drove into a fight having very little intelligence about the opponent or at least knowing how unpredictable the situation was; this situation is comparable for him. A hail came up on-screen in front of Stone's central system chair, "Talk to me!"

"Kid there?" Kraa-Nuve popped up on the two-dimensional screen.

Stone pointed a thumb in Driven's direction, "Right behind me. He's eager to get a piece of the Earth 11 scum."

"Should," Driven came close enough for Kraa-Nuve to see. "Gun pro."

"So I read," Stone pulled up his file nonchalantly and Driven was caught off guard.

"There's a file on me? Let me see that!" Driven leaned over and looked through it, making sure nothing majorly incriminating was in there. "I'm definitely not this boring!"

"If that's how you want to put it," Stone rolled the cigar from one side of his mouth to the other. The Gallyntheis flies up next to the Caracalla at the system's inner line, waiting for the security to approach for their usual checkpoint activities. In the midst of them approaching the Gallyntheis, several alarms went off inside their security gate offices. The small ships around the gate started to leave the gate, Spoilsport laughing as he pulls the strings on this complex puppet dance.

After their security backup had been summoned to another gate, the Caracalla moved in reverse, Stone following suit then waiting until the backup security is at a safe distance. "Kid?"

"Yeah?" Driven responded, mildly anxious about the situation.

Stone pointed to the station below him, "Have a seat down there for me. I think you'll find yourself at home."

"Have to hit, go," Kraa-Nuve spoke down to A'rris in the gunner's station chair. "Ever ready." The almost teen-looking merging of Proximity and Desha smiled and gripped the triggers.

Driven was as caught off guard with the Caracalla's barrage of fire as the checkpoint security that was basically rendered defenseless. Driven joined the party and bore down on them with laser fire. Once they have done enough damage, the Caracalla zoomed through the checkpoint as fast as their non-PSL engines could take them. Stone blasted forward as well, trying his best to keep up but the Caracalla is definitely a step ahead in the open-space speed category. Stone chuckled heartily, "Welp!"

"Looks as though we have some fun times ahead of us, aye captain?" Driven put his feet up on the weapons' control panel.

"Kraa is the captain, not me," Stone said with as little aggravation as he can, trying to remain affable.

Driven tried to recover, hearing the hint of annoyance and sensing his body temperature rise enough to show signs of it, "This is a beautiful interface you have down here, Stone! Who designed it?"

"Came wit' the ship, kid. And, nah, I didn't pick it out. Good try though," *at least he's trying,* Stone appreciates such things.

"On-planet seven eins," Kraa-Nuve told them through a mouth full of vittles. "Time snack."

That seven eins could not have gone slower for Driven as he watched Stone's closest TAT clock, his trigger fingers itching like they had been bitten. It was not long to Kraa-Nuve before they saw the glow of Earth 11, since he knows that time goes faster for him when he is chewing, closing on their target was fueling Driven's excitement.

About halfway to Earth 11, they met a fleet of ships they did not recognize. The fleet allowed them to pass through without any friction at all. Kraa-Nuve came over the communication, "Prophyrian. Clean later." They slide through inner space to the atmosphere and into Atlani airspace, not seeing the other members of the Vanguard as they survey the situation. Driven is immediately disappointed that there is no welcome force of guns and ships trying to destroy them.

"This sucks!" Driven complains until he sees the colossal Sukayishiru running. "Hey, Stone!"

"I already unlocked it, kid," the veteran expected the young Driven to be exactly the opposite of his father, attracted to the action. He does not waste time thanking Stone as he freefalls from nearly a thousand meters above the surface.

Stone follows Kraa-Nuve as he circles back around to the gate of the Sword, blasting the doors. A'rris drops out of the Caracalla and through the opening created by the gunfire. As A'rris gets into the halls, it splits into Proximity and Desha in a flash. They had practiced the transition from separate to together and separate again for days, enjoying the feeling of merging so much that they did it probably thirty times a day. They run through the catacombs of the Sword, racing to the entrance to the dungeon and blasting their way through the gate.

"Y'all ready to make a break for it?" Proximity grabs one of the inactive automatons' halberds and starts unlocking cells.

"We need all of you to keep some order!" Desha's plea falls on deaf, newly freed ears. It is not complete chaos as they are all going in the same direction, but a stream of inextinguishable excitement heading out into the free world. She stops letting them out and grabs her communicator, "Wait Prox! There are too many of them and they're overrunning us!"

"I thought it looked cool as shit to see 'em all runnin' around all crazy!" Proximity pauses the unlocking process as well.

"Captain," Desha speaks through, "we need someone else at the gate to round them up!"

"Wild good," Kraa-Nuve thinks it may be beneficial for the fight at the gate for them to be as untamed and disorderly as possible.

"The enemy isn't expecting a hundred slaves to storm out of those gates, Desh," Proximity reminds her. "We'll clean up after!"

Desha listens as he starts back freeing the slaves from their cages, enjoying the excitement and danger of it. None of the freshly freed beings attack either of them, fortunately, but they do continue in the same direction. They do not even show any unrest about the pause in their freeing process; they just appreciate the beings with the keys.

Every prejudice, every bit of stigma any of those slaves against each other disappeared as soon as they hear the beautiful song of freedom in their collective ears. Some of those races of beings truly do hate each other enough to where they would kill each other given the chance. However, they believe, with no prior agreement for this, that there will be time for conflict later and they should work together for the time being. There have not been any injuries so far during the exodus to freedom, so Desha reconsiders and returns to unlocking cells with the halberd. Freedom is much more important at this point for them than instruction and tidiness.

Outside of providing a portion of the cover for their escape, Desha feels an extreme gratification for becoming a part of the Vanguard. They have done truly great things as a group and individually, as history undoubtedly will read. She thinks back to when she first got to Atlan and how she thought it was a dismal and despicable place. If it was not for the Marks and the competition, she never would have come. Though the Marks became a nonissue fairly quickly, so did the IGS. Everything went to the backburner when Proximity entered her life and she appreciates every moment as if it was gifted to her by her own God.

She looks for her other half as he is opening the cells on the other side of the vast dungeon. They share their feelings as, even though they are not A'mal, she basks in feeling his elation come through her. It seems as though the more they connect with A'mal, the more their hearts grow together and the less separate they actually feel.

Proximity's happiness enhances Desha's and vice versa. He does not know it immediately but the more they experience things together outside of A'mal, the more fulfilling the connection is for the both of them. He feels her heart smiling and having fun along with him right now, new to this sense considering it is not his people who experience this type of connection regularly. He is indeed excited to the highest degree that they are together freeing hundreds of beings from the overt oppression of the Enslaver and Its minions.

After landing softly with parachuted assistance, Driven runs stride for stride with the giant Sukayishiru with absolutely no idea where they are running to. He is still amazingly excited about the next move, unable to wait much longer. He grabs Grace, beelines to the back of the giant foot and shoots through his Achilles. The Sukayishiru stumbles but keeps going as his blast is but a pinhole and not enough to stop him. "You're a stubborn one, huh?" He pulls Mercy out as well, aiming both of them at his huge heels. He fires off round after round until he sees the big foot start to overextend.

The Sukayishiru turns down another street as they pass into downtown Atlan, slipping as he tries to pivot. He catches himself against a building, crashing through some of the upper floors with his elbow and tons of weight. He recovers despite his injury and keeps moving towards the battlefield though not nearly as fast or efficiently as before.

Driven hops up through the rubble he caused from stumbling into a stone structure and keeps shooting at the same leg. The Sukayishiru gets annoyed enough to take a swing at Driven with his gigantic axe. *Wow*, he is surprised by how fast the Sukayishiru moves; even though the running was swift, he could not imagine someone that big still having normal dexterity. *No matter. I'm still much, much better than normal!* After that swing, the Sukayishiru keeps trying to move towards assisting his captain of the Black and Onyx team.

Unharmed, Driven does not even consider stopping, so he blasts rounds at the opposite leg. The Sukayishiru limps, actually feeling the shots sent through this time. Now, instead of trying to get back to the fight, he focuses on defending himself. So, he turns with his axe turning with him, the swing aimed at the pest. Driven rolls under it, passing through the sparks that fly from the black axe blade scraping the ground. He shoots up at the Sukayishiru's fingers as he gets ready to swing again. His grip is loosened by the sting of Grace and Mercy and the axe almost slips out of his hand but he switches to his left hand which is covered by the armored gauntlet.

Driven runs at his leg and blasts his toe, forcing him to step back on that bad Achilles. He puts his guns away and jumps at the giant leg that tries to kick him in midair. Driven instead catches his shin with both hands and rides it until he puts it back on the ground. The massive fighter tries to shake him off but Driven's grip is strong against the grooves of the custom armored shin plate.

Tobias's son starts to climb up the plate until its owner slaps at him. Fortunately for the normal-sized being, he felt it coming soon enough to jump out of the way and up to the next plate that covers his knee. Driven keeps climbing and jumping out of reach until he gets to his spine, right under the unreachable part of his back. The Sukayishiru drops to one knee and tries to scratch Driven off of him, which fails the same as every other attempt. He throws himself back-first into a nearby building but Driven jumps off over his shoulder in enough time to not get crushed.

Driven pulls his guns again and shoots in the gap between the ornate helmet and breastplate. He gets caught by the massive right hand and shoots down at his thumb and wrist, loosening his grip and letting Driven fall out of his hand. He tucks and rolls as the goliath grabs his neck from the pain of being shot. The giant starts to shrink, going from ninety-eight meters back down to seventy-two, and then stabilizes at that height again. Driven assumes he is getting the upper hand in the battle and gets even more enthusiastic about taking him down.

The colossus's strategy for getting smaller, however, is to make himself less vulnerable as his exposed areas are smaller and harder to shoot. This quickly becomes a double-edged sword as Driven's accuracy does not decrease in comparison, but the relative size of the bullets increases along with the holes they create. The shrinking is not something the Sukayishiru can quickly renege though as his power is in changing his size, regardless of the direction, and has to be used carefully. He pays close attention to his use or else he will either snap back to normal size without notice or be stuck in whatever size he is in as permanent until he can get enough energy to change back. Once, he was stuck at ten centimeters tall for several hecu after testing the limits of the technique.

The battle ahead of them continues to rage on as well, Arra heating up some clay that Gith creates. Together, across the entire field, they throw hardened spears, flaming discs and exploding bombs of dirt and mud. He puts up a little wall of mud and she bakes that too for him to use as a shield. She covers his approach with streams of fire, charring the ground in front of him.

Gith runs straight for the Sukayishiru with the shield as he keeps throwing wind blades. Arra runs to the side of him and leads him around the blasts with the marks burned into the ground. The two shields meet and Gith's cracks but then he falls backwards and covers the Sukayishiru in the same mud that he broke through. Gith pours it on heavily, the mound of mud coming from the cracks in the ground and coating the shield and the enemy holding it. Arra comes down by them and drops a firefall atop the pile of mud, hardening and heating it to a scalding temperature.

Lo is using all of his powers against the captain, the black lion sword in his right hand as he tries to cleave her to pieces, the hydra spear in his left hand to thrust a hole through her or drown her, and the polar shield on his back to keep her powerful whip at bay. Castra continues to box with the telekinetic, at a standstill similar to Lo and the captain.

Castra's division of the Vanguard finally understands that they have the upper hand in the battle until they see the giant, down to fifty meters again, stumble into the street. The moment they see him, Castra feels like everything is about to fall apart and they are going to be right back at square one, on the defensive at every turn. Gith thinks they might be in a better position with the one he and Arra have neutralized but this definitely puts a hamper on things, remembering how difficult it was at the beginning of the battle. Arra stops the firefall and prepares to focus on taking out the giant, ready to sacrifice everything as fire elementalists tend to be in life or death situations. Lo cannot and will not take his attention off of the captain, no matter how impossible the end may seem with that giant joining the fight again.

"That's a big problem," Castra says but all of these doubts are erased as the giant Sukayishiru keels over in front of them, shrinking methodically back to normal size. Driven runs and puts his foot on the fallen raisin of a warrior's chest, guns still hot from his assault.

"Problem solved!" Driven aims one at each of the remaining Sukayishiru to get a gauge of their movements through the sights of his weapons. He loves the captain's teleportation and notices a mathematical pattern to the way she defends and the way she places her attacks, something a being without his brain would probably never notice considering how complex it is, albeit predictable. He also enjoys the telekinetic's hand-to-hand fighting technique, something he has seen before and could probably trace whoever the being is behind the mask back to the gym he learned it in fairly easily but he saves that tidbit of knowledge for another time.

Driven decides to hop into the fight with Castra and the telekinetic first as he feels he can impact it the most in the shortest amount of time. He turns Grace away from the captain and aims it with Mercy at the telekinetic. Castra sees him aiming in his peripheral and leads the fight to a position he knows he cannot get shot in.

Driven takes a few shots to check the integrity of their armor; the bullets bounce off and ping into the ground. "I guess I have to be a bit more hands on with these guys, huh?"

"Pretty much!" Castra grunts out as he rolls out of the way as Driven comes in swinging and connecting with the side of the telekinetic's face, the aggressor reminiscing on how it felt to cross that wolfrat through the window back on Yar JK. He nearly sheds a tear of joy in remembering the good old days before he knew of this multiversal conquest that they have on their hands, before he knew he was almost obligated to be a part of this revolutionary defense of freedom.

Appropriately, the Sukayishiru does not drop nearly as easy as the wolfrat did. Driven throws a few more fists, some landing, some blocked, some missing altogether, to show he is more than a power puncher. Castra brings in his interpretation of fisticuffs as well, showing how good of a team they make as their timing with each other is pretty good considering they have never breathed the same Air before, if what Driven's respiratory system does could be considered breathing.

Skirting through the sky over them in the Gallyntheis, Stone circles back around to the gate and sits the ship on top of one of the buildings that remains standing. He gets out and looks over the situation below as well at the skies, trying to formulate some course of action quickly. He changes his mind when he realizes exactly who he is dealing with and how fluid this situation will be until the very end. He, instead, prepares for the worst and plots the fastest course to the safest place he knows then puts in a few calls to beings he knows will have their back on the way.

When Stone sees Psilos exit, he remembers that entire fleet of Prophyrian warships that is in position to come on-planet at any relevant point in time. One of the explosions from below makes him jump, the pyrotechnic Sukayishiru giving his best defense considering he is the only one left to defend the gate.

He does give a merry fight though, probably deserving to be the captain of a troop if he lives and if the Sukayishiru remain necessary as their subject to be protected is under siege by a very powerful foe. The Sukayishiru may not survive if they have nothing to protect. They are not the type of band to go adventuring or be proactive about sorties and campaigns. They must have a very specific job though they are not soldiers for hire. Their type must have a goal directed by someone else's ambitions or needs.

And the Vanguard has become quite the diversion from the Sukayishiru's overall task. Driven and Castra Nim's double-team of their Black and Onyx clad opponent ends successfully as Castra crushes the horn on his armor, turning his helmet and gauntlet to dust. Lo continues his clash with their captain as she is the last warrior left in their group. The captain of the Midnight and Diamond colored group and her remaining counterpart are in a stand-off against Synite and the rest of the crew. They do not quit but also have no suicidal tendency. They are not programmed to do so since, fundamentally, they cannot complete their task of protecting the Enslaver if they sacrifice themselves.

 # CHAPTER XXVIII

A rumble comes from the entrance into the Sword. Proximity and Desha run out, hand in hand, excited about their accomplishment. "This is gonna be good!" Proximity says over to his love. The freed slaves storm out in droves, the last fighting Sukayishiru's automatically trying to control them with explosions. He cuts a couple of them down but soon his aggression is met with a wave of freedom. They take his weapon, rip his cloak and he quickly disappears under the dogpile. Even the explosions, which go off randomly since he has no control over his fate at this point, cannot save him now.

Seeing that this fight is finished, Psilos has a moment to focus on the rest of the atmosphere. He feels that something terrible is about to happen somewhere near so he yells for his team, "Everyone except Proximity, Desha and the captain of the ship above us needs to meet in the arena immediately! You three must control the pack!" Before they can confirm or deny his request, Psilos is in the Air on the way to try to stop something though he is afraid he will not be able to change the outcome regardless of his effort.

This is one of the moments that Synite had dreamt of since he was dropped into the Sword's dungeon. As those warriors, those beings who were either taken from their homes or put in the worst of situations, flood the street, the purpose of them coming back to Atlan has been successfully completed. The death of the Enslaver, an eventuality at this point, and the unification of the Vanguard are beautiful pieces of lagniappe for him, Psilos, and Amethyst.

"It's a shame that neither of them are here to enjoy this scene," Desha keeps her eyes glued to the hundreds coming out of the Sword, clamoring for their first breaths of freedom. Though the few who are around to police the moment will surely tell them of it, this would have been something special to watch.

They come out like co-eds rushing their home field after a historic victory. And, surprisingly, Stone, Proximity and Desha's job is very easy right now. The golden dragon Porussa, one of the most beautiful beings in many universes, steps out in the middle of the throngs of others. They move around her as she steps out slowly, fearlessly, and with elation crossing her face. Stone looks down from under the Gallyntheis as the crowd builds in the street and the chants of freedom in twenty different tongues ring through downtown Atlan.

Those regular citizens who are still in the area watch on, those who were unaware of the true nature of the Sword frightened by the sight and those who were conscious of the Sate'Gran's nature elated. Both groups are overwhelmed by the earth-shattering enlightenment that is taking place right now: there is an entire population of beings that were being held in escrow like circus animals to later entertain the masses.

Another group is trembling in fear, the group that was intrinsically invested in the endurance of the Sword's enterprise. Their security has been compromised and, in order to salvage it, they have to move very quickly, although it is basically too late for most of them to do anything about it. These beings, peppered around Earth 11, will have their day in court very soon if the Vanguard does their due diligence, which Fabric had already been seeing to with the help of Spoilsport. These two, when they were working out other, more crucial details to the survival of this effort, had also been gathering lists of beings whose thumbs shall be drained the most by the toppling of the Sword. It was fairly easy for Spoilsport, given his talents, and should not be difficult to follow-up on those who live through this revolution.

However, this scraping of the underbelly of Atlan cannot take away from the celebration that is shaking the streets of the metropolis. The news breaks all media sources across the planet in moments and reaches a few of the other Earth planets soon after. This intergalactic wildfire spreads, reaching trillions of homes with the images of freedom and unity.

The actual Atlani police come down on the group finally, attempting to quell the excitement. As the members of the Vanguard expected, this peaceful demonstration of revolution after the real violence may take a turn for the worse. Proximity and Desha turn A'mal and emerge from the celebration to meet with the captain of this particular police force that has been on the Enslaver's payroll for decades. Stone drops down to the edge of the crowd as well, certain he can dissuade any outbreak of carnage.

"If things turn violent here," Stone tells him, "the consequences could be horrific. It'd be best for you to keep your distance and make sure nobody opens fire on them."

He looks Stone up and down, "Why should I listen to you? Who are you?"

A'rris giggles at him, "We freed 'em! Ya better leave 'em alone!"

"Then it's you that I should be taking into custody!" the police captain starts to reach for A'rris but Stone catches his arm.

"You don't want to do that," Stone puts the arm back by his side and pats him on the shoulder. A'rris sticks their tongue out at the police captain as Stone continues, "You wouldn't be able to arrest this rascal anyway. Do you remember the IGS? This is, umm, the child of the two beings who disappeared during that race," which is probably the easiest way for the feeble mind of the officer to understand exactly what A'mal is. "Do you think you'd be able to hold someone who could make a lap around this entire city faster than you could put the cuffs on 'em?"

After blowing the police captain's mind, his only response is canned: "What do you want?"

"We have what we want already," Stone motions towards the dancing crowd of free beings behind them. "You want peace and you have it right now. You don't want a thousand beings that have been trained to fight to the death to come down on your little squad here. So, let's be logical here. Your Sate'Gran has no power over this place anymore," Stone reports. "That's over, if you haven't noticed."

"Way over!" A'rris adds with a snicker.

"Things are changing in this world and you do not want to be the one who loses everything for fighting the fight that cannot be won," Stone looks deep into his eyes. "All you have to do is usher the crowd. You'll have help very soon, I assure you. Now," Stone looks at his credentials and smiles, "how do you want this to go, captain?"

Orbiting a moon at the edge of Earth 11's system, a message is relayed from a local satellite to a long carrier that has been prepared for such to come. The news alert comes up on several different screens in front of several different characters. The being that matters the most sighs and rubs his pale hand back across his pale, bald head.

From his throne, he turns on his communicator that speaks to the entire ship, "Giving all honor and understanding to Vxrasunin, General Animosity and I are going to pay a quick visit to our post on Earth 11. Remain ready for our hail if things take a turn. I am positive, by the Will of Vxrasunin," he stands and pulls his black cloak around him, "that we shall make it back very soon."

He hears someone enter his space, "Just us two, Lord Heresy?" Her voice is muffled by the device that covers her mouth. "Such a personal touch. I feel it."

"I assumed you would, General," Lord Heresy's dark, eyes shift. He is one of the most plain, unassuming looking beings one could ever imagine. His nose is regular; his eyes, ears, teeth and mouth are all regularly imperfect but not so much that one would notice; his head is shaped regularly and he is average height and weight. There is absolutely nothing special about the way Lord Heresy appears, nothing that would cause him to stick out in a crowd, which is exactly how he loves it. "Is your ship prepared?"

"Yes, my lord, always." Animosity turns to go to her cockpit.

In this dark room, Lord Heresy wraps his gauntlet gloved hand around something that is much blacker than the darkness of the room and the darkness of night. He and his tool fade into the shadows, the same as the Sukayishiru were made to do, and meet Animosity in the cockpit of her imperial ship. The ship breaks off from the carrier and quickly jumps into PSL.

The attendees' wailing turns to whimpering and crying as the crowd surrounds the wounded Enslaver. Amethyst feels no remorse as she floats to the ground and the ring disappears. The attendees start to kneel around their fallen leader, from the edge of the crowd on in.

Suddenly, It stands back up, groaning in pain, and locks eyes with Amethyst. The dragon's left eye goes completely black and the center eye glows, 'You are mine.' Amethyst freezes, unable to move or feel anything, her entire nervous system cut off from her brain and her memory wiped by the power of the dragon's eye. 'You have always been mine. Nothing has changed except the time.'

A few of the attendees get up and they clear a path between her and the Enslaver, "What's going on?" Amethyst tries to struggle but still cannot move as a couple of attendees retrieve her. "Where am I? Who are you?" They grab her under her arms, by her waist and lift her, the sight of the monstrous Enslaver frightening her. As they carry her to their leader, she looks afraid, more fearful than anyone has ever seen her look in a very, very long time.

'This is why no one opposes me, my prize,' the Enslaver tells her. 'This is why you never lifted a hand against me. You knew you could never win no matter how strong you are.'

"You," Amethyst cannot squeeze out many words, finding it harder to breathe the closer she gets to It. "What are you?"

The Enslaver's eye glows bright with the power of victory, 'There is nothing you need to say, prize. Once I take that bracelet from you and attach it to one of your copies, this game is all but over.' Her brow shows confusion and It reads that same feeling in her heart, 'Oh, you never knew?

Look around you. Pay attention to them, all of them, carefully. How they're all the same height, the same stature. How they all sound the same and have the same eyes, your eyes.'

Amethyst looks harder at the attendees, "What are they?"

'Still cannot tell? Even without any memory, you are less intelligent than I believed you to be when I brought you here, which is probably why I've had so much trouble,' all of the attendees start to take the wrappings from their faces, revealing themselves to their original. All of the females look almost exactly the same as her and all of the males look like masculine versions of her. 'The elders were made first and then I made hundreds of them at one time. The only reason they exhibit differing personalities is because I gave that to them. It is how I decide what to do. I drop different perspectives into their feeble emotions, which they inherited from you, and see who wins.'

"But," she mentally answers her questions of 'how' and 'why' before she wastes time asking them. She looks at them, stopping on a face that resembles her own as the rest of them do. She looks in her own eyes, nearly terrified at the sight of them, but also remembering herself.

During an excavation on the way to Atlan, the Enslaver and several of the others who are now in league with It discovered a scientist. That scientist was hiding from several Earth authority groups on this moon that the Enslaver had paid for a contract excavation. They were there to dig up a powerful elementalist energy source that was not attached to any specific element but had energy ratings off the charts in every pole. As they pulled the bracelet from the deepest crater on that moon, they made a deal with that scientist to continue his scientific exploits in cloning advanced beings. The scientist was paid with a pardon on Earth 11, which blanketed every Earth planet, and was allowed to go home to his family again.

'Even that mistake, the one I made train Synite into becoming a warrior, the one you grew to love. Do you remember Santhia?' *Santhia? Synite?* Amethyst could not have known, even with her emotional memory and the Will of the bracelet starting to click back in her brain. 'She was an experiment, one of the few given the opportunity to have their own personality. It was a partial success,' Amethyst's memory floods her as she tries to make sense of how she could not have noticed as they had similar features. 'She served her purpose as did many of the other more disposable copies of you,' the Enslaver chuckles from its actual mouth.

"You're pure evil!" Amethyst cries out, gulping down a breath as best she can. She feels her hatred again, the power of the dragon's eye not nearly strong enough to keep her at bay for long. Then, the avenue the Enslaver felt the need to take her down sparked a few things that refreshed her. Of course It could not resist cursing her before killing her.

'I am only a cog, my prize. I am only one of the four that are meant to rule,' if the Enslaver had a mouth, It would smile at her now. 'All praise has to be given to Vxrasunin, not me, though I am a large part of the plan.'

"What plan?" Amethyst turns as she hears Its hand rise from them behind.

'It does not matter to you since you will not live to see it!' the attendees put Amethyst into the Enslaver's hands and It starts to crush her. Even though her brain is still cut off from her body, she still has very powerful survival reflexes.

Things go dark for Amethyst as she is surrounded by the black palms of the Sate'Gran. Life has never been this dark for her before and she does not truly know how to respond to it. This darkness reminds her of times when she was a young girl, searching for approval from her cold father and deaf mother, of war and the despair she went through when they lost her grandfather. Then, she recalls how much she lost when the Enslaver took her from her home and destroyed it. The crushing sadness overwhelms her, this cocoon of blackness and pain swallowing her into the abyss that she assumes is her death. She imagines that this is how it felt for many of her friends and family as they were made into dust, as the lives of billions were silenced simultaneously. The same being who delivered the end to original versions of her race is finishing the job. Her sadness turns from a suffocating blanket to the hands of rage against her back, pushing her to something. The rage of those billions for the being that took the future away from them presses against her, begging her to impart the revenge that has been eating at her spirit for more cycles than she would admit.

That blackness that surrounds her starts to change. It brightens; gaining redness that gains a bit of indigo and turns a deep purple. Her protector, the band around her arm that has both protected and given her the power to protect, is now begging her to protect herself. She can feel it urging her. She can feel. She can feel her Will rise from the soles of her feet up to her knees and hips, through her heart to her shoulders and down to the tips of her fingers. The energy from the bracelet that is tied into her takes over her body for a moment and then gives her the control she needs.

Rays of amethyst glow from the Enslaver's hands and she spreads them apart with her usual ease. She floats there, her skin kaleidoscopic with a purple undertone, the bracelet's energy permeating and fueling her every cell. Amethyst looks straight into the Enslaver's eye as it rolls erratically, searching for an answer. She not-so-calmly breaks both of Its hands, "There is nothing here that can save you now."

The Enslaver stumbles back on Its heels, toes spread for balance and locks the dragon's eyes on hers. It concentrates as hard as It can, pushing every ounce of power It has drawn from the stolen eyes into trying to reclaim control over the prize. Unfortunately for those eyes, her rage over the betrayal trumps Its power so tremendously that one of the eyes ruptures in the struggle. It blankly rolls back and closes, dead to its user.

Amethyst rushes the Enslaver, a trail of light behind her in a pavonine pattern but still in the dark purple tint, and throws It through the wall to her right. As It is landing, she puts her foot in Its gut, crushing a few bones in the process. The ground below Ometku's back caves a little under the weight of the being and the force of the push.

The Enslaver rolls over on its elbows and swings Its teeth at Amethyst and she catches them in her right hand. It tries to pull back but her grip is too strong and, instead, she yanks out the tooth in her hand. It still amazes her by its tolerance for pain but she ups the ante: Amethyst reaches into the Enslavers mouth and rips an entire row out from the bone that holds it in. It spews gallons of thick acid at her but the substance beads off of her protective coating and melts the floor.

Amethyst's frustration from sitting idly as this poor excuse for a being has decimated cultures across the stars is apparent. The directed attacks from a nearly berserk warrior bleed with emotion. Her relatively new passion for the Enslaver's destruction, at least consciously new, has taken this mission to end a beings life and changed it into making a being suffer until the end.

During the beating, every strike gives her the opportunity to think even more about how angry she is and therefore get even angrier. For instance, while she crushes one of Its legs in several different places, she thinks about how her winnings from the arena were directly or indirectly used to continue the cycle of those clones of her that run every aspect of Atlan. She, in essence, actually helped fund the creation and employment of these abominations. Had they simply been families saved from her home that were brainwashed, it may have been a different story and she might be more merciful towards them. However, that not being the case, she has to destroy them all along with their creator and controller. These thoughts enraged her enough to pull that crushed leg off and toss it to the side.

As Amethyst throws the Enslaver back into Its hall through a different section of bricks in the wall, the hole reminds her of her door that led to her balcony; the balcony that was open out to her garden and the rest of the free world. She understands now that, even without an electromagnetic bar or lock in sight, It really had her in the perfect prison: the one in which the prisoner has the appearance of complete freedom as they are allowed to come and go as they please but are so loyal to their warden that they do not want to leave.

She had not known true freedom until she was placed under the limitations that their escape afforded. She was literally confined but spiritually freed by the Caracalla, allowed to become what she was born and built to be: the meaningful crux of a movement. Without her participation and ascension into freedom, there would be no Vanguard. Symbiotically, without the Vanguard, she would not be here now, ending the Enslaver's reign and changing the landscape of several universes.

The bracelet's energy spreads through the room and her appearance returns to normal. Her demeanor is calm, though, not her usual emotional rollercoaster after using that much power. It remains to be seen whether she either has full control now or it is a temporary high. All she feels now is destruction and the readiness to impart that desire on everything. Amethyst hovers forward and the Enslaver ducks lower to show Its remaining teeth but, before It can do anything, she grabs It by the collar and raises Its central eye up to hers. "I can see the fear of death in your eye," and can no longer hear Its voice in her head but if she could she would bet It was pleading for Its life. "It is well warranted."

She turns him so she can face the other dragon's eye and rips it out, blood and pus squirting everywhere from the socket created in Its shoulder. All of the attendees gasp as the Enslaver is taken apart, a timely reminder to Amethyst of their presence. She drops the monster, looks at Its underlings and then at the wet eye in her hands, thinking *This could be useful at some point.* She wraps the eye in the ring that would normally protect her and she shoots a hole out of the ceiling. The ring flies it out of the hole she created and the Enslaver gasps as the atmosphere seeps into Its foreign lungs.

"I nearly forgot about the aversion you have to what we breathe normally," Amethyst takes in a big breath and throws her arms upwards. The force from her movement blasts the majority of the roof off of that portion of the building and it crumbles behind her. An avalanche of dust rolls through but she blows it back so no one gets the opportunity to escape.

The Enslaver's breathing gets shallower by the moment as the elements in the Air rip through Its esophagus and digs into Its lungs. It drags Its one-legged, broken-armed, bleeding, toothless self on Its side, the same side she yanked the eye out of, thinking she would leave It there to die. The attendees surround Its deathbed and ignore Amethyst completely, comforting their dying master.

Now, there is a conundrum in her heart and it is right in front of her. They are only following Its orders, blindly doing what she would have done before Synite opened her eyes. *These puppets of the Enslaver, who is certainly dead, are living beings like everyone else but should they be allowed to live? For what reason should they live? They were made to serve that which they kneel before right now. That was their sole purpose and, now that It is gone, what is their purpose? Surely they cannot reproduce and if they did, it would be abominable.*

They are me, or at least what I used to be, but now that part of me is gone. And, now, they should be gone as well. Amethyst rises, her indomitable resolve is to destroy everything It has created. No matter how it feels later after having killed a multitude of beings that look identical to her, she knows she cannot allow clones of her to walk this Earth or any other.

  # CHAPTER XXIX

Promis barges in on Spoilsport watching split-screen footage of all of the fights, confident in herself and what she wants. "Take me to them," she demands, only met by laughter from Spoilsport.

"Who?" He points at his screens, "Them? You're a joke!"

"Do you think I'm joking with you?" her head tilts and her hands on her hips. "I'm serious!"

"That's what makes it so funny," he cackles even more.

Promis shows her fed up face, "This is my life and I want to be by their sides!"

Spoilsport turns away and kicks his feet back up on the table, "I saved your life. I'm not going anywhere. So, go back in there and get comfy," he reclines and she approaches but he stops her with one motion. "I would calm down before you do something you'll regret, Sarah."

"Don't call me that!" she yells. "You don't get to call me that anymore!"

He stands up and points at her, "Look!" he yells back, his yell much more frightening and bite-over-bark than hers. His lips pursed, "I understand your predicament and, honestly, I almost wish I had left you alone so your saviors could go on a merry chase to find you. But, you have no idea what they're getting into by even being here right now and neither do they. Your friend just killed the Enslaver," he points back at the screens, "and now we're all happy, but they're about to be in a universe of shit considering who is approaching this planet right now."

"What?" Promis is actually scared.

"You know they should've stayed away," he reminds her of her own words. "He shouldn't have opposed the Thorns, Sarah, because I call you whatever I want to call you."

She tilts her head, confused, her brow and raised hands confirming it, "Thorns? What are you talking about?"

"I know who you were, Sarah Cassidy," Spoilsport revels in making jaws drop for one reason or another. "You dealt with the Thorns before they were hunted. You know more about their history than even I know which is another reason you are so attractive to me. There are very few beings that know secrets I haven't learned and you have some things I'm quite curious about."

"I don't know what to say," Sarah admits after panting moments of hesitation.

"There is too much power within the idea of the Thorns," he reminds her, "which is why they were taken over to begin with. Cutting one thorn at a time does not kill the rose. It doesn't work, no matter how ugly it is."

Promis fights back her tears, "I can't even breathe the same without him," she admits. "I know I might end up dead but I would rather be dead in his arms than alive in yours." She walks away again, as she does best, and slams onto the chair she was sitting in before. Spoilsport does not take such ugly words to heart though considering he has heard them so many times. Instead, he relaxes back into his chair and looks back at the battles that wind down in front of his eyes.

He watches closely the footage of Amethyst as she rises above the house that the Sate'Gran built and looks down at the destruction. The Enslaver stops breathing, Its body limp and shriveling, hollow of whatever spirit It had left from all of the terrible things It had done.

She points down at the body and it starts to compress, crunching and curling into a purple marble the size of a large melon. It shoots up to her and she catches it, feeling the end in her hands. She takes that giant marble and flies to the coast, dropping it into the sea brusquely and coming to a stop for a moment. Her shoulders relax and she sheds a tear of relief as the marble sinks into the deep, their mission here finally complete.

She, however, sees one more objective: she flies up above the clouds in an instant and stops when she feels she is far away enough to do what she needs to do. She takes one breath and zips down, feet first, into the very foundation of the Sword of Atlan. The halls fall in on themselves, the skybox collapses, taking Synite and everyone else in the Sword off guard, the streets of the market split open and the entrance gate is obliterated. Every attendee around is killed in the quake and, fortunately, all of the civilians that were in the streets had gone out of range already.

The freed slaves and the police force surrounding them go farther out into the market and take cover with each other. Once things settle and the dust clears, the party continues to drive on peacefully, though much of the peace in downtown Atlan had been disturbed much earlier in the day.

The silence after her action is deafening, no sign of life coming from anywhere except for the members of the Vanguard, the slaves they helped escape and the Sukayishiru that are still conscious. Amethyst emerges slowly from the crushed buildings and flies down to the Sword, landing next to Synite as he stands at the edge of the rubble that used to be the skybox.

"It's done," she turns to him and sighs. "It's really done."

"I heard," he refers to the big hole in the earth she opened up and turns to the rubble behind him, smirking with pride. "How do you feel?"

Usually around this time, she is ready to give her life away from the post-usage depression but, right now she is ready to start her life anew. "Relieved."

"Amethyst, you did it," he makes a smile creep across her face, feeling the bond between them is stronger than ever, as though nothing can come between them now. "You remember the first time we met?"

"Yeah!" she laughs at the thought. "You were so weak and uncertain of yourself. I'm surprised I even let you in!"

Synite rubs the back of his neck, "So was I! I was so nervous to even be in the same room as you." He brushes the hair from his face, "I knew that there was no way I was leaving that room without at least a sliver of your confidence."

"You did exactly that," she tries to remember exactly what she felt. "Even with everything that was holding me back, I felt that you would be the one to change all of this," she puts an arm up to refer to the destroyed Sword behind her.

"What was it?" he steps closer to her, grabbing the same hand she had up. "What was it about me, me specifically, that drew you in?"

She searches between his eyes for the thing she has been looking for, "I don't know." She feels the warm breeze that continuously surrounds him, "I had never felt someone speak to me so honestly, not since I'd been here. It wasn't your words. If anybody else had come in there and said the exact same words to me, I wouldn't have budged."

"I see," Synite intertwines their fingers.

"Not that your words were meaningless, Cairo," she puts both hands on his face, looking up a little. "I knew that behind those words was the love that we have now. I know I didn't show any emotion then because it was still to be proven."

"I do remember that," he laughs, puts his hand on top of one of hers and puts the other hand on her waist. "You were cold!"

"I wish we cou--" The ground shakes below them, the epicenter of the quake coming from the coast where she dropped the Enslaver. Amethyst turns; Synite sees the concern on her face and is ready to do whatever she needs him to do. Assuming it is another transformation or something even worse, she releases him and goes to the sky without hesitation. Synite follows, ready to devote the rest of his time to finishing their job here. They blast over the majority of the Vanguard, unaware that their mates are converging into the arena as Psilos commanded.

What they do see, however, is the police surrounding the mob of free beings that are celebrating in the street at the gate of the Sword. Amethyst stops over it and Synite hovers next to her. They grab each other's hands and watch the moment that they came here for, the moment that they left here for together. "This moment," Amethyst says knowing the Enslaver is gone and that the revolution's presence in Atlan is solidified, "makes everything else worth it."

The pride that they are sharing right now is enough to make even the death of their friends and the separation from their families disappear for only this moment. Right now, there is no pain, no suffering, no anger, no guilt; there is only the happiness of this moment which wipes away any doubt either of them may have ever had about what they were doing. Living in this moment has immortalized them beyond the stars and beyond the words of those who run the press on Atlan. This is beyond politics, beyond Universal Marks, beyond value; this is the type of moment that many beings wish they were born to erect.

And moments only last as long as Time allows. This one is ended by another rumble under the city, a reminder of why Amethyst and Synite were in the sky going in this direction in the first place. They embrace and look at each other as Synite says, "Let's finish it."

Back when the slaves finished the pyrotechnic Sukayishiru, the captain with the whip teleported away and to the side of the only ones left. Rarely have they mixed groups but survival is the main objective for them at this point. The three of them look at each other and start to back away from the Vanguard; they seem to have gotten some sort of order from their commander. The Caracalla touches down in the sand of the arena, Kraa-Nuve stepping down to watch the last events of this battle from the front row.

On her way to the coast, Amethyst sees the marble in the air bulleting towards them. She pushes Synite out of the way and dodges accordingly. They turn and chase the whirring marble, Amethyst nearly catching up to it but not before it shoots above the clouds. She looks back and tells Synite to stop instead of trailing it with her. He and the demon inside him do not agree with the plan but they follow her directions, keeping an eye on her in case things take a turn for the worse. Synite does her a favor and clears the sky so the both of them can see exactly what is going on with this rogue marble.

It stops on the edge of the stratosphere and blinks once, flashing an ultra-bright light across the sky like an explosion without the destruction. Synite feels a shift in the Air, almost as if the entire area is flipped; then, he sees why. Clumps of earth rise slowly from ground zero of Amethyst's battle, headed towards that small orb in the sky. The chunks of the Sword, the Enslaver's throne and the hall surrounding it, the skybox and other pieces that have meaning to Ometku start to rise quicker.

Amethyst is flying towards the marble, surrounded in the energy of the bracelet, and does not see what is coming up behind her. The energy that also protects her in the vacuum of space and allows her to move independently of any outside force also renders her ignorant of the gravitational shift that occurred between the marble and the planet below.

She cocks a fist back and puts her all into the open-palmed punch she connects with the giant marble, trying to send it into space but with no success. She does succeed in cracking the orb though, not understanding why it would not move. The essence of death, from all the attendees and the Enslaver, begins to leak from the marble, strengthening its pull on the portions of planet even more.

Synite skies to try and save her from the storm of rock but stops as he feels the gravity pulling him out of control. He corrects his path and yells to her, "Get out of there!" A sinking feeling goes through his gut, unsure of how Amethyst will pull herself out of this, though his confidence in her is unwavering.

The ground continues to crumble upwards, sounding similar to a thousand horses herding through a field. Unable to hear Synite over the thundering gravitational pull, Amethyst turns and finally sees the pieces of earth coming at her, its range so wide that it is too late for her to get away from it in Synite's direction without being crushed. So, she tries going to the other side of it towards space.

The leaking substance from the marble suddenly expands into a giant black sphere, ironically screaming the same scream the Enslaver did during Its transformation. It keeps expanding towards Synite and, out of nowhere, Psilos flies up and yanks him out of the path of danger. The sphere stops its expansion, swirling like the jet stream that wraps around every Earth. It thumps the same as a heartbeat and then contracts powerfully, bringing everything within its circumference into a central point and vanishing. All of the pieces of the Sword, all of the crushed history, and all of Amethyst are gone in an instant.

Synite looks around after bouncing back from Psilos's maneuver, unable to believe what he saw and even more astonished by what he can no longer see. He does not feel Amethyst's presence anywhere on Earth 11 anymore. He does not sense any sign of a being more powerful than Psilos on Earth 11 anymore.

"She's gone. She was right here next to me," he turns behind him and back towards where she was. "Now, she's…" he cannot choke out the rest of the statement.

Psilos puts a wall around the feelings he has about their most revered idol turned friend being destroyed. He had prepared for something terrible but could not see past the Enslaver's transformation. And, even if he had left his fight to save her, at least thirty other lives would have been sacrificed as a result from what his allied selves informed him. Psilos has avoided so many terrible occurrences with his actions but could not save the lives two beings that meant a lot to him.

Psilos quickly urges Synite to join the rest of the remaining Vanguard as they move to meet in the arena. It is difficult for Psilos to pull him away as his eyes are still locked on the spot where Amethyst was. Synite has had his fair share of memorable moments over the last decade or so: his father getting killed, the battle royale, freedom with Promis, defeating Lord Qor, meeting Amethyst, their escape and losing Santhia, seeing Amethyst's power for the first time, fighting next to Psilos on Prophyria, losing Promis, seeing the Quiet Men, seeing the freed slaves and the moment before this one, when the darkness swallowed one of his dearest friends. Of all the moments, this one has him in the most disbelief. His father was a police officer and they die in the line of duty all the time. He had the feeling someone would be lost in the shuffle of the escape from Atlan. Promis was hardheaded and he knew she would slip up at some point, causing something extraordinary to happen. However, Amethyst was, to him, the denominator of the Vanguard. He does not feel as though the tether between them is broken; it is like it completely disappeared. He cannot feel any connection, her spirit, the warmth of her soul is nowhere to be found. Outside of his father's memory, she was his primary motivation to succeed. She became more than just a friend but someone he could truly count on no matter the circumstance. She was both a protector and a vulnerable jewel that needed to be protected at all costs. And she is now the reason those tears stream down his face as he feels completely helpless and vulnerable after having lost nearly every woman that has ever meant anything to him in his lifetime. His mother left, Santhia was killed, Promis is all but gone and now Amethyst. And then, it hits him.

Synite turns his head, finally hearing Psilos's pleas, and follows him away from the destruction. He tries his best to keep the noise of things he cannot control from his mind as he tries to continue leading. "We have to get everybody in the same place," he keeps close enough to Psilos to hear him over the wind.

"Where do you think the best place would be?" Psilos gives Synite another distraction. "All of the living enemy forces have gone away from the battlefield. I told Suubai, Coldsmoke and Orchanik G to go to the Sword where you were. The combination of Proximity and Desha are policing the freed slaves."

"Away from them," Synite suggests. "We do not want to think we are coming to threaten putting them back in."

Psilos keeps his thoughts ahead and on the innocent bystanders that are still roaming those streets. "Should we allow them to roam free in the wake of all of this destruction?"

"When we," Synite remembers the moment he had with Amethyst watching the freeing of the slaves, "when we passed over the gate where they were, the police and that other ship seemed to have them in control."

Psilos stays next to him, "Do you believe we should go to the edge of the city then?"

"Let's meet everyone in the arena and move from there," Synite and Psilos fly steadily over to the arena, passing over the gaggle of his ex-dungeon mates. Psilos drops down to Proximity and Desha, separated from their A'mal form, and tells them to push to the arena.

Back by the Gallyntheis, Stone sees their movement and gets back to his cockpit to do the same. When he steps in, he notices a call coming in from an unknown location. He picks it up and sees Spoilsport picking his things up like he is in a rush to leave from where he is at. "Did you mean to call me?"

"Of course I did!" Spoilsport continues to gather his items, Promis waiting for him at the door. "You have to get off this planet right now. He just got out of PSL and is thirteen eins away from you!"

Stone's heart drops, "Are you talking about who I think--"

"Get out of there! You don't have time for debate!" Spoilsport closes the call and leads Promis out to his car.

"Where are we going?" she asks as they rush out of the condominium. "Tell me something!"

"I can't be seen here with you right now by Lord Heresy," because if he was, the Thorns might think he has chosen sides against them and that would destroy some of the things he has put in motion. He has covered his tracks so far but being seen with someone who they know is loyal to the Vanguard would put him in a precarious situation that he may not be able to dig his way out of currently. "I don't have time to explain but maybe when we get somewhere safe."

The Gallyntheis darts over the city after Synite and Psilos, Stone calling Kraa-Nuve to no answer as he is still on the field. He pulls up next to them and opens the lower hatch to encourage them to come aboard, which they do.

"I'll explain on the way out but we have to get everybody off of this planet right now!" Stone's voice comes from a communication pad on the wall of the lower storage. "When we get above them, y'all have to go down there and get everybody on a ship. We have ten eins!" Stone notices a blip come into the inner space of Earth 11, near satellite orbit range so he speeds up and gets them over the black sand in less than an ein.

Proximity and Desha made it there a few eins before them and are heading to get on the Caracalla. Driven approaches Coldsmoke who sits on the rubble by himself. Castra, Lo and Lone tell each other about their experiences in the battle as Orchanik G joins them. Fabric introduces NanVash to Kraa-Nuve while Gith and Arra marvel at the Caracalla with Suubai coming up next to them. On the other side of the field, the last of the Sukayishiru are camped together, waiting on what the next move will be.

The bottom of the Gallyntheis opens up and the two founding members of the Vanguard drop down to the revelry of their team. There is applause and cheering which is quickly stopped by the waving hands and booming yell of Psilos: "We must exit this place. Now! Get on a ship and we will rendezvous with the Prophyrian fleet and decide what else to do from there!"

Sensing the urgency in his voice, everyone gets to the ship closest to them, the Gallyntheis lowering to meet everyone that crowded up next to Psilos and Synite. "Where is Amethyst?" Lone yells to Castra Nim over the exhaust of the ship but is only met with a shrug.

"She must be on the other ship," he yells back, Synite and Psilos are both unprepared to explain to them what happened to their leading lady.

In front of them, on the other side of the arena, one of the suns on the horizon is blotted out by a fairly large imperial warship drifting into the atmosphere. The Caracalla blasts off into the atmosphere as the Gallyntheis gets to a safe distance for everyone to board, Stone at the top of the hatch stairs. Synite and Psilos are looking directly at the ship that approaches, not moving to board. Their backs to Stone, they cannot hear or see his urges for them to board as quickly as possible.

The imperial ship lands swiftly and turns its engines off. The back hatch opens and digs into the sand, Animosity stepping down the ramp to meet the faces of the Sukayishiru that had been awaiting their arrival. She turns up to the entrance and says, "Only four survived. They must have met quite the battle!"

The vantablack spear, which looks curved in the light, taps the top of the ramp as the pale-footed Lord Heresy makes his way down to see his remaining creations. "They may still prove to be useful at some point." He hears the roar of engines coming from the other side of the arena and steps over to the side of their ship, his robes waving in the wind and the spear sucking in every bit of light around it. "Oh?"

Psilos watches Synite's body language, hoping that he does not attack. "We must go," he looks back up at Lord Heresy, seeing the figure but feeling absolutely nothing of his power. He can feel how dangerous the other being is that walks back up onto the ship with the Sukayishiru but has absolutely no gauge on the power of the new leader of the Eighteen Thorns.

Synite and Heresy meet eyes for the first time but certainly not the last, as they both know immediately. They see something very different in each other, something that neither one of them have ever seen in any other being in their lives. Synite feels that the being in front of him is the true cause of the great majority of his problems for the past few cycles and Lord Heresy feels the exact same way, though he has knowledge of who Synite is and what he has done here. Synite heard and ignored Psilos despite the powerful engines, but he still turns to get onto the Gallyntheis with Psilos's encouraging hand.

"The forces of Dark are much more active, zealous and conscientious, and determined than the forces of Light," Lord Heresy watches as the ship containing half of the Vanguard exit the atmosphere, noticing the crushed arena around him finally. He scowls, searching for the spirit of the Enslaver and feeling not even a glimmer or remnants of what used to be one of the most important members of the new Eighteen Thorns of the Rose. All he can see is what was a reliable source of income now crushed to pieces.

For a sec, Lord Heresy wants to go after them and take recompense for all of this destroyed property. Instead, he turns away and joins Animosity aboard their ship.

"They are heading to meet a fleet of Prophyrian ships, certainly there to either protect them or come down here and fix this," she tells her superior. "We would not be able to neatly finish a fleet that large."

"You're saying we should leave then?" Heresy asks for clarification.

"I'm not saying we would lose," she is aware of Lord Heresy's abilities as well as his plans for the future, "but it would be a while before our defense would arrive. Considering what we have yet to accomplish, I would not advise forcing the action yet."

Lord Heresy takes these things into account and takes a seat as a throne made of shadow catches him. "Outside of a few temporary and circumstantial quarrels," the bald figure looks down at the Sukayishiru that come to his feet, kneeling before him, "the naïve human race has never fully had any true enemies outside of their own kind," then he looks out at the destruction the Vanguard caused to the Sword on the horizon, "until now."

* * * * * * *

The labor of love is the only labor worth more than the hours (or hecu lol) you spend on it. That is what TVA will always be for me, a labor of love. These hundreds of thousands of words take a lot of work. A lot of exhaustion naps had to be taken in the making of this story. A lot of other things, going out with friends, mending relationships, traveling, were sacrificed for me to make my mark on history. Your support in this endeavor has been crucial to the worth of continuing to pursue its finish. I've spent a lot of words thanking you for it and will spend more as your support remains in my corner.

If you know me, you know that book 3 is the most crucial book in the series to me as it opens up the Pandora's Box of TVA and, as I've said to many of y'all, shows you how deep the rabbit hole goes. You know, that part of any story where it goes from being potentially really good to "Holy crap, this is more than I expected!"? My brother and I have had full confidence that introducing the Thorns and tying most of the mysteries in that I've only sort of mentioned would propel TVA into something beyond just a good couple of books.

And I hope you enjoyed it as much as I loved creating the story, weaving the plot and designing the fights. I knew before I started writing the first book that this would be the part of the story that REALLY hooked people in and it's my sincerest dream that it works!

And, if it doesn't, well, maybe the next one will!

-LDR
@TVABooks on Twitter
www.facebook.com/TheVanguardAnthologies
BOOK FOUR IS ON ITS WAY!

The Prophyrian fleet came down soon after everyone left and began the reconstruction of downtown Atlan led by Fabric, Synite, A'rris and their Psilosking. The Prophyrian engineers had their work cut out for them, having to adapt all of their techniques to the environment of Earth 11. They collaborated with local workers and engineers to boost their knowledge base and eventually hired mostly Atlani people to lead the projects. The cooperatives tried their best to make sure the style and functions of the new downtown Atlan molded well with what the world needed: something completely different from what the Enslaver had built. The automatons were broken down for parts and were a tremendously important part of the technological studies used to update the marketplace.

The Vanguard made sure to stay in the loop on the changes in society and the realpolitik of Earth 11 since the most corrupt and powerful figure in the planet's young history is out of the picture. After the exposure of the Enslaver's illegal dealings, many other arenas started to shut down after persecution by the Earth Union with the assistance of the Prophyrian fleet. Most of the leaders who are found guilty of unethical practices are put in Intragalactic prison. An investigation is opened against the entire arena system and the new ones that are opened afterwards do not allow for death matches.

Unfortunately, no efforts could have stopped the economy from crashing. From everyone who worked in the office buildings around the Sword to peddlers in the market to the anchors of the Sword report, over a thousand core workers' jobs were destroyed. The billions of Marks that went back into Atlan from the profits of the Sword are gone. The tourism industry from those that came around the arena during events is crippled. Even after the rebuild is finished, without the blood of the Sword, Atlan will never again be the bustling metropolis that it was with the arena.

In the meantime, Fabric and Psilos took the forefront in ushering in a new democracy, allowing even Prophyrians who wish to stay to run and vote on a new leadership board, similar to the one created to recover Earth Prime after the Cataclysm. That board's most important objective was to bring viable ideas to the table that can sustain the recovery of the economy and attract people back to Atlan. Despite having a tremendous influence, Synite avoided the political arena altogether, showing no favoritism to either side of the argument regardless of what he believed considering the weight of his favor to the public.

There was a meeting that took place after the board was established about what to do with the Sword's funds that had been sitting in limbo since the destruction. Approximately nineteen billion Marks, give or take, leftover from liquidating the Enslaver's properties were claimed and distributed to the thumbs of the members of the Vanguard and the slaves, not to the city itself. They made the decision to trust those thumbs to do the right thing with the Marks and it worked out well.

Fabric, Psilos and Coldsmoke all gave Synite their shares and he used half of everything he had to pay living wages to everyone who assisted in the rebuild, including the Prophyrian and Giarc immigrants. He donated another two-thirds of those Marks plus the M154 million share that was meant for Amethyst, the worth of her old estate, to several business owners so they could expand and hire more employees. All-in-all, he is left with less than five million Marks to his thumb.

After being the catalyst for a revolution, Synite decided the most responsible thing to do was to stay on the sidelines and protect the city as a sentinel instead of leading them philosophically. After going through so much turmoil with that same population, he did not feel capable of it. He would visit the countryside where he spent a few hundred thousand Marks to build obelisks as memorials for Santhia, Vulcarus, Amethyst, the Grujek family, the civilians lost in the battle and the attendees. The Enslaver's name is never referred to by any Atlani being ever again, Its era disappearing in the annals of history.

While they are still in Atlan, Synite delivered Porussa her surviving eye, putting the past behind them, glad to have seen her and had no regret about keeping her alive. She was more thankful than anyone else even though it was only one eye. After she got it surgically re-implanted, she spent a few days with him, recognizing that Synite is as beautiful as she had imagined. Even though only half of her sight and very little of her ocular prowess was returned, the space between being blind and being able to see is wide.

Every night, she, Synite and the teen A'aradon form of A'mal watched the moon for different reasons. Porussa enjoyed the light of the moon and the brightness of the stars after not seeing them for a very long time; one night she and Synite were there alone and she told him of the power of her eye outside of only beholding the beauty of things. He confessed to her about the demon inside of him and asked if she could free him of it or suppress it at least. They spent hecu upon hecu delving into his mind and emotions, her single eye not powerful enough to flush him of Thesia. They were able to weaken and suppress the demon's control over Synite as well as reconnect him with Gale. He was also able to confess to Gale of Thesia's presence, igniting better communication and forcing the three of them to remain aware of each other.

A'aradon and Synite were wondering if Promis would ever return to them one night as they basked in the moonlight. Spoilsport never attempted to make contact and Synite got so frustrated that he put together plans to leave. He even gave up on the little hope that Amethyst might have survived the crushing darkness that took her from them. There was too much pain left in this place for him, too much history to face day in and day out.

Despite the beauty that grew from the necessary destruction the Vanguard caused here, the place seemed completely empty for Synite as the two women that enriched his life the most were no longer there. Those around him are no less important but those losses were too much for Synite to stay around for. Fabric put him in touch with Alexander and they made plans for Synite to go through the shift doors to find a new home.

"As much as I…" Synite tells Fabric, Psilos and A'aradon as he and Driven gather their things in the cache room of the Weapons Rack, "I need to get away." They have learned that a champion's path is a lonely one. Beings like Synite have what some consider very strange destinies. They are in the vein of the old gamblers who would enter tournaments and win consistently despite the nature of the games. It is strange to see the same few make it to the top of such fields of play but, when you know that games are about more than odds but skill and choices, it is understood a bit better. "This life has done nothing except take things from me. If I could punch a hole through Time, just reach into it for a moment and get back everything I've lost, I'd give every ounce of energy I have to do it. I'd give up this elementalist shit," Synite sighs, "I'd give up the lightning, the wind…I'd hand this power to a stranger. I'd go back to being a slave to have my father, Santhia and Amethyst back."

"I can understand that," the more mature A'mal tells him. "We wish you all the luck in the verses."

"I love you all and I'll never forget everything we have been through together," they embrace for what some may think is the final time. Psilos and Fabric let him go through that shift door, Synite refusing to look back and Driven salutes. The door closes behind them and they are gone.

Psilos is glad Synite is going off on his own for a change despite feeling some sadness as he goes away. He recalls when he left and how they must have felt being separated from him for the first time. This feeling is a little different than when he went home to repair his world. Though the majority of the Vanguard is here on Earth 11 still, Psilos feels alone without Synite and Amethyst. He has no idea what to do but exits the cache room and goes out front.

Psilos tries his best to look at the bright side as everyone returns to a couple of things that they have not seen for a long time: normalcy and peace. Castra Nim, Proximity and Desha have moved to Nortghard with Arra and Gith who have started a life together. Umberito Ya-El, better known as Coldsmoke, remains in Atlan with Psilos and Fabric though he connected NanVash with his trainers in K'oma when he went home to announce his resignation. Along with the ex-Sukayishiru who had their powers taken away but did not die in the battle, Suubai and Orchanik G have started to build their own arena. Other past active arena fighters, Abo

Mimao, Soldati Dmittri and Korisong, joined them, using the training grounds outside of Atlan as their base of operations.

Again, Psilos is glad for all of the progress that has been made, between the people surrounding him and the land that has been recovered. The destruction of the Sword started a new era of prosperity that he has to attest to Synite's Will. There is only so much one being's Will can produce, though. This, the peace of Atlan, the freeing of the slaves, the revolution of the minds of much of the populace, this is enough to make anyone proud of their life and of the future.

On the other side of things, Psilos has to adjust to a lifestyle he did not expect. Fabric joins him outside, "I'm so glad you and Synite came to know each other."

"As am I," Psilos looks to the sky. "I have not felt so close to anyone as I do him in probably more than a century."

"That's quite a long time there sire," Fabric pushes his glasses up and joins him looking in the sky. "I wonder what the future holds for him."

"Beautiful things, I am certain," Psilos looks down as a beautiful thing approaches them.

Resembling a mirage, she strolls up to the two of them, words prepared for this moment, though she figured a few others would be around. Fabric looks down at her, wiping his glasses off, "Where is everybody?"

EL CORAZÓN DE UN HIJO

UNA TRAVESIA A TRAVES DEL CORAZON DEL PADRE

M. JAMES JORDAN

Fatherheart Media
www.fatherheart.net

Dedicado a Jack y Dorothy Winter

ÍNDICE

RECONOCIMIENTOS

No se le puede hacer justicia al reconocimiento que quiero hacerle a Jack Winter como la influencia más fuerte en mi vida. Cuando era un joven cristiano en la escuela bíblica, el Señor me habló con voz clara diciéndome que quería que fuera como un Josué para este hombre, para Jack Winter. Por los siguientes veinticinco años, Denise y yo fuimos primeramente discípulos de él, pero luego nos volvimos en hijo e hija de él respectivamente. Así como Josué asimiló todo lo que el Señor le había mandado a Moisés, yo traté de asimilar todo lo que el Señor le había impartido a Jack. Antes de que Jack muriera, impuso sus manos sobre mí y oró para que yo recibiera la impartición de su manto de unción. Desde que Jack murió, estoy tratando de continuar y entrar a la tierra que hay después del río Jordán, justo como Josué continuó después de que Moisés murió.

Quiero reconocer con gran afecto a John y Sandy Randerson, Jan y Sandra Rijnbeek, mi esposa Denise y mis hijos, a Jack Winter (de nuevo) y algunos otros que continuaron creyendo en mí, me sostuvieron y me llevaron cuando no era capaz de sostenerme a mi mismo.

Quiero agradecer a Stephen Hill por sus horas de trabajo sin las cuales éste texto no hubiera sido posible. Y gracias también a Wilson y Erica Sze por sus palabras de ánimo y su determinación de ver este trabajo impreso.

Quiero agradecer a la gente de *Fatherheart Ministries International* por la compañía y el aliento a través del camino mientras exploramos juntos el amor del Padre.

Por último – simplemente no encuentro palabras – no creo que existan aquellas que puedan decir - «Gracias» suficientemente a nuestro Dios y Padre por su maravilloso plan y su habilidad de cumplirlo en mi vida. Él estuvo conmigo antes de ser yo cristiano y desde que lo soy ha sido fiel a mi—sin impresionarse por mis éxitos ni asustarse por mis fracasos. Él simplemente me ama.

En 1977, Jack Winter vio algo en medio de una miríada de refracciones y reflexiones que estaba haciendo acerca del cristianismo de la época. Fue un destello fuerte de luz pura. El pudo observar al mismo corazón de Dios el Padre. Las consecuencias todavía están reverberando a lo largo de la cristiandad hasta el día de hoy.

Jack y Dorothy Winter habían vivido una increíble aventura hasta ese día. Llenos del Espíritu Santo y fe, habían empezado la travesía hacia lo desconocido, abandonando al mundo y sus afanes, y vivían con un nivel de dedicación al Espíritu y a la Palabra de Dios que es muy difícil de encontrar. Antes que pasara mucho tiempo, cientos de individuos de todo el mundo se les habían unido en lo que se denominó «Daystar Ministries». Fue en esa red de comunidades que Jack se topó con este encuentro con el corazón del Padre.

Por los últimos veinticinco años de su vida, Jack dedicó los recursos extraordinarios de su rica vida interior y su profunda experiencia ministerial, exclusivamente para ministrar el amor de Dios. Se había dado cuenta que este amor de hecho era una sustancia, una sustancia que podía ser impartida y que podía sanar al quebrantado de corazón. Entrecruzando el globo terráqueo, voló más de un millón de millas, y pasó de sol a sol sosteniendo a muchos miles de personas entre sus brazos, viendo la maravillosa sanidad de Dios. Yo fui una de esas personas. Jack había visto la realidad del amor paternal de Dios—la culminación de la revelación del Nuevo Testamento.

Este libro cuenta mi travesía personal hacia y dentro de esa luz. Jack fue un padre espiritual para mi, y antes de morir en agosto del 2002, él me impuso manos para recibir su manto. Pero aún la abrasadora revelación del amor del Padre que él había recibido había sido solo una parte. Siempre hay más. Este es el camino que yo he encontrado al Padre. Su amor al ser derramado en mi corazón me ha llevado de ser un simple cristiano a tener una vida como un hijo de Dios. Esto ha resultado ser solo el primer paso. Lo más emocionante es que siempre hay mucho más.

James Jordan, Taupo 2012

Cuando el Padre se revela

~

Durante los últimos quince años, he viajado alrededor del mundo más de treinta y cinco veces, hablando en incontables conferencias e iglesias, compartiendo acerca de la revelación del Padre. Frecuentemente siento que el Señor me lleva alrededor del mundo simplemente para contarle a la gente lo que me ha ocurrido en la vida. Alguien me dijo una vez, «James, pareces pensar que el amor del Padre es la respuesta a todos los problemas de la humanidad». ¿Que si realmente creo eso? Yo lo creo, con todo mi corazón.

Mientras más me adentro en esta revelación del amor del Padre, más me doy cuenta de la completa renovación que necesita el cristianismo. ¡Hemos tenido un cristianismo que está demasiado enfocado en lo que tienes que hacer, y no en lo que Dios ya ha hecho! Muchos de nosotros cargamos con el bagaje de una presentación falsa del evangelio. Se nos ha dicho lo que tenemos que hacer desde nuestra iniciativa en lugar de lo que Dios ha hecho desde *su* iniciativa.

Se nos ha dicho que hemos sido bendecidos para que podamos bendecir a otros. El hecho es que hemos sido bendecidos porque Dios nos ama y porque anhela bendecirnos. Se nos ha presentado un evangelio que nos dice que debemos trabajar para Dios—pero te puedo decir que esto hará, eventualmente, que colisiones y te quemes. Más y más cristianos están saliendo de este tipo de cristianismo y bajándose de la cinta de correr en donde continuamente hay que tratar de complacer a Dios y trabajar para Él.

De esto se trata el cristianismo simplemente: Dios te ama y Él quiere que continuamente vivas experimentando cómo Él te ama. Este es todo el punto del cristianismo. El llegar a este entendimiento nos lleva al reposo y al contentamiento, y a la paz interior que es tan contagiosa que la gente será impactada sólo por quienes somos. Estamos en una renovación, una reforma, una restauración del cristianismo que es, yo creo, tan importante como *la* Reforma misma.

CONOCER A JESÚS NO ES LO MISMO QUE CONOCER AL PADRE

Mucho de la impresión que he obtenido del cristianismo durante los años es que todo está centrado en Jesús. El Padre solo se menciona de pasada. De hecho, el Padre parece estar solamente en el trasfondo comparado con la persona de Jesús. Creo que esto es porque tenemos tanto enfoque en la persona de Jesús. Tenemos la idea de que si conocemos a Jesús y hemos experimentado a Jesús entonces automáticamente conocemos al Padre. Juan 14:7 es uno de los versos de donde la gente toma esta idea equivocada, cuando Jesús dijo, «Si me han visto a mí, han visto al Padre», pero necesitamos recordar que Jesús *no* es el Padre y que el Padre *no* es Jesús. Entonces Jesús *no* estaba diciendo «Yo soy el Padre». El nunca dijo que conocerle a Él era lo mismo que conocer al Padre. El dijo que el Padre estaba en Él haciendo las obras. El habló las Palabras que le fueron dadas para hablar. El dijo «Solo hago lo que veo hacer al Padre», pero Él *nunca* dijo «Yo soy el Padre».

Todo lo que enseñamos debe estar basado en la Escritura. Si vamos a obtener una revelación que no esté basada en la Palabra entonces no es una revelación de parte de Dios. Sin embargo, debe decirse que el caminar de acuerdo a la Escritura no es necesariamente lo mismo que caminar con Dios. Si caminas con Dios *automáticamente* caminarás de acuerdo a la Escritura. Caminamos en el Espíritu, no en la Palabra, pero el Espíritu nunca nos guiará a nada que no esté validado en la Palabra. Los discípulos nunca leyeron el Nuevo Testamento. ¡Lo escribieron! ¿Cuál fue su fuente de material? Caminaron con el Espíritu y el Espíritu les dio la Palabra para que la escribieran.

Una vez leí algo por Andrew Murray que me impactó grandemente y lo que me llevó a escribir este libro. Él lo puso así : «*Lo que el amor del Padre fue para Jesús, el amor del Padre también lo será para nosotros*». Verás, la falla enorme de nuestra experiencia cristiana es que aun cuando confiamos en Cristo, dejamos a un lado al Padre. *Pero Cristo vino para llevarnos al Padre*. Ese fue el punto de su venida – el llevarnos a Dios Padre.

Andrew Murray continuó escribiendo: «*Su vida de dependencia en el Padre fue una vida en el amor del Padre*». ¡Me encanta esa declaración! La razón por la que él fue capaz de depender del Padre fue porque Él sabía que el Padre le amaba totalmente y que podía depender en ese amor. En todo lo que pasó en su vida, Él tuvo dependencia total en el Padre. Luego Él hizo la declaración que me encanta más que todas ¡*Lo que el amor del Padre fue para*

Jesús, el amor del Padre también lo será para nosotros! ¿Qué lugar tenía el amor del Padre en la vida de Jesús? ¿Qué tan importante fue el amor del Padre para Jesús? ¡Tendríamos que decir que lo era todo! Él se deleitaba en hacer la voluntad del Padre. Vivía en la experiencia y el conocimiento del amor del Padre por Él. Estaba en el regazo del Padre, viviendo eternamente ahí, en el corazón del Padre. Ese era su lugar.

Creo que hoy en día estamos viendo cómo una revelación comienza a arrasar en el mundo, una corriente en el océano que va a levantarse en las playas como un tsunami y ese algo es la restauración del lugar que el Padre tiene en la vida cristiana.

Derek Prince, comentando acerca de Juan 16:6, (en donde Jesús dijo *«Yo soy el camino, la verdad y la vida. Nadie viene al Padre si no es por mí»*) hizo la siguiente afirmación: *«Este verso habla acerca de un camino y de un destino. Jesús es el camino, el Padre es el destino».* Luego él hizo esta observación *«¡El problema con la mayoría de la Iglesia hoy en día es que nos hemos quedado atrapados en el camino!».* ¡Nos hemos quedado atascados en el Camino! Hemos venido a Jesús pero no hemos seguido hacia una relación íntima con el Padre. Una de las razones de esto es que muchos de nosotros no hemos tenido relaciones íntimas con nuestros padres terrenales y por ende, cuando leemos versos como este, simplemente no lo podemos ver. Interpretamos nuestra teología como algo centrado solamente en Jesús. Yo creo, sin embargo, que Jesús hubiera dicho: «No todo es acerca de mí. Es acerca de mi Padre».

Estamos en un tiempo en donde el fundamento de nuestro cristianismo está moviéndose y pasando de ser una banca de dos patas, por así decirlo, a una banca de tres patas. Hemos tenido una revelación de Jesús y una revelación del Espíritu Santo y hemos basado nuestro cristianismo en estas dos realidades porque la revelación *es* realidad en nuestro corazón. Ahora, sin embargo, Dios está trayendo a nosotros una revelación del Él mismo como Padre, y ya que Dios es amor, ésta es una experiencia de amor. Está basada en una invasión personal e íntima del amor del Padre a nuestros corazones. Para algunas personas esto llega como una poderosa corriente, mientras para otros, esto es algo que gotea poco a poco. Realmente no importa como venga, siempre y cuando venga. De hecho, la revelación frecuentemente nos viene de forma gradual, como cuando amanece un nuevo día.

Al sentar el fundamento de lo que el Padre debe ser para la vida cristiana, quiero citar a San Agustín de Hipona quien dijo: «*La Biblia entera no hace nada más que hablarnos del amor de Dios. Este es el mensaje que apoya y explica todos los otros mensajes*». Todo tema cristiano que puedas pensar es una expresión del amor del Padre. De hecho, *todo* en el cristianismo es acerca del amor del Padre. El cristianismo sin entender y experimentar el amor del Padre es un cristianismo sin fundamento.

Algo estará desviado en nuestro concepto de lo que significa ser un cristiano si no tenemos el amor del Padre como fundamento. Aun la cruz es una expresión del amor del Padre. El amor del Padre no es una expresión de la cruz. Porque de tal manera amó Dios al mundo que dio a su Hijo unigénito, y su muerte en la cruz fue, en ese sentido, el mensaje más grande de cuanto Dios nos ama. Expresa cómo es el amor de Dios en realidad. Todo el punto del cristianismo es el amor del Padre, y la cruz remueve todo lo que se interpone entre nosotros y ese amor para que podamos venir confiadamente al trono de la gracia y subirnos a su regazo para conocerle como nuestro Padre. Nuestro cristianismo estará muy distorsionado si no entendemos que el amor del Padre es la revelación que sostiene y explica todos los otros mensajes.

San Agustín sigue diciendo: «*Si la Palabra escrita de la Biblia pudiera ser cambiada y resumida en una sola palabra y volverse una sola voz—esta voz clamaría más poderosamente que el rugir del mar: "¡El Padre te ama!"*».

Verás, ¡no conocemos lo que no conocemos! Conocemos la doctrina y aun podemos enseñarle a la gente acerca de conocer a Dios como Padre sin conocerle personalmente nosotros mismos como Padre. El tener una revelación cambia nuestra perspectiva de tal manera que, sin pensarlo, automáticamente empezamos a abordar a Dios como «¡Padre!». ¡Podemos conocer las Escrituras *acerca* del Padre, y podemos pensar que conocer las Escrituras es lo mismo que conocer al Padre mismo! ¡No conocemos lo que no conocemos!

Uno de los problemas más grandes en el cristianismo el día de hoy es la creencia de que si sabemos lo que dice la Biblia automáticamente tenemos aquello que la Biblia describe. Esta es una idea equivocadísima. Puede ser un problema particular para aquellos con una tendencia académica, como yo. Por muchos años pensé que el conocimiento de las Escrituras era lo mismo que tener la realidad de eso de lo que las Escrituras hablan. Eso me llevó a una creencia totalmente falsa con respecto a dónde estaba yo con Dios, lo cual a la larga se hizo pedazos con un fracaso personal. ¡Cuando eso pasó, de repente me di cuenta que todo mi conocimiento no me había cambiado ni un poco! Clamé a Dios para que me diera algo que me cambiara.

Estamos viviendo en un tiempo en el que Dios se está revelando a sí mismo como un Padre de una forma sin precedentes desde el tiempo de los apóstoles. Sea lo que sea que hayas sabido y experimentado en el pasado, hay un nivel sin precedentes del amor del Padre que todavía está disponible. Si podemos abrir nuestros corazones a ello, Él puede transformar toda nuestra experiencia del cristianismo y volverlo algo más grande. El cristianismo realmente comienza cuando llegamos a experimentar aquellas cosas por las que Jesús murió en la cruz para que recibiéramos: ¡el amor del Padre!

Déjame empezar la historia de cómo llegué a esta revelación. Cuando Denise y yo conocimos al Señor en 1972, vinimos desde un punto en donde no había nada remotamente cristiano. No habíamos tenido ninguna exposición al cristianismo. El edificio más cercano a la casa en donde yo me crié era una pequeña iglesia al tope de una colina. Solía ver a la gente llegando ahí. Algunos de ellos eran mis amigos de la escuela, pero no tenía idea del porqué ellos querrían pasar una hermosa mañana de domingo en una iglesia. Yo no entendía para nada. Nunca había escuchado el término «nacido de nuevo».

Cuando tenía casi veintidós años, le di mi vida al Señor. Mi salvación había sido un cambio monumental en mi vida, ya que desde que era un niño yo había sido una persona extremadamente solitaria. Vivíamos en un pueblito pequeño y por mucho tiempo yo nunca tuve a nadie con quien jugar. Los chicos más cercanos a mi edad vivían al menos a tres millas de distancia, así que después de la escuela, yo vagaba por mi cuenta alrededor de los campos y las fincas detrás de nuestra casa. Casi siempre después las clases, yo deambulaba en las colinas cercanas hasta que caía la noche y luego caminaba a casa cruzando el campo, en los caminos de las granjas, trepando las verjas y las puertas. Conocía muy bien todo el terreno, pero estaba muy solo.

Así que cuando Jesús vino a mi vida, a mi extrema soledad, se dio un impacto enorme en mi. De repente, esta Persona estaba entrando a mi corazón, alguien que me amaba, y me enamoré de Jesús debido a esto. Mi salvación fue literalmente una gloriosa experiencia a todo color. Nunca había sido el cielo tan azul ni el pasto más verde que en ese entonces.

NACIDO EN EL AVIVAMIENTO

Cuando fui salvo, Denise y yo empezamos a ir a una iglesia que estaba en pleno avivamiento. Muchos americanos usan el término «un avivamiento» de la misma forma que usaríamos el término «alcance» refiriéndonos a reuniones de evangelismo. Pero avivamiento, como lo he entendido, es cuando la presencia y el poder de Dios se manifiesta tan fuertemente que la gente lo experimenta de forma tangible. Cuando llega un avivamiento, siempre tiene un efecto muy importante en nuestra experiencia del cristianismo. Un verdadero avivamiento es cuando la presencia de Dios se hace presente con extremo poder. Es un desatamiento sobrecogedor de su presencia en un lugar en particular.

Cosas maravillosas sucedían en esta iglesia durante ese tiempo de avivamiento. Había una joven ahí que quería aprender a tocar el piano para acompañar la alabanza, pero nunca había recibido una sola lección en su vida. Un día, se sentó en el piano, uno de los diáconos oró por ella e inmediatamente pudo tocar en cualquier nota que ella quisiera. No podía tocar el piano excepto cuando estaba acompañando la adoración y empezó a tomar lecciones musicales dieciséis años después para descubrir qué era lo que había estado haciendo todos esos años.

A veces, la gente podía literalmente ver a Jesús caminar entre la iglesia, paseándose por los pasillos e imponiendo manos sobre la gente, solo tocándolos al pasar. Mucha gente tenía visiones grupales y veían exactamente las mismas cosas al mismo tiempo en los servicios. Uno de los ancianos recibía a los visitantes, luego invitaba al Espíritu Santo a venir, y nos dejábamos llevar por lo que ocurriera. A lo largo de cinco años no hubo necesidad de pastor o líder en las reuniones porque el Espíritu Santo era tan poderosamente evidente. Fue un período extraordinario. Produjo hambre en mí de experimentar continuamente avivamiento y desde ese entonces he tenido una expectativa y una esperanza de que tal vez vuelva a pasar el día de hoy. Sin embargo, yo no puedo hacer que suceda. Depende completamente de Él.

Viendo en retrospectiva ese tiempo, me doy cuenta de algo más. Cuando el Espíritu Santo de Dios se manifestaba poderosamente, yo hice la equivocada suposición de que la razón por la que Él estaba honrando a la iglesia con su presencia era porque la enseñanza era perfectamente acertada. Mucha gente a través de la historia y en todo el mundo hoy en día están haciendo la misma suposición equivocadamente. Asumimos que si obtenemos nuestra interpretación y aplicación de la Escritura de forma exacta, entonces Él vendrá y nos honrará con su presencia manifiesta. ¡Eso no es cierto! De hecho, esa suposición es la base de mucha disensión entre los cristianos el día de hoy. Sin embargo, la realidad es que Él no viene porque la enseñanza sea correcta, es su venida la que *corrige* la enseñanza. La Palabra solo se puede entender en su presencia. La biblia fue escrita en medio de avivamiento. Cada persona que la escribió estaba viviendo en un total avivamiento personal.

Así que estábamos experimentando un tremendo sentido de su presencia, domingo tras domingo, año tras año, y la gente estaba viniendo de todo el mundo. Antes de que pasara mucho tiempo, los ancianos de la iglesia decidieron organizar una conferencia. El único lugar en la ciudad lo suficientemente grande para acomodar a las multitudes era el hipódromo, en donde había una tribuna grande, y muchas personas asistían para escuchar a los mejores conferencistas del mundo de ese entonces. Fue una bendición enorme para nosotros el ser expuestos a los ministerios de algunos de estos oradores internacionales y a la unción que había en esas reuniones. Sin embargo, al funcionar bajo la suposición de que Dios estaba derramando bendiciones debido a lo correcto de la enseñanza, yo asimilaba absolutamente todo lo que estaba siendo enseñado y predicado. Nunca se me ocurrió cuestionar que eso pudiera ser cualquier otra cosa que no fuera la absoluta verdad.

Recuerdo que hubo un orador en particular en la conferencia que predicó un mensaje que me impactó mucho y el cual acepté totalmente sin cuestionar. Predicó del texto en donde Jesús tomó a Pedro, Santiago y Juan y los llevó al monte de la transfiguración. Habló acerca de cómo Jesús fue transfigurado y como la figura de su ser cambió al ser investido de la gloria del Señor, y cómo ellos vieron (al menos hasta cierto nivel) como Él se reveló como lo que había sido desde la eternidad. En medio de esto, vieron a Moisés y Elías apareciendo con Él. El Padre habló desde la nube: *«Este es mi hijo amado. Escúchenlo»*, y los tres discípulos cayeron al suelo inconscientes. Luego de un tiempo alzaron la vista y solo *«vieron a Jesús»*. Moisés y Elías se habían ido y habían dejado a Jesús ahora en su estado normal.

Sólo Jesús

El punto del mensaje del predicador podía ser resumido en esas dos palabras «sólo Jesús». El estaba diciendo en esencia: «Debemos ver a Jesús y sólo a Jesús. Él es el autor y consumador de nuestra fe, el Alfa y la Omega, el Principio y el Fin. Su nombre es el único nombre bajo el cielo por el cual podemos ser salvos. Él es la cabeza del Cuerpo, la Iglesia. Él es el Novio. Él es todo y su nombre es supremo». ¡Todo era acerca de Jesús y solamente acerca de Jesús!

Ahora, cuando él predicó eso, todo adentro de mi gritó «¡amén!» porque Jesús me había salvado y yo había tenido una experiencia poderosa de salvación. Jesús se había vuelto todo para mí. Cada vez que oraba, oraba a «Jesús mi Señor». Todo era Jesús. La adoración era acerca de Jesús. Las canciones que cantábamos eran acerca de Jesús.

Algunas veces poníamos un verso acerca del Espíritu Santo o acerca del Padre pero todo estaba enfocado en la persona de Jesús y yo pensaba que ese eral todo el enfoque el cristianismo.

«¿Has recibido el amor del *Padre*?»

Algunos años después fuimos a la escuela bíblica, y un hombre llamado Jack Winter vino a Nueva Zelanda y habló en una conferencia en la escuela. Jack empezó a hablar acerca del Padre y durante ese tiempo él empezó a recibir una revelación más grande del Padre. Nunca habíamos conocido a nadie con la unción de Dios como la que Jack tenía sobre él. Habíamos sido expuestos a muchos ministerios maravillosos pero, en lo que a mí concierne, cuando Jack Winter hablaba, era como escuchar a Jesús. Era mucho más que cualquier otra cosa que hubiésemos escuchado antes.

Jack solía decir algo maravilloso: «Mucha gente predica el evangelio *pero nosotros les damos la oportunidad de vivirlo*». Esa fue una declaración enorme. Para unirse al ministerio de Jack uno tenía que vender todo lo que tenía y darlo a los pobres o ponerlo a los pies de los apóstoles y seguir, junto al cuerpo de cristianos, lo que era llamado en ese entonces *Daystar Ministries*. Era el ministerio de fe más puro que yo había visto. Habían veces en las que ninguna de las doscientas personas en la base tenían comida alguna para el próximo día así que solamente oraban. Es una cosa orar e interceder por algo, pero cuando uno necesita comida en la mesa en las próximas dos horas, hay un nivel diferente con respecto a lo que está pasando con las oraciones.

La revelación acerca del Padre que había empezado a ocurrir en Jack en la conferencia en Nueva Zelanda ahora estaba en su plenitud y él se había dado cuenta que si la gente lograba tener una experiencia del amor del Padre, ellos recibirían sanidad emocional. Era un momento emocionante. Habían como cuatrocientas familias que habían aplicado para unirse a su ministerio ese año. Habían doce bases diferentes en todos los Estados Unidos y tenían seiscientas personas a tiempo completo, aún así , el escritorio de Jack era una pequeña mesa a la par de su cama. El no estaba buscando nada grandioso, en los absoluto.

Cuando llegamos ahí, todos estaban muy emocionados acerca de esta revelación del amor del Padre y empezaron a preguntarme «¿has recibido el amor del Padre?». ¡Yo me ofendí muchísimo! Yo tenía veintiocho años de edad y sentí que íbamos a pasar el resto de nuestras vidas en el ministerio de Jack. Vivía justo fuera de la campiña Neozelandesa, lo cual sería descrito por muchos como la jungla. Tres mil quinientos pies más arriba de la meseta el panorama se vuelve una gran mata de hierba lo cual se ve como océanos de pastos dorados. Esas colinas son lugares hermosos para pasar la vida, y yo venía de este tipo de vida al aire libre, un fuerte y saludable joven en la plenitud de su vida. Estaba acostumbrado a vivir en las montañas, dormir a cielo abierto, cortar mi propia leña para hacer fuego y cocinar mi comida, y me había endurecido por ese tipo de vida. Y ahora me preguntaban «¿has recibido el amor del Padre?».

Mi respuesta interior a su pregunta fue algo airada, «¡miren, estoy lleno del Espíritu Santo! He plantado una iglesia. Asistí a la escuela bíblica. Puedo profetizar, echar fuera demonios, sanar enfermos y predicar el evangelio en las calles. Soy un destructor de demonios. ¡Soy un hombre de Dios! ¡Dios me ha llamado a ser profeta, un instrumento afilado que divide entre el espíritu y el alma! ¡Mis palabras pondrán de rodillas a la gente! ¡Mi predicación sacará al justo de entre de los pecadores y hablará a las vidas de mucha gente! Estoy llamado a ser un profeta. No soy muy de "eso del amor". ¿Qué quieres decir con eso de que *si estoy lleno del amor del Padre"*?».

UNA PRIMERA LUZ

Luego de estar ahí por algunos meses me cruzó un pensamiento de repente. Recordé cuando tenía cuatro años, mi mamá (que tuvo que haber tenido un toque del Señor en su vida en ese entonces), por un período breve de tiempo, solía tomarnos a mi hermana y a mí a su recámara por la noche para arrodillarnos frente a un baúl en donde mantenía una cruz y una vela. Encendía la vela y luego nos enseñaba el Padre Nuestro. En los años siguientes ellos no lo recordaban pero a mi nunca se me olvidó porque dese ese entonces oré el Padre Nuestro cada noche antes de acostarme. Cerraba mis ojos, y en mi mente recitaba la oración. Al final siempre añadía «Dios, bendice a papá y a mamá, a mi hermano Bob, a mi hermana Sylvia y Señor, cuando crezca, dame salud, una familia feliz y un buen trabajo.» Oré eso todas las noches. ¡Algunas noches se me pasaba así que la próxima oraba dos veces! Nunca pasé por algo una sola noche.

Durante los primeros meses en Daystar, el Señor me recordó que cuando Jesús le enseñó a sus discípulos a orar, les enseñó a decir «Padre nuestro.» ¡Me di cuenta que había estado orando así desde que tenía cuatro años y seguí haciéndolo hasta que cumplí catorce o quince! Jesús le enseñó a los discípulos a hablarle a su *Padre*. Podía ver ahora que Jesús, desde el principio, estaba dirigiendo a sus discípulos directamente a una relación con el Padre, no solamente con Él mismo. Esta fue la primera grieta, por así decirlo, en ese mensaje de «sólo Jesús» que había escuchado. Yo había empezado a realizar que el cristianismo no era solamente acerca de Jesús.

Verás, cuando la gente me preguntaba «¿has recibido el amor del Padre?», mi pregunta para ellos era «¿Por qué estás hablando acerca del Padre? ¡Todo es acerca de Cristo! Él es el único nombre bajo el cielo en el cual podemos ser salvos. El es Señor de todo. El es el Rey de reyes. Todo es acerca de Él. Él es quien nos salvó, el que murió en una cruz». Yo no había realizado que el Padre también murió en la cruz en un sentido muy real; yo sólo seguía repitiendo «¡Todo es acerca de Jesús!».

Tenía el sentimiento de que si tenía una relación con el Padre, le estaría siendo desleal a Jesús. Pensaba «después de todo lo que Jesús ha hecho por mí, ¿cómo puedo volverle la espalda a Jesús y relacionarme con el Padre?». Ahí estaba la lucha para mí. Por supuesto que eso no tiene nada que ver, pero así me sentía. Este recuerdo de orar «Padre nuestro» fue el primera grieta en mis defensas. Jesús de hecho les dijo a sus discípulos que le hablaran a su Padre. El dijo,

«Pero tú, cuando te pongas a orar, entra en tu cuarto, cierra la puerta y ora a tu Padre» (Mateo 6:6).

De repente empecé a pensar «¡Oh, sí *hay* algo del Padre en esto». *Sí es* algo legítimo tener interacción directa con le Padre. Había yo empezado a ganar terreno.

ADORANDO AL PADRE

Algunos meses después, apareció otra grieta. Recordé el tiempo algunos años atrás cuando estaba en la escuela bíblica y había un orador Americano que se había mudado con su familia. Este hombre pasó once años en la escuela y enseñaba acerca del Evangelio de Juan. Había momentos luego de sus enseñanzas cuando, en vez de salir caminando de las clases, ¡salíamos flotando del aula! La reverencia y la adoración con la que enseñaba era una increíble bendición. Nos llevó a través del libro de Juan verso por verso durante todo un año. ¡Al final del año se disculpó que solo habíamos podido llegar hasta el capítulo 16! Había sido un año increíble profundizando en el libro de Juan.

Sin embargo, cuando llegamos al capítulo 4, él dijo, «Vamos a abordar este capítulo de forma diferente. En vez de que yo les enseñe, le voy a dar a cada quien uno o dos versos para que los estudie y luego regrese a presentar a la clase lo que ha aprendido.» Cuando él dijo eso, inmediatamente quise que me tocara un verso en particular. Pensaba que si me asignaba ese verso, no iba a tener que hacer ninguna tarea porque ya había recibido revelación de ese verso. Ya estaba ocupado con mi tiempo, así que si me tocaba ese verso en particular podía evitar el hacer la tarea y podría obtener más tiempo libre para mí mismo.

Así que él repartió versos a cada miembro de la clases y me dio exactamente el verso que quería. El verso era Juan 4:23, pero cuando lo había estudiado, pensé que quería decir lo siguiente:

«Un tiempo viene y ahora es, cuando los verdaderos adoradores adorarán a Dios en espíritu y en verdad, porque este tipo de adoradores busca Dios». No es exactamente lo que dice, pero eso fue lo que yo *pensé* que decía. Estaba tan contento de haber recibido el verso que quería. No necesitaba estudiarlo. Finalmente llegó mi turno para compartir mi revelación en frente de la clase. Yo estaba seguro de que había hecho un buen trabajo al comunicar el entendimiento del verso, y eso fue confirmado cuando algunos de los estudiantes me felicitaron después de que hablé.

Mi revelación era acerca de «la adoración en espíritu y en verdad» porque yo sabía lo que era la adoración. La adoración es cuando tu espíritu trata de salir de tu boca y es una expresión total de amor y afecto profundo. No hay mucho trabajo intelectual; es simplemente una conexión de espíritu. He descubierto que no puedes aprender a adorar. La adoración es una respuesta natural a su presencia. ¡*Eso* es adorar en espíritu y en verdad! Y eso fue lo que compartí al mundo como mi revelación.

Luego, ocho años después, descubrí lo que quería decir ese verso en realidad. En el verso, Jesús estaba diciendo *«Viene el día, y es ahora, cuando los verdaderos adoradores adorarán <u>al Padre</u> en espíritu y en verdad porque tales adoradores busca <u>el Padre</u>»*.

Hasta ese entonces todo mi enfoque de adoración estaba en la persona de Jesús y sólo Jesús. Todas las canciones que solíamos cantar en esos días, aun ahora, están centradas «sólo en Jesús». Usamos productos con las siglas WWJD *(en inglés* «¿Qué haría Jesús (en mi lugar)?). Cantamos «Todo es acerca de ti, Jesús.» De alguna manera, yo creo que Jesús no estaría de acuerdo con esas afirmaciones. Yo creo que Jesús diría «*De hecho*, es acerca de mi Padre».

Por supuesto, no está mal adorara a Jesús. Algunos de los versos más importantes acerca de la adoración en la Escritura son acerca de la persona de Jesús, particularmente en Apocalipsis, en donde los ancianos rinden sus coronas delante de Él, exaltando en adoración al Cordero de Dios. Pero el punto que deseo hacer aquí es que Jesús *mismo* dijo: «Los verdaderos adoradores adorarán *al Padre* en espíritu y verdad». En el momento en el que leí eso no podía imaginarme a mí mismo diciendo «Te amo, Padre.» Estaba conmocionado de que estas palabras estuvieran tan alejadas de mi perspectiva aunque podía ver lo que Jesús mismo las dijo. ¡Estaba empezando a entender que de hecho hay un lugar para el Padre en nuestras vidas! Mi postura de «Jesús y sólo Jesús» estaba empezando a cambiar.

A medida que toda esta revelación está empezando a venir a la Iglesia el día de hoy, y a medida que empezamos a ver al Padre de nuevo, hay gente que está luchando con este mismo asunto y frecuentemente hacen la crítica: «Ustedes parecen solamente ir al Padre y omiten a Jesús.» Déjenme decirles claramente: de ninguna manera omitimos a Jesús. El único Camino al Padre es a través de Jesús y es sólo en Él que tenemos relación con el Padre.

ESTAMOS EN CRISTO

Algunos dicen que las herejías se cantan antes de que se prediquen. Desearía que las personas que escriben canciones cristianas consultaran con alguien que de hecho tenga algo de entendimiento bíblico. Muy frecuentemente nuestras canciones dicen cosas que la Biblia no enseña para nada, y aun así cantamos más las canciones de lo que leemos las Escrituras. Por ejemplo, hay un viejo himno que habla acerca de «caminar con Jesús, la luz del mundo.» Muchas canciones hablan acerca de «caminar con Jesús» pero eso no es una declaración bíblica en realidad.

No caminamos *con* Jesús. Estamos *en* Cristo y Él está *en* nosotros. Nuestra vida ha sido absorbida en su vida. Hemos sido bautizados en Él y ahora...« *ya no vivo yo mas Cristo vive en mí, y la vida que ahora vivo la vivo por la fe en el Hijo de Dios quien me amó y se entregó por mí*» (Gálatas 2:20). Él se ha vuelto mi vida. Él vive *dentro* de mi y yo *en* Él. He sido bautizado *en* él. No es tanto que camine con Él lado a lado, sino que Él está *en* mi y yo en Él. La realidad es que caminamos con el *Padre* en Cristo. En realidad no es que sea *mi* relación con el Padre. Yo he entrado a la relación de Jesús con su Padre.

JESÚS ES EL CAMINO AL PADRE

En todo este proceso empecé a ver que de hecho es bíblico tener una relación personal con el Padre por quien es Jesús y quien soy yo *en* Él.

Y luego me crucé con Juan capítulo 14 y esto vale la pena sopesarlo porque hay algo aquí que frecuentemente se malentiende. Amo los versos que hablan acerca de los últimos días antes de que Jesús fuera crucificado. La observación de Jack Winter era que las palabras finales de una persona antes de morir son especialmente dignas de notar.

Jesús empezó diciendo,

«*No se angustien. Confíen en Dios, y confíen también en mí. En el hogar de mi Padre hay muchas viviendas; si no fuera así, ya se lo habría dicho a ustedes. Voy a prepararles un lugar. Y si me voy y se lo preparo, vendré para llevármelos conmigo. Así ustedes estarán donde yo esté*» *(v1-3).*

Jesús estaba anunciando que se iba a ir y aun así los discípulos seguían esperando un reino literal. Es un shock para ellos porque Jesús dijo «Me voy. Les dejo aquí». Puedo imaginármelos viéndose entre ellos diciéndose «¿Sabías tú de esto? Vine y le seguí porque pensé que iba a derrotar a los Romanos. Hemos dado nuestra vida y dejado nuestras redes de pescar. Vamos a levantar un reino como lo hicieron los Macabeos y vamos a volvernos soldados de un nuevo ejército para romper las cadenas y liberar a Israel. ¿De qué está hablando Él *ahora*?»

Pero Jesús estaba diciendo básicamente, «No, voy a prepararles un lugar pero no pueden venir conmigo ahora mismo.» Luego continuó,

«Ustedes saben a donde voy y conocen el camino» (Juan 14:4)

Recuerdo estar en la escuela junto a otros treinta estudiantes en la clase. Algunas veces el maestro hacía una declaración que ninguno de nosotros entendía, pero nadie decía nada porque nadie quería hacer una pregunta que le hiciera parecer estúpido. Me imagino que los discípulos tuvieron la misma reacción cuando Jesús dijo: «Ustedes saben a donde voy y conocen el camino». Puedo imaginarme a estos muchachos viéndose los unos a los otros diciendo: «¿Conoces tú el camino? ¿Te dijo Él algo? Él no me dijo nada a mí. ¿No vine yo el día que él habló de esto? ¿De qué está hablando?».

Estoy seguro que cada uno estaba avergonzado de admitir que de hecho no sabían. Tomás luego hizo esta bella, pura e inocente declaración, «Señor, no sabemos a donde vas. ¿Cómo podemos saber el camino?». Qué bueno que Tomás dijo eso porque si él no lo hubiera hecho no tendríamos el verso siguiente, el cual es uno de los versos más importantes del Nuevo Testamento.

«Jesús le dijo 'Yo soy el camino, la verdad y la vida. Nadie viene al padre sino por mí» (Juan 14:6).

¡Él les estaba diciendo cuál era el camino y cuál el destino! Cuando Él dijo: «Yo voy a prepararles un lugar para que estén donde yo estoy», lo que Él realmente les estaba diciendo es que iba a prepararles un lugar en el corazón del Padre. Nota que *no* dijo «Ustedes estarán donde yo estaré» sino dijo «Estarán donde yo *estoy*». Jesús vivió todo el tiempo eternamente en el regazo del Padre y mientras estuvo en la tierra todavía estaba viviendo ahí. Juan 1:18 dice,

«Nunca nadie ha visto a Dios. El unigénito Hijo que está en el regazo del Padre, Él se lo ha declarado»

Viene un tiempo en el cual el mundo solo escuchará a aquellos que estén viviendo en el regazo del Padre, en su amor. Porque solo es desde ese lugar que podemos realmente declarar a Dios, realmente revelarlo al mundo. El ser hijos de Dios va a sobreponerse a cualquier otra perspectiva del cristianismo. *Tiene* que hacerlo, y la razón es que sólo en ese momento la Iglesia se volverá finalmente la total representación del Hijo de Dios.

El Padre es el destino

Jesús dijo, *«Yo soy la verdad, el camino y la vida, nadie viene al Padre son es por mí»*, *Jesús es el Camino al destino. El destino* es el Padre. Luego Él añadió la siguiente,

«Si realmente ustedes me hubieran conocido, hubieran conocido a mi Padre también y desde ahora en adelante le conocen y le han visto»

Muchas personas han tomado estas palabras y han creído que si has visto a Jesús, si has tenido una experiencia real con Él, entonces automáticamente tienes una relación con el Padre. Ellos creen que no hay experiencias que se pueda tener del Padre separado del contacto con Jesús. Casi podría yo creer lo mismo si no fuera por el verso 8, y la pregunta de Felipe,

«Felipe le dijo, "Señor, muéstranos al Padre y eso será suficiente para nosotros."»

Lo que Felipe estaba diciendo básicamente es «Jesús, te he estado observando todos estos años. ¡Puedo verte a ti pero no puedo ver al Padre! Vemos que tienes una relación con Él pero sólo podemos verte a ti. ¡Muéstranos al *Padre*!».

Jesús respondió,

«¡Pero, Felipe! ¿Tanto tiempo llevo ya entre ustedes, y todavía no me conoces? El que me ha visto a mí, ha visto al Padre. ¿Cómo puedes decirme: «Muéstranos al Padre»? ¿Acaso no crees que yo estoy en el Padre, y que el Padre está en mí? Las palabras que yo les comunico, no las hablo como cosa mía, sino que es el Padre, que está en mí, el que realiza sus obras. Créanme cuando les digo que yo estoy en el Padre y que el Padre está en mí; o al menos créanme por las obras mismas.»

El le estaba diciendo a Felipe que los milagros de hecho eran señales de la presencia del Padre. En el verso 7, El dice «Si me hubieran conocido, hubieran conocido al Padre también». En otras palabras, «Puedes conocerme o puedes *realmente* conocerme, y si tú *realmente* me conocieras, conocerías la Padre también».

La verdad, querido lector, es que tú puedes tener una relación con Jesús—y aún así, no «ver» al Padre para nada.

EL PADRE DEBE SER REVELADO POR JESÚS

Déjame decirlo de otra manera. Jesús hizo otra afirmación en Mateo 11:27. Él dijo,

«Todas las cosas me han sido dadas por mi Padre y nadie conoce al Hijo excepto el Padre. Ni conoce nadie al Padre excepto el Hijo y aquel a quien el Hijo se lo quiera revelar.»

Esta declaración me tocó cuando era joven, porque siempre había pensado que la soledad es cuando no conoces a nadie. Sin embargo, descubrí que la verdadera definición de soledad es cuando nadie te conoce *a ti*. Cuando percibes que nadie realmente conoce lo que es ser tú entonces te encuentras de hecho en una situación muy solitaria. La soledad se rompe cuando dejas que alguien más sepa cómo es vivir tu vida.

Cuando Jesús dijo en este verso, «Nadie conoce al Hijo excepto el Padre», Él realmente estaba diciendo que Dios era el único que realmente le conocía. Jesús cargó con esta soledad toda su vida en la tierra. Ni aún su propia madre lo entendía. Ella «guardaba todas las cosas en su corazón» pero no le entendía realmente. El dijo «sólo el Padre me conoce *de verdad*». Luego le dio la vuelta a la declaración y dijo «y nadie conoce realmente al Padre sino el Hijo.»

Esta fue una de las razones por las cuales los líderes judíos se enojaron contra Él y le crucificaron. Fue porque Jesús de Nazaret decía conocer a Yahvé mejor que *ellos*, ¡la elite religiosa! ¡Esos líderes habían pasado su vida entera en el templo desde que eran niños y habían aprendido todo lo que era posible aprender acerca de Dios! Habían vivido en ese ambiente continuamente, memorizando vastas porciones de la Escritura, definiendo su conducta para nunca hacer nada malo, con el propósito de poder conocer a Dios y ser aprobados por Él.

Ahora este hijo de un carpintero, que muy probablemente era tachado de hijo ilegítimo, vino a ellos y les dijo: «En todo su aprendizaje ustedes no conocen realmente a Yahvé. *Sólo yo lo conozco*». Él condenó a todo el sistema religioso judío al decir que Él era el que la tenía correctamente, el único que realmente conocía a Dios.

Él tenía razón. Tal vez ellos sabían *acerca* de Dios pero no *conocían* a Dios. Verás, ya que Él no era un hijo nacido de Adán, el pecado no lo separó de Dios. Isaías 59:2 nos dice que el pecado nos separa de Dios ¡pero Jesús nació si pecado! Él no era un hijo de Adán. El era una concepción directa de Dios mismo en el vientre de María.

El tener contacto con Dios estuvo disponible inmediatamente durante toda su vida. Cuando él oraba, su Padre se le revelaba— *espíritu a espíritu*. El todavía tenía que caminar por fe justo como nosotros pero Él tenía una conexión íntima con el Padre. El fue concebido naturalmente del Espíritu así que Él fue lleno del Espíritu Santo desde la concepción.

Entonces cuando Él dijo, «Nadie conoce al Padre excepto yo», Él estaba de hecho diciendo: «¡Toda la raza judía y aquellos que han aprendido todo acerca de Él no le conocen de verdad pero yo sí!».

Él comprobó la verdad de esto por las obras que hizo y las

palabras que dijo. Las obra que hizo tenían que ser una señal de la presencia del Padre, no solo un ejercicio de su poder y autoridad. Sus milagros apuntaban a la realidad del amor que el Padre tiene por nosotros.

Mientras los líderes religiosos estaban tambaleándose por sus afirmaciones tan audaces de ser el único que realmente conocía a Dios, Él vino y expandió su declaración: «Nadie conoce al Padre excepto al Hijo *y aquel a quien el Hijo se lo quiera revelar*». Lo que Él quiso decir fue: «Conozco al Padre por conexión personal, y nadie le conoce como yo, *pero* yo se los puedo revelar. Yo puedo revelar al Padre a aquellos a quienes yo quiera.» ¡Es necesario que el Padre nos sea revelado por Jesús!

Es una revelación

Hay una *revelación* del Padre. No llegas simplemente a conocer al Padre porque tengas un deseo de hacerlo. No puedes venir a conocer al Padre porque te apropias de alguna Escritura o crees lo que la Escritura dice. El Padre tiene que ser revelado a ti por revelación, justo como Jesús fue revelado a ti por revelación cuando naciste de nuevo.

No naciste de nuevo por tu propio poder. No hay nada que hayas hecho que haya causado que fueras salvo. Respondiste a la iniciativa de Dios.

El arrepentimiento y la fe no causan por si mismas que nazcas de nuevo. Sin embargo, cuando Dios ve lo que lo estás haciendo de lo profundo de tu corazón, Él hace que se de una transacción en tu espíritu, haciendo que nazcas de nuevo por dentro. No solo es porque tu crees lo que la Biblia dice y entonces tú tratas de hacer lo que la Biblia dice. Te vuelves una nueva creación por medios sobrenaturales. Algo nuevo ha nacido en ti y tu ya no eres el mismo. Es la obra de Dios en tu corazón. La salvación de hecho es una revelación de Jesús y esa revelación es dada por Dios mismo. El nos muestra a Jesús.

Similarmente, el bautismo del Espíritu es cuando el Espíritu Santo es revelado a tu espíritu. La realidad del Espíritu Santo, la sustancia de su ser, es manifestada a la parte más profunda de quien eres tú en tu espíritu, y tú de repente conoces que el Espíritu Santo es real. Lo llamamos «bautismo en el Espíritu», o la «llenura del Espíritu», pero verdaderamente es tu espíritu obteniendo la revelación de la presencia del Espíritu Santo dentro de ti. Cuando eso ocurre recibes revelación y el conocimiento de algunas verdades automáticamente.

Cuando conoces a Jesús en la salvación hay algunas verdades que se imparten a ti sobrenaturalmente y en un momento no tienes absolutamente ninguna duda de la veracidad de las mismas. *Sabes* que Jesús nació de la virgen María. ¿Cómo sabes eso? Por *revelación* del Señor, porque así es Jesús. Conocerás que Él no es meramente *un* hijo de Dios. Él es *el* Hijo de Dios y sabes sin duda alguna que no hay otro hijo aparte de Jesús. Tu espíritu en su parte más profunda le ha conocido y tu sabes esa realidad innegable. Muchos mártires murieron muertes horrendas porque no podían negar la revelación y la realidad de Jesús.

El bautismo del Espíritu Santo también trae conocimiento de *revelación* de que él es el que da poder milagroso. Sansón derribó los pilares del templo. Elías corrió más que las carrozas y los caballos para regresar a la ciudad. Cuando el Espíritu de Dios viene sobre una persona, el poder también viene sobre ella porque el Espíritu de Dios otorga el poder de Dios. La Deidad estuvo personalmente involucrada en la creación del universo. El Padre inició, Él habló la Palabra, la cual es Jesús, y el poder del Espíritu Santo creó, la Trinidad obrando junta.

Si no estás lleno del Espíritu Santo buscarás explicaciones de los milagros que disminuirán su realidad, pero cuando estás lleno del Espíritu Santo, es diferente. Verdaderamente conoces, porque has tocado la realidad del Aquel que tiene el poder de Dios.

La revelación del Padre

Conocer al Padre no solo es un asunto de adherencia a una teología en el libro, sino que el Padre mismo se vuelve real a tu espíritu y su amor empieza a ser revelado en tu interior. Cuando Jesús dijo: «Nadie conoce al Padre excepto yo y aquellos a quienes yo escoja revelárselos», Él estaba hablando acerca de una *revelación* de Dios nuestro Padre a nuestros corazones.

Estamos entrando a un ámbito del corazón a medida que venimos a esto porque la *revelación* viene al corazón. Me encanta esto porque no es solo para los intelectuales o aquellos con una fuerza de voluntad para hacer las cosas que se supone que hagan. De hecho, esas mismas cosas casi siempre se vuelven un obstáculo.

Yo creo que Dios ahora está derramando una revelación de Él mismo como Padre de una manera sin precedentes desde el tiempo de los apóstoles. Todo el punto del cristianismo es conocer al Padre y conocerlo por revelación. Jesús es el Camino al Padre. La revelación del Padre es el destino.

Por qué importa el corazón

~

Déjame animarte a que permitas que el Espíritu de Dios alimente tu espíritu mientras lees este libro. Mi deseo es que a través de este libro Dios haga una obra en tu corazón. Este es mi enfoque al escribir. Dios generalmente no viene a re-adoctrinar tu mente. Sin embargo, lo que Él hace es venir a *cambiar nuestros corazones*, porque cuando tu corazón cambia te vuelves una persona diferente. Sin necesidad de hacer nada más, actuarás diferente y serás una persona diferente. Cuando el corazón es cambiado automáticamente actuarás diferente.

Estoy seguro que has notado que la Biblia no fue escrita como un libro de texto. No tiene un listado de temas con mayúscula enumerando los tópicos en orden. Fue escrita a propósito por Dios en una manera tal que las verdades han de ser descubiertas por aquellos que tienen ojos y oídos. ¡Una vez escuché a alguien decir que a Dios le encanta ser descubierto! Como un padre jugando a las escondidillas con sus hijos, Él ha planeado que sólo aquellos que vengan y pasen tiempo con Él, con hambre de encontrarlo, le descubran.

A medida que leemos la Biblia, buscándole con todos nuestros corazones ahí, Él nos enseñará grandes y maravillosas cosas que aún no conocemos. ¡Es cuando llamamos a Él que Él responde! Sus verdades están escondidas del observador casual. Esa es la razón por la que Él no nos ha dado su Palabra como un libro de texto para que el observador casual lo pueda descubrir. Sus verdades están escritas en palabras que parecen ordinarias, como las otras, pero no lo son.

He descubierto una maxi-verdad[1] escondida en Proverbios 4:23. Esta dice: «*Guarda tu corazón con toda diligencia, porque de ahí salen los asuntos de la vida*». Este verso se ha vuelto un enfoque esencial en nuestro ministerio y yo creo que es una de las declaraciones más grandes en la Escritura. La Biblia está llena de estas afirmaciones o maxi-verdades tales como: «Dios es amor», o «Dios es Espíritu». Estos son temas enormes - ¡son maxi-verdades! Yo realmente creo que este verso en Proverbios 4 es una de las maxi-verdades del cristianismo, la cual tristemente ha sido omitida por la mayoría de cristianos hoy en día.

Verás, tu corazón es la parte más importante de ti, y todo lo que experimentas en la vida debe ser experimentado a través de tu corazón. La manera en la que interpretas la vida, la forma en la que interpretas eventos y cómo ellos te afectan está todo determinado por la condición de tu corazón. La verdad es que, tu mente es tuya—tus emociones son tuyas—tu voluntad es tuya—¡pero tu corazón eres tú!

---

1 **Maxi-verdad** *es un término que mi esposa y yo hemos acuñado para referirnos a una verdad máxima.*

Lo ilustro de esta manera. Una persona puede decir algo a dos personas al mismo tiempo y aun así una de las personas puede interpretar algo totalmente diferente a lo que la otra persona interpreta. La persona que habla puede estar usando las mismas palabras, habladas al mismo tiempo a estas dos personas, y aun así pueden significar dos cosas diferentes para ambas. ¿Por qué? Es porque sus corazones han sido acondicionados diferentemente, y esas palabras pueden decirle cosas diferentes a diferentes personas. Dos personas pueden experimentar la misma mirada por parte de una persona e interpretarla completamente diferente.

De hecho, podrías decir que todos vivimos en diferentes mundos porque cada uno de nosotros ha sido condicionado a experimentar la vida diferentemente. Por ejemplo, cuando un chico que ha sido criado con un padre violento escucha la palabra «padre», su corazón se cerrará automáticamente a esa palabra. No escuchara lo que estás queriéndole decir. Pero cuando un niño que ha tenido un padre maravilloso escucha la palabra «padre», inmediatamente evocará sentimientos de confort y seguridad. ¡Dos mundos totalmente diferentes!

Cada uno de nosotros vive en mundos diferentes simplemente porque nuestros corazones han sido cambiados y afectados por las cosas que vivimos. Nuestro ambiente familiar, la parte del mundo en donde crecimos, nuestras actitudes culturales, educación, estatus intelectual, habilidad atlética y nuestras diferentes relaciones. Todas estas cosas han afectado la forma en que ahora tu experimentas la vida. Puede que no seas capaz de articular lo que piensas, pero ves la vida a través del acondicionamiento de tu corazón.

Cómo son cambiados nuestros corazones

Cuando nos volvimos cristianos queríamos cambiar y volvernos más como Jesús. La forma en la que Dios hace esto posible, sin embargo, no es a través de la educación de tu mente, o al motivarte a tomar mejores decisiones por determinación humana. Aun así, esta es la forma en que frecuentemente se nos es descrita la madurez cristiana. «Si quieres cambiar, entonces tienes que hacerlo de esta forma. Tienes que madurar. Necesitas crecer».

El entendimiento predominante con respecto al discipulado, como se nos dice a menudo hoy en día va algo así: *«Tienes que hacer esto, y tienes que hacer aquello»* o *«Debes de dejar de hacer esto, y debes dejar de hacer aquello»* o aun *«Tienes que desarrollar estos patrones y hábitos y desarrollar un comportamiento para poder cambiar».*

La verdad es que, ¡aunque tú puedas dejar de hacer ciertas cosas, esto no cambiará tu verdadero yo porque tu corazón es quien te hace quien eres! La forma en que tu corazón ha sido afectado por tus experiencias de vida determina quien eres tú en este momento.

Esta es la razón por la que Proverbios 4:23 dice,

«Guarda tu corazón con toda diligencia porque de ahí emanan los asuntos de la vida»

Todo lo que tú eres es debido a la condición de tu corazón. Puede que logres cambiar tu comportamiento por determinación y fuerza de voluntad, pero te puedo predecir lo que ocurrirá. Puede que hagas las decisiones correctas y hagas todo de la forma que se supone que lo hagas. Puede que hasta aprendas a sonreír de la forma correcta y actuar como un buen cristiano. Pero un día algo ocurrirá en tu mundo y de repente volverás a ser quien eres tú *en verdad*, a usar el lenguaje que no deberías usar. O te revertirás a la forma de pensar a la forma de tratar a la gente que sabes que está mal.

En un momento de stress extremo todo saldrá por tu boca. Puede que digas «lo siento, ese no era yo». Déjame decirte que... *ese eras verdaderamente tú.* Porque, cuando la presión está presente, lo que está en tu corazón saldrá en lo que dices y en la manera en la que la dices. Cuando todo está lindo y cómodo puedes hablar desde tu mente y saber qué decir, pero cuando hay presión, hablarás y actuarás según la verdadera condición de tu corazón. El cambiar tus acciones no cambiará quien eres en verdad. El cambio real y permanente viene de un corazón cambiado.

Afortunadamente, Dios está en el negocio de cambiar corazones. Me encanta esta declaración; es una verdad maravillosa. *Cuando Dios cambia tu corazón, esa parte de tu corazón automáticamente cumplirá con todo lo que Dios pide de ti. Automáticamente serás lo que un cristiano debe ser sin pensarlo, porque vendrá de tu corazón.*

En Fatherheart Ministries en Noruega, tenemos una pareja encantadora, Olav y Unni. Fueron salvos en los setentas y el impacto en su pueblo de Noruega fue muy notable. Una tercera parte de los jóvenes en el pueblo se volvieron cristianos. Primero los conocimos cerca de diez años atrás cuando ministramos en su iglesia y el amor del Padre les afectó profundamente. Toda la lucha de Olav por sobresalir, por ser el «buen hombre cristiano» , por ser «el buen pastor», se acabó cuando experimentó el amor del Padre y entró al reposo. El amor del Padre ha transformado sus vidas.

Olav y Unni ministran bastante en Kenia. Cuando estaban caminando a casa una noche en Nairobi luego de una reunión, nueve hombres los acosaron, les pegaron severamente y robaron todo lo que tenían. Los dejaron tirados en medio de la calle sucia en los barrios pobres de Nairobi. Cuando despertaron de la inconsciencia, Unni estaba llena de gozo al descubrir que todavía tenía su anillo de bodas pero todo lo demás había desaparecido. Solo pudieron arrastrarse para estar juntos, ¡pero a medida que empezaron a orar por sus atacantes fueron llenos de tal amor por estos hombres que los habían herido! Esto los maravilló. El amor fluyó de su interior. No podían pensar en nada más que cosas así: «Qué amables jóvenes, Dios ayúdalos y ámalos. Son jóvenes tan maravillosos. Dios los bendiga». Todo este amor salió de su corazón. Esta experiencia los convenció acerca de la absoluta realidad del amor del Padre, porque el amor fluyó de su corazón sin esfuerzo alguno. No tenían que perdonar a sus atacantes porque habían descubierto que poseían algo mucho más grande. Poseían un profundo amor por sus enemigos.

¡Así debería ser un verdadero corazón cristiano! No es que «debo perdonarlos» o «sé que lo correcto es perdonarlos». Para Olav y Unni era una sobrecogedora expresión de lo que ya había en sus corazones. No tenían que preguntarse qué era lo correcto en esa situación. ¡La misma clase de corazón que tenía Jesús se había hecho latente automáticamente en ellos!

Cuando Dios cambia tu corazón, serás diferente automáticamente.

El cristianismo no es acerca de aprender cómo actuar para luego actuarlo por determinación humana. Yo creo, por supuesto, que deberíamos resistir el pecado con toda nuestra determinación, pero dejar de pecar no nos hace semejantes a Cristo. Debemos de entender que sólo es Dios el que puede cambiar nuestros corazones para ser una persona como Jesús. Cuando Él te cambia, automáticamente serás diferente sin pensar siquiera en ello.

Necesitamos entender que el cristianismo se energiza a si mismo. Cuando vives una vida cristiana, esto te convertirá en lo que un cristiano debería ser. No serás tú el que lo haga. Ni tus esfuerzos, ni tu auto-control, ni la disciplina. Si desarrollas una vida que se vea cristiana, por tus propios esfuerzos, entonces *tú* te llevarás la gloria por ello. Sólo cuando Dios te ha cambiado es que le darás toda la gloria a Él. Dios obra en nuestros corazones para cambiar quienes somos, y sólo después de ello, todas nuestras conductas y formas de pensar cambiarán *automáticamente* para ser como Aquel que nos ha cambiado.

TEJIDO CICATRIZADO

Si has sido herido profundamente en tu vida, tienes una herida en tu corazón y permanecerá ahí hasta que Dios la sane. Siempre y cuando esté ahí, esa parte de ti estará doblada y torcida de alguna manera y no operará como se supone que lo haga.

Me caí de mi bicicleta cuando tenía nueve años y me quedó una cicatriz a lo largo de mi rodilla, justo en donde la manecilla oxidada cortó mi piel. Lloré y lloré. Cuando llegué a casa podía ver una cortada en toda mi rodilla. Cuando mi mamá la estaba limpiando, mi padre la vio y dijo «tendrás esa cicatriz por el resto de tu vida». La cicatriz sigue ahí el día de hoy pero es muy pequeña. ¿Sabes por qué? ¡Mi rodilla creció! Aun así la marca se quedó del mismo tamaño porque el tejido cicatrizado no crece. Cuando tu corazón tiene cicatrices, esa parte de ti no crece, sino que se queda como un niño. Es por eso que muchos de nosotros algunas veces tenemos reacciones infantiles de las que nos avergonzamos. ¡Estamos determinados a reaccionar de forma diferente la próxima vez pero invariablemente reaccionamos de la misma forma!

Dios está en el negocio de sanar las cicatrices de tu corazón. Cuando Él sana una herida en tu corazón, esa parte de ti vuelve a crecer a la madurez. Tampoco le toma mucho tiempo para crecer de nuevo. Afortunadamente, ¡Dios nos sana muy rápidamente!

Cuando tu corazón ha sido descuidado o no ha recibido el afecto que necesita, o cuando ha sido roto y herido, entonces esa parte de tu corazón permanecerá con una cicatriz hasta que Dios la sane. La obra de Dios es sanar nuestros corazones y Él lo hace al derramar su amor consolador.

TU CORAZÓN ERES TÚ

Cuando eres herido en tu corazón, es herida la parte más profunda de ti. ¿Porqué? Porque tu corazón no es tuyo. Tu corazón eres *tú*. Tu habilidad de tomar decisiones es una habilidad que tienes, porque tu voluntad es tuya. Puedes dirigir tu voluntad de la manera que quieras. Tú no eres tu mente, porque puedes cambiar de parecer. Puedes decidir pensar de forma diferente. Por lo tanto, lo que tú piensas no eres tú, porque tú tienes control sobre lo que piensas. Puedes educar a tu mente en formas diferentes. Puedes saber que algo está mal pero decidir creer lo contrario. Puedes dirigir tu propia mente. Tu mente no es tú. Es tuya.

Es lo mismo con tus emociones. Tus emociones son tuyas, pero no son *tú*. Mucha gente se queda atrapado en pensar que sus emociones son de hecho quienes ellos son. Cuando se sienten tristes, entonces el mundo entero está triste. Si se sienten felices, entonces la vida es maravillosa. Si se sienten deprimidos, entonces ven al mundo como un lugar deprimente. Tus emociones y sentimientos pueden ser tuyos pero tú no eres lo que son ellos. Solo porque te sientes de cierta forma, eso no significa que sea cierto.

Tu mente es tuya, tu voluntad es tuya, tus emociones son tuyas. *Tu corazón eres tú*.

AMOR SANADOR

Cuando Dios cambia tu corazón, empiezas a amar lo que Dios ama. Empiezas a sentir lo que Dios siente. Empiezas a pensar como Dios piensa. Empiezas a hacer lo que Dios hace-- ¡automáticamente! Así que este libro no es acerca de la educación, sino acerca de que Él vendrá a tu corazón a sanarlo y derramar su amor en él, y cambiar tu corazón para ser como Él.

Las maravillosa noticia es que cuando el amor llega, todo lo que ha producido la *falta de amor* es revertido. Algunas veces uso la palabra desamor, la cual no es una palabra real en inglés pero describe muy bien la realidad. Hay tantas cosas en este mundo que hemos experimentado las cuales no son amor. Puede que hayas tenido muchas experiencias traumáticas de desamor, las cuales han creado agujeros en el fundamento de tu vida. Cada experiencia de desamor es como una explosión en las partes más profundas de tu ser. Cuando Dios derrama su amor en ese fundamento, primero llena los agujeros automáticamente. Su amor corre hacia esos hoyos y los traumas de tu vida y empieza a restaurarte.

Aun así muchos de nosotros todavía no entendemos esto. El enfoque de la mayoría de las ministraciones de consejería que hicimos fueron para diagnosticar lo quebrada de la vida de las personas al intentar identificar e aislar los incidentes a través de los cuales fueron heridos. Luego orábamos por ese asunto, para que Dios lo sanara y Dios respondiera nuestras oraciones y viniera a derramar su amor sanador. Así que era exitoso. Lo que he descubierto ahora, sin embargo, es que si puedes abrir tu corazón y solamente permitir que el amor del Padre venga, ¡llenará todos los agujeros! Así que si podemos encontrar la llave para ayudar a cada uno de nosotros abrir nuestro corazón y permitir que el amor del Padre entre, mantenemos ese amor fluyendo, ¡vamos a ser sanados lo queramos o no!

Como verás, el amor del Padre se derrama en tu corazón y éste es el lugar en donde te encuentras con Él. Solíamos creer que el mensaje del corazón de Padre que tiene Dios es algo que sana a la gente emocionalmente, pero he descubierto que la sanidad del corazón es sólo la introducción para conocer al Padre. Cuando su amor viene de primero, ese amor sanará nuestros corazones. Si mantenemos nuestros corazones abiertos nos podemos convertir en hijos e hijas con una relación con el Padre, creciendo en el conocimiento y la experiencia de su amor.

Realmente la llave es abrir nuestro corazón. No sé como abrir mi corazón. No tengo idea de cómo sucede en verdad. Ojalá supiera. Pero lo que *sí puedo* hacer es simplemente rendirme delante de Dios y decir: «Dios, lo que quieras hacer conmigo está bien. Duela lo que duela, hazlo de todas maneras. Padre, confío en que eres un buen Dios y tú no me harás daño. Puedo rendirme a ti. Puedo confiar en ti porque eres bueno».

Muchos de nosotros tenemos razones por las que no podemos confiar en algunas personas en nuestras vidas. Nunca hay una razón para no confiar en Dios. Algunas personas dicen «Dios permitió que esto pasara en mi vida». Dios nunca te hizo nada malo, ni a nadie, ¡jamás! Él solo puede ser bueno. Él no puede pecar. Así que nunca hay una razón para que mantengamos una ofensa contra Dios ni de perdonarle por algo que sintamos que Él haya hecho. Puede que creamos que Él hizo algo malo, pero no fue así. Aun cuando no siempre entendamos lo que pasa en nuestras vidas, la verdad es que Dios siempre es solamente bueno.

A medida que lees este libro, te invito a rendirle tu corazón a él, tanto como sepas hacerlo. Puedes decir: «Padre, aquí estoy, para lo que quieras hacer». Tal vez tú estás leyendo esto con tus propias expectativas pero yo preferiría que las expectativas de Dios se cumplieran en vez de las mías. Puedes decir, «Padre, aquí estoy para lo que *tú* quieras para mí, no para que mis propias expectativas se cumplan».

El sólo puede ser bueno. Podemos confiar en Él.

Perdonando desde el corazón

~

Cuando Jesús murió en la cruz Él dijo: «¡Consumado es!». Todo lo que Dios tiene en su corazón para darnos ya ha sido provisto. La situación es que ahora estamos llegando a entender bien qué es lo que Él ha hecho. Lo que Jesús logró en la cruz está volviéndose real en nuestra experiencia. El proceso de crecimiento cristiano es acerca de que tú y yo entremos a la realidad de lo que Él ya ha hecho. Dios no necesita hacer nada más. Cristo lo ha hecho todo. Pero, ¿por qué no podemos entrar a la plenitud de esto? En los próximos dos capítulos quiero explorar la respuesta a esta pregunta.

EL YA NOS ESTÁ AMANDO

En toda esta revelación del amor del Padre, la situación no es que nosotros estemos tratando de que Él derrame su amor en nuestros corazones. Su amor está lloviendo continuamente sobre nosotros en todo momento. La pregunta es: «¿Por *qué no estoy experimentado más? ¿Por qué esto no es real para mí?*». El asunto principal que nos encara es que hay bloqueos dentro de nosotros que obstaculizan esa realidad para que no se materialice en nuestra vida. A medida que nos deshacemos de esos bloqueos, su amor por nosotros se vuelve más y más real en nuestra experiencia. El tema musical del avivamiento galés era un hermoso himno que decía: «Aquí está el amor, vasto como un océano, su fiel misericordia es como un diluvio». El amor de Dios es como un océano. Conozco como son los océanos. Se requieren casi doce horas para volar de Nueva Zelanda a Los Angeles y no hay nada en medio más que océano. Estamos apenas empezando a mojar nuestros pies en el increíble océano del amor del Padre.

Cuando entramos a una experiencia continua de experimentar a Dios amándonos, esto cambia nuestra personalidad. Cambia nuestra vida y nos transforma en la imagen de Jesús. *El amor mismo nos transforma.* La llave del crecimiento espiritual es deshacernos de las cosas que obstaculizan la experiencia de la realidad de su amor. Esa es la verdad más simple y más profunda a la vez.

El cristianismo se auto-energiza

El cristianismo se *auto-energiza* desde adentro hacia afuera. Si estás viviendo el cristianismo real esto creará un cristiano en ti, transformándote para hacerte todo lo que Jesús es. No tienes que *hacer nada* para que suceda. Si tú no estás siendo transformado en la semejanza de Jesús, la realidad es que de hecho no estás experimentando el cristianismo. La esencia del cristianismo es simplemente esta: Jesús murió en la cruz para reconciliarnos con Dios, para que podamos entrar a una relación con su Padre y vivir la experiencia del Padre amándonos continuamente. El cristianismo es infinitamente más que el conocimiento conceptual de que Dios te ama. Es la *experiencia misma* de ser *amados* por Él cada minuto de cada día. La diferencia entre estas dos realidades es monumental. Aun el diablo sabe que Dios te ama. Eso no es fe; es simplemente doctrina correcta. La fe es *conocer* cómo *El te ama*. Si no estás experimentando eso es por los bloqueos en tu corazón. Cuando estos obstáculos se remueven entonces el cielo se abre.

El cristianismo puede ser comparado a una persona que ha heredado mucho dinero de un pariente que ha muerto, pero no sabe que lo ha heredado. Hace algunos años la prensa neozelandesa publicó una historia de un hombre que había heredado una suma enorme de dinero de parte de un pariente lejano en Suramérica de quien nunca había escuchado. Le tomó a los ejecutores del testamento algunos años determinar que él era el único pariente vivo y subsecuentemente buscarlo. El había heredado la increíble suma de trece billones de dólares.

Imagínate el escenario. Un día recibe la llamada telefónica de un abogado convocándolo a una reunión. Llega a la reunión y se entera que esta vasta suma de dinero es ahora completamente de él. ¡Qué shock! ¿Qué crees que haría al próximo día? Esto cambiaría su vida dramática y permanentemente. Uno puede pasarse horas imaginando lo que él haría y cómo su vida cambiaría.

La verdad, querido lector, es que eso es exactamente lo que es el cristianismo. A través de la muerte y resurrección de Jesús hemos venido a heredar algo impresionante. Muchos de nosotros tenemos una idea muy pequeña de lo que realmente es esa herencia, pero estamos aprendiendo. Estamos descubriendo lo que realmente significa ser salvo. Es mucho más que simplemente obtener un pase al cielo, vivir una vida bonita, ser buena gente con los vecinos, ser un buen jefe o empleado, ir a la iglesia frecuentemente o tener un ministerio en la misma. ¡Muchos creen que esa es la suma total de lo que es el cristianismo! ¡Déjame decirte, el cristianismo es un poco más grande que eso!

¡El cristianismo es acerca de que tú y yo nos volvamos como Jesús! Ese es el propósito. El vivir una vida en la eternidad conformada a la vida que Jesús vive en la eternidad. ¡Es mucho más allá de lo que podamos imaginarnos! El cristianismo es algo enorme y nosotros hemos heredado todo el lote. La persona que ha sido cristiana por cinco minutos no tiene menos que la persona que ha sido cristiana por ochenta años. La persona que ha sido cristiana más tiempo podrá entender más de lo que es su herencia, pero todos de hecho poseemos lo mismo.

Einstein una vez dijo: «No sabes bien en verdad lo que no le puedes explicar a tu abuelo». Me gusta mucho ese concepto, porque cuando realmente sabes algo en la vida, ese algo vuelve más simple. Lo que yo estoy hablando no es complicado. El Padre nos ama y eso cambia quienes somos. A medida que conocemos ese amor, experimentamos ese amor y caminamos en ese amor, ese amor nos transforma en la imagen del Señor. Así que quiero decirte algunas de las cosas que han sido bloqueos en mi propia vida y señalar el camino que el Señor ha usado para llevarme ahí.

Un milagro incómodo

Conocimos a Jack Winter de primero en Nueva Zelanda en 1976 cuando él nos invitó a venir y ser parte de su ministerio en los EEUU, ministerio conocido como *Daystar Ministries*. Llegamos ahí en septiembre de 1978, volando a una ciudad de Los Angeles cuando había un calor sofocante, y luego nos dirigimos a Indianápolis. Habíamos venido con un boleto de ida, lo cual yo pensé que había sido un maravilloso milagro de Dios porque entrar a los Estados Unidos como un visitante a corto plazo sin tener un ticket de vuelta es difícil. Dorothy Winter nos recogió en el aeropuerto, y luego fuimos al centro del ministerio en Martinsville, Indiana. Fue ahí en donde empecé a escuchar acerca del amor del Padre.

Sin embargo, yo tenía un gran problema. Yo no sentía que había sido llamado a un ministerio de amor. Yo era un hombre de Dios, no un cobarde de Dios. Esta «onda del amor» definitivamente no era para mi. Para mi, el ministerio se trataba de ser un «instrumento trillador afilado» con palabras que cortan los poderes de la maldad, para llevar a los demonios a ponerse de rodillas. Cuando llegué a la base del ministerio de Jack, con Denise y los tres niños, para mi desaliento descubrí que se trataba acerca de este «asunto del amor». ¡Me temía que habíamos cometido un terrible error pero no podíamos ir a casa porque no teníamos un boleto de regreso! El Señor tenía propósitos en medio de mi incomodidad.

Así que estábamos atrapados ahí, y luego de un corto tiempo empecé a pensar que al fin y al cabo podría hacer que mi tiempo ahí valiera la pena. Entonces, estaba hablando con una de las intercesoras un día, la vi a los ojos y pude ver que sabía realmente como orar. Pensé «yo no tengo idea de cómo orar pero obviamente ella sí sabe». Así que decidí ahí mismo que trataría de aprender.

APRENDIENDO A ORAR COMO UN HOMBRE DE VERDAD

Me sentía muy motivado por una historia en el libro de Hechos en donde Pedro estaba en un techo y dice que mientras estaba orando, sintió hambre. Pensé: «¿Cuánto tiempo se requiere para que un hombre tenga hambre?». Por lo menos debería tratarse de algunas horas. Me identificaba con Pedro en el sentido de que él era un hombre que trabajaba mucho físicamente. Un hombre con manos callosas y rostro batido por el tiempo. Un tipo acostumbrado al aire libre como yo. El tipo de hombre que, si las cosas salían mal, se auto-medicaría con trabajo. El fue a pescar después de que Jesús murió. No se metió bajo su cama a llorar ni se encerró a leer poesía. Me encanta la poesía y he escrito algo de poesía, pero era el hombre trabajador en Pedro con el que me identificaba más. Mis manos también estaban callosas. Había pasado mucho de mi vida en las montañas como un cazador profesional y luego había trabajado como constructor después de que Denise y yo nos casamos.

Así que me podía identificar con este hombre rudo y duro, este Pedro. Aun una persona activa, acostumbrada al aire libre, trabajadora como él, aprendió a tener vigor en su vida de oración. Algunas veces asumimos que es más fácil para un introvertido o un intelectual orar con longevidad pero aquí estaba Pedro orando hasta que sintió hambre. Esto me retó muchísimo.

Otro personaje bíblico que me retó fue Elías quien evidentemente era un tipo de hombre duro. Es descrito como con «frente de pedernal». Se requiere cierto tipo de persona para ser alguien capaz de hacer las cosas que hizo. Si Elías entraba a un cuarto probablemente quedaríamos nosotros asustadísimos. Lo que me impactó fue que (en 2 Reyes 1:9) él se sentaba en una colina. Eso para mí, indicaba una vida de oración. El sabía cómo sentarse con Dios.

Me retó el hecho de que yo no sabía como orar por ningún plazo de tiempo. Así que quería aprender a orar. Mi objetivo era convertirme más como estos personajes inspiradores de los que había leído. En el sótano del lugar en donde vivíamos había una preciosa pequeña capilla que estaba decorada completamente de verde, así que decidí que iba a pasar un tiempo ahí cada sábado por la mañana cuando nadie más estuviera alrededor. Planeé cerrar la puerta, quedarme ahí y orar por tanto tiempo como pudiera.

A medida que el siguiente sábado se acercaba estaba creando listas de cosas para poder orar por ellas. Cualquier cosa que pudiera ser generalmente descrita como oración sería usada para hacer que yo permaneciera más tiempo orando. Pensé que si mi mente vagaba no me condenaría mi mismo, sino reenfocaría mis pensamientos. Tenía paz de no pedir perdón por mi fragilidad humana, me enfocaría en orar toda mi lista de peticiones y punto. El siguiente sábado por la mañana me encerré en la capilla y oré por todo lo que se me ocurriera.

Oré en lenguas, oré en inglés, oré cantando, oré postrado, oré sobre mi espalda, oré corriendo alrededor del cuarto. Oré tan largo como pude, y tan lento como pude solo para hacer que mi oración durara más. Tenía mi Biblia conmigo pero estaba ahí para orar, no para leer mi Biblia. Luego de lo que sentí como una eternidad, las paredes se estaban acercando para encerrarme. Estaba aburrido y claustrofóbico. Corrí a la puerta al corredor. Vi mi reloj y eran las 6:20 am. Había empezado a las 6:00 am.

Ahora, yo no me rindo fácilmente. Esa era la realidad de aprender a orar. A lo largo de la semana estaba pensando en más cosas por las cuales orar. Bajaba el próximo sábado porque me había comprometido a ir cada sábado. El siguiente sábado pasé por el mismo proceso, orando por todo lo que se me ocurriera, tan lento como fuera posible, en lenguas y en inglés, cantando, de pie, sentado, acostado, corriendo. Toda permutación posible de los diferentes métodos de oración. Finalmente, esa mañana cuando ya no podía más y salí de la puerta...habían pasado veinticinco minutos. ¡Pensé que eso era progreso pero iba a pasar mucho tiempo antes de que pudiera sentare en una colina como Elías lo había hecho! ¡Ciertamente no me había dado hambre como a Pedro!

Seguí bajando a la capilla cada sábado por la mañana. Era trabajo duro pero perseveré porque pensaba que si estas otras personas pudieron hacerlo, entonces yo también podría. Quería ser un hombre de Dios y haría lo que fuera para convertirme en un hombre de Dios.

Luego un día, algo pasó. Cuando estaba orando, de repente la presencia del Señor vino al cuarto. Sentí su presencia muchas, muchas veces antes pero nunca la había sentido a este nivel cuando estaba solo. Había experimentado un poderoso sentido de la presencia de Dios con otros en reuniones pero nunca cuando estaba a solas. Esto era sorprendente. Cuando su presencia vino, mi pensamiento inmediato fue que no debería hacer nada que causara que la presencia se fuera de ese lugar. Tenía mi Biblia en mi mano y tenía temor de abrirla. No pedí nada que, según yo, pudiera sonar egocéntrico o con un motivo equivocado. Estuve ahí delante de Él y solo hice lo que sentía totalmente cómodo en su presencia. Luego de un tiempo se fue, disipándose como neblina en una montaña. De repente me di cuenta que sólo yo estaba ahí. Él se había ido. Vi mi reloj. Más de una hora había pasado y había parecido como cinco minutos. No lo sabía aun pero estaba aprendiendo el secreto no solamente de la oración, sino de la vida cristiana.

La vida cristiana completa está enfocada en una cosa. Esa cosa es encontrar su presencia y permanecer ahí, aprender a vivir con una realidad consciente de su presencia. Cada vez que bajé a esa capilla luego de ese día, bajaba buscando su presencia. Algunas veces vino, otras no lo hizo, pero se volvió más y más regular. Estaba aprendiendo a cómo encontrar su presencia más y más.

Luego una vez cuando estaba orando algo ocurrió que cambió todo. Fue la última vez que llegué ahí. Su presencia vino y yo estaba con Él. Para ese entonces mis tiempos de oración eran de tres y cuatro horas. Estaba caminando alrededor de la capilla con mi Biblia abierta en mi mano. A medida que estaba llegando a la pared una de tantas veces para voltearme y caminar de vuelta, el Señor me habló de repente.

Ese momento ha afectado lo que soy el día de hoy. Más allá de eso, y sin saberlo yo en ese momento, ha afectado también la vida de miles. Me habló de forma extremadamente desafiante. Me hizo una pregunta que me sacudió hasta lo más profundo. La pregunta contenía cinco palaras, pero estaban cargadas de significado. Recuerda que estaba luchando con todas las preguntas acerca de haber recibido el amor del Padre. Él habló con comunicación perfecta, su presencia volviéndose lo que ahora solo puedo describir como altamente intencional. De repente estaba yo bajo los focos de atención. Sentí cómo Él me veía intensamente para ver cómo respondería a su pregunta.

De alguna manera yo supe que Él podía ver lo que yo estaba pensando y sintiendo. Cada respuesta mía estaba a simple vista de él. Temía el estar bajo el escrutinio del Señor. Sentí como una luz de búsqueda estaba sobre mí combinada con rayos-X. Hebreos 4:13 dice, «*Todas las cosas están descubiertas delante de los ojos de aquel a quien hemos de rendir cuentas*». Lo más atemorizante para mi fue que me volví consciente de esta realidad. Estaba expuesto bajo su mirada implacable. Estuve ahí tratando de salir con una respuesta para esta pregunta. Era algo muy simple el entender pero muy difícil el lidiar con ello.

Él simplemente me pregunto, «*James, ¿de quién eres hijo?*».

Si Él hubiera hecho una pregunta un tanto diferente, o si Él lo hubiese puesto de manera diferente, podía haber respondido más fácilmente. Si él me hubiera dicho: «James, ¿quién es tu padre?» Yo le podía haber dicho «Mi padre es Bruce Jordan». No había duda. Bruce Jordan *es* mi padre. Y yo le hubiese dicho: «Es Bruce. ¡Bruce Jordan es mi padre!» Pero Él no me pregunto quién era mi padre— el me preguntó de quién *yo era hijo*. Me percaté cuando Él hizo esa pregunta, que hacía mucho, pero mucho tiempo antes, yo *había dejado de ser* el hijo de mi padre.

CERRÁNDOLE EL CORAZÓN A MI PAPÁ

Recuerdo claramente cuando tenía diez años, sentado en una silla de barbero cuando me cortaban el pelo. Estaba con mis brazos sobre el descansadero de la vieja silla del barbero. Todos en nuestro pueblo tenían al menos un rifle de cazar y otras armas para participar en las competencias de tiro, las cuales se llevaban a cabo constantemente. El barbero era el cazador de más renombre en el pueblo. El salía a las colinas con nada más que su rifle, un bolsa de dormir, una bolsa con harina y algo de arroz y sal para comer, y se iba por semanas. Sin embargo, mi madre era la que tenía mejor puntería. Era una «Annie Oakley»[2] de verdad.

[2] *Annie Oakley fue una famosa tiradora de exhibición al principio del siglo pasado en los EEUU. Considerada primera «superestrella» americana.*

Ella salía a tirar conejos y regresaba con sesenta o noventa conejos en una sola tarde y todos ellos con un tiro en la cabeza. Hasta el día de hoy conservo su rifle.

Mientras todavía estaba cortándome el pelo, otro hombre vino y empezó a hablar con el barbero. «¿Cómo te fue en tu última ruta de caza?», le preguntó el barbero. El hombre luego dijo algo que cambió mi vida. Comentó que su ruta de caza no había tenido éxito porque los exterminadores de venados del gobierno habían pasado y no habían dejado venados para cazar. Estos exterminadores eran empleados por el gobierno para vivir en las montañas y cazar venados. Eso era todo lo que hacían, se quedaban en las casuchas y vivían debajo de las rocas. Cuando escuché esto entendí inmediatamente que estos cazadores tenían que ser mejores que el mejor cazador del pueblo porque habían cazado a todos los venados sin dejar uno solo para los del pueblo. Desde ese momento en adelante, todo lo que quería era vivir solo en las colinas y cazar venados para el gobierno.

Me encantan las montañas, pero lo que me atrajo fue el sentido de libertad que tendría al no tener que mantener ninguna relación dado el estilo de vida que prometía esta ocupación. Había descubierto que la gente podía herirme y pensé que, si podía vivir sin gente, podía vivir sin dolor. Mucho de mi dolor estaba conectado a mi padre. Cuando escuché acerca de los exterminadores del gobierno básicamente dejé de esforzarme en la escuela. Cada vez que venían las notas de las clases mis profesores les decían a mis padres «James tiene la capacidad más alta en el aula, pero no la usa». Podía salirme con la mía y pasar los exámenes sin tener que ir a la escuela tanto. Debido a esto pasaba la mayor parte del tiempo posible fuera de la misma. Estaba dejando pasar el tiempo hasta poder cumplir dieciocho años, la edad mínima para convertirme en exterminador. De hecho, me dejaron empezar cuando tenía diecisiete. Había sido tan herido por mi padre que había cerrado mi corazón a él antes de cumplir los diez años de edad, y no había podido ser un hijo desde ese entonces.

Ahora, cuando el Señor me encaró con la pregunta «James, ¿de quién eres hijo?» supe inmediatamente que Él estaba buscando un nombre. La pregunta fue extremadamente específica, «James, ¿de quién eres hijo? ¡Dame un nombre!».

Lo primero que pensé contestarle fue «Soy hijo de Bruce Jordan». Inmediatamente me di cuenta que no podía decir eso porque Él estaba viendo mi corazón y sabía que no había sido un hijo para mi padre.

La pregunta agitó cosas profundas en mí. Durante los mese previos a ello había estado leyendo el libro de Juan y había sido impactado por lo que Jesús dijo acerca de su relación con su Padre. Había resaltado cada declaración que había hecho. Declaraciones tales como: «*Me deleito en hacer tu voluntad*», o, «*Tengo una comida que ustedes no conocen. Mi comida es hacer la voluntad de mi Padre y terminar su obra*». De repente comprendí que hacer la voluntad de su Padre era algo que satisfacía tanto a Jesús que a veces ni siquiera sentía hambre física. Y cuando vi mi propia relación con mi padre, empecé a reconocer que era totalmente diferente. Entendí que lo que el Señor me estaba diciendo realmente era «James, ¿de quién has sido un hijo, así como Jesús ha sido un hijo para mí?». Eso es lo que él había estado preguntando.

El Señor estaba poniendo su dedo en un asunto importantísimo en preparación para que mi corazón pudiera recibir el amor del Padre. Mi actitud a mi padre terrenal era un bloqueo enorme en mi corazón para poder recibir la paternidad de Dios.

MI PAPÁ

Una de las memorias más fuertes que tengo de mi padre es que él tenía una capacidad enorme de hacer pelea, especialmente cuando estaba borracho, lo cual era frecuente. No importaba lo que uno dijera, él tomaba la contraria y provocaba contenciosamente. Cuando era un niño pequeño no entendía que mi papá tenía problemas a los que estaba atado. Simplemente pensaba que me odiaba. Solía provocarme al punto en que literalmente yo perdía control de mi cuerpo y explotaba con ira y frustración. Cuando él provocaba una pelea, todo lo que le escuchaba decir era que yo era estúpido. «*Hay algo muy malo con tu cerebro. Eres un idiota. No eres lo suficientemente bueno para mí. No puedes pensar claro. ¡Hay algo en ti que no funciona!*». Desde ese entonces he aprendido algo acerca de las peleas. Pelear no tiene nada que ver con el tema de la pelea. El tema de la pelea es meramente un instrumento que una persona peleonera emplea para lograr una ventaja. Una pelea es de hecho una lucha de poder.

Sin lugar a duda mi padre tenía problemas. Yo también, pero yo era un niño pequeño. Y cuando él usaba toda la fuerza de su voz adulta, su mente adulta y el poder de su personalidad en mi contra, había veces en las yo pateaba las puertas y las sacaba de sus bisagras. Casi podía ver todo de color rojo, somataba la puerta y corría a las colinas detrás de mi casa, humeando de cólera y llorando hasta que mi corazón se calmaba. Regresaba cuando habían apagado las luces, subía a través de la ventana de mi recámara y me dormía. Nadie venía a chequear si había regresado. Luego había tensión en la casa durante días. Y eventualmente poco a poco se disipaba hasta la próxima pelea. Crecer así hizo que le cerrara mi corazón a mi papá.

PERDONANDO CON TU VOLUNTAD

Poco tiempo después de que me volviera cristiano, un hombre vino a predicar a nuestra iglesia. El mensaje que predicó era básicamente este: «*Debes perdonar a otros que han pecado contra ti. Si no perdonas, Dios no te perdonará*». Entendía lo que estaba diciendo. Había leído las Escrituras muchas veces. Pero lo interpretaba como un asunto de seguridad eterna. Al no perdonar uno podía perder su salvación. No se me ocurría ninguna interpretación alternativa para ese verso.

¡Si hay un tema candente para mí es éste! Creo que muchos, muchos cristianos en todo el mundo han estado engañados acerca de lo que realmente significa el *perdón*. Muchos cristianos piensan que han perdonado a alguien cuando en su corazón realmente no lo han hecho. Creen que el asunto está cerrado porque han perdonado de la forma en que se les ha enseñado. A medida que escuchaba a este predicador me sentí bajo una presión enorme de perdonar a mi padre, o perdería mi salvación. ¡Estaba atrapado! Quería salirme del auditorio pero no podía. Pensaba que si me iba estaría dejando atrás también al cristianismo. Así que me quedé y la presión se volvió cada vez peor.

La cruda realidad es que no quería perdonar a mi padre. No había ni un hueso en mi cuerpo remotamente interesado en perdonarle. Pero el predicador estaba insistiendo en que lo hiciera.

No se trata de la voluntad

Finalmente, cuando terminaba la reunión, él dijo: «Cualquiera que necesite perdonar a alguien que pase al frente ahora». Así que pasé al frente, todavía batallando conmigo mismo, y uno de los ancianos vino y se paró al lado mío. Finalmente, después de mucho tiempo de no poder obligarme a decir las palabras para perdonar a mi papá, él me dijo: «James, usa tu voluntad».

Cuando él dijo eso yo supe que esa era la clave para que yo pudiera salir de ese lugar esa noche, porque yo sabía como usar mi voluntad. Hubo veces cuando estuve en las montañas y había un clima siniestro, los ríos se inundaban y yo andaba empapado y con frío. En esa situación, si no llegas a una cabaña al anochecer probablemente no sobrevives la noche. Así que haces funcionar tu voluntad y logras sobreponerte al viento y a la lluvia hasta llegar a la cabaña. Ese tipo de situaciones son muy reales, así que sabía lo que era poner a funcionar la voluntad. De manera que cuando este anciano dijo esto, apagué mis emociones y, como un acto de voluntad dije «Yo perdono a mi padre en el nombre de Jesús». Me sentí tan aliviado. Las lágrimas pararon. Yo estaba feliz. Sentí que mi salvación eterna estaba asegurada.

Luego de regreso en la capilla ese día, cuando el Señor me preguntó acerca de quien era yo hijo, me percaté de que todavía tenía asuntos enormes con respecto de mi papá en mi corazón. No había sido un hijo para él. No me había relacionado con él. Ni siquiera quería relacionarme con él. Las peleas entre él y yo todavía seguían de vez en cuando. No supe, hasta ese día, que mi anterior confesión de personar a mi papá no había sido nada más que una fachada.

Mucha gente ha sido guiada a creer que el perdón es una decisión. Puede que empiece como una decisión pero eso no es lo que es el perdón. Las palabras «te perdono» habladas meramente como un acto de voluntad no resultan en un perdón genuino.

Déjame poner pausa en mi historia acerca de lo que pasó en la capilla hasta el próximo capítulo para ir a la esencia de lo que quiero comunicar en este capítulo.

PERDONAR CON LA VOLUNTAD VERSUS PERDONAR CON EL CORAZÓN

Mucha gente cree que han perdonado simplemente porque han hecho una decisión, han usado su voluntad y han dicho las palabras de perdón.

La palabra «perdón» se ha convertido en un cliché que muchos cristianos asumen despreocupadamente pensando que saben lo que significa. Lo que quiero decir aquí es que en este libro ello significa algo muy diferente. De hecho, nunca he escuchado a otro predicador decir lo que yo voy a decir.

Vengan conmigo a Mateo capítulo 18. La primera parte de la historia comienza en el verso 21, cuando Pedro vino y le preguntó a Jesús acerca del perdón. Dice: «*Entonces se le acercó Pedro y le dijo: Señor, ¿cuántas veces perdonaré a mi hermano que peque contra mí? ¿Hasta siete?*».

Esa fue la pregunta de Pedro. Lo que estaba diciendo era: «Señor, ¿qué tan lejos va este tema del perdón? ¿Cuántas veces debo practicarlo?».

Detecto renuencia en Pedro en la forma en la que él formuló la pregunta. Muy probablemente Pedro había sido testigo de la gracia y misericordia en Jesús hacia la mujer hallada en adulterio y en muchos otros incidentes que pasaron. Cuando el hombre fue bajado a través del techo para ser sanado, las primeras palabras de Jesús a él fueron: «*Hijo, tus pecados te son perdonados*», ¡y el hombre ni siquiera había pedido perdón por sus pecados! Pedro había sido testigo de cómo Jesús había perdonado pecados y había extendido misericordia de manera libre y generosa. El habría visto esto durante un período de tiempo pensando: «Jesús, ¿ hasta donde llega esto? ¿Cómo reconcilias el perdón con las demandas de la ley?». A medida que Pedro hizo la increíble pregunta, también expuso su corazón. La respuesta de Jesús hacia él fue: «*No digo que hasta siete veces, sino hasta setenta veces siete*».

Yo no creo ni por un minuto que Jesús haya querido decir que hay que perdonar exactamente cuatrocientas noventa veces y nada más, luego de eso Pedro podría escoger. Jesús estaba diciendo que el perdón no tiene fin. Expuso el hecho de que Pedro no tenía idea alguna al respecto de lo que es el perdón.

Si entendemos el perdón como la mayoría lo entiende hoy en día, se puede ver también que perdonar a la misma persona por el mismo pecado siete veces es extremadamente difícil. Cuando alguien peca contra ti siempre duele. Siempre hay dolor de una forma u otra. Así que perdonarles y cancelar la deuda y dejarlos ir repetidamente dolería más y más cada vez. Lo que queremos generalmente es pedirle cuentas a la persona la segunda o tercera vez y luego la amistad se acabaría. Así que cuando Pedro dijo: «Señor, ¿siete veces?», él pensó que estaba siendo muy piadoso. Sin embargo, en la realidad, mostró que no había entendido la esencia. La gracia, la misericordia y el perdón que Jesús estaba enseñando estaba en una dimensión totalmente diferente.

AMANDO LA MISERICORDIA

Para demostrar lo que Jesús quiso decir veamos a Miqueas 6:8. Muchas personas tienen plaquetas con este verso colgadas en sus casas:

«Oh hombre, él te ha declarado lo que es bueno, y qué pide Jehová

de ti: solamente hacer justicia, y amar misericordia, y humillarte ante tu Dios»

¡Amar la misericordia! La misericordia tiene en el centro el ver al culpable liberado. Eso es perdón. El deseo de Dios es que *amemos* el perdonar. No se supone que sea algo que debamos hacer, sino algo que *amemos* hacer. El tipo de corazón que Dios quiere es un corazón que *ama* el perdonar.

Si amas algo, lo harás intensamente. Lo harás cada vez que tengas la oportunidad. Es más, estarás buscando oportunidades para hacerlo. Cuando Pedro dijo «Señor, ¿cuántas veces debo perdonar a mi hermano que peca contra mí?» lo que estaba diciendo es «esto es *trabajo duro*. No me gusta hacer esto, lo encuentro difícil. No quiero perdonar.» Pero la respuesta de *Jesús* fue «Pedro, no tienes idea de lo que es verdaderamente el perdón».

Jesús continuó contando una historia para ayudar a Pedro a entender la diferencia. Frecuentemente hemos pasado por alto ese punto. Pedro no entendió lo que era el perdón. Pensó que se lograba por determinación humana contra lo que una persona *realmente* quería hacer. He hablado mucho a las personas que me han dicho: «Alguien me hizo esto y me imagino que les voy a tener que perdonar todos los días». Sí, hay un proceso para perdonar. Me tomó seis meses pasar por esto con mi padre. No estoy diciendo que no haya un proceso porque ciertamente lo hay. El Señor empezó a llevarme a través de estos próximos versos en Mateo para que yo pudiera llegar a perdonar a mi padre de la manera en la que Él quería que lo hiciera. Él quiere que progresemos y vayamos de escoger perdonar, a perdonar con amor, y luego al punto de *amar* el perdonar. El anhela llevarnos más allá de solamente perdonar como un acto de la voluntad, y llegar al perdonar sin reservas desde un corazón que *ama* perdonar.

La mayoría en la iglesia hoy ha sido enseñada que el perdón es un asunto de escogencia y un acto de voluntad. Jesús no está de acuerdo. El dice que el perdón es un asunto del corazón.

El perdonar es cancelar una deuda

En este pasaje, Jesús dándose cuenta de que Jesús veía el perdón sólo como un mandamiento difícil que debe ser obedecido, contó una historia para explicar y guiar a Pedro a un perdón que él amaría practicar y que saldría de su corazón. Déjame parafrasear la historia

Había un rey que tenía un sirviente que desfalcó una gran cantidad de dinero del reino. Ya sea que lo haya apostado, haya hecho malas inversiones o lo haya gastado, el dinero se esfumó. Cuando fue descubierto, le rogó al rey que lo perdonara. El rey lo perdonó y canceló la deuda.

Este sirviente poco tiempo después salió y se topó con alguien que le debía una pequeña cantidad de dinero. El hombre también le rogó a él que le perdonara la pequeña cantidad de dinero pero el que fue perdonado de la deuda enorme no le quiso perdonar la pequeña deuda al tercero y lo echó en la cárcel hasta que le pagara. El rey se enteró y mandó a llamar al sirviente para decirle: «Te perdoné toda esa deuda, ¡y tú no perdonaste una pequeña cantidad!». Por esa razón el rey a su vez lo echó a la cárcel también en donde fue torturado y atormentado.

Esa es la historia. En el verso 34 dice «*Y en ira el dueño le entregó a los atormentadores, hasta que pagara toda su deuda*». Cuando

Jesús declara lo que es probablemente uno de los comentarios más serios en el Nuevo Testamento, *«así también mi Padre que está en los cielos hará a cada uno de ustedes, si no perdonan a su hermano de todo corazón».* En otras palabras, estarás atormentado hasta que perdones de tu corazón. Jesús contó la historia con un propósito. El enseñarnos cómo perdonar de todo corazón.

Debemos ultimadamente venir a este lugar en donde podemos *perdonar desde el corazón.* La verdad es, *tu voluntad no es tu corazón.* Tu voluntad es tuya. Tu corazón eres *tú.* Sabemos esto porque una persona puede controlar la voluntad. Tú puedes determinar tu voluntad para hacer algo o *no* hacer algo. Mucha gente que ha tomado la decisión de perdonar pero no ha perdonado de corazón todavía vive en un tipo de tormento, pensando *«esto no tiene que ser nada relacionado con falta de perdón porque ya he perdonado. He hecho la decisión, así que para mí, el perdón ya fue realizado. Los problemas que hay en mi vida ahora no pueden tener nada que ver con el perdón, porque ya he perdonado, tal y como me enseñaron».* De hecho, el perdón sigue siendo el meollo del asunto, pero no pueden encararlo porque creen que ya lo han practicado y lidiado con ello.

Así que regresemos a la historia a la cual el Señor me llevó verso por verso para ayudarme a perdonar a mi mamá. Jesús dijo,

«Por lo tanto el reino de los cielos puede ser comparado a un rey que deseó hacer cuentas con sus siervos».

Cuando leí ese verso, el Señor habló claramente y simplemente me dijo: *«James, mientras lees la historia, ponte en el lugar del rey».* Este rey tiene que perdonar a alguien, así que para entender cómo funciona, necesitamos ponernos en la posición del rey.

Al ponerme en el lugar del rey, mi padre se volvió el siervo quien me había robado tanto. El rey decidió, por razones desconocidas, el ajustar todas las cuentas de su reino y rectificarlas. Todo lo que estuviera incorrecto, quería arreglarlo. Quería que todo lo escondido saliera a la luz para ser corregido. Esto se volvió su determinación, el tener un reino que fuese justo.

A medida que lees esto puedes ponerte en el lugar del rey. Puedes decir: «Señor, quiero que todas las cuentas de mi vida se ajusten. Si hay cosas que no están realmente perdonadas, muéstrame qué son. Si he decidido yo mismo, o si no he podido ver, Señor, ¿me lo traerías a la atención para que aquí, hoy, yo pueda empezar a encararlo? Señor, quiero que las cuentas de mi reino estén en orden».

La historia continúa, «*Cuando empezó a ajustar cuentas, vino ante él uno que le debía diez mil talentos*». ¡Esto era casi equivalente a cien millones de dólares americanos en dinero de hoy en día! Este siervo obviamente era un hombre confiable, sostenía una posición de influencia en el reino.

Los peores pecados, los que nos lastiman más, usualmente son perpetrados por personas que están más cerca y en quienes confiamos. Generalmente, cuando no confías en alguien, lo que hacen contra ti confirma lo que te sospechabas, pero cuando confías en ellos, esto inflige una herida más grave. Este hombre tenía un lugar en el corazón del rey. El rey confiaba en él y se le sorprendió robando dinero de su dueño.

Esta es la razón por la que duele tanto cuando alguien peca contra ti. Porque cuando pecan contra ti ellos están robando algo de tu vida. Estás siendo robado.

No tienes que estar en el ministerio por mucho tiempo para descubrir que se ha pecado horrendamente contra algunas personas. El daño a sus vidas debido a lo que alguien más les ha hecho es absolutamente devastador. Cuando alguien peca contra ti siempre terminan robándote algo de tu vida.

Denise y yo estábamos ministrando a una dama una vez en Minnesota. Ella tenía ochenta y tres años de edad. Cuando era una niña de tres años, había sido violada. No pensaba que había tenido ninguna relación con respecto al asunto del que quería hablarnos. Su problema era el hecho de que se había casado cinco veces y cada uno de sus esposos se habían divorciado de ella. Tenía el corazón roto por el hecho de que estos hombres que ella había amado le habían rechazado. Todos habían dicho lo mismo, que ella no había sido una esposa afectuosa, y entonces la habían rechazado. Al escuchar la historia también descubrimos que había sido violada a los tres años. Ella no podía ver lo que era obvio para nosotros. El hecho de que sus problemas maritales eran causa y efecto y que ella estaba viviendo el legado de su abuso infantil.

Lo que le ocurrió cuando tenía tres años destruyó algo de su femineidad, de su habilidad de ser mujer. Destruyó su capacidad de poder relacionarse libremente de forma amorosa y de poder disfrutar una relación de intimidad. Le fue robada esa habilidad. Luego, me di cuenta de que lo que se le había robado no solamente era su capacidad de ser mujer, sino mucho más: la experiencia de tener un matrimonio feliz e hijos. El chance de volverse una abuela. Todos los beneficios que un matrimonio estable producirían durante toda su vida le fueron quitados. Como una mujer de ochenta y tres años, ella no tenía nada de esas cosas. Se las habían robado cuando era una niña de tres años.

Puse mis brazos alrededor de ella y le pedí al Padre que viniera a derramar su amor en esa parte en su corazón que tenía tres años de edad, y que sanara su herida. Un milagro ocurrió ese día. Esa anciana empezó a reírse como una niñita de tres años. Estaba riéndose incontrolablemente con gozo. Luego ella paró y nos vio con una expresión muy seria y dijo: «¿Porqué se tardó tanto Dios para sanarme?». Yo no tenía la respuesta a esa pregunta. Todo lo que podía pensar en decirle fue: «Bueno, más vale tarde que nunca, creo yo». Al escuchar eso ella inmediatamente siguió riéndose, «¡Sí, más vale tarde que nunca!». Fue un verdadero gozo para ella escuchar eso. Fue sanada.

Cuando la gente peca contra nosotros, el hecho es que *siempre* nos roban algo de más.

Si no entendemos lo que nos fue robado, no podemos cancelar la deuda.

Mucha gente pide disculpas superficial y rápidamente cuando han hecho algo malo: «Hermano, lo siento. Por favor perdóname.» ¡Sabemos que eso es «lo cristiano»! Y la respuesta cristiana es «sí, te perdono», y pensamos que ya se acabó. Sin embargo, en la mayoría de los casos, la relación nunca se sanó. No hay restauración de la relación porque expresamos palabras de perdón que no identificamos como equivocadas. Hay muchas relaciones superficiales en el cuerpo de Cristo por esta misma razón. Heridas de corazón que nunca han sido sanadas. *Si no entendemos lo que fue robado, no podemos cancelar la deuda.*

Así que, en esta historia, fueron robados diez mil talentos. Para que este rey perdonara, tenía que cancelar la deuda equivalente a cien millones de dólares. Eso es mucho dinero.

EL PERDONAR CON EL CORAZÓN TE COSTARÁ

Déjame usar este escenario. Imagínate que un día yo paso por tu casa y decido tocar y molestarte para que me prestes $20. Cuando llego a tu casa no estas en la casa pero la puerta está abierta y puedo ver tu billetera sobre la mesa. Veo dentro y pienso, «si él estuviera aquí me prestaría esa suma. Es mi amigo. Así que lo tomaré». Entro entonces y tomo los $20, los gasto, y así se esfuman.

Cuando regresas más tarde, notas inmediatamente que te hacen falta $20. Piensas «¡Alguien me robó! No debí dejar la puerta abierta». Sin embargo, al día siguiente el Espíritu Santo me redarguye y me doy cuenta que he pecado. Ese no fue un préstamo. De hecho yo robé ese dinero. Así que regreso a donde estás tú y digo: «Hermano, perdóname, pero ayer cuando saliste, vine a tu casa y tomé $20 de tu billetera y los gasté. Se esfumaron. ¿Me perdonas?».

Ahora tú tienes que escoger, pero tu decisión tiene que tener apegado una parte emocional porque probablemente estarás emocionalmente apegado a esos $20. Para poder dejar ir esos $20 tú debes cancelar la deuda. Si no me perdonas entonces la tengo que pagar en su totalidad. La falta de perdón demanda que le pecador restituya por completo. *El perdón cancela la deuda.* Lo que hace del perdón algo difícil para nosotros es el hecho de que el inocente debe pagar por el culpable. Siempre ha sido así. Lo vemos en Jesús. Cuando él perdonó a los pecadores, ¡A él le costó la vida! El perdón y la misericordia de hecho atentan contra la justicia. Te va a costar $20 el perdonarme.

Lo maravilloso acerca del perdón es esto: cuando perdonamos a alguien, esto nos hace más como Jesús. Cuando cancelamos una deuda, cuando estamos pagando por el pecado de otro, entonces nos acercamos más a Él y nos volvemos más como Él.

Entonces pensarás: «¿Qué son $20 dólares para James y para mí? No es un tipo tan malo. Cometió un error aquí. Ok, cancelo la deuda». Así que me dices: «Ok, te perdono». Salgo de tu casa y estoy libre y nunca tendré que pagar esa deuda.

Ahora, déjame cambiar la historia un poco. Cuando voy a tu casa y abro tu billetera y saco los $20 me doy cuenta que ahí está tu tarjeta VISA. Lo que es más, has dejado el número de PIN en la parte de atrás. Así que tomo la tarjeta de crédito y los $20 y voy al banco y saco $1,000 de tu cuenta de banco y regreso la tarjeta VISA a tu billetera. Me gasto todo, los $1020. Todo se esfuma. El próximo día me arrepiento. Sin embargo, cuando vienes a casa y la tarjeta VISA está ahí en tu billetera, solo te hacen falta los $20. No sabes nada acerca de los $1,000 dólares hasta después de que te llega la cuenta mensual.

Al día siguiente cuanto el Espíritu Santo me redarguye y vengo a decirte «Hermano, perdóname pero ayer vine y me robé un dinero de tu casa. ¿Me perdonas?». Nota que no dije los detalles acerca de tomar la tarjeta para que pienses que solo fueron $20. En realidad, te robé $1,020 pero estoy pidiéndote que me perdones por todo lo que te robé. Así que cuando te digo: «Hermano, te robé un dinero. ¿Me perdonas?» y tú dices «¿qué son $20 entre James y yo? Ok James, te perdono».

Déjame hacer la pregunta. ¿Fui perdonado? ¡No! *No* he sido perdonado. *¡No me puedes perdonar a menos que sepas lo que se te ha robado!* Tú me has perdonado por $20 pero cuando obtengas tu estado de cuenta de tu VISA vas a tener que pasar de nuevo por el proceso de nuevo. Y te sentirás mucho más emocional acerca de $1,000 que acerca de $20. Esto tocará tu vida de forma muy real. Tal vez tenías los $1,000 reservados para tus vacaciones o algo muy importante para ti. $1,000 no es una cantidad pequeña. Y así que en tu corazón, es un asunto más grande el tener que perdonarme por eso.

Verás, para muchos de nosotros, cuando perdonamos a alguien por algo, casi nunca hemos considerado bien lo que nos ha sido robado.

Estaba descubriendo esto cuando el Señor me estaba llevando por el proceso de perdonar a mi padre. Al frente de la iglesia yo había dicho con el anciano: «Perdono a mi padre en el nombre de Jesús» y tanto dolor había salido a la superficie de mi vida mientras trataba de decir las palabras. Pero, ahora leyendo esos versos, el Señor empezó a traer a mi mente la consciencia de que la inhabilidad de mi padre de ser el padre que yo necesitaba había tenido un costo inmenso para mí.

Empecé a entender que si mi padre pudiera haberme dicho, en medio de una pelea: «Hijo, no quiero pelear contigo. Te amo. Eres un buen chico. Tienes una mente genial. Te disfruto. Eres mi hijo», eso hubiese hecho una gran diferencia. Pero seguía tentando y tentándome, hasta que yo perdía el control.

A veces veo fotografías familiares viejas de cuando era un adolescente. En cada fotografía, sin excepción alguna, mi rostro estaba viendo al lado contrario de mi padre. Cuando veo mi rostro en esas fotos siento ganas de llorar. Era un chico pobre, partido por la mitad. Si mi padre hubiera simplemente puesto su mano sobre mi hombro cuando pasaba a la par mía eso hubiera hecho una gran diferencia en mi vida.

Si él me hubiera dicho que me amaba. Si solamente él se hubiera sentado a decirme: «Hijo, ¿cómo va tu día?». Mi padre no era un mal padre, pero la segunda guerra mundial lo dañó profundamente. Si hubiera podido ser un mejor padre, mi vida hubiera sido mejor. Mi padre nunca fue violento físicamente pero sus palabras eran constantemente crueles y cortantes. Yo empecé a familiarizarme con lo que me había costado el hecho de que mi padre haya sido el hombre que fue. Y empecé a enojarme mucho, pero mucho.

MI PADRE NO PODÍA PAGAR

A medida que Dios me llevaba por este proceso de realizar el costo, hubo veces cuando quise subirme a un avión y regresar a casa. Algunas veces me sentía tan enojado que quería pegarle a mi padre. Me sorprendí de toda la ira que estaba escondida profundo en mi corazón. Me sentí quebrantado. Estaba empezando a darme cuenta del costo real de la inhabilidad de mi padre de ser el padre que necesité.

Siguiendo con la historia en Mateo 18- en el verso 25 dice «*Y como él no podía pagar* (este es el hombre que había robado diez mil talentos), *su amo ordenó que fuera vendido junto a su familia e hijos, y todo lo que poseía, para que se realizara el pago*». Quería que mi padre fuera castigado. La falta de perdón quiere que la otra persona pague por lo que hizo. Pero las palabras que me quedaron grabadas fueron las primeras palabras del verso, «*como no podía pagar*». Este hombre había robado una cantidad masiva de dinero y todo se había esfumado. No podía regresarla.

Pasaron las semanas, y las palabra seguían regresando, «como no podía pagar». Y el Señor empezó a recordarme de cosas que había escuchado acerca de mi papá. La gente junto a la que había luchado en la guerra, mis tíos y tías. Empecé a ver su vida de forma diferente.

Recordé la forma en la que mis tías (sus hermanas) hablaban de él con un tono de voz burlón. Mi padre había dejado el hogar cuando él tenía dieciséis años. Había sido enviado a una ciudad que quedaba muy lejos en esos días, y se le permitía regresar a casa solamente una vez al año. El vivía con una anciana en una casa cerca de donde trabajaba, tenía una ocupación que odiaba y de regreso en casa no había ningún interés en él. Cuando regresaba cada año su mamá le daba la bienvenida con un apretón de manos y le decía adiós una semana más tarde con otro apretón de manos. Él me dijo algunos años después de que la única persona que le había dicho «te amo» había sido mi madre.

Cuando tenía diecisiete años, estalló la segunda guerra mundial. Se unión al ejército territorial inmediatamente para ser entrenado y fue enviado a pelear en las islas del pacífico. Luego fue a Egipto y fue parte de la avanzada de los aliados a través de Italia, en donde permaneció hasta el final de la guerra. Contó una vez como fue testigo de cuando su mejor amigo murió por un tiro directo de un disparo de tanque. Recuerdo que dijo «nunca encontramos ni un retazo de sus ropas». El era un observador de artillería pesada, localizaba posiciones del enemigo y ordenaba el fuego, dirigién- dolas al blanco. Casi nunca podían ver a donde habían disparado hasta que hubieran atravesado el pueblo que había sido obliterado. Una vez él vio pedazos de los cuerpos de mujeres y niños en las calles de un pueblo que bombardearon. No había hombres ni soldados ahí - ¡sólo mujeres y niños! Mi padre tenía diecinueve años y había sido el que había dirigido las bombas a ese pueblo.

Frecuentemente veo en retrospectiva y pienso que si yo hubiese sido Dios ese día, y hubiese visto el corazón de mi papá cuando atravesaron ese pueblo, ¿cómo me hubiese sentido con respecto a él? Yo pienso que hubiera sentido furia contra lo que pasó, pero pena por él, viendo lo que sus manos habían hecho y eso de lo que él había sido parte. Mi padre regresó de la guerra necesitando amor. Se casó muy rápido con mi mamá y en unos pocos años tuvieron tres hijos. Empezó a tomar tanto alcohol como pudo porque no podía manejar las emociones y las memorias que lo acechaban. Mi padre tenía una pelea con el mundo dentro de él por la injusticia de su vida. Consecuentemente él volvía todo una pelea porque había una profunda insatisfacción dentro de él. Había tenido tres hijos que necesitaban un padre que los amara. ¡Pero él no tenía nada de amor para dar!

Al leer esas palabras, *«como no podía pagar»,* supe que mi padre no tenía capacidad alguna dentro de él para ser un padre. No tenía amor para dar. No podía pagar lo que me debía.

No puedes dar lo que no tienes

Verás, no puedes dar lo que no has recibido – y aún así a veces podemos pensar que las cosas son tan simples, «¿por qué no pueden hacer estoy y lo otro? Es tan simple». Pero si nunca lo has recibido, no es tan simple. Mi padre nunca había escuchado las palabras «te amo». Nunca tuvo un padre que pusiera su mano en el hombre y le dijera «estoy orgulloso de ti, hijo». Todo lo que tenía en su corazón era una pelea con el mundo. *El no podía pagar.* Empecé a ver a mi padre simplemente como otro ser humano que había sufrido, que era imperfecto y quien, como yo, no podía manejar mucho de la vida que le había tocado.

«Luego el dueño del siervo fue conmovido con compasión, le soltó y le perdonó la deuda» (v27).

El dueño fue *movido a compasión*. Cuando vi que mi padre simplemente no tenía los medios para pagarme, por primera vez en mi vida tuve compasión por él. Nunca había visto las cosas desde esta perspectiva. Creo que si hubiera podido tener la perspectiva de Dios y hubiese visto las cosas que habían pasado en la vida de mi padre, hubiera tenido una actitud diferente para con él.

EL VERDADERO LADRÓN

Tenemos un enemigo de nuestra alma. Este enemigo viene a robar, matar y destruir. Pero no a robarte el auto, viene a robarte el alma. No viene a destruir tu televisión, viene a destruir tu personalidad. Viene a matar todo lo bueno en ti, todo lo piadoso, todo lo amable, todo lo placentero y todo lo gentil. Viene a destruir todo lo que tiene un dejo de Dios en ello.

Como cristianos, tenemos un escudo de la fe para protegernos de los darnos de fuego del enemigo. Pude ver que mi padre nunca había tenido un escudo, y entonces, los dardos de fuego del enemigo le dieron. Satanás no tiene escrúpulos. No se tienta en ninguna manera, ni ejerce ningún tipo de control sobre la maldad que quiere hacerle a cualquier persona. Hará las cosas más horrendas al niño más puro e inocente. El diablo había estado atacando a mi padre desde el momento en que mi padre nació, aun antes de que naciera incluso. Todos los que te han herido, han sido atacados también. El enemigo ha estado atacando y destruyendo a tu padre y madre de maneras en las que nunca podrás entender. Robándoles su potencial de ser las personas que soñaron ser, para dejarles incapaces de ser los padres que necesitaste.

Así que empecé a entender algo acerca de la vida de mi padre y empecé a ver que era un hombre tal y como yo lo era. Batallando con los problemas de este mundo, tratando de hacer lo mejor que podía, solo que no tenía la capacidad de ser lo que yo necesitaba que él fuera. Por primera vez en mi vida, oré por mi padre, y oré algo así,

«Señor, quiero que mi padre sea bendecido. Quiero que sea feliz. No quiero que cargue esta culpa ya más. No quiero que deje de ser amado. No quiero que siga estando solo. Quiero que sea amado. Quiero que sea perdonado por las cosas en su consciencia y todas las cosas de la guerra que lo perturbaron. No quiero que siga cargando con ellas. Todas las cosas que hicieron que bebiera tanto para adormecer su corazón. Señor, te estoy pidiendo que le perdones por todas esas cosas para que pueda rendirlas y dejarlas atrás para poder ser libre. Señor, ¿le perdonarías sus pecados, podrías perdonarlo por todo? Ni siquiera quiero que se sienta culpable por la forma en que falló en ser mi padre, porque eso es añadir a todos los problemas de su vida. Quiero que sea libre de los sentimientos de fracaso como hombre, como padre, como esposo. ¡Quiero que sea libre! Señor, quiero que sea bendecido. Señor, lo perdono con todo mi corazón. ¿Lo perdonarías tú también?»

Cuando hice esa oración pude sentir que quería genuinamente que él fuera perdonado por su propio bien. El estaba llevando tanto peso encima *y yo quería que él fuera libre.* Puedo decirte esto – con ese tipo de perdón, uno termina *amando* el perdonar. Cuando dije, *Señor, le perdono con todo mi corazón* , algo extraño pasó lo cual no me esperaba.

Repentinamente, me sentí increíblemente vacío. En mi corazón me sentí tan solo y vulnerable. Me sentí como un niño que estaba totalmente desprotegido. Cuando no perdonas del corazón estás guardándole la deuda a la persona que te debe. Cuando la dejas ir, te quedas vacío.

Perdoné a mi padre y cancelé la deuda. Lo solté de sus obligaciones como padre, y de ser lo que nunca pudo ser. Paré de esperar cosas de su parte porque eso era otro peso sobre sus hombros. Le solté de mi esperanza de que me pagara lo que me debía algún día. De repente, me sentí completamente vacío y totalmente solo. Me sentí como un niño sin nadie que me protegiera.

En ese momento, cuando ese sentimiento me inundó, tuve una visión extraña. En la visión, yo era un maestro de escuela en un aula de aproximadamente treinta niños. Les grité a esos niños de doce años: «¿Quién va a ser un padre para mí?». Los niños me vieron perplejos. Solo eran unos chicos. ¿Cómo podían ser mis padres? Volvía yo a gritar una y otra vez: «¿Quién va a ser un padre para mí?» pero por supuesto, no sabían que decir. Luego me di cuenta que atrás de ellos en la parte de atrás de la clase, una mano se levantó. Cuando vi más allá de las cabezas, sentado en el piso recostado en la pared estaba nuestro Padre celestial. Y Él me dijo: «James, yo voy a ser un padre para ti.»

El perdón hecho desde el corazón es cuando tu corazón deja ir a esa persona, les libera y los suelta. Cuando tu corazón está conectado a alguien a través de la falta de perdón, entonces no está libre para estar conectado con tu Padre celestial. Dios quiere conocernos de corazón a corazón, como un padre. Cuando desatamos a nuestra madre o padre con todo el corazón, entonces nuestros corazones son libres para estar conectados con nuestro Padre celestial quien está diciendo: «Yo los recibiré y seré un padre para ustedes... y ustedes serán mis hijos e hijas.» (2 Corintios

6:17-18). Tú tienes un Padre celestial que quiere conocerte profunda e íntimamente. Tal vez estés todavía atado a tus padres a través de la falta de perdón. Es hora de perdonarles desde el corazón y dejarlos ir.

El corazón de un hijo

~

Ahora quiero terminar de decirte lo que pasó en la capilla esa mañana. Esto fue crucial para llevarme a experimentar el amor del Padre.

Cuando el Señor hizo la escalofriante pregunta: «James, ¿De quién eres hijo?» ocurrió la comunicación más increíble. Sabía que él estaba preguntando: «¿Para quien has sido un hijo, como Jesús ha sido hijo para mí?». Había mucho más involucrado en este asunto, tanto que me quedé por largo tiempo tratando de encontrar la respuesta. Me quedé perplejo con la pregunta que me hizo el Señor, tratando de salir con una respuesta adecuada. Habían dos temas dándome vueltas en la mente al mismo tiempo, como dos discos rotando salvajemente en direcciones opuestas; estaba pasando a través de todo lo que podía pensar, tratando de encontrar una respuesta que pudiera satisfacer ambas situaciones. ¿Qué podía decir? Era un momento muy intenso y sabía que el Señor era capaz de ver y observar los movimientos internos de mi corazón, mente y emociones.

Como un reflector, Él estaba buscando dentro de mi para ver mi reacción a su pregunta.

Lo primero que se me vino a la mente en respuesta de: «James, ¿de quién eres hijo?» vino en la forma de un nombre, y el primer nombre que se me ocurrió fue el nombre de mi padre. Pensé que podía simplemente decirle al Señor: «Soy hijo de Bruce Jordan», pero tan pronto como me vino el pensamiento, me percaté que no podía decirle eso al Señor, porque había dejado de ser un hijo para mi padre hacía ya mucho tiempo. Por supuesto, era su hijo de sangre, pero no era un hijo para él de la misma forma en que Jesús era un hijo para el Padre. Así que tenía que borrar eso de mi mente y rápidamente encontrar otra respuesta.

La otra persona que vino a mi mente fue un anciano en la iglesia en donde fuimos salvos. El era un hombre impresionante. Su nombre era Ken Wright. Había estado caminando en el Espíritu por muchos años. También era el hombre que me había bautizado. Recuerdo ver su itinerario una vez cuando planeó un viaje ministerial alrededor del mundo. No iba a estar en ningún lugar por más de cuatro días, en la totalidad de los dos años, y visitó más de cien países diferentes. Cuando hablaba, bebíamos las palabras y el Espíritu que había en él fluía directo a nosotros. Estábamos muy impresionados con él y tenía un corazón paternal para con nosotros.

Así que cuando el Señor me hizo la pregunta « James, ¿de quién eres hijo?» de repente se me ocurrió que podía decir que era el hijo de Ken Wright pero de nuevo, en el momento en que me pasó eso por la mente, sabía que no podía decirlo, porque (aunque había aprendido todo lo que podía de parte de Ken) ciertamente no tenía el corazón de un hijo para con él. Jesús dijo a su Padre: «Me deleito en hacer tu voluntad» pero yo nunca había deseado complacer a Ken. Tomé todo lo que pude aprender de él para complacerme a mi mismo. Así que pensé: «No puedo decirle eso al Señor tampoco. ¿A quién más puedo nombrar? No puedo decir Bruce Jordan. No puedo decir Ken Wright, así que ¿Para quién puedo decir que he sido un hijo?».

El otro hombre que podía pensar era Neville Winger. Solíamos decirle tío Nev. El tío Nev era dueño de un negocio de venta de autos en Nueva Zelanda y lo vendió todo para comprar una granja en una isla cerca de la costa de Nueva Zelanda. Era una granja mal cuidada, de ochocientos acres de campo silvestre con una costa de mar hermosa. Se mudó ahí con su esposa Dot, y por muchos años llevaban a jóvenes necesitados a vivir a su casa. Nev y Dot tenían un corazón para los jóvenes y se llevaban a vivir con ellos a los que querían ayudar. Así que estaba buscando un lugar a donde poder llevar a estos chicos y sacarlos de la calle para cuidarlos en su casa. También quería un centro de conferencias y avivamiento para Nueva Zelanda así que compró esta granja con el propósito de alcanzar esta visión.

Nev era un hombre extraordinario, un verdadero padre espiritual en la nación. Cuando predicaba me podía conectar con él y pensaba que me gustaría asistir a la escuela bíblica que él empezó; lo cual terminamos haciendo. De alguna manera, Nev, tal y como Ken, tenía un corazón de padre con respecto a nosotros. Nos profetizó largamente una noche y todos estos años después, esa noche sigue siendo relevante.

Así que pensé que le podía decir al Señor: «Soy el hijo de Nev Winger», pero *de nuevo*, al estar bajo el reflector de Dios, me di cuenta que tampoco podía decir eso. La verdad es que nunca había sido un hijo para él en mi corazón. Yo había sido alguien que había consumido lo que él tenía, no le había dado lo que yo tenía a él. Un verdadero hijo, como Jesús, siempre está interesado en los negocios de su padre. Yo nunca estuve interesado con el negocio de mi padre ni con el negocio de Nev Winger. Nunca jamás consideré cómo podía ser una bendición o una ayuda para estos hombres. Tenía un corazón totalmente huérfano. Estaba intensamente incómodo y peleando y luchando cuando todo lo que tenía que hacer era decir: «Señor, no soy el hijo de nadie y *no quiero* ser el hijo de nadie». No podía admitir eso porque había algo más que estaba sucediendo. Cuando le había cerrado el corazón a mi padre había perdido completamente el corazón de hijo.

El espíritu de hijo

¿Cómo es el corazón de un hijo? Para entender esto veamos Gálatas 4:4, el cual dice,

«Cuando se cumplió la plenitud del tiempo, Dios envió a su Hijo, nacido de mujer, bajo la ley, para redimir a aquellos que estaban bajo la ley, para que pudiéramos recibir adopción como hijos».

Cuando nacemos de nuevo, nos volvemos hijos e hijas de Dios por adopción. Sin embargo, Dios va más allá de la adopción. La adopción es el primer paso. Pablo continúa,

«Y ya que son hijos, Dios ha enviado al Espíritu de su hijo a nuestros corazones clamando ¡Abba!¡Padre!».

Ya que son hijos de Dios legalmente, Él ha derramado el Espíritu de su Hijo. Él ha puesto ese Espíritu en nuestros corazones, el Espíritu que clama: «¡Abba! ¡Padre!». Un hijo adoptado no clama «¡Abba! ¡Padre!». Nuestros corazones humanos no claman «¡Abba! ¡Padre!». Es el Espíritu del Hijo en nosotros el que clama «¡Abba! ¡Padre!».

El Espíritu de su Hijo es derramado en nuestros corazones. Cuando le cerré mi corazón a mi padre, perdí el corazón de un hijo. Así que cuando el Espíritu Santo fue derramado en mí no había un corazón correspondiente de hijo. Ya que le había cerrado el corazón de hijo, el Espíritu Santo no podía sacar a relucir esa parte de hijo de adentro de mi. Este es un punto vital, el cual el Señor estaba exponiéndome cuando Él me hizo esa pregunta. El estaba buscando un corazón que estuviese abierto a ser un hijo.

Jesús experimentó esto cuando el Espíritu Santo descendió sobre él en su bautismo. Cuando Dios anunció: «Este es mi hijo amado en quien tengo complacencia», el Espíritu que nos hace capaces de ser hijos descendió sobre Él. ¡Desde ese punto en adelante Jesús proclamó al mundo entero que Él era el Hijo de Dios! Antes de eso, él era Jesús de Nazaret, el hijo de María y José, pero ahora él fue proclamado como Hijo de Dios. El mismo Espíritu Santo que vino sobre Jesús es el mismo Espíritu que nos hace hijos de Dios.

Muchos cristianos han conocido al Espíritu Santo como el Espíritu de adopción pero todavía no le han experimentado como el Espíritu que les habilita para ser hijos de Dios. Consecuentemente, podemos estar llenos del Espíritu Santo y no vivir como hijos. Cuando el Espíritu se derrama en el corazón de una persona que no sabe como ser un hijo o hija para con sus propios padres, entonces el Espíritu Santo no puede funcionar en esa persona para hacerle un hijo. *El Espíritu de Dios debe encontrar una armonía correspondiente dentro de ti para que eso sea real en tu propia experiencia de vida.*

Cuando le cerré mi corazón a mi padre, perdí el corazón de un hijo. Cuando le cerré mi corazón a mi padre, ya no tenía el corazón de hijo para ninguna figura paternal... incluyendo a Dios.

RELACIONÁNDONOS A UN PADRE

Ese era mi gran problema. Había mucha gente que vino a mi vida con algo de corazón de Padre para conmigo pero no tenía manera de relacionarme a ello. No me daba cuenta de que si uno no tiene corazón de hijo para con su propia madre o padre terrenal, entonces uno no tiene el corazón de un hijo para con nadie, y por ende uno no puede lograr una conexión con ningún padre. *¡Incluyendo Dios Padre!* De la misma manera en que hacer a Jesús el Señor absoluto es un prerrequisito para tener una relación con Él, el tener el corazón de un hijo o una hija es crucial para tener una relación con Dios el Padre.

Si quieres conocer a Dios el Padre, solo hay una forma. El no se va a relacionar contigo de ninguna otra forma que como un Padre. Muchos de nosotros nos hemos convertido en padres en algún momento de nuestras vidas, pero Dios nunca se *convirtió* en un padre, Él *siempre fue* un padre y Él siempre será Padre. Él creó el universo, pero él no es un creador por naturaleza. Si tu padre es un ingeniero, por ejemplo, no te relacionas con él en base a su ocupación, te relacionas con él en base a su identidad en la relación. Él se relaciona contigo como un Padre porque eso es lo que Él es. Padre es la esencia de su ser. Jesús vino a revelar que Yahvé es Papá, que Yahvé es Padre.

Yo creo que probablemente más de noventa porciento de nosotros en el mundo occidental le hemos cerrado nuestros corazones a nuestros padres. Hemos usado lenguaje sofisticado acerca de ello pero la realidad de la relación íntima es algo muy extraño a la experiencia de mucha gente.

Así que cuando estaba en la capilla y el Señor me habló esas palabras: «James, ¿de quién eres hijo?», él realmente estaba abordando el estado de mi corazón. No podía encontrar respuestas. Tenía que haber dicho: «Señor, no soy el hijo de nadie», pero tenía dificultad de decir eso. Déjame decirte porqué.

Todos los hombres de Dios son hijos de alguien

Desde que me volví cristiano había querido ser un hombre de Dios, como los predicadores ungidos. Siempre oraba: «Señor, hazme un hombre de Dios». Cuando estaba en la capilla ese día, tratando de encontrar un nombre que pudiera mencionarle al Señor, otro proceso mental estaba ocurriendo en mi cabeza. Tenía que ver con un tema favorito mío en esa época. Cuando estaba en la escuela bíblica había hecho un inmenso proyecto de estudios acerca de la cronología del Antiguo Testamento. Cuando estaba investigando los famosos personajes del Antiguo Testamento, algo continuamente me fastidiaba. Casi todos estos héroes eran descritos como «el hijo de...». Josué el hijo de Nun, Caleb el hijo de Jefone, David el hijo de Isaí. Cada persona que leía era descrita en términos de ser hijo de alguien.

Esto me molesto mucho. ¿Por qué no David el poeta, el rey guerrero? ¿Por qué no Isaías el gran profeta? ¿Por qué no Caleb el hombre de fe? Yo era tan independiente que pensaba: «¿Por qué no pueden estos sujetos pararse sobre sus propios pies? ¿Por qué no podían ser hombre de verdad? ¿Por qué necesitaban a su papi para ayudarlos?». Esto revelaba el verdadero estado de mi corazón en relación a mi padre.

Ese día en la capilla sentí que Dios me estaba diciendo: «James, te he escuchado pedirme que te haga un hombre de Dios. ¿Quieres ser un hombre de Dios? ¿Es eso verdad? Bien, *todos* mis hombres son hijos de alguien. Así que si quieres ser un hombre de Dios, James, ¿de quién eres hijo?».

JESÚS FUE EL HIJO DE UN HOMBRE IMPERFECTO

Yo *sabía* el daño que los padres pueden causar. ¿No sabían estos héroes bíblicos el daño que los padres causan? ¡Deben estar locos para ser hijo de uno de ellos! Yo sabía que Jesús es el Hijo de Dios pero lo podía perdonar por eso porque su Padre es perfecto. ¡Los padres perfectos no son el problema, sino los imperfectos! Luego me di cuenta que Jesús será eternamente conocido como el hijo de David. De hecho, su ministerio está basado en el reinado de David. ¡Y David no fue un hombre perfecto!

Muchas iglesias hoy, basados en los fracasos del célebre rey de Israel, impedirían que David ministrara o tuviera algún lugar de autoridad en la iglesia. ¡Pero a Jesús no le importaba el ser conocido como el hijo de un hombre imperfecto! ¡Eso me retó muy literalmente! Si Jesús fue capaz de ser un hijo para un hombre imperfecto, entonces seguramente había algo equivocado en mi perspectiva. No quería ser un hijo de alguien imperfecto, pero Jesús estaba feliz de ser conocido como el hijo de un hombre imperfecto. No podía yo escapar a esta realidad. ¡Estaba atrapado!

No lo sabía en ese entonces, pero ese día iba a determinar el resto de mi vida. Finalmente, tenía que ser honesto y admitir: «Señor, no soy el hijo *de nadie*. Y lo que es más, no quiero serlo. Me atemoriza. ¿Me ayudarías?». Cuando dije: «¿Me ayudarías?», su presencia inmediatamente dejó el lugar y me quedé solo en la capilla. Sentí que el Señor se había ido para empezar a trabajar en mi problema.

ENCONTRANDO EL CORAZÓN DE UN HIJO

Luego de este encuentro, el Señor empezó a obrar en mi para restaurar el corazón de un hijo. La primera cosa que pude hacer, como describí en el capítulo anterior, fue perdonar a mi papá desde el corazón. Cuando llegué a este punto mi corazón fue libre y empecé a preguntarme cómo podía ser restaurado el corazón de hijo en mi propia vida.

No podía encontrar ninguna respuesta a esa pregunta. Pensé y oré bastante acerca de ellos pero nada parecía ocurrírseme. ¿Cómo recupera uno el corazón de hijo después de haberlo perdido? Bueno, cuando uno pierde algo, ¿dónde lo encuentra? ¡Lo encuentra en el lugar donde lo dejó! ¿Cierto? Si puedes regresar a donde lo perdiste, ahí estará. Es tan simple como eso.

Así que había perdido el corazón de un hijo en mi relación con mi papá. Ahí era donde había cerrado mi alma, así que, para obtener de vuelta el corazón de hijo, pensé que iba a ser algo relacionado a mi papá, pero no sabía qué. No podía pensar en ninguna manera en la que pudiera encontrar de nuevo el corazón de hijo. Luego de un tiempo empecé a descubrir que había una cosa que podía hacer. Había perdonado a mi padre por todas las cosas que hizo y las que no hizo, sin embargo, realicé que también le había tratado de una manera inapropiada. Había cerrado mi corazón hacia él. Podía haber tenido más misericordia y haberle honrado. Fue mi decisión el cortarlo de mi corazón. Luego se me ocurrió que le iba a escribir una carta para pedirle perdón por todas esas cosas.

Cuando era un chico en mi hogar, una de mis tareas era podar el césped en la parte trasera de la casa. Nunca lo hice sin que mi papá tuviera que presionarme para hacerlo. Nunca lo hice de buena gana y necesitaban ser cortadas. También evitaba mi responsabilidad al salir después de llegar a casa de la escuela y quedarme afuera hasta que el sol caía y no había ya tiempo de podar el césped. Me ponía feliz cuando llovía porque lo usaba como una excusa. Si no llovía bajaba al riachuelo a nadar o capturar anguilas. Finalmente mi padre me hacía presión y me amenazaba, como por ejemplo, con prohibirme salir a jugar así que a regañadientes podaba el césped. Nunca lo hice de buena gana. Pensaba entonces que podía pedirle perdón por esto y por otras cosas similares.

Sin embargo, había un problema con esto. En nuestra casa, nadie nunca pedía perdón porque era percibido como debilidad. Nunca nadie pedía perdón y nunca nadie decía «te amo». Esos eran señales de debilidad y por ende yo tenía miedo de pedir el perdón de mi padre porque solía usarlo contra mí para la próxima pelea.

La carta

Decidí redactar la carta para ver cómo se podría leer pero no sentía que podía dar el paso de mandarla. Eventualmente expresé en la carta lo que quería expresar. Pedí su perdón por nunca haber podado el césped de la forma en la que él quería que lo podara. Pedí perdón por no tener la actitud correcta con respecto a él. Pedí perdón por las peleas. Pedí perdón por cosas que le dije. Pedí perdón por no hacer muchas de las tareas que él quería que hiciera en la casa. Al final de la carta le puse: «Pido tu perdón por cerrarte mi corazón cuando tenía diez años y por ya no haber sido un hijo para ti». Luego puse la carta en una gaveta donde estuvo por dos semanas hasta que se la mencioné a Jack Winter quien me contestó:

«Bueno, ¡más vale que la mandes ya!», y se fue.

¡Ahora sí sentía la presión! Compré un sobre y una estampilla, puse la dirección en el sobre, y la volví a guardar en la gaveta en donde estuvo por otro mes. Sabía que cuando la escribí puse lo que quería decir pero no quería re-leerla porque estaba acobardándome. Finalmente, sabía que la tenía que mandar. Sabía que Jack me iba a preguntar si había mandado la carta y quería poder decirle que sí, así que decidí llevar la carta «a dar un paseo». Me dije a mi mismo que no la enviaría. Solo iría a caminar hacia la oficina postal.

Cerca de donde nos estábamos quedando había un buzón rojo al lado del camino. Caminé hacia el y puse la carta pensando «si la dejo aquí le va a llegar». Rápidamente la saqué del buzón y seguí caminando. Seguí por treinta yardas, pero sabía que tenía que mandarla. ¡Regresé, la puse en el buzón y la solté! Inmediatamente sentí como si me hubieran pateado en el estómago. Lloré el resto del camino de regreso a donde nos estábamos quedando, fui directo a la recámara, me acosté y lloré amargamente. Sentía temor por la reacción de mi padre cuando leyera la carta.

Luego de eso fuimos a Minnesota a un lugar de retiros que el ministerio de Jack Winter había comprado. Estábamos manejando a este nuevo centro ministerial y le dije a Denise: «Cuando lleguemos a este lugar, me gustaría ser un hijo para el liderazgo de ahí». ¡Nunca había pensado en esos términos y estaba sorprendido de que las palabras estuvieran saliendo de mi boca! ¡Era la primera evidencia de cambio! Fue mientras estábamos ahí que Jack Winter vino y predicó de nuevo acerca del amor del Padre. Le había escuchado hablar muchas veces pero nunca lo había entendido de verdad. Me arrodillaba a la par de él muchas veces mientras oraba por la gente para experimentar el amor del Padre. Veía como los demás lloraban a medida que el dolor de sus corazones se sanaba, y estaba sintiendo la unción pero no entendía lo que estaba sucediendo.

UNA IMPARTICIÓN DEL AMOR DEL PADRE

Luego de escuchar predicar a Jack acerca del amor del Padre esa noche, le dije: «Jack, finalmente entiendo lo que estás hablando. ¿Orarías por mí?». El había estado buscando una oportunidad de orar por mí así que estuvo de acuerdo. Me llevó a un pequeño cuarto detrás del centro y me senté en una silla. Jack se arrodilló a la par mía y me vio directo a los ojos: «¿Puedes ser el pequeño niño que necesita ser amado?», me preguntó. Pensé: «Soy un hombre de veintinueve años. ¡No soy un pequeño!», pero cuando vi a los ojos de Jack, de alguna manera supe que me estaba viendo realmente como era. Por fuera era fuerte, esbelto y capaz, pero por dentro era un niñito que necesitaba ser amado porque nunca había conocido el amor de un padre.

La verdad es que, aun si has conocido el amor de un padre, igualmente sigues necesitando el amor de un padre día con día. Así que le dije: «No sé Jack, pero puedo tratar». Me pidió que pusiera mis brazos alrededor de su cuello como un pequeño que necesitaba abrazar a su papá. Nunca había abrazado a un hombre en toda mi vida, pero puse mis brazos alrededor de su cuello. Se sintió extremadamente raro y quería escaparme de eso y correr pero él rápidamente puso sus brazos alrededor de mí y me abrazo muy fuerte. ¡Me estaba dando un mensaje claro de que no iba a salir de ahí hasta que todo hubiera terminado! Luego él oró una oración muy simple: «Padre, vendrías y harías de mis brazos tus brazos alrededor de este joven». En ese momento ya no estuve siendo abrazado por Jack, estaba siendo abrazado por Dios. El continuó:

«Derrama tu amor en este corazón porque nunca ha conocido a un Padre como tú». Luego de dos o tres minutos él acabó y se puso de pie.

Desde ese momento y en adelante todo parecía diferente. Cuando empezaba a orar, la palabra «padre» salía de mí espontáneamente. Sentí como si mi espíritu hubiera tocado al Padre. En la realidad era el Padre el que había tocado mi espíritu.

Algunos meses después volamos de regreso a Nueva Zelanda. Fuimos a quedarnos con la mamá de Denise en Taupo, en donde ahora vivimos. Nos quedamos ahí por dos semanas pero no quería visitar a mis padres porque tenía temor de descubrir la reacción de mi padre a esa carta. Luego de un par de semanas finalmente le dije a Denise: «En realidad tenemos que ir. Vamos y salgamos de esto de una vez por todas». Así que nos subimos al auto, manejamos y pasamos la tarde con mis padres para luego regresar a Taupo. Mi padre nunca mencionó la carta.

Les visitamos de nuevo algunos meses después pero seguía sin mencionarla. Una tercera visita unos meses mas tarde, y seguía sin mencionarla. Pasaron cinco años. Ahora tenía yo treinta y cinco años, mi padre nunca había mencionado la carta y empecé a preguntarme si la había recibido siquiera. Luego un día le dije a mi madre: «Cuando estábamos en los EEUU algunos años atrás, le escribí una carta a papá. ¿Sabes si la recibió?». Mi madre contestó «¡Oh sí! ¡La recibió! De hecho, todavía la tiene. La mantiene en la gaveta en su mesa de noche». Cuando dijo eso me percaté que la carta era preciosa para mi papá. Era demasiado preciosa como para sacarla a relucir en una pelea. Mi padre nunca había sido capaz de decir «te perdono, hijo». Nunca le había escuchado decir «lo siento» o «te amo» ni nada por el estilo. Nunca había hablado de esa manera pero realicé que la carta era preciosa para él y asumí que me había perdonado. Los años pasaron y luego decidí un día que iba a decirle a mi padre que lo amaba.

No sentía amor por mi padre en mi corazón, pero mi pensamiento era que si lo decía por fuerza de voluntad, luego Dios honraría eso con sentimientos de amor. En la misma forma en que los constructores ponen concreto en un marco de madera que han puesto, mi declaración de amor proveería el marco para que Dios pusiera lo que tenía que poner. Yo diría las palabras « te amo» y confiaría en que Dios me daría los sentimientos de amor por mi padre. La verdad, es que yo hubiera escogido escalar en Monte Everest en vez de esto. Era algo monumental lo que estaba tratando de hacer. Pero en todos las peleas que tuve con mi padre, él me había enseñado una cosa y esa cosa era decir cosas que pudieran ser difíciles de escuchar para la otra persona. De hecho, era muy fácil para mí en esos días. Así que tomé la decisión de decirle que lo amaba.

«¡TE AMO, PAPÁ!»

La próxima vez que les visitamos estuve buscando una oportunidad para decirlo. Estaba esperando que él fuera a la cocina para luego seguirlo, servirme un vaso de agua y decir «por cierto, papá, te amo» y salir de vuelta a la sala, pero nunca fue a la cocina y no había manera de tenerlo a solas. Finalmente estuvimos por irnos para manejar de regreso a casa y pensaba que había perdido mi oportunidad. Mi papá tenía un hábito particular. Cuando la gente le visitaba siempre se paraba en la cocina, a través de la cual tenían que pasar los invitados para poder salir de la casa. Se paraba dándole la espalda al refrigerador y le daba la mano a la gente a medida que salían. Mi papá no me enseñó muchas cosas en la vida pero cuando tenía cuatro años me enseñó a dar un apretón de manos. Todavía puedo recordar palabra por palabra con un detalle exacto. Dijo: «Cuando le das la mano a un hombre – haz un apretón firme – nada de este saludo aguado por favor. Aprieta dos o tres veces y luego suelta la mano. ¡No toques a ningún hombre por demasiado tiempo!».

Así que estábamos saliendo de la casa y le di la mano a mi padre – dos o tres veces, apretón firme, le solté—y salí de la casa. El le dio la mano a los otros y dejamos la casa. Cuando llegué a la esquina de la casa pensé: «¡Lo haré ahora!» así que vi de reojo a mi mamá y papá y les dije: «¡Adiós mamá y papá. Te amo, papá!» y doblé rápido la esquina. Denise y los niños siguieron rápidamente, se subieron al carro y nos fuimos. ¡No escuché ningún golpe ni grito así que me salí con la mía!

La *próxima* vez que los estábamos visitando hice lo mismo. Le dije «te amo» de nuevo. Esta vez cuando apretaba su mano en el refrigerador hice lo mismo - apretón fuerte, dos o tres veces— pero esta vez no lo solté y el me vio. Le vi directo a los ojos y le dije «te amo papá» y luego le solté y salí de la casa. Cuando salí al césped, volteé a ver y mi papá estaba ahí, viéndose la mano. Mi padre nunca había escuchado esas palabras habladas a él en toda su vida, particularmente de parte de un hombre. Mi madre las había dicho por un tiempo cuando se acababan de casar pero luego dejó de decirlas. Con una valentía creciente, decidí que haría lo mismo la próxima vez que visitara.

Cuando llegó ese día y estábamos saliendo, me dio la mano para que se la apretara y pensé que eso ya era un avance. Esta vez, sin embargo, en vez de tomar su mano, puse mi brazo dentro del suyo, le abracé por la primera vez en mi vida y le dije «te amo, papá» a sus oídos. Asintió con la cabeza casi imperceptiblemente pero yo sentí como si estuviera abrazando a un árbol. Cada músculo en su cuerpo estaba rígido. Luego de esa vez, aprovechaba cada oportunidad para decirle «te amo, papá» cada vez que visitábamos.

Fue tres años después que mi padre me llamó por teléfono una noche. Mi mamá era la que siempre había las llamadas, y esta era la segunda vez en mi vida que mi papá me marcaba. Me dijo «hay un juego de rugby cerca de tu ciudad y voy a ir a verlo. Me pregunto si puedo quedarme contigo esa noche». Luego añadió «hay algo que quiero decirte». Mi padre nunca se había quedado en nuestra casa antes. Solo había visitado una o dos veces y ya habíamos estado casados por dieciocho años para ese entonces. Vino después del juego y Denise preparó una buena cena. Comimos y luego dijo «hay algo que quiero decirte», así que Denise se ocupó al otro lado de la casa para dejarnos a solas.

Nos sentamos ahí toda la noche y no podía decirlo. Traía el tema una y otra vez. Decía «he venido porque quiero decirte algo. Quiero decirte esto». En medio de todo me miraba, como si estuviera desesperado por decirlo pero no podía así que empezaba a hablar del juego de rugby otra vez, o acerca de otra cosa. Fue ahí cuando me dije «nunca he escuchado estas palabras dichas hacia mí excepto por tu madre». También dijo: «Tengo entendido que los hombres no se dicen este tipo de cosas». Y luego también dijo: «Durante la guerra, uno no se hace amigo de nadie, porque cando mueren, no puedes hacer tu trabajo.» Todas estas cosas salieron mientras estábamos sentados ahí.

Yo soy el más joven de mi familia. Mi hermano es un científico y mis padres muy orgullosos asistieron a todas sus ceremonias de graduación. ¡Fue el primero en mi familia que fue a la universidad, probablemente desde Adán en el jardín! Mi hermana trabajaba en la televisión y mis padres miraban los créditos al final del programa televisivo todos los jueves en la noche solo para ver su nombre. Estaban muy orgullosos de ella. Yo tenía el potencial académico más grande en nuestra familia, pero todo lo que quería ser era exterminador de venados y un recluso, y vivir en las montañas. No hice nada para que mis padres estuvieran orgullosos de mi. El sentía que yo le había fallado. Cuando me volví cristiano, la cosa se puso peor. Se volvió un punto de pelea. Sin embargo, esa noche, cuando se quedó con nosotros después del juego de rugby, dijo: «Hay algo más que necesito decirte».

Se puso muy serio. Era muy difícil para él hablar de estas cosas pero me dijo «puede venir un momento en que solo uno de nosotros esté vivo, hablo de tu madre y de mi», y eso fue todo lo que dijo. Me vio como diciendo «por favor entiende lo que estoy tratando de decir. ¡Por favor no me hagas decirlo!» Estaba en shock por lo que me estaba pidiendo. Yo era su hijo más pequeño y había fallado en llenar sus expectativas. Todo lo que pude decirle fue: «Papá, si en algún momento te quedas solo, puedes venir a vivir con nosotros». Sus hombros se relajaron visiblemente como si un peso se le hubiera quitado de encima, pero todavía no había dicho lo que había venido a decir.

Las horas pasaron y era ya casi media noche y sacó el tema otra vez. «He venido porque quiero decirte esto». Se acercó mucho pero no pudo decirlo. Finalmente dijo «Quiero que sepas», me seguía viendo con ojos suplicantes. «¡Ayúdame a decir esto!». No había nada que yo pudiera hacer para ayudarlo. Todo lo que podía hacer era estar sentado y esperar y finalmente... Nunca lo dijo pero casi: «Quiero que sepas que tu madre y yo amamos a todos tus hijos». Yo respondí: «Yo también te amo papá» y él asintió su cabeza como afirmando que eso es lo que había querido decir.

«¡TE AMO, HIJO!»

Pasaron los años y eventualmente el me dijo «te amo, hijo». Fue en el año 2001 y había estado hospitalizado por seis o siete años. La diabetes le había costado su pierna derecha y su vista se había disminuido grandemente. No podía ver televisión. Todo lo que podía hacer era ver la brillantez en la ventana y no había nada interesante fuera de la ventana. Había tenido una serie de derrames pequeños y había perdido su memoria a corto plazo aunque su memoria a largo plazo seguía intacta. Fui a verlo porque íbamos a salir a un viaje ministerial largo a Europa y, por primera vez en mi vida, pude tener una conversación con él en donde no se puso peleonero. Todos sus argumentos habían acabado.

Le dije cómo me sentía cuando era un niño y peleábamos todo el tiempo. Estaba escuchando y entendiendo, sin ningún argumento de respuesta. Cuando estábamos hablando me dijo tres veces: «¡Lo siento tanto!». Mi padre nunca se había disculpado con nadie. Tres veces ese día me dijo: «¡Te amo, hijo!» y cuando estaba cruzando la puerta me dijo: «Oh y por cierto» y yo me volví para verlo: « ¡Tu sabes que siempre te he amado!».

Recuerdo haber pasado por la casa de mi mamá después de dejar a mi papá en el hospital y haberle dicho de lo que habíamos hablado con papá, y lo que él había dicho, y ella me dijo: «Cuando tú somatabas la puerta y salías a la noche, ¿sabes lo que tu padre solía hacer? El se encerraba en el cuarto con llave. No me dejaba entrar ahí, porque se quedaba llorando».

Poco tiempo después estábamos en Inglaterra y estábamos terminando lo que había sido una agenda agotadora de reuniones. Era la reunión final y estábamos orando por las últimas personas presentes. Uno de los hombres de la iglesia se me acercó y me dijo «James, hay una llamada telefónica de Nueva Zelanda. Es tu hermano». Yo sabía de qué se trataba, por supuesto. Me había preguntado qué haría si mi padre moría cuando yo estuviera de viaje. ¿Cancelaría las conferencias? ¿Regresaría? ¿Importaba en lo más mínimo? ¿Qué debería hacer?

Así que hablé con mi hermano y me dijo que mi padre había fallecido media hora antes y que había insistido en que viniera a casa y hablara en su funeral. Volé de regreso a Nueva Zelanda mientras Denise se quedaba en Inglaterra. El funeral fue un día después de que había regresado y expresé mi sorpresa de que papá hubiera querido que yo lo oficiara. El siempre había peleado conmigo y me había dado la impresión de que se había opuesto al cristianismo fuertemente.

Recuerdo estar de pie en el frente hablando en el funeral. Habían bastantes personas asistiendo y al ver el cuarto me pregunté si había alguien que genuinamente amara a mi padre. Había peleado con todo el mundo. Al ver la caja funeraria a la par mía pensé: «Tal vez quería que oficiara el funeral porque sabía que tenía el corazón de un hijo para con él, que yo era verdaderamente su hijo».

El corazón de ser un hijo

Esa fue mi vida con mi padre. Al ver atrás, la parte más maravillosa acerca de ello para mí fue el momento cuando puse esa carta en el buzón. ¿Porqué? Porque cuando puse ese sobre que contenía la carta, Dios me restauró el corazón de hijo y esa fue la puerta para que yo pudiera conocer a mi Padre celestial.

Creo que la mayoría de nosotros hemos perdido el corazón de

hijo con respecto a nuestros padres naturales o nuestras madres en lo terrenal. ¿Cómo lo recuperamos?. Lo encontraremos de nuevo en el lugar en donde lo perdimos.

La verdad es que, no puedes conocer realmente al Padre a menos que tengas el corazón de un hijo o una hija. Puedes recibir un toque de Él. Puedes experimentar más de su amor. Podrás incluso conocer su amor cuando toca tu corazón y tus emociones. Pero no puedes tener una relación íntima con Él como Padre a menos que tengas el corazón de un hijo. Muchas personas encuentran al Padre celestial pero solo aquellos que tienen el corazón de un hijo o el corazón de una hija pueden vivir en relación con Él como padre. A medida que le conoces como padre y su amor empieza a llenar tu corazón, ese mismo amor, con el tiempo, continuamente sanará tu corazón. Ese amor disponible, continuará derramándose al suelo de tu ser hasta que llene todos los agujeros y cuando haya llenado todos los agujeros empezará a subir en nivel y llevarte a un lugar en donde su amor será como un poderoso océano en el que nadas.

Ya que muchos de nosotros hemos cerrado nuestros corazones a nuestros padres terrenales y hemos perdido el corazón de hijos e hijas, tal vez tú también tienes una carta que escribir a uno de tus padres o a los dos. Tal vez una llamada, o una plática cara a cara es más apropiada. Te lo dejo a ti para que decidas, pero hay dos cosas que sé sin lugar a duda. Primero: si no tienes el corazón de un hijo para con los padres que Dios te dio, no puedes tener una relación verdadera con Dios como tu padre, y vivirás tu vida atrapado en tus perspectivas y formas de ser teñidas de orfandad.

Lo segundo es esto: si estás en alguna forma de ministerio cristiano continuamente enfrentarás barreras a tu efectividad porque para ser como Jesús de primero tienes que ser un hijo de corazón. Si no tienes el corazón de hijo, tu capacidad de hablar y actuar como Jesús desde tu corazón será limitada. Hebreos 1:1 dice: «En el pasado Dios habló a través de profetas pero hoy Él ha hablado a través de su Hijo». ¡El sigue prefiriendo hablar a través de hijos! Esta revelación del Padre y su amor es crucial para el futuro de la Iglesia, así como para nuestras vidas individuales.

Dios es nuestro Padre de verdad

~

Como un joven cristiano empecé a orar y pedirle al Señor que Él me permitiera ver las cosas en la forma en las que Él las ve. Quería verdaderamente entender la vida en la forma en la que Dios la ve. Proverbios 14:6 dice: «*El conocimiento es fácil para aquel que tiene entendimiento*». Muchas personas buscan conocimiento, pero si tienes entendimiento, el conocimiento viene por añadidura. Yo quería vivir mi vida desde una perspectiva lo más cercana posible a la forma en la que Dios vive. El ver todo desde la perspectiva de Dios trae el descubrimiento de la paz real y duradera en nuestras vidas. El conocimiento puede traer confusión pero cuando tienes entendimiento tienes paz porque puedes ver el propósito de Dios tras de todo.

EL PROPÓSITO DE LA VIDA

Cuando tenía doce años, mi familia se mudó lejos del pequeño pueblo campestre en donde había crecido. Me encantaba vivir ahí y detestaba tenerme que mudar, pero en medio de mi tormenta interior empecé a tener hambre por descubrir el propósito de la vida. Recuerdo haber salido a ver las estrellas una noche, escuchando en mi cabeza las palabras de mi maestro de escuela quien nos había dicho que la luz de las mismas duraba para siempre. No había ningún muro de ladrillos pesados alrededor del espacio exterior. «Aún si lo hubiera», decía él, «¿Qué piensas que habría tras de ese muro?». Eso me voló mi pequeña mente en pedazos llevándome al pánico, porque estaba pensando que aun *si había algo* allá al borde de todo lo que existe, *¿qué podría ser eso? ¡Tiene que durar para siempre!*

Recuerdo cuando le pregunté a mis padres cual era el propósito de la vida. ¿De qué se trata? ¿Quiénes somos en realidad y qué estamos haciendo aquí? ¿Qué significa todo esto? ¿Por qué estamos vivos? ¿Cómo es que podemos pensar y estar conscientes? Cuando era un chico me consumían estas preguntas. Un hombre me dijo «no te preocupes. Cuando creces, ya estas cosas dejan de importarte». Esa fue la respuesta más inútil que haya escuchado. Falló completamente en satisfacerme. Pensé: «Este hombre obviamente hizo las mismas preguntas cuando era joven y ahora está viejo y *aun* no ha encontrado las respuestas». Todo el asunto conmovió cosas dentro de mí. No se ha hecho más fácil articular esas preguntas ahora de lo que lo fue antes.

Cuando estaba en la escuela se me enseñó que la evolución es la respuesta a esas preguntas. Muchos de nosotros fuimos enseñados que aparecimos en esta tierra como resultado de una serie interminable de accidentes raros al azar. No hubo propósito alguno detrás de ellos. La vida fue meramente el efecto de las condiciones climáticas, combinadas con reacciones de minerales, y lentamente, de esta serie de ocurrencias extrañas, nosotros los humanos llegamos a existir. Por encima de nosotros, el tiempo está pasando y la tierra continúa en su órbita alrededor del sol y está continuamente rotando sobre su eje. Con el paso del tiempo esto se hará más lento. El sol perderá su calor y todo en la tierra morirá. En el análisis final, la suma total de propósito para toda esta cosa llegará a ser... absolutamente nada.

Por esto, me preguntaba cual era el punto de siquiera ir a la escuela. Mi pregunta era: «¿Por qué habría de ir y aprender a ganar un mejor ingreso? ¿Para tener hijos que seguirán sin respuestas a ninguna de estas preguntas? Sí, serán educados pero habrán vivido una vida de lucha y supervivencia financiera – ¿y todavía van a llegar al final de sus vidas sin propósito? ¿Y finalmente el sol se apagará y se enfriará y todo desaparecerá y el propósito de todo es absolutamente nada?». Luchaba con la idea de motivarme a mi mismo para lograr cualquier cosa. Cuestionaba el derecho de otros para decirme lo que era correcto o incorrecto o cómo vivir mi vida.

Hace algunos años hubo un reportaje de noticias que decía que (de entre todas las naciones de primer mundo) Nueva Zelanda tenía la incidencia más alta de suicidio de adolescentes. De repente, la pantalla de televisión se llenó de gente dando opiniones acerca de este reportaje. Los políticos estaban dando entrevistas y ventilando sus opiniones. Muchos psiquiatras y psicólogos ofrecieron varias teorías. No estoy diciendo que mi opinión sea más válida que la de ellos – pero creo que si los adolescentes se enteran de que el propósito de su vida es prácticamente nada, y la vida es solo un evento biológico sin valor, entonces ¿por qué prolongar el sufrimiento? Yo puedo entender completamente porque la gente joven se suicida si cree que la evolución es cierta. ¿Por qué no acabar con todo ahora? ¿Por qué esperar a que todo termine naturalmente?

Todos somos linaje de Dios

Lo que quiero ver ahora es algo que me ha traído una paz tremenda. Me ha dado una capacidad sin precedentes para tener paz en mi corazón con respecto a las situaciones que tengo que enfrentar en la vida. A medida que pasan los años, he venido a entender un poco más y ver cosas desde una perspectiva diferente. Hubo un tiempo en mi vida cuando sentí que realmente tenía un entendimiento completo del evangelio. Todo parecía lógico para mí cuando veía mi propia vida y había una grieta en mi credibilidad. Podía ver que mi vida carecía de suficiente autoridad y poder para verdaderamente bendecir la vida de aquellos con los que entraba en contacto. Si tenía la correcta visión del evangelio, ¿por qué no estaban pasando más cosas? ¿Por qué no veía frutos y efectividad como en la vida de Jesús? Así que tomé tiempo para estar a solas con el Señor. Le entregué todo lo que me habían enseñado y le pedí que purificara mi entendimiento y abriera mi corazón para que se me enseñara más. Le pedí que las verdades que yo había recibido fueran puestas en un proceso de filtración utilizando su amor y su perspectiva. No es necesario recalcar que Él empezó a enseñarme mucho más de lo que sabía.

Una de las cosas que empezó a cambiar mi entendimiento fue leer el mensaje que Pablo le dio a los filósofos atenienses en Hechos capítulo 17. Creo que si puedes llegar a algún entendimiento de lo que estoy escribiendo en este capítulo, ello podría hacer una diferencia increíble a la forma en que vives tu vida y cómo experimentas tu relación con Dios. A medida que lees a través de este pasaje nota que no había un solo cristiano entre los que estaban escuchando a Pablo. En su discurso, Pablo dijo:

«El Dios que hizo el mundo y todas las cosas que en él hay, siendo

Señor del cielo y de la tierra, no habita en templos hechos por manos humanas, ni es honrado por manos de hombres, como si necesitase de algo; pues él es quien da a todos vida y aliento y todas las cosas. Y de una sangre ha hecho todo el linaje de los hombres, para que habiten sobre toda la faz de la tierra.» (v24).

Ahora, esta es una declaración itneresante. *«De un hombre Él ha hecho toda nación de los hombres, para que habiten sobre la faz de la tierra.»* (traducción literal de la versión en inglés NKJV). El poblar la tierra fue de hecho una comisión en el jardín del Edén. La humanidad tenía que expandirse y llenar toda la tierra. Luego el apóstol continúa,

«...y les ha prefijado el orden de los tiempos, y los límites de su habitación»

Déjenme hacer un breve comentario aquí: este no es el punto principal que quiero hacer, pero es una afirmación interesante la que Pablo hace. Dios predeterminó el tiempo de nuestro nacimiento y el lugar de nuestro nacimiento. Venimos de diferentes naciones que no estaban necesariamente tratando de hacer la voluntad de Dios, pero en medio de todo, de alguna manera, el tiempo y lugar de tu nacimiento fue parte de su plan para toda la humanidad. No es por accidente que soy un Neozelandés y que tu seas de la nacionalidad que eres. No es un error porque fue *Dios* quien determinó los tiempos para ti y los lugares exactos donde deberías vivir. Hizo esto para que toda la humanidad le buscara.

Luego Pablo hace otra declaración interesante en donde cita a un poeta griego secular. Necesitas entender que Pablo era intelectual-mente brillante. Como estudiante se sentó a los pies de Gamaliel quien era el maestro principal de su secta particular de fariseos.

Era nivel tope de los estudiantes de su época. El dijo que había sobrepasado a otros que estaban en su clase (Gálatas 1:14). En otro lugar (2 Corintios 11:5) él declara que él no era «inferior» a nadie. Creció en un pueblo llamado Tarso, la cual era una ciudad universitaria del imperio romano. Sin lugar a dudas él había alcanzado el zenit de la conducta y el conocimiento religioso.

Para cuando tenía doce años había memorizado vastas porciones de los libros de Génesis, Éxodo, Levítico, Números y Deuteronomio. Esa era una expectativa normal de un chico en este lugar en particular. El era un chico brillante, y yo imagino (que como fue criado en una ciudad universitaria) que él y su familia habrían tenido exposición a las muchas culturas el imperio romano. Sin lugar a dudas también había tenido exposición a la cultura griega, la cual probablemente fue la cultura dominante de ese tiempo y había aprendido un poema griego (de Aratus, un poeta que había vivido en su pueblo de Tarso), el cual él pudo recordar. En este pasaje, Pablo estaba hablándole a un grupo de griegos que eran los filósofos principales de la ciudad de Atenas. Sabemos que estos griegos estaban ansiosos por no ofender a ninguno de los dioses. Eran muy religiosos en su filosofía y querían cubrir todas las bases, por así decirlo. Así que construyeron un altar para honrar al «dios desconocido».

Estos filósofos escucharon que Pablo estaba predicando en la ciudad así que le pidieron que viniera a hablarles a ellos. Mientras les estaba hablando citó este poeta griego en particular. Me sorprende que un poeta griego tenga al menos una de sus líneas del poema registrado en las Sagradas Escrituras. Estoy seguro que no sabía que estaba escribiendo Escritura cuando ideó este verso. Lo que es más, Pablo lo citó como verdad, la cual es de hecho sabiduría de Dios. Es Escritura inspirada y como tal, está inspirada por el Espíritu de Dios. En algún punto Dios dio aliento sobre lo que este poeta griego había escrito, y Pablo lo usó para ganar a estos filósofos griegos. Él dijo:

«En Él (refiriéndose al Dios judío) *vivimos y nos movemos y somos. Como algunos de vuestros propios poetas han dicho: "Porque linaje suyo somos"».*

En el verso 29 él continuó: *«Siendo pues , linaje de Dios...».*

Ahora, había leído este pasaje muchas veces antes de realmente notarlo. Cuando noté esto, me llegó como un dilema porque Pablo estaba hablándole a un audiencia *totalmente no cristiana* y les dijo: «Somos linaje de Dios. Somos hijos de Dios». Verán, se me había enseñado que me volví hijo de Dios cuando *me volví cristiano.* Me volví su hijo en el momento en que nací de nuevo, y a menos que nazca de nuevo no puedo entrar en el reino de Dios. Y eso es absolutamente verdad. Sin embargo, parece haber un problema aquí a medida que leía esto porque Pablo le estaba diciendo esto a los filósofos griegos: « Por lo tanto, ya que somos hijos de Dios, ya que somos su linaje, venimos de Él, ya que somos sus hijos...». ¡Mi problema era que no podía entender como pablo le podía decir a estos filósofos griegos y no cristianos que eran hijos de Dios!

Quiero decir claramente en este punto, que nunca experimentaremos ninguno de los beneficios de ser hijos de Dios a menos que nazcamos de nuevo. Eso es absoluto y no hay argumento contra ello. Pero hay algo más en lo que Pablo estaba diciendo ahí para que esto sea Escritura y pueda ser verdad. Siempre se me dijo que antes de que fuera cristiano yo caminaba en oscuridad. Se me dijo, de hecho, que Satanás mismo era mi padre porque estaba caminando en sus caminos. Pero aquí Pablo dice que *todos somos* hijos de Dios, aun aquellos que no son «nacidos de nuevo». Esto me tomó por sorpresa, porque se me había enseñado que éramos nacidos del Espíritu de Dios, y que el nacer del Espíritu de Dios es nuestra entrada a ser hijos de Dios. Pablo estaba diciendo algo más, sin embargo, lo cual sonaba como algo que consideraríamos doctrina cristiana no convencional. Suena como una forma de universalismo.

Así que estaba tratando de entender esto y el Señor me dio algo de vislumbre.

Al considerar esto, es crucial entender algo: Cuando Dios creó a Adán y Eva en el Jardín del Edén, su propósito para ellos era que *no pecaran*. Los teólogos han argumentado por siglos en este tema de si Dios sabía antes de tiempo que Adán y Eva terminarían pecando. No hay consenso para esto para nada. Sin embargo, lo que sabemos es que el plan de Dios para Adán y Eva era un plan *real*. Su propósito era que *no pecaran*, así que para que entendamos este asunto de que cada persona en el mundo es un hijo de Dios, necesitamos entender el significado de la palabra *redención*.

REDENCIÓN

Lo que significa la palabra redención es «comprar de vuelta».

Estoy usando un reloj que recibí para Navidad como un regalo. Fue comprado para mí, así que no puedo decir que este reloj ha sido redimido. Fue comprado, pero no fue redimido. Cuando Jesús nos compró con precio, Él nos compró *de regreso*, Él nos *redimió*. El comprar mi reloj nunca puede ser descrito como «redención» por una simple razón. Solo puedes redimir algo que has poseído antes. La redención que Jesús logró a través de su muerte en la cruz por ende, fue el comprar de vuelta lo que Dios había poseído previamente. ¡Jesús no solo nos compró, nos compró de vuelta!

Por lo tanto, en un sentido real, el cristianismo es verdaderamente descrito en términos de redención cuando entendemos que *antes* de que fuéramos pecadores *de hecho le pertenecíamos a Dios.* Esa pertenencia no se originó durante el tiempo de nuestra vida, sino que empezó en la vida de nuestros ancestros, Adán y Eva. Cuando estaban en esta tierra todos y cada uno de nosotros estaba en ellos porque todos venimos de ellos. Toda la raza humana estaba contenida en Adán y Eva y le pertenecía a Dios, antes de la caída. ¿Cuál era el propósito de Dios para nosotros? Su propósito fue que Adán y Eva no pecaran nunca y continuaran multiplicándose como Él mandó. Se multiplicarían y llenarían la tierra y la sojuzgarían. Esta fue la comisión que tenían que cumplir. Su propósito (y era un plan real) era que la humanidad llenara la tierra sin que Adán o Eva pecaran.

EL PLAN ORIGINAL

Imagina lo que el mundo hubiera sido si Adán y Eva no hubieran pecado. ¿Puedes imaginar lo que tu vida sería? Sería muy diferente de cómo la experimentas ahora. Si Adán y Eva no hubieran pecado, ¡estarían vivos el día de hoy! Podrías ir a su casa y tocar la puerta, y Adán te contestaría y te invitaría a pasar. Estarían ya vivos por mucho tiempo, pero todavía estarían en la plenitud de sus vidas. Creo que si Adán entrara en un lugar el día de hoy todos los presentes se postrarían y le adorarían por su apariencia. Pensaríamos que es Dios, porque Adán fue hecho a la imagen de Dios.

Si el pecado no hubiera entrado, Adán y Eva hubieran visto al rostro mismo de Dios todos los días por cuatro mil años. No sería una revelación limitada, sino podrían contemplar la total revelación de quien Dios es. Cuando Moisés subió a la montaña y volvió a bajar, su rostro estaba tan lleno de la gloria de Dios que gran temor se apoderó de la gente. Tuvo que cubrirse a sí mismo con un velo para que pudieran soportar la forma en la que se veía luego de estar cuarenta días en la montaña. Adán y Eva hubieran caminado con Dios por *miles* de años. Lo que es más, cada persona que hubiera nacido todavía estaría viva el día de hoy—lo cual se traduce en tus padres, abuelos, bisabuelos y más allá. Cada ser humano estaría vivo porque no habría tal cosa como la muerte.

La muerte es una cosa con la que es muy difícil de lidiar porque no hay nada en nosotros que haya sido creado para lidiar con ella. Toda forma de rechazo , soledad o trauma es difícil de manejar porque no tenemos un recurso interno para hacerlo. No fuimos diseñados para el mundo como está en estos momentos. Fuimos diseñados para un mundo en donde Adán y Eva no hubieran pecado nunca.

Considera otra diferencia enorme. Toda persona que hubieras contactado en tu vida entera *solamente* te hubiera expresado amor y aceptación absoluta, maravillados de verte. Estarían llenos de la realización de tu hermosura y lo emocionante que es estar contigo. Celebrarían los increíbles dones y recursos que hay en la tierra porque tú estás en ella. La forma en que te darían la bienvenida cada vez que te ven te afirmaría tanto, y tendría un efecto tremendo en nosotros.

No podemos siquiera imaginar el sentido de gozo que hubiéramos experimentado si Adán y Eva no hubieran pecado. Es difícil imaginarlo pero *esa es la vida* que Dios diseñó para que tuviéramos. Imagina cómo era para Adán el ser formado como un ser humano adulto con toda la capacidad mental, emocional, de corazón y voluntad, así como la habilidad total de entender y pensar apropiadamente. Su intelecto hubiera sido mucho mayor a cualquiera de nosotros. De acuerdo a los científicos, solo usamos un diez porciento de nuestra capacidad cerebral. Adán tuvo que tener el 100% de su capacidad mental e intelectual. Vino a este mundo e inmediatamente recibió la totalidad del amor de Dios derramado en su corazón sin obstáculos.

La entrada de su vida en este mundo tuvo que estar saturada de un sentido de lo maravilloso y amado que era, porque vio directo a los ojos de Dios el Padre inmediatamente después de obtener la conciencia. Cuando Adán abrió sus ojos, los cuales son las ventanas de su alma, y vio el rostro de Dios el Padre, su alma tuvo que haber sido saturada con la persona del Padre. Verás, Dios es amor y su propósito fue que cada hijo e hija de Adán y Eva estuvieran llenos del mismo amor, la misma revelación, la misma substancia, cada día de sus vidas en toda la historia de la humanidad y hasta la eternidad.

Fuimos diseñados para este tipo de existencia. *Fuimos diseñados para que nuestro nacimiento natural fuera nuestra entrada a una experiencia completa de Dios como nuestro Padre.* Nuestro nacimiento natural nos llevaría hacia la bendición de conocer a Dios como nuestro Padre y a la experiencia de nosotros ser sus hijos e hijas. Nunca tendríamos necesidad de una palabra para «seguridad» porque nunca tendríamos la habilidad consciente de concebir nada que no fuera total paz y seguridad. El concepto de temor no existiría. Tu madre y tu padre no serían las personas que has conocido. Hubieran sido tus padres de una forma muy diferente. Sus padres (tus abuelos) habrían estado saturados del mismísimo amor de Dios Padre, para que de la misma manera su amor por tus padres hubiera sido la perfecta expresión de Dios, mucho más allá de lo que has experimentado. Déjame repetirlo una vez más. *Nuestro nacimiento natural hubiera sido la entrada a todas las bendiciones de Dios como nuestro Padre,* y a la experiencia de su presencia, su provisión, su amor, su cuidado y su guía hacia cada una de las bendiciones que hay en su corazón para nosotros.

Segundo nacimiento

Sin embargo, como sabemos bien, Adán y Eva *sí pecaron.* Y ya que Adán y Eva pecaron, Dios tuvo que diseñar un *segundo nacimiento* para llevarnos al conocimiento de su amor como nuestro Padre, y traernos a toda la experiencia que implica el que Él sea un padre para nosotros. Así que, cuando envió a Jesús a morir por nosotros, el Padre abrió una puerta y Jesús se volvió esa puerta. Jesús no abrió la puerta. Él *es* la puerta.

Dios el Padre abrió la puerta para que regresáramos a Él. Para que pudiéramos ser *comprados de vuelta* y pudiéramos tener acceso a todo lo que perdieron Adán y Eva. ¡Eso es lo que significa ser redimidos! Todo el propósito de Dios al enviar a su Hijo a la tierra para nosotros era para *redimir* todo lo que se había perdido cuando Adán y Eva pecaron. De hecho, Él ha redimido *más* de lo que se perdió. Eso es porque en vez de ser hijos e hijas de Dios como Adán, en Cristo hemos participado de la vida de Dios mismo. ¡Qué maravilla! Cuando nacemos de nuevo es para que viniéramos a conocerle como nuestro Padre de la misma manera que Adán y Eva le hubieran conocido si la caída no hubiera ocurrido. Cuando vemos esto, obtenemos una vislumbre de lo que realmente significa ser cristiano. Nos da una vislumbre a nuestro destino y la obra de Dios en nuestra vida.

Este entendimiento completo de la redención es crucial para ministrar efectivamente la vida de otras personas. El propósito máximo de Dios es restaurar tu vida y mi vida a lo que *hubiera sido si Adán y Eva no hubieran pecado*. Ese es el propósito de la cruz y el propósito de la redención. Es el propósito de volvernos cristianos. El propósito de *todo* lo que Dios está haciendo en nuestra vida es restaurarnos al estado sin pecado de Adán y Eva. Vale la pena que meditemos en cómo sería la vida para nosotros y como nos sentiríamos acerca de nosotros mismos si hubiéramos nacido en ese mundo. Dios quiere que conozcamos su amor por nosotros porque el amor pone un fundamento profundo dentro de nosotros que nos da seguridad absoluta del alma.

Cuando sabes que Dios te ama, no hay lucha con la doctrina de que Dios es tu proveedor. Frecuentemente puedes luchar para creer que Él proveerá para tus necesidades materiales. Puedes pararte en las promesas de Dios, puedes ejercitar fe y puedes creerle a Dios tan intensamente como quieras. Puedes hacer confesiones positivas y repetir afirmaciones personales para obtener esta verdad adentro de ti. Sin embargo, si no conoces verdaderamente en tu corazón que Dios el Padre te ama, tendrás gran dificultad para poder aferrarte al hecho de que Él va a cuidar de ti. Pero cuando tienes el fundamento profundamente dentro de ti de que Dios es tu Padre y que él te ama, entonces no vas a tener ninguna dificultad en creer que él va a cuidar de ti en esta vida. El amor es el fundamento de la fe; de hecho, el amor es el fundamento *de todo* en nuestra vida cristiana. El experimentar y caminar en el amor de Dios el Padre es de lo que todo esto se trata.

Mucha gente está diciendo que el camino a la piedad es apropiarte de ello al recitar declaraciones verdaderas a ti mismo. Nunca serás convencido de esa manera. Pero cuando su amor llena tu espíritu y tu *sabes* que Él te ama, la Biblia se vuelve un libro diferente. Hemos sido escogidos antes de la fundación del mundo. ¡No le escogimos a Él, en vez de esto Él nos escogió para una vida increíble que es eterna y ya ha empezado! *Esta es* la eternidad para nosotros, ¡ahora mismo! El propósito, el plan, la dirección que Dios tiene para nuestra vida es redimirnos para que nuestra vida sea todo lo que Él planeó para nosotros *antes* de la caída. ¡«El paraíso perdido» ha sido recuperado en Cristo!

El Señor te concibió

El profeta Jeremías dice,

«La palabra del Señor vino a mí diciendo: "Antes de que te formara en el vientre, te conocí, antes que nacieras te aparté, te puse como profeta a las naciones"» (Jeremías 1:4).

No podemos asumir de esto que todos somos profetas para las naciones. En un sentido general eso es verdad y puede ser más específicamente para alguien de la misma forma que fue para Jeremías. Yo creo, sin embargo, que la primera parte del verso es relevante a cada uno de nosotros porque está hablando de la creación de Jeremías. *«Antes que te formara en el vientre, te conocí».* Me costaba entender esto. *¿Qué quiso decir* el Señor? *¿Cómo* podía conocer a Jeremías antes de que estuviera en el vientre de su madre? Si lo ves desde un punto de vista puramente biológico, Jeremías no existía antes de estar en el vientre de su madre. Esto no está hablando de re-encarnación tampoco. La re-encarnación no es parte del entendimiento bíblico de la vida humana. Así que, ¿cómo podía el Señor conocer a Jeremías antes de que él estuviera en el vientre de su madre? Ni te atrevas a dudarlo. *El verdaderamente* conocía a Jeremías.

Solo hay una forma en la que esta declaración pueda ser verdadera. Mucho tiempo atrás, antes de que Jeremías estuviera en el vientre de su madre, Dios concibió en su mente a la persona que sería Jeremías. Él diseñó la persona completa de Jeremías, su ser físico, su capacidad mental, su estructura emocional y espiritual, los dones y talentos que tendría. Dios podía decir, antes de que Jeremías estuviera en el vientre de su madre, «sé exactamente la persona que vas a ser».

Querido lector, creo que es lo mismo para cada uno de nosotros. Mucho tiempo atrás Dios *te concibió* en su corazón y en su mente.

El creó a la persona única que tu eres con las habilidades naturales específicas que tienes. Tu madre y padre probablemente no sabían si ibas a ser hombre o mujer pero Él conocía todo de ti hasta el más íntimo detalle. El sabía qué tan alto serías, el peso que tendrías (más o menos algunas libritas), Él sabía que color de cabello tendrías. El conocía tu personalidad y los talentos que tendrías. El le dio a cada uno de nosotros ciertas habilidades que otros no tienen. Nos limitó en otras habilidades. Él diseñó *exactamente* a la persona que serías. Él te conocía. Tú necesitas entender que Él es tu Padre *de verdad*, porque Él te concibió en su mente y corazón antes de tu concepción natural.

Lo que es más impresionante es que Él concibió a cada uno de nosotros en amor, porque él es amor. En otras palabras, cuando Él decidió que te iba a crear, en su mente Él pensó: «¿Cómo puedo hacer a éste absolutamente hermoso?». Él diseñó a cada uno de nosotros con amor absoluto. Alguna gente piensa que son un error, y que no deberían estar en esta tierra. Esto es muy personal para mí. Mi madre me dijo: «Cuando tu papá y yo nos casamos realmente queríamos tener a un niño de primero. Así que cuando tu hermano llegó estábamos muy contentos. Luego pensamos que sería maravilloso tener una niña y llegó tu hermana. Estábamos tan contentos que decidimos que no queríamos tener más hijos». Ella continuó «Luego descubrimos que tú venías». Hizo una pausa y siguió, « pero cuando *tú* llegaste, trajiste tu amor bajo el brazo». En otras palabras: «¡Durante nueve meses en realidad no te queríamos mucho!».

Mucha gente ha tenido una experiencia similar y constantemente sienten que no deberían estar en esta tierra. Puede ser que sus padres se *tuvieron* que casar porque había un embarazo y consecuentemente sintieron como si hubieran tenido un problema desde ese entonces.

La maravillosa realidad es esta: Dios nuestro Padre concibió a cada uno de nosotros en su amor antes aun de que hubiésemos estado en el vientre de nuestra madre. ¡Eres una concepción de amor de tu PADRE DE VERDAD!

No hay tal cosa como un hijo ilegítimo. Solo hay padres ilegítimos, porque cada hijo que ha venido al mundo ha sido amado y querido por Dios nuestro Padre. Esa es la razón por la que Él puede decir por el Espíritu a través de Pablo en el libro de Hechos, *que todos nosotros* (cristianos o no) somos su linaje. Él pudo decir esto porque en su plan original para la humanidad, Él diseñó a cada uno de nosotros.

Me he preguntado varias veces: «¿En qué punto me diseñó Él? ¿Cinco minutos antes de que fuera concebido?». ¿Se sorprendió Dios cuando dijo «¡Oh, no! ¡Aquí viene otro! ¡Rápido! ¡Produzcan a otro!»? ¿Por cuánto tiempo me diseñó realmente? ¿Fue durante cinco minutos antes de mi nacimiento? ¿Se tardó años? Yo creo, de hecho, que Él diseñó a cada uno de nosotros antes de crear un solo átomo de este universo, porque Él no estaba buscando un universo, Él estaba buscando una familia. Su propósito no fue que Él tuviera una maravillosa creación. En vez de esto, Él hizo la creación como un ambiente para que nosotros pudiéramos vivir en él. Vemos a las estrellas e imaginamos que durarán para siempre. ¿Sabes por qué creó todo de esa manera? No para que nos abrumáramos con desesperanza acerca de nuestra existencia, sino para que pudiéramos ver todo y decir «¡guau!». Para que todo en nosotros estuviera lleno de maravilla con respecto a Él. Él hizo el universo para darnos una impresión acerca del Padre que tenemos en verdad. ¿¡No es Él bueno!?

Hechos a su imagen

Mucha gente va por la vida sintiendo que no pertenecen a ningún lado o que no deberían de haber nacido. Algunas personas sienten fuertemente como si fueran intrusos en su propia vida, tanto que no sienten que siquiera pertenecen a su propia casa. Pasan su vida entera trabajando y ahorrando para pagar la hipoteca para poder ser dueños de una casa y finalmente obtienen su certificado de ser dueños de la casa pero siguen viviendo como si no deberían estar en esta vida. La plena y simple verdad es que somos los chicos de nuestro Padre celestial.

Hace mucho tiempo Él decidió que te iba a tener a ti, y *el día en que viniste a este mundo fue el día que Él había estado esperando por miles de años.* Lo único que lo tiñó todo para Él era saber que, por la caída, tu nacimiento natural no te otorgaría la bendición de que Él fuera también tu Padre. El nos sigue amando como Padre pero a menos que nazcamos de nuevo nunca experimentaremos ninguno de los beneficios de que Él sea verdaderamente nuestro Padre. El envió a Jesús para morir por nosotros para que pudiéramos nacer de nuevo y nuestro *segundo nacimiento* nos llevará a la bendición de tener a Dios como nuestro Padre.

Veamos también el Salmo 139:16. La Nueva Versión Internacional lo pone así,

«Tus ojos vieron mi cuerpo aún sin formar».

Hace mucho mucho tiempo, antes de que tu cuerpo fuera formado en el vientre de tu madre, Dios lo vio. Él sabía cómo se iba a ver tu cuerpo físico antes de que el mundo fuera hecho. No eres el resultado de procesos evolutivos y por lo tanto resultaste siendo un accidente de la naturaleza sin propósito ni razón de existir. Tus padres no sabían si ibas a ser niño o niña o al menos no pudieron escoger qué serías. Pero mucho antes de eso, cuando Dios determinó los tiempos para ti y los lugares exactos donde vivirías, Él supo cómo sería tu apariencia.

Sé que algunas personas nacen con malformaciones físicas o ceguera, sordera o cosas peores. De alguna manera, el que la humanidad le haya abierto las puertas al pecado y a su vulnerabilidad a la destrucción de Satanás, ha permitido que estas cosas pasen. Algo de la culpa la tienen los errores en la medicina, y tal vez descubriremos más en el futuro acerca de las cosas que los humanos hacemos para causar que otras cosas pasen también.

Sin embargo, la verdad es que antes de que estuvieras en el vientre de tu madre Dios sabía cómo sería tu cuerpo físico y Él dice que somos hechos maravillosamente.

Nuestra hija fue modelo internacional por diez años. Siempre pensé que era hermosa, aun cuando se levantaba en la mañana.

Me recuerdo que le pregunté una vez: «Estas supermodelos, ¿creen ellas mismas que son hermosas?» y ella me respondió «ni una sola de ellas». Cada una diría que había una parte de ellas mismas con la que no estaban contentas. Sus rodillas eran muy redondas, su nariz muy grande o sus ojos muy pequeños. Esto solo sirve para demostrar el sentido innato de que algo de la increíble creación de Dios en nosotros ha sido robado.

Aquel quien es en sí mismo belleza no puede hacer nada feo. La esencia de un artista es expresada a través de sus pinturas y no hay nadie más hermoso que Dios. Por lo tanto, cuando Él te hizo a ti y a mí, Él estaba expresando su propia naturaleza. Él nos hizo hermosos. Mucha gente pasa toda su vida sin sentir nunca que son suficientemente buenos para el escrutinio público, nunca pueden estar pie frente a otros. Tienen un sentido profundo de culpa acerca de ellos mismo. Se sienten tímidos. Se cubre a ellos mismos con velos de separación porque no sienten aceptables en su apariencia, sus intereses o su estilo de vida.

Dios nos hizo a cada uno y concibió cada aspecto de nuestro ser. Mucha gente siente que Dios hizo al hombre a su imagen y que la mujer salió nada más ahí para ayudar, por así decirlo. Ella fue creada para ser esclava, para trabajar junto al hombre. Lo que no vemos, sin embargo, es que la mujer *también* fue creada a la imagen de Dios. Ellos no realizan que la femineidad esa parte de ser mujer (de la misma forma que la masculinidad) es una expresión de la naturaleza misma de Dios.

Lo femenino también es una expresión de cómo es Dios. Yo conozco a una mujer que no tiene espejos en su casa porque está convencida de que es fea y el espejo parece solamente confirmar esa percepción. El hecho es que Dios nunca ha hecho nada feo, y si la gente no puede ver lo hermoso o hermosa que eres eso solo demuestra la diferencia entre ellos y Dios, ¡porque Él piensa que soy hermoso y Él piensa que tú lo eres también!

De alguna manera toda esta cultura de celebridad de Hollywood ha presentado un ideal de belleza y una percepción de lo que significa ser bien parecido, que nadie puede llenar de ninguna manera. Nos roba el sentido de confianza acerca de nuestra apariencia. Dice el dicho: «Si el granero necesita pintura entonces lo pintaremos». No estoy en contra de el uso de maquillaje. Cuando he sido entrevistado por televisión me dijeron que necesitaba ponerme maquillaje. ¡La primera vez que eso pasó no podía creerlo! ¡Tuve que lavarme la cara muchísimo para que se me quitara! El simple hecho es este: Dios te ha hecho con hermosura y si la gente no puede verlo, no es tu problema; es problema de ellos.

Dios mismo es el que me conoce mejor que nadie y Él es el que me ama más que nadie. El conoce todas mis faltas y aun así Él me ama absolutamente. No podemos decir: «No amo a esta persona porque tiene tantas fallas.» Cuando no somos capaces de amar a alguien o cuando somos incapaces de expresar amor a otros, eso solo resalta la diferencia entre nosotros y Dios. Dios nuestra Padre nos concibió a cada uno en su mente y en su amor, y Él nos creó para ser completamente adorables. Él *es nuestro Padre de verdad.* Él es y *siempre ha sido* tu *Padre de verdad.*

Solamente has sido un préstamo para tus padres. Ellos no sabían nada de ti, pero Dios sí. Él concibió los rasgos únicos de cada ser humano individual. Él diseñó todo acerca de nosotros. Él es nuestro Pare real, y si recibimos a Cristo y caminamos en su vida, conoceremos a nuestro Padre celestial por el resto de la eternidad.

RESTAURADOS PARA SER HIJOS E HIJAS

Cuando estamos hablando acerca de Dios siendo un Padre, o acerca de recibir el amor del Padre, no estamos solo hablando acerca de Dios viniendo a nuestra vida y dándonos la experiencia o un toque de su amor para sanar nuestro dolor emocional. Esas cosas ocurren, pero lo que realmente se trata es que Dios está restaurándonos para ser sus hijos e hijas. Él está redimiéndonos para venir a conocerle a Él como nuestro Padre, justo como Adán le conoció, y más que eso, como Jesús le conoció.

Es la intención de Dios el Padre que nosotros viniéramos a caminar con Él en la eternidad como hijos de acuerdo a quien Él es. Ahí es a donde nos está llevando. Para mí, este es el asunto más emocionante de realizar de que Dios es mi Padre. El conocer que todo lo que soy fue diseñado por mi Padre celestial y que yo soy su hijo. Desde la eternidad hasta la eternidad, soy su hijo. Por supuesto, no soy Jesús, pero la verdad gloriosa es que «en Cristo» Él se ha vuelto *mi* Padre y yo soy su hijo ahora y para siempre . Él siempre ha tenido el propósito de que fuera de esa manera. Él tenía que redimirme por lo que pasó en el jardín, pero siempre fui su hijo, y siempre lo seré.

El Padre ha estado esperando por miles de años por el momento en que viniste a este mundo. Cuando naciste, Él celebró porque te conocía mucho antes de que estuvieras en el vientre de tu madre. Él ha estado esperando por el día en que tu espíritu finalmente recibiera la revelación de que Él es tu *Padre de verdad*. Como todo padre amante que tiene la expectativa del día en que su hijo le dirá «¡Papi!» por primera vez, Dios el Padre ha estado esperando por miles de años para que tú veas para arriba y le veas, y clames de las profundidades de tu corazón: «¡Papá!».

El espíritu de orfandad

~

Escuché por primera vez el término «espíritu de orfandad» en una conferencia en Toronto en el año 2002. Escuché al Señor decirlo quince minutos antes de que tuviera que hablar. Rápidamente abrí mi Biblia y un verso que había leído muchas veces antes me impactó y todo cambió. Subí al podio y todo el mensaje surgió a medida que hablaba. No sabía cual iba a ser mi mensaje pero este verso se me iluminó y ha sido uno de los mensajes más conocidos en esta revelación del Padre. Podrías decir, de hecho, que se ha vuelto una enseñanza insignia de nuestro ministerio, proveyendo el paradigma fundamental desde el cual enseñamos.

El verso que me impactó está en Juan 14, el cual Jesús habló en sus últimos días, aproximadamente una semana antes de ser crucificado. Jack Winter una vez dijo que las últimas palabras de un hombre seguramente terminan estando entre las palabras más importantes que dirá jamás. Cuando leí este verso en particular en Toronto ese día, sentí que la gravedad cambió y que la tierra se movió. Mi vida cristiana nunca ha sido la misma desde ese entonces. He recibido una cantidad de revelaciones – pero ésta ha sido la que más significantemente ha cambiado la perspectiva de cómo vivo mi propia vida. Viniendo yo de una teología pentecostal/carismática, este momento de repente me llevó a una perspectiva del Padre que nunca antes había visto.

UN PEQUEÑO VERSÍCULO CURIOSO

Antes de decirte cuál es el verso quiero darte un poco de trasfondo. El Evangelio de Juan fue el primer libro de la Biblia que leí. Así que leí este verso muchas veces previamente y aun así no había entendido su significado. De hecho, pensé que era un pequeño versículo curioso y extraño, un verso que realmente no entendía. Contenía una palabra que no es usada en ninguna otra parte del libro y es usada en solo otro lugar en el Nuevo Testamento completo. En esa reunión en Toronto, sin embargo, el verso saltó de la página y cambió todo para mí. Dios abrió mi entendimiento para hacer algo que no había sido visto antes.

Déjame darte una idea de porqué me impactó tanto. Cuando estaba en la escuela bíblica, se nos dieron las palabras clave para cada capítulo del libro de Juan. Al memorizar una palabra, podías recordar de qué se trataba todo el capítulo. Había un verso en particular que era clave para entender todo el libro de Juan. Ese verso (Juan 20:31) dice: «*Estas cosas están escritas para que ustedes crean que Jesús es el Hijo de Dios, y que al creerlo, tengan vida en su nombre*». Eso me hacía sentido completamente porque cuando el Señor abrió mis ojos a este otro verso en Juan 14, vi que este verso podría ser la clave para *todo el Nuevo Testamento, tal vez la Biblia entera*. Es increíble lo que pasa cuando un «*pequeño versículo curioso»* de repente adquiere un significado increíble.

El verso que ha cambiado todo para mí es Juan 14:18. Es un verso pequeño pero contiene tanto. Jesús lo dijo y Juan lo escribió,

«No los dejaré huérfanos. Vendré a ustedes».

Cuando esta perspectiva me iluminó, por primera vez en mi vida, empecé a entender el problema básico de la humanidad. El problema básico no solo de nuestras luchas individuales sino también de las luchas que tenemos en relación los unos con los otros. El problema básico de la vida en iglesia, la fricción entre denominaciones, las disputas familiares y aun las guerras entre naciones. De repente vi el problema de raíz de la lucha de la humanidad en esta tierra en toda la historia. Fue un cambio total de paradigma.

Alguien me dijo una vez: «James, pareces pensar que el amor del padre es la respuesta a todo el problema de la humanidad». Yo lo creo con todo mi corazón, porque todo problema tiene su fundamento en el hecho de que Adán y Eva perdieron su lugar en el Edén, ¡Perdieron su lugar en la experiencia del amor del Padre! Cuando eso pasó, la raza humana se quedó corta de la total provisión de Dios y perdió relación íntima con Él.

Así que cuando Jesús dijo las palabras: *«No los dejaré huérfanos, vendré a ustedes»*, ¿qué quiso decir exactamente?

TODOS SOMOS HUÉRFANOS

De primero debo decir que estas palabras no se originaron en el corazón o mente de Jesús. Él las dijo pero no vinieron de su pensamiento o teología. Vinieron de su Padre. Jesús dijo: «*Las palabras que hablo no son mis palabras sino solo digo las palabras que mi Padre me ha dicho que diga. No solo digo lo que mi Padre me ha dicho que diga sino lo digo en la forma en la que Él me ha dicho que las diga*» (Juan 12: 49-50). Estas palabras vinieron del corazón del Padre.

Cuando Jesús dijo las palabras: «No los dejaré huérfanos», necesitas entender que no estaba hablando estas palabras en un orfanato. La mayoría de la gente escuchando no era huérfana en el sentido natural. Sabemos de hecho que Pedro y Andrés estaban ahí. Habían estado pescando con su padre cuando Jesús los llamó, así que sabemos que tenían padre. Santiago y Juan también tenían papá. Eran los hijos de Zebedeo (conocidos también como hijos del trueno). Sabemos que su madre estaba viva porque vino a Jesús y le pidió que sus hijos se sentaran a su derecha y a su izquierda en el reino venidero. Era una seguidora de Jesús, creía que Él era el Mesías, y obviamente amaba a sus hijos y quería lo mejor para ellos. Así que está claro que no eran huérfanos.

Solo un pequeño porcentaje de la audiencia ese día eran huérfanos de verdad, y aun así las palabras del Padre para ellos fueron: «No los dejaré huérfanos. Vendré a ustedes». Esta es la palabra de Dios para nosotros a lo largo de las eras y ha quedado registrada para siempre.

Por lo tanto, nuestra conclusión es que el Padre *ve a toda la raza humana como huérfana. Él nos ve a todos como huérfanos.*

EL ESPÍRITU DE ORFANDAD ORIGINAL

¿Por qué ve Dios a toda la humanidad como huérfanos? Para

entender esta cosmovisión, de que todo el mundo está en un estado de orfandad, necesitamos regresar a su origen. Veamos a Isaías, capítulo 14, la cual nos abre la cortina (por así decirlo) y nos da una vislumbre hacia algo que ocurrió antes de que la humanidad hubiese sido creada. Esta es una profecía dada por el profeta Isaías al rey de Babilonia y fue una palabra contemporánea para su propia época. Sin embargo, muchas profecías tienen más de una aplicación y pueden ser interpretadas en una multiplicidad de niveles.

Desde el verso 12 en adelante es claro que hay otra aplicación que va mucho antes que el tiempo de Isaías y el rey de Babilonia. De hecho, algunas versiones de la Biblia preceden esta sección con un título que lee *«La caída de Lucifer»*. Muchos académicos creen que este pasaje es acerca de los orígenes de Satanás.

La sección empieza *«Oh Lucifer, ¿Cómo caíste del cielo, hijo de la mañana?¿Cómo fuiste cortado hacia la tierra, tú que debilitabas naciones? Porque has dicho en tu corazón...»* Luego siguen estas aseveraciones que empiezan con las palabras «Yo» (haré, subiré, etc..). Así que vemos que la caída de Lucifer empezó cuando decidió en su corazón «Yo haré estas cosas».

«Tú que decías en tu corazón: Subiré al cielo; en lo alto, junto a las estrellas de Dios, levantaré mi trono, y en el monte del testimonio me sentaré, a los lados del norte...» (Isaías 14:13).

No estoy completamente seguro del significado de esto, pero *entiendo* cuando dice que él dijo «subiré, haré esto o aquello». El dijo *«subiré al cielo; en lo alto, junto a las estrellas de Dios,»* y su ambición final era: *«Y seré como el Altísimo»*. La ambición que surgió en el corazón de Lucifer era reemplazar al Dios Altísimo, tomar su lugar y ultimadamente volverse como Él. No estaba diciendo «voy a estar a la par de Dios», sino, «¡*voy a ser como Él!*». ¡La ambición de Satanás no era volverse como Dios sino *reemplazarlo*! Si esto ocurriera Satanás mismo sería la máxima autoridad del universo.

Creo que esta ambición continuó creciendo en Lucifer al punto en donde él realmente creyó que había tenido éxito cuando el Príncipe de la Vida fue crucificado. No entendió que había (en las palabras de C.S. Lewis) una «magia más profunda» operando que resultaría en su caída y ultimada derrota.

El punto más importante que quiero hacer aquí, sobre lo cual descansa todo esto es éste: cuando Lucifer formó su oscura ambición para reemplazar al Altísimo, lo que estaba diciendo era esto: «¡No tendré a ningún padre sobre mí!». Dios es «padre» por naturaleza y el cielo siempre estuvo lleno de su paternidad. Por lo tanto, Lucifer estaba efectivamente diciendo: «No quiero un padre sobre mí, *yo* quiero ser el padre. Nadie va a estar sobre mí. No soy un hijo. Nadie estará por sobre mí».

Hay un pasaje muy similar en Ezequiel 28: 12-19. Esta vez es Ezequiel quien estaba profetizando sobre el rey de Tiro, y de nuevo hay otra capa de significado, la cual va más allá que el contexto del tiempo en la que la profecía fue dada. Podemos tener información acerca del origen de toda esta orfandad. Hablando acerca de Lucifer, el verso dice:

«Tú eras el sello de la perfección, lleno de sabiduría, y acabado de hermosura. En Edén, en el huerto de Dios estuviste; de toda piedra preciosa era tu vestidura».

Cuando leemos esto vemos que Satanás no fue creado como

una vil criatura. Fue conocido como «el brillante». Estaba lleno de sabiduría y era perfecto en hermosura. *«En Edén, en el huerto de Dios estuviste; de toda piedra preciosa era tu vestidura».* Estaba adornado con increíble belleza, el más hermoso de todos los seres. También estaba lleno de sabiduría pero, por su propio amor a su belleza, su sabiduría fue corrompida. En su estado original tenía un lugar de proximidad cercana al trono de Dios.

«Tú, querubín grande, protector, yo te puse en el santo monte de Dios, allí estuviste; en medio de las piedras de fuego te paseabas. Perfecto eras en todos tus caminos desde el día que fuiste creado, hasta que se halló en ti maldad...» (Ezequiel 28:14-15).

Esta iniquidad era la ambición de corazón de reemplazar a Dios y deshacerse de Dios. Era la ambición de Dios el desplazar el lugar de Dios en su vida para poder hacer lo que él quería hacer y ser la máxima autoridad en su propia vida. Esta todavía es la base de todo pecado el día de hoy.

El verso 16 dice: *«A causa de la multitud de tus contrataciones fuiste lleno de iniquidad, y pecaste»* y luego vienen estas palabras, *«por lo que yo te eché del monte de Dios, y te arrojé de entre las piedras del fuego».* El verso 17 dice: *«Se enalteció tu corazón a causa de tu hermosura».* Nota que no dice que su hermosura fue removida. *«Corrompiste tu sabiduría a causa de tu esplendor; yo te arrojaré por tierra».*

Otras versiones usan el término «te expulsé» o «te arrojé a la tierra». Jesús mismo vio a Satanás caer como un rayo desde el cielo. ¡Tuvo que haber sido muy dramático! Fue echado a la tierra, fuera de la presencia de Dios, expulsado del Monte de Dios, fuera del cielo y hacia la tierra, y él tomó a los ángeles con él.

EXCOMULGADO DEL AMOR DEL PADRE

No sé como es el cielo. No he estado ahí. Todo lo que sé es lo que las Escrituras me dicen, que en el cielo no hay necesidad de sol o de luna porque Dios mismo es la luz. Dios llena los cielos. Y ya que Dios es amor, esto significa que el cielo está lleno de amor.

Imagina como será. Vamos a vivir en un ambiente en donde cada aliento que tomemos será como respirar amor líquido. Viviremos continuamente en un ambiente de amor total. No habrá la posibilidad de rechazo porque la aceptación total será respirada cada segundo. Amor absoluto que lo satura todo.

No solo el cielo está saturado de amor, sino que está lleno de un amor específico. Está lleno del amor de un padre porque Dios es Padre. De Él, todo lo que existe ha nacido. No podemos iniciar una sola cosa. Él inició nuestra salvación y nosotros solo respondimos a la invitación. Él inició la creación y nosotros entramos a todo lo que Él nos ha dado. Por su misma esencia y naturaleza, Dios *es* padre. No es algo en lo que Él se convirtió. Antes que todas las cosas, más por encima de todo, y en el sentido más profundo, su amor es un amor paternal.

Satanás, habiendo rechazado a Dios como padre, fue echado del cielo y exilado de toda paternidad. El *quería* estar sin padre. La misma esencia de su ser es que *no tiene padre*. Es un huérfano *y quiere ser un huérfano*. Por eso es que no hay redención para él. Tenía la perfecta revelación de quien es Dios y escogió rechazarle. Y al ser enviado a la tierra se volvió la máxima expresión del *espíritu de orfandad*.

El apóstol Pablo tenía conocimiento de lo que estoy diciendo.

En Efesios 2:2 él escribió: «*en los cuales anduvisteis en otro tiempo, siguiendo la corriente de este mundo, conforme al príncipe de la potestad del aire, el espíritu que ahora opera en los hijos de desobediencia*».

En otras palabras, antes de volverte cristiano, había un espíritu operando en ti que te estaba guiando al sistema del mundo. En ese sistema del mundo estabas pecando, fuera de los propósitos de Dios y necesitabas ser revivido. El príncipe del poder del aire estaba guiándote a su forma de desobediencia y en sus caminos hay orfandad.

El mundo es un orfanato

Cuando entendemos que Satanás es un espíritu huérfano vemos que los caminos de este mundo son, de hecho, caminos de orfandad. Satanás engañó al mundo entero. Nos ha guiado en el camino de *su* sistema de valores, así que todo el sistema del mundo funciona en las formas en las que un huérfano funciona. Cuando definimos el pecado como «fallar en dar al blanco», es de hecho fallar en alcanzar al padre y vivir una vida de orfandad.

Considera cómo es para un huérfano vivir en un orfanato, y lo que es para un hijo vivir en un buen hogar con padres amantes. Hay una inmensa diferencia entre estas dos cosas.

Déjame delinear algunas de las características de la orfandad. La realidad más básica de ser un huérfano es esta: un huérfano no tiene nombre. Frecuentemente el nombre de un huérfano es cambiado o se les abandona sin que nadie sepa su identidad. No hay un sentido de historia, no hay un sentido de venir de algún lugar. No hay sentido de que tu nombre signifique algo para ti.

Cuando eres criado en una buena familia tu nombre es el nombre de tu padre, y el padre de él, extendiéndose hacia atrás en la historia. Tu nombre es compartido por tus hermanos y hermanas y hay un sentido de identidad familiar que viene al tener el mismo nombre. En el mundo vemos gente tratando de crear un nombre para ellos mismos, tratando de ser importantes, tratando de hacer algo que les dé un lugar en la sociedad. La orfandad no solo es algo que tiene que ver con el mundo. Es un estado fundamental del corazón humano.

Aun en la iglesia vemos la orfandad en primera plana. Vemos a gente en el ministerio tratando de crear un nombre para ellos mismos, tratando de hacer una «obra importante», queriendo involucrarse en un «ministerio significativo». Recuerdo haber tenido esa misma ambición. La motivación tras de esto es que si hago algo importante significa que *yo* soy importante. Uno de los dichos del mundo es «si quieres sentirte importante, empieza a hacer algo importante». Esa es una característica de un huérfano. Un hijo o una hija encuentra su importancia en la familia, de ser amado y atesorado simplemente por quien es él o ella.

Otra cosa acerca de los huérfanos es esta: nadie les da nada. No hay regalos de Navidad o de cumpleaños. Si hay un regalo, ha sido dado al orfanato y distribuido al azar. Solo por causalidad recibirías algo que de verdad querías. Tal vez un pequeño niño quería un bote de vela, pero recibe un tractor. Un regalo al azar sin significado personal. Los cumpleaños o la Navidad no significa nada para un huérfano. La lección es esta—no obtienes nada sin ningún esfuerzo. Esa es uno de los distintivos de este mundo. Te las tienes que ver por ti mismo, nadie te va a dar nada, no hay ninguna «comida gratis», así que más vale velar por tus propios intereses.

Para un huérfano no hay herencia, así que tienes que pelear por lo que sea que vayas a obtener. ¡Y no dejes que nadie te lo quite, porque podrás estar seguro que tratarán de hacerlo! Esa es la vida en un orfanato. Al pequeño niño le quitan su comida los niños más grandes. El mundo funciona de esta manera. Solo mira nuestros sistemas financieros. Dicen: «Es negocio, nada personal», pero es *muy personal* para la persona que está perdiendo. Para un huérfano es difícil ser generoso porque siente que nadie jamás le dará nada y si da algo, nunca lo va a recuperar. Un hijo, en cambio, tiene un punto de vista diferente: «Mi padre es muy generoso y extremadamente rico y él da buenos regalos».

Los sistemas por los cuales este mundo es gobernado son sistemas huérfanos. Por ejemplo, ¿sabías que la democracia no es del reino de Dios? La democracia podrá ser la mejor forma para que los huérfanos gobiernen a los huérfanos en un mundo caído pero sigue siendo un sistema huérfano. Así no es como Dios gobierna su reino. Tristemente, muchas iglesias se rigen por los principios de la democracia. Si tienes un liderazgo de la iglesia que tiene un corazón de orfandad, todo el ministerio tendrá el mismo sentido de orfandad. Esto lo permea todo.

Otro ejemplo: el capitalismo. El capitalismo podrá ser la mejor forma en la que los huérfanos aprenden a negociar con los huérfanos, pero ciertamente no es un sistema basado en la justicia. Está basado en valores huérfanos de comprar y vender para obtener una ganancia – y una ganancia que sea la más grande posible independientemente de lo que es justo y bueno. El reino de Dios es diferente. El reino de Dios trabaja sobre el principio de dar *todo* lo que tienes – y *recibir* todo de parte de Dios. Si alguien te hace ir una milla con él, ve más distancia. Si alguien te golpea en una mejilla, pon la otra. Si alguien toma tu ropa, dale también tu abrigo.

No estoy en contra de hacer negocios. No estoy hablando contra hacer una ganancia. Esta es la forma en la que el mundo corre y necesitamos funcionar dentro de ello, pero también necesitamos entender que esta no es la forma de hacer las cosas en el reino. El reino de Dios tiene valores diferentes, y tanto como sea posible para nosotros, necesitamos funcionar dentro del reino de Dios para operar en sus principios. ¡Algunas iglesias operan todo su presupuesto sobre principios de capitalismo y esto los ata! Dios puede ir mucho más allá de lo que pensamos, y si limitamos nuestro pensamiento a lo que puede ser logrado dentro del sistema de capitalismo entonces estamos limitando lo que Dios puede hacer. Pero cuando creemos por la provisión de Dios en sus sistemas financieros, ¡salimos de la orfandad y nos volvemos hijos!

La diferencia entre el cristianismo y el no-cristianismo es la diferencia entre ser un hijo y ser huérfano.

Una travesía imaginaria

Quiero que hagas una pequeña travesía imaginaria conmigo. Quiero que intentes imaginar como fueron las cosas cuando Adán fue creado. Solo tenemos algunas palabras en Génesis 3. Dice: «*Dios formó al hombre del polvo de la tierra, sopló en su nariz el aliento de vida, y el hombre se volvió un ser viviente*». Imagina si fueras un ángel viendo cómo Dios crea todo el universo. ¿Cómo se hubiera visto esto?

Frecuentemente me he preguntado porqué Dios no hizo al hombre en el primer día, para que él pudiera ver a Dios crear todo. Eso hubiera sido extraordinario ¿no crees? ¿Por qué esperó Dios hasta la tarde del sexto día para crear al hombre? La única razón que se me ocurre es porque *no quería que el hombre le conociera como un padre trabajador*. Si el hombre hubiese presenciado el acto de la creación, hubiera sido empujado a trabajar y a lograr cosas. Hemos sido hechos para el reposo de Dios y a menos que vengamos a un lugar de reposo dentro de nosotros mismos nuestra relación con Dios será obstaculizada. Esa es la razón por la que las Escrituras dicen: *«Estad quietos y conoced que yo soy Dios»* (Salmo 46:10).

Dios formó al hombre. Él habló todo lo demás para que fuera creado por la palabra de su mandamiento, pero Él formó al hombre esculpiéndolo con el polvo. Debió llegar el momento cuando los ángeles respiraron con sorpresa a medida que empezaron a entender que Dios estaba haciendo una copia de Él mismo. Era una creación perfecta.

A medida que Él estaba formando este hombre, llegó el momento en el que el cuerpo fue finalmente completado. Un cuerpo masculino adulto perfectamente formado pero sin vida. Dios luego sopló en la nariz del hombre. Tienes que estar muy cerca de alguien para soplarles en la nariz. Si tu hubieras estado observando esto, ¿qué habrías visto? *Se habría visto como si Dios estuviera besando a Adán.*

Cuando una madre sostiene a su hijo recién nacido hay una mirada de maravilla absoluta en su rostro. Todo el dolor del parto se olvida, y el amor y ternura, y la maravilla se unen en su expresión. No creo que haya ninguna mujer que no haya tenido este sentido cuando dio a luz a su primer hijo. Ella sabe que un milagro impresionante ha ocurrido.

Dios el Padre es el prototipo de padre todos los tiempos. Él es el máximo progenitor y nosotros somos copias de Él. Cuando Él estaba soplando en la nariz de Adán estaba dando a luz a un hijo.

Me imagino que este fue uno de los momentos más increíbles de la historia. Si tu hubieras estado viendo eso hubieras visto todo el amor y la ternura de un padre en su rostro.

¿Pero qué hubieras visto si estuvieses observando a Adán? Hubieras visto su pecho moverse con su primer aliento a medida que sus pulmones se inflaban. Luego el corazón empezó a latir. Hubieras visto una repentina ola de color llenar su cuerpo, cuando la sangre empezó a bombear a través de todos los músculos, los tejidos y la piel. Todo en el cuerpo empezó a funcionar. Tal vez a medida que los músculos empezaron a tener oxígeno hayan habido pequeños movimientos en los dedos de las manos, de los pies, y en los párpados. Todo se empezó a mover porque el cuerpo estaba cobrando vida. No solo está el cuerpo cobrando vida sino que el cerebro también habría estado volviéndose operativo. ¿Cómo habrá sido para la mente el estar funcionando pero no tener nada que pensar? ¡Y la memoria empezaría a funcionar pero no habría memorias! ¡Nada de nada! Su personalidad estaría ahí pero no habría input. Como una computadora que está encendida pero no tiene sistema operativo. Está vacía.

Luego llegaría el momento cuando Adán recibiría su primer input. ¿Cuál piensas que fue ese momento? ¿Qué hizo que él tuviera el primer registro de información? Yo creo que fue el momento en el que abrió sus ojos. ¿Qué crees que vio en el momento en que abrió sus ojos? El amor expresado a través del tacto, a través de la voz y a través de los ojos. Los ojos son las ventanas del alma.

Así que Adán estaba empezando a abrir sus ojos. ¿Crees que el Padre había salido a leer el periódico, ver televisión o jugar futbol? ¡Nunca! Él estaba intensamente amando a su hijo y le estaba trayendo a existencia. Dios no es un padre a tiempo parcial. Él está ahí todo el tiempo. Nosotros nos preocupamos con otras cosas, pero Él no tiene nada más con lo cual estar ocupado. ¡Nosotros somos su ocupación! Cuando Adán abrió sus ojos, estaba debajo de un torrente de amor del Padre. *El estaba recibiendo todo el amor que hay en el universo entero.* ¡Qué pensamiento maravilloso! No puedo imaginar lo que fue para él, que la primera cosa que experimentó fue el amor total del Dios Altísimo. Adán sabía que era ser total y completamente amado por Dios.

Pensé que yo era el único que había pensado en esto pero un día descubrí que Pablo el apóstol también lo había visto. Cuando el verdadero importe de este verso me capturó yo pensé «¡Pablo, eres un pillo! ¡También lo sabías!», escucha lo que dice:

«Por esta causa doblo mis rodillas ante el Padre de nuestro Señor Jesucristo. . . para que habite Cristo por la fe en vuestros corazones, a fin de que, arraigados y cimentados en amor, seáis plenamente capaces de comprender con todos los santos cuál sea la anchura, la longitud, la profundidad y la altura, y de conocer el amor de Cristo, que excede a todo conocimiento, para que seáis llenos de toda la plenitud de Dios» (Efesios 3:14-19).

Arraigados y cimentados en amor. El fundamento mismo de la vida de Adán estaba *arraigado* y *cimentado* en amor. ¿No es eso maravilloso? Esta herencia de cada cristiano es el tener nuestros ojos abiertos para ver el amor increíble que el Padre tiene para nosotros. Esto no es un cristianismo extraordinario. ¡Este es el fundamento! Este no es un libro nuevo en el estante, por así decirlo. ¡Este es el estante mismo! No es una nueva experiencia añadida a mis otras experiencias de vida. ¡Esta es la base de todo! El asunto fundamental, a través del cual yo interpreto todo es que *el Padre me ama.*

Un hombre vino a mí luego de una reunión hace años y me dijo: «James, dices que el amor del Padre es el fundamento, pero de verdad... la cruz es el fundamento, ¿no es así?». A mi no me habían hecho esa pregunta antes y no lo había pensado. Pero en un segundo vi algo y respondí: «La cruz es una expresión del amor del Padre. El amor del Padre no es una expresión de la cruz».

Déjame ponerlo de esta manera. Cuando naces de nuevo te sumerges al pozo de salvación, encontrando el amor de Jesús. Sigues buceando más profundo, ¡y eres lavado por la sangre! ¡Sigues profundizado y Él se vuelve tu Señor! Sigues yendo más lejos, ¡y eres lleno del Espíritu Santo! Sigues más adentro, y empiezas a moverte en milagros. Sigues aún más profundo, ¡y empiezas a ministrar con unción! Sigues más profundo y profundo hacia la justificación y la santificación. Luego llegas al fondo del pozo, desde donde sale *todo*. El amor del Padre. ¡Ahí está! Él es la fuente. Su amor es el amor por sobre todos los otros amores.

PARAÍSO

Adán estuvo arraigado y cimentado en amor desde el momento en el que abrió sus ojos. Luego Dios creó una esposa para él. Ella no tenía ningún nombre en ese punto. Los dos fueron llamados Adán. El amor es unidad. Adán (y Eva) tenían esta unidad, justo como nosotros deseamos ser uno solo. Dios había creado un ambiente maravilloso en donde los colocó a ambos.

Adán (y Eva) vivieron en el jardín, totalmente saturados del amor del Padre. Él comulgó con ellos todos los días. Necesitamos entender que la relación de Dios con Adán era la de un padre con su hijo. La Escritura llama a Adán «hijo de Dios». He tratado de imaginar cómo era su vida pero no la puedo comprender. Ellos tuvieron que haber vivido en una paz continua. Una paz *más profunda* que la paz. No había una palabra para la paz porque no había nada diferente a ello. Vivían en gozo total y completo. Podías haberte sentado con ellos y tratar de explicar el concepto de inseguridad y ellos no hubieran entendido de lo que estabas hablando. El temor estaba completamente fuera de su marco de referencia. Esta vida en el jardín del Edén era inocente pero en otro sentido era también era la personificación de la madurez. Aspiramos aquello que ellos tenían naturalmente.

Sabemos que Satanás puso una trampa para ellos y cuando lo hizo, lo hizo bien. De joven pasé un tiempo poniendo trampas, vendiendo piel de animales para subsistir. Puse muchas trampas en el bosque y sé muy bien que tienes que hacer que se vean atractivas. No atraparás nada si una trampa se ve peligrosa al animal que estás tratando de capturar. Tiene que verse *mejor* de lo normal y aparecer más atractiva que lo ordinario. Luego la presa quedará atrapada por sus propias acciones.

La primera parte de la trampa de Satanás fue el prometerle a la mujer que si ella comía del árbol ella sería como Dios. Eva *amaba* a Dios. ¿Cuántos de nosotros hemos orado para que Dios nos haga como Jesús? ¿Por qué oras esto? ¡Porque lo amas! El amor quiere ser como eso que ama y estar incorporado en ese objeto de su amor. Por supuesto que estaba ella interesada en la promesa de Satanás. Quería ser como su Padre. Ella *amaba* a Dios.

Luego Satanás le mostró que el fruto era hermoso. Una cosa que sé es que las mujeres aman la belleza. Me he quedado en lugares en donde solo viven hombres y la casa no tiene belleza, era solamente funcional. Las mujeres aman la belleza.

Eva vio el fruto y vio que era hermoso. Ella vio que era bueno y nutritivo. El nutrir puede ser expresado en muchas formas, pero una de las formas más comunes es a través de la creación y la provisión de buena comida. Puede ser una expresión de amor, cuidado y provisión para la familia. Eva extendió su mano, tomó el fruto y lo comió. Cuando comió el fruto, ¿qué pasó? *Nada.*

Adán y Eva estaban tan unidos que no podían pecar individualmente. No fue hasta que él también comió que los ojos de ambos fueron abiertos y la trampa se cerró... ¡BUM! No había forma de regresar. No podían escapar. Las consecuencias quedaron escritas en concreto. No creo que ellos hayan tenido idea de las consecuencias que existirían. Sabían que si comían del fruto morirían, pero esa sería, según ellos, probablemente la última de las consecuencias.

La unidad entre ellos se esfumó. «*Y Adán llamó a su esposa Eva, porque ella era la madre de todos los vivientes*» (Génesis 3:20). Aquí es donde Eva obtiene un nombre diferente. Se volvieron dos, cuando previamente habían sido uno. C.S. Lewis dijo que una espada había separado a los sexos ese día, una espada de enemistad entre lo masculino y lo femenino, lo cual todavía tiene que ser restaurado. Dios luego hizo túnicas de piel y los vistió. Ahora ellos fueron testigos del derramamiento de sangre. «*Luego el Señor Dios dijo: "He aquí el hombre se ha vuelto como uno de nosotros, conociendo el bien y el mal. Ahora, para que no tome también del árbol de la vida , y coma, y viva para siempre". . .*»(v.22). Luego los expulsó del jardín.

Atrapados en la trampa, el pecado se volvió su capataz. El problema con el pecado es que te agarra y ya no puedes escapar por ti mismo. El pecado te domina. La única forma en que el poder del pecado puede ser roto es a través de la sangre de Jesús. No puedes romper el poder del pecado al decidir vivir de forma diferente, pero cuando la sangre de Jesús es aplicada, eres libre el las garras del pecado. Adán y Eva entraron a una vida de pecado pero la sangre de Jesús no había sido provista aún.

DOS OPCIONES TERRIBLES

Dios tenía que tomar una decisión increíble. Recuerda que Él los amaba y quería solo lo mejor para ellos pero ahora ellos habían tomado un camino en donde solo hay dos posibilidades. El podía echarlos o dejarlos en el jardín viviendo como pecadores para siempre.

Dios estaba viendo a Adán y Eva a medida que el peso del pecado descendía sobre ellos. Ahora ellos iban a descender más profundo en la desesperanza, cargando un peso de culpa que crecía y crecía constantemente. Sus personalidades se pudrirían en el interior, envueltos en avaricia, inseguridad y temor. Lo único en lo que puedo pensar, que me da una idea de cómo sería eso, es el personaje de Gollum en el film *Señor de los anillos*. Esa criatura se asió de algo poderosamente malvado. No podía soltarlo, no podía parar de perseguirlo aunque lo estaba destruyendo desde adentro hacia fuera. Se volvió grotesco, una criatura parecida a un gusano, degradada de su sentido original de ser, y esa degradación tenía un efecto constante en él.

Yo creo, que a medida que Dios veía a Adán y Eva, Él vio que ellos ya habían empezado un proceso de degradación. Y el corazón del Padre dijo: «¡No podemos dejar que esto continúe para siempre! ¡Diez mil años pasarán y ellos estarán vivos y *todavía degradándose*! No podemos permitirles que vayan coman del árbol de la vida. Necesitamos expulsarlos del jardín. ¡Debemos evitar que tengan acceso a ese árbol!». Así que les dijo «¡Se acabó, deben irse!».

Es imposible imaginar lo que Adán y Eva habrán sentido cuando escucharon esas palabras. No podían culpar a Dios por su dilema. El hecho de que ellos se habían buscado lo que les estaba pasando solo hacía la desesperación aún peor. Dios vino a ellos como un Padre amante. El no los estaba expulsando como una retribución o un castigo. El enviarlos fuera del jardín fue escoger la maldad menos severa de las dos opciones. Cuando Él los expulsó, Adán y Eva probablemente eran las personas más devastadas de corazón que el mundo ha visto.

Hay dos cosas diferentes que determinan cuanto dolor experimentarás cuando alguien te rompe el corazón. De primero, mientras más fuerte sea el amor que has experimentado, más grande será el dolor. ¡Adán y Eva habían sido amados por el amor más grande en el universo! De segundo, si tu corazón ha sido roto previamente, generalmente serás más reservado la próxima vez. Previo a esto, Adán y Eva nunca habían *sentido* dolor alguno. No sabían lo que era el dolor. Y ahora, creo estaban experimentando el dolor emocional más grande que alguien haya sentido jamás. Ellos tenían que haber sido las personas más tristes y desesperanzadas que el mundo haya visto. Ahora Él los empujaba hacia la puerta para salir del jardín. Parecía como si Adán y Eva no podían sostenerse sobre sus piernas ni caminar hacia fuera del jardín y el Padre tuvo que forzarlos físicamente. Él no lo hizo para castigarlos. Ni porque los estaba rechazando. El lo hizo *porque Él los amaba.*

Dios nunca ha hecho nada que no fuera una expresión de su amor y Él les echó fuera *porque* los amaba. Puedo imaginarmelos arrastrando sus pies, tratando de prolongar los momentos en el jardín porque por primera vez estaban experimentando temor.

¿Cómo será allá afuera? ¿Qué quiso decir cuando dijo que la tierra produciría espinos y que tendrían que trabajar con el sudor de su frente? ¡Quería decir que Él no iba a seguir proveyendo! ¡Todo lo que necesitaban estaba en el jardín! ¿Cómo vivirían ahora? Ellos tendrían que construir una vida diferente para ellos mismos. Nunca le verían como le veían en ese momento, ya no más. ¡La vida como la conocían había llegado a su fin!

LA RAZA HUMANA SE VUELVE HUÉRFANA

A medida que los echaba del jardín, lo que estaba pasando en realidad era que Él los estaba empujando lejos de una experiencia de su amor. Nunca experimentarían su amor de nuevo. El pecado siempre crea separación y ahora su pecado les había separado de Él. Ellos tenían que haber sabido esto a medida que dejaban el jardín que la relación como había sido estaba llegando a su fin. Al dejar el jardín ellos estaban dejando el ambiente del amor del Padre y volviéndose más como el que fue echado del cielo. Ellos estaban volviéndose huérfanos. Toda la raza humana, incluyéndote a ti y a mi, estaba en ellos cuando estaban saliendo del jardín. *En ellos la raza humana se ha vuelto huérfana.*

Algo todavía más siniestro estaba ocurriendo para agravar todavía más su miseria. El que había sido echado del cielo a la tierra como un rayo empezó a crear engaño. Una alianza profana empezó a desarrollarse entre el espíritu de orfandad echado del cielo y este hombre y mujer con corazón huérfano que ahora estaban totalmente ignorantes acerca de cómo vivir fuera del jardín. Así que Satanás empezó a guiar a la raza humana al engaño que continúa estando activo en toda la humanidad hasta el día de hoy. Todos hemos caminado en estos caminos, como dice Efesios 2:2. El mundo se ha vuelto una sociedad huérfana. El ser salvos, llenos del

Espíritu Santo y el conocer a Jesús íntimamente no cambiará esto. ¡Solo un Padre puede eliminar la orfandad!

Por un largo tiempo nunca siquiera pensé en lo que tuvo que haber sido para Dios. Él los amaba con un amor paternal y sabía lo que ocurriría. El sabía que la avaricia envolvería el corazón humano y toda persona se volvería en contra de su prójimo. El podía ver la espada entre los sexos, la barrera invisible entre el hombre y su mujer a medida que dejaban el jardín. Ahora ellos eran huérfanos en el sentido más amplio de la palabra.

Hace algunos años estaba en San Petersburgo en Rusia. Era noviembre y estaba muy frío. Cuando caminaba una noche, un niño, como de nueve años, pasó corriendo a la par mía. No tenía nada puesto más que unos pantalones cortos de algodón y una camiseta de manga corta de algodón. Tenía los pies descalzos, las piernas sucias y el cabello sin cortar. Tenía un pequeño bolso lleno de palos sobre su hombro. Presumí que iba a encender una fogata en algún lugar para calentarse un poco. Cuando corrió a la par mía, paró y me vio sobre sus hombros. Nunca olvidaré la imagen de su rostro. ¡Fue como ver el rostro de un hombre maduro pero en el cuerpo de un chico! Su mirada me dijo: «¿Qué me vas a hacer?». Luego se dio la vuelta y siguió corriendo. Hay muchos chicos como él en todo el mundo. Hay tanto sufrimiento en el mundo. Sufrimiento más allá de lo que podemos imaginar.

El Padre sabía cómo iba a ser cuando Él miraba a Adán y Eva salir hacia esa vida huérfana. Pero también sabía que era mejor que la alternativa, la cual era vivir por siempre en una degeneración eterna. Creo que un gran clamor empezó a surgir en el corazón del Padre en ese momento. Un clamor de agonía. Una cosa que sé como padre es esta: cuando mis hijos sufren, yo preferiría estar yo en su lugar. Es más difícil ver a tus hijos sufrir que sufrir tú mismo. Es casi intolerable el ver a tus hijos sufrir y no ser capaz de hacer nada al respecto. Y ahí estaba un Padre enviando a sus hijos fuera, conociendo el sufrimiento que vendría inevitablemente. Creo que un clamor salió de las profundidades de su ser. A medida que el mundo siguió, el sufrimiento se incrementó, y ese grito se volvió más y más intenso. Él podía ver a todos sus hijos, a toda la raza humana, en una vida de sufrimiento. Su corazón paternal se extendió a ellos, sabiendo que pronto olvidarían que Él existía y que les amaba.

El plan de rescate del Padre

Desde su corazón de absoluta compasión, Él envió a gente a hablarles de su amor. El envió legisladores y jueces, envió reyes y sacerdotes a expresar su corazón y mostrar una forma de vivir libre de sufrimiento. El llamó a una nación, un pueblo que fuera un testigo pero todo esto fue inadecuado. Toda la raza humana estaba descendiendo hacia una vida huérfana, una vida de sufrimiento, experimentando un nivel extraordinario de soledad y quebrantam-iento. El vio a sus hijos sufrir y un gran clamor salió desde dentro de Él. El envió profetas. Envió madres a Israel. Envió salmistas y poetas que pudieran hablar sus palabras elocuentemente. Ninguno de ellos pudo expresar perfectamente su corazón. ¡Ni uno de ellos!

Finalmente Él envió a su propio Hijo, quien sería la perfecta representación de Él mismo, su imagen exacta – su Hijo, quien no solo diría lo que Él quería que dijera sino lo diría *exactamente en la forma en la que Él quería decirlo.* ¡Él envió a Jesús! Jesús el Hijo vino al mundo, totalmente desconectado del sistema huérfano, y empezó a vivir una vida como Hijo. Estaba libre del engaño de orfandad que infectaba a toda la raza humana. ¡Vino como un Hijo! Sus palabras, que vinieron de un Padre perfecto, sorprendieron al mundo. Él, libre de los efectos del pecado, fue capaz de extender esa libertad a otros. Él dispensó su libertad de la enfermedad, su libertad de Satanás. Pudo asegurarle a un pecador que sus pecados eran perdonados. Él mandó a que el cojo se levantara y caminara. Él escupió en los ojos del ciego y fueron abiertos. Él vino a la tierra totalmente libre de la naturaleza huérfana caída del mundo para mostrarnos cómo es el Padre, para restaurarle al mundo el conocimiento de que el *Padre nos está amando.*

En los últimos días, antes de ser crucificado por el mundo, Él *finalmente* pudo decir lo que había estado ardiendo en el corazón de su Padre, como un volcán, por generaciones. Él finalmente pudo expresar lo que su Padre quería que expresara. Este clamor estaba en el corazón del Padre desde el momento en que Adán y Eva salieron del jardín hacia una vida sin padre, engañados por el espíritu huérfano que fue expulsado del cielo en las eras pasadas.

Finalmente Jesús fue capaz de expresar directo desde el corazón de Dios, las palabras que el Padre le dijo que dijera, diciéndolas en la forma en la que el Padre quería que las dijera,

«¡No los dejaré huérfanos, sino vendré a ustedes!»

A medida que el Padre los veía salir del jardín hacia una orfandad, Él tuvo que quedarse atrás. Pero Él envió a su Hijo a romper todo lo que se interpone entre Él y nosotros y nos hace la promesa: «¡*Yo seré un Padre para ustedes y ustedes serán mis hijos y mis hijas, dice el Señor Dios Todo poderoso!*» (2 Cor. 6:18). Esta orfandad que está en toda la raza humana no puede ser echada fuera. No es demoníaca en ella misma. Es el estado del corazón *humano.* Pero cuando el corazón humano se encuentra al Padre, deja de ser huérfano. Y sus caminos de orfandad empiezan a desaparecer.

Jesús no es la puerta para llegar *al* cielo. ¡El es la Puerta para que el Padre pueda venir a nosotros! El velo del templo que se rasgo de arriba hacia abajo no fue para que nosotros pudiéramos entrar. ¡Fue rasgada para que Él pudiera venir! Él la separó y salió, ¡y en ese momento toda la estructura religiosa colapsó! El reino de Israel se acabó. Antes de que pasaran cuarenta años el templo fue destruido y el linaje real de Israel desapareció. ¡Ahora el Padre sale del templo para ser un padre para todo el mundo!

El evangelio simplemente es esto. Es acerca de un Padre que perdió a sus hijos y los quiere de vuelta.

El envió a su Hijo a traerlos a casa. El dijo: «Hijo, ve y tráelos a casa. ¡Quien quiera venir, tráelo a casa!». La obra del Espíritu de Dios es sacarnos de la orfandad y hacernos hijos. Jesús vino como el Hijo para volverse el Camino al Padre. Cuando tú te conviertes en un hijo, puedes conocer al Padre más y más. ¡Eso es el cristianismo! ¿No es maravilloso? ¡Casi no puedo creer que Él sea tan bueno! Su intención en ser un padre para nosotros y deshacerse de nuestros caminos de orfandad. Él nos está trayendo, a sus hijos, a casa otra vez para estar con Él.

El secreto para ser un hijo

~

Desde que estaba creciendo como un joven cristiano, se me ha dicho que tengo que madurar y crecer. En nuestro cristianismo estamos tratando de volvernos fuertes, educados, competentes y seguros de nosotros mismos—cuando el Señor está tratando de llevarnos a ser como niños. En el mundo necesitas volverte educado para sobrevivir y ser exitoso pero en el ámbito del dominio de Dios necesitamos ser como niños pequeños. Por años, estaba yo tratando de hacer todo este trabajo duro hasta que descubrí de qué se trata todo *realmente*.

El Señor ha cambiado radicalmente toda nuestra perspectiva de la vida cristiana. Cuando Denise y yo estábamos en nuestros treinta y tantos, estábamos pastoreando una pequeña iglesia en Nueva Zelanda. Era la segunda vez que pastoreábamos una iglesia y nos manteníamos muy ocupados. Pasábamos nuestras tardes y cada fin de semana aconsejando a la gente. Llegó un punto en el que no nos habíamos ido a la cama hasta después de la noche durante dos semanas seguidas. También teníamos visión para construir un centro ministerial. A un amigo le habían regalado cien acres y nos habíamos mudado ahí para ayudarle a construir. Estábamos construyendo casas, instalando cables eléctricos y sistemas de drenaje, así como mejorando el camino de acceso al lugar.

Luego el Señor nos habló acerca de construir una casa grande de ocho dormitorios ahí. Oramos y recibimos el cuarto de millón de dólares que costaba el construir la casa. En adición a esto, estaba empezando yo a recibir invitaciones para hablar fuera de Nueva Zelanda, así que por cuatro años estuvimos extremadamente ocupados haciendo la obra del Señor. Desde el momento en que nos despertábamos hasta que nos íbamos a acostar (y luego orábamos por sueños en la noche) estuvimos viviendo, comiendo, respirando y durmiendo el reino de Dios. Estábamos haciendo todo lo que podíamos, laborando para la obra de Dios.

Luego de repente ocurrió un cambio. Una mañana, estaba esperando en la puerta de entrada para que Denise bajara las escaleras para que pudiéramos ir a la iglesia. Luego ella llegó al fondo de las gradas y se sentó, y empezó a llorar. Cualquiera que conoce a Denise sabe que ella no llora por nada. Si estaba llorando, tenía que haber algo *muy serio* y urgente. ¿Hubo una llamada con noticias terribles? Ella estaba llorando tan fuerte que no podía decirme por qué estaba llorando. Le seguía preguntando «¿qué pasa?» pero no podía hablar. Todo lo que pudo decir al final fue: *«Simplemente no puedo enfrentar a esa gente una sola vez más».*

Quemándonos

Estábamos emocionalmente exhaustos después de diecisiete años de Servir al Señor a todo vapor. Estábamos viviendo, comiendo y respirando vida ministerial. Yo estaba enseñando en escuelas de JUCUM, y estábamos orando por mucho dinero para diferentes proyectos, teníamos compromisos para hablar en Asia, Corea, los EEUU y Canadá, así como las islas del pacífico. Estábamos trabajando muy duro sirviendo al Señor y de repente nos topamos contra el muro.

Esto pasó en 1988. Decidí que no podía permanecer en el ministerio con Denise así. En ese momento pensé que yo estaba bien. Tenía invitaciones para hablar en cuatro escuelas de JUCUM en Australia, así que le dijimos a nuestra iglesia que íbamos a tomarnos un descanso de seis meses, cumplir con nuestros compromisos en Australia y luego tomar un tiempo fuera del ministerio. ¡Tan pronto como llegamos a Australia, sin embargo, yo empecé a llorar! Me sentaba en el sofá por horas, viendo al piso con lágrimas corriendo por mi rostro. Estábamos exhaustos emocionalmente.

Por ese tiempo, Ken Wright y su esposa Shirley vinieron a vernos. Él era el hombre que me había bautizado, uno de los hombres que le podía llamar algo así como un padre, hacía tiempo cuando el Señor me había preguntado de quién era hijo. Cuando se estaban yendo para regresar a casa, Ken se subió al carro, luego bajó la ventana unas pulgadas para decir algo. Fue bueno que haya hecho esto porque lo que me dijo me hizo sentir que quería pegarle en la cara. Con un ojo medio cerrado, me dijo: «Por supuesto que te das cuenta, verdad James, que sólo tu carne se puede quemar». *Y estábamos* quemados, completamente exhaustos.

Cuando escuché a Ken decir esas palabras, todo en mí se levantó con ira «¡no he estado trabajando en la carne! Hemos estado orando para que *todo* se mueva en el poder del Espíritu, ¡buscamos hacer todo en el poder de Dios!». ¿Cómo podía decir eso? EL problema era que su declaración era completamente incuestionable. No había forma que pudiera decir que estaba exhausto si era la obra del Señor hecha en toda su fuerza. Si te quemas, es un indicador claro que mucho de *"ti"* ha estado involucrado en la obra. Ese fue un hecho difícil de encarar para mí. Todo en mi vida, en lo que respectaba al Señor, estaba motivado por el deseo de que el Señor se moviera por su poder y su Espíritu. Siempre cantamos esa canción *«No es por fuerza ni poder, sino por mi Espíritu, dice el Señor»*. Yo descubrí que mucha gente cantaba la canción y luego salía y usaba su propia fuerza y su propio poder para hacer la obra de Dios. Cantar la canción no hacía una diferencia muy grande.

Por lo tanto, con todas nuestras ocupaciones, nos habíamos vuelto completamente exhaustos. Estuvimos fuera del ministerio por dos años. Estuvimos fuera de todo. Denis pensó que nunca regresaríamos a trabajar a ningún tipo de ministerio de nuevo, y yo no tenía idea de lo que haría con el resto de mi vida si no volvía. Por dos años hicimos muy poco. Tratamos de hacer algunos trabajos, pero las cosas más simples se volvieron difíciles. Pensar en secuencia lógica por media hora era extremadamente difícil. Una tarea simple como podar el césped era un esfuerzo extremo para mí. Regularmente necesitaba dormir después de cortar el césped. No porque estuviera físicamente cansado sino porque estaba mentalmente exhausto debido al esfuerzo.

A través de toda la experiencia, empecé a re-examinar muchas cosas acerca de la vida cristiana. Siempre había hecho una prioridad el llenar toda obligación y tarea, en mis tiempos privados y quietos, mi preparación de sermones y el visitar a los enfermos. Cuando era un pastor había un flujo constante de personas que venían a mi oficina a compartir sus problemas conmigo, y ahora estaba cargando los problemas mientras ellos se sentían muy bien. Esto se acumuló en los años hasta que ya no podía manejarlo. Empecé a pensar que tenía que haber una forma mejor.

Presión para crecer

Luego de un par de años, recibí una invitación para ser pastor de una pequeña iglesia carismática en Auckland. Fui a visitarles y les conté acerca de mi estado de salud. Les dije lo que mi doctor y amigos cercanos pensaban. Ellos respondieron: «No te vamos a pedir que hagas mucho. Si tan solo puedes trabajar un par de días a la semana, ese sería un buen comienzo». Tuvieron tanta consideración para con nosotros. Pasamos los siguientes siete años ahí y ellos nos sanaron, nosotros les sanamos a ellos porque ellos también habían pasado por un momento difícil después de que sus ancianos y el pastor se habían ido. Fuimos capaces de enfocarnos en la gente para que regresara el Señor en vez de quedarse atascados en los problemas, y el Señor nos sanó a todos durante todo ese tiempo juntos.

En 1994, escuché acerca del avivamiento de Toronto así que fui a Canadá y fui movido profundamente por lo que Dios estaba haciendo ahí. Tenía el sentimiento de que una nueva vida estaba siendo soplada en mí. Podía sentir la bendición del Señor y sentí que estábamos empezando un nuevo día. Luego, en 1997, compramos un ticket alrededor del mundo para viajar con Jack Winter y ver lo que Dios podría hacer a través de nosotros. No desempacamos nuestro equipaje por los siguientes cuatro años y medio y todavía seguimos viajando en este ministerio, viviendo en el nuevo día.

Cuando me volví cristiano, el mensaje predominante que aprendí sonaba algo como esto:

«Ahora que te has vuelto cristiano, debes crecer en el Señor. Ahora tienes que madurar. ¡Tienes la victoria hermano! Sea lo que sea que venga, tienes que sobreponerte. Tienes que buscar a Dios y encontrarlo en medio de la situación, ¡debes ser victorioso!».

Así que había una presión continua para madurar. En aquellos días cantábamos una canción en particular, la cual odiaba cantar. Mucho de la letra es tomada de la Escritura pero había una línea que distorsionaba el significado de las Escrituras que había en la canción. Me disculpo con la persona que la haya escrito, pero la canción va algo así: *«Soy conquistador, soy victorioso, estoy reinando con Cristo. Estoy sentado en lugares celestiales con Él».* Ahora, todo eso es escritural. Pero luego viene una línea que yo no podía cantar: *«No conozco la derrota, solo destreza y poder».* Sé que se supone que sea una confesión positiva pero si tenía que decirla, sería una mentira porque había conocido mucha derrota en mi vida, no solamente destreza y poder.

El mensaje era continuamente reforzado: *«Tienes que pensar positivamente. ¡No puedes permitir ningún pensamiento negativo porque eres un vencedor! Debes caminar en fe y aferrarte a la victoria. Debes tener todo en orden, ser competente y lleno de fe. Debes conocer la Palabra, escuchar todos los mensajes, escuchar a todos los predicadores, y leer todos los libros. Necesitas volverte un cristiano que tiene-todo-lo-que-se-necesita, ¡un hombre de Dios maduro!»*

Había un dicho: «Cuando te vuelves cristiano, ¡tienes que tener todo en orden, bajo control!», me doy cuenta ahora que aún si tienes todo en orden, ¡sigue siendo solo una fachada! Mucho de nuestra confesión positiva es solo una fachada en vez de fe. Si podemos ser honestos acerca de dónde nos encontramos en vez de negar las realidades que vivimos, podemos ganar terreno espiritualmente. Muchas cosas que se nos fueron enseñadas a hacer fueron un tipo de negación y la negación no es victoria .

EL CABALLERO SOBRE EL CABALLO BLANCO

Hacer algunos años tuve una visión que resultó siendo un encuentro que transformó mi vida. En esta visión, estaba de pie en un bosque ancestral. Sabía que era un bosque ancestral por los árboles, eran cedros enormes con ramas enormes extendiéndose a lo ancho. Me recordó de los bosques de Sherwood en la historia de Robin Hood. Estaba ahí de pie sobre el suelo lleno de grama, y cuando miré, de repente vi que estaba parado en un camino antiguo que ya no era usado y tenía maleza cubriéndolo. Podía ver el rastro del camino doblándose alrededor de los árboles. De pie ahí, noté que algo más estaba saliendo del bosque acercándose a mí.

Cuando estuvo más cerca pude ver a un caballo blanco, y montado en el caballo blanco había un caballero medieval. Su armadura era brillante, de un blanco traslúcido o plateado. El caballero estaba sosteniendo una espada en el airc mostrando la parte plana de la cuchilla en vez de estar listo para el ataque. Su otro brazo estaba extendido con la mano abierta. ¡Lo extraño fue que no estaba sujetando ninguna rienda! A medida que se acercaba, podía ver que el caballo estaba *danzando*. Dos pasos hacia delante, dos pasos hacia atrás. Unos pasos hacia la derecha, otros hacia la izquierda. Repetía este movimiento una y otra vez. No había prisa. El caballero estaba ahí, con las manos levantadas, levantando la espada.

El caballero se acercó a mí despacio en su caballo danzante y mis ojos empezaron a apreciar otros movimientos. De la oscuridad del bosque había gente saliendo hacia el camino. El deslumbre de la luz que rodeaba al caballo y al que lo montaba estaba extendiéndose hacia la oscuridad del bosque. Algunas personas estaban llorando y algunas estaban riéndose. Otros estaban heridos y estaban gateando hacia la luz, siendo llenos de gozo. Algunos estaban danzando como pequeños niños, tomados de la mano, danzando en círculos. Algunos estaban de rodillas a la par del camino con sus manos levantadas a medida que pasaba el caballero, adorando al Señor. El caballero no era el Señor pero estaba llevando la gloria de Dios y estaba pulsando fuera de él e irradiando la oscuridad del bosque.

De repente me percaté que estaba parado en medio del camino. Pero no tenía nada que temer y no sentía que tenía que hacerme a un lado para dejarles pasar. Estuve ahí y el caballo llegó hacia donde yo estaba y paró. El caballero tenía abajo el visor en su casco así que su rostro estaba escondido. Parecía ser que no estaba interesado en mi ni había notado que yo estaba ahí. Simplemente se sentó ahí sin hacer movimientos. Luego sentí intuitivamente que había yo sido invitado a poner mi pie en el estribo en donde estaba el pie del caballero. Así que puse mi pie en el estribo sobre su pie cubierto por la armadura y me empuje para pararme a la par de él. El no había cambiado de posición para nada. Su espada todavía estaba levantada y su mano extendida. Le miré pero no podía ver su rostro por el visor, ya que las rencillas en el mismo no eran grandes, no se podía ver nada a través de él.

Extendí mi mano y levanté el visor para ver su rostro. Pero cuando lo hice, ¡no había rostro ahí! Ningún rostro en lo absoluto. ¡Levanté el casco y para mi sorpresa, ¡no había cabeza tampoco! Luego vi abajo por el cuello y adentro de la armadura había u pequeño niño --¡solo un pequeño niño! El pequeño niño tenía una gran sonrisa en su rostro, como diciendo: «¡Esta es la broma del siglo! Yo estoy solo sentado en este caballo y estamos danzando y todas estas cosas están sucediendo alrededor de mi, y la gente está saliendo a encontrarse con el Señor, la gente está siendo tocada y salva y sanada y bendecida y todo está ocurriendo—y ellos piensan que soy un gran caballero de Dios. ¡Pero solamente soy un pequeño niño!». Cuando vi eso, y vi el rostro del niño con la gran sonrisa, y por primera vez en mi vida empecé a entender de lo que se trata el ministerio cristiano.

La Iglesia es una fiesta

En los años, la iglesia ha sido descrita en muchas formas diferentes. Ha sido descrita como un ejército. Alguien escribió una vez un libro titulado *La Novia con las botas de combate*. Aun cuando nunca leí el libro, debo admitir que no me gustó el título. Imagínate yendo a una boda y la música empieza para que la novia camine hacia el altar. Aquí viene la novia . . . toc, toc, toc, toc. Los invitados se voltean para ver a la novia desfilando, sus botas de combate haciendo un ruido incómodo sobre el piso de piedra. No puedo llevarme a mi mismo a creer en esa descripción de la novia.

Hemos pensado que la iglesia es un ejército y que todos tienen que marchar en la procesión militar. La iglesia es una extensión variada de dones y libertad de cualquier cosa que hayamos soñado. La iglesia no fue diseñada para contener el mismo tipo de personas. Es un lugar donde la individualidad puede ser totalmente expresada en síntesis perfecta con otros. La iglesia es una sinfonía de dones bajo la dirección del Espíritu Santo. Algunos han descrito a la iglesia como un hospital, en donde todos estamos en camas hasta que alguien nos compone. Esa es una idea dominante en círculos eclesiales pero yo he descubierto la verdad. ¿Sabías lo que es la iglesia? *La iglesia es una fiesta.*

Como joven cristiano, a mi se me exhortaba constantemente a salir y salvar al mundo. ¡Por supuesto que el mundo necesita ser salvo! La respuesta es Jesús. Sin embargo, no es mi conocimiento o entendimiento (*aun* del cristianismo) lo que salva al mundo. Cuando salí de un período de desgaste, la gente venía a verme con su problemas. Les escuchaba, seguía repitiéndome en mi mente «este no es mi problema. No tengo que arreglar esto». Oraba para que el Señor les ayudara y les ministrara, porque no podía tomar esa carga yo mismo. Hay cosas que van a suceder en nuestra vida que son primordialmente entre el Señor y nosotros. La gente puede ayudarte pero no pueden cargarte. Así que aprendí a cómo evitar ser cargado con estas cosas y a ser como un pequeño niño.

SIENDO COMO NIÑOS

He descubierto una característica particular de la gente piadosa. Lo más maravilloso acerca de la gente que se parece a Cristo es que también son la gente más parecida a los niños. Jack Winter era como un niño de una forma increíble. El solamente creía en la biblia, y como resultado vio a Dios hacer muchas cosas sorprendentes.

Jack tenía una intercesora llamada Amy que oraba por él y subsecuentemente intercedía por nosotros. Tenía como ochenta años cuando la conocí. Vino a Nueva Zelanda, e intercedió por mí por dos semanas, por ocho horas al día, en lenguas. Esa fue su asignación. Trajo un amiga con ella y entraban a este cuartito, cerraban la puerta y escuchábamos los sonidos más increíbles saliendo de ese cuarto. Oraban con gran autoridad. Sin embargo, cuando paró de orar y salió del cuarto para sentarse a almorzar con nosotros, ¡era como una niña de tres años! Estaba bromeando todo el tiempo. Era tan divertido estar con ella y su risa tenía una pureza inocente sin sofisticación en lo mínimo. Justo como una niña pequeña que no tiene idea de cómo ser dignificada o sofisticada, así era ella. Era como una niñita.

Se nos había dicho tanto que necesitábamos crecer. Se nos había dicho que necesitábamos volvernos competentes y maduros, llenos de fe y poder. Se nos ha dicho que necesitamos aprender todas las lecciones y acumular conocimiento para que podamos dar siempre respuestas a las preguntas de la gente. Los predicadores frecuentemente me decían: «Si la iglesia está haciendo su trabajo verdaderamente, estaríamos haciendo esto o lo otro porque es nuestra responsabilidad arreglar este mundo». ¿Sabes en donde nos encontró Dios? Nos encontró en drenajes, en las cloacas y en callejones – a algunos literalmente. Teníamos vidas rotas y destruidas. No somos los nobles de este mundo. No somos los que se las saben todas. Somos los que no tienen esperanza, que no podían hacer nada bueno. El me encontró bajo un árbol en algún lugar del desierto. No sé por qué me escogió. Soy lo peor de la sociedad. ¿Por qué vino a buscarme?

Todo el propósito del hombre es *adorar a Dios y disfrutarlo por siempre*, dice la confesión de Westminster. Eso es suficiente. No necesitamos nada más. Esto aplica al ministerio tanto como a nuestras vidas personales. El cristianismo no es un camino a la eficacia sino *un camino hacia el volvernos como niños*. Mientras más nos volvemos como niños, más cerca estamos a Él. Y mientras más cerca estamos de él, más nos volvemos como niños. ¿Crees que Jesús nos dijo: «*A menos que sean como niños no podrán entrar al reino de Dios*» cuando en realidad había otro camino?

Los niños saben cómo disfrutar la vida. ¿Quién tiene más gozo? ¿Un abogado o un niño? ¿Quién puede reírse a carcajadas de una forma más libre? ¿Un arquitecto, un policía o una pequeña niña? La respuesta siempre es, un niño. ¿Por qué? Porque no están preocupados por la eficacia de los asuntos de la vida. Se reirán y reirán por algo por lo que nosotros ni siquiera sonreímos. Tienen una capacidad increíble de disfrutar el momento presente. En muchos casos el cristianismo como lo conocemos ha añadido a nuestras vidas la seriedad. Podemos caminar en la cuerda floja del temor de para no hacer las cosas incorrectamente o vivir de forma equivocada. Con razón los no creyentes nos ven y piensan: «¡*Yo no quiero ser así*!»

JESÚS ERA COMO UN NIÑO

Jesús mismo era extremadamente como un niño de corazón. Mateo 11:25 dice: «*En aquel tiempo Jesús dijo: "Te alabo, Padre, Señor del cielo y de la tierra, porque habiendo escondido estas cosas de los sabios e instruidos, se las has revelado a los que son como niños"*».

Me tomó varios años darme cuenta de que Jesús está de hecho hablando de sí mismo aquí. ¿Cuáles son «estas cosas» de las que Él habla aquí? Él está hablando de las cosas que ha estado enseñando en los capítulos precedentes. Si no se les eran reveladas a los sabios y prudentes, ¿*a quién* se les eran reveladas? *Se le fueron reveladas a Jesús*. Él era el que las estaba enseñando. *El Padre le enseñó estas cosas porque tenía el corazón de niño*. Él dijo: «*Mi doctrina no es de mí mismo*» (Juan 14:10). En otras palabras, «no he obtenido esto de deducciones teológicas. No tengo opiniones acerca de todos los temas doctrinales».

El también dijo: «*El hijo no puede hacer nada por su propia cuenta*» (Juan 5:19). En otras palabras «Hay algo en mí que puede hacer esas cosas que hago o enseñar lo que enseño. Los milagros que hago están sucediendo a través de mí, no de parte de mí. Las palabras que hablo no son mis palabras. Es el Padre viviendo en mí el que lo hace todo».

Él no dijo: «El Hijo *no quiere* hacer nada por su propia cuenta». Ni tampoco dijo: «El Hijo *ha escogido* no hacer nada por su propia cuenta». Él dijo «El Hijo no puede hacer nada por su propia cuenta». ¡Qué declaración tan sorprendente!

Yo digo esto con reverencia, pero Jesús era increíblemente incompetente.

Él tenía el corazón como de niño, no actuaba como los adultos de hoy en día.

Frecuentemente el día de hoy aspiramos a lo que es sabio y prudente. Jack Winter solía decir que esta revelación es frecuentemente difícil para pastores y líderes. Habiendo sido un pastor yo mismo puedo entender las presiones que líderes y pastores tienen. Los pastores frecuentemente reciben este mensaje como bueno para la congregación pero no aplicable al liderazgo. Los líderes de la iglesia necesitan abrir su corazón para lo que Dios tiene para darles.

La sabiduría es actuar correctamente en cualquier situación mientras la prudencia es tomar decisiones correctas por un bien futuro. Frecuentemente los pastores pueden estar enfocados en tratar de hacer cosas de la forma correcta -- «¿Cuál es la cosa correcta para decir? ¿Cuál la forma correcta de abordar esto? ¿Qué hacemos en una reunión de liderazgo? ¿Cómo nos preparamos para los siguientes cinco años? Lentamente se vuelve más y más acerca de cómo vivir tu vida ahora y cómo hacer todo "de la forma correcta". Jack creía que los pastores frecuentemente se habían vuelto "sabios y prudentes" y habían cerrado su corazón de niños.

No estoy diciendo que no deberíamos hacer estas cosas, pero no asumas que esto es madurez. Cuando empezamos a pensar en las líneas de *«así se ve la madurez, ahora soy un cristiano maduro porque hago estas cosas»*, lo que pasa es que tener sabiduría y prudencia se vuelve nuestro objetivo de vida, lo cual de hecho actúa como un bloqueo para recibir revelación. La revelación es dada a un corazón *como de niño*. Yo creo que esa es una de las razones por las cuales el Cuerpo de Cristo en el último siglo han hecho pocos avances hacia la revelación e intimidad con Dios. Nos hemos estado enfocando en volvernos sabios y prudentes, cuando el Señor de hecho nos está guiando en el camino de volvernos como niños.

El saberlo todo no es la felicidad

Hace algunos años estaba en Holanda en un lugar llamado Vlissingen. Mientras estaba tomando café con mi anfitrión una mañana él me dijo: «James, he descubierto algo. *El saberlo todo no te hace feliz»*. Esta declaración me afectó tremendamente. Desde que me volví cristiano me han recalcado que tenía que saber todo y ser un líder cristiano, tenía que tener una opinión acerca de todo. Tenía que saber lo que cada Escritura quería decir o al menos estar informado en todas las opiniones diferentes que están allá afuera. La presión era por *saberlo todo*.

Un tiempo después, mientras estábamos todavía en Holanda, yo era el conferencista en un campamento para hombres y estaba compartiendo un cuarto con un robusto holandés que hablaba con voz resonante. Subsecuentemente nos volvimos buenos amigos. El domingo, luego de que la última sesión había terminado, estábamos sentados en nuestra cama de literas esperando a que nos llevaran al aeropuerto de Ámsterdam. Al estar ahí sentados me hizo una pregunta acerca de un asunto de liderazgo, o algo que tenía que ver con un ministerio cristiano. Respondí: «Oh, pues no sé». Sus ojos se abrieron perceptiblemente, luego cayó acostado en su cama en una carcajada. Luego de un par de minutos me vio y dijo: «¿No sabes?». Yo dije: «No, no sé». El volvió a caer de espaldas sobre la cama, muerto de risa. Toda la cama temblaba cuando él se reía. Me senté ahí, impresionado de su reacción. Finalmente se volvió a sentar: «James, eres el predicador. *¡Tienes que saber!*». Verás, esa es la presión que recae sobre nosotros. La presión de acumular conocimiento, obtener sabiduría, y volvernos los expertos.

La canción de Paul Simon

Luego de que Denise y yo sufriéramos ese desgaste, nos fuimos a Australia a cumplir con los compromisos de hablar en JUCUM. Fue un tiempo horrendo en nuestras vidas. Estábamos totalmente exhaustos, pero el Señor nos ayudo en todas las cosas que necesitábamos hacer. Estábamos un día manejando a través de la parte salvaje desde Adelaida a Brisbane y acabábamos de pasar por un pueblo en New South Wales llamado Bourke. Hay un dicho que dice que si estás regresando "desde Bourke", quiere decir que estabas realmente hasta la parte más remota de la región. Así que estábamos conduciendo por esos caminos en los que puedes manejar durante doce horas sin que el panorama cambie.

Al conducir escuchábamos el álbum de Paul Simon titulado *Graceland* en el estéreo del auto. Una canción empezó a sonar con letra acerca de un personaje llamado Fat Charlie el arcángel. La letra decía «*Fat Charlie el arcángel irrumpió en el lugar. Dijo "no tengo ninguna opinión acerca de esto o de aquello"*». De repente

Denise y yo empezamos a reírnos. ¡Ni siquiera un «arcángel» tiene una opinión! ¡Está bien el NO saber! ¡Aún si eres un arcángel! Cuando nos empezamos a reír, la presión de crecer y ser fuerte, maduro y tener todo en orden empezó a disiparse. Luego de luchar por cinco años para volverme un hombre con conocimiento, la idea de que un «arcángel» no tenía idea fue de hecho un gran alivio.

«Ocupados, ocupados, ocupados»

Frecuentemente cuando visito iglesias, tengo la oportunidad de pasar tiempo con el pastor antes de la reunión en donde voy a predicar. Cada iglesia tiene su propia cultura, tal y como cada nación tiene su propia cultura. Visito muchas iglesias diferentes, así que cuando llego a un lugar por primera vez las antenas espirituales están listas, tratando de descifrar lo que la cultura y las creencias son de manera que se pueda construir una fluidez con ellos para comunicar efectivamente. Muchas veces le pregunto al pastor algunas cosas, las respuestas a dichas preguntas me dan mucha vislumbre. Una pregunta que le hago al pastor es «¿Cómo va tu iglesia?». Muchas veces, escucho algo parecido a lo que sigue:

«Oh, estamos muy ocupados. Aquí todo es "acción". Hay tanto ocurriendo, la iglesia está creciendo. Tenemos esta conferencia y aquel predicador por venir. Estamos extendiendo el estacionamiento y necesitamos ampliar la cocina. Hay viajes misioneros para África este fin de semana. El grupo de jóvenes está creciendo. De hecho, está tan grande que tenemos nuevos pastores viniendo para dedicarse a ellos. Y también necesitamos más servidores en el estacionamiento. Estamos reuniendo dinero para esto y para aquello. Queremos plantar una iglesia nueva aquí y otra por allá. El ministerio de mujeres ha despegado y estamos haciendo actividades de alcance el próximo mes».

Todo lo que escucho es «ocupados, ocupados, ocupados». Muchos pastores piensan que eso es lo que quieres escuchar. Si eres un conferencista invitado, quieren dar una buena impresión. Cuando escucho acerca del activismo pienso «Oh, oh. ¿Qué está ocurriendo de malo aquí?».

Imagina que vas con Jesús un día en el cual Él está caminando alrededor de Nazaret y le preguntas «¿Cómo va el ministerio, Jesús?»

«¡Oh, todo está muy ocupado, ocupado, ocupado! Nos vamos a Capernaúm esta tarde; necesitamos organizar un bote para que nos lleve porque la multitud va a ser muy grande. No podemos tener micrófonos pero podemos usar el agua. Y Lázaro acaba de morir así que se supone que vaya a Betania, y María y Marta están muy mal. Tuve que haber ido hace días pero ha habido tanta actividad. He estado hablando y enseñando en todos lados, y estoy trabajando con los discípulos, pero Pedro es un pequeño problema. Así que necesito solventarlo. Y luego estuve ocupado sacando a los cambiadores del templo. Ya sabes, alguien murió y quedé un poco retrasado y tuve que ir a otro lugar a levantar a otro de los muertos. Así que eso nos atrasó el calendario un poco, pero ya compusimos a la señora con el flujo de sangre así que vamos de camino –¡todo es vamos, vamos, vamos! Hay que entrenar a estos discípulos!

Si tú le hubieras preguntado a Jesús cómo estaba su ministerio, ¡no creo que Él te hubiera respondido con algo así! Probablemente habría respondido algo como: *«Padre es verdaderamente maravilloso. Hemos visto como Él ha hecho cosas sorprendentes. Solamente estamos participando de esto, tú sabes. Es increíble lo que Él está haciendo. No soy yo, ¡es Él! Él me dice qué decir y lo digo. Es increíble ver lo que pasa cuando digo lo que Él me dice que diga. Cuando toco a la gente, veo cosas espectaculares ocurrir. Vimos a este sujeto con un brazo lisiado y todo su brazo fue restaurado. ¡Fue simplemente maravilloso! ¡Este es un tiempo increíble!»*

Yo creo que Él hubiera estado lleno de gozo. Cuando los discípulos de Juan Bautista vinieron a Él con la pregunta: *«¿Eres tú el Mesías o estamos esperando a otro?».* Su respuesta fue: *«Vayan y díganle lo que escuchan y ven. Los ciegos ven, los cojos están caminando, los sordos están escuchando».* Él no sentía la necesidad de reafirmarle a Juan que Él era el Mesías. Yo creo que lo que Él estaba diciendo *verdaderamente*: «Lo que está ocurriendo es maravilloso. No estamos haciendo nada. Dios está haciendo todo. Solo somos niños pequeños jugando en el lodo y esto es tan divertido».

Como dije antes, he aprendido que el reino de Dios es una fiesta. Muy frecuentemente lo hemos convertido en un alcance evangelístico o una causa. Lo hemos vuelto en algo que es serio y pesado. Nunca es un problema invitar a nadie a una fiesta pero tendrás dificultad haciendo que vengan a la iglesia.

TU DEBILIDAD ES TU FUERZA

Pablo el apóstol sabía cómo era vivir en la paradoja de la debilidad. Él habla acerca de ello en su segunda carta a la iglesia de Corinto. Coincidentemente, encuentro muy interesante lo mucho que Pablo habla acerca de sí mismo. Sería fascinante estudiar las veces en las que Pablo usa las palabras «yo, mi, mío» en todos sus escritos. Seis veces en sus epístolas escribe «imítenme a mí». Yo sugeriría que cada vez que Pablo habla acerca de sí mismo hay que poner atención especial. En 2 de Corintios 12:7, Pablo empieza a hablar acerca de él mismo, diciendo:

«Para evitar que me volviera presumido por estas sublimes reve-laciones, una espina me fue clavada en el cuerpo, es decir, un mensajero de Satanás, para que me atormentara..»

No sabemos exactamente lo que era la espina en el cuerpo, pero lo que sabemos de seguro es que Pablo tenía un problema. No era un problema simple. Algunas personas han bromeado que la espina en su carne era su esposa. ¡No le doy nada de credibilidad a eso! Encuentro generalmente que los esposos son más una espina en la carne de sus esposas que al revés. Algunas personas han dicho que la espina en la carne era que él era corto de estatura porque el significado de su nombre es «pequeño». Para alguien de su calibre eso hubiese sido algo de muy poca importancia. No pienso que ser "algo bajito" habría afectado a Pablo para nada. Algunas personas han dicho que la espina en su carne era que Pablo se estaba quedando ciego. Ahora, esa es una posibilidad. Él dijo en Gálatas 4:15, *«sé que de haber sido posible, ustedes se hubiesen sacado los ojos para dármelos».* Él conocía el amor que le tenían porque había compartido el Evangelio con ellos. Sea cual sea la espina en su carne, él ciertamente tenía un problema. Lo que es más, él lo describe como siendo «un mensajero de Satanás», así que tuvo que ser algo muy perturbador para él.

En el siguiente verso, él dice:

«Con respecto a esto, le he pedido al Señor que me quite (esta espina)».

Ahora, Pablo había pasado por muchas cosas y había experimen-tado la gracia de Dios en todo ello. Pero sea lo que sea que eso haya sido, le causó el rogarle a Dios tres veces para que se lo quitara. Esto era obviamente algo muy difícil para él. Cuando le pidió al

Señor que lo librara, su petición fue denegada. Sin embargo, Dios le estaba diciendo «mi gracia es suficiente para ti, porque mi poder se perfecciona en la debilidad».

Mi poder se perfecciona en la debilidad. La verdad es, si quieres tener el poder de Dios reposando sobre ti y eres fuerte en ti mismo, de hecho te descalificas a ti mismo de tener el poder de Dios en ti. El poder de Dios viene sobre gente débil. La fuerza de Pablo no era que se había vuelto fuerte, competente y tenía todas las respuestas. De lo contrario, la gracia de Dios vino sobre él *debido* a su debilidad. El Señor dijo: «Mi gracia es suficiente para ti porque mi poder se perfecciona en la debilidad».

Lo que he descubierto es esto, si crees que Dios te usa porque oras mucho, o que te usa porque has hecho esto o aquello, *entonces tu corazón se quedará con la gloria para él mismo.* Puedes aún decir: «Te doy toda la gloria Señor», pero no es tu forma de hablar lo que el Señor toma en cuenta. Él ve tu corazón. Cuando tu corazón se queda con la gloria, Dios cortará el poder. No compartirá su gloria con nadie. Se requiere fe para saber que no hay nada que nos califique para que Dios nos use. Se requiere más fe para salir y confiar en que Dios nos usará. Se requiere mucha fe para dar un pazo en Dios cuando tienes un sentimiento sobrecogedor que no hay nada de valor en ti para Dios.

SÉ UN PEQUEÑO NIÑO

Un ejemplo más de la debilidad de Pablo puede ser vista en 1 Corintios, capítulo 2. De acuerdo a los académicos, la iglesia corintia era la más carnal de esa época. Esa era su reputación. Y aquí está Pablo, el estudiante rabínico por excelencia. Era académicamente brillante y lleno de celo religioso. Ahora, él ha recibido una increíble revelación del Señor, tanto que necesitaba una espina en la carne para evitar que se sintiera exaltado en su propio corazón. Aun el apóstol Pedro no pudo entender muchas de las cosas que Pablo dijo. Escribió (en 2 Pedro 3:16) «...(Pablo) *en casi todas sus cartas, donde habla de estas cosas, aun cuando entre ellas hay algunas que son difíciles de entender*». Pedro tenía dificultad para entender lo que estaba hablando Pablo. La profundidad de revelación de Pablo era obviamente increíble y aquí estaba él llegando a la iglesia en Corinto para tratar de poner orden.

En el capítulo 2 y versículo 3, escribió a la iglesia en Corinto, «*Yo estuve con ustedes en tanta debilidad que temblaba de miedo*».

No se apareció en Corinto diciendo: «Sé exactamente lo que está pasando con este sistema de crecimiento de iglesia. Sé cómo hacerlo. Puedo venir a arreglar todos sus problemas. Sé qué decirle a los líderes de la iglesia y al equipo. Tengo experiencia y práctica. Me sé el modus operandi. Arreglaré su iglesia en una semana—no hay problema—dos semanas a lo máximo». Él no dijo nada por el estilo, en vez de esto dijo «Vine a ustedes con tanta debilidad que temblaba de miedo». No sabía que hacer.

Pablo había aprendido el mismo secreto que Jesús sabía. Ser como un niño pequeño. Cuando pensamos que sabemos qué hacer, nos descalificamos.

Dios viene a nosotros en nuestra debilidad. No necesitas sabértelas todas todas para ser hijo o hija de Dios. Una de las mejores amigas de Denise, Katie, dio su testimonio en una reunión hace años y nunca he escuchado un testimonio tan devastador en toda mi vida. Mientras más compartía más sentía que era mi hermana. No había experimentado el mismo tipo de dolor pero podía identificarme a la realidad de su historia. Cuando la gente da una presentación de fuerza cómo se las saben todas, no tengo absolutamente ni idea de cómo identificarme con ellos. Sé que hay veces en las que *parece* que yo me las sé todas, y cuando viene la unción parece que yo tengo puesto una armadura reluciente. Puede verse como si yo fuera un caballero de Dios. *Pero quita el casco y ve hacia adentro.*

Ya no estoy en el juego

En el pasado solía pretender ser una persona competente y aprendí todos estos pequeños trucos para parecer fuerte. Luego empecé a ver que mi debilidad es de hecho mi mejor posesión. ¡Yo era un cazador que llegó a la salvación por error! ¡No era mi culpa! Una persona muy valiente profetizó sobre mí que me iba a convertir en un maestro de la Palabra. Esa fue la profecía más valiente que cualquiera pudo haber hecho si tú hubieras visto como me veía ese día en particular. Y yo estuve lo suficientemente loco como para creerlo. Así que me imaginé que, si iba a ser un maestro de la Palabra, mejor si la empezaba a leer lo más pronto posible. La he estado leyendo desde ese entonces y ahora siento como si estuviera parado en un río de revelación, sabiendo muy bien que no es por mi competencia.

En estos años recientes de nuestra experiencia cristiana, hemos estado disfrutando de la vida. Solo podría disfrutar esa libertad y gozo una vez que estuve libre para desatar todo lo que sentí que tenía que llegar a ser y volverme solo un pequeño niño en los brazos de mi Padre.

¿Sabías cual es la llave hacia esta revelación del amor del Padre? Vuélvete como un niño. *Un pequeño niño.* Mientras más trates de ser sofisticado y saberlo todo, leer todas las Escrituras, escuchar a los sermones y leer libros; mientras más quieras ser grande, fuerte, adulto, un hombre o una mujer de Dios con reputación, menos capacidad tendrás de conocer al Padre como un Padre que te ama.

En mi visión del caballero montado sobre el caballo en el bosque, me sentí como un pequeño niño...*pero estaba sentado en un caballo blanco.*

El caballo blanco representa al Espíritu Santo. Por eso es que si vas a transportarte de esa forma no puedes tomar las riendas. Tienes que ir a donde sea que Él dance. Y es una danza. Dios quiere usarnos. Él quiere que su poder sea revelado a través de nosotros pero la paradoja es que *tu debilidad es tu posesión más grande.* ¿Tienes debilidades en tu vida? ¿Tienes problemas que no sabes cómo componer? Son tus activos más importantes. Muy frecuentemente estamos esperando a que Dios los arregle antes de poder usarnos. Déjame decirte algo. Él te usa en medio de tu debilidad. Mientras más débil estás, más puede Él usarte. El obstáculo más grande es nuestra propia fuerza, nuestra propia competencia, nuestra acreditación y logros. El estar "lleno de fe y poder" y "tener todo resuelto" es nuestro bloqueo más fuerte.

Si tú tienes tu fuerza, Él te dejará obtener el producto de tu fuerza. Sin embargo, si puedes ser débil, obtendrás el producto de la fuerza de Él y eso es infinitamente mejor.

La gloriosa libertad de los hijos

~

Con todo mi corazón deseo que seas ayudado a abrir tu corazón para recibir el amor del Padre. Es el deseo más profundo del corazón de Dios el que sus hijos se acerquen a Él, que vivan en ese lugar de intimidad, escondidos en Cristo en el corazón del Padre. Pero hay más que solo esto. Hay una herencia mucho más gloriosa en la que podemos entrar, la herencia que le pertenece a los hijos y a las hijas. Él es nuestra herencia, pero más glorioso que eso es que, nosotros somos la herencia de Él. ¡Ahora, qué culminación! Esto es lo que nos espera. Es el panorama abriéndose de una forma tan amplia como la eternidad misma. Así que ajusta los cinturones de seguridad, y prepárate para la aventura de tu vida.

La forma en la que ministro ha asustado a algunos. Watchman Nee dijo que hay dos formas diferentes de hablar con unción. Una es dar un mensaje en donde sabes exactamente lo que vas a compartir de principio a fin y luego eres capaz de desatar la unción. La otra forma es seguir a la unción de manera que no sabes a donde vas o lo que vas a decir, lo cual es mucho más temible pero también más divertido en el sentido de que no estás seguro lo que el Señor va a decir de un momento a otro. Algunas veces me encuentro hablando, sin saber lo que estoy diciendo, y me encuentro siendo sorprendido por las cosas que oigo salir de mi propia boca. Muchas veces me encuentro diciendo algo y no tengo idea de lo que estoy hablando. Esto me pasó una vez en Alemania y, por supuesto, trabajando con un intérprete no tenía tanto tiempo de orar entre las frases que decía. Dije algo y no sabía porqué lo había dicho y sentí como que era el Señor. Estaba hablando acerca de cómo Dios ama venir y ser un Padre para todos nosotros en el día a día de nuestra vida. Él ama mostrar su amor al proveer cosas ordinarias como espacios de estacionamiento, por ejemplo. Cuando estaba predicando me escuché a mi mismo decir: «¡*Pero eso no es lo que Él está buscando*!».

¿QUÉ ESTÁ BUSCANDO ÉL REALMENTE?

Cuando lo dije, inmediatamente pensé: «Bueno...¿qué está buscando? » ¿Qué más podía haber? ¡Sentí que era el Espíritu Santo hablando pero no tenía la idea más remota de lo que Él estaba buscando! Dentro de mí mismo estaba diciendo: «Señor, ¿qué estás buscando en realidad?». Él no dijo nada, así que seguí hablando y dije: «A Él le encanta venir a la iglesia y ungir nuestra adoración. . .¡pero eso no es lo que Él está buscando!». «¿Qué estás buscando Señor?» ¡gritaba mi corazón!

Mi mente aceleraba pensando «¿qué voy a decir?», sentí como si estaba cavando un hoyo más y más profundamente, ¡y no iba a poder salir del mismo! No tenía idea de lo que iba a pasar, pero no había otra opción más que seguir hablando. Así que empecé a contar una historia acerca de una experiencia que Denise y yo habíamos tenido.

Conté la historia de cómo estuvimos en Holanda un par de años antes, conduciendo hacia la estación de trenes con mucha prisa. Los trenes en Holanda corren muy puntuales; no se retrasan ni por unos segundos. Si no estás ahí en el minuto exacto, pierdes el tren. Así que estábamos conduciendo a la estación para alcanzar nuestro tren. Teníamos cuatro minutos para estacionar el auto, salir de él, tomar nuestro equipaje, comprar el pasaje, ir a la plataforma y subirnos al tren. Así que estábamos sufriendo. Llegamos al garaje y estaba lleno. No solo eso, había cientos de bicicletas recostadas sobre las paredes del estacionamiento y nos dimos cuenta que era la hora más ocupada del día. Estábamos yendo arriba abajo por los corredores del lugar buscando un espacio vacío pero no había ni uno. Estaba totalmente lleno. Así que Denise oró: «Padre, ¿nos darías un espacio para estacionar?». Ella había empezado a orar en cuanto entramos al garaje porque pensó que necesitaba darle tiempo al Señor para enviar a alguien de vuelta a su carro. Requiere un poco de tiempo aun para Dios organizar estas cosas.

Así que al conducir y dar vueltas ella añadió: «¡Señor, haz a alguien sentir *solo un poco* enfermo hoy como para no ir a trabajar!». No conozco acerca de este tipo de teología pero así fue como ella oró de todas maneras cuando estábamos conduciendo por otra fila de espacios – y ella vio a un sujeto en el tope que había parqueado su carro y caminaba hacia nosotros. De repente paró, se volteó y regresó a su auto. Denise le gritó a Vince, quien estaba conduciendo: «¡Sigue a ese hombre!». Así que lo seguimos. Al dar la vuelta en la esquina, se subió a su auto, retrocedió y se fue. ¡Un espacio vacío! Nos metimos ahí inmediatamente y Denise dijo: «Está bien Señor, ¡ahora lo puedes hacer sentir bien!». Era el espacio más cercano a la puerta de la estación. Salimos rapidísimo, compramos los tickets, nos apuramos en la plataforma arrastrando nuestro equipaje, bajamos las escaleras y cruzamos la otra plataforma, subimos otras escaleras hacia la plataforma en donde nuestro tren estaba esperando, y nos subimos al tren. ¡Las puertas se cerraron justo detrás nuestro! ¡Apenas y lo logramos!

Así es Él. Él ama ser un padre para sus hijos de esa manera. Pero, al estar hablando ese día, seguía diciendo: «¡Pero eso no es lo que Él está buscando. Él ama ungir nuestras cruzadas, nuestros alcances, nuestros planes misioneros a las naciones, ¡pero eso no es lo que Él está buscando!». Esa frase seguía viniendo y podía sentir como la tensión subía en el auditorio. Todos estaban pensando: «¿Qué es lo que Él está buscando?». . . ¡y yo no sabía! Finalmente, cuando lo estaba diciéndolo de nuevo, Él me mostró.

Verás, Él ama venir y ser un padre para nosotros en todas las cosas en nuestras vidas, pero lo que Él realmente está buscando es que nos volvamos hijos e hijas de Él en todo lo que Él hace. Él está queriendo que no solo le conozcamos como padre en *nuestro* mundo, sino que nos volvamos hijos e hijas de Él en *su* mundo, en *su* perspectiva de vida.

Una cosa que había notado acerca de padres y madres es que ellos quieren que sus hijos experimenten la calidad de vida similar o *mejor* que la suya propia. Sea cual sea el nivel de educación que tengan, quieren que sus hijos estén aún mejor educados. Siempre quieren lo mejor para sus hijos. Él es nuestro Padre y su deseo es que nos volvamos hijos e hijas *apropiados* a quien Él es.

Cuando empezamos recién a escuchar acerca del amor del Padre, pensamos que solo era para sanidad emocional. Luego nos dimos cuenta que hay mucho más que eso de lo que había pensado jamás. Él derrama su amor en nuestros corazones y nos sana de los traumas de nuestras vidas pero ese solo es el punto de comienzo.

Muchos de nosotros empezamos a experimentar el amor de Dios y pensamos: «Oh, ahora estoy sano y puedo regresar a hacer lo que estaba haciendo antes porque ahora soy una persona que ha sido sanada». El propósito de Dios es mucho más que eso. Él quiere que aprendamos a caminar continuamente delante de Él en debilidad. Su deseo es que nos acostumbremos a tener el mismo sentido de vulnerabilidad y dependencia que tenía Jesús. Uno de los secretos más grandes de la vida cristiana es aprender a estar cómodos con las debilidades en lugar de luchar contra ellas.

Muchas veces nos humillamos para ser débiles *en privado* para obtener sanidad pero nuestro Padre quiere que aprendamos a vivir en ese lugar. La vulnerabilidad se siente muy arriesgada. Dios no quiere que hagamos una visita esporádica a la humildad, sino que *vivamos* ahí. A medida que aprendemos a vivir en ese lugar vulnerable de necesitar constantemente su amor y de identificación creciente con las palabras «el Hijo no puede hacer nada por sí mismo», entonces Dios nos puede usar. Puedes alcanzar las alturas en Dios que no han sido alcanzadas antes lejos de la humildad. Así que cuando aprendemos a vivir ahí, Él puede obrar en nosotros como hijos e hijas. Esto es lo que empecé a ver. El Padre quiere que nos volvamos e hijas *apropiados* con respecto a quien Él es.

Cuando me encontré a mi mismo hablando esto en Alemania por primera vez, fue en los comienzos de una revelación que no solo empezó a cambiar mi vida, sino también mi identidad. En ese momento de mi vida había estado pensando «bueno, tenemos un éxito relativo como ministerio itinerante, lo cual estoy disfrutando más que cualquier otra cosa que haya hecho en la vida. Tenemos suficiente dinero para vivir. Está funcionando para nosotros de manera práctica». Estaba pensando: «¡Esto es! Soy un predicador itinerante viajando alrededor del mundo hablando acerca del

Padre; luego me voy a casa, descanso, y vuelvo a viajar. ¡Está funcionando bien!».

Pero cuando vi que Dios nos estaba llamando a ser hijos e hijas apropiados a quien Él es, en *su* perspectiva del universo—fue ahí cuando empecé a pensar que necesitaba encontrar una dirección en la vida apropiada a un hijo de Dios y no solo a un predicador itinerante. ¿Qué podía hacer con mi vida para que eso me convirtiera en un hijo *apropiado* a mi Padre?—Porque mi Padre resulta ser, ¡el Dios Altísimo! Ahí fue cuando empecé a vislumbrar todo este sueño de ver el amor del Padre salir de toda corriente del cristianismo, a toda cultura, a toda nación, y a toda persona en el mundo. Así empezó la historia. Empezamos a desarrollar escuelas en las cuales la gente pudiera ser impactada tan profundamente como fuera posible con una experiencia del amor del Padre, porque una vez llega a tu corazón, todo tu mundo cambia.

¿Cómo es Dios?

Cuando empiezas a considera lo que significa ser un hijo o una hija apropiada a quien el Padre es, esto te lleva a otra pregunta. ¿Cómo es mi Padre? ¿Cuáles son los conceptos más grandes que describen quien es mi Padre? Estos son los atributos que necesitamos explorar para movernos a ser hijos apropiados a quien Él es. ¿Cuáles son unas de las palabras más importantes o conceptos que le describen? Déjame describir algunos atributos familiares que me vienen a la mente. Dios es verdad, es compasivo, es relacional. ¡Sí! Es salvación, fe, esperanza y gozo, todo esto describe su naturaleza. ¡Absolutamente! Otros que se me ocurren como, misericordioso, glorioso, santo. Luego podíamos mencionar los «omnis». Omnisciente, omnipotente, omnipresente.

Estaba pensando acerca de estos atributos de Dios y otra palabra me vino a la mente. Era una palabra que no había considerado como describiendo la naturaleza de Dios. Lo que es más, nunca había escuchado a ningún conferencista cristiano usando esta palabra tampoco. Era la palabra "libre". Dios es LIBRE.

La libertad es probablemente una de las cosas más preciosas para el corazón humano. Vemos cintas acera de la libertad, leemos libros acerca de la emancipación, escuchamos música que expresa libertad. ¿Por qué el personaje de William Wallace en el film *Braveheart* captura nuestra imaginación? Es porque todo en nosotros responde a un hombre que daría su vida por su propia libertad, la de su gente y su nación. La libertad es uno de los problemas más grandes que encaramos como raza humana. Más que cualquier otra cosa, la gente quiere ser libre. Lo opuesto a la libertad es la esclavitud. No puedo imaginarme nada peor que la esclavitud. ¡Preferiría estar muerto! La esclavitud tiene que ser una de las cosas más crueles que la raza humano haya diseñado. No hay decisión que tú o yo podamos hacer como individuos, para nada, si somos esclavos. No tienes control sobre lo que haces de un momento a otro. No tienes control sobre lo que comes, o lo que te pones como ropa. Si te casas, podrías terminar separados de por vida si uno o los dos son vendidos a lugares diferentes. La esclavitud de niños es aun peor. Va contra todo lo que es libre dentro de nosotros. Hay algo en nosotros que tiende hacia la esperanza, que cree en algo mejor.

La libertad es intrínseca a la naturaleza y al corazón de Dios. Él es *libertad total*. La libertad siempre es medida por limitaciones. ¿Tiene Dios limitaciones? El puede hacer cualquier cosa, ¿no es cierto? Él puede crear cualquier cosa que quiere. No hay límites para su libertad. Bueno, hay una cosa que no puede hacer.

Él no puede pecar. Eso no es una limitación aunque solía pensar que la era, hasta que entendí la naturaleza del pecado. La gente me decía: «el pecado es una cosa horrible, terrible. ¡No lo hagas! Dios lo odia. Está mal. ¡Es malvado!». Pero estas explicaciones no satisfacían mi alma para nada porque eran comportamientos los que estaban siendo etiquetados como pecados que no parecían lastimar a nadie más. ¿Por qué eran estas cosas en particular tan malas? Hay muchas cosas que son malas obviamente pero habían otros pecados en los que honestamente no miraba mal alguno. Hay cosas que permitimos en nuestras vidas porque no entendemos completamente lo que está mal acerca de ellas o no vemos la maldad en ese comportamiento en particular. Por eso es tan malo el pecado. Como le dijo Dios a Caín: «*el pecado está a la puerta y su deseo es dominarte*» (Génesis 4:7). El deseo del pecado es siempre dominarnos y cuando nos involucramos en el pecado, sus cadenas nos enredan y empiezan a arrastrarnos y a botarnos. La razón por la que Dios no quiere que pequemos no es tanto porque el pecado sea «malo» (por así decirlo) sino porque él sabe que destruirá nuestra alma. Nos arrastrará más y más profundo a una atadura de la cual no hay escape si no es por la sangre de Jesús.

Así que cuando decimos que Dios no puede pecar es porque Él no pierde su libertad. Él no será dominado por nada. Él siempre será libre. Nunca había realizado que la libertad era tan importante para Dios. Lo que es más, empecé a ver esto cada vez que leía la biblia. Pasajes tales como Romanos 8:15, 2 Corintios 6:18 y Gálatas 4:6 todos hablan acerca de nosotros como hijos e hijas de Dios llegando a esa misma experiencia de *libertad* que Él disfruta.

LAS LIBERTADES DE ESTE MUNDO

Cuando vemos la libertad desde nuestra perspectiva humana,

parecería que aquellos que poseen más libertad en este mundo son probablemente los más ricos. Si tienes mucho dinero, puedes hacer lo que quieras. Mientras más dinero tengas, más libertad tendrás también. Hace algunos años el actor John Travolta voló a Nueva Zelanda en su propio jet, el cual él piloteó. Estaba volando al aeropuerto de Auckland y estaba llegando al punto en donde tendría que entrar a un patrón de aterrizaje. Por capricho de repente decidió no aterrizar sino volar a lo largo de Nueva Zelanda y admirar el país de primero Así que voló por sobre toda la isla del norte, y la del sur, viendo a las montañas y luego regresó a Auckland. ¡Solo para ver! Tuvo que haber costado decenas de miles de dólares solo el ver por la ventana y observar lo que quería. Si tienes el dinero puedes hacer casi todo lo que quieras.

Imagina por un momento, que te despiertan una mañana con una llamada telefónica. Al contestar, descubres que has heredado una cantidad enorme de dinero. Tanto dinero que, si empezaras a gastarlo todos los días por el resto de tu vida, nunca lo agotarías. Imagínate eso. Podrías comprar cualquier cosa. No tendrías limitaciones. Si tuvieras todo ese dinero, ¿qué harías? ¿Viajarías alrededor del mundo? ¿Irías a ver los parques más hermosos para explorarlos? ¿Comprarías una isla? ¿Qué pondrías en la isla? ¿La mansión más lujosa que puedas imaginar? ¿Te irías de compras? ¡Por supuesto que sí? ¡Todos nos iríamos de compras! Imagina que quieras ir a Hawái pero todos los pasajes estaban agotados, ¡entonces podrías comprar la aerolínea misma! Y podrías ir a donde quisieras, cuando tú quisieras. Tal vez te podrías quedar en el hotel más fino de Mónaco durante algún tiempo. Tal vez sería posible comprar el hotel entero. Las opciones y oportunidades son casi ilimitadas. ¡Si eres lo suficientemente rico, tienes toda la libertad en el mundo!

Uno de mis sueños era ir a Alaska. Eventualmente reuní suficientes millas aéreas para ir. Así que, empezando en Fairbanks, pedí aventón hasta Anchorage, lo cual me tomó nueve días. Un fulano me llevó a volar en su Piper Cub de dos asientos, sobrevolando por bosques, buscando alces y osos desde el aire. Fui a pescar salmón con otros amigos y ahí estaba yo en el agua, capturándolos uno tras otro. ¡Habían huellas de oso en la arena detrás de mí, lo cual fue un poco desconcertante!

Cuando cumples un sueño, tienes un sueño menos. Eventualmente te quedarás sin sueños. Si tienes todo el dinero en el mundo para hacer lo que quieras, fácilmente cumplirías tus sueños en tal vez, cinco años. Pero te acostumbrarías a ello y lentamente tu perspectiva cambiaría y la vida perdería su emoción y su diversión.

Hace muchos años leí un artículo en la revista *Time* escrito por un psiquiatra de los archi-millonarios. Declaró; «*La desesperanza de la gente ultra rica es impresionante*». ¿No es eso interesante? Los ultra ricos pueden tener toda la libertad de este mundo, pero su desesperanza es increíble. Si todos tus sueños se cumplen, luego ya no hay nada por lo cual vivir. Tengo sueños que sé que no se cumplirán pero disfruto el sueño porque el mismo acto de soñar te da vida. Si no tienes sueños y no hay nada más que quieras hacer, tu alma se muere. Los sueños son increíblemente importantes para nosotros. *Lo que esto revela es que el corazón humano tiene la capacidad de soñar libertades que van más allá de lo que el mundo tiene para ofrecer.* Este mundo no puede llenar tus sueños y este mundo no puede darte la libertad para la cual fue diseñado tu corazón. No fuimos diseñados para la libertad limitada de este mundo. Fuimos diseñados para la misma libertad que Dios experimenta.

¿Hacia donde vamos?

El capítulo número ocho de Romanos explica cosas acerca del cristianismo que nunca había considerado antes. Habla de ser hijo y muestra a donde nos está llevando Dios. Muchas veces solo vemos los beneficios de una verdad en particular pero no la base de toda la realidad. Por ejemplo, podemos pensar que echar fuera demonios es el propósito de ser llenos del Espíritu, en vez de ser un producto de lo que nos estamos *convirtiendo* en Dios. Nuestra identidad en Dios es mucho más grande que la habilidad de hacer grandes cosas para Él.

Desde el capítulo 1 hasta el capítulo 8, Pablo está dando un panorama general de los propósitos de Dios en toda la historia, mostrando cómo Él está obrando en el mundo. Él termina esta imagen con la culminación en medio del Romanos 8. Luego de eso, hace una maravillosa declaración: «*Si Dios es por nosotros, ¿quién contra nosotros?*» y «*¿Qué nos puede separar del amor de Cristo?. . . Ni lo alto ni lo profundo ni ninguna otra cosa creada nos puede separar del amor de Dios en Cristo Jesús Señor nuestro*». Estas son declaraciones maravillosas y poderosas.

Deseo llamar tu atención de regreso al verso 22, a la declaración que dice «*. . . porque sabemos que toda la creación gime a una con dolores de parto hasta este día*». Como hombre, no sé mucho de los dolores de parto. Sin embargo, estaba con Denise cuando estaba dando a luz a Mathew, nuestro hijo menor. Pasó por todo el parto sin hacer un solo ruido. Tampoco usó ningún tipo de analgésico. Yo me sentía tremendamente orgulloso de ella pero me enfermé al verla, viendo la agonía que ella sentía. Y aunque no emitió sonido, casi rompió un hueso de mi mano-- ¡Así que sí se un poco acerca de los dolores de parto! La gente me dice que el parto es una experiencia completamente absorbente. Es imposible pensar acerca de algo más cuando estás dando a luz. Pablo usa esta metáfora para describir la intensidad del deseo de Dios de dar a luz a algo. ¡Toda la creación está en dolores de parto tratando de dar a luz algo! Hay un deseo increíble en Dios de que su creación sea desatada de las consecuencias de la caída y obtenga la libertad.

Dios es extremadamente intencional con lo que Él está haciendo en nuestras vidas. Algunas veces podemos ver nuestra fe como un apéndice de nuestras vidas. Estamos ocupados llenando otros roles: «Soy un arquitecto, un banquero, un policía, un contador, un líder en los negocios, un miembro de equipo, una mamá, un papá, un mentor, un atleta...oh, y también soy cristiano». Pero ser cristiano significa que Dios tiene la alta intención de completar una obra en ti, convertirte en eso que Él diseñó. El está obrando muy intencionalmente. No es un hobby. Lo es todo para Él. Él está lleno de propósito en lo que está haciendo.

Si regresamos al verso 19, hay una declaración hermosa que no captura toda la intensidad de esa verdad, «...*porque con fuertes ansias la creación tiene expectativas de la relevación de los hijos de Dios*». ¡El enfoque de Dios en todo el curso de la historia humana es ver a sus hijos e hijas surgir! Yo creo, que a medida que la gente que vaya más y más adentro en la revelación de Dios como nuestro Padre, experimente su amor y camine con Él de la misma manera en la que Jesús caminó, vamos a ver más hijos e hijas de dios surgiendo, *con una autoridad más allá de lo que has visto o experimentado antes.*

Esta será una clase de autoridad diferente. Hemos experimentado la autoridad de la Palabra. Hemos experimentado la autoridad del Espíritu. Hemos experimentado la autoridad de los dones ministeriales. Hemos experimentado la autoridad del oficio del ministerio. But there is a greater authority. The authority of the Father! ¡Y solo viene sobre los hijos! Cuando la autoridad del Padre viene, será totalmente inyectada con amor, verdad, poder, gracia, ternura, amabilidad, sabiduría, y todos sus atributos paternales. Será una autoridad que el mundo no podrá soportar. Cuando esa autoridad venga, vamos a ver a *hijos* e *hijas* de Dios saliendo de toda nación.

LA AUTORIDAD DE LOS HIJOS E HIJAS

Ahí es hacia donde va el cristianismo. Ese es el objetivo más grande de la creación. Cuando los hijos de Dios se revelen en la imagen de Cristo vamos a ver a hombres y mujeres surgir de toda nación con una capacidad increíble de hablar desde el corazón del Padre.

Más allá de la autoridad de simplemente creer la palabra, más allá de la autoridad de ser lleno del Espíritu Santo, pero con la autoridad de la persona del Padre estampada en sus corazones y reveló a su semejanza.

Beyond the authority of simply believing the Word, beyond the authority of being filled with the Holy Spirit, but with the authority of the personhood of the Father stamped into their hearts and revealed in His likeness. Dice que «*...toda la creación gime esperando la revelación de los hijos de Dios*». *¡De esto se trata!*

¡Él nos está llamando a ser hijos e hijas apropiados a quien Él es! Llevando la marca, la estampa y la *autoridad* del Padre sobre nosotros. Los dos testigos en Apocalipsis 11 son un buen ejemplo del resultado del propósito del Padre. Ellos atormentaron a los líderes del mundo con su predicación y nadie los podía matar

con ninguna arma que el mundo pudiera idear hasta que Dios lo permitió. ¡Los líderes del mundo están tan aliviados de su muerte que celebran con una fiesta! Pero Dios los levanta de los muertos a la vista de todo el mundo y los lleva al cielo. Te animo a que leas acerca de ellos para obtener una vislumbre de lo que es tener autoridad como hijo.

Cuando vemos lo que Pablo está diciendo, que «... toda la creación está gimiendo por los hijos de Dios sean revelados» vemos la descripción de esto en el verso 21, «... porque la creación misma será liberada de la atadura de la corrupción hacia la gloriosa libertad de los hijos de Dios». ¡La gloriosa libertad de los hijos de Dios! Cuando vemos a lo que significa ser hijos e hijas del Padre, esto nos muestra que su llamado hacia nosotros es que seamos libres como Él es libre.

Esto es lo que todo buen padre quiere para su hijo—tener el mismo nivel de experiencia de vida que él tiene. Tenemos un Padre que no es comparable con un padre humano sino que Él es el Padre de la cual todas las familias de la tierra toman nombre. En otras palabras, todos tomamos nuestra identidad como familia y como seres humanos del hecho de que Él es nuestro Padre. ¡Somos parte de la relación de familia que existe en la Trinidad! Él es el Padre, el Padre de verdad y ahora somos sus hijos e hijas, parte de la realeza. Él ha puesto su Espíritu en nosotros y nos está llamando a venir a su amor, a experimentar su paternidad hasta que crezcamos en hijos e hijas apropiados a quien Él es.

Hubo un movimiento hace algunos años llamado «los hijos manifiestos de Dios» pero no tenían la revelación del Padre. No puedes ser un hijo si no tienes una revelación del Padre. El ser hijo no es acerca de ser hijo. El ser hijo es acerca del Padre porque tú solo eres un hijo o hija verdadero cuando tienes una relación con un padre o una madre. Eso es lo que significa ser hijo. Y así, a medida que crecemos en este asunto de ser hijos, Él nos está trayendo a la *libertad gloriosa* de los hijos de Dios.

¿QUÉ TAN LIBRE ES DIOS?

El tipo de libertad a la que somos llamados va más allá de lo que pensamos. Cuando le das tu vida al Señor, Él te perdona tus pecados y eres libre. Juan 8:36 dice «Si el Hijo te hace libre, eres verdaderamente libre». Muchas veces relacionamos eso a ser simplemente libres de pecado y ser nacidos de nuevo, pero esa libertad va mucho más allá. ¡Ese es solo el comienzo!

Hay un verso en Gálatas que nunca he entendido en realidad, no hasta que empecé a ver este tema de la libertad. En Gálatas 5:1 dice: *«Es para libertad que Cristo nos libertó»*. Siempre me había preguntado acerca de eso, porque no sabía lo que significaba. ¿Por qué repitió Pablo dos veces la palabra "libertad"? ¿Por qué no decía solamente «Dios nos ha llamado a scr libres»? El era muy deliberado acerca de su uso del lenguaje porque es *para libertad* que Cristo nos libertó. Solía pensar que la razón principal por la cual hemos sido hechos libres era para ser libres de las ataduras del pecado. No es así. Es *para libertad* que Cristo nos libertó. ¿Por qué? Es porque *la libertad es nuestro destino*. El nos ha hecho libres porque la libertad es tan maravillosa, no porque la atadura es tan terrible. Quiere que caminemos en su libertad y esta libertad es una cosa increíble.

Soñamos acerca de esta libertad. Creo que nuestros sueños salen del jardín del Edén, del mismo corazón de Dios. Hay un eco del jardín del Edén adentro de nosotros. Nuestras expectativas de cómo nos debería de tratar la vida en términos de justicia llegan hasta el mismo jardín del Edén. A pesar de las injusticias que abundan en este mundo presente habrá un día de justicia perfecta.

Somos llamados a ser libres como Jesús, como el Padre. Pero, ¿qué tan libre es Dios? Aquí es donde todo se pone mejor.

Una cosa que me gusta de Jesús es que Él estuvo libre de impuestos. Más precisamente, Él pagaba sus impuestos, pero era libre de *los métodos del capitalismo por los cuales obtuvo el dinero para pagar sus impuestos.* En Mateo 17, Pedro fue a Jesús con una pregunta. Voy a parafrasearlo: «Señor, el cobrador de impuestos está a la puerta. ¿Pagamos *nosotros* impuestos?». Jesús básicamente respondió: «Sí, los pagamos, pero no estamos limitados a los caminos del mundo». Luego le dijo a Pedro que fuera a pescar, diciéndole: «Cuando pesques algo, el pez tendrá una moneda en su boca y será suficiente para ti y para mí». Me fascina que Jesús no haya incluido a los otros discípulos en este milagro. Solo fue Pedro el que le preguntó a Jesús y pudo ser testigo de la libertad en la que operaba Jesús. Así que Jesús fue libre de los sistemas de impuesto de este mundo.

Los dones del Espíritu en los que Jesús operaba eran una demostración de su libertad de las limitaciones del entendimiento humano. No era tanto que Jesús tenía un ministerio de sanidad, ¡sino que Él era *libre de enfermedad*! Él era libre de todo lo que el enemigo tenía. Él no solo sanaba a la gente sino les daba libertad de la enfermedad. Él los liberaba de su prisión de dolor y enfermedad porque Él caminaba en esta libertad.

También fue *libre de los límites de la educación*. El sabía cosas que no se pueden aprender en un aula de colegio. El era libre para funcionar en la perspectiva de Dios con respecto al conocimiento. La Escritura dice que «*Jesucristo fue hecho sabiduría de Dios para nosotros de parte de Dios*» (1 Corintios 1:30). Podemos entrar a la sabiduría de nuestro Padre. Podemos apropiarnos del conocimiento que Él tiene.

Jesús fue libre de las limitaciones de nuestro conocimiento terrenal. Fue libre de la información que entra por los cinco sentidos, a través del aprendizaje y la educación. Fue libre del conocimiento generalmente aceptado y obtuvo el conocimiento que fue más allá del entendimiento terrenal. Caminó sobre el agua, no porque Él haya querido caminar sobre el agua, sino porque era libre de la gravedad. Pedro no era tan libre. Él vio al agua y pensó «Aaargh, ¡me voy a hundir!» y se hundió hasta que vio a Jesús para que le liberara de su incredulidad. Jesús era libre de ese tipo de pensamiento. Vemos esto cuando fue tomado por las nubes y ascendió a su padre. ¿No te gustaría volar? ¿Por qué sueñas volar si es imposible que alguna vez lo harás?

We see this when He was taken up through the clouds and ascended to His Father. Wouldn't you like to fly? Why do you dream of flying if it is impossible that you ever will?

NACIMOS EN UNA PRISIÓN

Imagina a un niño que ha nacido en una prisión sin ventanas. Crece en una prisión, entre otros prisioneros, nunca sabiendo que hay una vida fuera de la prisión. Toda su perspectiva de existencia es el sistema penitenciario. No conoce nada más. A medida que el tiempo pasa, se familiariza con todo el sistema de prisión y aun aprende a usar algo de ello para aventajar a otros y tener beneficios que otros no tienen. Aprende a manipular el sistema porque se ha vuelto tan inteligente acerca de la forma en la que opera la prisión y acerca de lo que puede y no puede hacer para salirse con la suya. Pero todo lo que hace *sigue estando dentro de la prisión*. El nunca ha ido al océano, nunca ha visto las montañas, no sabe nada de las granjas. De hecho, no ha visto nada excepto barras de prisión, muros de piedra y el régimen de la prisión. El podrá pensar que tiene una buena vida pero sabemos que él no sabe mucho acerca de las maravillas de la vida.

El punto es que cada uno de nosotros ha nacido en esa prisión. Sir Walter Raleigh hizo una declaración increíble: «El mundo no es nada más que una prisión gigantesca». Se llama «este mundo», esta realidad física y pensamos que esto es todo lo que hay en la vida, esta es toda la extensión de la existencia. Algunos de nosotros nos hemos vuelto diestros en manipular los sistemas de este mundo. Pensamos: «Si puedes hacer que la vida sea mejor para ti y puedes obtener cosas mejores del sistema del mundo, ¡bien por ti!». Vivimos nuestras vidas creyendo que esto es lo mejor que la vida tiene que ofrecer—pero no es cierto.

La realidad, querido lector, es que somos hijos e hijas de Dios. Pero cuando Adán y Eva pecaron un velo cayó sobre la raza humana y obscureció la realidad de quienes somos. *Somos hijos e hijas del Dios Altísimo y Él nos está llamando a su libertad.* El nos está llamando a ver a quien es nuestro Padre y a estar vivos a una vida apropiada a quien Él es. Cuando empezamos a vivir expectantes, creyendo y viendo lo sobrenatural, viendo más allá de lo que percibimos como «real«, más allá de lo que está frente a nosotros, más allá de los sentidos, y empezamos a soñar acerca de lo que podemos ser en Él, empezamos a alcanzar nuestro estado de hijos. La maravillosa verdad es que dios nos está llamando a algo más grande de lo que realizamos. El mundo tratará de encerrarte.

Algunas veces aún la iglesia tratará de encerrarte en las limitaciones de trabajar dentro del sistema. Pero somos hijos e hijas del Dios Altísimo.

Experimentando la libertad gloriosa

Déjame terminar contando unas historias. Estas historias muestran como esta libertad gloriosa opera y nos da un vistazo en el tipo de vida que podemos esperar como hijos e hijas apropiados del Padre. Dos de las historias son de experiencias de amigos y una es de mi propia experiencia.

Una de las amigas de Denise estaba sentada en su casa cerca de Toronto, orando. De repente se dio cuenta que estaba gravitando sobre el suelo. Salió del techo de su casa hacia la noche estrellada. Las paredes tampoco pueden retener a Jesús. Salió hacia el cielo y empezó a caminar a través del aire, moviéndose a una velocidad tremenda sobre el océano Atlántico, luego a través de Europa. Podía ver cómo todo pasaba debajo de ella. Era tan real como cualquier otro momento de su vida. Cuando llegó a Rusia, empezó a descender hasta que atravesó el techo de una pequeña casa, atrás de los bosques de Siberia. Se encontró de pie en el piso de una cocina y un anciano estaba recostado sobre la mesa—llorando. Puso sus manos en sus hombros y empezó a orar, y al orar por él, el gozo del Señor vino a su corazón.

Cuando él estaba llorando de gozo, ella salió por el techo otra vez y voló a Suramérica, se encontró orando por alguien más ahí y luego voló de regreso a su propia casa. Nunca había experimentado nada como esto antes. Estaba tan maravillada. Un día le dijo a Bob Jones el profeta acerca de esto y le preguntó: «Bob, ¿qué piensas de esto?» y él le dijo: , solo te estas volviendo una cristiana de verdad, ¡eso es todo!».

Otro amigo de Minneapolis estaba orando en su cuarto una noche cuando sintió una corriente de aire contra su rostro. Abrió sus para encontrarse de rodillas sobre un embarcadero. Había estado orando en las horas tempranas de la mañana, pero en el muelle la luz del sol brillaba con fuerza. Sorprendido, vio a su alrededor, preguntándose qué estaba pasando. De repente vio a una muchacha gritando, en pánico, así que corrió hacia ella y descubrió que su amiga se había caído al agua y tenía dificultad para salir. Ninguna de las dos podía nadar pero este hombre resultó ser un buen nadador, así que saltó del muelle y la sacó del agua. La levantó sobre el mismo y pasó unos minutos calmando a ambas amigas. De repente se encontró de regreso en su cuarto en Minneapolis, ¡su ropa estaba empapada en agua salada! El no tenía idea de donde había estado. Unos años después él estaba en un campamento cristiano cuando dos chicas vinieron corriendo a través del gentío. Una estaba gritando: «¡fuiste tú! ¡Tú eres el hombre que me salvó! ¡El hombre en el muelle cuando me caí al agua! ¿A dónde te fuiste?». El les preguntó: «¿Dónde fue eso? ¿Dónde ocurrió eso?». Ellas estaban incrédulas: «Tú sabes donde fue, ¡estuviste ahí!». El les contó que no tenía idea, y les relató la historia. Ellas dijeron: «Bueno, eso fue en Florida».

La última historia es personal. Algunos años atrás estábamos en una reunión familiar en el hogar de la madre de Denise. Llegó la noche y todos estaban hablando de qué íbamos a cenar. Finalmente se decidió que cenaríamos pizza, y era mi turno el ir a traerla. Salí a la entrada de la casa, le quité el seguro al carro. Cuando estuve a punto de subirme me di cuenta que había olvidado mi billetera. Estaba en el cuarto. Pero cuando iba a entrar a la casa, una vocecita dentro de mi dijo: «No te preocupes acerca de ellos». Yo pensé: «¿No te preocupes? ¡No tengo dinero conmigo! Hay suficiente en mi billetera. No hay problema, voy y agarro mi billetera. ¡La necesito!». Pero otra vez oí: «No te preocupes».

Así que cerré la puerta del carro y empecé a manejar hacia la ciudad – como cuatro millas de distancia. Todo el tiempo estaba pensando: «¿Qué estoy haciendo? No conozco al sujeto de la pizza. No me van a dar la pizza sin dinero. ¡Debería regresar por mi billetera!», pero de alguna manera mi cuerpo seguía conduciendo el auto. Llegué a una esquina en donde tenía que doblar a la derecha, así que paré y vi hacia la calle. No venía nada. Vi hacia la otra – tampoco. Y cuando noté, volando directo hacia mí, venía una nota de $10. Nunca había visto dinero volando por la calle antes de eso y nunca lo he vuelto a ver. Voló directo hacia mí y una corriente de aire lo levanto por sobre el capó del auto. Pensé: «¡Voy a agarrarlo!» así que abrí la puerta justo cuando voló del capó y paró justo a la par de mi puerta. El auto que manejaba era bajo así que solo tuve que abrir la puerta y recoger el dinero. Cerré la puerta y fui por la pizza. ¡El total fue de $9.95! Tenía suficiente dinero en mi billetera en casa, pero era el Padre diciendo: «Tu piensas que eres el padre de familia, pero te estoy mostrando que yo soy tu Padre». Ese fue un gran milagro para mí, aunque haya sido un acosa pequeña. Me dejó ver que realmente no somos de este mundo.

Somos hijos e hijas de Dios. Cuando aprendamos a caminar en la continua experiencia del amor de Él todos los días, nos volveremos libres. Todas las cosas que pensamos que son maravillosas, dones sobrenaturales de Dios, son solo expresiones de quien se supone que seamos. A medida que los hijos e hijas de Dios sean revelados, el reino va a ser establecido y este mundo cambiará. Todo lo que ha sido de Satanás será echado fuera. El día vendrá, el día de las bodas del Cordero y todos estaremos ahí. El Padre vendrá y se arrodillará a la par nuestra para enjugar toda lágrima de dolor. La Escritura dice: «Ahora somos hijos de Dios pero no se ha revelado lo que seremos» (1 Juan 3:2). Cuando estemos en las bodas del Cordero nos diremos los unos a los otros: «¡¡Sólo sabíamos la mitad!!».

Vivimos en un tiempo en donde la Novia se está preparando para las bodas del Cordero. Seremos la Novia de Cristo en el día de la boda. Tradicionalmente en las bodas judías el Novio no ve a su Novia hasta el día de las bodas. Antes de eso ella está siendo preparada para él. Un día veremos a Jesús cara a cara pero ahora estamos siendo preparados para ese día.

Abraham (tipo del Padre) envió diez camellos llenos de dones de su casa con su siervo (tipo del Espíritu Santo) para que Rebeca se acostumbrara al amor y al ambiente familiar que Isaac (Jesús) había tenido toda su vida. Ahora es Dios el Padre quien está derramando sobre nosotros todo lo que Él es y lo que Él tiene para que estemos preparados y seamos apropiados para casarnos con su Hijo.

«AHORA SOMOS HIJOS DE DIOS»

Siento por primera vez en mi vida que realmente he venido a entender lo que significa el evangelio. Es acerca del Padre que perdió a sus hijo y Él simplemente los quiere de vuelta. Ya que la mayoría de la raza humana tiene gran dificultad para amar a las figuras de autoridad (la caída ha causado que la mayoría de la gente en el poder haya sido corrompida por ese poder), el Padre no vino Él mismo, sino que envió a su Hijo a representarlo perfectamente y llevarnos de vuela a Él.

¡Qué persona tan increíble es Dios! ¡Y somos sus hijos y sus hijas! Espero or el día en que veamos a hijos e hijas en su plena expresión de libertad, siendo levantados de todas las naciones del mundo, exhibiendo y expresando la persona, naturaleza y las obras del nuestro Padre, y caminando como Jesús en este mundo roto.

RECURSOS

Derek Prince, *Boletín de febrero 1998*.

C. S. Lewis, *A Grief Observed*, Faber and Faber, London, 1961.

Andrew Murray, *Permaneciendo en Cristo*, Bethany House Publishers, Minneapolis, Minnesota, 2003, publicado en Inglés (*Abiding in Christ*). Originalmente publicado in 1895 por Henry Altemus *Abide in Christ*.

Agustín de Hipona, citado por Fr. Raniero Cantalamessa en *Life in the Lordship of Christ*, Sheed and Ward, Kansas City, 1990.

UNA INVITACIÓN...

Si disfrutaste leyendo este libro te invitamos a las escuelas "A" de Fatherheart Ministries 'A' Schools. Son una semana de un ambiente de revelación de amor.

Los dos objetivos de las Escuelas 'A' son:
1. Darte una oportunidad para que tengas una mayor experiencia del amor de Dios el Padre.
2. Darte un entendimiento bíblico robusto acerca del Padre en la vida y el caminar cristiano.

Durante la escuela serás introducido a la perspectiva total de la revelación del amor del Padre. A través de vislumbres de revelación y enseñanza bíblica contada a través de las vidas de los que te ministrarán, serás expuesto a un mensaje transformador de amor, vida y esperanza.

Se te dará la oportunidad de remover los obstáculos principales para recibir el amor del Padre y descubrir tu corazón como un hijo o hija verdadera. Jesús tenía el corazón de un hijo para con su Padre. Vivió en la presencia de mor del Padre. El Evangelio de Juan nos dice todo lo que Él dijo y lo que ÉL hizo , lo que vio al Padre hacer. Jesús nos invita a entrar al mundo como hermanos y hermanas del Unigénito.

Al abrir nuestros corazones el Padre derrama su amor en nuestro corazón por el Espíritu Santo. En un corazón transformado por el amor, pueden ocurrir cambios verdaderos y duraderos. Luego de años de luchar y querer lograr cosas, muchos están finalmente encontrando el camino a casa, hacia un lugar de descanso y de pertenencia.

Para enviar una aplicación para una Escuela A visite 'Schools & Events' en **www.fatherheart.net**

Copias adicionales de este libro y otros recursos de Fatherheart
Media están disponibles en:

www.fatherheart.net/store - Nueva Zelanda

www.amazon.com - versiones impresas y de Kindle

FATHERHEART MEDIA

PO BOX 1039 Taupo,
Nueva Zelanda 3330

Visítanos en www.fatherheart.net